D1016961

# WORK AND PLAY

MEN OF GOOD WILL • VOLUME ELEVEN

Book XXI. MOUNTAIN DAYS
Book XXII. WORK AND PLAY

For a full list of the books in

Jules Romains's series

MEN OF GOOD WILL,

please turn to end

of this volume.

# WORK
# AND PLAY

by **Jules Romains**

Translated from the French by Gerard Hopkins

Alfred A. Knopf · New York · 1944

# DRAMATIS PERSONAE

Since a number of the characters of *Work and Play* were introduced in the earlier volumes of *Men of Good Will,* the reader may find it convenient to refer to a list of Dramatis Personæ, with a short summary of the antecedent action in which each has participated. It is suggested that the best way to use the Dramatis Personæ is to refer to each character in turn when the reader reaches the point in the narrative where that character makes his first appearance (as indicated by the page numbers following the names below). Historical characters, of whom several have been introduced into the action of the novel, and characters appearing for the first time in *Work and Play* are not included in this list.

JERPHANION, JEAN (p. 4), one of the central characters, not to say heroes, of *Men of Good Will,* came to Paris in 1908 to study at the Normal College in preparation for a career as a teacher. He brought from his home in the mountains of southern France, and from his peasant background, an honest ruggedness of character, an independent mind, a vigorous sense of humour. He is a tolerant sceptic who, like other young men of his time, saw all too clearly the shadows of coming events that were to immerse Europe in chaos. His long conversations with his friend Jallez (see below), with Clanricard (see below) and Laulerque (see below), centred on the question that has occupied the minds of thoughtful young men throughout the civilized world in this century: What can we do about it? Jerphanion saw some of his fellow students throw themselves into causes and movements of various kinds, and he himself considered joining both the Freemasons and the Socialists. He gained considerable insight into the nature of parliamentary democracy as secretary to the Marquis de Saint-Papoul (see below) during his campaign for election to the Chamber of Deputies by a provincial constituency. Shortly before the war he married Odette Clisson (see below). As an infantry lieutenant he was at the front during the greater part of the war, and was in the thick of the Battle of Verdun, with some particularly awful experiences in the Valley of Haudromont. The war revealed Jerphanion as a brave soldier, a conscientious and considerate officer, and a brilliant observer of human nature under stress of battle. After the war he served with the Army of Occupation in the Rhineland, writing frequently to Jallez to give him his impressions and ideas. Subsequently he became chief assistant to Bouitton (see below), whom he accompanied on a brief trip of observation to the Soviet Union.

SAINT-PAPOUL, THE MARQUIS DE (p. 6), won a seat as a provincial member of the Chamber of Deputies at a time when Jerphanion (see above) was his secretary. He is now a Senator.

BONNEFOUX, DR. (p. 6), was the leading opponent of the Marquis de Saint-Papoul in the election.

CASTAING, DR. (p. 6), was the retiring deputy for whose seat Saint-Papoul was a candidate.

CRIVELLI, HECTOR (p. 6), a Corsican, was the political expert in charge of the Marquis's campaign.

SOULARD (p. 7) was president of the Republican Club of Bergerac, supporting the Marquis's candidacy.

GOUZENNES (p. 8) was another candidate opposing the Marquis in the election.

JALLEZ, PIERRE (p. 8) is the best friend of Jerphanion (see above).

They are the two most important characters of *Men of Good Will,* and are good foils for each other: where Jerphanion is objective, normal, sceptical, Jallez is introspective, poetic, subtle. In many long walks together Jallez showed his friend the Paris he genuinely loves, and evoked, from a lyrical memory, the story of his childhood friendship with Hélène Sigeau (see below), which ended in Hélène's disappearance. Less successful than his friend in emotional relationships, because he demands more of them, Jallez has had a love-affair with Juliette Vérand, not knowing that she was married to Maurice Ezzelin (see below). The affair brought unhappiness on both sides, and Jerphanion tactfully intervened at one point to straighten out the matter. But in their long conversations it is Jallez who reveals not only a deeper emotional nature, particularly in the memories of his adolescence, but also a greater originality in ideas. After taking his degree at the Normal College, Jallez became a free-lance journalist and, before the outbreak of war, made a tour of Alsace and the Rhineland to write a series of articles on the frontier. A conscientious objector during the war, he was put to work repairing army boots. After the war he went to Nice for a few perfect months while he was still young and independent. He has been an occasional correspondent for a Chicago newspaper and now holds a position with the League of Nations. In 1922 he went to the U.S.S.R. in company with Stephen Bartlett (see below). After various adventures he became involved with the Cheka, and a letter and telegram from Jerphanion, then in Moscow, were of help in releasing him from prison.

CABIROL, ABBÉ (p. 24), of the Catholic Institute, and LEBAIGUE, MONSIGNOR (p. 24), are two influential Catholics whose support of Saint-Papoul was solicited in his election campaign.

LAULERQUE, ARMAND (p. 31), first appeared as a young radical, who joined a secret society organized for violence in political action, for which he carried out several missions, one of them involving the purchase, in his own name, of a mysterious property in the south of France.

The society's part in the attempted assassination of Briand, together with various suspicious matters which he learned, undermined Laulerque's confidence in its revolutionary effectiveness. He was at one time in love with Margaret-Desideria Kreuz (see below), a Croatian girl who was a fellow member of the secret organization; also he had a brief love-affair with Mathilde Cazalis (see below), which he has since resumed. A latent tubercular infection led him to Switzerland, where he admires the way of life of the people and has advanced to an important administrative position at a mountain sanatorium.

JERPHANION, ODETTE (*née* Clisson) (p. 84), was married to Jean Jerphanion shortly before the war. She received long letters from him at the front, met him in Paris when he was there on leave. They are deeply in love.

GRIOLLET (p. 93), owner of a small tannery in Paris, one of Jerphanion's company at Verdun, to whom Jerphanion felt that he could talk more freely than to most.

JERPHANION, JEAN-PIERRE (p. 136), son of Jean and Odette, now nearly seven years old.

BOUITTON (p. 136), a member of the Chamber of Deputies, who has resigned as Minister. During his Ministry Jerphanion became his chief secretary and assistant. Bouitton has a warm affection for Jerphanion and his family, and relies on him heavily in practical details. In 1922 they made a brief trip to the U.S.S.R., where they were keen and open-minded observers of the Communist way of life.

GURAU, MAXIME (p. 161), mentioned only incidentally in this volume, has been a prominent figure in several earlier ones. He is an honest politician with slightly tarnished ideals. Beginning as a member of the Chamber of Deputies and an independent journalist, he served as Minister of Labour in Briand's Cabinet, as Minister of Public Works under Monis, and finally as Foreign Secretary under Caillaux. A man primarily of action, he is "practical" in the sense that he has learned the uses of hypocrisy; but fundamentally he is a man of good will. In or out of office, he works consistently for peace.

QUINETTE (p. 222) first appears in *Men of Good Will* as a humdrum bookbinder, who becomes obsessed with the idea of committing a murder for its own sake. His first victim was Augustin Leheudry, an obscure young man, with no connexions, whose confidence he proceeded to gain step by step, and whom he finally killed in a quarry, making identification impossible. In order to lay a red herring across his trail he made friends with an inspector of police, whom he has assisted as a spy. Subsequently he committed other murders. After the war he returned to his former bookbinding shop, which he had left for some mysterious activities during the hostilities. Still later he opened a bookshop in Nice under the name of Quinette-Descombles.

VIAUR, DR. ALBERT (p. 229), was first introduced as resident physician at Celle-les-Eaux, a spa built and popularized by Haverkamp (see below). By a series of unusual experiments he was led to a general theory of the part played by the nervous system in living organisms, opening up an enormous field involving the whole subject of biology. His experiments were frowned upon and he himself cold-shouldered by his more prominent colleagues. Jallez (see above), in the course of writing a series of articles popularizing certain recent scientific theories, interviewed Dr. Viaur and witnessed some of his experiments. He was struck by Viaur's simplicity, sincerity, and disinterestedness in connexion with his researches.

STRIGELIUS, MARC (p. 250), a minor poet and essayist, introduced briefly at a literary party which Jallez and Jerphanion attend. He has written several long literary letters to his sister.

# DRAMATIS PERSONAE

FACHUEL, GASTON (p. 258), an assistant magistrate of the Paris area. He has questioned Quinette (see above) about the mysterious disappearance of a woman, and later is induced by one of his friends to give a dinner for Quinette. He is struck by Quinette's resemblance to the notorious Landru.

LENGNAU (p. 266), an authority on Freemasonry, who talked on the subject with Jerphanion, Laulerque, and others of their circle before the war.

CHAMPCENAIS, HENRI, COUNT DE (p. 266), a former oil-magnate, who has invested in Haverkamp's enterprises. More recently he established connexions with a ring of international munitions-makers. Episodes from his sex life have revealed him as a sentimentalist and perhaps a masochist. He has betrayed and been betrayed by his wife. In Moscow in 1922 he was present at a supper party given for Bouitton (see above) by Haverkamp (see below).

HAVERKAMP, FRÉDÉRIC (p. 266), as a real-estate promoter, managed to build up Celle-les-Eaux, a highly profitable "health" spa near Paris, with a fashionable hotel and casino; his success arose from advertising the local waters, practically without distinguishing mineral properties, as being medicinally valuable. Later he induced the Army to take over Celle-les-Eaux for convalescent officers. He has also participated in an undercover deal in the disposition of disestablished religious properties. A man without a trace of sentimentality, he is hard-boiled but not ruthless; he conducts his love-affairs on the animal level, and with the same satisfaction that he gets from a good dinner; but he is genuinely in love with Paris. Before the outbreak of war he made the mistake of overreaching himself, and was involved in financial difficulties as a result. He is by no means without scruples, but he is an opportunist, and it was the most natural thing in the world for him to stumble, more or less by accident, into war profiteering. In 1922 he paid a visit to Moscow, where he entertained Bouitton (see above) and Jerphanion at supper.

TURPIN, RAOUL (p. 273), has figured principally as architect of Haverkamp's spa, Celle-les-Eaux. Since then he has built Haverkamp an ultra-modern studio, largely with a view to hanging his paintings.

WAZEMMES, FÉLIX (p. 291), was killed in a courageous counter-attack at Mort-Homme. Previously he had been a small patron of the turf, had had a pleasant love-affair with an older woman, and had spent several years in the employ of Haverkamp. A typical obscure son of the Parisian lower bourgeoisie, he was useful to his employer in a minor capacity, and had no higher ambition than to be rich and have a famous actress for his mistress. Shortly before the war he had joined the reactionary, proto-fascist *Action Française*.

MIRAUD, VICTOR (p. 291), a philosophical craftsman, now retired, who has taken pride in his work and followed the progress of revolutionary syndicalism. He was the uncle by marriage of Wazemmes (see above).

CAULET (p. 295), a comrade of Jallez and Jerphanion at the Normal College, fond of practical joking.

GENTICŒUR, MME (p. 311), has been mentioned only twice before in *Men of Good Will*: once when she became Haverkamp's secretary; once, very casually, when she became his mistress.

BERTRAND (p. 318), motor-manufacturer and affiliate of a group of oil-monopolists.

SAMPEYRE (p. 377) is an intellectual liberal, now noticeably ageing, a follower of Jaurès, and mentor of a group of young idealists who formerly met at his house on Wednesday evenings to discuss peace, politics, and labour. Since the war he has been obliged to give up his house and now lives in an apartment on a small pension.

SAMMÉCAUD, ROGER (p. 387), is a leading figure among the oil-dealers. He has seduced the Countess de Champcenais, with whom he had once been to the Fôret d'Othe (alluded to here), to see her subnormal son.

COPTIC PRINCESS, THE (p. 387), is called Eugénie. She purports to be a Christian Egyptian Princess, of Coptic family. Four days of love with her in Bruges make up one of the "chapters" into which Sammécaud's life is divided.

SAMMÉCAUD, DIDIER (p. 395), is a young man of the times, a pal of Marc de Champcenais's. (Marc is the subnormal son of Henri and Marie de Champcenais. See under SAMMÉCAUD, ROGER, above.)

SAMMÉCAUD, BERTHE (p. 396), wife of Roger Sammécaud, has appeared only briefly.

LAFEUILLE, PIERRE (p. 397), was a brilliant law-student before the war, and worked on the staff of Gurau's newspaper (see above). His articles campaigning for a state monopoly in oil were used by the oil-magnates to pull the wool over Gurau's eyes. In the war he served as a captain, and we have seen him, while touring the line, caught by a bombardment and telephoning information back to headquarters.

CLANRICARD, ÉDOUARD (p. 404), is an idealistic young Parisian schoolmaster. Out of his genuine goodness of nature, which might be mistaken for naïveté, he has been a good Samaritan to one of his pupils, a poor boy whose father was unemployed. Through an article he wrote on the loneliness of the young intellectual, he came to know Jallez and Jerphanion; and when he joined the Masons for spiritual refuge, he tried unsuccessfully to influence Jerphanion to follow his example. At a political discussion group led by his friend Sampeyre (see above), he met and fell in love with Mathilde Cazalis (see below). Jerphanion, unaware of Clanricard's feelings, almost became Mathilde's lover, but broke off the relationship when he learned of his friend's unhappiness, and Clanricard subsequently married her. An infantry officer during the war, he was given an order to attack which was impossible to carry out; after a struggle with his conscience, the dilemma was solved by a fellow officer who countermanded the order and made a false report to headquarters. Before the Armistice Clanricard lost an arm. More recently he has learned of the treachery of Mathilde and Laulerque, and this, combined with other bitternesses, led him to plan a trip to the Soviet Union, which, however, he gave up.

SUZANNE (p. 404) is Bouitton's competent stenographer and secretary. She accompanied Bouitton and Jerphanion on their trip to the U.S.S.R.

CLANRICARD, MATHILDE (*née* Cazalis) (p. 405), a young school-teacher who formerly frequented the Wednesday evening discussion group led by Sampeyre, where several young men were attracted to her. Almost engaged to Clanricard (see above), she jilted him for Jerphanion, who later gave her up; then she had a brief affair with Laulerque. Sampeyre advised her to come to an understanding with Clanricard, whom she married shortly before the war. Later she resumed her affair with Laulerque on one of his visits to Paris. This led to rancour with her husband.

KARL, MONSIEUR (p. 409), a member of the secret society to which Laulerque belonged before the war. Laulerque worked with him in connexion with the purchase of real estate in the south of France.

MASCOT (p. 412), Laulerque's superior in the secret society, who gave Laulerque instructions, and later announced his intention of retiring from the organization.

KREUZ, MARGARET-DESIDERIA (p. 444), a Croatian girl whom Laulerque met on missions for the secret society in Amsterdam and later in Paris. In the course of their intimacy she told him of certain suspicious and unsavoury matters connected with the society.

SIGEAU, HÉLÈNE (p. 446), the little girl whom Jallez loved in childhood. She enters the story only in his recollections.

EZZELIN, MAURICE (p. 446), a dull office clerk, the husband of Juliette Vérand, with whom Jallez has had a love-affair, continued after her marriage. Ezzelin learned, by means of an anonymous letter, who his wife's lover was, and went to the Normal College to see Jallez. Not finding him, he told his troubles to Jerphanion, who handled the case adroitly. Jallez, who had not known of Juliette's marriage, then broke off the affair.

FABRE (p. 450), an amusing fellow officer of Jerphanion's at the front during the war.

BARTLETT, STEPHEN (p. 474), an English journalist, pages of whose travel-diary have been quoted, giving his impressions of Paris, the French people, and various events. He met Jallez in a café in Rome in 1922 and they became warm friends. They made a trip to the U.S.S.R. together, where they experienced various difficulties, adventures, and amusing episodes.

TORCHECOUL, ERNEST (p. 474), an amateur economist, is a friend of Bartlett's (see above) and introduced him to Paris. When the war came, he retired to his native district, where he married a somewhat older woman who was owner of a château.

MARCHAND (p. 475), a fellow officer of Jerphanion's, killed in the war.

POLIAPOF, DMITRI (p. 475), serving as a waiter in a *trattoria* in Rome, overheard Jallez and Bartlett discussing their plans for a trip to the U.S.S.R. He introduced himself to them as a former member of the Duma, an anti-Bolshevist, and arranged to meet them in Russia. A great air of mystery surrounds him and his connexions. Once in Russia, they saw him, in disguise, on a boat on the Volga.

DUROURE, GENERAL (p. 511), when a Lieutenant-Colonel, predicted the coming of war several years before its outbreak. As an expert on artillery, he was present at a pre-war dinner-party given by the Count de Champcenais (see above) in honor of a munitions-manufacturer. During the war he made several appearances. He was offered command of the Verdun sector, but refused to give up his own for it. His billet was destroyed by a Zeppelin bomb and, taking this almost as a personal affront, he went to lodge a complaint about it with General Joffre.

TELLIÈRE and GENTILCŒUR (p. 559), two friends of Jallez, who admires their lyrical, humorous attitude towards life.

# Contents

## 21.
## MOUNTAIN DAYS

| | | |
|---|---|---|
| I. | A Winter Drive | 3 |
| II. | Jerphanion's Full-dress Speech at the Le Puy Luncheon | 25 |
| III. | A House of Gentlefolk | 74 |
| IV. | How Monsieur Pouzols-Desaugues would have Established the Peace | 89 |
| V. | On the Road to the Mountains | 103 |
| VI. | The Story of Saint François-Régis | 107 |
| VII. | The Deaths at Vaurevauzes | 110 |
| VIII. | Letter from Jerphanion to Odette: Mountain Thoughts | 133 |
| IX. | Of Poisons | 143 |
| X. | A Visit to the Curé | 154 |
| XI. | The House at Vaurevauzes | 170 |
| XII. | An Orator's Day-dreams | 188 |
| XIII. | Odette's Answer | 193 |
| XIV. | Snowscape, and a Chat about Crime | 199 |
| XV. | The Landlord and the Good-Looking Concierge | 212 |
| XVI. | Society Is Slow-moving | 221 |
| XVII. | Jallez Enjoys a Sensation of Well-being | 224 |
| XVIII. | Reappearance of Dr. Viaur | 230 |

| XIX. | The Bitterness of Success and the Disappointments of Fame | 233 |
| XX. | A Magistrate Who Won't be Rushed | 253 |
| XXI. | Pull Yourself Together | 263 |
| | Summary | 267 |

# Contents

## 22.
## WORK AND PLAY

| | | |
|---|---|---|
| I. | Haverkamp Sets About Refurbishing | 273 |
| II. | Henry de Belleuse is Taught a Lesson | 290 |
| III. | A Roof-Top Pilgrimage | 294 |
| IV. | Husband and Wife | 301 |
| V. | Haverkamp Wishes to Carry Out Repairs in His Private Life | 307 |
| VI. | The Story of a Mistake | 311 |
| VII. | Half-Measures Are Never Satisfactory | 323 |
| VIII. | A Plan of Action | 331 |
| IX. | Haverkamp Discovers That He Has Been Rather Stupid | 338 |
| X. | Advice from an Old Hand | 343 |
| XI. | To Which the Newcomer Replies | 346 |
| XII. | The Future of France | 354 |
| XIII. | Thoughts of a Soft-Hearted Judge | 364 |
| XIV. | Jerphanion Writes to Laulerque | 377 |
| XV. | Back from the Countess's | 379 |
| XVI. | In the Forest of Ardennes. A Lover of Islam | 387 |
| XVII. | Sammécaud at a Turning-Point | 395 |
| XVIII. | En Route for a New Life | 400 |
| XIX. | Jerphanion Consults Laulerque and Finds Him Almost Too Much Disenchanted | 403 |
| XX. | Odette and Jallez Have a Confidential Talk | 422 |
| XXI. | A Party of Four. Missed Opportunities | 433 |
| XXII. | Two Men at Odds with Themselves | 438 |

| | | |
|---|---|---|
| XXIII. | Monsieur Pouzols-Desaugues Gives Signs of Life | 452 |
| XXIV. | Just Like the Old Days. The Exposition of 1900, Lengnau and the Future of the World | 456 |
| XXV. | Happiness, Too, Is Worth Defending | 468 |
| XXVI. | A Tempting Proposal | 474 |
| XXVII. | Laulerque Repents | 478 |
| XXVIII. | Haverkamp, Confronted by the Work in Progress, Realizes That There Is a Limit | 480 |
| XXIX. | Mistress and Wife | 488 |
| XXX. | A Theatre Deal | 494 |
| XXXI. | Haverkamp Entertains Jerphanion | 508 |
| XXXII. | An Offer out of the Blue | 520 |
| XXXIII. | Jerphanion Makes His Report. Algebra à la Haverkamp. Bouitton Loses His Temper | 524 |
| XXXIV. | The Exquisite Delight of a Project Realized | 531 |
| XXXV. | All Set for the Counties and the Kingdoms | 538 |
| XXXVI. | Château d'Aubepierre by Grosbois-sous-le-Mont | 544 |
| XXXVII. | Ernest Torchecoul Does the Honours of His Château | 547 |
| XXXVIII. | A Family Party | 551 |
| | Summary | 560 |
| | Index | *follows page* 562 |

# BOOK TWENTY-ONE:

# MOUNTAIN DAYS

# Chapter

## 1

### A WINTER DRIVE

There must have been a just perceptible frost during the night. When, at a turn in the road, the car ran into a patch of shade, the air struck suddenly raw; but no sooner was it left behind than the day took on a surprising quality of happy lightness. The sun, as cloudless and unencumbered as on a morning of high spring, imparted just the right degree of cheerful warmth with no hint in it of uncomfortable fierceness. "I'm not going to put up the top," Grousson had said as they started from Saint-Julien; "with this sun we shall be warm enough." And he was right. Only one's feet remained frozen in spite of the heavy rug. Little drops of water hung from the bare twigs of the leafless undergrowth. The whole arc of the sky, shimmering and brilliant, echoed their lyrical freshness. If one was but fifteen again, and a peasant boy (and, after all, one's grandparents had been peasants), one would yield to the temptation, even now stirring somewhere in one's chest, to break into a mountain song and keep it going endlessly.

"What a lovely countryside it is, even at this time of year!" thought the traveller. "I always laughed at Mother when she used to write: 'It's Christmas week, but the weather is so mild that I took my lace out into the meadow yesterday, and sat working there for hours.' I'd forgotten. Christmas is almost on us, but there's really no reason why she shouldn't spend the afternoon in the doorway with her lace pillow —for she's still got that. What a pity that she hasn't still got the meadow too!"

Félicien Grousson, the driver and owner of the car, could scarcely be called a disturbing element in his passenger's day-dreaming. That he was taciturn by nature seemed improbable; in fact, his prominent, lively eyes and mobile lips gave the lie to any such supposition. But he was a man of strong common sense. Since M. Jean Jerphanion was going to have to make a long speech at this Le Puy luncheon, it was but natural that M. Jean Jerphanion should want to do a bit of silent thinking, all the more because he was to address no ordinary listeners, but an audience comprising all the clever fellows who ruled the roost in this part of the world—not just a few dozen easy-going chaps such as you'd find at a village meeting. So conscious was he of the need for discretion that even when M. Jean started turning his head from side to side, quite obviously on the look-out for something to take his mind off the matter in hand, he still wasn't sure whether he ought to venture a remark or two. When he did finally take the plunge, he was careful to say something appropriate.

"Well, sir, chance does sometimes play us a good turn after all. They've been saying for years hereabouts that sooner or later you'd be running for Parliament. Naturally you could have your pick of constituencies, though I don't suppose you found it difficult to choose. And then, just at the right moment, comes this illness of Monsieur Pagès-Vernet. It wouldn't have been easy for you, in a way, to stand against him, and a good number of people would have felt badly about leaving him in the lurch. He's been our representative now for a long while. When the new registration came into force in '19, it didn't really alter things; we still felt that he was *our* man, and so did he. He was a decent sort of fellow, though he'd become a bit reactionary by modern standards. In his time, though, he was a sound republican, and among the first to oppose Boulanger, even before Clemenceau."

"You're talking of him as though he were dead!"

"Oh well, he might just as well be. He's not good for much now. His housekeeper was telling me the other day that he doesn't recognize her now. And there wasn't much he didn't know about her once, I can tell you. He was a terrible one for the ladies, for all his la-di-da airs! Bonial, a chap I know, was saying awhile back: 'If all the women he's flirted with could make their husbands and sons

vote for him, there'd be a good pack of stuff in his ballot-boxes. . . .'
Ah well, I shouldn't be surprised if that's what he's paying for now—
that and all the hunt dinners he's put away. He can't say he hasn't
had a gay time, and that's more than one can claim for most men
between seventy and eighty. He must be getting along in years."

"How old do you think he really is?"

"Oh, sixty-eight, going on sixty-nine. . . ."

Grousson started to laugh. "That reminds me of something I heard
about the Protestants 'way up in the hills—you know those I mean?"

"I know."

"Of course you do—why, there were several villages of them close
to you when you were living with your parents at Boussoulet. . . .
Well, poor old Pagès-Vernet had some in his constituency—not a lot,
but, from what I'm told, he never knew which way they were going
to vote. You see, pretty advanced ideas run in those families on the
whole, and he was a bit reactionary for their taste; on the other hand,
the local parsons seem to have thought that his behaviour to the
women of their flocks hadn't been all it should be."

"I hope he didn't play any tricks with the Protestants!"

"I shouldn't think so, but one never knows. . . . He was probably
more careful, that's all. . . . The only real difference it would have
made is that if he'd been to bed with a fair Protestant, she'd probably
tell her man *not* to vote for the old rascal! . . . Well, to go back to
what I was saying, this illness of old Pagès-Vernet's a lucky thing
for you. It's made things smooth all round."

There was a hint of anxiety in Jerphanion's next question. "Would
you say," he asked, "that my chances are pretty good?"

The immediate reply was a jovial roar. "If," said Grousson, "you
mean of being elected next spring, I should say you've as good as got
the whole thing in your pocket! You'd have to make a pretty good
fool of yourself between now and then not to. . . . In the first place,
you're a local man. People know you, or at least they've heard of you.
Your father's well thought of. I'll go further than that and say he's
loved. Everyone realizes you're an educated chap with his head

screwed on right, and you can talk. The only people who are going to
vote against you, as far as I can see, are the real old die-hards."

Jerphanion felt no desire to question such encouraging sentiments.
The words gave him much the same delicious sensation as a cool
drink on a summer's day. He lacked the courage to ask: "But what
about the rest of the constituency?" and confined his response to a
contented smile and a faint shake of the head. Silence fell between the
two men.

An entirely irrelevant thought began to tease Jerphanion's mind:
"What was that doctor's name who sat for Bergerac before Saint-
Papoul, in 1910? Bonnafous? No, Bonnafous was the fellow who stood
against him. Castaing, that was it, Dr. Castaing. . . . I remember
how Hector Crivelli, that old Corsican brigand and former student
of Saumur, made the last syllable ring. The situation was much the
same as it is here. Saint-Papoul was lucky enough, in his case too, not
to have to fight against a sitting member. It really is a curious coincidence."

There was something at once funny and humbling in the thought:
"One's got to take one's models as one finds them. Here am I starting my political career not like a Gambetta or a Jaurès, but like a
Marquis de Saint-Papoul. How Jallez would laugh! . . . After all,
the Marquis hasn't done too badly when one thinks of his natural
endowments. He's a Senator, he's president of his local Council . . .
the big man of his department . . . a respected ornament of the
Senate. . . . He doesn't open his mouth much, to be sure, but he's a
member of the chief committees, and he's consulted at moments of
crisis. He could have been a minister, of Agriculture, say, if he'd
wanted to. But the Marquise probably shied at the expense and the
responsibility. No, come to think of it, the comparison is not too
odious."

It was not the first time since his campaign started that he had been
reminded of Bergerac in 1910—April 1910. He had been forced more
than once to realize what a useful apprenticeship that amusing incident of his past had been. Situations and occurrences which might

otherwise have disturbed or disgusted him appeared now in the guise of familiar experiences, caught up and exhibited in the light of boyish laughter. He had learned not to take things too hard. The pleasant vaccine with which, in 1910, he had been inoculated ensured immunity now. Suppose, for instance, that some village mayor gave vent, in a rich local accent, to some stupid gibe which, in other circumstances, might have hurt his feelings, at once the orchestra of memory took it up pianissimo on a Périgord oboe, and forthwith the whole incident became just amusing, an intellectual joke. He found, in a number of constant features, much food for thought. Certain minor twists of French politics, recurring at different times and in different places, could not, for all their appearance of spontaneity, be entirely without significance; comic they might seem, but, for all that, they must, he thought, respond to some universal and profound need of the French character, to something which a candidate must take into account and understand more fully than a mere political theorist. Even the variations, when they occurred, could not be ignored. He found himself, willy-nilly, tracing their origins further and further back into the remote corners of past centuries. Le Velay and Périgord he saw as two deep channels graven in the stuff of history, as dwindling perspectives at the end of which he could catch a glimpse of Romano-Gallic villas, of Gaulish huts, of Celtic Stone Age dwellings.

"If anyone had told me in those days, when I was pounding away at Hector Crivelli on one side and Monsieur Soulard, the local undertaker, on the other, that a time would come when I should be doing the same thing in my own interests, should I have been surprised? Honestly, now. . . . No, I don't think I should. Disappointed, perhaps, at the thought that I should have made so little progress in fifteen years. It's awful the years and years one can lose out of a comparatively short life, almost without noticing. And when one takes into account five years of war on top of two years of military service, it's simply appalling! . . . How well I understand the impatience of some of my contemporaries who scrambled out of the mess with their lives. They've lost the gift of patience. . . . And if the same person had said to me: 'The cream of the joke is that you'll be a Radical-Socialist candidate—you, who had hammered out such a fine-sounding formula for old Gouzennes . . .'—and it *was* fine-sounding, though I'm hanged if I can remember how it went—'you and your Socialists, just playing into the hands of a party the sole object of which is to fling a monkey-wrench into the wheels of the social revolution!' Well, by and large, I told Gouzennes the truth, but it was no part of my job to instruct him in the subtleties of political theory. To be fair to myself, I did at least know that I was young in those days, that I could treat myself to a little over-simplification, to a certain amount of intolerance. . . . A crafty old mountaineer, Jallez used to call me. Well, that's not true, at any rate in matters of politics. From a purely worldly point of view I should have done better for myself by joining the Socialists, who were short of men. I should infinitely have preferred not to have to choose. A composer has got to write for the orchestra of his day. A man who wants to be politically active can only make use of the instruments to his hand. What's the alternative—make my own party, based on a lot of nice, neat, rational ideas? What could I have hoped for?—a mere handful of followers. And the result —another tiny party to add to the list, a penny whistle giving out a little note which would be lost in the general hullabaloo. Or, I suppose, I might play to the gallery, appeal to the confused thinking and hysterical passions of the mob, like Mussolini. But no, that's not my line; and, besides, French people would never stand for it, thank God! Far better to throw in my lot with something already firmly established, with a party having a long tradition behind it, a party which is based on certain clear-cut, rational ideas and is still powerful, can still command the means to action, is still worth while, a party which never, on principle, says no to anything until it has tested it, but has always, as Herriot is never tired of pointing out, remained Cartesian. . . . Why should one reject it? True, it's not very revolutionary, not very satisfying for a young fellow who used to thrill at the very mention of the word 'revolution.' . . . But one of the lessons I brought back from Russia is that once revolution takes on a quality of mysticism, it becomes as dangerous as any other fetish. . . . And, after all, one can make a political movement mean anything one likes by just changing its nomenclature. Hasn't Mussolini christened his gangster plot 'national revolution'? . . ."

The car stopped. Jerphanion roused himself from his day-dreaming, the form of which had been subtly influenced by the long vistas of leafless trees, the distant shoulders of sun-drenched mountain-sides, the close proximity of houses roofed with semi-cylindrical tiles, so that fresh ideas kept rising and dissipating in his mind, taking new stresses and a fresh direction from the play of light and the flickering movement of ever changing symbols.

"What about stopping for a drink?" asked Grousson.

"Just as you like." Jerphanion recognized the Pandreaux inn. It stood half-way between Saint-Julien-Chapteuil and Le Puy. Often, in the old days, when he had been travelling with his parents, the local bus had stopped there. But the drivers then had had good reason for the halt, for the long pull had given them a thirst, and the horses needed a breather. Did motorists today keep up the ancient tradition even though the excuse had vanished? He put the question to his companion.

"It all depends," was the answer. "When one's in a hurry, of course . . . but we're well on time. I think you ought to shake hands with the landlord. He might be useful to you. He sees a lot of people in the course of a day, and of all sorts too. Besides, a glass would warm us."

Jerphanion had no objection to performing a duty of that kind. At the worst it could only mean swallowing an apéritif. Like the sailor who in moments of danger invokes the patron saint whose courage under martyrdom may serve him as an example, Jerphanion let his thoughts turn to the Marquis de Saint-Papoul and his digestive troubles.

"What a life!" he sighed, but the sigh was little more than a tribute to convention. He could not pretend that he had not been fully warned when he chose it. As a matter of fact, he had laid in a good store of patience, but so far he had not had to draw upon it. Which was just as well, because this tour which he had undertaken with the object of seeing "how the land lay" was only the first step. There was a good deal worse to come once the electoral campaign started in earnest, with all its handshaking and canvassing. So far he had had a good deal less to put up with than he had expected. Whenever he felt tempted to indulge in depressing thoughts, he had a sure counter-irritant ready: "Remember," he only needed to tell himself, "Haudro-mont Valley." Freshly shaved and well dressed, he ran no worse danger now than that of hearing some jolly shirt-sleeved voter cry in his local singsong: "This is on me! I must be allowed to offer our future deputy a drink!" Similarly placed, the haggard, muddy lieu-tenant of Verdun would scarcely have felt inclined to indulge in self-pity.

On the whole he was quite pleased by the way he managed to deal with these situations. The great thing was to avoid any suspicion of being awkward or stand-offish. On the other hand, he would have hated to put up a show of coarse heartiness and hail-fellow-well-met ebullience. As it was, he smiled rather more than he wanted to, spoke when he would rather have been silent, asked questions about the answers to which he was completely indifferent. But with it all he succeeded in remaining natural. The experience was not a wholly novel one. Formerly, when he had had to break down the apathy of a pupil or stiffen the morale of one of his men, he had not always found it easy to put much enthusiasm into his words. In such cases he had generally fallen back on a sense of goodwill, rather too facile perhaps, but devoid of pretence, and on a quiet acceptance of the thing as a duty, which meant really no more than recognizing that the boy or man in question *needed* him. Similarly now it was enough to say to himself: "I am going to ask all these people to trust me. I have not the least intention of taking advantage of them. They are my kind; they come from my part of the world. They are just like my uncles and my cousins. It's all rather as though I were paying a round of visits to a lot of rather distant relatives, with the object of offering to represent them in some matter affecting the family interests. . . ." This thought enabled him to adopt the right attitude, and he realized that no more was expected of him. These people were sensitive enough to see that an educated man who had already seen a great deal of the world and had had dealings with highly placed persons could scarcely be expected to indulge in the buffoonery and back-slapping proper to cattle-dealers, or to employ the loud-voiced familiarities and greasy solicitations of a travelling salesman. Such conduct would merely have lowered him in their estimation. Nor did they expect him to know all their Christian names and surnames or to remember the ages of their children. After all, when a bishop came to conduct a confirmation no one expected him to know that Félicie's boy had died of measles the year before. M. Jerphanion did not put on airs; nor, on the other hand, did he set himself to flatter his constituents. And they liked him the better for it. A flatterer, they argued, is usually a man who is trying to get the best of a bargain, whereas M. Jerphanion always seemed to be saying: "I hope you'll vote for me, because, you see, I've got an idea that I should like to sit in Parliament. You, on the other hand, won't be the loser, because in that way you'll be sure of having a good member instead, perhaps, of a bad one." That was the kind of talk a serious-minded man could appreciate.

When they got back into the car, Grousson seemed readier than before to chat. He assumed, quite rightly, that the fifteen minutes they had spent in the inn with the landlord, his wife, and the two wagoners on their way home from Le Puy had set M. Jean's mind working, and that he was not so anxious now as he had been to be left to his own thoughts.

"I thought your father was looking very well this morning," he said. "Last summer he seemed to have grown a bit thinner. But he looks strong enough now. . . . He's nothing to complain of, I hope?"

"Goodness, no . . . though, in any case, he's not much given to complaining. . . . He's apt to get a touch of bronchitis in the winter, but it doesn't bother him much. . . . He used, too, to suffer from indigestion, but he never mentions it now."

"It may be that the teaching tired him, being shut up indoors, and not getting enough exercise."

"Quite possibly. He loves walking, strolling casually through the fields and along the river. And he enjoys picking mushrooms when they're in season."

"You don't need to tell me! Many's the time I've seen him at it. It shows he's not troubled with rheumatism. All that getting about and bending at his age. . . ."

"Yes, he's still pretty upright. But his memory's not what it was, more's the pity. There's nothing wrong with his mind, it's just that he can't remember. He knows it, and it worries him. But I think my mother alludes to it rather too often, which is wrong of her. You see, he tells himself that he's not going to remember things, and the fear paralyses his faculties. And if he doesn't, poor man, my mother very soon reminds him of it. As it is, whenever she mentions something that happened awhile ago, sometimes in the distant past, sometimes more recently, she more often than not begins by saying: 'I know you won't remember, but—' and then she gives a sigh and goes on."

"Your mother's brain is still so active . . . she remembers everything, down to the smallest details. I can't help laughing sometimes when we're having a chat. She can always dot the i's in talking of things that concern me, even when I've half forgotten them myself. She finds it difficult to realize that your father can't do the same. She thinks he just won't make the effort. . . ."

"Yes, she treats him like a lazy child. And in a way she's right in holding that the memory tends to get slack, like any other function, if it isn't exercised. I've known men in politics, quite elderly, well past sixty, who, when they've got an important speech to deliver, write it all out first. Then they learn it by heart, sometimes a matter of twenty or thirty pages! Sometimes it involves a lot of hard work before they succeed, but they manage it all right. And yet another man, no older, who has lost the schoolboy habit of using his memory would groan and grumble if he were asked to learn even one of La Fontaine's fables" ("but that's not true of the Marquis de Saint-Papoul," he reflected). "All I complain of is that my mother goes the wrong way to work. Shaking people's self-confidence is not the best way of helping them to overcome a disability. . . . What worries me is that it makes my father sad and taciturn. He was never much of a talker . . . but don't you think he's become rather melancholy?"

Grousson, who felt touched by these confidences, and remarked to himself that "Monsieur Jean is a good-hearted chap—not like some people I know who think of nothing but their own ambitions," replied in tones of cautious friendliness:

"I must say I always find him very nice. He never forgets to smile when we meet. Sometimes he has a good laugh. He still enjoys his little joke."

"You two are old friends."

"That's true enough. . . . I talk to him of the old Boussoulet days, of the people we used to know up there, and I can't say I find much wrong with his memory."

"But you don't start by making him nervous, you see. On the contrary, you give him confidence."

"Of course, I don't get round to Saint-Julien more than about once a fortnight, and when I do, I'm off again almost at once. When we meet it's usually for five minutes' gossip in the street. I don't notice his ways as I should if I lived in the same house with him."

"Naturally."

Grousson thought for a while; then:

"I never went to see them when they were living at Saint-Pierre," he said. "There was a very good reason for that in the early days; you see, I was called up. And then, later . . . they didn't lose much time about leaving the place, did they?"

"No. . . . It must be three years this Michaelmas since they moved down to Saint-Julien."

"Do you think it was a wise step?"

"It was I who suggested it."

"I'm told they had a nice little place up there. I rather think I know what it looked like."

"It was a pleasant little cottage. I always used to find it very picturesque. It had a magnificent view over the Saint-Julien Valley, with the Cévennes on the southern horizon. My mother inherited half of the house, and, on my advice, they bought the other half. That was a short while before my father retired. I thought they'd like to feel that the place was their own if they didn't find something they liked better somewhere else, and in fact they did settle down there. In addition to the yard, there was a kitchen garden and a meadow—enough land to grow vegetables, rear poultry, and keep a goat. Unfortunately, my father doesn't care about gardening. I'd hoped that he'd get to like it when he had plenty of time on his hands . . . though I know nothing about it myself. I've never really fathomed what sort of hobby he'd care about. . . . As things turned out, he was thoroughly bored up there, and so was my mother, more or less. And there were other disadvantages, as they soon discovered. It was impossible to keep their bedroom warm; for weeks on end during the summer the spring in the yard went dry, so that my father had to make quite a journey every time they wanted water. . . . I realized, after talking with them, that their dream was to settle in Saint-Julien, where they would find well-stocked shops, friendly neighbours with enough time on their hands to be sociable, and all the life and bustle of a market town. . . . So we set about finding the house where they live now. Its chief defect, in my opinion, lies in the fact that it is wedged in between a lot of others, and has a front garden no bigger than a handkerchief."

"Just what I thought myself."

"Though I don't suppose they feel that as much of a hardship. . . . They've let the Saint-Pierre house to a farmer. . . . I sometimes wonder whether, after a lifetime spent on the mountain, surrounded by peasants, they're not hankering after a real city—somewhere not too hectic; whether, in fact, they wouldn't be happiest living in an apartment at, say, Le Puy."

"Do you think so? It seems odd to me!" Grousson said in a thoughtful tone. "Not, of course, that one doesn't sometimes wonder where one would like to live if one could choose. When the day comes for me to hand over my present house to my son, I'm not at all sure that I shall know what to do. What I should like best would be a nice little well-wooded estate with a certain amount of pasture and moorland. There are plenty of the sort of thing I mean up on the high land. I should shoot, and I should breed horses, just for something to do. On the other hand, I should miss Le Puy, and my wife would say I wanted to kill her with boredom."

"Is your son in business with you?"

"The elder, yes. . . . In a way, I'm less concerned about his younger brother. In a bit under two years he'll be qualified as a doctor. He's a hard worker. All he'll ask of me will be a little help in setting himself up in practice—a matter of fifty thousand francs, I suppose, at most. Always shy about asking me for too much. But the other's quite different. It's always been my notion that he should carry on the business. He was never one for his books—never even matriculated. Not that that's likely to bother him much."

"I can't help laughing when I think of you with a couple of grownup sons. You look so young."

"People married young in my day." He started to chuckle. "I've got a pretty shrewd idea, from studying the dates, that the wife and I started our family the very first night. And we went to it again the next year. Well, nothing like that for keeping a couple level-headed. To go back to what I was saying about my older son, I've made him go right through everything from the bottom, so's he can get the hang of it all—mail, book-keeping, and all the rest of it. This autumn I've sent him down south to do the wine-buying; sent him to a few of the growers I'm on really good terms with, because I know they won't take advantage of him. The only thing I've not put him on to yet is making the round of my customers in the district."

"Why is that? Do you regard it as a specially ticklish job?"

"Oh, I don't know about that. I suppose the real reason is that it's the part of the business I've organized most thoroughly along my own lines. It's become very much a personal matter. You see, I'm only in a small business. All my customers are local men, and I've no intention of expanding it. I deal almost exclusively with hotel-proprietors, innkeepers, and the smaller retailers . . . with a few grocers thrown in, though nowadays, what with the competition of the large chain-store concerns—the Casino at Saint-Etienne, and places like that—the grocers' single-bottle business has dropped almost to nothing. The bar trade's what we live on."

"Do you sell much wine in the cask to private persons? I think my father has always got his stuff from you."

"Oh yes, to be sure. But it's not like it used to be; the profit's very small. What I really make a profit on is bottled wines and liqueurs, and even with liqueurs we have a hard battle to fight against the large producers who sell direct and employ their own travelling salesmen."

All the while he was listening, Jerphanion could not help pondering the fact that his companion was precisely one of those middlemen about whom there had been so much discussion ever since the cost of living had taken an apparently permanent upward trend. It was generally held that people like him were mainly responsible for the increase. "And yet he's not what you'd call a post-war product at all, not one of those men of my age, or a little younger, who, having decided that there's nothing in life worth taking seriously, have determined not to do a stroke of work for their living. He takes his business very seriously indeed. But is he performing any really useful function in the community? He has just admitted that one of his chief objects in life is to prevent the producer and the retailer from doing business direct. Would it be fair to call him a perfect example of the social parasite? Is he just one sprout of the enormous fungus that is slowly eating away the life of the body politic? Before answering that question one would have to do a little figuring, discover, for instance, whether the producer who employs his own travelling sales-men and sells direct runs up higher overheads in time and money than our friend, and whether in the long run the consumer pays more or less for what he buys. The odds are, I'm afraid, that he pays much the same, and it's pretty certain"—he remembered the Moscow shops of the Soviet régime—"that he'll pay a good deal more when the bourgeois parasites of the wine and spirits trade, like my friend Grousson here, have been replaced by what Jallez would call 'the officials of the Bistrokomprol.' "

"From the moment I started in business," went on Grousson, "I've always insisted on seeing how things were for myself. That's why I've succeeded. I've got a good nose for a deal. A lot of my competitors in Le Puy used to say: 'Our local customers know what we have to offer them. All we've got to do is to see that they get our price-lists, and that their mail orders are promptly attended to. Once or twice a year we look in on them just to keep things friendly, but that's all.' Well, I don't do things that way. I make a point of going round the district each week. I was one of the first hereabouts to have a car, and I don't mind telling you I've had my share of breakdowns and blow-outs on these damned roads of ours! When I had only my horse, I used to put up each night on the road. The only times I stayed at home was when snow made travelling impossible. At first my customers were pretty well staggered: 'Why, it's only three weeks since he was here last! What in the world can he want to talk about now? Seems like he's plenty of time to waste.' But soon they got used to seeing me, and they found my frequent calls a convenience. If a delivery had gone wrong, there I was on the spot to put things straight. If they ran short of something, even though they had always got it up to then from one of my competitors, they soon learned to say: 'Grousson'll be along, and we'll ask him to get it for us, or something as good.' A country innkeeper is always too lazy to write letters; besides, he prefers to do business by word of mouth. I carry round samples of most of my stock in the boot. If someone mentions crème de menthe, for instance, I say: 'Just take a taste of that and tell me what you think.' Eight times out of ten I go off with an order in my pocket. But the great thing is that I give my customers the feeling that I'm really prepared to take trouble about them."

Jerphanion listened very carefully. He tried to imagine the details of this man's life. It seemed to him sober, full of variety, and, when all was said, just as legitimate as many others.

"What it comes to," he said, "is that you are your own travelling salesman."

"Got to be; I certainly couldn't afford to support one. And there'd be no point in it, seeing I don't do business outside the district. Besides, a salesman who turned up as often as I do wouldn't get the same sort of welcome. The customers would begin to find him too much of a good thing."

"But what's to stop you from expanding your business further afield?"

"Just think for a moment. What's the point in my offering southern-grown wines or Charente brandies to people living in the Lozère or the Ardèche? They'd say: 'The fellow's crazy! What on earth good's he to us?' Besides, if I was to deliver goods as far away as that I should have to build up a whole subsidiary organization, which would cost millions. I haven't got the necessary capital, and if I had, I should be the worst sort of lunatic to try to run a show like that from Le Puy, which is about as badly placed as it could be both for getting goods by rail and for delivering them by road. You may have noticed that if you start out from Le Puy to drive into any of the neighbouring departments, you just can't avoid, at some point or other, having to climb above the three-thousand-foot line. And I don't think," concluded Grousson on a note of pride, "that you can say the same for any other prefecture in France."

"True enough, and what with snow . . ."

"Snow and everything else—gas-consumption, wear and tear, loss of time . . ."

"Yes, you're perfectly right. But there's something else I didn't quite understand. You said just now that you looked in at Saint-Julien about once a fortnight. But you only make your round once a week, don't you? . . . How is it that every other trip leads you to Saint-Julien? I can't believe you cover half the department each time you go out."

"No. Let me explain. . . . I didn't want there to be any bad blood between me and my competitors—especially the two chief ones. Gradually, therefore, I sort of staked out a claim to the eastern section, or rather the south-eastern, which is the most difficult and least rewarding of the department. Naturally, I take orders if they come my way from anywhere, but I don't look for 'em in the other fellows' country. There's nothing like a regular written agreement. I've made no promises, and neither have they. It's just that we try not to cut each other's throats."

"I understand."

"Well, of course some of my trips are more worth while than others —better customers and all that—so I'm naturally more careful to nurse them. It so happens that Saint-Julien comes within two—or rather three—of those itineraries."

Jerphanion had given up pondering the purely economic aspect of the matter, preferring to concentrate his attention on the actual existence led by the man sitting at his side. "It's the personal element that really interests human beings. Not that the economic machinery isn't important, but by itself it has no more appeal than a mathematical sum. What is really absorbing is to see what emerges from the arrangement in terms of actual life, of hours lived in a recurring sequence, day after day. A beggar hanging about the Naples quays, seen as an economic formula, has scarcely any appreciable value at all, is as near as can be to nothing. But regarded as an element of living flesh and blood, he can often give points to many a great thinker or master of human endeavour like Aristippus, Epicurus, or Epictetus. Yet this superiority of his can never have a money equivalent. Economically his value will always be in the neighbourhood of zero. The American phrase: 'So-and-so is *worth* so much' must surely be one of the crudest figures of speech ever imagined. The great thing is to try to get a clear picture of Félicien Grousson opening the door of his garage in the morning, checking the water-level in his radiator, making sure that the sample bottles are all safely stowed in the boot, starting the engine. If the cylinders fire at the first touch he feels in a

good mood. He fills up at the pump down the street, and after a word
or two about the weather, off he goes along the same road by which
we shall soon be entering the town. His clothes vary with the season,
but are on the warm side, and he takes a rug with him just to be safe.
If it looks like rain, he puts up the top; otherwise, he likes to feel
the rush of air on his face, and one of his chief amusements is to notice
from week to week the greater or less degree of cold or heat, of dry-
ness or dampness, and to judge the angle at which the sun strikes
familiar landmarks. When he crosses the bridge at Brives—which we
shall soon be crossing, but going the other way—he never fails to
glance up-stream at the distant line of mountains which he knows
so well. He loves them, and gets a little thrill each time he sees them.
How could he help loving them? Is there anywhere in the world a
view more completely satisfying, no matter what one's mood, than
that from the bridge of Brives, looking towards the distant mountains, ethereal, wise, remote? From there he turns up the valley of
the Gagne, having on one hand the volcanic cliff, on the other a line
of little fields running down to the stream. The rock, to which cling a
few pine trees, stunted and almost rootless, is a medley of many
colours—tannin, rust, purple, red lead, and blood. Its texture is like
nothing so much as that of some metallic sponge. Through what
æons of antiquity has this narrow gorge been formed! Grousson
draws up at the Pandreaux inn. After a short halt he sets off again,
this time perhaps along the road to Lantriac, stopping first at that
place, then at Laussonne. (How I love the place-names of this countryside! They breathe the very air of Gaul, the flinty smell of Rome;
they are at once taut and deep-mouthed, long-suffering and unyield-
ing, worn but indestructible.) At each stop he is greeted by name,
cordially but in tones of deference, like an old relation who is also a
great man in the city, head of an honoured and well-established firm
about the conduct of which no customer has ever had a serious complaint to make. 'You always bring fine weather, Monsieur Grousson,'
they say; or: 'You don't seem to bother much about the rain!'—for
it does rain sometimes, and the water has a disgusting habit of blow-

ing in through the cracks in the top of the car. At midday he probably
eats his lunch at one of the upland inns, where he is offered some of
his own wine. 'Not too bad,' says the landlord with a wink; and he
answers politely, if possible in the local dialect: 'No, not bad at all.
But what I like is the way it improves by being kept in your mountain cellars. It's got quite a different taste from what it has at home.'
A pleasant enough life, when all's said; unhurried, with just the
right amount going on, secure and free of anxiety; plenty of variety
in the faces he sees, and yet with a sort of recurrent pattern in their
arrangement, so that they recur with the regularity of the seasons,
and never become mere incidents in an anonymous mass. He probably
has to do rather too much eating and drinking—that's the danger of
such an existence; but, as he said himself, he hasn't much to lose from
that point of view—ten years or so of old age one way or the other. In
the trenches no one bothered much about whether one was going to
make old bones or not. Besides, one never knows; nature is pretty
arbitrary in her distribution of pains and penalties."

The car was just running into the outskirts of Brives, past the remains of the Roman road and the ruins of the old bridge with its
beautifully composed curves, reeking of "poetry" and looking like
some ruin in an old engraving. It turned on to the new bridge.
Jerphanion saw once again on his left hand the view up-stream, dominated by the mountains, ethereal and wise, not very high, indeed, but
infinitely remote. They wore a cap of snow, but the patch of whiteness was so much diminished by distance, so much toned down by the
paradisal light—the sky was just such as one sees in Primitive versions
of the Annunciation or the Marriage of the Virgin—that it gave no
sense of edged and bitter cold. Only the clearness of the air told of
winter, and the almost tangible freshness that lay in the depths of
the shadows. The rectangular houses, tall and narrow, coloured a
golden pink beneath their low pitched roofs of semi-cylindrical tiles,
were such as might have figured in pictures three or five centuries
back. They had replaced others just like themselves between which

had ridden the men of the Crusades coming in from Notre-Dame du Puy. In sober fact, they, or others indistinguishable from them, had stood there ever since the days of Roman Gaul, since the days of that Roman road past the remains of which the car had just been driven.

"From the moment that I first read Virgil," thought Jerphanion, "the hill of Brives has always seemed to me the most Virgilian scene that one could ever hope to see. Now that I have been to north Italy, I know that there are other places just as Virgilian, perhaps even more so, because they are without that little extra something that one gets here. But, for all that, the feeling I had then is just as strong as it ever was. The only difference is that I should perhaps describe it rather differently, should be tempted to say that it was a scene from Virgil overlaid with the slow accretions of the French Middle Ages, a sort of added quality of spirit that breathes of mountain songs and stained-glass skies."

"You see," said Grousson, "we're really a bit ahead of time. I'll drop you at the Hôtel de la Loire."

"Won't you come in and meet these gentlemen?"

"No . . . it would look as though I was begging an invitation. I get along with them pretty well in a general way, although I think there's rather too many of them, especially the younger ones, who like flirting with Bolshevism. If you can give them a word of warning on that score, some of us'll feel grateful. It will be better, I think, if I don't butt in today. . . . I'll look in at the committee rooms. . . . Too late to go back to the office; most of the staff will probably have left by this time. . . . We've fixed things up for tomorrow, haven't we? I won't bother you in the morning, because I know you've got an appointment with the prefect. After lunch we'll start out on the Monastier road. I'll call for you at the hotel."

"You know," said Jerphanion very earnestly, "I really feel rather guilty about all this. I accepted your offer without thinking. But I realize now what a change in your plans it must mean. There's no particular reason why you should make a trip tomorrow—you wouldn't normally have gone until next week."

"Bah! What does it matter when I go? It's glorious weather, and next week it may be snowing. . . . I'm my own master. . . . My work isn't a matter of ruled lines like a sheet of music-paper."

"Well, but you wouldn't have waited until afternoon to start, and now, because of me, you'll have to sleep on the road."

"It makes a change from time to time . . . and it'll please one of my customers. I'll probably stop at Vidal's place. . . . Besides, even granting that it does mean altering my plans a bit, you wouldn't like to stop me doing my bit for the republican cause, now, would you?"

Confronted by such an argument, Jerphanion felt that he could only yield gracefully. But there was one more thing he felt he must mention.

"I've promised, you know, to lunch with this Monsieur Pouzols-Desaugues. . . . Perhaps I was a fool to accept."

"Do you want me to drive you there?"

"Certainly not. He's going to send his car to the hotel for me."

"Then I'll pick you up at his place. It won't be more than ten minutes out of our way. I think you said your first meeting was at half past three?"

"Yes—or three forty-five."

"Then I'll be there at half past two. That'll give us plenty of margin for the climb. You know where he lives?"

"On top of the spur that rises above Brives, isn't it?"

"Yes. But it's not so much a spur as a plateau."

"I didn't realize that. But tell me—don't you think it may have been rather foolish of me to say I'd go—from the political point of view, I mean?"

Grousson's expression was eloquent of broad-mindedness:

"He's looked on as rather reactionary. He still sits as a member of the general council over at Saugues, where his wife comes from. But he doesn't play much part in local affairs. He wants to be on good terms with everybody. You can speak quite freely about him to the prefect, and I should be very much surprised to hear that he'd raised any difficulties about your going."

He thought for a moment or two, then: "I said he didn't play much part in local affairs; but he's pretty well thought of in some quarters, for all that—in the Bishop's palace, for instance. I'm pretty sure that if he talks of you later on as a capable and intelligent young fellow, rather too far to the Left, perhaps, but with a wide outlook, it'll have a very different effect from what it would if he said he'd thought you a doctrinaire and fanatic. There's ways and means in these matters, and if the parish priests and the members of religious bodies don't vote for you, they can at least be persuaded to—well, to moderate their opposition. A thousand votes are very easily diverted. . . . No, on the whole, I can't see that it'll do you any harm. . . . Well, then, half past two tomorrow. I'll ring the bell, but I won't bring the car inside his gate."

Jerphanion smiled. He couldn't help thinking of the Abbé Cabirol and Monsignor Lebaigue.

# Chapter

## 2

### JERPHANION'S FULL-DRESS SPEECH AT THE LE PUY LUNCHEON

As soon as coffee had been served, the chairman of the luncheon committee, who happened also to be president of the Haute-Loire Teachers' Association, introduced Jerphanion to the company in a few words and called on him to speak.

Jerphanion had given a great deal of thought to what he should say. He had not, however, prepared any sort of set speech, nor even jotted down any consecutive notes. Five or six main headings, which he regarded as essential to his argument, he had got firmly fixed in his mind; for the rest, he was determined to rely on the inspiration of the moment. A few phrases had suggested themselves to him, and these he would introduce as he went along, provided they did not lead him too far from his main theme. An audience likes a carefully thought-out piece of oratory, but what it likes still more, what gives it a sense of conviction, is to feel that it is listening to the natural and spontaneous development of the speaker's thoughts. Besides, if one is not too straitly confined within the limits of a prearranged plan, one need not be too cautious. The prejudices of the various listeners are, as it were, in abeyance. No one is likely to take offence at what may, after all, be no more than a casual sally, and the more conversational the tone, the greater is this margin of freedom.

He rose, glanced round the room, and tried to calculate how many there were present. "About two hundred," the chairman had told him a few minutes earlier. "A hundred and fifty to a hundred and eighty," was his silent correction of that total. It comprised about thirty women, most of them young.

All the faces were turned towards him. "A thoroughly nice lot," he hurriedly decided. "They mean well by me. There may be a few fanatical extremists among them, but taken by and large, they are a thoroughly decent, well-educated lot, who take their job seriously and have a sincere respect for honest thought. I feel in tune with them, and I shall speak to them only of what I hold to be true and just."

He began slowly, and in a conversational tone:

"My dear friends, you know, or if you don't, your chairman has told you, by what right I use that word. I was born in a village of this, of your, countryside—a village no different from those in which most of you live and work. My father was the local schoolmaster, and I began my education under his care. I continued it at the secondary school of this town. I was intended for the teaching profession, and actually followed it for a number of years. I still, officially, belong to it. . . . So, you see, there is every chance that we shall understand one another.

"I am very grateful to you for having invited me to this luncheon. Why? Because it is a private and intimate entertainment organized by yourselves. The fact that you have asked me, an outsider, is, I consider, a mark of confidence. You all of you know that I am standing as a candidate at the next Parliamentary elections. Such a mark of confidence on your part, therefore, takes on a particular significance.

"I fully realize that you are free men, and that by welcoming me among you here today you are in no way committed to become my supporters. I want to make that point quite clear. By so doing I hope to put you at your ease. . . ."

He had been careful to maintain a light, friendly tone, letting his eyes wander over the faces nearest to him as he spoke. His auditors responded with a little ripple of laughter which showed them to be in a sympathetic mood.

"Whatever line of action you eventually decide to adopt, you will be able, this afternoon, to get a pretty good idea of me—of me, I mean, in my role of prospective candidate, of the political faith which I now hold and which I shall maintain in the Chamber in the event of my being elected. This will be all the easier for you to do since it is my intention to speak with complete frankness. . . . Oh, I don't mean to say that in my ordinary addresses to voters I shall indulge in lies, of course I shan't. . . ." The laughter was more marked this time, and the women audibly contributed to it. "But you must realize that I shall not always have time to work out my thoughts in detail, that I shall have to simplify if I am to make myself generally comprehensible, and that at times I may even have to refrain from dwelling on certain subtleties for fear that they may be misunderstood. This is a point which I need hardly stress in speaking to you, since it is precisely your job to formulate abstract and not seldom very complicated truths in such a way that they will be capable of assimilation by listeners whose degree of education differs very considerably. . . . No one, I feel, will be better suited than you to pass judgment on my ideas in general and on my political program in particular."

Once again he glanced round the assembled faces. Already he was beginning to pick out a few from the crowd, by reason of the particular kind of interest that they expressed. He had time to notice a wave of encouraging assent, and set himself to cultivate it.

"As a matter of fact, your opinion is of considerable importance. That it should be is a cause of very real annoyance to those who don't happen to like you, but that it is remains an undoubted fact. You may not set out deliberately to exercise influence, but you do, and it is a continuous influence. I don't say that you could, in the course of a few months, succeed in changing the attitude of those who are opposed to you in principle—and would most certainly be opposed to me. But I do say that any opinion you may form today with the scrupulous honesty of mind for which you are renowned will stand a very good chance of being shared, in a few months' time, by the great majority of republicans living in this department."

He got the impression that his listeners were by this time in a most favourable state of mind. He stopped speaking and for the next few seconds appeared to be sunk in thought.

"You may be saying to yourselves: 'Why should this young fellow, who could have done so many things with his life, who had'" (he spoke the next few words with great emphasis) "'a fine profession waiting for him, one of the finest in the world—why should this young fellow start messing about with politics?' I will answer that question. In the first place I have not said good-bye to my profession. I have merely been granted a period of leave 'for personal reasons.' I am sure, dear friends and colleagues, that you have no difficulty in recognizing the phraseology of officialdom." The kind of pleased laughter with which people in the know greet an esoteric reference ran through the room. The women's voices seemed to predominate. "Well, politics, I know, don't have any too good a press in these days. Rightly or wrongly we think that our political chiefs have led us—or let us slide—into disastrous adventures, and that later, when it became a question of getting us out of them, or of doing their best to liquidate the consequences, they gave no sign that they had become either more clear-sighted or abler." This passage produced considerable applause, which Jerphanion interpreted as an invitation to indulge in hostile and facile criticism. "I'm afraid," he thought, "that they are going to be disappointed. Well, so much the worse!"

"I am prepared to admit," he went on, speaking now more quietly and very much more slowly, "that many of them carry the weight of a grave responsibility. It may be with the idea of lessening that weight, or of putting off the evil day when they shall have to give an account of their stewardship, that they have agreed—sometimes in a rather unusual fashion—to resume the 'burden of power.'"

This reference to Poincaré was received with the same type of applause.

"But what would you have? Those who blackguard all political leaders in general, and, in fact, the very idea of politics, seem to forget that a country can scarcely avoid having some sort of public life, and, consequently, men ready to conduct that public life. When we are satisfied with the men who conduct our public life, we call them representatives of the people and statesmen. When we are not, we refer to them as politicians." This time the applause was punctuated by laughter. "I am afraid that only the very simple-minded really believe that we can do without them.

"Oh, don't misunderstand me! I perfectly realize that among those who cry the loudest about the necessity of 'getting rid of the politicians' there are many who are very far from being simple-minded." The tone of his voice was slowly rising. "The politicians whom *they* want to get rid of are precisely those who are elected and controlled by the people, and their object is to replace them by others who shall be nominated either by the arbitrary will of one man or by the sinister machinations of a clique." The room burst into loud and appreciative applause. "In short, what they are after is not to take the goods off the market, but merely to change the shop that supplies them." Renewed applause, half drowned in laughter, greeted these words. "The manœuvre is not unknown to us. We have heard it described by our fathers and grandfathers. There was once a man called Louis Napoleon who made himself famous by replacing 'politicians' called Lamartine, Ledru-Rollin, and Victor Hugo by nominees of his own who bore such names as the Duc de Morny, Rouher, Tom, Dick, or Harry. And we know too what happened then. . . ." He paused.

"There is in the world today a certain Benito Mussolini who is well on the way to making himself famous by just such a performance. He, too, claims to be ridding his country of the politicians. What is Fascism if not an attempt to place the whole public life of a country in the hands of a faction and its leader, or, if you prefer, to substitute for freely elected representatives a gang of uniformed politicians trained to obey orders, men in whose eyes the people are no more than a flock of sheep to be directed hither and thither at will? The results in this case, no less than in the former, are rapidly becoming visible. The odious act of aggression against Corfu, the latest stroke of armed force at Fiume, are a timely lesson to us that though our own political leaders were unfortunately incapable of saving us from a war, we should be ill advised to rely on the power of a collection of dragooned politicians to maintain peace in the Europe of tomorrow —to say nothing of their activities in their own country against the liberty and dignity of individuals and of groups."

He had delivered this portion of his speech in a loud voice and without a break. It was greeted with what the newspapers call "noisy and prolonged applause." Mussolini and Fascism were already becoming a red rag to audiences of Left sympathies.

Jerphanion now changed his tone, and when he resumed, it was on a solemn, muted note, as of a man engaged in searching his conscience. Nor had he ceased to be aware of his surroundings. Among the few faces which he had already picked out from the mass, one in particular riveted his attention. It was that of a man of about forty, with a moustache, a pair of eyeglasses, and eyes that impressed by their air of thoughtful honesty. He was sitting at the corner of a table to the right of the room, full in the light of a window.

"But we should never forget that even we, living in a country where political leaders are freely elected and where government is controlled by the representatives of the people, are not wholly guiltless of hypocrisy and cowardice if we try to fasten on them alone responsibility for the faults that they commit. It was always, remember, open to us to choose better. It was always open to us to exercise more effective control. I will go further and say that it was within our power, whenever opportunity arose, to open our neighbours' eyes to the faults which were about to be committed, and in that way to bring public opinion to bear upon our leaders and our governments. I will go further still. It is hardly fitting for those of us who, knowing themselves to be gifted for political life, abstained, whether because they wanted to lead a quiet life or from any other motive, from entering the arena, to cast the first stone at the 'politicians.' The 'politicians' can always counter by saying: 'What proof have you that in our place you would have done any better? If you felt so sure that you could, it was your duty to come forward.'

"Speaking for myself, I have always, since before the war—that is to say, since the days of my earliest youth—recognized the necessity of political action, and it was always my dream—a very vague dream, I admit—that I might some day play a part in public life. The war, in which I served like many of you under conditions of great hardship, forced me to realize a number of truths, the first being that the sole advantage of such disasters is that they may teach us to inquire into their origins and make it possible for us to avoid their recurrence. It was driven in on me too that only those are entitled to inveigh against the horror of events and the mad devastation of fate who can honestly say that they did everything in their power, when the opportunity was theirs, to control the events and to counter with intelligence and good sense the operations of fate. Finally, I was forced to recognize that my own generation would carry a particular load of responsibility if it ever again allowed history to be made according to the dictates of blind chance."

Jerphanion was still conscious of a general attitude of sympathy among his listeners. This atmosphere of support was concentrated for him in the few faces which he had picked out, and particularly in that one which had become for him the central point of reference of the room. A sudden thought flashed into his mind: "Whatever the future may hold, I shall never regret having been present at this meeting, having spoken as I have done to these people. My words will not be entirely lost. My concern is to be of service to the truth and to the future. . . . After all, whether or not I am elected is a matter of very secondary importance." He continued:

"And now I am going to confess to an error of judgment of which I was guilty in the days of my youth. I had a friend in those days, a school-teacher of Paris, a year or two older than myself, called Laulerque. I was at that time a student at the École Normale in the rue d'Ulm. What I am going to tell you happened in what is now, alas, the distant past—twelve years ago. . . . I was full of liberal ideas on all sorts of questions—we all were. . . . This teacher friend of mine used to say to us: 'It's all to the good that you should be generous-minded about the various problems of the day. But the only really important problem at the moment is whether the world war which is due to make its appearance within the next two or three years will or will not break out. If it does break out, then our possible attitude to the other problems of our day will cease to be a matter of any interest to anybody. When a fire which has been smouldering in the woods reaches your house, the pleasant plans which you had been turning over in your mind for repapering the walls or changing round the furniture in your bedroom look like so many bad jokes.' Perhaps I ought to point out, to avoid misunderstanding, that my friend Laulerque had no belief whatever in the advantages of war. He did not even believe in it as a valuable prologue to revolution. From his point of view, war could have no other result than the piling up of devastation and the recrudescence of a state of barbarism." He changed his tone and fixed his gaze deliberately on those among his auditors who were wearing the ribbon of the Croix de Guerre. "And what, may I ask, do *you* think? Should you say that my friend Laulerque was very far wrong in his diagnosis?" There was an outburst of applause, started by the wearers of the Croix de Guerre and spreading to the rest of the room.

"His final attitude may be summed up as follows: 'Seen in terms of action, the only urgent problem today is how to prevent this war from occurring, how to stamp on the sparks before they set the wood on fire. All other questions can wait until later. . . .' The actual means that he himself took to prevent war and extinguish the sparks were, perhaps, of a rather romantic and fanciful kind. They are another story, and it is not my intention to say more about them now. The point I want to make is rather different. He got into the way of repeating his warning in and out of season until we were sick of it—it became like old Cato's '*delenda Carthago.*' Speaking for myself, I considered that the thing was becoming a mania with him, an *idée fixe.*" He let his voice take on a note of self-mockery. "I found his attitude too strictly limited. . . . You see, I did not share his certainty about the threatening proximity of war. For me war was merely one possibility among others—a possibility, moreover, of which I had formed but a pale and colourless image. At heart I was an optimist. I hoped, without giving the matter too much thought, that everything would turn out for the best. There were so many more exciting problems to be considered, so many questions which, in my view, were filled with a positive content and might be regarded as of enormous significance for the future. My friend Laulerque reminded me, with a difference, of those nationalists of a past day for whom all political and social questions faded into insignificance before the one vital necessity of being armed and ready. The only difference between them lay in one word of the refrain which they both sang. 'We must prepare for war' became, in his mouth: 'We must prevent a war.' Otherwise his attitude seemed to me to be just as narrow as theirs. I refused to treat the problem of peace or war as something which could be considered in isolation. To my mind, the causes of armed conflict had to be sought in the profundities of the social and economic order. I thought it superficial and out of date to behave as though one could take action against threats of war which were of a more or less episodic nature, instead of first attempting to modify the permanent and essential causes of armed struggle which are inseparable from the social and economic organization of the community. . . ."

A good deal of emphatic applause came from a table to the right of the room. Apart from this there was no general display of feeling, but it was clear that the audience as a whole was showing increasing interest in his words.

"This attitude, let me say, astonished me the more as coming from one whose ideas were, for the most part, extremely advanced, who was never averse to entertaining the most extreme of the Left-wing theories. . . . He was on terms of far greater intimacy than I had ever been with men in the revolutionary movement. His chief grievance against them had always been that they were lacking in a spirit of genuine audacity. For instance, he regarded the Unified Socialists as a lot of old women." A certain amount of mocking laughter came from the table on the right and seemed to be deliberately prolonged.

Jerphanion paused, and when he resumed, the tone of his voice had once more changed.

"A few years later, when I was in the trenches—and I don't think I need remind you that one had a good deal of time for thinking in the trenches—" (more laughter, this time marked by sympathy, came from the wearers of the Croix de Guerre) "my mind turned more than once to Laulerque and that mania of his. I think I was better able then to appreciate it. You, ladies, can have no idea how a certain amount of frozen mud round one's feet and the sound of shells going to and fro above one's head render one susceptible to thoughts of that nature. . . ." Most of the laughter this time came from the female element in the audience and seemed to hold a hint of grateful recognition. "The more conscious I became of the spreading disease of destruction, of the growing devastation, both material and moral, the more sure I was that he had been right, and that his outlook had been marked by vigour and depth. It became clear to me that the relative urgency of problems have, in practice, what may be called a hierarchy of their own, which is quite different from the hierarchy adopted in the text-books of philosophy. He would be but a superficial writer who should, in a work on theory, presume to discuss the problem of war without first analysing the influences—so various and so hard to apportion justly—which combine to produce a state of war in the modern world. The student cannot but realize that, for instance, the problem of capital, the problem of large-scale industry, the problem of over-population, or, in a field with which you are familiar, the problem of forming the minds of children and adolescents, are each, and together, of greater importance than the actual problem of war itself, because they dominate and condition its every aspect. But at any given moment of history what counts is the relative degree of urgency. The urgency of a problem may be so acute, so vital, that all other problems have to be relegated to the background. When that is the case, the search for underlying causes becomes merely a Byzantine futility, to be considered only later when time allows."

He broke off, busily searching in his mind for some concrete instance of what he meant, the sort of instance employed by school-masters. But those which first occurred to him, all of them drawn from history, lacked in themselves that weighty, schematic quality which they should have to be really illuminating. Like all examples taken from history, they were controversial. He chose, therefore, to fall back on analogy, since an analogy, like a magnifying glass, has the property of enlarging the object looked at without overmuch distorting. He remembered that he was dealing with listeners who were familiar with the powers of the magnifying glass and, though they were not fooled by the part played in its employment by illusion, could appreciate its proper uses.

"Take, for example, the case of a doctor some sixty years ago, called in to treat a patient suffering from an acute attack of typhoid. He would be ignorant of the real cause of the disease, because the theory of microbes had not then been developed, and, unless he was a fool, he would be fully conscious of his ignorance. Would he, before embarking on a course of treatment, say to himself: 'It is essential that I first discover the underlying cause of typhoid. It is no good merely attacking the symptoms . . .'? No, he would do nothing of the kind, unless he was quite mad. He would deal with the case in the best way he could, and without wasting a moment; and if he was a good doctor, he might even save his patient's life.

"The situation in politics is much the same. The statesman must be able to see clearly what matters most at any given moment; must be capable of grasping the relative degree of urgency, of recognizing the hierarchy. Political genius consists primarily in just that—the power of summing up a situation . . . at a later stage it must also be gifted with the power of grasping imaginatively the way of dealing with it. No doubt you teach your pupils that Henry IV, Richelieu, and Louis XI were all great statesmen. But what precisely do you mean by that? You mean that they could, each of them, approach the problems of their times with a keen sense of their relative urgency and could then go straight to the point instead of aimlessly beating about the bush. Why was it that Napoleon, for all his military genius, was never a great statesman? Because, except on the battlefield, he never had any conception of the relative urgency of the problems with which he was faced. He never, for example, saw that the really important thing for France in the years following the Revolution was, not to conquer Europe, but to remain the strongest and most modern power on the

Continent, and so to act that she might extend the influence of her example and her ideology, while discouraging her enemies from attempting to attack her. What it certainly was not was to rouse a feeling of hatred so violent that sooner or later it was bound to issue in action. . . . Your answer will be that that wasn't what interested Napoleon. . . . I am inclined to agree with you."

There was some applause and a certain amount of laughter which sounded as though it were inspired by thoughtfulness. Jerphanion paused, then continued, with a return to his confidential manner:

"I met my teacher friend Laulerque again a short while ago. He is no longer a teacher. He has had all sorts of adventures. But I am not here tonight to tell you about him. He said: 'Well, was I right?' 'Yes, you were.' 'Unfortunately,' he replied, 'I rather think I still am.'

"I see exactly what he meant. Undoubtedly the situation today differs in a great many particulars from the situation in the years immediately preceding 1914. But the order of urgency is, alas, the same now as it was then. I repeat, alas! The millions of dead have not sufficed radically to change it. I agree with my friend Laulerque that in 1923 the one problem that dominates all others is the same as in 1910: how to prevent war, the recurrence of war; how to eliminate the fear, the obsession of war. If we can succeed in establishing for Europe, for the world, a long period of peace, and in giving to the peoples of the world a feeling of genuine confidence in the power of that peace to last, the solution of all our other difficulties will be comparatively easy. For instance, the present financial embarrassment of governments is due to the fact that no long-range plans are possible. As things are, if such plans are produced, no one believes in them. Money is perfectly willing to be employed in short-term operations at, if possible, a very high rate of interest, but it mistrusts the future. And it mistrusts the future primarily because it mistrusts the duration of the peace. This state of financial stringency results too from the lack of enthusiasm shown by the nations of the world to help one another. The victors are afraid that if they help the vanquished, they may be providing them with the means of preparing a war of revenge. Among the victors themselves the richer nations are afraid that if they help their poorer or more exhausted nighbours, they may see their subsidies used for the purpose of building up a military hegemony, or to strengthen one of yesterday's allies who may be among tomorrow's foes. It would be very foolish of us to underestimate the importance of this condition of financial stringency, or to hand it over, scornfully, for treatment by the professionals of capitalism. For this stringency is as much a cause as an effect. It is perpetuating the morbid conditions which gave it birth, and is increasing the chances of a new war by making impossible the development of normal relations between the countries of the world. As a result of it we see arising on all sides policies of isolation and even of economic hostility. The severity of this economic struggle is growing daily, and in the long run it is bound to produce a struggle of a different kind. Finally, it makes it impossible for the various governments to realize, within their own frontiers, those reforms without which our form of society cannot long continue."

The attention of his audience was now deeply engaged. The restrained nature of the applause was not due to any lack of approval, but rather to a desire not to disturb the general intellectual response of the audience.

"I mentioned reforms . . . and I maintain that the mere existence of a durable peace would go a long way to solving, or at least modifying, most of our social difficulties, in fact if not in theory. In this connexion let me tell you of another of my friend Laulerque's pet ideas. He explained it to me when I saw him again after my return from Russia." There was a noticeable movement among his hearers. "What it comes to is that we must take into consideration the immense technical resources of the modern world. Never let us forget, ladies and gentlemen, that the money, the labour, and the technical equipment expended during one single day of the late war would have sufficed to establish and endow any one of those social enterprises which we have been demanding for the last twenty years. A world at peace would soon accumulate all the resources it needs, and these it could scarcely help distributing widely and in accordance with a carefully

planned program. For even the greediest capitalist could hardly con-
sume unaided all the hams or keep for his own use all the sewing-
machines which he produced. Even without any modification of our
present social structure—and I by no means exclude the possibility
of a good many modifications—a large number of reforms would
automatically ensue. But so long as the governments and peoples of
the world live in constant fear of a new war, whether in the near or
the distant future, any such expansion remains impossible. The nations will continue to live from hand to mouth and in a constant state
of alarm. In such conditions any modification of structure can be
brought about only by violence, and at the risk of imperilling the very
existence of the countries which may undertake the experiment. . . ."
His words were greeted by what, in press reports of public meetings,
are called "varying degrees of response."

"You have all seen for yourselves what has happened since the
war. . . . Five years ago, ladies and gentlemen, five years and one
month, to be precise, the bugles sounded the armistice! While we
were fighting we were given solemn promise that the first, the main,
result of victory would be to slay the giants of war and of militarism
once and for all. We were to see the birth of world peace. . . . Let
us not be too hasty in assuming that we were the victims of lies.
Many, if not all, who talked in that way were perfectly sincere. From
time to time I am brought into contact with some of those who played
an important part during those years, who still play an important part
in the councils of Europe. . . . I hear them speak in their unguarded
moments, listen to their real thoughts. Sometimes what they say has
a strong smack of cynicism—they are not, remember, carefully choos-
ing their words as they would for a public utterance. . . . But this I
will say, I have never yet come across one who did not, in his heart
of hearts, long for a durable peace. Even the most aggressive confine
themselves to some such fairly moderate statement as: 'We must see
to it that the people are not lulled into a state of excessive tranquillity,
for that would result in a loss of virility, and, in addition, make it
impossible to govern them.' The same idea can be expressed in an-

other way by interpreting their words as meaning: 'By all means paint militarism as black as you like, but see to it that you keep at least a small standing army. Standing armies are indispensable as schools of discipline for the young, and as a guarantee of order at home.' So widely held is that idea that even when the peace treaty was drawn up, no one seriously denied even to the conquered countries the right of maintaining small standing armies. The only points in dispute were the actual numbers to be permitted and the method of their organization.

"I have spoken of the peace treaty. My words applied to those responsible for it. Almost all those—and I refer now to the victors, who drew up and imposed its terms—almost all, the French, their European allies, the Americans, were sincere. They honestly wished to build a durable peace, and they were animated by no love of militarism. Let me add—in reply to certain lines of criticism, and to tendencies in some quarters to attach excessive blame to its authors— that though it was their declared object to make the Central Powers pay for a disaster the responsibility for which they all shared to at least an equal degree, the negotiators were not animated by any deep-seated sense of hate or by any strong desire for vengeance. There was nothing particularly villainous in their intention. The misfortune was that within any given country, such as France, and between the various countries concerned, there existed a division of opinion as to the best means of ensuring a durable peace. This lack of unity resulted sometimes in feeble compromises, sometimes in inconsistencies and even in deplorable changes of attitude.

"It is essential to realize too that though the war may have resulted in a victory over militarism, it did nothing to diminish the fever of nationalism. So far from that being the case, the nationalistic movement of the older countries was scarcely even weakened, while the world had now to take into account the new-born and intractable patriotism of a dozen or so freshly organized nations.

"All things considered, the Treaty of Versailles was not too bad a document. Of course it contained mistakes and injustices. But it is right that we bear in mind the number of mistakes and injustices which it tried honestly to clear up. It is attacked on the ground that it was not constructive. That is a stupid criticism. The treaty which established the League of Nations was most certainly a constructive instrument, one of the most constructive instruments known to history." The applause was on a much modified scale, and this time was a fair indication of the lack of enthusiasm in the audience. Jerphanion was quite aware of this and had, indeed, expected no less.

"I know," he continued with a smile, "that the League of Nations, like the politicians, habitually gets a bad press. Attention is concentrated on its sins of omission or on the obstacles it is said to put in the way of international understanding. Some go so far as to accuse certain governments of making use of it in a spirit of insincerity and without any real wish to see it succeed.

"I hardly imagine that you expect me to embark on a pæan of praise in honour of the various governments which have successively come to power in France since the armistice, and in particular since the resignation of Briand, which was brought about by an actual trial of strength." Here he was interrupted by a loud burst of applause. "My impression is that our feet are set on a dangerous road." The applause redoubled. The audience seemed pleased to be able once again to show its entire approval of the speaker.

"But we must not forget the faults committed by others. The most extraordinary of these faults, the most demoralizing, let me say, and, I am inclined to add, the one that will entail the most serious consequences in the long run, was that committed by America. You, my friends who were in the trenches at the same time as I, will remember the wave of encouragement which swept over us when we heard President Wilson's messages and knew that the Americans had intervened. By entering the war, President Wilson's America made available for us powerful material resources, and later sent us a fine body of men who, though they may have had·rather too much baggage—" the wearers of the Croix de Guerre grinned broadly— "and were rather too much inclined to take their time and perfect their precautions, did give us assistance which, in the long run, could not be overestimated. We were terribly tired, and America set the scales of war tipping in our favour. But, above all, she gave us a new faith, made it possible for us to believe in the value of what we were doing, to hope that the appalling massacre would not be entirely in vain. Wilson had behind him, without, perhaps, altogether realizing it, millions and millions of Europeans, men who were themselves engaged in the struggle and for whom his voice spoke in the name of the future. Unfortunately, he had behind him only a section of the American public. You know the whole sorry tale. The League of Nations, proposed, not to say imposed, by America, suddenly found itself repudiated and abandoned by her. America, which had dictated so many of the clauses of the Treaty of Versailles, refused to sign it. But that was not the worst. America, having induced us to renounce certain territorial guarantees of security in exchange for a guarantee given by herself in partnership with Great Britain, went back on her word and refused to implement that guarantee. . . ."

This time the audience, instead of applauding, marked its agreement by a scarcely perceptible murmur which was like nothing so much as an audible drop in the temperature of the room.

"We are all so grateful to America, are all so conscious of the old bonds of friendship which unite us to her, that we feel a certain embarrassment about what we think of her behaviour, and especially of the terrible short-sightedness from which it sprang. . . . Clemenceau tried to put something of our feelings into words in the course of his tour through the United States last winter. . . . My admiration for Clemenceau is not without reservations. . . . I am not at all sure that he found the right way of dealing with Wilson at Versailles, or that he was really whole-hearted in his attempts to smooth the President's path . . . and I am inclined to accuse him of still more serious errors; I think that he lacked faith in our ideal of international justice, that he never believed sufficiently in those generous impulses which are to be found, side by side with others, deep down in human nature, impulses to which Jaurès, up to the end of his life, never failed to make such stirring appeals—" the whole room broke into enthusiastic clapping—"impulses in which *we* believed even while we fought. If we had not so believed we should have stopped fighting . . ." (another burst of clapping led by the group of veterans). "It is such impulses which France, true to her traditions and to her sense of mission, has always sought to enlist on her side" (renewed applause). "Clemenceau is a pessimist, a misanthrope, a cynic. He is also a man of yesterday. It is probably true to say that he was supremely fitted to win that particular war, which struck the death-knell of an old world. He certainly was not fitted to achieve the peace —this particular peace, the function of which was to ring in a new world." (A note of solemn enthusiasm was audible now in the applause.) "But I read in *L'Illustration* the text of his American speeches, or rather of the single speech which he delivered with variations wherever he went. Read it for yourselves. He said a number of very true things, made several simple and forcible points. He said, for instance, to his American audiences: 'You came too late and left too soon.' He pointed out that their present policy of isolation is not only an offence against the duty which they had themselves recognized and voluntarily shouldered, but a source of danger to them in the future. He tried to make them understand that the situation of France is not an easy one, and that if she seems to have the idea of security on the brain, there is every reason for it. . . . The Americans welcomed Clemenceau, the Tiger, with brass bands and acclamation. I am far from certain that they paid much attention to his words. That is to be regretted. . . ." He smiled, and a new note came into his voice.

"It is my intention, provided my political life is not cut short—and that depends upon my neighbours of the district of Velay—to make a trip to America in the near future, just as I made a trip to Russia, with the object of satisfying myself about just what we can and cannot expect of its inhabitants. . . ." He broke off, only to continue a moment later on a note of light badinage: "Don't encourage me to talk fatuous nonsense. . . . It is not my expectation that I shall get results where Clemenceau got none, but, as I said before, I want to see for myself what France has to hope for from that side of the Atlantic, to say nothing of what there may be for us to learn in the matter of industrial methods and technique, since I understand that the pace of American production is so very much in excess of our own. . . .

"To go back to what I was saying. There were faults committed by America. There were faults committed by England. The latter were of a different kind, but the picture which they offer is scarcely more agreeable to contemplate. Here too we present the unpleasing spectacle of people hanging on to the coat-tails of friends who have had enough of us. . . . I do not know England well. I had no opportunity of going there before 1914, and since the war I have paid no more than three visits to London, all of them short, all of them of an official nature, so that though I came in contact with a number of leading personalities, it was not possible for me to study the life of the people at close range. . . ." He had resumed his air of confidential friendliness. "I went in company with the political leader with whom I was at that time, with whom I still am, working. In short, what it comes to is that my ideas about England have been mainly formed by that aspect of her conduct which it has been open to all to see and ponder. Let us not go back to the period before the war—there is no end to the amount of digging up the past in which we might indulge. During the war itself she was a firm ally—slow, perhaps, but firm—and far from easy to handle. . . . I will put the whole thing in a nutshell and say that she rendered us a great service, not so great a service, possibly, as we rendered her, but still of the same general nature. . . ."

His listeners were following him with the most careful attention, marking their agreement by little grunts and movements of the head.

"Since the war the general impression she gives is that she has seen enough of us, that she finds us tedious and tiresome and for ever putting forward ridiculous claims, ready to exploit the situation in our own favour, and not altogether beyond suspicion of wishing to immobilize the poor old Continent beneath the armed might of the Republic. . . ."

"And she is perfectly right," said a quiet voice speaking from that table to the right of the room to which his attention had already been drawn more than once.

"No, my dear sir," replied Jerphanion just as quietly, "I do not agree. She is not perfectly right. . . ." A considerable portion of the audience applauded. ". . . In any case England started to attribute these sinister motives to us and to use them as a justification of her own attitude a considerable while before our policy took the direction which we all know it has taken, and which I disapprove no less than you. As a matter of fact, she is herself largely responsible for what has happened in France." (Sporadic applause.) "There seems to be a feeling in England that the country really deserving of sympathy, compassion, and encouragement is Germany. I don't say that such an attitude is general, but from what I heard in influential circles, it certainly does exist. There are people there who hold the view that Germany has been victimized. They are within measurable distance of regretting that they ever helped us to fight her. I got an impression that England is indulging in a good deal of quiet encouragement of Germany against us, against honestly carrying out her part of the treaty. Across the Channel all sorts of old anti-French prejudices are raising their heads. . . . If there is one man I detest—I can mention his name here because this is a private gathering—it is Lloyd George. He seems to me to embody the least admirable characteristics of the British, with a few unpleasant qualities of his own added. You no doubt remember the ridiculous bombast in which he indulged during the war—stuff about hanging the Kaiser, and similar nonsense. . . . At the peace negotiations he certainly did more than Clemenceau to wear Wilson out and make a fool of him, and to prevent any frank and constructive solutions from being adopted. No one was more ingenious in laying traps for his colleagues, no one took more delight in flinging monkey-wrenches into the machinery. . . ." (Laughter and applause.) "One could go on for ever enumerating the dirty tricks he has played on us since Versailles, or tried to play, or got his tools to play for him. . . . There are moments when I am inclined to think that his whole political program might be summed up in the words: "pin-prick the French"—but not openly, oh no, always in an indirect and underhand manner. Why? Well, in the first place France was England's friend and ally—yesterday—and there is a good deal of the weathercock about Lloyd George. We have a weakness for thinking of our own politicians as weathercocks, but it would be a serious error to regard them as the champions of that particular type of acrobatics. No weathercock of the calibre of Lloyd George would ever make a career in France comparable to the one he has made in England." The audience relaxed in a burst of delighted laughter.

"There is, too, a permanent feature of the English character, of English politics— How can I best describe it without being unfair? . . . The English by and large are fond of their friends and would like to be loyal to them. But they don't like their friends to have overmuch good luck; they don't like their friends to reach a point at which they can do without them, and they dislike it still more when their friends depend too much on them. . . . At the very moment when one begins to feel sure of their friendship they like to make one feel that there are others also with a claim on them, that they can give their favours as they please, and scatter largesse in more directions than one. . . . They like playing seesaw—keeping one guessing. . . . It is all very complicated, and leads, naturally, to much complexity of behaviour. . . . The English have an inbred dislike of putting their cards on the table—or their hands either. I suppose it has something to do with their national character; I am quite sure that it has something to do with their history. England has never—or not, at least, for several centuries—been in a position to impose her unaided will on the other great peoples of Europe, or even on one of those peoples. She has never been strong enough, has never felt sufficiently sure of her unsupported power to take the risk. France has. Under Louis XIV she stood alone, during the Revolution, and under Napoleon. . . . So, unfortunately, has the Germany of Bismarck and William II—has, I mean, felt that she could take the risk. When a nation has, for several hundred years, felt itself in a position to take risks, it learns, under certain circumstances, to speak its mind, and when that country happens to be Germany, to speak with brutal frankness. England has always had to act with others, by means of others, often a large number of others, each one of whom, taken in isolation, was small or insufficient. No nation can speak frankly either to an enemy whom she cannot face alone, if it turns nasty, or to those she may eventually require as allies, and whose minds are not yet made up. . . . In such circumstances a country has got to manœuvre continually, sometimes with her enemy, sometimes with her allies, sometimes with both . . . and manœuvre means dissimulation. . . . When one is manœuvring with several persons at the same time it is difficult to be loyal to all—and even wholly loyal to any one of them." The smiles of the audience showed its appreciation of this piece of analysis.

"What the wisdom or the spite of the world has chosen to call 'English perfidy'—and such reputations are never wholly without cause—one hears a good deal of talk about French irresponsibility and French vanity, and charges of that kind irritate us—but there are such things as French irresponsibility and vanity. . . . Well, what is called English perfidy seems to me to be the effect of historical causes. . . . It should be noted in passing that the same world-wisdom has a good deal to say about German deceit and German brutality . . . and it would be strange indeed if we protested against such language! . . . Now, ladies and gentlemen, deceit is shown at the expense of the enemy, of the stranger, of Tom, Dick, and Harry, whereas it is the characteristic of perfidy to be exercised against friends, against intimates, against members of one's own family. . . . You will, I think, agree, ladies, that when one accuses a woman of perfidy—and I believe that does sometimes happen" (the ladies of the audience laughed unreservedly) "—one means that she is perfidious at the expense, not of the grocer at the corner, but of her husband or her best friend. . . . It looks as though perfidy were a poison produced by the same glands as are responsible for the emotions of friendliness . . . as something that occurs when those glands become worn out or undergo a change in their composition" (general laughter). "By behaving to us as they have done since the Treaty of Versailles the English have given ample proof that they regard us as their friends." The laughter broke out afresh, accompanied by a burst of lively applause.

Jerphanion began to realize that, if he continued at this rate, his speech looked like being a very long one. Not that he had noticed the slightest sign in his hearers either of weariness or of impatience. Far from that, the audience appeared to be delighted. There were signs that it felt particularly flattered to think that a future representative of the people, and in all probability a future statesman whose career might be watched by the whole country, was at such pains to make it the honoured recipient of his first public declaration. This was no mere after-dinner speech, but a long and serious address. Those present were, after all, teachers who knew from daily experience that no speaker with a due regard for his subject and for his audience could deal shortly with even the most elementary questions of policy.

"Unfortunately," thought Jerphanion while the applause was dying down, "I've still got a great deal to say. There are certain points I must touch on even though they are only the commonplaces of electioneering. If I didn't, they might later remember my omissions and draw injurious conclusions from my silence. . . . They're not going to complain about being kept rather a long time. . . . Still, there's a limit. I must try to work off the inevitable routine stuff as quickly as possible and without going too much into detail. That done, my conscience will be at rest and I can see how much time I've got left. . . . It'll play the devil, of course, with the orderly arrangement of my speech, but that can't be helped. . . . And it isn't, if it comes to that, a regular speech at all, and anyhow I can put more life into the business like that. . . . But I must find some plausible way of making the transition and of convincing them that if I make hay of logical sequence, I do so deliberately. . . . I mustn't forget that these are people who have learned how to order an argument."

"My dear friends," he resumed in a quiet and confiding tone, "I feel that I am taking an unfair advantage of your attention" (murmurs of protest), "that I am, perhaps, laying too much stress on what must seem, after all, to be nothing but generalities somewhat far removed from those questions of immediate interest which I shall have to deal with in Parliament—if I ever get there. . . . But I am sure you realize that our fate, and the fate of our children, are involved in these problems and in the way they are handled by those who represent us. That is something of which I need hardly remind the veterans of the last war, or you, ladies and gentlemen. Had anyone come forward while you were in tears because your husbands, your fathers, your brothers, your fiancés, were in the trenches, leaving you without news, and remarked that foreign policy was a subject little likely to interest you and better left to specialists, he would not have been very kindly received . . ." (loud applause). "That such would have been your feelings, my friends, is the meaning of democracy, the achievement of democracy . . . and it is this truth that you, particularly you educators of the young, have got to instil into the minds of the people. . . . Democracy is still in its infancy; its task has not yet been completed. In its early days it was held to apply only to certain spheres of our community life. For instance, between 1870 and the last war there were many excellent republicans, especially in the provinces, who would have said: 'Foreign policy is a matter for the Quai d'Orsay. What interests us is internal administration—the problems that are live issues in various parts of the country. . . . It is not the business even of our deputies, except of those few who have specialized in the subject, to get themselves mixed up in all this foreign business, all this diplomatic plotting and counter-plotting. Still less is it fitting for a simple citizen who is not a fool or a faddist to bother his head about what schemes the German Emperor or the King of England is hatching. His job is to see that a new railroad is installed in his own department, or a tax on doors and windows repealed. We have a Minister and a staff of civil servants whom we pay to concern themselves with the activities of foreign governments.' Such an attitude was a left-over from an earlier period, from a period when the people had not yet attained its majority, but was kept tied to the apron-strings of guardians and tutors who were not in the habit of asking its advice in matters of business. But now by stages we have reached a time when the people is no longer *in statu pupillare*. The people understand, for instance, that since they pay the taxes, they have a right to some say in matters of public finance. . . . That is one of the lessons they have not been slow to learn" (laughter). "Well then, as soon as the realization became widespread that it was the people without distinction of age or sex who made war—and it was not until 1914 that that truth was forced on them—they began to discover that the whole question of war, of the way it was planned, provoked, or avoided, was one of immediate and very real concern for them. The temptation to regard those who dealt with the problem as mere bores or as astrologers who went through life with their heads in the clouds ceased to be operative. Yes, my friends, so long as the man in the street or the peasant in the fields is not prepared to regard his country's foreign policy, at least in its wider aspects, as his own peculiar concern, as something in which he should be prepared to take an intelligent interest, just so long shall we be living in a bygone day. The moment he wakes to the fact, then and then only shall we be riding on the full tide of democracy" (loud applause). "One of the many proofs of Jaurès's greatness," continued Jerphanion, pressing his advantage, "was that he never ceased urging that truth on the working classes, even at times when the working classes would much rather have listened to inflammatory speeches about the inadequacy of wages or the eight-hour day. I don't mean that Jaurès was not interested in wages or the eight-hour day—his every action proved the contrary— but he had an eye for what I have called the hierarchy of problems, and since, whatever he was, he was not a demagogue, he had the rare courage to take the people into his confidence and make them see with his eyes." (Renewed and enthusiastic applause.)

Jerphanion glanced towards the gentleman with the moustache and the eyeglasses and fancied that he read in his face the evidence of quiet but whole-hearted agreement.

"Please don't think that I am not fully aware of the problems that affect you, and the people of this department, more particularly. To begin with yourselves: it is essential that steps be taken to defend your interests as a professional and corporate body. Your scale of salaries must be revised, and the same holds good for all officials and the members of the public services. The actual rate of pay is far from bearing a proper relation to the cost of living, and machinery must be set up to safeguard it in the future against further inconsistencies of the same sort. In this matter your professional organizations should be given the opportunity of examining the facts in conjunction with the representatives of the State. It is of the first importance that your unions be not only tolerated but recognized, and that, speaking generally, the right of officials to trade-union representation be no longer a matter of controversy."

Several of the tables expressed full-throated approval; others adopted an attitude of greater reserve.

"Please do not think that by confining my remarks to sectional interests I wish it to be understood that I am not fully aware that the whole vast problem of the relations subsisting between trade unions and the State has got to be reconsidered. . . . To mention only the most urgent and tangible aspect of the matter, it is intolerable that while whole sections of the population are busy amassing personal wealth at an indecent speed, those who directly serve the interests of the community should be reduced to want. Still less is it tolerable that veterans of the last war should be left in a condition of grinding poverty. I am all in favour of revising the law of pensions, and I should view with sympathy any general proposal tending to provide maintenance for the ex-soldier, provided always"—he repeated the phrase with impressive emphasis—"provided always that the self-respect and moral influence of the recipient are not impaired. Neither disability pensions nor maintenance grants, however right and proper in themselves, must be allowed to deteriorate into instruments of bribery or blackmail. It would be a national scandal should the past services of our veteran fighters be allowed to dwindle in their own eyes, or in those of the nation, to the stature of an unimportant item in the life of the community. The claims of these men, and I feel sure that you will agree with me, are outstanding, but they cannot be considered in terms merely of cash, nor can they be balanced by a simple award of material benefits and then comfortably forgotten. My own hope is that these men will remain always the creditors of their country, and that the moral element in their claim will never cease to be recognized. I will go further and say that these veterans of ours have a right to be consulted in the affairs of the nation, a right conferred on them in the hard school of experience. It is within their competence to see that certain errors of the past are never repeated, to prevent the progressive lowering of the standards of political and, more generally speaking, of public life, to insist that our governors and administrators be imbued with a spirit of far-sightedness and altruism, to remind the younger generations that the life of any nation is difficult, and subject always to external threats, to convince them that the future of the world cannot be planned in dance-halls and cabarets. As they grow older they will form a kind of Council of Elders, rich in numbers. Such a Council of Elders will be able to command the respect of the community only if no one can stand up and say: 'You cashed in to the last possible penny on your position as war veterans. From now on we don't want to hear you so much as mentioned.'"

Each one, almost, of his sentences had been followed by applause. Whenever his words had touched on material interests which were more or less those of his listeners or of a section of them, there had been in this applause a note of relief as well as of convinced approval, a sort of immediacy which was expressed by an increase of tempo, as though to say: "It was time someone mentioned that. We're always the ones to get fooled—and don't forget it." But these outbursts soon died down. When, however, the speaker turned to moral values, treating of what are generally referred to as "higher" interests, the applause, though perhaps less noisy, was steadier and lasted longer.

It was as though the audience felt that it could let itself go with an easier conscience.

"There is something fundamentally sound about the people of France," thought Jerphanion as he noted the subtle differences in the response evoked by his words. "Their instincts are noble. What chivalrous, what arduous tasks they can be induced to undertake if only they can be first persuaded that one doesn't take them for a pack of fools!" And he registered a silent oath that he would be one of those who should make his countrymen conscious of their own fitness for hard trials and deeds of chivalry. Enthusiasm for the life of politics caught at him suddenly with all the freshness and splendour of a new revelation. "Never let the element of bigness be absent even from practical affairs and the matters of every day. *Memento Magnitudinis.* The only difference between what I feel now and what I felt in the old days on the college roof and in our study is that then everything was vaguer, more in the air. . . . The artist must never let the great lines of his composition be swamped by detail. . . ." And then what he had just been saying about the war veterans and their rights reminded him of a conversation he had had with Jallez at a café on the Boulevards at the time of the Battle of Verdun . . . about the way in which the soldier gradually acquires a sense of caste, and how he reckons, if he comes through a war alive, on establishing his claim to privileges that shall be more than merely of the moment, as others had done in the old days with that acute nose of theirs for the actual and the possible. It was only human, after all, and, if one thought back to Haudromont Valley, not much more than just. Might it be that politics, too, were but the art of conveniently deleting considerations of truth, humanity, and justice if they cluttered up the picture overmuch, or if there was a risk that they might bring grist to the enemy's mill? But, thank God, there was no time now to indulge in private examinations of conscience. One of the advantages of action is that no sooner do things look like working up to a debate about matters of conscience than it is time to apply the closure.

"The same concern for justice," he went on, "compels us to inscribe upon our banner not only the revision of retirement pensions, but also a measure to ensure an improvement in conditions for all old people, whether in our cities or our countryside. We have a special duty to see justice done to the claims of the agricultural labourer. You who live, for the most part, in small hamlets, passing each day the humble war memorial, where such exists, or the simple marble plaque on the wall of the local mayor's office, know what the war cost the country folk of France. On this point it may be said with justice that three categories in particular of those called up for active service suffered more than average losses—the peasantry, school-masters, and—the students of the École Normale Supérieure in the rue d'Ulm."

The room burst into loud applause. There was a feeling in the air that by these words he had acknowledged the existence of a sort of moral debt, but the response had also in it an undercurrent of good-natured irony. Here and there, even, could be heard the sound of laughter.

"We owe it to the peasants in particular that some protection be given them against the middlemen, who alone are benefiting from the rise in prices. We owe it to ourselves, moreover, to see that they share less inadequately than in the past in the material rewards of modern civilization, such as roads, water-supply, and, more especially, the electrification of the countryside. . . . That is a by no means utopian program, and one that it should be possible to set in motion almost at once. I have no time now to go into its details. I shall have occasion at future meetings, both here and elsewhere, to discuss it more thoroughly. The point I want to stress now is that I am well aware of the problems involved, and that the summary way in which I have touched on them must not be taken as the measure of my interest in the subject, or of the care that I have taken to master it."

The sober applause which greeted these words was evidence that the audience was satisfied with the tone of this passing reference.

"As, no doubt, you will have noticed for yourselves, these remarks of mine are not to be regarded as part of a set speech. We are merely chatting here in an intimate and desultory fashion. Unfortunately we have not the time to cover the whole ground, and it should to some extent be covered if we are to avoid misunderstanding on the essential points. It must seem that I am doing all the talking. But in fact that is not so. Your reactions are not hard to gauge. I am, believe me, deeply conscious of them. I, too, am being taught a good deal today."

A ripple of contented laughter showed that his hearers were conscious of being subtly flattered.

"I should, for instance, have liked to go with you into the whole question of what sums will have to be found if this program of reforms—and it by no means covers the whole ground—is to be put on a practical footing. It is not an easy question—these things never are easy when one discusses them seriously with intelligent people and is not content merely to indulge in tub-thumping. In my opinion there are several ways in which the State might increase its revenues. Take, for a start, the organization of the taxes. There are a great many taxes, as I think you will agree, and they constitute a very heavy burden on those who pay them. But there are very many people who don't pay and who ought to. There are those who would raise the rate of the inheritance tax, the transfer tax, and the income tax. That is all nonsense. The rates in question are already excessive. By raising them still further you will only succeed in piling a still more crushing load on the back of the honest citizen. What is necessary is to devise some method by which people are prevented from slipping out of their responsibilities and cheating the community. I would take as a glaring example the present state of the income tax. The way it is levied is a crying scandal. With the exception of State officials, civil servants, and a few other unfortunate categories, no one pays the full amount, and that is especially true—it's no good blinking the fact—in the provinces."

There was a good deal of laughter at this, and marked applause. The audience seemed to be feeling proud of its courage in showing its support of the statement just made.

"And while we are on this subject of revenue, there is another scandal to which I should like to draw your attention—the scandal of war contracts. Not enough energy has been shown in having them revised. . . . Last year I happened to be dining one evening in Moscow with one of our old established war contractors—I had had to keep the engagement for professional reasons, and I trust you will forgive the lapse—who told us quite calmly that the State still owed him a trifle of eight millions. . . . He seemed to be rather less put out about it than I should have been if I had suddenly discovered that I was twenty francs short of what I thought I had in my wallet. . . . Apparently he felt pretty sure that he would get paid sooner or later. . . . If I was the State, I know well what I'd do. . . ."

The audience showed its approval with the high spirits of a lot of children at a Punch and Judy show.

"And then there is the scandal of reparations and war damage." ("I'm on safe ground," thought Jerphanion; "people here are not directly concerned. If I were standing for a Reims constituency, it would be quite different.") "We are full of love and respect for those who live in the devastated areas . . . but it is a matter of openly acknowledged and notorious fact that hovels worth no more than seven thousand francs have been replaced by neat, smart houses costing anything round fifty thousand to put up; that owners of out-of-date and tumbledown factories are receiving in compensation—and without putting their hands into their pockets for a penny—superb premises equipped with the latest thing in plants, so that we see what as a liability often amounted to barely a hundred thousand being suddenly transformed into an asset worth millions. . . . We know perfectly well, you and I, that a vast conspiracy is going on in that part of the world between contractors, architects, war victims, and experts. Since we know, too, in spite of anything the ineffable Monsieur Klotz may say, that it won't be Germany that does the paying, we feel a natural disinclination to foot the bill for this gigantic program of graft" (loud applause). "But I go further than that. I say that the whole principle of complete compensation is thoroughly unsound. I entirely fail to see in what way the small investor of Le Puy or Perpignan who has lost two thirds or three quarters of his capital as a result of trusting the State or the great public combines is less worthy of consideration, and less to be pitied than the small landed proprietor of Reims—to say nothing of those unfortunates who, with the intention of supporting our foreign policy, put all their savings into Russian bonds. . . . When the theory of reparations was worked out, did anyone give a moment's thought to these poor members of the public? . . . The problem should have been treated as a whole. A sort of national balance of profits and losses should have been struck, and partial but equitable compensation should have been assured to all these various categories of citizens, the money for which should have been found by a tax on all profits, added to the amount of the German payments. Is it too late now? To realize such a plan in its entirety, yes; but not to establish the principle for all future dealings."

The audience approved with much murmuring and shaking of heads. Its members, including the ladies, seemed delighted to think that the speaker was capable of dealing with all these thorny questions, and, better still, take up a personal and clearly defined attitude towards them. The eyes of the gentleman with the pince-nez and the moustache, as well as other eyes behind other pairs of glasses, seemed to be saying: "He's not just a phrase-maker. Obviously he's stuck his nose into all sorts of out-of-the-way corners, and he knows what he's talking about."

"You will say," continued Jerphanion, "or at least some of you will say"—and he addressed himself more particularly to one or two tables at the right side of the room, filled mainly by young people whose political sympathies had never for a moment been in doubt—"that measures such as I have outlined are possible only where a far more advanced collectivist system is installed than is the case in France. The same objection might be made to several of the reforms on which I have touched in passing, as well as to others which I have not had time to mention; if, that is to say, we really mean those reforms to be more than mere eyewash election slogans. . . ."

He stopped, sweeping the room before him with his gaze.

"My dear friends," he said with happy nonchalance, "I don't think I need be on my guard with you, and that is more than can always be said at a public meeting. Well, I am going to take advantage of the fact. I know that you will not twist my words. I know too that, whatever your personal views, you are not the kind of people to be easily frightened by phrases or by ideas. . . ."

There was a noticeable increase of attention.

"It would be childish to start talking of the social problem, or of particular social problems, and to pretend ignorance of the existence of a political theory the very essence of which is to provide a complete and systematic solution of all these separate problems as well as of the central problem itself: I refer to the theory of socialism. It would be no less childish to make a pretence of forgetting that at this very moment there is in existence a form of socialism which has shouldered vast responsibilities; which is in process of conducting a huge experiment, which for the first time in history on such a scale is setting the living facts of actuality against the dead facts of printed theory: Communism. The whole of Russia—that is to say, the largest country in Europe, occupying, if we add its Asiatic possessions, the sixth part of the land area of the world—forms the stage on which this experiment is working itself out. Russia is, from this point of view, in all minds. People respond to the challenge differently. According to their temperaments, they see Russia as a laboratory, as a model, as a threat. . . . I have no doubt that among you, and especially among those of you who are young, there may be found a number of Communists, or of sympathizers with Communism." He was being listened to now in complete silence. "If it were not so, I should be almost tempted to think it a pity, for it would prove that the younger generations of Frenchmen were inclined to settle down too soon, were lacking in any real interest in the movements now at work in the world." This sally produced a faint titter of laughter. "So you see, if I am elected, I am not likely to trot off to the prefect with a request for a strong hand with the hot-heads." There was another burst of laughter, and even those who did not share in it could not keep themselves from smiling.

"Well, I can hear you saying: 'We let you drivel on when you told us that the task of preserving peace, of establishing peace, took precedence of every other consideration, even of social problems . . . and later still when you enumerated a list of moderate reforms, which obviously would never come to anything. But our real opinion is that your attitude is a purely superficial one, and that your suggested remedies are like nothing so much as the steps taken in the story by the doctor who applied a poultice to a wooden leg. And ten or fifteen years ago you would have agreed with us, wouldn't you? In those days perhaps your friend Laulerque was right and you were wrong, and on two separate points: the threat of an imperialist war was both enormous and imminent; the breaking-point was actually at hand. But today the situation is different. The imperialist governments are exhausted. If they are thinking of war, it is not of a war between themselves but of a war against the U.S.S.R.—a very different affair. In the second place, ten or fifteen years ago the socialist solution was still only a theory. It had a long way to go and many obstacles to overcome before it could become a historic, an active, reality. But the war has changed all that—the war and the Russian Revolution. Communism can point, not in some remote future, but here and now, to the real, the final remedy, to the treatment which attacks not the symptoms but the underlying causes of the disease. The Communist remedy is not content just to keep peace alive, as a doctor keeps a patient alive, by drugs. It destroys the essential cause of wars by destroying the capitalist system, of which militarism and imperialism are but two expressions. It does not confine itself to introducing into the social order—or, rather, disorder—a number of desultory palliatives which the mere process of capitalist development is bound to leave without effect. It tears up inequality and injustice by the roots by suppressing the exploitation of men by their fellow men, and by assuring a fair distribution of the products of labour. . . . And this is not something that might be happening in the moon, that may happen on earth in the year 2000, but something that is going on almost next door. What is to prevent you from acting like the Russians? If you let the chance slip, if you let our present discontents become permanent, you will have no one but yourselves to blame. You are like the doctor who would try to cure a case of typhoid in the year 1923 with compresses and infusions.'"

Jerphanion allowed his listeners time to appreciate the complete objectivity of his words. There was no applause this time, not even from the tables where the young extremists sat. When he resumed, it was in a tone of frankness, with the air of a serious seeker after truth.

"Please don't think that I've been indulging in a display of oratorical fireworks, that I've been behaving like—oh, you know the kind of thing I mean—like the lawyer who states a case quite quietly and reasonably, while all the time he's hugging himself with delight to think what a mess he's going to make of it in a moment or two. . . . No, that's not the sort of game I like, and I don't suppose you do either. You are in the habit, when talking to your classes about some difficult and controversial subject, of putting certain questions to yourselves. The clever lawyer, the kind of man I've just been describing, has all the appearance of doing the same thing, but actually he does nothing of the sort. . . .

"My mind has been deeply troubled by the experiment, by the example, of Communism. It still is. It was because I was so passionately interested in the whole thing, so full of curiosity, that I went to Russia."

Jerphanion looked at his audience, which might now be said to be "devouring him with their eyes."

"You see me in a position of considerable embarrassment. It would need a whole lecture to give you any idea of my trip, though it lasted a bare three weeks, and though I saw only a tithe of what there was to see. For not only is the field a vast one from the mere point of view of its physical dimensions, but the subject itself swarms with contradictions. I defy any honest man to make a definite statement upon any point connected with Russia today without being immediately aware of objections, modifications, counter-facts. From what I have seen of the few poor remains of czarist Russia, I feel pretty sure that it too must have been full of contradictions, that in the old pre-Revolution days the charming and the exciting must have rubbed shoulders with the hateful, and that any two travellers, each with the same cultural background and an identical degree of intellectual honesty, might easily have brought back from a visit conclusions that would have seemed to be diametrically opposed to one another. A mere difference in sensibility would have been alone sufficient to cause the clash in their reactions—you know how it is when we feel our teeth set on edge by some detail of daily life which others just don't notice at all —there's a friend of mine who can never think of England without a little spurt of anger, because when he was there he had to do a lot of travelling by train and was always being half frozen because of the draughts. Or the difference could easily be accounted for by the fact that they happened not to have seen the same things, met the same people, experienced the same incidents. . . . I don't see how it can be avoided. We who know the history of our own country, and are not, in spite of what the gentlemen of the Right may say, particularly sectarian in our responses, are perfectly well aware that two travellers might, for instance, have driven through France from end to end in the reign of Louis XVI, and one of them noticed only its pleasing and gracious aspects, the elegancies of the *ancien régime,* which he would have found reflected even in the life of the people, while the other took account only of the blemishes, the injustices, the instances of corruption. Neither of them would have been necessarily either dishonest or stupid. . . . But in the case of Soviet Russia the difficulty is infinitely greater because—as no doubt you realize— nothing has yet assumed its final form, nothing has settled down . . . because there are ruins cheek by jowl with scaffolding, and examples of failure, perhaps merely temporary, perhaps final, inextricably mixed with experiments which are full, or seem to be full, of promise for the future. What right has one to draw conclusions, to make pronouncements upon what may or may not happen? How is one to choose between two pieces of evidence each pointing in an entirely different direction? I myself heard a Russian Bolshevist on Lunacharsky's staff say: 'Your League of Nations and your plans for disarmament are a joke. We are the only people capable of putting an end to militarism.' And another, no less ardent a Bolshevist, and one of Trotsky's most admiring colleagues: 'Just wait; in five years we shall have the most powerful army in the world.'"

There was a burst of loud laughter in which almost everybody joined, each expressing by it, at will, his sense of irony or of intellectual satisfaction.

"To treat the subject in any really useful way, I ought to quote a large number of my impressions and experiences, giving them in as great detail as possible, and taking pains to avoid any suspicion of tendentious choice . . . leaving on you the onus of weighing the evidence and drawing conclusions. But in fact all I can do is to offer you a number of generalizations which I have not the time to support with argument, which I must ask you to accept on the strength of my unsupported word, and about which I am far from feeling any too sure myself. . . . So you see what an embarrassing position I am in."

A ripple of sympathetic gaiety made it clear that his hearers were fully alive to his scruples, and that his voicing them had but increased their confidence in him.

"The conclusion to which I have come—or rather the general impression which I brought away with me (though I may have cause to revise it later)—is this— Please don't be surprised at the care with which I pick my words. I should hate to let my tongue run away with my thought. . . . Well, then, I should say that some sort of revolution would have been inevitable in Russia even had there been no war. Abuses had been so deeply rooted, and in the governing and administrative classes there had been, despite the presence of many persons of undoubted integrity, so much rottenness and such a legacy of bad tradition, that no attempt at progressive reform could probably have succeeded, and might even have resulted merely in the quickening of the revolutionary tempo. . . . Was the Bolshevist revolution the only type of revolution possible, the only type that could succeed in getting the necessary foothold? On this point I do not feel nearly so certain; in fact, I am inclined to think that it was not. Or let me put it this way: the course taken by events seems to me to have been determined less by any profound necessity than by circumstances and the human element. Russia was far from being one of those over-industrialized countries in which the concentration of capital and the increasing numbers of a proletariat formed the seed-ground for a Marxist revolution. . . . Military defeat need not have been so complete as in fact it was, or might have taken a different form. . . . It would probably have needed only a show of greater energy on the part of the Emperor or the presence in the field of a few good generals for the story to have developed differently. Even when a country's governmental system is corrupt, it is not impossible, at moments of crisis, for an emperor to be energetic or a general to possess genius. Situations are judged after the event, and it is only natural that chatterers and historians should set about discovering something that shall satisfactorily explain cause and effect. If France had been beaten— thoroughly beaten—at the Marne or at Verdun, the 'wise guys' everywhere would have found it only too easy to prove that France had been predestined to defeat by reason of the rottenness of her parliamentary system and the decadence of her political leaders. . . . In the Russia of '17 the parties of the Left, comprising the men who were neither reactionary nor Bolshevist, could have been better manned and better led. . . . We must hand it to Lenin and his friends that at one particular moment, which happened to be the decisive one, they showed more energy than anyone else, were less hampered by scruples, and that in the midst of the general confusion they had the presence of mind to occupy, at once, the strategic points which no one on the other side had the elementary sense to defend. . . . But, ladies and gentlemen, all that seems to me to partake far more of the nature of historical accident than of historical necessity. . . . I was quite a small boy when that well-meaning fool—I was about to say lunatic—Déroulède leapt at the head of General Roget's charger crying: 'March on the Élysée, sir!' If the general's courage had not failed him, if the movement, long plotted, had succeeded, we should probably have been saddled with a Cæsarian dictatorship for the next ten or fifteen years. If anyone maintained now that round about 1895 some such system of government was a historical necessity for France, shouldn't we think that he was pulling our leg?"

There was a great deal of delighted applause.

"The Bolshevists have a better argument—or rather, as they put it, the historical circumstance is still recognized as such, but so much extended and enlarged that it almost takes on the appearance of historical necessity. What the Bolshevists say is that immediately following on a catastrophe for which, as I think we must admit, they had been in no way responsible, Russia found herself in a state of collapse so complete that only leaders of outstanding energy and ruthless determination could prevent her utter break-up. Such energy they, as a party, possessed; and, I must say, the facts seem to bear them out. They owed it to their chief, perhaps also to their political dogma, to the fanatical conviction with which it inspired them. And that is something that should give us pause. In the course of history there have been many dogmas which bred such energy in their holders that no one could stand against them, so that they were able to expand enormously and fight great wars of conquest. Islam is a case in point. But the conquering energy of Islam has never served as a proof that the dogma in itself is *true*, or that the peoples of western Europe were wrong in refusing to adopt it. The point merits attention. There is no reason at all why there should not arise somewhere, tomorrow, a dogma still more full of vitality than Lenin's Bolshevism, even though it may be a hundred times less true; and such a dogma might well inspire the faithful with a still stronger passion for power, a still sterner concentration of will, so that they, in their turn, would win through to victory. . . . What I'm getting at is this: it may very well be that the Bolshevists were the only people capable of setting up any kind of government in Russia as they found her. But that fact does not prove that their dogma was in any way better than (or perhaps even as good as) any other. The great point to remember is that their argument has no validity whatsoever outside Russia, and outside the particular concatenation of circumstances which then existed in Russia. Particularly I would point out that it does not apply to countries like France and Great Britain. France has not suffered an overwhelming military defeat; she is not breaking up, nor is she a prey to nation-wide anarchy. She has a Parliament which still functions, a government—whether good or bad is beside the point—which can command obedience. She has not been reduced to crying: 'We must accept these people because there is no one else . . . we must do what they tell us to because we have no alternative.' What is still more important, our 'man of the people,' workman or peasant, is not in a position of having to look to a Communist revolution for one half, for one quarter, of the moral and material advantages with which it dazzles Russian eyes, and that for the very good reason that he has been actually enjoying most of these advantages for a good many years.

"You will say: 'All this business about Russia is old history. What interests us is to know what Communism has accomplished, what it is worth . . . and what it promises for the future.' I find it extremely difficult to answer that question. Communism in Russia has been guilty of certain errors that stare you in the face. What is worse is that it has been responsible for much destruction and cruelty and many massacres. It has suppressed almost all civic liberties. It imposes on its subjects a way of life which, you can take my word for it, is not very pleasing. On the other hand, it has undoubtedly put an end to abuses and it has liquidated a feudal system which was utterly out of tune with the times. It has awaked in the breast of the workman and the muzhik a sense of human dignity which centuries of slavery, more or less patriarchal, had deadened. It has taken up arms against drunkenness and illiteracy. In fighting religion in the name of a materialism which has itself become an official religion it has certainly overstepped the limits laid down by the natural feelings of reverence which inspire the individual conscience, but it has, at the same time, probably checked the growth of a number of very crude superstitions, and prevented the exploitation of the people by a clergy with a low standard of morality. In fighting capitalism in the name of a Marxism which has been erected into a dogma, it has certainly overstepped, once again, the limits laid down by man's natural respect for individual liberty and by his feeling for life. Nevertheless, it has shown that even the most strongly entrenched citadels of capitalism are not invincible, and that the life of a community can go on without their presence in its midst."

There was loud applause from one side of the room.

"Among its minority populations it has favoured those national cultures which were oppressed under the old Empire. Already they have been granted independence and are showing a renewed vitality. In the economic field it has done little so far beyond repairing a very small part of the ruin caused by the war, by the Revolution itself, by the years of civil strife, and by its own mistaken methods. The standard of living seems still to be lower than that of the most backward among the other countries of Europe, a great deal lower, certainly, from the purely material point of view, than it was in the old Russia of the czars before 1914—even for the proletarian class. To what extent does that class find compensation in the consciousness that it is now not only the equal of every other class, but, in theory at least, the ruling element in the country? That is a question to which I think it impossible to give a definite answer.

"There is another question which I have tried to face honestly; it is this: How much of the progress that has undoubtedly taken place would, in fact, have been achieved without any Communist revolution? Might it not be argued that another political system, another type of revolution, would have produced almost precisely the same results without the cost of so much destruction and suffering, without having to pay so high a price in terms of the happiness and freedom of the individual? It is a question that I hesitate to answer, but if I did so, it would, I think, be in something like these words: 'Some other, some gentler system, some other kind of revolution, more liberal in outlook, more merciful in its operations, would have been slower-moving. But is time saved really worth all these sacrifices? Almost certainly fewer mistakes would have been made and, consequently, there would have been less reconditioning to do than at present.'

"What is to happen in Communist Russia is still a matter of considerable doubt. Some there are who say: 'Communism was a war measure. The system can endure only if it returns to a more normal attitude—and that's already beginning to happen with the NEP. The purely theoretical side of the business will just be quietly shelved, and we shall see all the old features come slipping back without any fuss—private property, inheritance, individual enterprise in business, and so on. Russia will establish a form of social democracy much as we know it here, much as it exists everywhere. The whole huge country burned and fought over for—just that! . . . What fools we should be to tread in the footsteps of people who are now realizing that they took the wrong road!' But there are others who maintain that the NEP proves nothing but that a period of rest is necessary after a hard march, and that once it is over, the Communist Revolution will resume its interrupted course, in better shape than ever, and that after coming first to flower in Russia, it will ultimately sweep in triumph through the world. Which are we to believe?

"We are not prophets. What characterizes contemporary Europe, no matter where you look, is the swarm of movements and tendencies to which it has given birth. Many of these movements are diametrically opposed. We believe that there is a future for those among them which happen to reflect our own preferences. But never has it been more difficult to make a rational forecast."

("I really must finish with Communism and shut up," thought Jerphanion. He began to be conscious of certain familiar symptoms in his head which betokened fatigue. They had had a way, in the old days, of appearing during the last few minutes of some lesson on which he had expended too much mental energy. They comprised a lack of lucidity, giddiness, and a sudden loss of all interest in what he was saying. "Buck up!" he adjured himself. "I shall soon be on the last lap.")

He swallowed some water, and began again:

"What I have just been saying does not, I need hardly point out, mean that we have nothing to learn from the Communists, that there are not certain points of achievement and method of which we should take careful note. It does not mean that the criticism of the capitalist system, formulated and pursued for the last seventy-five years by so many fine minds, is fundamentally false, or that it is not our job to achieve, by slow degrees, a new form of society in which money shall no longer be allowed to accumulate in the hands of a few, in which every man and woman shall embark on life with the same chances, and in which gain shall have ceased to be the sole end of the citizen's activities. Nor does it mean that we ourselves stand in no need of revolution. It is up to us to make our own revolution in our own way.

"And now, if you will permit me, I will indulge in a few words of personal reminiscence.

"I have told you that before the war I had never had any very accurate or vivid idea of what war was like. Naturally, I didn't want it, but I was very far indeed from realizing the accumulation of every kind of horror that in fact it is. Now that I have seen war at first hand, I am ready to maintain that there is no greater good fortune for a country, no better proof of its collective wisdom, than, whenever possible, to avoid the experience of war. If I was in a position of power, there is nothing I should esteem a greater glory than to be able to spare my country the ordeal of battle.

"When I was about twenty or twenty-five, not only did the idea of revolution fail to frighten me, but I found it actively pleasing. I used to say to myself: 'We shall never establish a new order, never know better days, unless we have a revolution.' Now—well, I have seen a revolution, though not in the same way as I have seen war. My view of it was limited to a tour lasting less than three weeks in a country which had just had its revolution. What, I wonder, would have been my feelings if I had lived for whole months and years under revolutionary conditions, if I had seen the daily toll of violence and destruction, if I had paddled through warm blood and wandered among still smoking ruins? . . . Even what I did see, empty though it was of actual horrors and cooled of its pristine heat, was enough to fix in my mind a second idea heardly less firmly than the one of which I have already told you. It was that the experience of revolution must be avoided save in circumstances which make such avoidance absolutely impossible. But I believe that the way to avoid revolution is by making revolution unnecessary—that is to say, by suppressing by peaceful and progressive means the injustices and abuses which revolution sets out to remedy."

A considerable section of the audience broke into applause, though its reasons for doing so appeared to differ.

"So there! Now you know the full extent of my thought. I believe that we Frenchmen ought to avoid a revolution; and all the more because we have not, unfortunately, managed to avoid a war. Having emerged exhausted from the one, we have no call to plunge what is left to us of youth and strength into the other.

"That, too, is why I shall offer myself next spring bearing the label and inscribed on the lists of a sound, sensible, and what we old soldiers would call a thoroughly 'snug' party, the party of the Radical-Socialists. If anyone had told me when I was twenty that I should one day come forward as a Radical-Socialist candidate, I should have laughed in his face. It would have seemed to me so lacking in every quality of heroism, so flatly respectable! I don't want you youngsters who are listening to me to think that I have become an old man. It is not that. But I have seen war at first hand, and I have seen revolution. It is my profound conviction that given good will, good sense, and determination, both war and revolution can be avoided. However that may be, let us at least have nothing with which to reproach ourselves, should either break out.

"I chose the Radical-Socialist Party, lacking in dash though it may be, because I recognized in its attitude both good will and good sense. In the quality of daring it may not, perhaps, be so strong—from the very nature of its composition one could hardly expect it—but there is no reason why that particular lack should not be made good. It would not be too much to say that it holds to no fixed body of dogma. It is bound by no one system. If one gets down to brass tacks, it has actually very few prejudices. It believes in the principle of private property, and I believe that it is right in doing so. That belief is based less on material than on moral, on, I might almost say, intellectual, reasons. But it is not closely bound up, has not even a tacit understanding, with large-scale capitalism. Its rank and file is composed of decent, honest folk who are the heirs of a tradition which has its roots far back in the life of the French people. It is the representative of those who, since the days of the Communes, have founded our liberties and patiently extended them in the course of centuries. It is prepared to keep an open mind. You young men can rely on us to see to it that you have a fair hearing.

"We shall do our utmost to win the next elections. By 'we' I mean the Radical-Socialists in coalition with the republican parties of the Left. At a single blow we shall put an end to the Poincaré government, and, I hope, to Millerand's Presidency."

There was an outburst of enthusiastic applause, which, except for a few abstentions, appeared to come from all corners of the room.

"In internal affairs it will be our object to carry through a program of democratic reforms—those that I have mentioned casually in the course of my remarks, and others—reforms as extensive and as daring as the state of our finances will permit. Step by step we shall move towards a new society conceived as the fine flowering of democracy and republican government—that is to say, without involving us in the sacrifice of any of our essential liberties, of any of the 'rights of man.' It will be our ambition to reconcile the working population of this country with the general structure of republican society, and our first step towards this end will be the reconciliation of trade-unionism and the State, since the present divisions existing between these two elements, and the internecine struggles to which they have given rise, cannot continue much longer without imperilling the very life of the community. We shall do our best to establish a charter of organized labour within an organized society—organized but free—as our ancestors did their best to establish a condition of harmony, combined with a reasonable degree of independence, between the executive, the legislative, and the judiciary.

"In foreign affairs we shall begin by liquidating this business of the Ruhr on the most advantageous terms possible . . ." (loud applause, and varying degrees of response). "I say 'on the most advantageous terms possible' because I do not believe that the agreement reached in the course of the last few weeks, and in conditions well known to you, was the most advantageous possible. But we are not children, we are not fools . . . and we are not fanatics. It is not our way to say automatically that France is wrong every time she does or says anything. I spent several months with the Army of Occupation, and I have no exaggerated ideas about German good faith, or about the sincerity of the German governing class in a policy of co-operation, whether that governing class be composed of Junkers, Social Democrats, or middle-class politicians like Herr Stresemann. I do not forget what happened at Oppeln; I do not forget that Rathenau was murdered. Let me add that should the separatist movement in the Rhineland show signs of genuine strength, we should be fools if we helped a Prussianized Germany to stifle it. German unity has done enough harm in Europe. Let it be sufficient that we have not actively assailed it. It is no part of our duty to preserve it. Should a Rhenish buffer state, a kind of larger Belgium, come into existence, oriented towards the west, and with the old Gallic, Latin, and Catholic elements (of which there are a considerable number) in control, it would, I think, be an important trump card in the hand of peace. And anything that can help to ensure peace has my unstinted loyalty. . . . But whatever happens, whatever gestures of friendship may be made by any future government of the Left towards Germany, there must be no question of France backing down, and any settlement must be accompanied by ample guarantees."

There was a fresh burst of applause. It was approximately of the same volume as before, but was spaced rather differently. Most of the war veterans seemed to join in it both times.

"When all is said, however, this business of the Ruhr is but a single detail in a whole composition. Our job is to find some solid basis for peace, some solid basis for Europe. We must strengthen the League of Nations, give it arms, a more genuine authority, a more democratic constitution, and influence that shall be more definitely of and over the *people* of Europe. The question of admitting Russia will arise in the near future. That will be followed, a little later, by the question of admitting Germany. In my opinion it is our duty to help Germany, and at the same time to watch her; to help every decent and honest element within the country, every element that is prepared to work for democratic liberty and international agreement; to watch, to denounce, to discourage every dubious movement, and even at a distance the stirrings of such movements are not difficult to detect. In my opinion it is up to France to take the lead in this matter, to show herself generous and daring, to speak in no uncertain tones whenever she is sure of the justice of her case, never to be guilty of meanness, never to rest contented to cry out like a village lawyer whenever some tiny detail in a legal document is omitted, but not to stint her voice when it is a matter of imposing constructive ideas and of rallying round them whatever of faith and enthusiasm still burns in the hearts of the peoples of the Continent. Thus and thus only can she justify her victory."

As Jerphanion sat down, his brain was in a whirl of contradictory thoughts. "Thank God, that's over! . . . It didn't go too badly. . . . I was too long. . . . I didn't say half what I wanted to. . . . There was a lot of applause. . . . They look as though they liked it. . . . Still, I think they might have clapped a bit more. . . ."

71

The chairman leaned towards him. "Splendid! It really was a great success. . . . We're not much given to making a noise down here. We're not southerners, you know."

The chairman rose.

"I wish to propose a vote of thanks to the speaker."

The vote was duly given and the applause kept up by wave after wave of renewed clapping, mingled with which could now be heard cries of "Bravo!" and other exclamations not clearly to be distinguished. A feminine voice was distinctly audible calling gaily: "Long live Jerphanion!"

Jerphanion rose in his turn, waved his hand in greeting and thanks, and resumed his seat.

A little later he found himself once more on his feet, confronting, one after another, different groups drawn from his audience. He answered questions, or rather said laughingly:

"It's too difficult! If I was to answer you properly I should have to make another speech! . . . And I'm really tired, you know."

A young woman intervened. "Of course he's tired. Why can't you leave him alone?"

Another young woman came up. "Will you come and have a look at my little village, Monsieur Jerphanion? You'll find it full of a lot of old oddities, but I undertake to organize a meeting which may give you something to think about."

He found himself facing the man with the moustache and the eyeglasses.

"I noticed that you were listening very attentively . . . and I thought you looked as though you approved of what I said. . . . That encouraged me a good deal, and I'm grateful."

The next to beard him were three or four of the young fellows who had been seated at the "extremist" table. They crowded up to him. A young woman elbowed her way through to the front. One of the little group said:

"We don't agree with everything you said, Monsieur Jerphanion, but we should like to thank you for speaking as you did. . . . We'd heard you were rather reactionary."

"I hope you don't think so any longer?"

"No, we don't. . . . Of course there's no chance of getting a candidate here whom we could really support . . . so we'll try to get our people to vote for you."

"But we mustn't do it too obviously," said one of the others, laughing. "Otherwise we might spoil his chances."

Jerphanion allowed himself to indulge in the thought that, generally speaking, he was having a thoroughly good time.

# Chapter

## 3

### A HOUSE OF GENTLEFOLK

The chauffeur brought the limousine to a standstill and sounded his horn several times. Jerphanion put his head out of the window. He saw a fairly high wall, constructed, like so many in this part of the country, of pieces of volcanic rock set in cement. But here the red or reddish stones predominated over the blue which were to be found in great profusion higher up the valley, and the cement was more plentiful. Probably at some time or other it had formed a complete coating of rough-cast. Midway in the wall's length was a crude rustic carriage entrance, the wood of which showed but few traces of paint. The rounded lintel was composed of three unusually large blocks of granite, grey in colour and much weathered. The gate opened with a faint grinding sound, and the car drove into the sort of courtyard which one would expect to find in front of the dwelling of an old-fashioned country gentleman. The roundness of the steel-coloured pebbles with which it was paved had nowhere been worn down, and grass sprouted plentifully on the uneven ground. The business part of the premises lay to the left. Country carts and agricultural implements lay about in the open air in front of a row of small outhouses which, though distinct from the main farm buildings, obviously belonged to them. The farm itself showed only its back. Clearly it faced the other way, its stable, yard, and separate exit being, for the moment, invisible. To the right—that is, to the south-west—lay the manor-house proper. It was a square, massive pile, differing only in size and in the possession of a square tower, which occupied the south-east corner, from any peasant dwelling. Its only exterior ornament was a sort of fluting cut in the freestone stringcourse which framed the windows. The walls showed a mosaic of volcanic stones in which, as in the wall of the park, the red and reddish variety predominated. But here the stones were larger, and the pointing of the cement was neater. Close to the house and in the near distance towards the south-east could be seen a number of large old trees, at present leafless—chestnuts, walnuts, ash—while farther off, to the north-east, there was visible the foliage of pines and firs. One got the feeling that the plateau extended on out of sight in a series of woodlands, meadows, and ploughed fields. Walking there, no doubt one would be conscious only of the quiet sense as of illimitable plains and be no longer aware of the steep escarpment which lay in fact on every side. The air was mild. There was a complete absence of wind. The only sounds that broke the stillness were the occasional cry of a winter bird and now and again a hint of cackling from the farmyard, for all the world like the creaking of a cartwheel.

Jerphanion saw coming towards him a gentleman whose only noticeable feature appeared to be a monocle. He was a man of middle height, aged about sixty, wearing a suit of thick brown cheviot. His bare head showed a forehead from which the hair had receded. He had a small tooth-brush moustache.

He held out his hand, smiling.

"How do you do, Monsieur Jerphanion? It is a great pleasure to make your acquaintance. You're lucky in your weather. I'm glad. It's only really nice here when the sun shines."

His voice was that of an educated man with an underlying hint of natural harshness. Of local accent there was scarcely a trace.

They walked towards the house, mounted a flight of low steps, and found themselves at first in a large hall which clearly occupied the whole depth of the building, though it was divided in two by a cumbersome staircase built of some very heavy wood, and so wide that four persons could easily have climbed it abreast. It reminded the visitor of the main staircase of some old college. There was nothing remarkable about the furniture, the pieces of which might have been found almost anywhere scattered about corridors and waiting-rooms.

Some were middle-class nonentities; others the product of country carpenters. On the walls, rather unexpectedly, a number of rare fabrics and knick-knacks rubbed shoulders with many trophies of the chase. The general air was one of neglect.

M. Pouzols-Desaugues helped Jerphanion off with his overcoat.

"You seem to have been prepared for a regular Siberian trip!" said he, weighing it in his hand. "Aren't you a bit hot in it today?"

"I did find it rather too warm coming from Le Puy, but the car that is coming for me is an open one, and besides I'm driving up into the mountains. . . ."

"Naturally, naturally. . . . Shall we go into my study till lunch is ready? Don't worry; I'll see that you're not late."

They went down a passage which led from the foot of the staircase into the left-hand wing of the house. The study was situated in the ground floor of the tower. It was a charming room, square in shape, with windows in three of its four walls. Those facing south-east and south-west were double. The one to the north-east was single and set close to the angle made by the forward thrust of the tower where it joined the main façade of the house. The ceiling was beamed, the bookshelves well filled, and the furniture had at first sight the air of being old and comfortable. A number of engravings and odds and ends of virtu gave an impression of refinement. A large square, earthenware stove, set beneath the mantel of an old open fireplace, occupied the middle of the one wall that had no windows. The warmth that came from it, combined with the sunshine streaming in through the panes, gave to the room a sense of cheerful cosiness.

"Lovely views, don't you think?" remarked the host.

To Jerphanion they seemed superb. The general impression was quite different from the one he had got from the bridge at Brives. The main scenic elements were the same, but here they were quite differently arranged, broken up and regrouped, with changed perspectives, while others which had been invisible, or only to be guessed at, from the bridge now made their contribution and lent a richness of detail to the composition. Height and distance combined to reduce almost to pin-points the details of the lower valley, the immediate surroundings of the bridge, and the scattered houses of Brives itself. But the general character and tone of the scene were in nowise changed, nor did the valley seem dwarfed. The river, looking far narrower from here, gave off a more dazzling brightness, reflecting the sky so vividly that it was almost as though a strip of sky had fallen to earth. Beyond the valley's farther wall, range after range of heights appeared, plane after receding plane, piling up into great mountain walls that occupied the different sectors of the far horizon, picked out surprisingly by running lines of light just where the watchful eye might have expected to see earth and sky lost in all-veiling mist. Far to the south-east the Mézenc chain, with its snow-capped peak and high summits secret with the wisdom of eternity, still remained the dominant note of the great panorama; while to the right, through the window that pierced the wall close to its point of junction with the main front of the house, could be seen, if one stood at the proper angle, Notre-Dame-du-Puy and the crags of Corneille, so foreshortened that they looked like a single vast votive offering, an object of brooding mystery, set as the furnishing of some solemn rite above the roof-tops of the town. This section of the view, with its alternation of light and shade, its wealth of detail, its houses and roads looking like things read of in a story-book, the foreground and the distance, the near and the far, catching the eye wherever it might range, and holding the imagination; this visionary sweep with its hint of meanings unexpressed lurking in familiar things, as though every tree and hill and patch of light were, in some strange way, symbolical, reminded the gazing Jerphanion so poignantly, this time, of a landscape seen in one of the Primitives that the sense of it was pain, as though some movement of folk memory had overpowered his puny singleness of apprehension with the battering breaker of some re-lived past.

"How happily could I spend the rest of my life here," he thought, "reading, thinking, working . . . at something I could take my time over, at something of lasting value! . . . Gladly would I wave farewell to all ambitions, only—well, I should have to have private means, or have married an heiress."

"So you were a great success . . ." said M. Pouzols-Desaugues, waving his guest to a chair.

"You've heard about the luncheon?"

"It was only necessary to read this morning's *Tribune*."

"Oh, is there an account of it?"

"Indeed there is, and not too badly written up either." With a rather too conscious smile M. Pouzols-Desaugues added: "But, you know, I have my own spies as well."

When next he spoke, it was in a serious and thoughtful tone:

"You gave them a lot of good sense. There are plenty of thoroughly decent chaps among 'em—I know 'em well. . . . A glass of port?" He went over to a chest on which a bottle and some glasses were standing. "But there's also a good many young hot-heads—too many of 'em by far—fellows who'd be better off doing an honest job of work herding cows. It's all this damned education—puts ideas into their heads. One of these days somebody'll have the bright notion of getting out a balance-sheet showing how all this compulsory education has worked out, and then you'll see the number of undesirable subjects it has forced into the curriculum and, by so doing, made dangerous. And in the case of teachers the damage may go far. Once they have imbibed the poison, they give it out, and the youth of the countryside furnishes the first victims."

"All the same," said Jerphanion quietly, "I doubt whether they would have been contented with cow-herding at any period of our history. They would have become priests and curés. . . ."

"That may be, but their surroundings would have been different; they would have been subject to another kind of discipline. They might have amused themselves with their housekeepers, but from the point of view of public morals they would have been far less dangerous. . . . Their teaching would have been limited to dogma . . . not that I'm much in love with dogma myself, but, all things considered, I find it a good deal less undermining than Bolshevism. . . .

Still, I must say you pricked the Bolshevist bubble pretty successfully. Coming from you like that—well, I don't say that it will make them change their minds—not the real extremists—that would be expecting too much. But you've shaken their self-confidence a bit. They'll find fewer persons to listen to them."

Jerphanion felt half inclined to correct this rather one-sided view of what he had said. But "What would be the use?" he reflected.

M. Pouzols-Desaugues changed the current of his thoughts. "You seem to be particularly interested in foreign affairs, or am I mistaken?"

"I admit it; I am."

"And you're quite right. Unfortunately—" he pulled a thoughtful face and shook his head—"it's all very difficult. Knowledge in these matters can't be faked. Take Briand, for instance. He's for ever just missing the point. To know a country thoroughly a man must have lived there."

"Of course that is a very important element in the education of a statesman. But it's no bad thing to have given some thought to the matter and to have a clear idea of the goal to be attained."

M. Pouzols-Desaugues appeared not to have heard this reply. He went on pursuing his own thoughts, emitting a little spurt of laughter and readjusting his monocle. "I gather that nowadays a man needn't waste his time running about Europe or travelling round the world —he can go to Geneva instead. . . . that makes it much more comfortable."

"If only," answered Jerphanion very calmly, "the countries of the world would agree to do their business in Geneva, it would simplify a great many things."

"Oh, no doubt," said the other with a world-weary and slightly patronizing smile; "but, you know, there's nothing really new about the League of Nations. Just cast your mind back to the Congress of Vienna and the Holy Alliance . . . or to the Congress of Berlin and the Triple Alliance, to which it gave birth. The only difference is that the League is more hypocritical, because it was devised by Anglo-Saxons."

"I'm dealing with a complete fool," thought Jerphanion. "Quite useless to argue. . . . Why on earth did I come here? To see the view, I suppose. Well, at least I've had that pleasure. But how comes it that such a brainless ass lives in so divine a spot?"

"People in general," went on M. Pouzols-Desaugues, "are always suspicious of peace treaties. . . . And it has ever been the habit of the conqueror in any war, the man who, for the time being, is master of the situation, to attempt to consolidate his position by building up a system of alliances. When there is more than one conqueror, it is the shrewdest brain among them that takes the lead and twists matters to his own advantage . . . even if it was not he who won the battles or made the greatest sacrifices. . . . Metternich and Austria at the moment of the Treaty of Vienna . . . England now. . . . If the others are fools enough to let themselves be taken in, so much the worse for them. . . . Naturally, there is no law against—what was the word you used at the front?—against 'camouflaging' all this beneath a lot of parsonical talk—just to impress the simple souls. . . . The style of doing things changes a little with the period, that's all. The Holy Alliance was all right for the simple souls of its day. Now things have to be smothered up in humanitarian sauce. And because it happens to be France who is to have the wool pulled over her eyes, special care is taken for those simple souls whom we know as free-thinkers and socialists. . . ."

"The man's not such a fool as I thought," reflected Jerphanion. "It's a hateful point of view, and terribly petty-minded; but it's not the point of view of a stupid man. It's the sort of stuff he gets from the papers. He must have plenty of time to read them."

Aloud he remarked, without the faintest hint of irony:

"Your attitude is curiously reminiscent of that taken up by the *Action Française.*"

The slightest possible flush showed on M. Pouzols-Desaugues's cheeks. His eye-socket worked away at the monocle.

"Can't say I read it much," he said. "Generally speaking, I don't read a great deal of what's written today. . . . Most of my ideas are based on personal experience."

Jerphanion remembered that the prefect had told him as recently as that morning that M. Pouzols-Desaugues had once been "some sort of embassy attaché."

Feeling his way very carefully, he said:

"I believe you were formerly in the diplomatic corps?"

A smile fluttered about his host's lips. There was something in it of pride as well as of regret. He removed his monocle, replaced it, and raised one arm, the hand drooping in a soft gesture that was eloquent of scorn.

"Oh, that was fifteen years ago—roughly speaking," he said. "I did scarcely more than climb the first few rungs; I was young. . . . But chances did come my way—I don't say I didn't go out of my way to look for them—of filling a number of different posts . . . some of which were not without a certain importance. . . . The actual importance of a post, as no doubt you realize, does not always correspond with its place in the hierarchy. Although I entered the service by the front door, I elected to work in the consular division. I was a Consul, and later, though still young, a Consul General. It meant a less brilliant career than I should have had as a junior in an embassy, and it was a great deal more exhausting; certainly less sought after by my colleagues. . . . But I preferred it. I had to work ten hours a day; I had to handle vast questions involving important trade matters; I had to make my own decisions and shoulder my own responsibilities. There was no one I could hide behind if I made a blunder . . . very different from making myself agreeable at teas and balls. But I learned a lot . . . and I served my apprenticeship. If I had been handed a legation in one of the smaller Balkan countries, or in South America, I should, of course, have had to find my feet, but I should not have run the risk of finding myself out of my depth."

He sighed. "And that, in fact, is precisely what happened. Monsieur Hanotaux was good enough to take an interest in me. Monsieur

Charles Dupuy, too, who was the big man in my department."

"But you—left the service?"

M. Pouzols-Desaugues smiled. "Life, you know, is an odd business. . . . I married." Into his voice there crept a note of provocative directness, almost of flippancy. "I won't say that I married my wife for her money—absolutely not. . . . But it so happened that she had some. At the time I am speaking of, the life of a diplomat was expensive, and the higher one rose in the service, the more expensive it became. It was only natural that I should say to myself that my wife's money would help me to occupy, in a becoming manner, the posts to which I might one day be appointed. . . . Well, as things turned out, my wife developed a hatred of living abroad. Most of the time she spent in tears, writing despairing letters to her mother. Whenever we had to give a party, no matter how small, or a dinner, there was a first-class scene. . . . She was quite a young girl, and consequently had been very little into society. Besides, she had a temperamental dislike for it. . . . To cut a long story short, the business never even looked like working, and at the end of a year I resigned."

Jerphanion felt touched by this confidence. The figure in front of him became suddenly much more human. In accents almost of friendship he said:

"The sacrifice must have cost you dear . . . I can see that."

"It certainly cost me something. But it does, you know, sometimes happen that a perfectly quiet, ordinary fellow finds himself cast for the leading part in a tragedy by Corneille. I was deeply in love with my young wife . . . and my love was returned, though that, I think, is rather an understatement of her feelings. But what she loved in me was not the diplomat, the budding ambassador. There could be no question of our going our separate ways, nor could I dream of ruining her life."

"So you chose to ruin your own . . ." said Jerphanion quietly.

"It was the easier alternative."

"Wouldn't it have been possible to find—some temporary solution? . . . Couldn't you, for instance, have got a headquarters job in Paris, which might have given your wife time to get used to the idea? . . . She might have grown accustomed to diplomatic circles, seen other women perfectly at their ease in that sort of life, managed, perhaps, to overcome her earlier repugnance."

M. Pouzols-Desaugues shrugged his shoulders. "Possibly. I confess my nerves were all on edge. It seemed to be a case of all or nothing . . . I was young, remember. . . . Either give up my career or my wife. . . . Even if my feelings had allowed me to consider the second of those alternatives, divorce then was not the easy thing it is now. My wife being the kind of woman she was, a separation—I in Stockholm, perhaps, she here—wasn't feasible. Anyhow, that sort of compromise wouldn't have done my career any good."

He stopped. Both men sat for a while thinking silently. Jerphanion remembered something else that the prefect had told him: "You'll find his wife a queer fish. Must have been pretty once. Comes of a large landed family—plenty of money. There was only one other child, a son, who became a priest and didn't care a bit if his sister got everything. . . . The father's name was something like Boyer or Bollier—nothing very distinguished. One of their ancestors had got into the habit of sticking the territorial appellation onto the end of his name. Saugues was where they came from, and Bollier de Saugues was what he called himself. Then after a while they dropped the Bollier and became just simply de Saugues, spelt in two words like that, which gave an aristocratic air. When young Pouzols married the heiress, he joined the two names. It's quite a usual thing in this part of the world—I needn't tell you that. But one must admit that he showed considerable discretion in writing hers as a single word and dropping the particle." To this, Jerphanion had replied: "Perhaps he was afraid that his son might follow the family example and drop the Pouzols, in his turn, as being too plebeian." "Perhaps," the prefect had agreed; "still, you must admit that Pouzols de Saugues, spelt in three words, would have looked a good deal grander than the hyphenated form. . . . That would have flattered his natural snobbery. . . . Pouzols-Desaugues, with the hyphen, is the kind of thing I always expect to see over a shop front when I'm taking a stroll in the market square at Breuil."

M. Pouzols-Desaugues, with the hyphen ("a hyphen that has cost him a pretty penny," reflected his visitor with a flash of untimely humour), began to talk again:

"If things had gone differently, I suppose I should have been just about retiring with an ambassador's pension—or a minister's at the very least." Once again he let his hand flutter rather helplessly at the end of his outstretched arm. "So that's that!"

On a note of irony, he added:

"Well, I'm councillor in the domestic service, and that's something, after all." Then: "I suppose if I'd tried, and hadn't minded putting up with my share of rebuffs, I might have done more in the political way . . . stood for Parliament . . . got caught up in the machine. But there are some people I hate rubbing shoulders with, some forms of drudgery to which I will not submit. I'm not one of those who find shaking hands easy."

Jerphanion was on the point of interrupting rather sharply. But he stopped in time, with the reflection that there was nothing personal in M. Pouzols-Desaugues's remarks, and that, generally speaking, there was a good deal in what he was saying.

"I'm not much of a hand with words," went on the other, "but this I will say: when I plump for a thing, I go all out. Once I'd chosen a career, I considered my whole future, my whole life, as settled. Good-bye to that, good-bye to everything. I'm not the sort of fellow who can switch from one thing to another. I've often said to myself, since: 'If I'd been a jockey by profession, and then gone and got my leg smashed in a fall, I'd have been just about finished.'"

"And what about myself?" thought Jerphanion as he listened. "Am I the sort of fellow who can switch from one thing to another? What happens if I fail in politics? . . . But, setting that aside, how should I have acted if I'd been in his shoes? Well, in the first place, I should not have married Mademoiselle de Saugues. . . . Easy enough to say that, and, after all, how easily Odette could have misled me about her character when she was a young girl. Women in love, women on the look-out for a husband, are capable of taking on any kind of protective colouring. . . ."

M. Pouzols-Desaugues seemed to notice that his guest's mind was elsewhere. "I'm afraid you're worried about the time. Lunch'll be ready in five minutes, and I guarantee there shan't be any delay about serving it."

"Oh, that's all right. The car's coming to pick me up at half past two. I've plenty of time. . . . To return to what we were saying a little while ago, are you sure that the ideas you hold now about the League of Nations, and other things, are really derived from your experiences as a young diplomat, however instructive those may have been? Conditions have changed so since then."

M. Pouzols-Desaugues's right hand adjusted his monocle with as much care as though it were a complicated screw.

"Naturally, naturally. But the experience I gained then makes it possible for me to interpret facts. . . . I learned a number of fundamental truths which are as valid now as they were then. . . . During my fifteen years in the service, I managed to live in seven different countries—very different, believe me—including Germany. I was in touch with colleagues drawn from every nation. I had a smattering of all their languages."

"And what were those truths?"

"That all peoples, after a while, dislike one another. Foreign countries don't really improve by being known, nor does knowing one another do much to help. That was where the value of the old diplomacy came in. It managed their affairs with as few blunders as possible, and kept them apart . . . in the manner of lawyers with difficult and quarrelsome clients. . . . Second truth: all France's neighbours hate or envy her, even those who owe her a debt of gratitude. Why? That would take too long to explain. . . ."

"Don't bother about explaining—stick to your generalizations."

"Thirdly: official friendship between nations is so much eye-wash for the mob. Unscrupulous governments make use of it to deceive or paralyze those more simple-minded than themselves. A simple-minded government is one that depends upon, and reflects, popular opinion. It is easier, as no doubt you realize, for an autocratic government to be unscrupulous—that is to say, to make a great show of eye-wash—while all the time it is doing and thinking precisely what it likes, or, in other words, making the advantage of its own country its sole criterion of conduct. Other kinds of government are more or less bound to turn the eye-wash into reality, to avoid irritating public opinion."

"Which means that you condemn the Republic. . . ."

Once again a faint flush betrayed M. Pouzols-Desaugues's embarrassment.

"Not necessarily. She has a more thankless task, that's all. Even in a republic it ought to be possible to free the conduct of foreign affairs from the shackles of public opinion. It's been done successfully more than once in the past."

Jerphanion could not keep himself from laughing. "Nobody could accuse you of being a modern! . . . Everything we're trying to do runs exactly counter to your ideas."

"I know it very well."

"I might answer you in the first place by arguing that the particular peril to which you have drawn my attention—that of the simple-minded government with its popular backing finding itself up against an unscrupulous neighbour—will disappear entirely or be much diminished as soon as all governments tend to become the mouthpieces of public opinion, which is what is happening to-day. . . ."

"That's all very well, but you'll always have countries like England and Germany, for example, where the strings will be pulled, in the future as in the past, by men who can afford to laugh at public opinion, or who know how to form it. Whereas in France . . ."

"But the real case against you—and I can make it with added conviction, having had five years of war, including the Champagne and

Verdun—is that the results of the old diplomacy were not what you might call brilliantly successful. It may have prevented the peoples of Europe from getting to know one another, but it certainly didn't prevent them from bashing one another's heads in. I really don't know what the simple-minded, popular governments and the League of Nations could do that would be much worse than that!"

M. Pouzols-Desaugues's expression underwent a marked change. He seemed to be suffering considerable discomfort. For a while he was silent, apparently seeking for the words he wanted, while the fingers of his right hand worked away at the imaginary screw.

"I am quite appalled," he said, "to think of what a wrong idea I've given you of what I think. . . . I'm not much of a hand when it comes to talking, and I've grown unaccustomed to discussing serious questions with anyone who might make discussion worth while. . . . The kind of people I see here . . . my loneliness. . . . I do a good deal of thinking here, in this room, for instance, with that lovely view before my eyes . . . but I rarely have anyone to talk to. . . . I have a pretty shrewd idea when I'm right, when my reasoning is correct . . . or at least I think I have . . . but I've lost the ability to communicate my thoughts."

"I can't say I've noticed it. . . ."

"But it's true! I seem to be putting things into words, but somehow they are not the things I had in my mind. . . . If I could show them to you as they developed in the course of my thinking, they wouldn't seem so stupid. . . ."

"But it never occurred to me for a moment . . ."

"Take, for instance, this question of the last war, on which you have just touched. I've been over it in my mind again and again during the past few years . . . here, in this very room. . . . There's nothing much else, unfortunately, for me to do with my time, apart from a few odd jobs now and then. . . . It would take me a whole evening of talking to explain my point of view, and even then I should do it badly. . . . On certain points we should probably agree, on others we should differ. . . . To me the whole business seems terribly complicated. . . . I just can't answer you in a few neat phrases, as I ought. . . ."

Jerphanion was acutely aware of the man's obvious good faith, of the meticulous care, even, which he devoted to the subtler shades of his own thinking.

"I realize that," he said in soothing tones, "but—"

"Don't think," broke in M. Pouzols-Desaugues almost violently, "that I congratulate the old diplomacy on having let us in for that war. Heavens, no! But a tool isn't necessarily bad because it is badly used. What I mean is . . ."

The door opened. A stout—what might almost have been described as a very stout—woman came in. Her contours were heavy, her arms enormous. Her large face must have been beautiful before it had become swollen to its present size, and her big eyes were still fine, though now distinctly cowlike.

Jerphanion was introduced in the minimum of words. The lady gave vent to a few dull commonplaces in a voice that bore strong traces of a brogue. There was a sort of stolid uneasiness in the glance which she directed towards her husband, who, in his turn, showed signs of embarrassment.

"Let's go in to lunch," he said as soon as he caught a glimpse of the butler through the open door. "Monsieur Jerphanion is rather pressed for time."

To the butler, whose hands were those of a gardener, and whose get-up had obviously been assumed for the occasion, he said:

"Make the meal as quick as you can. We must have finished our coffee by a quarter past two, by twenty past at latest."

# Chapter

## 4

### HOW MONSIEUR POUZOLS-DESAUGUES WOULD HAVE ESTABLISHED THE PEACE

The dining-room was huge. Being situated at the north-east corner of the house, with one window overshadowed by the tower, and the other giving onto a cold patch of sky criss-crossed by a tangle of branches, it was filled with a rather melancholy light. It was without the fine old pieces of furniture which might have given it an inner glow. A wood fire, lit too recently, warmed one side only, and that not very successfully.

Mme Pouzols-Desaugues, speaking in the same heavy, bored tones which she had already used, gave vent to a series of remarks, some of which referred to the weather and might have been intended for the guest, while others, called forth by the absence of some dish, by the state of the fire, or by something that had happened that morning in the wood-shed, might equally well have been intended for the master of the house or the gardener-butler, though never by a single sign did she make it clear which of them she was addressing. Even the anxious glances which previously she had cast in the direction of her husband had now ceased to operate. The stout lady was a gloomy if quiet presence.

At first M. Pouzols-Desaugues showed a reasonable degree of patience. Possibly he considered his wife's economy of words as an inevitable precaution demanded by her state of health, and felt it to be unwise to rally her on it. There was about him an air of absent-mindedness, as though he were pursuing a difficult and elusive line of thought. Now and then he lowered his face and peered into his plate as though he had suddenly become very short-sighted.

The lady, turning without warning to Jerphanion, and speaking in the same emotionless voice, astonished him with a series of questions:

"I believe you have come from Paris? Are you a schoolmaster? Do you always get such a long vacation at this time of the year?"

M. Pouzols-Desaugues clicked, as it were, into life.

"My dear"—his voice had a cutting edge—"Monsieur Jerphanion, who is honouring our table with his presence, can boast the highest university honours. He is qualified to instruct, not in a school class-room, as you suggest, but as a member of one of the faculties. But his business is not instructing—no, not instructing at all. . . . He has chosen to occupy his mind with politics. He is already an important figure in his party, and he is paying us the compliment of standing as our prospective member at the next elections. It goes without saying that he will be elected. When, my dear, at some future time, we have a favour to ask, it is to him, probably, that we shall have to go."

Jerphanion took refuge in a smile as shy as that of a young girl. He was not without a feeling of gratitude to M. Pouzols-Desaugues for speaking as he had. At the same time he could not help wondering whether the lady had not done him a considerable service by forcing her husband to declare himself so definitely, and as he probably would not have dreamed of doing five minutes earlier. He was now, to some extent, committed.

At this moment M. Pouzols-Desaugues turned towards Jerphanion and went on with what he had been previously saying, just as though nothing had occurred to interrupt their conversation:

"I was, you know, far from being one of the 'It'll all come right in the end' school during the war. . . . I was in a constant state of fright about what was going to happen. Naturally I didn't say so, but I was genuinely terrified. . . . I had too clear a vision of the strength of our enemy and the inadequacy of our allies. I kept on saying to myself that if some fluke gave us the victory, it would be almost too good to be true . . . that should such a thing happen we must exploit it as much as we could, must make sure of having fifty years of peace—I am, you see, just as great a pacifist as you—for, said I to myself, if we miss this chance, we shall never get another. And it *ought* to be easier than winning pitched battles. When the armistice was declared, I was torn between joy, naturally, and anguish. . . . You at the front had had enough of the whole business—it didn't take much imagination to realize that. . . . But here it was easier to take a more detached view; here it was difficult not to say to oneself: 'We're letting go too soon. The Germans don't really feel that they've been beaten. We ought to crush their Army—go right on to Berlin." To have done so would not have cost the hundredth part of the sacrifices we have already made, whereas now we run the risk of losing all we have gained just for the sake—if you'll forgive the phrase—of a candle's end.' But what would the soldiers have had to say about it? Well, they might have kicked a little at first, but I believe that later developments would have made it up to them—which is more than you can say now. They would have had the feelings of conquerors. They would have come home in far better heart, with tales to tell of triumph and not merely of hideous slaughter just brought to an end one fine day by a bugle. Even then we were beginning to experience the difficulties of peace. If we had led the Allied Armies to Berlin—for I think you'll agree that it would have been the French who did the leading—we could have spoken in no uncertain voice, could have dug our toes in. . . . I had a great deal of confidence in Clemenceau. The great thing about him was that he had no use for humanitarian nonsense. He knows that most of mankind is bad, ungrateful, and mean; and such knowledge is strength. He knows that foreigners have no love for us, and that if we allow ourselves to depend upon their good feelings we shall get it in the neck. Unfortunately he had a weakness for the English . . . and behind him, always ready to twitch his coat-tails, were those simple-minded fools who had taken Wilson's sermonizing at its face value. The real trouble was that he was never in a position to say to his partners: 'My troops are in Berlin. If this is all I can offer them in the way of peace, much though I regret having to say so, they will refuse to come home.' Foch and the Army ought to have been trump cards in his hand, but they were not.

. . . For the moment the balance of strength lay with us, possibly for the last time in history . . . but even so we couldn't so much as guarantee ourselves three years of peace. No, not three years! for scarcely were those three years over when we had to march into the Ruhr!"

"But what then," asked Jerphanion in tones of genuine interest, "would you have done if you had been in charge of the peace negotiations? Don't forget that we had partners to consider, and not the easiest of partners at that."

"Oh, I know. . . ." M. Pouzols-Desaugues laid down his fork. The quick, jerky movements of his head, the uneasy way in which he kept playing with his monocle, showed clearly that he was repeating no ready-made phrases, but that he really was trying to express in the best possible way, and for a listener who deserved his most serious attention, the results of long hours of solitary brooding. "I know! . . . So far as those partners were concerned, I should have enlisted the full sympathy of Italy instead of treating her in the offhand manner that Clemenceau adopted. . . . I should have patted Wilson on the back instead of giving him the impression that I was hand in glove with Lloyd George with the object of putting him in his place. Then I should have insisted on having the left bank of the Rhine and sticking to it . . . and on Italy having the Dalmatian coast. I should have bargained like a hard-headed old peasant. . . . 'That or nothing,' I should have said. 'For all I care, the conference can go on for years. Until I am given the left bank of the Rhine with the right of occupying it with French troops and French troops only, I shall refuse even to discuss any of the other clauses.' Naturally, all this would have meant careful manipulating of French public opinion, and a policy dominated by the Army. I should have been in favour of wholesale re-enlistment. I should have begun to build up a large professional army. Many of those who had been mobilized were already completely out of touch with their former ways of life. . . . Many of the younger men—I could give you plenty of examples—had been in the Army for six or seven years. . . . It was true to say that, practically, they had known nothing but the Army. I believe that with good pay, good prospects, and the certainty of leading a far more amusing life than they had had at the front, one could have got them to sign up again without any difficulty. Was I wrong? After all, you were one of them and should be able to say."

"On that point, probably not. . . ." Jerphanion remembered how his own mind had worked as he lay in his dug-out in Champagne, with its dry, glittering walls, or on the crowded roads leading down into the furnace of Verdun, with Griollet beside him, that "Legionary" of the granite face. "But," he went on, "it wasn't exactly what we were fighting for!"

"Not exactly? Naturally . . . but I'm being, you know, perfectly consistent. France today is no longer the France of Louis XIV, nor of Louis XV, nor even of Napoleon. She can't afford luxuries . . . can't afford to throw away her trumps. It was up to us to do whatever might serve the country best, odd things though that might involve—considerably odder than Verdun."

"Don't I know it! . . . But Clemenceau could have carried out a policy like that only by extending and strengthening his dictatorship. A huge professional army, such as you envisage, would, in the long run, have upset the equilibrium of the régime. We should have ended by killing democracy, even though we mightn't mean to; and don't forget that it was precisely in order to protect democracy, in order to extend democracy, not only in our own country but all over the earth, that we had been fighting. The future must mean that for us, or nothing."

M. Pouzols-Desaugues slowly raised his shoulders. He seemed anxious not to be drawn into making any general statement on this particular point, not to be forced into a direct contradiction of anything his visitor might say.

"It is difficult," he said mildly, "to insure against all risks. The great thing is to know from what direction the greatest threat of danger comes."

"Besides," continued Jerphanion, who had not been slow to realize that M. Pouzols-Desaugues's argument had close affinities with his own "hierarchy of urgency," but who was in no mood to be brought up short by any such consideration, "we rely—I mean I and those who think with me—on one fact in particular, which is this: that up to now the people have never themselves controlled foreign policy. You, I think, would agree. But we don't draw the same conclusions from the evidence as you. It is *our* convinced belief that in no country does the mass of the population want war. . . ."

M. Pouzols-Desaugues raised his hand in interruption, but Jerphanion went on: "Please let me finish. I may be wrong in my psychology. I confess that I had doubts myself when I used to think about all this at the front. But the thing has got to be tried. Never, in the whole course of history, have the great masses of the people ever been so near, in all countries, to controlling what is done in their name. . . . I think you must admit that. It may not, so far, have been always very successful, appearances may not always have corresponded to the reality . . . there may even, here and there, be signs of a partial reaction, as in Italy. . . . But taking it by and large, you cannot deny that there has been a change. Merely by deploring the fact you have yourself admitted that it exists. . . ."

"Certainly. . . ."

"Well, it's on that we take our stand. What we say is this: Aren't all these people, now that the old dynasties and ruling classes are no longer there to impose on them a line of conduct which they must follow blindly, going to find some way of getting together for the purpose of establishing peace, since it is certain that they prefer peace, even a poor peace, to war . . . and especially to modern war and its horrors, of which they have had their fill? I go further and say that we have no right to shirk the experiment, or to cut it short. To do so would be ridiculous. The alternative, after all, took centuries to reach its predestined end, which was a system built up of recurring periods of massacre and destruction, and catastrophes involving more and more of the earth's surface. . . . The least we can claim is that we should be allowed to see what democratic principles can achieve when applied on a large scale to the affairs of the world. That, in my opinion, is precisely what the League of Nations is doing. . . . Why should you assume that democracy will fail? You can have no certain knowledge, since in fact the experiment has never before been made."

"Maybe, maybe," said M. Pouzols-Desaugues without much enthusiasm, and making a face. "I am a fanatical supporter neither of the Right nor of the Left. I only hope you are right. . . . All I want for France is peace and tranquillity. . . ."

"Which is precisely why I feel justified in saying that your peace plan, with its accompaniment of mailed fist, professional army, and all the rest, even if it succeeded, would in all probability set us off on a new period of imperialist expansion. . . . You must know how difficult it is to apply the brakes, nor can you doubt whither such a policy would lead our country, even were it relatively stronger than it is today. The end of that road would be another Malplaquet, another Waterloo, another Sedan. . . ."

"Oh no, no! You mustn't for a moment think any such thing!" exclaimed M. Pouzols-Desaugues with vehemence. "I was about to say that, on the contrary, my idea would be, having made France as safe from attack, as invulnerable, as possible, to see that she withdrew from the arena, abandoned her alliances, gave up her various commitments, refused to embark on any fresh ambition. . . . Then, and then only, could we set about a leisurely program of reform, and be no longer obliged to waste our moral and material resources on foreign adventures. We need them badly at home. . . . And since I am in the mood to tell you all my secret thoughts, let me admit frankly that, to my mind, a strong professional army would have one very great advantage—and a double-edged one at that. . . . After the kind of peace I had dreamed of, the one great danger still to be feared would have been in the domestic field—social agitation, the infection of Bolshevist ideas, and so forth. . . . My professional army would have absorbed the unemployed, and so reduced the causes of social unrest . . . not to mention the fact that it would have served to intimidate all would-be disturbers of the peace at home. With six or seven hundred thousand men, including two hundred thousand coloured troops, at its disposition, a government could breathe freely."

"Six or seven hundred thousand men!"

"I have gone into the figures rather carefully . . . my facts are by no means all drawn from a single source. I need scarcely add that the costs of upkeep would be defrayed by Germany. That would be something far more tangible than a hundred, or even than fifty, years of reparations running into astronomical figures, not one single pfennig of which we shall be getting in ten years' time. . . . Besides, it would be the best possible way of making them take us seriously."

Jerphanion restrained his laughter with difficulty. His mind was sufficiently elastic to realize that what his host had put forward had the merit of being systematic, methodical, and possessed of a logic of its own. Merely from the standpoint of historical realism it would obviously be far better to carry out such a policy in its entirety than to make a half-hearted experiment with his own—which was, in all probability, what the present rulers of Europe would do. But his temptation to laugh sprang from other causes: from his realization of what a vast abyss could lie between the points of view of two men both of whom had started from the same facts; of two men, both belonging to the same period and the same country, both enjoying the benefits of education, both entirely free from the suspicion of being either mad or dishonest, and neither merely concerned to generalize the ideas and interests of the class to which he belonged. There was really no reason at all why Jerphanion should not have chosen to make a career in the party of the Right. In what way could his acts be said to depend upon class-consciousness? (Class must never be confused with social origins.) His class, in so far as he had one, was that whose members retain complete freedom of action, a party composed of men unfettered by preconceived notions. It is only after such men have chosen on which side of the barricade they are to be found, have taken sides for deliberate and well-weighed reasons, that one can try to guess why they have chosen just that. On the other hand, he could have mentioned, without any difficulty at all, ten or twenty landowners within the ranks of the radical party more keenly alive even than M. Pouzols-Desaugues to their class interests, who nevertheless, animated by the same kind of sincerity—men, that is to say, of an honourable, not to say heroic cast of mind—were prepared to manifest their faith in democracy, both national and international, by supporting the power of the people to control foreign policy, by urging the substitution of collective security for militarism —in short, by upholding all that the League of Nations stood for and promised for the future, even if it could not point as yet to any actual achievement. As for M. Pouzols-Desaugues, it was pretty obvious that class-consciousness was but one ingredient of his philosophy; he owed that philosophy quite as much to a medley of circumstances operating over a considerable number of years: to his birth and upbringing in the conservative and provincial middle class, of course, but also to a natural temperament which probably inclined him to adopt a pessimistic and suspicious attitude; to a profession which he had followed for fifteen years, and as a result of which he had lost all romantic illusions about foreign lands; to a number of other purely personal experiences, the most bitter of which must have been his marriage and his interrupted career; perhaps, also, to a feeling of superiority which the conditions of his life no longer justified; to an absence of friends with whom he could have conversed on terms of intellectual equality, to excessive solitude, to an over-indulgence in books which he could not discuss, with the result that their stimulus had turned sour within his mind. . . . The sum total of all these things was something now too deeply inwoven into the fabric of his being to be loosened by a single hour's argument. All one could do was to note the abyss lying between two representative men of the same period, and it was surely better to recognize its comic aspect than to waste one's energy in vain recrimination, better to find some way of maintaining unbroken the frail bridge of personal sympathy which, paradoxically enough, seemed to have been thrown from side to side of the sundering gap.

M. Pouzols-Desaugues must have been thinking along similar lines.

When, just before half past two, he slowly accompanied Jerphanion to the front gate, he said:

"I can't tell you what a real delight your visit has been to me. It was very kind of you to come. It is a long time since I had such an interesting conversation. I shall give a lot of thought to what you have said. . . . We may look at things differently, but that does not prevent me from expressing a very sincere hope that you will be successful in your campaign. It is always good to be represented by a man of intelligence and, I need not add, of honesty. I do not suffer fools gladly, and if, by chance, they share my point of view, that only makes them the more tiresome. . . . You can scarcely need my modest powers of assistance, but what little I can do is yours to command."

In the middle of the courtyard he stopped and looked at his watch.

"Your car's not come yet; we should have heard it climbing the hill. I hope that coat's thick enough to keep the cold out?"

"Oh, I'm all right; but what about you?"

"Don't feel it. . . . I'm delighted to have these extra few minutes with you."

Suddenly his face took on an amused expression. He touched Jerphanion lightly on the arm and said, with an air of easy intimacy:

"Are you going into the mountains when you've finished with Monastier?"

"I thought I'd go up to Saint-Front and come back by Fay."

"Would you, by chance, be passing anywhere near Bournac?"

"I might—though I really can't say for certain. . . . Why?"

M. Pouzols-Desaugues's air of amusement grew more marked. "It was only that I thought if you had an hour to spare—but obviously you won't. The place I had in mind is not Bournac itself, but roughly between Saint-Front and Bournac, out on the moor—only a mile or two off the road."

"I am all curiosity!"

"I own some property up there, a largish farm—a very remote place. It's let to a local family—they've been there for years—extraordinary people. . . . I have a liking for anything that's out of the usual and mysterious, especially in these old and hidden corners of the country, with their atmosphere of other days. To cut a long story short"—he lowered his voice—"I am quite convinced—what I'm going to tell you is strictly between ourselves and has nothing at all to do with politics—that this farm of mine is the scene of a crime—perhaps even of two crimes! Not bad, eh? The first of them must have taken place about six, no, seven years ago, during that particularly hard winter we had while the war was on—the second, the last winter. The circumstances of both were identical—heavy snowfalls, communications cut for weeks together, the house half buried, the people as completely isolated as though they were living at the North Pole. Naturally, a death would pass unnoticed . . . the only available doctor would have been several miles distant and cut off from the house by a barrier of impenetrable snow. There could be no question even of sending for him. The corpse was put up on the roof, packed in snow, wrapped in a clean sheet, and left to wait. . . . Later, when the thaw came, it was shoved onto a bier and taken off to the nearest cemetery."

"Wouldn't a burial permit have been necessary?"

"The local mayor would have given that; he wouldn't have bothered much about such a trivial matter."

"How about the death certificate?"

"What busy doctor, who can barely manage to get all his childbirths and cases of serious illness into his professional day, is going to waste six hours or so just to make sure that some fellow who's been lying out in the snow for more than a month is really dead? . . . Nothing short of a police inquiry would make him do a thing like that."

"Or serious suspicions."

"In a countryside like this, mere suspicion counts for very little. The general attitude is that people should be left to mind their own business. Neighbours don't go shoving their noses into one another's affairs if they can possibly avoid doing so. . . . The first of the two incidents concerned the old father."

"Was it he who died?"

"Yes. The second time it was the elder son. The younger is living up there now with three women—the old lady, his own wife and his brother's widow—and with his children; the elder didn't have any."

"If I understand you aright, you think it was the younger who . . ."

M. Pouzols-Desaugues played with his monocle, and, in a voice which must have been the result of ambassadorial training, remarked:

"Say, my dear sir, am inclined to think." Then: "The first time there may have been some kind of understanding between the brothers. The second—well, the elder happened to be out of luck. . . . No doubt the women played a part in the business, but what exactly it was I'm not sure."

"And you have proof of this?"

"Yes—and what I don't know I can guess. I can't explain it all now; there isn't time. When the first of the two deaths happened, I did whisper something of what I suspected in the ear of a young magistrate whom I know, and he went so far as to set some sort of inquiry on foot. But it was already too late—nearly six months after the business had occurred. I hesitated a long while before speaking— didn't feel quite sure that it was altogether playing the game on my part. They couldn't lay their hands on anything in the nature of evidence, needless to say. The local policeman scribbled a page of notes. The justices didn't think it necessary to order an exhumation. My magistrate friend, whose calling-up had been deferred, was sent off to his regiment. No one lodged any complaint with the authorities, and so the whole matter was allowed to drop. When things began again, I confess I did nothing about them . . . or rather I contented myself with paying one or two calls at the farm on various excuses and nosing about on the spot. . . . It would entertain me considerably to think of you turning up there as though by accident and forming your own opinion—no more—about what has been going on. . . . You could take stock of the place and of the dramatis personæ, you could have a good look at the man in the case . . . and then, when you got back, we could talk the whole thing over, if, as I hope, you will do me the honour of taking pot luck again at my table. . . . It would be a change for you from politics. . . . But perhaps you are not interested in that sort of thing?"

"I should hardly be human if I wasn't. . . . As a matter of fact, on the rare occasions when I have come across them, I have found them fascinating—some of them, that is—and this case of yours seems to be among the number. The only thing I'm afraid of is that I may not have time. But if you'll tell me exactly how to find the place, and will furnish me with some plausible excuse for my visit, so that they won't take me for an escaped convict, I promise to do what I can."

M. Pouzols-Desaugues, now thoroughly excited, took a large notebook from his pocket. "You're really too kind! I'll draw a map showing how you reach the place from the Laussonne and Saint-Front road. . . . There, now. The name of the house, by the way, is Vaurevauzes. . . . I've made it as plain as possible."

"What an odd name!"

"It's pronounced: Vaoûrevôzes. . . . This piece of the road is pretty bad, but quite practicable for a car if there's no snow. It's really no more than a track across the moor, but the surface is hard and pebbly. I'll scribble a few words for you on my card, too. Make up any sort of story—that you want to buy a horse—something of that sort. . . . They've got some of my horses up there. . . . Just ask to see them."

"I find this all the more interesting," said Jerphanion, "because it has points of resemblance with something that has been occupying my mind recently—something that happened almost under my very eyes in the block of flats where I live in Paris. I had to play a part very similar to yours, and with just about as little success, so far."

"Oh, but that's extraordinary!" cried M. Pouzols-Desaugues in delighted tones. "Do tell me about it, quite briefly. . . ."

A motor horn sounded from the near-by hill.

"How unfortunate! Here's your car. Never mind, you must tell me about it the next time you come—about that and everything else. . . ."

"Everything else being, I suppose, the curious impression I shall get from sitting between four walls which have witnessed several out-of-the-usual occurrences, with a man who may well be a murderer—that is, if I go at all. I imagine that's the total of what you expect from me?"

"Why, of course. All I want you to say is, roughly: 'I was conscious of a perfectly definite smell of crime,' or 'I'm sorry, but I smelt nothing.' It'll be a thrill for me, and we can go into the whole matter together."

The horn sounded again, this time nearer.

"Have you any suspicion of motive?"

M. Pouzols-Desaugues's fingers went through the traditional pantomime:

"Money . . . love, too, perhaps. . . ." He gave a great bellow of laughter. "All very complicated and full of harrowing details, quite like one of the old Greek tragedies. Pay particular attention to the woman who's the elder brother's widow . . ." he started to laugh again. "I talk like this because I'm sure now that you will go there."

"I'll do my best. . . . And—should I happen to run across anyone on my road, or in the environs of the farm, whom I might think it worth while questioning, have I your authority to do so?"

M. Pouzols-Desaugues seemed not altogether to catch his meaning. "I don't quite understand."

"What I mean is, do you mind my seeming to know all about this little matter, without, of course, giving you away as the source of my information?"

"Mm—I'm not quite sure. . . . Oh, I leave myself entirely in your hands. I rely on your tact. Naturally, I don't want to get mixed up in the business . . . but I can't be the only person who's had suspicions, and I expect others have been a good deal freer with their gossip. . . . And now here *is* your car. . . . It really has been delightful. . . . You mustn't fail to come to lunch again before you go back to Paris. . . . I count on you, mind. Just give me a ring, and I'll send my car for you."

# Chapter

# 5

## ON THE ROAD TO THE MOUNTAINS

"I put up the top," said Grousson, "because I thought it might be a bit chilly up in the mountains. But I'm afraid it will rather get in the way of the view."

"Oh that doesn't matter. You were perfectly right."

The sky had become overcast. The position of the sun, which had declined from the zenith, could be gauged only by reason of the pools of molten silver which were visible here and there among the clouds. A coolness, closely akin to cold, seemed to emanate from earth and rocks, and filled the valley with a sense of peace.

Jerphanion sat swathed in his big overcoat, his hands in its pockets, the lower part of his body wrapped from waist to feet in one of Grousson's rugs, his back pressed against the padded rotundity of the seat. In the confined space above the floor-boards he was conscious of the warmth of the engine. Only on his chest and face could he feel the keenness of the air. The general impression was one of agreeable coolness, against which he felt no need to fortify himself. It had something in common with those swaddled, cosy sensations of bodily well-being of which our memories of childhood are full, and disposed his mind to rest and reverie, tempting him to indulge in pleasing and rather fruitless thoughts.

"The one thing I don't want to do," he told himself, "is to chat about politics and my chances at the elections. What I'd really like would be to listen to old stories. This ancient countryside with its hidden valleys must be full of them. Getting about as he does, Grousson probably knows a good many. . . . All that stuff Pouzols told me about the house of crime and the corpses in the snow hangs about my consciousness and echoes in my ears, not so much like some actual drama as some legendary tale. I rather think that if I gave my fancy rein I could embroider on it. There could be no better place for day-dreaming than this car, rolling along, not too fast, through the cold air and the wintry valley."

He glanced at Grousson out of the corner of his eye. "I wonder whether he's heard any vague talk about it."

Deliberately he set himself to savour the curious quality of his contentment. It occurred to him that its rather complex charm was largely due to what, for want of a better name, he might call reminiscence. But if reminiscence it was, it was of no personal experience. This past which seemed to touch him gently with its fingers, if it had been ever really lived, had been lived by others now long since dead. This awareness of his was due, as likely as not, to imagination. But if so, it was skilled in concealing its workings and keeping itself well in hand. It did not force itself into the foreground, but was content to supply an occasional fugitive flash that was like a hint emerging unsummoned from the depths of memory. The air of truth which hung about these glimpses gave them a sharpness of definition. In the intervals between their occurrence he was free to indulge his thoughts without confusing what was arbitrary in them with these flashes from a past far older than himself which seemed to force upon his mind a reality that belonged to them alone.

"Off to the mountains. . . . Those words recall something of the good old days which I myself have never known. This car is going a little too fast. One misses the sound of horses' hoofs, the friendly companionship of horses, the tinkle of bells. Still, once upon a time there must have been two men sitting as we are sitting side by side in a carriage, headed for the mountains. Once upon a time, and more than once. I can feel in my own person their chilled contentment, the way they snuggled against the seat, their shared desire for dreaming and for talk. . . . It must all have happened at some time when the last of the great historical misfortunes was already a distant memory, when as yet there was no slightest hint of other misfortunes still to come. And often all that can have reached them from those remote tragedies would be a faint, scarcely perceptible stirring of men's minds. No local troubles important enough to spoil the mood of the day. Not since the childhood of the oldest inhabitants had troops been seen in these valleys. Stories there might be of bandits, but the scenes of their enterprises lay far beyond the mountains. No wolves in the high woods, or none to be seen except after heavy snow. A recurring round of harvests, good, middling, bad—a natural system of compensations. Above all, no questioning of the basic structure. . . . Society was like the earth, the weather, the seasons. Every man had the right to complain, to grouse, to pray for better times, but no one was such a fool as seriously to wish the world other than it was. No one was going to cudgel his brains in an effort to think out something better. As well dream of a universe in which it never hailed, in which girls were always twenty years old. . . ." Jerphanion pulled the rug closer round him.

"What utter peace!" he thought; and the sense of it seemed to come to him across the centuries. "How we torment ourselves from morning to night, we moderns, arguing about the basic structure! Each generation is worse than the last. At one time it was: 'Which is better, a king or a republic? Universal suffrage or limited suffrage?' Then there was all that business about rights of inheritance, private enterprise, property. . . . 'Isn't this house with its garden,' men wondered, 'this baker's shop at the corner of the street, an offence against the true doctrine? Have we a right to be happy so long as such things are allowed to be?' Today those old problems are still tormenting us, but we have added others of our own: 'Is the proposed frontier for Czechoslovakia rightly drawn? Isn't the Danzig Corridor a dangerous mistake? Won't the unanimous-vote clause condemn the League of Nations to impotence?' What a game it all is! Take my own case, for instance. Not content with bothering my own head, I'm insisting that others bother theirs. What was it I was asking those schoolteachers to do yesterday if not to do their best to see that the humblest peasant in the most remote village should addle his brains not only about the suffrage and the problem of private property, but about the

Danzig Corridor as well? . . . Years ago, at this very spot, there
were two men, well wrapped up, in a carriage, telling each other
stories. . . . Politics? Why, they didn't even know that such things
existed. What does this job of mine amount to? I want to make sure
that anxiety about politics, about social questions, about international
affairs, percolates into every corner of the community—if need be,
to spread these things far and wide. . . . I am to be the man who
provides this three-headed trouble, its agent. . . . That is to be the
spring and centre of my being. . . . I know perfectly well that— Oh
well, no more of that now. Time enough to think of it an hour from
now. Meanwhile I don't want to lose that impression of setting out
for the mountains, with a good companion at my side, not today, in
the turmoil of the present, but on some afternoon of long ago, with
nothing about us but the stories of the countryside, the more or less
vagrant secrets of the highlands and the valleys, the whispered intimacies awaiting us in the roadside ale-houses. . . . I want Grousson
to tell me a story. I want to know whether he has heard of that house
with its snow-enshrouded corpses, or of something else of the same
kind, some other secret crime."

# Chapter

## THE STORY OF
## SAINT FRANÇOIS-RÉGIS

At that very moment Grousson, who was sick of saying nothing, put his curiosity into a not very original question:

"Weren't too bored at Monsieur Pouzols-Desaugues's, I hope?"

"Far from it! I found him a thoroughly agreeable fellow. He can be great fun, too. We talked of all sorts of things. Just before I left he told me some local stories."

"Ah! . . . by chance, that one about Saint François-Régis?"

"No. Why? Is it one of his favourites?"

"I should say so . . . and he keeps it as a rule for republicans, just to show 'em he's not so pious as people make out and doesn't mind that kind of joke."

Jerphanion wasted a couple of seconds wondering whether he really wanted to hear the story of Saint François-Régis.

"Is it a particularly good one?" he asked.

"That's a matter of taste."

"Well, let's have it."

"All right, then. You remember we were talking yesterday about the Protestants in your part of the world, up there in the mountains?"

"Yes."

"You must have noticed an odd thing about their villages. Except for one or two fairly concentrated groups, they're scattered more or less anyhow. A couple of miles from a Catholic village you may come on a Protestant one, with another Catholic one a little farther on. And in each of these places the inhabitants will be either all Catholic or all Protestant. It's odd, you'll admit, when one thinks that all those folk come from the same stock and have lived cheek by jowl for centuries."

"I confess I'd never given it much thought, but I suppose you're right."

"Well, it seems that once upon a time they all became Protestants, all the highland and mountain folk—even perhaps your own forebears."

"What's so unusual about that?"

"It annoyed the King, who made a number of threats, sent a force of police and clapped a lot of the villagers into jail. Others had their houses burned, as an example to their neighbours. But they stuck to their guns just the same. And so it went on."

"Yes?" And Jerphanion thought: "I'd forgotten all about that, forgotten that among all men's other anxieties the religious played a large part; that no matter how obscure a mountain peasant might be, he'd got to have views about predestination. That was something even more remote from his experience than universal suffrage . . . and something, too, that involved terrible penalties if he happened to give the wrong answer."

"Now, there was a certain Monsieur François Régis—Régis's a well-known name in these parts, one's always coming across it—who was a priest, and who had taken it into his head to convert the people hereabouts. He used to make his rounds, by road, going from village to village, staying in each just so long as the work demanded. In fact, his job was very like mine; but, so far as I know, he didn't have a carriage. Consequently, his movements were strictly limited. He made the most of what opportunities came his way. If he was given a lift by Peter or Paul, he couldn't very well ask Peter or Paul to go out of his way just for him. No, it was up to him to find out whether where Peter or Paul was going there happened to be some Protestant village for him to pop into his bag. I think he must have done a good deal of walking. Sometimes, no doubt, he had to change his plans when snow and bad weather made travelling too difficult, and then, probably, he tried to find work for himself elsewhere. The roads weren't so good, either, in those days, you know. I don't suppose his trips were as well organized as mine. It was a one-horse sort of job. But I don't think he much minded. He argued that his time was all his own, and that by dint of zigzagging about as he did, he would eventually cover the whole ground. However that may be, he was obviously a good deal better at the work than the King's police, because, from all I hear, the Protestant villages just dropped into his sack like swarms of bees being smoked out. At that time, and in the depths of the country, no one played a lone hand. If there was a change of religion, it affected all, or there was none. So, you see, he had a terrific success. But one day, when he was at Louvesc—you know the place?—at the lower end of the Vivarais Valley, not far from the highest point in the range—some time towards the end of August it must have been, he caught a chill. I suppose he'd been doing too much and was dead beat. Anyhow, he got a dose of the grippe, and a pretty bad dose it must have been, because, damn it, he didn't last long. He's buried up there, as you know. He was canonized later, and his grave became a place of pilgrimage. They say that there have been one or two small miracles. But the trouble, from his point of view, was that, working in the conditions he did, he was still a long way from completing his task when he died, and that even in the districts he had visited more than once, there was still a lot to be done. There were still a number of Protestant villages scattered up and down in the very heart of his reclaimed territory. No doubt he had set himself to do a good work, but it can't have been an altogether satisfactory one. I suspect that he thought about it, in his last moments, with rather mixed feelings. . . . And so what it comes to is this: if this Monsieur François Régis had not got a lift one particular morning, or if there had been a heavy fall of snow the night before, you'd just have been born a Protestant! . . . And that's the story of Monsieur François Régis; and I expect I've made rather a mess of it."

# Chapter

# 7

## THE DEATHS AT VAUREVAUZES

"It's a charming story," said Jerphanion, "and it makes one think. There's no one I'd have rather heard tell it than you; you gave it an added flavour. . . . But you say that Monsieur Pouzols-Desaugues keeps it for his republican friends. . . . I should have thought that its lessons would really have been more useful to the other side."

"I've done him wrong. As a matter of fact, I've only heard him tell it twice, and one of those times was at the prize-giving at the Catholic school at Le Puy, in the course of his speech. Two of my wife's nephews were pupils there and I had to. . . . At the end of his remarks, Monsieur Pouzols-Desaugues said: 'And so you see, boys, several of you must have been perilously near not being born in the true religion at all. And if you hadn't been, you'd have been quite sincerely convinced today that it was the others who were wrong, and that you were right. Let us, therefore, learn from this story to be both tolerant and modest.' I don't think the good Fathers quite knew whether he was fish, flesh, or fowl."

"Not too bad though, coming from him. Who knows, he may be blessed with a spirit of contradiction; there are times, you know, when it *is* a blessing."

Jerphanion stopped talking for a minute, tried to find some plausible way of changing the conversation, and finally, in an indifferent tone, he said:

"He told me he had some property up there, somewhere between Bournac and Saint-Front."

"Ah, you mean Vaurevauzes," said Grousson with a knowing smile. "Did he tell you—what had been going on there?"

"Vaguely." Jerphanion settled himself more snugly into his seat and drew the rug close. He was conscious of a little icy stab of pleasure. There was something about the coldness of the air between the rocky walls of the road that reminded him of the interior of a church, and of, he would have liked to add, days gone by. So Grousson did know something. Grousson was more or less aware of the story that was going about. No reason, then, why they shouldn't discuss it. . . . The rest of the drive promised plenty of entertainment. Without betraying his curiosity, he continued: "All I remember his saying is that two rather odd cases of death took place in the house—odd and not altogether dissimilar. There was, I believe, an interval of some years between them. Has he ever spoken to you about them?"

"No, *he* hasn't," replied Grousson, trying, like his passenger, to sound as uninterested as possible; "but I know what he thinks about it all from his chauffeur. Besides, this isn't the first time I've heard the matter talked about."

"Really? So others have had their suspicions too?" (And Jerphanion thought happily: "No need to bother any more about old Pouzols-Desaugues; we can leave him out of it."

"They couldn't very well not have, seeing the circumstances," said Grousson. "Besides, as you no doubt noticed, Monsieur Pouzols-Desaugues is not one for keeping a good thing to himself. He'd only got to drop a word here or there for it to be repeated. It doesn't take much to set people wondering."

"It was a question, originally, of the father, I believe, and then of one of the sons?"

"Yes, the elder."

"Do you know the place?"

"A little. I used to have dealings with them once. Before the war I supplied them with a small cask three or four years running."

"So they drank wine, did they, in an out-of-the-way corner like that?"

"Oh, they were comfortably enough off, if that's what you mean."

"But . . ."

"Even before the war livestock-breeding brought them in a tidy sum, and since! Well, with the rise in prices, they're not the only ones round here who have made a good thing out of farming."

"I don't doubt it."

"What I let them have didn't amount to much—small casks, holding about thirty gallons. They drank the stuff with water when they were working in the fields. It wouldn't pan out at much per head, even if the women didn't drink any. . . . So, you see, I got a chance of going there once or twice. Then came the war; I was called up, and I suppose they got what they wanted from one of my competitors. When I came back, I went up to see them one day to offer them my services again."

"By that time the father was already dead, if I've got the facts right?"

"Yes. He died during the winter of 1916–17; at the beginning of '17, to be precise."

"When you went up to see them, were there already rumours going round?"

"Yes. There'd even been an attempt to get some sort of inquiry going. But that may have been merely as a result of gossip. You know what people are. It was said that, especially since the end of the war, money had been pouring into the house as a result of stock-breeding. Everyone knew the exact number of animals they'd sold, and since they spent next to nothing and had not bought any land, it wasn't difficult to lay a pretty safe bet on how much the old man had saved. For it was he, one gathers, who held the purse-strings. Naturally, I can't speak from first-hand knowledge, but it all seems pretty likely. When the old man died, there wasn't much difficulty about who got what, because, you see, the house and land didn't belong to him. No one, naturally, clapped eyes on his savings. It's obvious that the two brothers had come to some arrangement."

"Very probably; but that doesn't prove they did their father in."

"No, I agree. . . . But people were saying too that the old man was as strong as an ox . . . that they'd met him a short while before it all happened—just before that heavy snowfall—and that he showed no signs of dying. . . . It wasn't so much what they said, you understand, as what they hinted. That's how folks are, especially up in the mountains. They don't say: 'This is what happened, and then that. . . .' Oh no, what they like doing is to let you see that in their view things aren't quite what they seem. That's why the authorities gave up the inquiry as a bad job. Everyone they questioned said: '*I* don't know nothing. All I said was that something of that kind might have happened, that it seemed odd to me when I heard that the old man was dead. I've a right to my thoughts. But I don't know nothing.' If ever you see the place you'll understand it all a great deal better. There are no neighbours for nearly a mile, and just think what that would mean with six feet or so of snow on the ground. There couldn't have been any eyewitnesses except among the people in the house; that's obvious. The assumption is that they weren't giving anything away or that the police didn't press them very hard."

"Or that they were innocent."

"Yes, there is that possibility."

"But what was your impression, when you went up to see them?"

"What do you expect! It was more than two years since it had all happened."

"Nothing unusual in their looks?"

"They'd always seemed odd to me, and there was nothing to make me change my mind. Everyone's a bit odd in the mountains, especially when they live in lonely houses out on the moors. But those people at Vaurevauzes were about as odd a lot as you'd find anywhere."

Jerphanion was agog with curiosity. "In what way?"

"Difficult to explain; but, for one thing, the father looked like a regular old brigand. He was black as black!"

"What do you mean by that?"

"What I say, black! You know what it's like when a fellow's black."

"How—his hair, his beard?"

"Yes, he had the kind of beard you don't see any longer, and it had white hairs in it, because he was getting on in years, but the rest of it was, oh, so black! . . . His hair, too, and as shining as though he'd oiled it. But the most striking feature of all was his eyes—real coals they were, and coals with the glow of fire in 'em; and did they glitter! His face, too, was unusually dark, but one notices that kind of thing less in people like that who show the effect of sun and wind easily in any case. You'd have taken him for one of those old gypsy men who come up from the south each spring with their caravans."

"He may actually have had gypsy blood in his veins."

"Well, I've come across more unlikely things than that. I never asked where he was from, but he can't have been of respectable mountain stock because he had no land of his own—just worked as a tenant farmer. His wife, I believe, was a local woman, perhaps even from Bournac—probably the daughter of poor peasants, one of seven or eight brothers and sisters. If she brought him as much as an animal or a few farm implements, he'd have been lucky. But there's no reason why one of his people, a grandfather, say, shouldn't have been a gypsy, one of those fellows, for instance, who settle down near some village for the summer and scrape a living by doing odd jobs of tinkering or the like. Easy enough for a girl to get her head turned by one of 'em. I shouldn't say he'd have let much grass grow under his feet. It had never occurred to me before, but it would explain a lot. . . . Or one of those Spaniards who used to come north for the harvest; though as a rule, I must say, they didn't get so far into the mountains."

"What was his name?"

"Wait a moment—it's just on the tip of my tongue—Leblanc!" Grousson burst out laughing. "Comic when you come to think of it, though it had never occurred to me before. Funny thing for the blackest man in the countryside to call himself Leblanc."

"It may have been a nickname given with the deliberate intention of making fun of him," said Jerphanion, delighted by the perspectives opened up as a result of this conversation. "You often get cases like that. But since, as I gather, it was his legal name, it must have dated from pretty far back. . . ." Jerphanion conjured up a picture of the sunburnt, oily-haired gypsy man, with his "glittering eyes," 'way back in the time of Louis XVI, happening on this village of blue-eyed mountain folk, seducing some neat local maiden, getting himself accepted by some miracle, or because the girl was with child, and being called Leblanc by his blue-eyed neighbours who could think of no other way of paying him out.

He went on: "How old was the father when you knew him?"

"About sixty. But what a figure of a man! He wasn't very tall or big. But you should have seen those impudent eyes of his, and the airs he gave himself! When you met him in his own house, believe me, he looked like the king of the mountains."

"Sixtyish. . . . Well, but—his sons, then, must have been comparatively young. . . . Hadn't they been called up at the time of his death?"

"Ah, but thereby hangs a tale," replied Grousson, dropping his voice to a more confidential tone. "Let me see, now; how did it go exactly? Yes, I've got it: the younger—but first I must tell you that there was very little difference in age between the brothers, not more than two years, and they must have been born while their father was still quite young. Warm-blooded he was, not the kind that waits till he's over thirty before he marries. . . . Well, this younger boy would have been about thirty-five when the war came. He'd never been very strong, I gather, so he got into an auxiliary service. Later, being a father of a family, he was given long leave and sent back to work on the land. . . . Probably Monsieur Pouzols-Desaugues had something to do with that. . . . The elder was in the infantry, and had been at the front almost from the beginning, although he belonged to one of the older classes. They say that he just worried himself sick thinking about his wife."

"About his wife?" (Jerphanion remembered what M. Pouzols-Desaugues had said: "Have a good look at the woman who was married to the elder son.") "But why? I suppose he was very much in love with her, and jealous, eh?"

"That's right. . . . They say the trouble started when his brother got that long leave of his; that was more than he could stand."

"Why? Was he envious of his brother's good luck—going back like that to his own wife?"

"In a way, yes . . . but I don't think that was the only reason. Well, the story goes that though he was in a pretty quiet part of the line, he did his best to get hit, probably arguing that either he'd stay there for keeps or get crippled and be sent home. At last he managed to get his leg smashed, just above the ankle. It was just about the time of Verdun. He always limped a bit afterward. Eventually he got his discharge, and here again, I don't suppose that a word from Monsieur Pouzols-Desaugues to the medical board exactly injured his chances."

"You said something just now about there being other reasons."

"Yes. . . ." Grousson showed signs of embarrassment. "My own private opinion is that he didn't much like the idea of his wife living in the same house as his young brother when he wasn't there to keep an eye on them."

"So that's how it was."

"But he already had pretty good cause for anxiety even before his brother went back home."

"Anxiety? On whose account?"

"Why, the old man!"

"Oh, come now!"

"Someone from up that way said to me one day, joking like: 'When his sons went off, the old man had three women instead of one; and it was none too many for him either, especially since his own wife wasn't much good to him by that time.' I know it was said in fun. But when you've seen the old man at home, as I've seen him, with his eyes like hot coals and his king-of-the-mountains airs . . . and when you've seen the wife of the elder son—because the other—well, the other was just ordinary—but *her,* even today she could turn most men's heads, and that was eight or nine years ago . . . having her there, within reach like that, every day from morning to night, in a lonely house of which he was lord and master, with no neighbours and no witnesses . . . and at a word from him the other two women would scuttle along to their burrows . . . well, I don't think he was the man to cheat himself of a good thing when the fancy took him. . . ." Grousson paused, adding a moment later in jocular tones: "Not that I think there was much need of a word to the other two . . . he'd probably fixed things up pretty satisfactorily with them. After all, that kind of thing was common, so we are told, in the days of the patriarchs, and even now it's not unknown among the Arabs. . . . In such cases a working arrangement's always possible, so long as there's no other man in the house."

Jerphanion felt almost overwhelmed by the abundance of material offered him.

"What marvellous twists and turns! If I get you right, it would not be absurd to assume that the elder son got his leg smashed in order to be sent home because he was jealous—first and foremost of his father . . . and secondly, as an afterthought, let us say, of his brother?"

"Yes, you see he probably argued something like this: 'It's not just that there's one of them; there are two; and me stuck here like a fool.'. . ."

"But tell me this—do you think that this uneasiness was born in him simply as a result of his knowing what his father and his brother were capable of, and because he realized that men found his wife attractive? Or do you think someone helped him a bit? I knew fellows at the front who used to get letters, usually anonymous, about their wives. Until then they'd have been pretty easy in their minds, but those letters would put them in hell. There were others too, of course, who just took no notice of them."

"I've come across the same kind of thing too." Grousson pondered awhile; then: "There's no way of telling, is there? But one may assume that the old mother or the younger son's wife wrote to him secretly . . . though without, necessarily, dotting the *i*'s and crossing the *t*'s."

"It's rather interesting, isn't it, to try to imagine the family's state of mind?"

"It certainly is."

"Especially if one bears in mind what happened later."

"It certainly is," repeated Grousson, who, though he never forgot for a moment to keep his eyes on the twists and turns of the road and to change gear every minute or so, was taking an obvious delight in telling his story, a delight to which the presence of so receptive a travelling companion gave an air of novelty.

"And now," went on Jerphanion, "we come to the old man's death. Let us assume, for the time being anyhow, that there was a crime committed. When the death occurred, both brothers were present in the house with the old man and the three women. In view of the place and the circumstances, we are forced to the conclusion that the crime—if crime it was—can only have been committed as the result of some understanding between the two brothers."

"Yes, that's obvious."

". . . And with at least some degree of connivance or willingness or passive acquiescence on the part of the women?"

"Of the two younger ones anyhow, I should say. . . . Quite probably they left the old mother out of the business altogether. That would be perfectly possible if all four were in agreement," said Grousson.

"But why the old mother especially? I find it easier to imagine her egging the elder son on in revenge for the insults to which she had been exposed . . ."

". . . Leaving the two younger ones out? It's difficult to believe that. . . . Or one of them? But which? . . . The old man may have had both of them. And even if he only had one, the prettier, the elder son's wife, he may have had to force her, in which case she too would have had plenty of motive for vengeance. It's a regular teaser, isn't it?"

"But why assume," said Jerphanion, "that any of them were left out? To diminish the chances of treachery? But the best way of doing that would have been to see that everyone in the house was compromised."

"True enough," agreed Grousson, "and that's probably what actually happened. . . . The way I looked at it was this: they'd have had to keep the younger son's kids—I'm not sure, but I think there are two or three—in the dark, and we may assume, therefore, that they arranged to strike the blow while the old lady, maybe, was busy looking after them, or possibly their mother. . . ."

"But don't you see that the woman in question—whether it was their mother or their grandmother doesn't much matter—would have found it far easier to divert the children's attention, or to see that they didn't wake or get up—the whole thing probably took place at night —if she'd known what was in the wind? Of course, I'm arguing a bit in the air. You have the advantage of knowing the house. Is it, for instance, large enough, with rooms far enough apart, to make it possible for a murder to be committed in the dead of night without some of the inmates knowing anything about it?"

"Yes, I know it—in a way. I've never been over it. It seems to me pretty big, though none too big for all the people who've got to live in it. Where do they all sleep? I've seen beds there, in the large ground-floor room. But what about the other rooms? Several of them must have slept together in one of them."

"Which, leaving the children out of it for the moment, would have made it all the more difficult for them to have committed a crime unknown to one or more of their number. I am inclined to argue in this way: This kind of business could quite easily have been plotted between three or four, or even between two—the two brothers, for example; why, after all, shouldn't it just have been the two brothers? Why, if it was to be kept from some of the women, shouldn't it have been kept from them all?—why shouldn't the whole thing have been carried through in such a way that the rest of the household should notice nothing, at first? But if that was the case, how would they have been able to answer the inevitable questions, explain their actions? 'You saw that he was at his last gasp, and you didn't call anybody? How was that?' I'm talking now only of the adults. Even if they'd pretended to be satisfied with the answers, that wouldn't have stopped their thinking. And the guilty, instead of sharing their knowledge with accomplices who, just because they were accomplices, would have to keep mum, would know that there were possible accusers in the house who, at the first hint of a difference of opinion, would make it clear that they had the whip hand. How was the death explained, do you remember?"

"I think—yes, that was it—they said he'd gone out of doors for a moment one night when there was a heavy frost—I believe that was the story—and that the cold had got hold of him, and that he'd fainted almost as soon as he got indoors again. Something like that, anyhow. I don't think much more was ever said. In cases like that it's a great advantage not to do too much explaining, or at least to seem not to be doing too much. Country folk know that all right—you ask the lawyers."

"Or army officers," said Jerphanion. "But what I should particularly like to know is whether the stage was set for his death with some illness, either genuine or faked. That might have increased or diminished the difficulty, according to circumstances, especially in the matter of keeping the business from certain members of the family. . . . No, the more I think of it, the more convinced I become that a crime committed under such conditions must imply a state of general complicity . . . though I will, under pressure, admit one possible alternative, that of the two brothers alone having been concerned. Two men in complete collusion might, given the particular setting, say to their womenfolk in a meaning way: 'That's what happened, and that's enough for you. No more questions.' Apart from those two possibilities—"

"By Jove!" said Grousson, anxious to conciliate, but, all the same, with sincerity, "I believe you may be right."

"To sum up, then, if there was a crime we can be at least sure of one thing: that the two brothers were in full agreement."

"Yes, one is forced to that conclusion."

"Which of them took the lead? Which first had the idea? The elder, according to you?"

Grousson made a face expressive of perplexity.

"Not necessarily. It's difficult to say."

"All right, then. Let us ask rather what their motives may have been. In the case of the elder it was probably jealousy of his father, a wild desire to avenge himself, perhaps as the result of a confession forced from his wife. . . . But I gather from you that he may have had equal grounds of jealousy against his younger brother?"

"Yes, although that's less certain. When a man is jealous by nature, and has a wife like that, it goes without saying that he'll be jealous of any man. But as I see it, his chief grudge would have been against his father—wrongly or rightly. . . ."

"So far so good. And here's another point. Might the younger brother, on his side, have had reason to believe that the old man, while he was alone in the house and could do as he wished, had treated himself to his second daughter-in-law as well? If he had, that fact alone would have united the two brothers in the same motive of jealousy, the same desire for vengeance, and might have led them to drop any disagreement there may have been between them."

"It's perfectly possible!"

A tree slipped past them as they drove, the corner of a field, a boulder jutting from a low hill, a slope rough with broom. And at each moment an idea, a character, a scene, slid similarly through Jerphanion's mind, seeming in a curious way to be linked with some feature of the scenery, as though there existed a pre-established harmony between the unfolding panorama of the road and the unfolding secrets of Vaurevauzes. He was still greedily intent on this diversion that had come his way. He refused to think of the village meeting lying ahead. (What drudgery it was! What joyless, dogged courage he would need! Would to God this drive could last for hours! How badly arranged life was, and what a mess one made of it!)

Rather disingenuously he said:

"It's a long climb; don't strain your engine. There's no need, we've plenty of time. Besides, it won't matter if I'm fifteen minutes or so late; they'll wait for me."

Then he went on with their previous talk:

"There's one detail—of the greatest importance too—which we're leaving out of account: the 'savings,' the famous savings. . . ."

"I was just going to say," Grousson interrupted him, "that the savings alone would be enough to explain everything."

"Anyhow, they wouldn't clash with the jealousy motive. How much do you think they amounted to?"

The wine-merchant pondered his reply. "It wouldn't surprise me to learn that at the time of the old man's death they amounted to sixty or eighty thousand." He shook his head. "Perhaps even more."

"The devil they did! In gold or notes?"

"Both. . . . Taking into account the period from which they dated, a pretty high proportion of gold."

"No bonds?"

"What do you think!"

"If you're right," said Jerphanion, "and if the women were made privy to the affair, even if at first they didn't much like the idea, the amount of money involved was enough to make them keep their mouths shut when it was over. A murder that brings in profits on that scale sets its authors beyond the reach of any ordinary moral condemnation, and creates solid links of self-interest between those who share the benefits. The old lady's the only one who might have thought differently."

"I'm not so sure even of that! For all we know, the old man may have kept her pretty tight, and it's quite possible that she was fonder of her sons than of her husband."

"Yes. . . . And so far as you know, there was no sign of any quarrel between these five persons? When the inquiry took place, none of them behaved in an odd way, none of them struck a false note?"

"Presumably not; otherwise—"

"Well then," concluded Jerphanion, "the whole affair must have been arranged between them . . . and this touching family singleness of heart brings us to—to the beginning of last winter? It was last winter that the elder son died?"

"Yes."

"And since we have agreed that on the first occasion a crime *was* committed, we are driven to conclude that a crime was committed on this one too?"

"I would go so far as to say," said Grousson with emphasis, "that if, by chance, one of the two deaths was natural, it was more likely to have been the first."

"Why do you say that?"

"Because, don't you see, having been an eyewitness of what had happened, the younger brother would have said to himself: 'It wouldn't be so difficult to get rid of someone when there's plenty of snow . . . no troublesome questions to be afraid of. . . . I've only got to wait long enough for it not to seem odd . . .'—always assuming, of course, that he had his reasons for sending his brother to join the family ghosts. . . ."

"An assumption which we can hardly avoid."

"But you can't make me believe that a fellow who's already put through one murder in the house, or at least had a hand in it, and has had to give evidence at an inquiry, would allow a natural death to take place in his house, and of a remarkably similar kind too, without kicking up a hell of a fuss and rushing off, even if the snow was six feet deep, for the mayor and the police just so as they should be able to satisfy themselves that this time the death really was natural, that everything was in order . . . and that there should be no question of lending willing ears to gossip or opening any more inquiries."

"That's true enough," said Jerphanion. "As a matter of fact, it's a particularly ingenious piece of reasoning. Thinking it over, I'm inclined to believe that you've found the best argument we could have to prove that murder took place both times. Yes—at an interval of six years!" He wagged his chin. "Six years! Have you been back to Vaurevauzes since the elder brother's death?"

"I have not. Can't say I was particularly anxious to. Anyhow, I hadn't the face to try—shouldn't have known how to look."

"So it's a long time since you set eyes on any of the family?"

"I met the younger brother once on the road, and the elder last summer at Saint-Front. I thought he'd aged a lot. He seemed as secretive as ever. As to his wife, I rather think I caught a glimpse of her this very year at Le Puy fair."

"In mourning?"

"Yes. Her veil made it difficult to see her face, but I think I recognized her."

"Still handsome?"

"She certainly seemed so, though I didn't see her close to."

Jerphanion indulged in a few moments' silent thought; then:

"There's one thing you haven't told me: what explanation did they give of the elder brother's death?"

"I've rather forgotten . . . but wait a moment—I'm inclined to think it was attributed to pneumonia. . . . It was said, too, that he'd been gassed during the war . . . as we all were, more or less. I suppose they put it down to that."

"The irresponsibility of the authorities is really extraordinary."

Grousson pulled a face. "They don't much care about these cases where they have to take God knows what amount of trouble and probably find nothing at the end of it all. Don't forget too that they were dealing with a family two members of which had been called up, one of whom was a member of the war veterans' association and had been wounded and discharged; and that if they had pressed things to their logical conclusion, they might have discovered a number of not very pretty things, however you look at them. . . . I may be wrong, but I have a feeling that the authorities fight shy of mixing themselves up in that sort of thing." He started to laugh. "Where war veterans are concerned, you know, things have a way of getting themselves hushed up."

"True enough!" said Jerphanion, laughing in his turn. Then, after another thoughtful pause, he went on:

"You're right. The second crime must be considered even more of a certainty, if that were possible, than the first, and this time there

can be no conceivable doubt about who instigated it. But the explanation, the logical sequence of events, is, don't you agree, a great deal
less easy to imagine? What was going on between the two men over
that period of six years? What motives did the younger have? And
had he been brooding on them all that while? Or— The part played
by the women is very much more mysterious."

"Yes . . . but if it's a question of motive, there was one that had
lost none of its validity—the money."

"How do you make that out? The situation had entirely changed."

"I venture to differ. Don't forget that the elder boy was childless.
Allowing that everything had been settled to the satisfaction of the
law, a considerable part of the estate, in the absence of a will, would
have gone to his brother's family, and to his old mother, which would
in fact have meant his brother, because the old lady would hardly
have had the effrontery to claim her share . . . and the same holds
good of the widow. But that would have been so much eyewash. The
lawyer would have had to concern himself only with the part of the
inheritance that couldn't be hidden, as, for instance, the animals and
the furniture. As I see it, after having done in their old father, the
two brothers would have kept the 'savings' from going into the common pool—you may think such an arrangement odd, but they may
well have had good reason for it—and hidden them in some spot
known only to them. During the last years of the war, and after
peace was declared, the price of livestock must have added considerably to the total involved. Vaurevauzes is a large farm; at any one
time there were probably as many as eighteen or twenty cows, to say
nothing of horses and other beasts. I mentioned sixty or eighty
thousand as the sum represented by those savings at the moment of
the old man's death. Six years later you'd have had to multiply that
amount three or four times."

"Aren't you exaggerating a bit?"

"Certainly not. You see what I'm getting at? The money had
always been a private matter between the two brothers. Well, it's not
difficult to imagine the way things went. There would have been

endless argument: 'I did most of the dirty work, but I didn't get anything like most of the profit'. . . and one or the other may actually have accused his accomplice of pocketing the bulk of what had been sold at market . . . or even of having dipped into the hidden hoard. One of them may quite probably have insisted on settling the matter once and for all—on having a proper share-out—while the other, let us say the elder, not wanting any such thing, may have argued to himself: 'My brother's a sickly creature; one of these days he'll kick the bucket. I'd much better grab the whole lot, or most of it, before I've got to render an account.' But what probably happened is that neither of them wanted to have a regular share-out. They'd each got into the habit of staking a claim to the whole amount. What a temptation it must have been for, say, the younger to make himself master, for good and all, of such a fortune merely at the cost of getting rid of his brother!"

"You make it all sound very plausible," Jerphanion agreed. "You've got a pretty shrewd idea of how the minds of all the people involved worked, and of the tangle in which their conflicting interests were involved. . . ."

"Well, I know them, you see."

"Another great point about your theory is that it explains why the whole business should have gone on simmering all those years. . . . One can see the motive of the crime slowly growing, like the money in the hoard."

Grousson once more took up the argument, speaking with considerable vehemence, but still in the rather confidential tone of a man trying to put into words, for the benefit of his companion, the result of much silent thinking:

"I've got another theory about the younger boy. . . ."

Jerphanion burst out laughing. "When we started on this subject," he said, "you seemed to have a pretty good idea of what had been happening. I see now that you'd been chewing on it for some considerable time. You're never going to make me believe that you've worked all this out in the course of our talk!"

Grousson smiled and shrugged his shoulders. "I'm alone in the car a good deal, you see, and I like having something to think about. . . . It helps to pass the time. A story like this doesn't come one's way every day, and keeping my thoughts to myself as I do, no one's the worse."

"But hasn't your conscience as a good citizen ever pricked you a bit when you thought of that fellow up there calmly enjoying the proceeds of two crimes? Have you never been tempted to impart some of your ideas to those who have a right to be put wise? You've been into the whole business so thoroughly! Even if, as you say, the authorities aren't any too keen. . . ."

The other shrugged again. "Whom should I tell? Any old police sergeant? He'd have to be pretty intelligent to follow my argument. The only way of getting to the bottom of a thing like this is to talk it over as we've been doing, taking one's time, and turning each point over and over. All the sergeant would say would be: 'Have you got any proofs? No? Well, if you ask me, it's just a lot of nonsense.' He wouldn't even bother to listen to me. Or do you suggest that I take what, after all, is pure supposition to a magistrate? He'd just look at me over his spectacles and think: 'The man's a fool! What on earth does he think he's got hold of?' You see, I could never make my meaning clear if I had to do all the talking as though I were presenting a report. . . . No, no . . . one would have to be on terms of intimacy, be in the habit of taking a drink with him at the café, and then, one day, when no one else was by, give a turn to the conversation. . . . But I'm not enough of a bigwig for that. I know the local magistrate by sight. I meet him occasionally at the Café de Paris, bow to him, and he bows in return. I don't suppose he even knows my name. . . . Besides, Monsieur Pouzols-Desaugues, who's an important man and has all sorts of ways of finding things out, and every reason for taking a hand, since the thing happened on his own estate, must have told you what it's all amounted to. After all, it was he who set the inquiry going."

"Oh, I realize that . . . but he probably didn't push it very hard

. . . and when the second death occurred, he played dead. . . . But don't think I'm denying that you were fully justified. If we've got time, I'll tell you about something that once happened to me. . . . To resume, I do see that the rest of them—the neighbours, I mean— even allowing that they'd gone a little way, a very little way, along the same road as you in the privacy of their own minds, would have been even more embarrassed by the idea of making their conclusions public . . . and would have had even better reasons than you for doing nothing. And that, of course, explains how it is that so extraordinary a situation could develop and could continue for so long. It is one of those cases, too, which almost make one understand how it is that anonymous letters come to be written. You and I, naturally, would never write such letters under any provocation whatever. But put yourself in the position of more simple-minded people. I don't say that even for them the sending of anonymous letters is a heroic procedure, but it is not necessarily the result either of cowardice or even of malice. It is the only way they have of easing their consciences and saying to the authorities: 'You are not doing your duty. You are allowing something monstrous to be carried through with impunity.' By the way, do you think that anyone up there thought of sending such things?"

"Possibly; but remember, it represents an enormous undertaking for people like that. And since, in such cases, they merely lay charges and are quite incapable of making their meaning clear, any letters they may send are entirely unproductive of results and simply get thrown into the waste-paper basket."

"That's true. It has taken us three quarters of an hour's discussion to get the facts clear, and we should need three or four hours more to get them down on paper. . . . But forgive me, I interrupted you. You had some theory about the younger brother, I believe? Tell it to me quickly, because I'm afraid we're almost at our journey's end."

"It's just this—I'm afraid you'll think I'm just imagining things— that after the younger brother got back from the war, and before the elder followed him, which didn't happen till 1916, something must have taken place between the older one's wife and his brother."

"Without affecting what was already going on between her and the father?"

"Perhaps—I can't say . . . maybe when the boy came back, she sent the old man about his business."

"So, according to you, the older son may have had some justification for suspecting his brother too? It's becoming pretty complicated." Jerphanion smiled. "What it comes to is that during the earlier period the situation took a most intriguing turn: the younger man comes back from the war because he's afraid that his father, taking advantage of the circumstances, may have stolen his wife. But once safely home, it isn't his wife but his sister-in-law who fills his mind, and it's he who starts playing the situation for what it's worth. The answer to such a supposition, of course, is: he'd been living in close proximity to his sister-in-law for years; why hadn't he fallen for her before?— To which, no doubt, you reply that the circumstances were new and exciting; that the husband was away, and that he had before him the example of his father. It sounds confused put like that . . . but in the warm reality of life—I'm sorry, I've gone and interrupted you again! Please go on."

"Well then, when the elder brother returned, his wife said nothing. The young man was careful not to seem as though he took any particular notice of her, and it's quite possible that his elder brother didn't think that anything much had been happening between the two. His whole resentment was concentrated against his father. Then followed the murder of the old man, and all the business between the two brothers that it involved. But the fact remained that the younger of the two had got the woman in his blood. He couldn't forget her, and perhaps she couldn't forget him. She may have gone on encouraging him and deliberately provoking his advances. . . ."

". . . So that the desire to have as an undisputed possession the woman for whom he'd fallen would have provided him with one more motive?"

"Yes; and that would explain, furthermore, how it was that she didn't kick up a fuss last winter when her husband was killed. . . ."

"And why she may even have had a hand in the business? I find this lady a very curious study."

"It makes one think, too," went on Grousson, "that on the first occasion it wasn't, after all, the elder who had been the leading spirit, as we had been tempted to suppose, but even then the younger."

". . . Urged to it by a burning passion for his sister-in-law and a retrospective jealousy of his father (his own wife no longer playing any part in the affair). He may, too, have said to himself: 'Let's get the old man out of the way for a start; I can settle her husband later.' Unfortunately, that raises a good many difficulties: in the first place, the length of the intervening period. A man may wait six years patiently for a hoard of money which he sees accumulating under his eyes. Would he wait six years for a woman?"

". . . whom he sees getting older every day?"

"Precisely."

"They may have found ways of temporarily slaking their thirst."

"That's possible . . . but it gives rise to still other problems—that of the younger man's wife, for example. What kind of woman is she?"

"Rather a dim sort of creature, so far as I remember. Not the kind to put herself forward or make a scene."

"Ugly?"

"No—mousy, rather. The kind of person one doesn't really notice."

"A woman who might have seen what was going on and have put up with anything from either of them without showing fight?"

"Exactly."

"But in that case, our two assistants—the younger brother and the other one's wife—at once take the front of the stage. In your original story I understood that he played rather a secondary part."

"As a matter of fact, of the two he was much more like his father. He has the same eyes, and he is almost as black. He's an impudent, possessive fellow, like his old man."

"But of a weak constitution?"

"Not so weak as all that. Besides, weakness has nothing to do with it. It may even add fuel to a man's will to mischief. I should say that, fundamentally, he's more capable of malice, slyer, than his father ever was."

"Malicious and sly, quite likely. I think you said that the elder, too, was a sullen sort of chap?"

"Not markedly so—merely the kind of man who doesn't wear his heart on his sleeve."

"I must say," laughed Jerphanion, "they do sound like a jolly family! And now tell me something about the fair lady. Is she really, or was she, as fair as all that? How old should you say she is?"

"Forty at most. She was younger than her husband."

"When the war started, then, she couldn't have been thirty yet. Probably younger than the young brother's wife?"

"I should say yes."

"And handsome?"

"I certainly thought so, though I suppose it's a matter of taste. . . . But I'm not sure that it is. A woman like that just makes one think of sex. It's written in her eyes, in her mouth, in the very way she looks at one. One gets a feeling that she never thinks of anything but men and of the effect she has on them. I've often said to myself that if I'd lived for months and months under the same roof as that woman, I should probably have wanted to go to bed with her. Most likely I should have controlled the desire, if I'd had good reasons for doing so, but the desire would have been there all the same. . . . I don't know whether she was on the scene when they wrapped the old man's body in a blanket before shoving it in the snow, but I'd bet that if she was, she gave the young man a glance or two that would have set his heart turning over in his body."

In the evening light they saw a stocky church tower and then some houses, the roofs of which were covered, some with iron-grey slates, others with cylindrical tiles of a faded brown.

"How high up in the hills one finds those old-fashioned tiles in this part of the world!" thought Jerphanion idly. Then, with a sigh, he said:

"Here we are. I expect they're waiting for me at the school. It would be simplest, I think, if you dropped me at the end of that lane. I shall be through in half an hour—forty minutes at most. How long would it take to get from here to Monastier?"

"It'll be dark by that time. My lights are pretty good, but I should have to drive slowly. Thirty or thirty-five minutes, I should say. . . ."

"Fine. Sure you're not going to be bored?"

"Oh no. I'll drop in on the local publican and try to sting him for a delivery of assorted bottles."

Jerphanion got out.

"Now that I've got a clearer idea of the younger brother and the handsome widow, it occurs to me that it may be somebody else's turn soon."

"Eh?"

"The younger brother's wife, my friend."

Grousson nodded his head and pursed his lips as though he were giving weighty consideration to this remark. "I hadn't thought of it that way, but it's damned likely!"

"We'll discuss the possibility this evening."

They separated, but between them there seemed to hang a furtive and conspiratorial air of mutual understanding.

# Chapter

## 8

## LETTER FROM JERPHANION TO ODETTE: MOUNTAIN THOUGHTS

My dearest dear:

I know you'll forgive me for not having written yesterday from Le Puy. I'm not sure that even this evening I've got energy enough to make this letter as long as it should be. I'm terribly tired, and to add to my troubles, this room is icy, in spite of the wood fire which they've tried to get going. The little hotel at Monastier in which I am staying is clean and the food is good; but it is hardly what you'd call luxurious. I've had to take to my bed in order to write at all without having my feet frozen, and the only light comes from a single almost exhausted bulb hanging from the ceiling.

Yesterday at Le Puy I had to sit up late talking business with two of the suggested candidates on the party ticket and their supporters. It's the part of the job I like least. I have to try to explain to them that in making this tour of reconnaissance on my own I am not trying to push them into the background, but rather to prepare the ground in the interests of the common cause. Luckily, they're not the kind of men to take offence easily, and are perfectly willing to accept me on trust. Unfortunately, however, one of them in particular is so utterly colourless that I don't really see how we can keep him on the list. I shall have to go into the whole question with the Paris committee. But that means that I can't mention either of them by name at my meetings, and have to content myself with vague generalizations. If that comes to their ears, as it's bound to do, they'll probably suspect me of disloyalty. It's all very tiresome. I'd give a good deal to have made my début in political life under the old system, too readily condemned, by which candidates were chosen locally.

Yesterday, at my school-teachers' luncheon, things went very well.

I gather that my speech was generally regarded as good (though I felt myself that it was too abstract and diffuse); anyhow, it produced its effect, and I'm pretty sure that the occasion will prove to have been more useful than any number of village meetings.

I've met the prefect, who is a pleasant, intelligent fellow in whom experience has bred a certain scepticism. He could hardly be more sympathetic. He pointed out that, with the present government in power, he can't support us too openly. However, he is going to do his best to explain to the authorities that the wisest course would be to move with the tide—which means me. I got the impression that he feels pretty certain that I will be elected, and is probably reckoning that if he can get permission from those in power to back me indirectly, he will establish, at small risk, a certain claim on my gratitude and on that of any future government. The trouble about this is that it puts me in a delicate position with the other men on the party ticket.

I had lunch with some rather odd people called Pouzols-Desaugues who live in a small château at Brives, high up above the Loire. The view was beautiful and romantic beyond all belief. My host sees himself very much as a grandee of the old school. He was once in the diplomatic service. His wife is a real old museum piece. It was he who wanted to make my acquaintance. He is a member of the general council and has a good deal of influence with the Church party and the moderates. He can more or less see to it that this or that candidate is accepted or rejected by the electors who, generally speaking, follow his lead. At heart he is a reactionary, but by no means stupid. I talked perfectly frankly to him, and I think he rather liked it.

This afternoon I had two meetings, the more important at Monastier; the other, a few hours earlier, in a village which you don't know. I was struck once again by the seriousness with which these people listen to me. At first they were a bit put out by my manner, which is not what they expect of a candidate. But gradually they came to realize that I had come there to discuss serious matters with which I should have to deal in their name should I be elected. They regard me in the light of a doctor who has come from the great city, very wise, but very simple of speech, not to flatter them, but to give his advice for what it is worth. They left the meeting with a considerably enhanced idea of their own position as electors and of mine as their possible representative. There would still be a brilliant future for the parliamentary system if more people would take that view. True, I'm not yet clear in my mind how to produce the same effect in the great centres, where the meetings will be noisier. But the real problem is how to get enough people of honesty and ability to offer themselves as candidates. As a rule it's an ungrateful job, and it means constant hard work. Meanwhile, the men who have failed in every other walk of life seem to regard Parliament as their happy hunting-ground. The real point (and that is where Péguy went wrong) is to prevent the mystical view of life from degenerating into bastard politics (to the advantage of the second-rate), and to raise politics (to the advantage of really worth-while minds) into a true mystery, in the sense of a genuine science. And there I think you'll agree.

I made my rounds yesterday and today in the car belonging to Félicien Grousson, whom I've told you about already. He is an excellent companion, gay, discreet, and always ready to help. He tells me local stories with humour and a knowledge of human nature and its workings which is far from superficial. I find this an admirable distraction. In particular he furnished me with the details of an obscure crime—the details of which have never come to light. (M. Pouzols-Desaugues had already mentioned it at lunch.) It is a superb specimen of the kind, and reminds me very much of the one you and I have so frequently discussed recently, for, like it, this one is twofold and has evolved slowly over a long period of time. But it has a far more impressive setting, and the persons involved are more clearly defined and a great deal more richly coloured. The incidents, too, are touched with a curious savagery, a massive sort of grandeur, and have given rise to a rich complexity of events although the initial facts are as simple, the unrolling of the story as inevitable, as in a Greek tragedy. The complications of the affair are internal; they owe nothing to outside events, to accident or coincidence. Indeed, there is about the whole business an almost classical bigness. The passions that motivate the whole—if my hypothesis is correct, and at present the whole thing is a matter of hypothesis—would bear comparison with the darkest inventions of the romantic or naturalistic schools, though there is nothing extravagant, nothing deliberately abnormal or "forced" about them. One is tempted to say: "If I had been in the same situation as these people, I should probably have behaved in the same way." I will tell you all about it when we meet (if, that is, I can, because it's not easy to explain). Between now and then I may be able to get together a few more details, one or two touches of first-hand local colour, since in the course of my wanderings I may have a chance of paying a call (in all apparent innocence) on the people concerned, seeing that they live quite close to the road I shall have to travel.

I constantly regret, darling, not having brought you with me. True, you'd have had to put up with a good deal of boredom, with a lot of hanging about, much fatigue, and an absence of comfort. On the other hand you'd have loved these trips up into the hills in the still mild winter weather, with no trace of snow except on a few distant peaks, the pine forests, the deep vistas of sky, while you sat all muffled up in the car listening to stories that seem born of the very shape and colour of the surrounding earth.

I'm worried by what you tell me about Jean-Pierre. For some time now I've noticed, and pointed out to you—sometimes at the risk of incurring your displeasure—that his fits of temper were over-frequent and, for a child of his age, a good deal too readily indulged in. I've no reason to believe that the approach of his seventh birthday is a particularly critical period for a young boy. He probably inherits the tendency from his parents. Both of them, I admit, have admirably regulated temperaments on the whole, but both, were it not for their excellent upbringing, might at times be tempted to fly into rages. I am willing to admit that in his case some small organic trouble may be involved, and as soon as I get back I will ask Bouitton to put me in touch with that children's doctor he knows (Veil-Berger is his name, I think). But, quite between ourselves, I have a feeling that Jean-

Pierre is a bit spoiled. The distance which temporarily separates us gives me courage to say this. He is spoiled, in the first place, by you, by your parents when they come to Paris or when he goes to stay with them, and by me, hard though I try to resist the temptation. He is still a little frightened of me. You tell me that since I went away and since your parents have been with you, his apparently baseless fits of temper have been much more frequent, so much so that even they, ready as they are to make every allowance, have remarked on them. My not being there has, of course, a good deal to do with it, and still more their being in the house, but I'm not sure that their indulgent admiration really explains it all. Let me tell you something else that I've noticed. It seems to me that these outbursts of temper have a close connexion, whether in Paris or in the country, with the presence not only of your parents, but of any casual friends or strangers —in other words, of witnesses. I suspect that there's some exhibitionism involved. He's probably delighted by the sight of the consternation and concern on your three faces whenever he stages one of his little scenes. Think this over seriously, and don't put it down to mere masculine lack of sensitiveness.

The situation is by no means unusual (though I don't put that forward as an excuse for doing nothing about it). The position of an only child is, it seems to me, difficult. Either he's neglected or he becomes more or less spoiled. Or perhaps it would be fairer to say that an only child tends to exaggerate his own importance and to look on himself as the centre of attention. You had only one sister (your brother was so much older that he didn't really count as a child at all when you were young); but even her presence helped to modify the situation. Children have a way of putting one another in their places; they learn from one another the lesson of modesty and of—relativity (that's the modern jargon, isn't it?). I know that I was an only son, but I was brought up among people who were accustomed to families of seven or eight, and were not in the habit of considering a brat's tantrums as signs and portents from heaven to be studied carefully by priests and soothsayers. The village school was not calculated to encourage my narcissistic tendencies, nor, alas, were the years that I later spent at boarding-school. There's another point too, which is not generally recognized: as a rule, school-teachers bring up their children, even only children, better than do other parents of roughly the same social standing. Why should that be? Is it that they are imbued by their calling with deeper knowledge or greater practical ability? I don't think so. The reason, to my mind, is that as a result of having always to do with children, they are, as the saying goes, "saturated" with them—know, almost to excess, their faults, their tricks, their ways of putting themselves across—with the result that when they get back to their own families they are in no mood to give in to any snivelling exhibitionism of the same sort. Similarly, the child of such parents knows full well that the false coin of sentimentality will not pass as current with the tired father who spends all day handling and rejecting that kind of money. Unfortunately, but quite naturally, this profound remark is a great deal less to the point in the case of teachers having to deal with senior classes, and still less in that of those who, after having had the supreme happiness of becoming fathers, were caught up in the activities of war or politics.

In short, the best cure for Jean-Pierre's nervous fits would be to have a little brother or a little sister, or perhaps one of each. The resulting friction would take off the rough edges. Neither you nor I would be able always to find one of them in the right at the expense of the others. There would be in the happy atmosphere of the home that element of almost military discipline which makes itself felt when there is more than one individual, whether young or old, to be looked after.

I can hear you exclaim: "What cheek the man has! It's all very well for him—" Oh, don't think I forget. I remember every detail of the talks we have had on the subject—that time, for example, after I got back from the Rhineland, when we discussed the whole problem frankly and honestly, when suddenly, in a burst of temper, I said, almost clenching my fists in spite of myself: "No! A thousand times no! I have no belief in the future. We've been born into too rotten a time in the world's history. The only reason I wasn't overcome by despair or fury when I spent those long months in the trenches was that there was always at the back of my mind the thought that things might settle down after the war. But I know now that things are not settling down. I can't see the future clearly, or rather I'm afraid of what I see. I'm just not brave enough to pitchfork a lot of new lives into the smoke-filled and quite possibly burning tunnel which stretches before us, nor yet to add to the burden of responsibilities and risks which the men of my trapped generations have got to bear. Our little Jean-Pierre is there, he's a fact in our lives, and we'll manage somehow to take him with us through the flames if the house collapses round us. But are we really prepared to add other complications? Frankly, I'm frightened. I'm not adducing arguments, I'm merely saying that, like a terrified animal, I've got a feeling of panic. . . ."

So, you see, it's not that I've forgotten or changed my mind. (You, too, felt the same.) Nor have I any regrets. I'm trying to develop a feeling of confidence. I'm doing better than that, because I have deliberately struck out on this new line in order to breed confidence in myself by doing something, by exerting all my strength to ward off the very things that make me frightened, to charm away, with the help of others, that very future at the prospect of which I stand trembling like a hunted beast. I'm neither a coward nor yet a passive onlooker. I am doing my duty as I see it. And if those of us who are all working to the same end do ultimately succeed in saving the peace, or in establishing it as a reality (which comes to the same thing), we shall, in the long run, have done our duty to better effect than if we had set about furnishing as large a population as possible from which to provide cannon fodder for the next world war.

That is the sort of thing that is going on in the minds even of the humblest inhabitant of France. Let me give you an instance. At the end of one of my meetings a peasant, quite young, who had been listening with the most flattering and intelligent concentration, came up and said very solemnly: "I want you to give me your advice, sir. I already have one child, a little boy" (see how true the analogy is).

"I should like another, but can you assure me that there won't be any more war?" He went on to explain to me that he was called up in 1911. After a few months he was sent to Morocco, where he saw a good deal of fighting. Later, as a result of the Three-Years Act, he was kept there, still on active service, until 1914. In that year, just as he was coming due for discharge, the World War broke out. He was brought back to France and sent to the front, where he saw many long months of fighting. Then he was transferred to Greece and Serbia. He has seen everything—the desert, the trenches, the Macedonian veldt: bombardment, torpedo attack by submarines, wounds, hunger, malaria, a casualty clearing station in the open field, the inside of a hospital ship. . . . He was finally demobilized in '19 after eight years, or almost, of that kind of life! The stretch of time between his twenty-first and twenty-ninth birthdays! A whole slice out of his poor little ration of living, and what a slice!—the only one which might have brought him a little happiness, a little light. His eyes are still bright; his face still wears the frank, open look of a man from the mountains of Gaul. And there he stood asking me for advice, waiting anxiously for my reply, hoping for some word that might help him to decide. One thing he didn't want, and that was to make a present of eight such years as he had known to his future son.

Well, not being a dealer in soothing-syrup, I faced him with a heavy heart. "My friend," I said with considerable hesitation, "I simply dare not advise you. It's too serious a matter. You must decide as your own heart bids you." I could have said: "Have a little faith. Only if we have faith can we force the hand of the future. If we produce a lot of children we shall intimidate our enemies, whoever they may be; and in that way we shall keep the peace."

It may be that the wisdom of our people is a source of weakness, the folly of others a source of strength—in a world that is the plaything of blind chance. But if this world of ours is to remain for ever the plaything of blind chance, it holds no further interest for me. It holds no further interest for me because in that case everything that has happened in it since the beginning shows up as false and sterile.

If it remains the plaything of blind chance it will quickly perish. The only reason why blind chance has not caused its complete collapse before now is that the available resources were far less formidable than they are now, and have operated only on a restricted scale. But the relative impunity which it has enjoyed in the past proves nothing. It was due to an accident which will not recur indefinitely. My only hope lies in the possibility of producing a reaction against blind chance. It is not by mass-producing children that we shall avoid war. Have Russia, China, Japan, Italy, where mass production has been the rule, been less exposed to the horrors of war than ourselves? Was the Germany of yesterday, which certainly practised such mass production, preserved from its dangers? Can it be said that a democratic and pacifist German of 1900—and there were democrats and pacifists in Germany then—helped to prolong the peace by begetting an extra child? All he did was to play his small part in increasing the sense of pressure within his country, in adding to that feeling of power and insolence and to the intoxicating mania for expansion which sooner or later was bound to emerge from it. For a world that remains subject to the blind laws of chance finds itself in an inevitable dilemma. On the one hand are the countries which by refusing to resort to a mass production of population may tempt the greed of an aggressor, on the other those who, as a result of doing so, run the risk of being cast for the role of aggressor and of starting a war from which their teeming nurseries will not save them—and eventually of losing it. (For the lessons of history show that aggressors do lose wars, even though they may start with an initial advantage.)

Stated in those terms, the problem becomes one of sheer lunacy. And if humanity continues to state it in those terms, then humanity is lost. We're not going to frighten away the spectre of war by producing children for the eventual stocking of the world's barracks. Only by abolishing war, as definitely as we know how, can we be sure of having a world in which it will be worth while to rear children at all.

Well, I've travelled a good way from Jean-Pierre's tempers, haven't

I? Give that insufferable brat a lot of kisses from me, all the same. To your parents I send my warmest good wishes. Don't let them go before I get back. I'm sure it won't upset their plans to stay a bit longer. You know how fond I am of them. Kiss them for me, and keep for yourself, my dear, darling Odette, any number of fond kisses from your

JEAN

who is almost falling asleep.

Address your next letter Poste Restante, Le Puy.

# Chapter

## OF POISONS

"What's the program for today?" asked Grousson, while he ran over the car to see whether everything was in working order.

"The only actual fixtures are two meetings, one at Saint-Front this afternoon, the other in the evening at Fay-le-Froid. If I meet anybody on the road who might be interesting, I should like to stop and have a chat with him for a minute or two; otherwise, nothing."

"Saint-Front this afternoon," Grousson repeated, with a somewhat worried look.

"Of course," Jerphanion added hastily, "only if it's convenient for you. I can adopt any itinerary to suit your arrangements—so long as I'm in time for my meetings. . . ."

"All I meant was that I should have liked to go to Saint-Front this morning. There's a customer I want to see, and I can't be sure of catching him unless I get there before eleven."

"That's all right! Let's go straight to Saint-Front."

"But there's no point in that for you, since you've got to be there again later. You'll find it an awful bore hanging about while I do my business."

"I'll go and look at the church. It's a particularly fine specimen, and I've not been inside it for years."

"You might have a chat with the curé. Do you know him?"

"No."

"He's a fine old chap—not one of the fanatical sort who'd tear you to bits as soon as look at you. It's a pleasure to talk to him. . . . They're a bit Church-minded, you know, in this part of the world, and it wouldn't do you any harm if they got to know that you'd paid him a visit. . . . It's not a bad idea. . . . Besides—" He broke off, with a smile.

"What?"

"I was going to say that when we'd finished, I with my customer, and you with your curé, why shouldn't we take a look at Vaurevauzes? Monsieur Pouzols-Desaugues gave you his card, didn't he? So that makes it all easy. Doesn't the prospect tempt you? Don't say you've lost interest since last evening."

They started off. The engine, which had been running for only a few minutes, was missing a good deal, and the car progressed in a series of jerks.

"If this goes on," said Grousson, "we're going to have a fine time of it on the hill. It was pretty cold last night. There's quite a lot of ice on the ground. I ought to have emptied the radiator last evening and filled up again this morning with hot water."

"Run her in second for a bit on the level," said Jerphanion. "She'll soon warm up." Then: "No, I've not lost interest, and if we've got time to have a look at Vaurevauzes, there's nothing I should like better. . . . I thought a good deal about that business in bed. . . . Before I turned in I was dropping asleep, but fatigue acts in an odd way; as soon as I shut my eyes, I felt as wakeful as a bushel of fleas. . . . If I do call on those people, it'll be out of pure curiosity. Still, the clearer I can get the whole thing in my mind, the more interesting the interview will be. There's one point we didn't discuss: if the father was killed first and the elder brother afterwards, which I'm more and more inclined to think was the case, how was it done? It can't have been as easy as one thinks. Even allowing that they managed to make away with the body, it wouldn't have done to leave visible traces of violence."

"Certainly not."

"If they'd wanted to make people believe that he'd died of a congestion brought on by the cold, or something similar, they must have realized, even though they weren't experts in pathology, that it would be a mistake to let the corpse show an entirely different set of symptoms—even if those symptoms did show death by natural causes. There was always the off chance that a doctor might get a glimpse of it."

"They probably hoped to get away with the business without calling in a doctor."

"Very likely, or say, rather, without having to have a post-mortem. But they could hardly have avoided one if their version of the matter had been too palpably false. You agree that the whole thing had been carefully thought out?"

Grousson shrugged his shoulders. "I agree certainly that they're not likely to have bashed his head in with a hammer."

"People of that kind would hardly have used poison. Where could they have got it, to begin with?"

Grousson pulled a face. "I wouldn't like to take my oath on that. If you or I wanted poison for any purpose, we should go to the druggist's for it. They, on the other hand, would see whether they couldn't manage somehow on their own."

"But how?"

"You've walked over the moors in summer time, haven't you?"

"Oh yes, often."

"And you've noticed, I expect, what a number of herbs and flowers and plants there are growing wild. Any number of 'em. I have an idea the doctors don't know everything."

"You mean that some of them contain poison?"

"Poison or something else which has much the same effect. It's just there for the picking. No need for a prescription."

Jerphanion's smile was eloquent of polite incredulity. "There can't be many herbs of that kind, and what there are must have been pretty exhaustively catalogued and analysed by the scientists."

Grousson was stubborn, but no less polite. "Maybe; but—well, look here. When anyone's bitten by a mad dog nowadays, he's rushed off to the Pasteur Institute, isn't he?"

"Yes."

"But that's a fairly recent development. Do you remember what used to happen when you were a child?"

"Let me think. . . . Yes, I know, the victim was taken to the blacksmith, who cauterized the wound with a hot iron."

"Precisely, that's what happened as a rule. But once the dog's saliva had got into the blood-stream, cauterizing wasn't any good. Have you never heard of the cure practised by the nuns of Saint-Julien-Chapteuil? You ought to, because you come from that part."

"I've forgotten for the moment."

"Ask your mother; she'll remember. She'll tell you that no one belonging to the canton of Saint-Julien has ever died of dog-bite within living memory. Not that there was any lack of mad dogs. The fact is that as soon as anyone was bitten, his friends sent a messenger into town, and the nuns gave him their cure. They always kept a supply ready."

"What was it?"

"A kind of blackish liquid, or so I've been told; very thick, and with a perfectly disgusting taste. Those who've had it, and I've known more than one myself, will tell you that it was all a man could do to swallow the stuff, even half a glass of it. For hours after they'd got it down they would be—very appropriately—as sick as dogs. Obviously it didn't act merely on the bite, but on the whole system. Something like a cure, eh?"

"Did they never say what it was made of?"

"I should think not! Certain herbs and plants, I suppose, pounded with a pestle and possibly set to simmer over a slow fire, or stewed— I really don't know. . . . However that may be, the resulting decoction must have been terribly strong. It was their secret. Now, who taught it to them? I gather that a number of offers to purchase it from them have been made from time to time, probably by druggists in Le Puy. Just think what a specialty it would have been before the days of Pasteur! But the nuns have always refused these offers. Even in recent years many people bitten by mad dogs have deliberately fixed matters so as not to be sent to the Pasteur Institute, either because they were frightened, or because of the waste of time involved, especially in the harvest season, when the chance of being bitten was greatest. These people would creep off secretly to the nuns, who have more than once been embarrassed by the popularity of their treatment."

Glancing at his companion, Grousson noticed that though he seemed deeply interested, he was still not wholly convinced. He returned to the charge.

"Look here, I don't want you to think I'm just telling you a pack of old wives' tales. I've given you the facts. I've met people as far afield as the canton of Yssingeaux who had gone to Saint-Julien for that cure. If I took the trouble, I could find among the old people of over seventy a good half-dozen who have had personal experience of the thing. It may all be very unscientific, still . . ."

"No," replied Jerphanion in conciliatory tones, "it's not unscientific at all, only rather surprising. I am perfectly ready to admit that among these carefully guarded country secrets there may be, along with a lot of nonsense, a great deal that is of real value which we have allowed to get forgotten."

"Ah, now you're talking! I once told what I have told you to Dr. Lézarnauds of Le Puy, who has the reputation of being a very advanced thinker. He just laughed in my face. 'But, doctor,' I said, 'it's something you ought to take seriously. I guarantee to produce people who have taken the stuff 'way back in the old days. Even though you may not know what herbs the nuns used, how can you be absolutely sure that it's all bosh?' He just said: 'We have a thorough knowledge of all the herbs that might have been used by these good women. . . . There isn't the faintest possibility that what you tell me can be true.' I wanted to say: 'If you know so much about herbs, why don't you try to make the stuff yourself and then give it to a few of these people over seventy to see whether they recognize the taste? . . .' It's silly to pretend to know everything like that."

"Then, according to you . . ."

The wine-merchant, hot on the track of his argument, immediately continued:

"It's not a question of 'according to me'; I've no particular theory to put forward. All I say is that if I wanted to get hold of some rather obscure poisonous herb on the Mézenc moors, I'd rather take the word of a local peasant than that of a doctor from Le Puy. And then again, leaving aside the question of genuine poisons—for there can't be many of them, and what there are must be pretty well known—it should be possible to find certain herbs which are not generally regarded as poisonous, but, on the contrary, are reputed to have curative properties when taken in a not too concentrated form, though when administered in a very strong brew they may well be capable of doing a man in, especially when mixed with other elements. Who'd ever suspect anything wrong? Take my own case. One day I happened to be at La Champ-Raphaël—you know the place? Well, I must have caught a chill, like Saint François-Régis. Anyhow, I felt so bad that I had to do something about it. That evening I went to bed without eating a thing in the little shabby inn where I happened to be staying. My teeth were chattering. The woman of the house said: 'If you like I'll get my neighbour to make you one of her infusions. You drink it with a lot of rum and sugar. It's not really very nasty, and you see if you're not all right tomorrow morning.' I drank the stuff, which, as she said, when taken with a lot of rum and sugar didn't taste too bitter; if anything it was rather too sweet, rather syrupy and sickening. At first I felt as though I'd got a hot stone in my stomach, or had eaten something that wouldn't go down properly. I still went on shivering. Then my heart started to beat like nothing on earth; there was a humming in my ears; I felt as though my head was going to burst; I no longer knew where I was. I can tell you I thought I was in for it! At the end of fifteen minutes or so I started to sweat—and did I sweat! . . . The whole of my body was streaming. My pillow and mattress were sopping wet—as wet as a piece of bread dipped in soup. I lay like that for hours, completely exhausted. Next morning, though I still felt a bit weak, I was able to continue my journey. The chill had vanished."

"Yes—but . . ."

"You see my point? Suppose the good woman, instead of wanting to help, had intended to harm. Suppose she'd made the infusion stronger, using the same herbs, but, say, two or three times stronger. Judging by what I went through, I really should have kicked the bucket."

"Oh, it's certain that once a man is past his first youth, this or that organ may very easily become fatally affected."

"And then, if they'd called in a doctor to give a death certificate, wouldn't he just have said: 'Obviously he died of his chill'?"

"It seems probable enough."

"Finally, let's assume for the sake of argument that they'd sent my body back to Le Puy and that my wife had insisted that death was due to something other than natural causes—which is not very likely, because she's not the kind of woman to make unnecessary trouble. Well, she'd have demanded a post-mortem, and what would they have found? Answer that if you can!"

Jerphanion took refuge in a grimace.

"I know I'm not an educated man like you," went on the wine-merchant, "but I always imagine, when I hear of doctors discovering traces of poison in a dead body, that they must begin by saying to themselves: 'Let's see whether there isn't some indication of arsenic, or of cyanide'—or any poison you like to name. It's the way I go to work when I'm not quite sure of a wine I'm sampling. I say to myself: 'isn't it over-sweet, or doctored, or treated with colouring matter?'"

"I think you're probably right, though I fancy one must also take into account the probability that direction is given to their suspicions by some appearance in the corpse, or in the organs that they are examining, in the same way, I presume, as you are put on your guard against this or that wine by something suspicious in its colour or taste."

"True enough. But nothing in the colour or taste of a wine is ever going to put me on the track of a concoction which nobody, normally, ever uses in faking wine, the very name of which I may not know."

"Remember, too, that when doctors want to have organs analysed, they send them to a laboratory which is properly equipped for that kind of work, where a list is kept of all probable poisons, far more exhaustive than any doctor could carry in his head, and where they have processes for quickly discovering them."

"Yes, but to go back to my own case, assume that what might have killed me in the good woman's infusion from being taken in too concentrated a form had been—I mention the first things that come into my head, for the sake of argument—a mixture of borage and verbena. Would it ever occur to your laboratory experts to think of borage and verbena? Would they be likely even to have them on their list?"

"I should be greatly surprised if they had," said Jerphanion, with a laugh. "For in that case I can see no reason why they should not suspect ten thousand other varieties of the vegetable world . . . the list would be endless. Besides, any given analysis would take them about six months to complete, even allowing (and I speak in complete ignorance) that they could succeed in isolating the active principle of borage and of verbena, to take your own examples. After all, there may be many different principles in the same plant, all of which may be known though there may not be any quick method of detecting their presence in a body. . . . It sometimes happens, too, that a substance may have left no trace, or only in one particular part of an organ, and that that part may not have been sent to the laboratory, or the analyst may not have thought it worth examining. The men who do that kind of job are, in their own way, officials with a great deal of work to get through in a short time. They can't waste weeks and months on a single case. An analytical laboratory isn't, after all, an institute of advanced scientific research."

"So, on the whole, you agree with me?"

"Speaking generally, I suppose, yes. But what's bothering me is this: does your theory really apply to people like the farmers up at Vaurevauzes? Any such secrets about the properties of herbs are known, as a rule, to the old. But both the crimes were committed by young people."

Grousson put on a knowing look. "Why shouldn't it have been the old girl who had the knowledge of herbs? There's no reason why she shouldn't, for years past, have been teaching her secrets to her daughter-in-law, the wife of the elder brother."

"And neither the father nor any of the men need have known anything about such things?"

Grousson shrugged his shoulders.

"It's just the kind of thing," he said, "that women do plot among themselves. There are plenty of families in which the man of the house couldn't tell you what goes into his soup, and couldn't brew an infusion to save his life."

"Then it must have been the older brother's wife who concocted the father's fatal drink? . . . Knowing the recipe already, there would have been no need for her to get the old woman's help, or even to confide in her, when the moment for action came?"

"Why not?"

". . . And she repeated the dose a few years later for her husband?"

Once more Grousson shrugged his shoulders.

"Yes, but," went on Jerphanion, "we still agree, don't we, that it was the two brothers who took the lead on the first occasion? They can hardly have been ignorant of the part played by the infusion, even if they couldn't make it themselves. How then can one explain the fact that the elder unsuspectingly drank the stuff six years later?"

Grousson proceeded to hedge. "As I said," he replied, "the whole thing's confoundedly complicated. One can suspect almost anything, one can be sure of nothing. But there's one thing, as I said before, that we can regard as more or less certain: they didn't shoot the old man or bash his head in, because, even assuming that their neighbours weren't going to ask awkward questions, they wouldn't have been such fools as to leave such an obvious piece of evidence. . . . But apart from that, anything is possible. It's often easier to kill a man than you'd think. I remember a chap at the front whose pals had made him blind drunk one very cold night. He slipped away from the dug-out to vomit, the cold got him, and he never came back. The old man up at Vaurevauzes may have been really ill, though not so bad as to prevent his coming and going. In fact, he may have pretended deliberately to be more sprightly than he felt. It wouldn't have been difficult to persuade him to go out after dark, his teeth chattering with fever, when the ground was covered with snow, and the thermometer showed four degrees below zero. Let us assume that when he came in they gave him an infusion, or some mixture of infusion and brandy, strong enough to floor an ox. When a man's mind is a bit wandering, as it would be if he had a fever, it would be fairly simple, if he didn't die quickly enough, to finish him off by, for instance, smothering him, eh?"

Jerphanion saw rise before him, etched against a crackling background of sunlit frost, the picture of this death-scene thus reconstructed. It seemed plausible enough. He found himself seized with admiration for Grousson's unusual gift of lucid exposition, combined with a daring inventiveness, plenty of sound common sense, and a flair for guessing how events came about. "Many a historian, trying to reconstruct some little-known incident, might well envy him," he thought.

"Yes," he said aloud, "yes—I see what you mean. But don't forget that we've still got to explain the elder brother's death. Is it conceivable that, after sharing in the old man's murder, he should have let himself be taken in by the same trick? Whether or not he was himself already a sick man, he would surely have had his suspicions aroused. It's hardly likely that he would have taken a possibly doctored drink."

"That's true," said Grousson, "but remember, no man can be on his guard at every moment of his life. Six years is a long time. In the course of those six years he would probably have drunk any number of infusions prepared by his wife, and even if he had begun by being suspicious, he would have been reassured by the fact that his health showed no signs of deteriorating. . . . It is possible, too, that his wife and his younger brother, who were already in a plot together, may have asked him to help them in getting rid of the old man, but without mentioning the infusion. They may simply have said: 'He's very ill. Now's the time to act. He could be strangled as easily as a chicken. He's so weak that it could be done without leaving any marks. . . .' "

Jerphanion made no reply. He felt that the hypothesis had been carried so far that there was considerable risk of losing the main argument in a mass of unnecessary subtleties. Anyhow, it was not up to him to confuse the issue by being too clever.

He found the noise of the engine delightful. The car was running at full power. It seemed to rejoice at putting forth its utmost. The explosions were as rounded and as closely packed as the kernels in a healthy ear of corn. The rapid succession of their detonations merely lengthened a bit—like an elastic band suddenly expanded— as a corner was rounded and the hill grew steeper. A moment later came that deepening note that makes one think of an outburst of temper without malice, when a car picks up easily. He couldn't, however, help thinking fondly of his own car, though not without a touch of anxiety. "I should like to try her out on this hill. . . . I hope she'd take it as easily as Grousson's . . . though, of course, the carburetor needs regulating. . . . I can't get it out of my mind that that fool of a mechanic at the garage fitted too small a jet."

Half-way up the slope on the other side of the valley two very old thatched houses shared the expanse of a rocky terrace. In front of them a little army of fir trees, or rather a squad, so few they were, dominated the next turn of the road. It was probably freezing out of the sun, though there was no hint of frost on the ground.

# Chapter

## A VISIT TO THE CURÉ

Coming out of the inn kept by M. Astier, where he had been spending a few minutes, the wine-merchant said to Jerphanion:

"Perhaps you could manage your visit to the curé while I'm busy with my other customer?"

"I've been thinking—won't the mayor be annoyed if I pay my respects to the curé first?"

"Not a bit. As a matter of fact, the mayor's pretty Church-minded —and then, the curé's a much older man than he is. He'll understand all right. Besides, it's not sure that you'll find him in this morning. You can call on him this afternoon, before the meeting."

Jerphanion was not altogether reassured. He was too old a hand at the business of politics not to know that the most innocent acts often lead to trouble.

"All the same, it's rather tiresome. My original idea was just to have a look at the church. If I'd happened to run into the curé, all would have been well. But he's not likely to be there at this time of day, is he?"

"Since he's not been warned of your visit, I doubt it. He's probably in his house, which is next door."

"That means I shall have to knock at his door, which puts quite a different complexion on the matter. It might occur to the school-master, too, that I was showing rather overmuch friendliness for the other camp. It's tiresome, as I said before."

Grousson had a sudden idea. "Look here," he said, "I tell you what. Take a turn round the church. Just manage to potter about for a bit. I'll send word to the curé that you're there; better still, I'll tell him myself. He's sure to go and look for you. You'll find it pretty chilly hanging about, though; you'd better button your coat. But what are we to do about your head? Damn it, you don't want to go catching a cold just now. You can't keep your hat on—I tell you what, I'll lend you my beret, it's knocking about somewhere in the car. . . ."

"Are you sure that would be all right?"

"Of course it would. Pull it well down and it'll make a sort of skull-cap."

"You make me think I ought to have brought my own; not specially for going into the church, but because it comes in useful so often. It's a sort of badge among the war veterans."

"Well, here's mine. I only hope it'll fit you."

"Splendid. It's a bit tight, but I can pull it up like this—that'll make it look better in a church. In any case, I won't put it on unless I feel cold."

"Good. Then we'll meet here at the car about a quarter to eleven. It won't take us more than fifteen minutes to get to Vaurevauzes."

"Do you think we'll find them all there?"

"Where should they be? There's no market here, and no fairs in the neighbourhood."

"That's true."

Just as he was moving away, Grousson said:

"I've told Madame Astier that we shall want lunch. . . . She was a bit put out, because she's not got much in the house."

"I bet she'll be able to give us something."

"Of course she will. An omelet to start with followed, I need hardly say, by sausage. After that, well, some lake trout, fresh caught this morning, with potatoes, and a dish of jugged hare—a hunter brought her a hare yesterday evening, so I expect it'll be a bit tough. Then, some mushrooms. . . ."

"Do you really think we'll want the mushrooms?"

"The way she does them makes your mouth water. We must just taste them."

"Oh, all right."

"She wanted to give us a roast to follow. She says that a dinner without a roast isn't a dinner at all—say a small leg of something— leg of lamb is specially good in this section, because of the grazing hereabouts. But she says she's not sure she'll be able to get one from the butcher at such short notice. If she can't, she'll be awfully put out. . . ."

"It doesn't look as though we should starve."

"She suggested veal cutlets instead. She says the butcher's out of veal for roasting, but she thinks he can manage some veal cutlets. . . . I told her not to bother."

"I should think not!"

"She can let us have a nice piece of blue cheese, but she can't manage much in the way of a sweet."

"What a tragedy!"

"She did murmur something about a rum omelet, but I thought that as we were starting off with omelet—"

"Really, she mustn't bother."

"We'll probably have to make do with dry cakes, but we can dip them in our wine. She's put aside two bottles of a sound Côtes-du-Rhone. I'll answer for it, it's stuff I sold her myself. . . . And she's going to light a wood fire in the small dining-room. We shan't do too badly."

"Oh, why aren't Odette and Jallez here?" thought Jerphanion. "What a lot we should find to amuse and astonish us, if only we were together!"

He could not make up his mind to take Grousson's beret out of his pocket, though the cold, striking down from the vaulted roof, went right through his hair to the scalp beneath and gripped his shoulders, in spite of his thick overcoat, in a way that he found it increasingly difficult to ignore. Quite a lot of sunlight streamed through the stained glass of the windows, but not enough, for it was concentrated into narrow beams which fell obliquely high above his head, so that they never actually reached his body and were productive of cheerfulness rather than warmth.

After a while he heard the sound of footsteps over by the main door, and saw, coming towards him, the figure of a short, thickset man.

The curé was very old and very small. His hair was quite white, and he carried himself with a slight stoop. His face was round, pink, fresh-complexioned; his expression at once smiling and reserved. His soutane had seen many long years of service. Beneath it there appeared to be many thicknesses of woolen undergarments.

Jerphanion broke the ice with a few polite phrases. He spoke in the low voice that seemed appropriate to the place in which they found themselves. The curé interrupted him in loud and resonant tones. He spoke with a strong local brogue which contained an attractive sing-song undercurrent.

"I'm very glad indeed to meet you, sir. Monsieur Grousson told me of your welcome presence. I hope you haven't caught cold waiting for me."

Jerphanion thought at first that the old man must be slightly deaf. But he soon realized his mistake. It was simply that the curé was accustomed to speak in his church, when there was no service going on, as he would have done in any other familiar spot. He saw no reason to employ a hushed tone of voice.

He went on:

"You have had a good look round?"

"Yes, indeed. But I am no stranger here. . . . I used to come here a lot."

"Well, then—let's go somewhere else. You'll catch your death."

"But how about you? After all, you say Mass here."

"Oh, I'm used to it. Come, let's go to my house. I can offer you some sloe gin. I'm afraid you'll find things in rather a mess, because the woman who does my housekeeping doesn't come in till later. But it'll be warmer than here."

There was a quickness, almost a gaiety, of movement about him, though from time to time there came into his eyes a look of nervous anxiety.

Nor was Jerphanion entirely at his ease. "Some of the neighbours are bound to see us," he thought. "Things like this get about so easily, and the most awkward inferences might be drawn. What will the schoolmaster think? . . . I don't want to be thought an extremist, but there's a limit to everything. It's all very tiresome. I don't think this was a very good idea of Grousson's."

Luckily it was not far to the curé's house, and the way led along a little-frequented lane. By his gait, by the way in which he glanced to left and right and looked at his watch, Jerphanion did his best to give the impression of a man who had picked up a casual acquaintance and was going along with him because he could not very well help it.

The curé's house was tiny. Like the rest of the near-by buildings, it was constructed of six-sided blocks of basalt very neatly laid. The edges were clear-cut, the cement in good condition. Not for the first time Jerphanion found himself thinking: "This is the stuff, the only stuff, for permanence; the basic material of our planet, indestructible. Nothing can injure it, not rust nor frost nor the effects of time. If ever I build a house of my own, this is what I should like to use. Compared with it, granite is mere rubble that would crumble at a touch."

The front door was reached by an outside staircase of ten steps or so, with an iron hand-rail fixed to the wall. "To keep the door well above snow-level," he reflected.

"I'm tempted to entertain you in the kitchen," said the old man. "The other room is more presentable, to be sure, but there's no fire in it. I've had one burning in the kitchen grate all morning."

"Let's go wherever you think best, sir. There's nothing I like better, in this part of the world, than a good kitchen. It's always the best room in the house in cold weather."

It was smaller than it would have been in most cottages, and many of the objects normally to be found in them were absent, the churn, the great kettles, the various household utensils. Otherwise it was a typical mountain kitchen. Two of its four walls—the one facing the fireplace and the one opposite the window—were occupied by an unbroken range of wooden furnishings forming a right angle and comprising two dressers, a cupboard with solid doors, and a clock. The cupboard and the clock stood each at one end. The pendulum of the latter, a large copper disk, adorned at its centre with an enamel plaque so much worn as to be scarcely distinguishable, could be seen swinging behind a circular glass panel. The narrow window, pierced in the thickness of the wall, showed, across a huddle of tiled roofs, to a patch of sunlit country. In the middle of the floor stood a table of rough country make, the dark brown of its wood seamed with ancient scars. A few odds and ends of crockery were visible on the shelves of the dresser, the empty spaces being filled by statuettes and pious objects. Some sacred pictures were pinned to the panelled walls. The edges of the woodwork had been worn smooth by age; its smooth, dark surface was slightly lighter in tone than the beams of the ceiling. In the fireplace, which was as big as the entrance to a small cave, two logs still smouldered, though almost on the point of extinction.

The curé added two more, poked the fire, and stuck the flattened, twisted nose of a large pair of leather bellows into the ashes. There was a little shower of sparks, cinders, and aromatic smoke. Tiny flames began to lick the sides of the fresh logs. The temperature rose by very little, but the room, in its protective shell of wood and stone, produced an impression of dry and healthy warmth. A faint smell as of sour milk was just discernible above the long-established, age-old atmosphere of burning wood.

The curé took a bottle of sloe gin from the cupboard.

"A present from Madame Astier," he said.

He went on to say how kind the neighbours were, how attentive to their old pastor. He owed the very wood for his fire to the generosity of his parishioners. Often, when Mme Astier had to cook a meal for visiting travellers, she sent him over something. Even the poachers remembered him.

"I don't encourage them, but I can't be too hard on their activities," he said in his singsong voice. "They mean well."

He looked at his visitor with eyes that betrayed a hint of anxiety. There was in his glance something of humility and apology.

"You see," he said, "I am more or less dependent on charity. It could hardly be otherwise, could it? . . . There have been bad times, very bad. . . . Just after the Separation was the worst. People weren't used to the new arrangement. . . . They were asked to contribute to the upkeep of their priests. Any sum, however small, would have seemed big to them, and that's hardly to be wondered at. But gradually things settled down. Then the war came, and with it a terrible rise in prices all round. People were just thoughtless, that's all. They made us gifts in kind. They couldn't know that we lacked, inevitably, certain commodities, things that no one would think of giving. . . . Very often there were days when they quieted their consciences with the thought that somebody else was looking after us."

"And then, of course," Jerphanion put in, "there are all the things that are not produced locally, things that it needs money to buy."

"There you have struck the nail on the head, my dear sir . . ." sighed the curé. Slowly he raised a pink and white hand knotted with veins and marked, here and there, with faint whitish stains. "I must seem like a beggar complaining that trade is bad. It's a distressing state of affairs, but, you see, it's not our fault if man cannot live without money. And that's truer than ever in the present state of the world. There are priests I know who don't hesitate to say as much from the pulpit, and in no uncertain tones. I've tried to do the same, but I'm afraid I'm not much of a hand at speaking in no uncertain tones. My voice is too mild. . . . The trouble is, I'm too shy. I never get beyond a few vague allusions. Taking them all round, they're very decent folk, but they can't be expected to guess right every time. . . . My main objection to the Separation Act is that it forced us clergy into this particular relationship to our flocks. . . ."

"But what about those special church services for which you can charge—isn't there some special name for them?—occasional wind-falls—don't they help a little?"

"A little . . . but the scale of fees is very low, and we can't raise them like stall-keepers at a fair. Besides, the services you mean are few and far between. And then, in a parish like this there are scarcely any really rich people who are used to making up deficiencies without any fuss. . . . But, really, you must forgive me for airing my griev-ances like this. I don't know how I came to get so talkative."

"There's nothing in the world to forgive. All this interests me enormously. Please believe me when I say that I find the whole situa-tion deeply distressing. It's right and proper that we should know about it. I can assure you that the men of the Left—even of the ex-treme Left—are far from being as anti-clerical now as they once were. To speak only for my own party, I am pretty sure that if I spoke of this visit of mine, and of what you have been good enough to tell me, to some of our leaders—friends of mine—like Bouitton or Herriot—or Painlevé, or to the men of my generation like Daladier or Delbos, even to Socialists like Léon Blum, or to independents like Gurau—they would see matters in precisely the same light as I do. They would be full of sympathy for you."

"So much the better, so much the better," said the old priest. But there was a hint of incredulity in his honest, wide-eyed glance.

"The difficulty is to find a workable formula which won't at the same time call in question the general principles which we have no intention of going back on . . . something which could be interpreted as just a gesture of national sympathy. There are so many things call-ing for attention. . . . Still, I don't despair."

Not but what he was silently thinking to himself: "Isn't there any little thing I could do to give this worthy man a treat? What about asking him to lunch? No, ten to one the schoolmaster would mis-understand my motives, and I certainly can't ask them both. That would be too much of a good thing. Even tolerance should be tactful.

Well then, couldn't I slip him a little money on my way out, on some pretext or other? But that might create a precedent which I'm not rich enough to follow up. Besides, it might look like an attempt to buy his support. . . ."

To rid himself of his sense of embarrassment, he said out loud:

"Do you look after the parish all alone?"

"Oh no, that would be impossible. I have an assistant. There was even a time when I had two. . . ." He sketched a gesture with his arms. "From one point of view it was a great convenience . . . but there was another side to it. . . . Luckily, the man I have now is not without private means. He is the son of a peasant in a big way, at Vorey, down in the lowlands. An able fellow. He even writes a bit, takes an interest in local dialect and folk-songs. . . . He is a friend of the Pouzols-Desaugues."

"I suppose you know them too?"

"Oh yes. . . . Madame is very charitable, a true child of the Lord. She never passes my door without leaving me a little something, and she always remembers us at Christmas-time. But, after all, this isn't her parish. There are claims on her at Saugues and Brives . . . to say nothing of the cases that are brought to her notice by her brother the canon. But of course you know all about that?"

"To some extent; I lunched with the Pouzols-Desaugues at Brives. . . ."

"So Monsieur Grousson told me."

". . . And I'm on my way to visit a property they have near here—to have a look at some horses they own there. . . . I take some interest in horses."

"Vaurevauzes?"

"That's the place, yes."

The curé opened his eyes still wider, almost imperceptibly shook his head, and scratched the wood of the table with the fingers of his right hand. He said:

"So you're going to Vaurevauzes?"

He appeared to be the prey of some repressed excitement. He reminded Jerphanion of an old maid who has suddenly caught a proper name.

"Shall I try to make him talk?" thought Jerphanion. "Why be shy?" He went on:

"I rather gathered that Monsieur Pouzols-Desaugues had had a bit of trouble up there—I mean, with the people who farm his land?"

"There may have been a little something."

The old man's face had grown calmer; he seemed to be on his guard. Jerphanion, kicking himself for a clumsy fool, fell back on conventional generalities:

"It's not very nice for a landowner, even when he doesn't listen to gossip, to feel that—well, that things are going on among his tenants which might be described as rather more than odd, is it? . . . Anyhow, that's the impression I got."

The curé had half-closed his eyes, and his lips assumed a faintly mischievous expression.

"One can't always choose one's tenants," he said, "any more than one can choose one's parishioners. Should Monsieur Pouzols-Desaugues take it into his mind to give that particular lot notice, I can scarcely see his neighbours flocking to the house to ask him to change his mind. I, certainly, should not head the deputation!"

Jerphanion refused a second glass of sloe gin. After a few moments' silence he went on, as though changing the subject:

"Although I was born near here, I know a good deal less than you do about the mountain folk—the real native inhabitants of the high valleys. I've always seen them from the outside. When I want to get a true picture of them, I think of the people I knew in my childhood and imagine them back a couple of generations or so. But maybe that's all wrong. There are certain clues that no layman can get hold of, unless he happens to be a doctor, in which case he may know a thing or two. For instance—" he tried to make it plain by the tone of his voice that the example he was about to produce had occurred to him quite casually—"for instance, I've often wondered whether the conditions of life in really remote mountain places encouraged normal moral standards or the reverse. I suppose you've lived in other parts of this department?"

"There's hardly a corner of it I don't know, except the district of Brioude."

"Then you're well placed to make comparisons. Where should you think that vice, or crime even, is most prevalent, in the lowlands or the highlands?"

There was an air of subtlety about the smile with which the old man replied:

"No doubt you are thinking of the really isolated farms, of the kind of houses one comes across here and there. . . . On the whole, morals in the mountain villages are pretty good, certainly better than in many other places. Faith is a more living reality. . . . As to the lonely farms, well, I won't say that remoteness doesn't encourage certain types of irregularity, where there's been a lack of good, pious upbringing."

"I've been told," said Jerphanion, deciding to take the plunge, "that incest in particular is far from uncommon in families that are thrown a great deal on their own resources."

To his surprise, his host took this remark as calmly as though he had been asked about the comparative frequency of the measles.

"Quite probably. It should never be forgotten that sin, and temptation to sin, tend to take the road of least resistance. I don't suppose that there's any more real evil in such places than elsewhere. But the opportunities for sin are of a very special nature, and more to be feared than most. . . . Fathers, in particular, are more than usually exposed to temptation in regard to their daughters. . . ."

"More than the brothers in regard to their sisters?"

"Yes, I think so. And then, you see, the sin of the father, being more horrible, causes a much greater revulsion in the victim, and consequently is more likely to be concealed. Usually, though not always, a daughter will yield to her father only after a struggle. And they brood on it afterwards, often with a feeling of vindictiveness. Very often, too, the wife grows suspicious and starts talking. But in the case of a brother and sister it's usually a matter of common consent. Gradually the bad habit grows on them, especially when they've begun it young. On the whole, they take very little more notice of it than they would of any other bad habit incidental to their age. They get into the way of considering it as the kind of trivial misdoing that's not worth bothering about."

"That's very odd, and very interesting," said Jerphanion.

"And let me add that when the mothers get to know of it, they too, unfortunately, regard it as merely one case of irregularity among many others, no better and no worse. They don't worry much about it unless it threatens to have unfortunate consequences. Then, too, there are some—remember I am speaking only of families living in really remote places—who argue that whatever the consequences may be, they are easier to conceal, or even, alas, to obliterate, when the whole business has taken place in the bosom of the home."

Jerphanion sat brooding on the curious perspective conjured up by the old priest so calmly, so, one was almost tempted to say, unconsciously. "The fact of the matter is," he thought, "that his experience of these people, and of human nature in general as exemplified in these people, has been so long and so intimate that nothing now surprises him. He does me the honour of believing me capable of understanding it too. He has spared me the usual shamefaced lies, the usual outbursts of affronted morality. He assumes, very rightly, that I stand in no need of a sermon upon the heinousness of incest. I am a man who is anxious to get at the facts, and he is doing his best to give them to me. This matured wisdom that has come to him as the result of a long life, he owes in part to a gift of observation which he shares with many others, but certainly, to an even greater extent, to the incomparable opportunities presented by the confessional. I can hardly ignore that fact, but that does not mean that I need make a parade of my thoughts on the subject. The secrecy of the confessional is probably applied collectively as well as individually. I must be careful not to awaken his scruples in the matter."

With an air of detached curiosity, he said: "And how about what we are accustomed to think of as the crime par excellence, murder, I mean, attempts on human life?"

"What is it you want to know on that score?"

"Would you say that the highland solitudes provide favourable conditions for it?"

There was something almost cunning in the sidelong glance which the curé directed at his visitor.

"I don't think," he answered, "that the commandment: 'Thou shalt not kill' is often violated in the mountains. At any rate," he added, "the papers have very little to say about it."

"If I was evil-minded I might reply to that by saying that human justice, lame enough in the valleys, finds itself almost without any legs at all when it comes to climbing the hills, and that it prefers to leave the punishment of crime in the hands of God."

The curé permitted himself a discreet laugh. For the first time he took from his pocket a horn snuffbox, the rich, smooth colour of which gave it the appearance of amber or onyx. He offered it to Jerphanion and then took a pinch himself.

"Possibly," he said in high good humour, "possibly."

"In this connexion," went on Jerphanion in the playful tone of one about to indulge in a piece of philosophic humour, "there is a question which I have often asked myself, but without finding any answer. . . . Take the case of people like those who live hereabouts, people among whom, as I think you would agree, religious faith has remained a living reality . . ."

"Certainly it has. . . ."

". . . among whom the believer is the rule rather than the exception. Let us assume that some man has committed a crime for reasons of greed or vengeance. . . . Very naturally he does all he can not to be caught by the police. But would he confess his crime to his parish priest, as we are told the bandits used to do in the old days?"

"If he was a true believer, yes; why shouldn't he?"

"In theory, I agree. But would he do so in fact? May it not be that the general attitude in such matters has changed in the course of the centuries? Isn't it possible that a modern criminal might hold that his crime had broken all links that bound him to the rest of the world, even to religion? . . . In the first place, would he have sufficient confidence in his priest?"

The curé's answer to this took the form of a non-committal gesture.

"Do you see what I'm after?" went on Jerphanion, stressing his point. "There was a time, apparently, when the criminal, and the ordinary man too, for that matter, found no difficulty in distinguishing between the laws of God and the laws of man. He thought it wise to keep on the right side of the former while doing his best to avoid falling into the clutches of the latter. The two things were regarded as being totally different. Can one say that the modern criminal has the same attitude—the genuine criminal, I mean, the author of a planned and premeditated act, not the mere casual and accidental murder? In his heart of hearts doesn't he, almost in spite of himself, really regard the priest and the policeman, the priest and the judge, as belonging to the same general type? Once he has made up his mind to embark on a crime, isn't he almost bound to cut completely adrift, to break with the whole system of civilized society, to let everything, deliberately, go hang? Wouldn't he think it a pretty bad joke, and the sign of an almost unbelievable simple-mindedness, to attempt to reconcile his conscience by confessing to a priest what he had done? Perhaps I'm explaining myself badly. Knowing, as I do, something about country people, I can't help admitting that the point—which is one of what you might call social psychology—fascinates me, though I despair of ever finding the answer by my own unaided efforts."

"There's one essential fact that you mustn't forget," replied the curé with some caution and hesitation, "and that is this. The man in question wouldn't be in a position to reconcile his conscience—quite so easily. I can't say, with any accuracy, how confessors may have regarded their duty in the old days. . . . There are stories I know. . . . Quite probably the procedure varied with the man." A more decided note crept into his voice. "Speaking for myself, assuming that someone came to me and confessed to having committed a crime—of the type you have in mind—I should definitely refuse him absolution unless he was willing to give himself up to the authorities."

"Do you really mean that? Wouldn't you consider that the penance you might lay on him would be punishment enough?"

"The fact of giving himself up to the authorities would in my eyes constitute an essential part of the penance. Naturally, I am speaking only in general terms. I'm willing to admit that there might be exceptional cases."

"Such as?—if you'll forgive me for asking."

"I can think of only two or three possible ones. . . . Take, for instance, the crime that has been committed from genuinely good motives—misguided, perhaps, but good—and with no intention of offending God. In such a case there might be reason to believe that the court would refuse to take any account of motive. I don't say that such a situation would be of frequent occurrence, but it very well might exist. . . . Then there's the case of a crime committed a long time ago. Where a guilty man has afterwards lived honestly, it is conceivable that there might be no good reason to cast him back into the slough of infamy. . . . A severe penance worked out far from the public eye, and accompanied, if possible, by compensation and restitution, might be the better course. . . . Finally, there's always the problem of the penitent who happens to be on his death-bed—" He paused, and fixed Jerphanion with his small and piercing eyes. "One such instance came my way many years ago. . . . I first of all asked the doctor, who luckily happened to be on the spot, how ill he thought the man really was . . . and then I gave absolution."

"But what if there had been no doctor there?"

"I should have done my best to decide, unaided, the degree of urgency."

"To go back for a moment. Let us assume that you have refused absolution to a self-confessed criminal unless he is willing to give himself up. . . . Well, he doesn't give himself up. What happens then?"

"If he came to confession again, I should repeat my exhortation, very solemnly. If he came a third time without having obeyed, I should refuse to hear his confession."

"Would he still go to Mass?"

"I could hardly stand at the church door and keep him out. But he most certainly would not be given the sacrament at Easter. . . . Besides, I rather think that if I saw him coming to Mass Sunday after Sunday, sitting and kneeling in a congregation of honourable neighbours, not from any motive of true piety, but as a hypocrite intent only on keeping up appearances—well, I rather think that I should be tempted to take homicide as the subject of my sermon. And more than once, if need be. Either God would permit me to touch his heart, or the odds are that we should see very little more of him."

They became aware of somebody shouting beneath the window:

"Are you there?"

"That's Grousson come for me," said Jerphanion. He looked at his watch and got up. Then, speaking as lightly as possible, as though in reference to some jest that had cropped up in the course of their conversation—

"Is it, may I ask, some time since you preached on the subject of—homicide?"

The old curé half-closed his eyes and smiled very faintly. Raising his right hand, he said:

"You know, my memory's terribly bad. . . . I have a way of entirely forgetting my sermons. . . . They are so unimportant."

The tone of his voice made it abundantly plain that he would say nothing more, at least on that subject. Jerphanion made a gesture of polite resignation.

The curé accompanied him to the top of the steps. He nodded his head towards Grousson and waved his hand.

"You've got a fine day for your trip to Vaurevauzes," he said.

# Chapter

## THE HOUSE AT VAUREVAUZES

When they got back to the car, Jerphanion said to Grousson:

"Just wait a second."

Entering the inn, he sought out the landlady, who was busy in the kitchen.

"A word with you, madame. I should like to show the curé some little kindness, but I don't want him to know anything about it. I should be very much obliged if you would set aside an extra portion of each dish—to be charged, of course, to me. I'd like the meal to be taken across to him—so that he can have exactly the same lunch as ourselves—and to be kept as hot as possible. With a bottle of the same wine as we have. But you mustn't tell him that it comes from me. No, really, I'd rather you didn't."

The good woman appeared heartbroken. "Oh, Monsieur Jerphanion, what an idea! It'll spoil all his pleasure. In any case, I must warn him what to expect, otherwise the poor man will have already had his little meal. . . ."

"But won't he think it odd that I didn't ask him to join us?"

"Leave it all to me. I'll tell him that you had to talk political business with your friend, and that you felt shy about inflicting that kind of conversation on him. He'll understand all right; don't worry about that."

"Your good curé gave me a lump in the throat."

"Why?"

"A lump in the throat, and something like remorse. The position of these village priests is wretched. We conveniently avert our eyes, and so avoid the necessity of pitying them. Oh, I know; religion is not one of the public services—or rather is so no longer. If there are not enough of the faithful to maintain their priests, or if the faithful are too stingy, that is not our business. But the State argues less rigorously when it is a case of keeping industries going whose usefulness is not particularly obvious, and of saving their personnel from dying of starvation. I am not myself a believing Christian, but millions of Frenchmen are. If I could, by my unaided efforts, tear religion out of their lives, I am far from certain that I should do so, because I have no love of destroying what I am not sure of being able to replace. I should be afraid, given the present state of the world, of doing more harm than good. Speaking from a purely selfish point of view, I should be heartbroken to think that the churches might disappear, or cease to be centres of living influence; to think that they might come to be regarded as mere relics, objects of sightseeing to be classed according to their varying æsthetic merits. . . . I feel distinctly uneasy. . . . I can't help thinking that we have shown a lack of graciousness. . . . But it's all very difficult."

Grousson said nothing. Not that he condemned his companion for feeling as he did. Far from it, for he was by nature both tolerant and given to compassion. "Live and let live" was, in his opinion, a maxim of sterling worth. Though he might hate monks, he had nothing against priests and would have been only too glad if they could be assured, by some discreet action of the State which would not endanger basic principles, of a reasonable and decent standard of life. But he did not regard it as his business to discover how this was to be done. He thoroughly approved of Jerphanion's behaviour in secretly performing an act of charity in regard to the curé of Saint-Front which could have none but the most favourable results. At the same time, he would have deplored the public confession of such scruples as his companion had just been voicing.

After maintaining some minutes of polite silence, he said:

"This road is in an awful state; just look at all those loose stones. When you're elected, I hope you'll have the decency to bear us in mind and do something to ginger up the Department of Roads and Bridges."

Then:

"Does he know that we're going to Vaurevauzes?"

"Yes, I told him."

"Did he make any comment?"

Jerphanion hesitated a moment before replying:

"He didn't say anything very definite—naturally enough. But I've got an idea—though I may be wrong—that he did give me a little hint. If I can follow it up, I will."

A stone set up on the right of the road marked the entrance to a track into which the car turned.

The earth was so hard that scarcely a rut was visible. Here and there the processes of nature had produced hummocks or depressions. The track was sown with little slithers of basalt, not unlike the fragments of tile that warn the traveller that he is approaching some house where roofing is in progress. Out on the moor, to left and right, glittered a few puddles covered with a skin of ice which cracked and oozed in the heat of the sun, and looked like rubbish of a different kind, broken glass the fragments of which had been swept together into the same hollow. Away in front the track crossed a rise in the ground behind which the house must surely lie hidden. The vast sweep of grassland, still green despite the season, but marked here and there with large reddish patches, stretched on every hand without visible limits. A line of stones set at wide intervals served to mark the course of the track when the country was under snow. A second similar line, but of smaller stones, branched off to the left and curved away over the down in the probable direction of the house. It was probably an emergency track, or the remains of an ancient roadway. There were few signs that it had been used by traffic.

Far away to the right, they noticed, close to a clump of trees, a group of horses, comprising, so far as they could make out, three or four full-grown ones and two or three foals, which were grazing and frisking at some distance from one another.

The car climbed the rise and the house came into view. It was a low building of very strong construction and considerable length. It was surrounded, or rather, companioned, by a number of trees markedly taller than itself. Each one of these displayed a few enormous branches, twisted and seemingly tormented, the extremities of which were adorned by a complexity of small twigs that stood out, etched like filigree, against the blue-grey of a north-easterly sky of infinite remoteness.

The house and its outbuildings presented to the eye a single line, though the roofs showed two distinct levels. The lower was that of the dwelling-house proper, the higher belonging to the stables and barns. Half-way along the frontage, which was pierced sparingly by narrow windows facing due south, what looked like the section of a tunnel projected from the façade, heavily vaulted with basalt blocks and carrying its own separate roof. It dominated the front entrance like the postern gateway of a fort.

The roofing throughout was of tile set at a moderate pitch, which was slightly flatter on the dwelling-house than on the neighbouring buildings. On what exact point of this roof had the two corpses lain? And had the same place served on each occasion? What had been the position of the bodies? Had they been arranged along the axis of the slope, with their feet resting in the gutter? In any imagined reconstruction of the scene the strange and the ordinary were curiously intermingled, so that the whole picture took on an almost burlesque character. True, in order to obtain any convincing representation of the event as it must have appeared at the time of its occurrence, it was necessary to envisage the roof as lying beneath a thick cushion of snow, to see the whole house as buried window-high in it, to abstract from the present view of it every actual element save that of the black, yawning tunnel. The corpses could never have looked like a couple of dolls perversely exposed to the view there on the tiles.

They had slept in the deep secrecy of the snow. This great mass of whiteness, so strongly wrought above the dark throat that opened at its base, must have formed an impressive tomb.

The car slowed down while its driver looked about for a convenient parking-place. From behind a slope thickset with shrubs, a child emerged for a moment, then turned and ran towards the house, disappearing into the tunnel.

A semicircular mound, surrounded by a low wall, did duty as a yard, over which half a dozen fowls were strutting. They made no sound. An unusual silence reigned. It was curious to hear no barking of dogs, no noise of lowing cattle from the cavernous cow-sheds.

Grousson pulled up on the right-hand side, the front wheels of the car resting against the low wall. As the two men got out and turned, they saw the figure of a woman standing motionless in the entrance to the tunnel, distinct against the deep shadows behind her, framed in the heavy vaulting of basalt. At her back the obscurity grew deeper as it receded, and it was impossible to make out clearly the exact position of the door. Dressed as she was in black, she gave an impression of slimness. Her face was rather pale, and upon the well-marked curve of her bosom there glittered a small golden jewel. As they approached, Jerphanion saw that her face, though no longer young, retained traces of beauty. It was not that of a countrywoman, being neither tanned nor marked by those deep lines usually to be seen among those who live hard lives in the high, bright spaces of the mountains.

"It's she," he thought, and for the benefit of his companion he murmured:

"It's she, isn't it?"

"Yes."

Her eyes, of periwinkle blue, were so wide open as to seem slightly dilated. They looked the two strangers straight in the face, and there was in their stare a hint of distress. The impression they made was not so much aggressive as pathetic. She wore a small lace cap, without ribbon, seemingly perched on the very top of her head. Her auburn hair, carefully curled, lay in a thick disorder about her face. Clearly, it had not been cut definitely short in the fashion of the city, but trimmed with care, and the coils into which it was gathered in the nape of her neck had the effect of slightly raising the lower edge of the cap. On her feet she wore black clogs, with ornamental bands, and elegantly shaped. Her skirt hung clear of her slim ankles in their black cotton stockings.

The general appearance of this woman, framed in its setting of shadow, set the mind playing with comparisons both strange and fleeting. It was not that of a peasant girl of today, nor yet that of a countrywoman aping the manners of the town. Something about her face and her hair held memories of those prints so popular at the time of the Revolution. But in her expression, in the actual shape of her features, so immature, so evocative of a spiritual delicacy, of an almost childish innocence, there was something of the Middle Ages. It was the type of face that one might have seen painted on wood and set against a porch not of black basalt but of gold or marble; the face of a saint or, maybe, of some resplendent sinner. The dark shadows of the tunnel thrust it forward in high relief. It was not difficult to imagine dark secrets lurking in the deep shadows, a creeping horror of sin and evil within the house, stealing along the floor that might have been that of a dungeon, a dank exhalation of black magic seeping through the shadows to the tunnel's mouth, touching in its passage the thin, taut body, the delicate ankles, the airy tissue of lace upon the head held high.

"You're looking for someone?" said the woman. "Oh, it's you, Monsieur Grousson; for a moment I didn't recognize you."

Her voice was soft, with a hint of resonance kept carefully in reserve. When she stopped speaking, her lips twitched slightly as though the words had set moving some deep eddy of emotion now concealed. Seen thus in movement, her mouth showed as well shaped, tender rather than sensual. The nervous movement which followed her speech contributed to the childish quality of her face.

Grousson introduced his companion, after which he proceeded to explain their presence:

"This gentleman is a friend of Monsieur Pouzols-Desaugues. . . . They were talking the other day about this farm and about the horses here. Monsieur Pouzols-Desaugues, on learning that he was coming in this direction, suggested a visit."

Jerphanion produced M. Pouzols-Desaugues's card. The woman glanced at it and then looked at Jerphanion. Her lips twitched again, this time with the hint of a rather puzzled smile.

"Come in," she said.

They advanced down the three or four yards of tunnel. Towards its far end they noticed a long stone trough standing against the right-hand wall. The woman went ahead of them. She said:

"We have had no snow this year, but there is a light frost."

"Quite a change from last winter," said Grousson, "though it's not over yet."

She pushed open the left-hand section of the double door which closed the end of the tunnel and in old days, before the neighbouring buildings had been constructed, must have served as a common means of access for man and beast. The opening revealed a reddish glow caught faintly into a spiral eddy. They entered a large room. It was warm and moist, and smelt of smoke with a just discernible tang of horse-dung added, though this seemed natural to the place, evidence of long-established function rather than of dirt and negligence. There were the usual clothes-presses and cupboard-beds built into the panelling, to be found in any local farmhouse, and a large clock. The attention was drawn, however, not to the furniture, but to a number of utensils which seemed to belong to an earlier age, such as would not have been found in any of the lowland villages: a kneading-trough, a spinning-wheel, a churn, all obviously made long ago. Age had given to the wood of which they were constructed a black colour and a smooth patina marked here and there by dents and scratches. In addition there were spoons, copper ladles, pots, and cauldrons reminiscent of the objects to be found in the pictures by the Le Nain brothers.

Two women were seated in arm-chairs between the large table and the hearth. "The mother and the wife of the younger brother," thought Jerphanion. The small boy had disappeared. Two varieties of sound could be heard coming from the recesses of the house: one set, distinct and close at hand, might conceivably have been produced by children at play on the stairs or in the corridors; the other, more distant and of a deeper pitch, could obviously be traced to the cattle-sheds.

The two visitors were offered straw-bottomed chairs. On the hearth two logs were slowly burning away. They gave off hardly any smoke, were partly covered with slabs of dried earth, and lay in a wilderness of ashes and embers. An iron pot, standing on four feet set amid the ashes, was simmering at some distance from the logs.

There followed an intermittent conversation the main weight of which was borne by Grousson and the widow of the elder brother. It dealt with such subjects as the weather, the roads, and Grousson's itinerary. Jerphanion only half listened. He was looking at the three women seen in the almost subterranean gloom of the vast room; three women, and somewhere outside, the man who was the sole survivor of another three. He drifted into a day-dream. He let the details of the great room vanish from his consciousness. He saw nothing any longer but the essential features of the place, the mingled play of light and shade, the glow of the hearth, the three women, one old, the other two still young. Vaguely there emerged before his mind's eye a scene from some drama of the cave-men. At first he saw three women and three men. Then one of the men succeeded in exterminating the two others. The women remained, submissive, silent. Whether they had merely acquiesced, or whether they had given active assistance, and what part each had played, remained undetermined.

To some question of Grousson's the widow replied:

"He's working at the bottom of the big meadow with his son Claude."

"He" was the brother-in-law, the sole surviving male.

Grousson continued: "It's not worth disturbing him; we'll go and find him."

But to Jerphanion's way of thinking Grousson's tact was out of place. What he wanted was to get his first impression of this surviving male, not in a meadow with his horses, but here, with the three women, in this cavernous interior where light played hide-and-seek with darkness.

What were the relations subsisting between these three women? According as one imagined what had gone before, and the role filled by each of them, so did these relations vary. The possible combinations, it was obvious, were endless. The mind soon lost its way in the complexities of the situation. If, on the other hand, one tried to get some positive pointer from the faces, the attitudes of the three women, the resulting evidence was so indeterminate, so deliberately induced, perhaps, that all conclusions seemed equally probable. One of the most likely hypotheses was that the passage of time and the sequence of events now so dominated the scene that there remained only a sort of dense atmosphere in which all personal emotions were reduced to an indistinguishable mass controlled, as it were, and set to a seemingly peaceful rhythm, by the dead weight of the authority exercised by the sole surviving male.

This atmosphere of submission was most evident in the expression on the face of the mother. She was working at a piece of coarse lace. It would have been too much to say that she was smiling, but her features were marked by a certain tranquillity. A network of fine wrinkles was visible between deeply etched lines, no one of which had a definitely tragic significance. She seemed unaware of anyone else in the room, to be intent only on attracting neither curiosity nor questions.

The wife of the younger brother began to cough. There was a hollow quality in the sound that set Jerphanion thinking. "She's probably consumptive," he reflected. "That wouldn't fit too badly into the general scheme. They needn't bother about killing her."

The handsome widow got up, opened one of the doors, and called out something. Even when raised, her voice remained pleasing. It was one of those voices that can make even an order delightful. One felt that one would have enjoyed being called to in those tones, to be in a position to obey its summons. There was a noise of running footsteps on the stairs. A young boy entered the room. He must have been the same young boy whom the visitors had seen outside the house and who had run away at their approach. His complexion, his hair, his eyes, all were markedly dark. He was as far removed as possible in appearance from his little mountain companions. Nor did he bear the slightest resemblance to his mother, who looked at him, said nothing, and had another fit of coughing.

"Go and get your father," said the handsome widow, speaking in the local dialect. "These gentlemen want to speak to him."

After this the conversation dwindled. Jerphanion was free to indulge his dreaming. "Do the explanations," he wondered, "which we found it so easy to elaborate in the car really hold water now that we're here? In the first place, what was the motive of these crimes? They don't seem to me any longer to have been necessary. Yesterday, when we were driving, we could take them apart and put them together again like the pieces of a well-designed machine. When one of us picked out some part that had been forgotten, it was as though it gave a little cry of pleasure. But today, with the flesh-and-blood actors before us, it all seems to have been no more than an ingenious game."

He noticed, fastened to one of the panels, a large crucifix, and below it a holy-water stoup, with a sprig of boxwood above it. His attention was drawn to the ticking of the clock, which was at once very slow and quite extraordinarily intense, sounding as though the pendulum, at each end of its swing, released a small hammer which struck on a thick metal plate. The noises coming from the cattle-sheds, too, were more audible than before. They had a muted quality, repetitive, and seemed to echo in the beams and walls and framework of the house, though without causing any definite vibration—as though, in the distant hold of a ship, slaves were jangling their chains.

There came next to his ears the barking of a dog and a man's voice calling it to order. Then the door which led out in the direction of the cattle-sheds opened, and the man appeared. He was of middle height, and both face and body appeared on the thin side. He was more blond than Grousson's description had led Jerphanion to expect. His eyes, narrow-lidded and piercing, were of an indeterminate colour. He took off his hat and laid it on top of a chest. His hair was black streaked with grey, not very thick and rather straight. It had receded slightly from the forehead, which was markedly narrow at the temples. The whole face was elongated and bony, with a long chin. "He reminds me of somebody," thought Jerphanion.

The wine-merchant introduced them, repeating the explanations which he had already given. The man listened with an expressionless gaze. He gave the impression of the care-taker of an estate called from a piece of work by tiresome visitors whom he cannot refuse to show round, and accepting the necessity with an affectation of indifference.

"I'll take you to see the horses," he said.

To his great relief, Jerphanion remembered whom it was he reminded him of. It was of a former Sorbonne friend reading for a degree in literature. This friend was called Delhuis, from French Flanders. His eyes were blue-grey, but he had always boasted that he had Spanish blood.

The younger brother led them through one corner of the cattle-sheds to a door opening from the back of the estate onto the moor. They had just time, as they passed, to glimpse the long row of animals, their round backs moving in the semi-darkness. The impression was one of rich luxuriance, and there hung in the air that smell of cattle-sheds in winter which seems so much more dense and soft than in the warmer months and evokes the picture of a world shut in and secure.

Jerphanion imagined that the horses which they were on their way to inspect would turn out to be those they had noticed in the distance as they drove up. But if that were so it seemed surprising that the man should have taken them this roundabout way by the cattle-sheds instead of by the more direct one through the tunnel. Perhaps he wanted to impress them by this vision of his prosperity. Jerphanion wondered, too, why the cows were confined to their stalls on this fine day instead of being outside like the horses.

This last question was innocent enough to be given expression in words. It might succeed in putting their relations on a warmer footing.

"There was a good deal of white frost this morning," replied the younger brother. "I thought it better to leave all the animals inside. But an hour ago, when I went to work, it seemed warmer, so I took the horses out. . . . They don't catch cold so easily . . . they move about more. . . . Not that they can find much to eat in the fields at this season, but they suffer more than cows from being shut up."

He had lost a little of his earlier constraint, though even now he was scarcely what could be called friendly. He made no attempt to conceal his interest in the subject of their talk, but he adopted a sort of ironically deprecating air. He was the sort of man who answers the questions put to him, but with an unexpressed comment that seems to mean: "I'm not such a fool as not to see that this doesn't really interest you." At moments his voice took on a refinement of inflexion strange in a man of his class.

Jerphanion complimented him on the cows which they had seen in passing. He replied with a little upward movement of the lips which raised his small moustache.

"Oh yes, the animals aren't too badly off—a good deal better than the humans."

"But I thought you'd had a series of good seasons hereabouts."

"Good enough so far as sales go. But the work's too heavy, especially now that I'm the only man on the place."

There was nothing in his tone beyond a hint of quite natural grievance. Jerphanion, glancing at him out of the corner of his eye, went on:

"Can't you get somebody to help you?"

"My eldest boy's beginning to be a bit useful. . . . The younger looks after the cows. I have a day-labourer from Bournac. It's not easy to find workers; the local boys have got enough to do at home, or else they go off to the towns. It's hopeless to try to get fellows up from the lowlands. You might as well ask them to emigrate to a savage island—and, if it comes to that, conditions here are a bit rough."

Grousson observed pleasantly that the problem of man-power was much the same everywhere, but added that the peasants had never had less ground for complaint than now.

". . . And that's more than ever true of you mountain people. . . . After all, the grass grows of its own accord, and you get almost as good a price for your milk as I do for my wine. Each time you sell a cow you rake in a small fortune."

The younger Leblanc showed by the half-polite, half-scornful face he made that he preferred not to discuss the matter further. He only said:

"Well, that may be. All I know is that when my lease runs out I shan't renew it." Turning towards Grousson with a faint air of defiance, he added: "And you can tell Monsieur Pouzols-Desaugues that I said so."

Grousson and Jerphanion exchanged a look. The man's remark seemed to them both exceedingly odd. It's meaning was not very easy to catch. For the moment they said nothing more, but merely grunted sympathetically.

The young man continued on a more sullen note than before:

"To begin with, the house is damned unhealthy. It's no better than a grave. If we're not careful, we shall all leave our bones here."

The two visitors were quick to seize the reference and hastened to take the opportunity thus providentially offered. Were they to understand that he attributed the sad losses which his family had suffered —about which M. Jerphanion had heard a certain amount of talk— to the house? That was really very odd, and very distressing. At first sight one would have felt inclined to blame the climate, and, so far as concerned the younger of the two dead men, the state of exhaustion due to prolonged war service. Could a house which, when all was said, was much like any other house really have so deadly an effect?

With the air of a man primarily interested in this problem of the house and anxious to get to the bottom of it, Jerphanion asked how precisely the two unfortunate fatalities had occurred. Unfortunately, almost before he had ceased speaking, and before the other had shown any sign of replying, Grousson, carried away by a private thought of his own, put quite a different question. Was there anything in the past history of the house to justify their host's contention?

Either because Grousson had been the last to speak or because his question was the least embarrassing to answer, it was to him that the young man replied. Without going into details, and in extremely non-committal terms, as though he were afraid of spreading disagreeable rumours at the expense of his predecessors or doing some injury to M. Pouzols-Desaugues by referring too openly to some blemish on his property, he gave his visitors to understand that the people who had farmed the place before he came had left behind them, after long years of occupancy, a veritable army of lethal germs. Two of their number had died of lung trouble, and their end had been accompanied by all the horrible symptoms of festering corruption traditionally associated with consumption. The house had never been thoroughly disinfected or even properly cleaned. Young Leblanc showed a surprising knowledge of the matter under discussion. He said that he remembered having read somewhere that the germs of tuberculosis can remain active almost indefinitely in buildings like the one he lived in, ill-lit, ill-ventilated, and full of dark corners, in which people lived in a condition of overcrowding during the interminable months of winter. He had read too that it is never easy to disinfect ground used for building-purposes, the surface of which remains impregnated with the filth it has absorbed, the noisome activities of which develop unseen and unchecked like mites in a piece of cheese.

Jerphanion could not make out whether the speaker was producing long-pondered arguments in defence of a carefully prepared case or whether he was merely expressing a personal conviction. Grousson, too, seemed surprised and puzzled. Jerphanion put a question:

"Have you never spoken of this to a doctor? When your father died, for instance—and that was some years ago, I understand. . . . Or, even more naturally, when your brother followed him—last winter, wasn't it? . . . You seem to be a man of education and intelligence who can see a problem pretty clearly. I should have thought that in a serious matter of this kind you would want to set your mind at rest."

The young man shrugged his shoulders. His nostrils twitched in a thin smile. "Didn't Monsieur Grousson tell you? The snow kept the doctor away."

"Yes, he did say something of the kind. . . . But why didn't you say something to him when it was all over? . . . I'm not suggesting that the body ought to have been exhumed . . . but I should have thought you might have asked him to examine the house and tell you what ought to be done. . . . Even if complete disinfection was impossible, he could surely have suggested something you could do. And anyhow he could have told you"—here Jerphanion and Grousson exchanged glances—"whether there was anything in your theory. After all, a matter of this kind can't just be left in the air. . . . There are the lives of others to be considered."

"I know that," said the man. "You heard my wife coughing?"

"Yes, that's precisely the point. . . . Her condition may not have reached a serious stage . . . quite possibly it may not be due to what we think. But you've got no right to let things slide. . . . Has the doctor examined your wife?"

"Yes, once, last spring. At the end of May."

"Then he has been here?"

"Yes."

"Did you talk to him of your brother's death?"

"I just mentioned it."

"And didn't you tell him that you thought the house unhealthy?"

"He was in a hurry. I'd caught him on his way to town. Doctors don't like being waylaid like that. They prefer being called in from a distance so that they can run up a big bill."

They had reached the spot where the horses were grazing. Jerphanion felt that he had not conducted their conversation very skilfully. He had certainly failed to get the sort of light on the situation which he had expected. So far from letting himself be driven into a corner, the young farmer had considerably strengthened his own position.

They looked at the horses. Three of them belonged to M. Pouzols-Desaugues. Grousson discussed their condition with a good show of knowledge.

"I used to be pretty well at home with horses," he said; "but it's extraordinary how quickly one forgets. I should feel a good deal more sure of myself nowadays if you asked me to tell you whether an engine was running smoothly."

Jerphanion was thoroughly discontented with himself. "I didn't even succeed in following up the hints dropped by the curé," he thought. These, as a matter of fact, he believed, were of very doubtful value.

Grousson turned to the young man. "Have you any idea where you'll go if you leave this farm?"

"I haven't thought about it yet," replied the other; then, rather cautiously, he added: "If I could find a nice little piece of property going, I might buy it—assuming that I could lay my hand on the money."

"And you would take all your family with you?"

The young man shrugged, narrowed his eyes, and let his mouth fall open. His look was that of a man hearing a problem expressed with which he is only too familiar.

Jerphanion risked a plunge. "That old curé of yours at Saint-Front seems to be showing his age a bit."

Leblanc, who had bent down to feel the pastern of one of the horses, looked up with sudden surprise.

"So you saw *him* this morning?"

"Yes." Jerphanion broke off for a moment before adding casually: "Were you in church last Sunday?"

"Last Sunday?" A faintly ironic smile showed on Leblanc's lips. He pretended to be pondering the question. "Let me think, now. . . . No, I don't think I was."

"Someone told me that he turned faint in the pulpit, just before the sermon. Surely you wouldn't have forgotten a thing like that. But, of course, it may have been the week before."

The young man seemed to be searching his memory. But the trick was a little too obvious. It was clear that a good deal more than one week had elapsed since he had last been to church.

Trivial though the success of his manœuvre had been, Jerphanion could not restrain a movement of satisfaction. He even glanced at Grousson as though to say: "Did you see that?" Then he remembered that Grousson, not knowing what he himself did, could scarcely have understood. Besides, the "curé's lead," if one could call it that, might be quite valueless.

They went back to the car. Jerphanion tried not to feel disappointed. "Life's like that," he reflected, forcing himself to smile. "One builds up all sorts of grand theories, and then one comes down to earth and finds oneself bogged in a clutter of perfectly ordinary events and petty details, all pointing in different directions. That is where fact and fiction part company."

In spite of everything, however, he refused to let himself be argued out of the belief that their visit had been extremely interesting, unexpectedly rich in its revelations, even if those revelations were of a purely negative kind. Probably, even though not realizing it at the time, they had picked up all sorts of significant details which no amount of reasoning would have supplied. It would be great fun getting them straight as they drove along or sat over an inn table and drew their conclusions. He let his mind play round the prospect of his next luncheon with M. Pouzols-Desaugues. Would the account of their visit and the suppositions which his own and Grousson's ingenuity had constructed from that event satisfy the curiosity manifested by the "squire" of Brives? Whatever happened, he must retain his self-confidence. Jerphanion saw in a flash the account he must give of the matter. . . . Yes, undoubtedly, his self-confidence must not be permitted to be in doubt for a single instant.

# Chapter

## 12

### AN ORATOR'S DAY-DREAMS

All the time that he was talking to his audience of forty constituents, he kept his eyes fixed on the moorland view which he could see through the small window to his right. Since morning the sky had become overcast. Moist clouds hung about the mountains. Darkness would fall earlier than usual. There was a threat of snow in the mild air, a threat borne out by a certain degree of physical discomfort. More than likely he would awake next morning to see the glare of snow reflected from the pine boarding of the ceiling, and to a realization that winter had come suddenly in good earnest.

It was not really cold. Mme Astier had lit her great stove, and the crowded room had developed a faint byre-like warmth (roughly about two "cow-power": forty men, two cows). But it was too much to expect that the chilliness in his feet, of which he had always been conscious since the days of his childhood—whether in the trenches or in the anterooms of ministers—should leave him now. Jerphanion mitigated its effect by walking up and down as he made his speech. It put him at his ease and had long been a habit of his. In the old days, when conducting a class in school, he had cultivated the art of pacing to and fro, with his hands in his pockets, between the blackboard and first row of desks. The only difference between then and now was that these new pupils had a somewhat odd look. They had heavy moustaches and tanned faces. They had kept their hats on, and now and again they spat. They gave off a strong smell (smell was a more accurate description than warmth). But, for all that, the expression of their faces was at once studious and friendly. Very likely they did not understand everything he was saying, but their wide-open eyes never left his lips. They certainly could not be accused of letting their attention wander, of idly watching the flies, not but what there were a good many flies, large, buzzing flies, almost as many as in summer; flies that had definitely come indoors for the winter and meant to spend it with human beings for company. Nor was there reason to complain on the ground of whispered asides. Another old habit which had reasserted its hold over Jerphanion was that of thinking, while he continued to talk, of some subject quite different from the matter in hand—of carrying on with himself a sort of spasmodic and private dialogue. This peculiar kind of counterpoint is possible, or rather is easy of achievement, only in certain circumstances. The question under discussion must not be one with which he had not already dealt, nor must the scene of his address be so strange (even if he had never been there before) as to monopolize his attention. Casual interruptions, if such occurred, must be of an easily recognizable type and not more frequent than usual.

The conditions today were perfect. This meeting at Saint-Front was like any other village meeting. He had merely to sketch the main lines of his electoral program, and to answer questions which, ten to one, would be perfectly familiar. This did not at all mean that his heart was not in his subject, or that he was dishing up a lot of ready-made twaddle. Not for a moment did he lose sight of the special nature of his audience. He watched his every word and was quick to note the reactions, however subtle, of his listeners. Not only did he keep his attention from wandering away from the matter of his discourse, but he was acutely alive to his own eloquence, and, in addition, to the attention paid to him, to the expression of gravity, not to say of anxiety, which his words brought to the surrounding faces, by the confidence in himself which he felt to exist in this close-packed stuff of humanity in which he was working. But it was all a matter of degree. So long as his mind could be relied upon to follow the lines laid down for it by long training, so long as the circumstances of the moment did not necessitate a continual tension of improvisation, he could still, while carrying on with his task, indulge in a certain amount of day-dreaming, entertaining some private part of himself with stories and even with acrimonious discussion. The only trouble was that this, as one might say, marginal play of the mind was too often interrupted, too often forced to deviate from its straight line of development, and repeat itself in a way that detracted to some extent from its charm. The effect was somewhat that of a dream that marks time in the brain of a sleeper.

Today this marginal play of mind was composed of three distinct elements: day-dreaming, narrative, and debate. In a series of flashes Jerphanion saw again the house at Vaurevauzes, the widow set in her niche of shadow, the three women slightly distorted by the uncertain light of the interior, the young man with the Flemish face, and heard the conversation which they had carried on while they looked at the horses. By fits and starts he recovered fragments of the amusing case which he and Grousson had built up while they drove along in the latter's car. He remembered the actual arguments they had devised, the very words, even, in which they had clothed them. He could examine them now in a light that differed from the one in which they had appeared that morning and last evening. He would have liked to recapitulate the whole case from the beginning. Even while he completed a phrase designed to embody a cautious condemnation of the government in power, he was conscious of a quite different, though no less carefully devised, phrase taking shape in his mind. "If this fellow is really a criminal, there is every reason to suppose that he is a liar as well. But can we be sure that he is a criminal without first establishing the fact that he is a liar?" Unfortunately, at this point he had to start a new passage about Poincaré's policy, which meant that for some moments his mind was fully occupied. So much the worse for the conclusion to which he had probably been working as to the double approach to young Leblanc as suspect and as witness.

But he had plenty of time in which to realize that this particular marginal play of mind was giving him distinct pleasure, and to administer to himself a sharp rebuke: "Isn't such childishness really absurd? For there can be no denying that it does help me to go on living, does give me courage to face the demands of every day, does bring me an added keenness. If I hadn't got this Vaurevauzes business to chew at secretly like a cigar, this room, these forty poor devils, might suddenly become an immense bore; my words might quite unexpectedly stick in my throat. And yet those familiar words which I am trying to get across have to do with something that I happen to regard as enormously important, as terribly urgent, terribly serious for all of us, and terribly difficult as well. Would a really serious-minded, a genuinely strong man feel as I do the need for this extra little bit of stimulant, for this shot of a drug in the other part of his mind? Perhaps, if the truth were known, I am neither serious-minded nor strong."

Ten minutes later, while some local notable was giving vent, with tiresome iteration, as though he were reciting the Litany, to a number of grievances, now entirely destitute of any practical value, on the subject of the new Monastier railway line, whose route it was too late to alter, Jerphanion, having found in a second the perfect answer which would silence the interrupter, took time to say to himself: "One's got to accept oneself as one is. After all, I've always been like that. It was just the same when I was supervising literature classes. . . . I might be taking my pupils through some text which I was passionately fond of—a scene from *L'Avare* . . . Hugo's *Expiation*. I would be trying to communicate some of my enthusiasm to them. And all the time I would be thinking, intermittently, and with a sense of delicious satisfaction, of my fine little car, of my recent highly successful valve-adjustment, of the brilliant hill-test I had carried out the day before, of the gear-change I had made, smooth as a sigh, and the exact tree at which I had made it. . . . If such thoughts were ill-timed, so much the worse. Maybe that's the way I keep young, alive, human. My childishness is part and parcel of my enthusiasms, and prevents them from becoming boring and inelastic. No doubt Poincaré is a great deal more serious-minded. That, unfortunately, is obvious. . . . All the same, one can never be quite sure."

While darkness fell over the landscape, Jerphanion managed to see life, especially his own, as a rich variety. He felt no desire to discipline himself. Given his temperamental feeling for order, and the way in which he and others had developed that feeling, he decided that he had had more than enough of discipline. Nor did he feel any desire that the details of his private meditations should take on a more respectable complexion.

# Chapter

## ODETTE'S ANSWER

When he got back to Le Puy, where the pavements were already covered with melting snow, Jerphanion found a letter from Odette:

Jean, dearest:

I was glad to get your letter. Time was beginning to drag, and I confess I was almost anxious. I do understand how difficult you must find it sometimes to write me a real letter, but please send me a short postcard or even a telegram.

Now I've got that off my chest—and you musn't think I'm blaming you—it's only fair to say that the length of your letter made up for everything. Thank you for telling me about all the little things that are happening to you. I've got a feeling that what you call your "reconnaissance patrol" is going very well and that the people of your own native province will be only too glad to elect you. To persuade them is the least of your problems. It's when it comes to dealing with the other men on the party ticket that you're going to find your real difficulty, especially if they are as "brilliant" as you say they are. What a ridiculous system it is, since what in fact it amounts to is that all the genuinely able men have got to work themselves to the bone in order to assure the success of a lot of nobodies! Do you remember what Bouitton said, half in fun, one day when he was dining with us?— that quite a number of clever persons are a great deal less put out by it than they pretend, because it enables them to surround themselves with the second-rate, who ever after will be entirely in their power. That, unfortunately, is not your line; you lack the special ability that can mould nobodies to your will. Your trouble will always be how

193

to keep them from noticing that their mere existence irritates you.

Do try not to overtire yourself. What with all this running about from meeting to meeting in the depth of winter, you'll come home with a whacking great cold, and I needn't tell you what a mass of work you'll find when you get back. Bouitton rang me up yesterday, bubbling with laughter as usual, to say that the Radical Party was relying on you to draw up a general plan of campaign. It wants one badly, I gather. It was said jokingly, but I think you ought to be very careful. They'll abuse your good nature, in the name of party loyalty. They'll argue that since your own seat is safe, you can give all your time to the general strategy of the campaign. Bouitton complained of his health. He's having trouble with his liver and kidneys. He eats too much and is too fond of the good things of this world, vintage wines and old brandy—to say nothing of other things which haven't, perhaps, quite the same effect on his liver and kidneys. And while I'm on this subject (I refer to the first part of the above sentence), do please watch your food. Going about in the cold and tiring yourself out must give you an abnormal appetite. And with all the different people you're meeting you must have to take an awful lot of drinks, and mix your drinks, which is worse. Be careful, dear.

I too wish that I was with you. I could have been such a help in getting you out of unnecessary invitations and stopping you from sitting up too late. I am sure, too, that we should have been amused by the same things. I have never seen "your" countryside at this time of year, and it would have interested me to look about, even though you tell me that there isn't any snow. Not that staying at home hasn't certain compensations. It's a great joy to me to have my parents here for a bit. They adore being in Paris. It's a kind of holiday for them. They make me take them about, and Papa overloads us with treats. He takes us to cafés and drinking-places and restaurants and cinemas —even to the theatre. The other evening he took us to see *Knock*,[1] which is having an extraordinary success. He had an awful job getting a box, which, when he *did* succeed, was tucked away in a corner so

_____

[1] *Dr. Knock*, a comedy by Jules Romains.—TRANSLATOR'S NOTE.

that one could hardly see the stage at all. Some extra chairs had been put in it, and we had to share it with another party. I enjoyed the play enormously for its biting wit and really terrifying sense of comedy. The style, too, has all the slickness and brilliance of a demonstration car at the Motor Show. Jouvet is marvellous. In the intermission, people were going into ecstasies about it and comparing it with Molière. I see what they mean, though it isn't a bit like Molière on the surface. We must go and see it together; I should like to know what you think.

I am sorry that what I wrote about Jean-Pierre worries you. I agree that there's nothing at all unusual in his nervous fits. I should say it would be found that eight out of ten boys of his age go through the same sort of difficult time if only their parents would take the trouble to note the fact. The real reason I feel concerned is that he happens to be *my* son.

Of course we spoil him, all of us. It's largely because of the way we treat him that he loves to hear the sound of his own voice, and knows only too well that he is the apple of our eye. If he had four brothers and sisters older than himself, his own concerns would have less importance even for himself. I confess that I find it very hard to imagine the atmosphere that must have obtained in large families of the kind that used to be common and to which you refer—families, I mean, of seven or nine children. What kind of importance can any single child, with the possible exception of the eldest son, have had for the mother and father? Each must have grown up quite independently and as best he might. If he died, he was mourned, perhaps, for a week, after which, if he was lucky, he might be remembered occasionally and at long intervals. I can't even believe that there can be any resemblance between the sort of way parents in those days thought of their hordes of children and that in which we feel for ours, because ours are quite irreplaceable, are our *only* children, even when they are not "only children" in the legal sense. In the old days, too, the sons made no bones about hating their father and wishing for him to die, while the daughters had only one thought, how best they could make fools of their mother with the clandestine assistance of the servants. One's only got to see the plays of the period to realize that. I think we should find it difficult to recapture a taste for that kind of family and family life even if the present weren't so full of threats, even if once again we had some right, in your own words, to trust in the future.

If you ask my opinion, I do not think that our habit of "spoiling" children—I use that rather simple word for lack of a better—results merely from the disappearance of the large family. I think it is due even more to the different attitude of the present generation, to a progress in the parental attitude. As a result of reading so many books about unhappy childhood, of listening to the grievances of misunderstood young people whose parents thought they were doing their duty, but whose agonies and miseries (and they could be infinite in number) no one ever bothered about, the parents of today and tomorrow have become a great deal more conscientious. That's what one means when one says that literature has an educational value. They have been led to recollect their own childhood, have been forced to admit that very often their parents, not from evil intent but from pure absence of mind and lack of intelligent concern, abandoned them to the privacy of their own adolescent troubles and to fits of despair quite as fearful, if not more so, and just as lasting, whatever one may think, as those of grown-ups. Consequently they have registered a solemn promise to do better by their own children, whether they are few or many. I know that is so from my own case. When I was a young mother, or just on the point of becoming one, I thought things out in a way I never should have done if I had been a young middle-class matron of an earlier age. I was much struck, too, by something Jallez said to us one day. I wonder if you remember. I think it must have been during the Victory Parade in '19. I had been speaking about Jean-Pierre. Jallez told us that his parents had been very good to him and very loving; that he had been devoted to them. His mother, in particular, he said, had been very sensitive, very tender, and extremely intelligent. Moreover, he had been brought up almost like an only son. Nevertheless, both as a child and later as a young man, he had gone through long periods not only of nervous restlessness but of moral agony that at times amounted to something like insanity, without either of his parents taking the slightest notice. In the case of his father this may have been due to a sort of shyness, a dread of infringing on the child's liberty, of seeming to play the spy on him. His mother was probably afflicted by another kind of shyness—a fear of discovering unpleasant truths, facts that cannot be discussed between mother and son. His parents would have felt criminally guilty if they had failed to note and treat the slightest physical trouble in their child, but would ignore his far more serious moral ills, or pretend to do so. The result was that our friend felt himself as much abandoned as though he had been an orphan.

The long and the short of the matter is that as parents we belong to a more advanced stage of evolution. It may well be that our children are not more nervous or more complex than those of earlier generations. But we pay more attention to them. We attach more importance to them. We don't believe that their troubles will cure themselves. It follows naturally that to some extent our children are less self-conscious about letting us see their little unhappinesses, and are readier to make themselves objects of interest. This is especially true where simple nervousness, capriciousness, and temper are concerned. And that, I think, is all that is wrong with Jean-Pierre. But should graver moral troubles lie behind what is, after all, mainly physical, we stand a much better chance than the parents of an older generation of realizing what is wrong. And in curing such things early recognition of the symptoms is half the battle.

Talking of Jallez, I've just had a letter from him. He talks of coming to see us about New Year's or perhaps a little later. He's leaving Italy. According to him, the new Fascist regime is by no means solidly established. He says that even the dramatic stroke at Fiume was received with a good deal of mocking laughter, and that if only

Mussolini's opponents could show a little more solidarity and decision, they could overthrow him the very first time he, or his followers, commit any glaring blunder.

Don't bother about your correspondence. In the case of urgent letters I reply myself, either giving the required information, when I know it, or saying that you are away and will reply when you get back. I can assure you, I'm extremely cautious. So far there has been nothing of importance.

A dinner invitation has come for you from a certain Comtesse Foulion, who lives in the rue Léonard-de-Vinci. The lady seems to be as ignorant of my existence as I was of hers. I replied that "my husband" was away, but that he would be shown the invitation on his return, and that he would answer it himself.

That is the end of my news. My parents would very much like to stay until you get back, but they have arranged to pay a visit to some friends in the Seine-et-Oise and can't very well get out of it. They send you much love. You know how deeply they value your affection. Jean-Pierre talks of you incessantly. He asked me this morning whether I was going to write to you, and asked me to send you a kiss. He says that next time he will enclose a line written by his own hand. As to myself, I can never tell you enough how much I adore you. I think of you all the time, I am longing for you to get back, and I send you a thousand kisses.

Your

ODETTE

# Chapter

## 14

### SNOWSCAPE, AND
### A CHAT ABOUT CRIME

As well as this letter, Jerphanion had found awaiting him a note from M. Pouzols-Desaugues:

Dear Sir:

I am going to hold you to your promise. I don't know on which day precisely you intend being back in Le Puy, but I hope it is clearly understood that as soon as you arrive you give me a ring and propose yourself for luncheon the day following. My car will fetch you and take you back, so that you will lose no more time than if you had taken your meal at the hotel.

Yours very sincerely,

HENRI POUZOLS-DESAUGUES

PS. I learn from my spies that you have already quite won the heart of our mountain folk. A certain visit paid by you to the old curé of Saint-Front has had the best possible effect. But it is not your account of that visit that I am anxious to hear.

As a result of this message, Jerphanion found himself next day welcomed in the courtyard of the manor-house by a M. Pouzols-Desaugues who was as prodigal of attentions as though he had been meeting an old friend from whom he had been many years parted.

They proceeded to the study. The landscape was still lovely, but so different that it was only with an effort that Jerphanion recognized it as the same. It was composed now of a patchwork of snow-covered fields divided by the familiar colours of the earth that, by contrast, seemed to have taken on a darker tone. The more distant features of the view were covered now by what appeared to be an unbroken blanket of white undulating with the rise and fall of the ground until it met the distant mountains, which today seemed nearer and much more clearly defined, their peaks wreathed by the woolly vapours of a greyish sky.

These reflecting surfaces of snow, widely scattered over the countryside, filled the room with the sharp, cold light far more penetrating than any summer sun. Distant corners of the ceiling, the upper portions of various pieces of furniture, never reached by the glare of August, showed clearly now, displaying a wealth of detail in splashed patches of this strange, fantastic illumination. Even the backs of the books standing on the shelves that faced the light emerged from their customary shadow and seemed to stand out in an icy glow.

In the faintly mischievous tone of a declared conspirator, M. Pouzols-Desaugues said:

"We'll stay here just long enough to take a glass of port. I know that after a tour like yours you'll have a lot to do. I don't want to cause a longer interruption to your day than would have been necessitated by lunch at your hotel. I've arranged for us to be alone. A relation living at Le Puy, discreetly canvassed by myself, has invited my wife. Before picking you up, the car dropped her, and will fetch her again after taking you back."

He winked as he spoke, dropping his eyeglass much as he might have done in the old days when he told his chief that he had "done the Germans in the eye."

Consequently, their talk took place at table, in the course of a meal consisting of fish and game. The only weak spot in an admirably thought-out menu was the wine, a Sauterne of a good year which Jerphanion found to be a great deal too sweet for his taste. (It was Jallez's influence which had sent him back to the dry white Bordeaux on which he had been brought up.)

"Please don't keep me on tenterhooks," said M. Pouzols-Desaugues. "What was your impression of Vaurevauzes—though I'm counting on something more definite than mere impression?"

"Before I start telling you about my visit, I'm afraid I must indulge in a longish preamble. You'll see why as I proceed. . . . You remember, of course, that I am touring in my friend Grousson's car. . . . Well, it appears that he knows all about the happenings at Vaurevauzes."

"I hope you didn't commit me too deeply."

"Never fear; we didn't mention you. Grousson, as I say, knew all about it; but, better still, he had devoted more than merely casual attention to the matter. I think I may say that for years he has been thinking about it at odd moments. Spending his life, as he does, driving about the countryside, he has plenty of odd moments to fill up, and being anything but a fool, he has built up an extremely ingenious and detailed theory about which you shall judge for yourself."

"I am all ears!"

"I need hardly say that he keeps it to himself. I had to worm it out of him bit by bit. We discussed it at great length. Perhaps I ought to add that in the course of our talk I suggested one or two new ideas, or, rather, dotted his *i*'s for him. Between us we have, I think, worked out a fool-proof case, so far, that is, as the present state of our knowledge permits."

"How I should have loved to be with you. It must have been terribly exciting. Why didn't you bring him with you?"

"I was very much tempted to . . . but I didn't dare."

"That was foolish of you."

"I'm not so sure. I don't think he would have felt at ease. He's a shy sort of chap. With me in the car, he could talk away in his own time. With you, he would probably have given a confused and incomplete account even of his own theories, and I could hardly have kept putting him right. I think you'll agree that we shall do better without him. Besides, you can always meet him later if you want to."

Thereupon, Jerphanion proceeded to recapitulate, as accurately as possible, the talks they had had in the car, doing his best to follow the original line of development. Pouzols-Desaugues listened with an expression of entranced delight. Now and again he ventured an objection, or asked for a point to be elaborated, begging Jerphanion's pardon for doing so. It was clear that he did not mean to miss a single scrap of the pleasure offered for his consumption. Argument could wait until later. What particularly called forth his admiration was the analysis of the situation and the attribution of motives.

"Where shall we find psychological imagination next!" he exclaimed. "Who would have supposed that an honest wine-merchant would be blessed with a knowledge of the human heart such as should by rights be the monopoly of a Balzac or a Paul Bourget?"

When Jerphanion went on to relate the discussion he had had with Grousson on the question of the material means necessary for the commission of the crimes, and especially on the existence of a "folk-lore type of poison," M. Pouzols-Desaugues broke in on him:

"I could have told you a lot about that. In the course of my life, as you may imagine, I have seen many odd things, and heard a good many country stories. I am inclined to think an explanation along those lines more than likely. But I don't want to delay what I still regard as your prize piece: I mean, the account of your visit to Vaurevauzes."

"I'm afraid you'll be disappointed about that," said Jerphanion. "But you must judge for yourself."

He described how they had driven up to the house, how the small boy had run away, how they had seen the widow standing in the frame of the tunnel.

"I wasn't so far wrong when I said she was interesting, eh?" exclaimed M. Pouzols-Desaugues. "Turned out by a good dressmaker, properly made-up and perfumed, she would stand comparison with most women—don't you agree?"

"I most certainly do."

"Well now, is she to be regarded as the *femme fatale?* And if so, in what way? Because, you see, I believe that there are at least two varieties of the *femme fatale*—the woman for whose favours men will commit crimes, but who demands nothing and even pretends to be ignorant that any crime has been committed; and the woman who issues orders or suggests what should be done. . . ."

"I am inclined to agree," said Jerphanion, "though I have had little personal experience of the *femme fatale*."

"Same here! She has not been a habit of mine, even in her more exotic manifestations. . . ."

"... I willingly admit your classification. But let me say this—I gave a good deal of careful attention to that handsome widow of ours, not only when she was standing in the frame of the tunnel, but afterwards, in the 'cave'—which is how I think of the big room. Grousson had spoken a lot about her, and it was clear that she had roused his admiration. Though he hadn't actually said so, he had certainly suggested to me that she belonged to the *femme fatale* class, and, if anything, to your second subdivision of that class. He had made a great deal of her power to obsess men's minds, to awaken in them a sort of sexual fever— "she's the kind," he said, "who gets one's mind working in one way and one way only"—and of the fact—the two things go together—that she was obviously preoccupied with the idea of the opposite sex. I had imagined her as a woman with loose lips and restless eyes, the kind of woman who always seems to be saying: 'Wouldn't you like to go to bed with me?' "

"I certainly didn't give you any such idea. . . ."

"No, I know you didn't . . . all you said was: 'Look at her carefully; she's worth studying.' It was Grousson's description that gave me the idea. Imagine my surprise. I saw before me at Vaurevauzes a woman of mystery—using 'mystery' in its subtlest meaning. There was nothing coarsely sexual about her. She was as far removed as might be from the type of country Messalina. I don't want to exaggerate, but I found something almost angelic about her—in the Lamartine or de Vigny sense. I don't mean that she seemed unacquainted with the passionate manifestations of love, but only that she gave the impression of one who would always transmute them to a spiritual plane, with 'that pure smile of yours, that tells at once of love and suffering.' There was no looseness about her lips, but a sort of quiver, and in her glance no provocation, but a hint of wounded innocence—the look of a frightened child. Perhaps I have said rather more than I mean, but that was roughly my impression."

M. Pouzols-Desaugues smiled. He seemed amused, and not wholly in agreement with his visitor's views. Jerphanion continued, this time more deliberately:

"You must have met, as I have done, in the course of your life, perhaps quite casually, plenty of women whom you suspected of being pretty dissolute at heart . . . women to whom you certainly would not have given absolution without confession . . . women who made no bones about assuming a virtue when they had it not . . . but who, for all that, had retained a kind of virginal air. Normal men, when they fall in love with women like that, feel tenderness and compassion as well as desire. Of course, there's nothing to prevent such women from rousing blind passion in a man, and no reason why blind passion should not result in tragic action should the man's temperament be of a particular kind. I have an idea that there are men, rather complex men as a rule, who find women of that kind a great deal more exciting than the loose-lipped and restless-eyed variety. . . . I am perfectly ready to admit that behind their appealing exterior they often conceal a calculating hardness, an ability to plot deliberate horrors, a willingness to lead men on to commit crimes for their sake. That's another question altogether. All I mean to stress is that if they happen to play the part of a *femme fatale* in a man's life, it won't be in any ordinary way. In spite of everything, I am inclined to believe that they differ from most women in the complexity, the subtlety, the frightening quality of their psychological make-up, and in the way they make their influence felt . . . nor has it got anything to do with their social class."

M. Pouzols-Desaugues still smiled as he listened, faintly but continuously nodding his head, his monocle firmly fixed in his eye. His attitude was that of a connoisseur of life who employs all his gifts of observation, every lesson of a long experience, in an effort to deal with the problem at issue.

"I see exactly what you mean," he said, "though I won't pretend that my own impressions agree with yours. I don't mean that I took her, as your friend Grousson seems to have done, for the kind of woman who turns a young man's head. That seemed to me too simple an explanation. But I can't say that I was conscious of that young-girl effect. . . ."

He broke off while the footman handed the dishes.

"I thought it better," he went on, "to wait till that fellow had left the room. Not that I think him more than usually inquisitive or particularly intelligent. But there is no point in letting him know what we are talking about. I am not the kind of man who doesn't mind what he says in front of the servants, just as though they were bits of furniture. That has always seemed to me to betoken a curious lack of imagination. I had one or two unpleasant experiences when I was in the diplomatic service—cases of servants who spied on me. . . . Well, what I was going to say was that you probably brought a more acute observation than I did to bear on the fair lady in question. In particular, you reached Vaurevauzes after long hours of super-subtle discussion, with the result that your mind was wide awake and you were prepared to do a good deal of hair-splitting. . . . I am prepared to admit, on general principles, that you are right. . . . I was about to add that it probably doesn't very much matter, but I should have been wrong. In one way or another that woman is the centre of a mystery. Everything depends on the idea we form of her . . . to a very large extent, at least, don't you agree?"

"Entirely."

"Good. . . . And what happened then? I am burning with curiosity to know what happened then."

Jerphanion described how they went into the house. He described the three women, the atmosphere of the big room, his own reflections.

"Nothing in all that to attract your attention particularly?"

"Nothing. I am not even sure that I got any clear idea about the arrangement of the house, or how the family lives. What, for instance, is there on the first floor?"

He went on to tell how the younger son had come in.

"Ah!" exclaimed M. Pouzols-Desaugues. "The other star performer! And what did you make of him?"

Jerphanion admitted that he presented an even greater problem, if possible, than the fair widow. "If I hadn't been warned in advance, I should have taken him for the normal peasant type, physically rather delicate perhaps, not very friendly, and of a quick, quarrelsome temper. I should never have suspected him of being either passionate or violent. Certainly not sinister or frightening."

"I trust you drew him out—though without appearing to do so, of course?"

"I would hardly go so far as to say that. . . . Taking advantage of some remark he let fall, I did try to get him to talk about the two deaths . . . but the results were scarcely brilliant."

Jerphanion repeated the complaints made by the young man about the unhealthfulness of the house, and the arguments he had adduced in support of his contention.

M. Pouzols-Desaugues stopped eating, laid down his knife and fork, raised his eyeglass, put both hands on the table, threw himself back in his chair, and in a half-angry, half-startled voice, said several times:

"God bless my soul! God bless my soul!"

Then:

"I must say the fellow's got a pretty good cheek!"

And finally:

"So *I'm* to be held responsible for all these deaths in his family!"

He moved irritably in his seat.

"I suppose he found out that it was I who more or less set the inquiry on foot after his father's death, and now he wants a little revenge."

He screwed his monocle into his eye again and leaned forward, his elbows on the table, his chin resting in his hands.

"Let me think. I want to get this business straight. . . . The Leblancs have been farming that place for me since—I suppose it was about 1904 that the old man first settled there. . . . Before that there'd been another family, but they only stayed a couple of years—impossible people who just hung on long enough to steal my timber and the lead of my roof gutters . . . so nothing much can have happened to them. . . . Before that—well, before that I had no tenants for the simple reason that the place wasn't mine. I bought it in 1902; and I remember that there was no tenant when the previous owner sold it. The farmers who had been there before were gone when I took possession and, if I'm not wrong, when I looked over the place for the first time. . . . There was only a sort of caretaker there—no trace of a farmer. . . . I can still remember how spacious the empty outbuildings seemed. . . ."

"Do you know anything about these farmers who were there before?"

"Precisely nothing at all. The man who sold it to me may have mentioned them . . . I think he told me they had made their fortunes because it was such marvellous land—or some nonsense of that sort. But I can't remember any details."

M. Pouzols-Desaugues remained lost in thought.

"Do you think," asked Jerphanion, "that what young Leblanc said about the earlier deaths that had taken place there may have had something in it?"

"That's a difficult question. Speaking offhand, I should be very much surprised if there were. Naturally, of course, I shouldn't have heard anything of it at the time of the sale. The vendor wouldn't have been likely to cry stinking fish, and in cases like that, any outsider with the requisite information is apt to keep it to himself for fear of being thought to have put a spoke in his neighbour's wheel out of spite. But it's odd, isn't it, that no one dropped the slightest hint to me in the course of twenty years? . . . There's nothing people love so much as to let you feel that you've made a bad bargain . . . to let you see that you weren't as clever as you thought you were. . . ."

"And now, I suppose, if one wanted to find out more—from pure curiosity, or just to satisfy oneself about how much lying has been going on—there's no way of verifying these rumours."

M. Pouzols-Desaugues showed considerable embarrassment.

"In theory it ought to be possible . . . but how is one to set about it? It would mean hunting through the legal records, and to do that one would have to know the name of the former tenants. . . . That could be managed, I suppose . . . but how about the dates? . . . We don't know them. . . . And how are we going to discover anything about the deaths that are said to have taken place there? Of course, we could always question the neighbours, but the curé is the only person on whose word I should be inclined to rely, and at the time this business may be presumed to have taken place, he wasn't there. He was appointed, I remember, just before the law relating to the Separation was passed. . . . He came and called on me. . . . As for anyone else, in the first place people's memories aren't what they were. That may seem an odd thing to say, but it's true. You won't find today any of those oldest inhabitants who used to be able to recount local history from the days of their childhood. I've had plenty of opportunities of proving that. They don't get asked about it, with the result that their memories become rusty. When young people to-day want to know anything, they look for it in papers or books, or else they go to the Mairie and ask. It never occurs to them to interrogate their nodding elders. That is more the case now, since the war, than ever, because the break with the past has become sharper. . . . But quite apart from all that, you would hardly expect me, as owner of Vaurevauzes, to go nosing about among all those forgotten horrors, assuming that they ever existed, would you?—reviving all the talk of galloping consumption, spreading the idea that my property is rotten with infection through and through? The fuss caused by old Leblanc and his eldest son dying one after the other is quite enough! . . . Our young friend can clear out when the lease is up, with his whole family, for all I care. . . . But once he starts saying that people were dying off like flies there from consumption even before these mysterious disappearances, it's all up with Vaurevauzes. It'll be a house under a curse. . . . I shall never find another tenant, to say nothing of a purchaser."

After a pause he went on:

"Of course, if I really thought there was anything in the business, I might feel bound in conscience to do something, because there might still be some infection hanging about. But I'm pretty sure the whole thing's pure invention—the invention of a criminal anxious to cover his tracks. . . . But the fact remains, my dear sir, that whatever the result of our investigations might be, the damage, from my point of view, would have been done. No one would believe that I'd started a hare like that without very good reason. I should merely have depreciated part of my patrimony to satisfy the probably passing whim of this fellow . . . for, after all, who's to say that he won't have changed his tune next week or the week after?"

After pondering for a while he continued:

"The more I think of this business, the shadier it looks. I don't now remember all the details of the version they put out after the old man's death, and more or less stuck to at the police inquiry. But it certainly didn't square with this tale of a plague-stricken house. The main point of it was that he had got congestion of the lungs, or had caught some sort of a chill, probably on top of a previous illness. . . . No, our friend certainly had not invented his little fairy-tale at that time. . . . Quite likely he improvised it in your honour."

M. Pouzols-Desaugues was obviously anxious that his guest should not regard him as one of those hard-hearted landowners who care nothing for truth or human life when their private interests are at stake. He continued after a short pause, on a note of puzzled amiability:

"Probably the least bad way of proceeding now would be, since you have confidence in your friend Grousson, who's a fairly responsible sort of person—by the way, I suppose he knows all about this?"

"Certainly he does. He was there all the time young Leblanc was talking. . . ."

"Good. . . . Then he might do a little discreet scouting up there in the neighbourhood, just to see how the land lies . . . nothing crude, you know. . . . He might pretend, for instance, that he had

met someone who had happened to mention some family or other—
'Didn't the So-and-so's live here once? What's become of them?' With
a little careful handling it's always possible to get people to tell what
they know, without putting ideas into their heads and starting a general rumour. Don't you agree?"

"Yes, and I'll mention it to him."

"But be careful to tell him not to repeat what this fellow Leblanc
said. You'll warn him, won't you, of the harm it might do me?"

"I think he'll be quick enough to see that."

M. Pouzols-Desaugues seemed to have recovered his cheerfulness.
Nevertheless, a moment or two later he said:

"There's another moral to be learned from this business: to wit,
that it's never any good handling fellows like that with kid gloves.
After all, I might have gone all out to get rid of him at any price;
I might have nagged at the legal authorities to do something or demanded a new inquiry, but I didn't. . . . And now not only does he
talk of clearing out, but he does all he can to blacken my property. . . .
There's one thing I'm strongly tempted to do. . . . I'm on very good
terms with one of the local magistrates, Monsieur Doublet, a charming man and quite young. Why shouldn't I ask him to go through
the files which he took over from his predecessor, and see what story
the Leblancs concocted about the old man's death? I could say: 'My
tenant, one of the dead man's sons, says now, it seems, that his father
died because the house was unhealthy. I don't like it at all. I want to
find out whether he aired this particular grievance at the time of
the inquiry, and, if need be, to stop his mouth by quoting his own
statement.' If Monsieur Doublet shows signs of curiosity and of wanting to hear more of something he doesn't know about already, well
then, I'll put him wise bit by bit. It all depends on his reactions.
Anyhow, we shall get some amusement out of the business. If your
name happened to come up in the course of our conversation, would
it be a great inconvenience for you to meet him, say, at the Brasserie
du Théâtre? . . . Quite apart from all this, I should like you to know
each other. He's really delightful. Don't you think it might be rather

fun? After all, what risk do we run? We're not accusing anyone. We're just telling a rather romantic and highly flavoured story. It can just remain an anecdote."

Jerphanion readily agreed. He was quite glad to think that his mountain adventure was to have a sequel, and he was anxious to see what a professional would make of the matter.

The point settled, they said no more. Their silence corresponded with the arrival of dessert and the reappearance of the footman.

# Chapter

## THE LANDLORD AND
## THE GOOD-LOOKING CONCIERGE

The man left the room, and M. Pouzols-Desaugues resumed his talk.

"I'm afraid you're going to find out, my dear sir, that I have a terribly retentive memory, and that as a creditor I am quite without mercy. You promised—surely you remember what it was you promised—on the occasion of your last visit—just as you were going away?"

"Let me see now—"

"Some story about an experience you had had not unlike mine, something that had happened quite recently. . . . I'm afraid I must hold you to your bargain. . . . You will admit, I think, that I have discharged my part of the debt in making you a present of this Vaurevauzes business—it's entertaining in its way, isn't it? Well now, I'm asking for a *quid pro quo.*"

"I'm sorry, but you'll find you've had the worst of the deal. My story's very small beer compared with yours. It's a crude little anecdote, without any amusing twists and turns. It is set in the murk of the Paris streets, and, worst of all, it is hopelessly flimsy, consisting, as it does, of a lot of pretty wild guesswork and a few attempts at action—that came to nothing. The only thing in its favour is that it doesn't take long to tell."

"I must begin by explaining that we live on the stretch of the boulevard Saint-Germain that faces the Île Saint-Louis, in a rather old-fashioned, though eminently respectable block of flats consisting of six floors. Our own apartment is not very convenient, and now that we have a child it is much too small for us—but you know what a business it is trying to find somewhere to live in Paris, and how shockingly one's exploited by landlords. Most people just hang on to what they've got. The man who owns our block has two or three other houses in the neighbourhood, and manages his affairs himself. I saw him once or twice when I was negotiating the lease. At that time he was something under fifty, a decent-looking fellow, comfortably off, living in one of his other houses, probably a retired business-man. We moved in shortly before the war. At that time there were a couple of concierges, perfectly ordinary, the kind you'd scarcely notice. The husband was a thickset sort of chap who was employed, I think, on the tramway. But when I got back from the army, a new pair had moved in, of quite a different type. The husband was thinnish and refined-looking, with a rather stupid face. Like his predecessor, he worked away from home, in some near-by bank. His wife was a woman of about forty, plump but good-looking, well built, and very careful of her appearance, rather above her station in manners and general get-up. She didn't, I need hardly say, do any of the heavy work. She had a woman in to help her, and what she couldn't do, the husband looked after in his free time. His wife confined her efforts to sitting in her lodge and answering inquiries in an affected voice. Very occasionally she brought the mail up.

"The husband looked as though he had a secret sorrow, and I rather liked him. There was an appealing expression in his eyes. Now and then I exchanged a few words with him. He confessed that he was worried about his health. In particular, he complained about the state of his stomach.

"We noticed that gradually he grew worse. His complaints became more frequent. He began to take days off from the bank, and we didn't at all like his looks.

"This state of affairs went on for several months, with alternations of improvement and relapse. Finally his absences from the bank became longer; he kept to his room; he took to his bed. And then, one fine day, he died.

"You probably know what middle-class tenants in Paris are like. They have no more than a nodding acquaintance with one another.

The death of the concierge, however, led to a good deal of stopping on the stairs and discreet chatter.

"All the next day his affected widow stayed in the privacy of her lodge. It was a fine chance for her. Her clothes and her attitude betokened the stricken sufferer. At the end of a few weeks she vanished, not, I should say, without announcing her impending departure in very refined accents to those of the tenants who invaded her seclusion. There was nothing surprising about her decision to go, since, obviously, she was not temperamentally fitted for the job.

"Quite soon we learned that she had retired to a small apartment in the rue de Pontoise. The building in which it was situated was, we were told, of a very good class, and, since the apartment itself was not a furnished one, it was obvious that either she had furnished it herself or that someone else had for her, and at pretty short notice too. This information reached us through the medium of various servants, with the collaboration, I suspect, of a woman who sold papers. She had a stand situated on the ground floor of the house next door, much patronized in the neighbourhood.

"It was not long before the facts began to be accompanied by comments, hints about what had been going on before the man's death. The servants, and the news-vendor, too, I am quite sure, made it clear that they had long suspected our handsome concierge of being on more than friendly terms with the landlord. The little flat in the rue de Pontoise had almost certainly been furnished at his expense. How could she have raised the necessary sum otherwise? If the couple had had to take on a caretaking job in order to live, it was hardly likely that the lady could have retired as a result of her husband's death. The small pension paid by the bank would have been wholly insufficient for her needs. Our spy service soon found out, too, that the landlord was paying frequent visits to the apartment in the rue de Pontoise. He was frequently seen going in and out quite openly.

"Very soon people were saying freely that the poor fellow's death had been highly convenient. There was a lot of talk about the progress of his last illness, which had been matter of common knowledge to the tenants.

"I ought to say that, at the time, I got wind of all this in a very fragmentary fashion. I had come to hear of it more or less by a fluke, and paid very little attention to what was being said. It was only later that I began putting two and two together.

"A further rumour, started probably by other servants and other news-vendors, was soon added to the original one. It was said that the landlord's wife had fallen ill in her turn, that she was sinking gradually for no very good and sufficient reason, and suffered a great deal of pain.

"I need hardly add that the mere fact was enough to set tongues wagging. The coincidence of the two illnesses was, as the papers say, 'highly disquieting.' . . . There was no need for the ingenuities of gossip. . . . It was all rather like a laboratory experiment: no need to do more than establish the facts and let them tell their own story.

"But did no one, you'll ask, think that something ought to be done to save the life of the landlord's wife? About that I can't say. You know how shy people are about taking the initiative in such cases. Most of them were content to regard the whole affair as a play they were seeing or a book they were reading. They wanted to know what was going to happen, and since the majority thought they knew what that was likely to be, and desired the expected dénouement as something æsthetically right and proper, they felt no temptation to spoil the issue by taking a hand in the development themselves. It was about this time that I began to find the situation somewhat odd, and to listen in a rather half-hearted way to the various echoes which reached me. But I still looked on the whole thing as a piece of servants' gossip. It never occurred to me that I ought to take any action.

"Several months passed. From time to time I learned that the landlord's wife was far from well, and that the good-looking widow was getting along very comfortably in her flat in the rue de Pontoise, where she seemed to live a far from forlorn existence. I can imagine that at the lower level of servants and news-vendors the current of information flowed more strongly, and that the situation was being followed, from day to day, with scrupulous attention. Everywhere in the neighbourhood a host of spectators must have been waiting in a state of feverish excitement to see what would happen. For all I know, there may have been arguments and bets on the issue: 'She'll die!' 'She won't!' To cut a long story short, after keeping everyone on tenterhooks, the lady did eventually die."

"How amazing to think," exclaimed M. Pouzols-Desaugues, "that such a situation could develop in the middle of Paris, at this time of the world's history, with so little fuss, with, as one might say, such effrontery!"

"Wait till you hear the rest. The landlord's wife died last spring, in May to be precise. At the end of September we learned that our landlord had just married our ex-concierge, and that the newly united couple had decided to exchange the noise and bustle of Paris for 'a château in the Seine-et-Marne.' The 'château' may, in fact, be little more than a comfortable villa, but the news was highly significant. This time the audience had been well rewarded for its patience."

"But was nothing done? I always imagined that city-dwellers were, on the whole, less shy than their country cousins about setting the police in motion, and that in cases of this kind, the authorities' lives were made a misery by anonymous letters."

Jerphanion shrugged his shoulders.

"I was given to understand later that one or two such letters had been sent. But the setting counts for so much in such matters. My impression is that in Paris the anonymous letter is confined to the lower and lower-middle classes. The front-row spectators at this particular play, the people whose indignation might most likely have found such expression, were primarily our co-tenants, and in the second place the tenants of the building in which the landlord had been living; in other words, middle-class people, who, with very rare exceptions, have a rooted dislike of that method of procedure. Apart from them there were those in the neighbourhood, of course, who had heard about the various goings-on, but only in a vague way, and as a series of rather remote events. . . . What about the servants, you'll ask. Well, I won't say that a servant isn't capable of writing an anonymous letter to satisfy a personal grudge, but I can't see her doing it in the interests of pure justice. Besides, to whom should the letters be sent? To the local police commissioner, I suppose. They would not be opened by the commissioner himself, however, but by some bored, uninterested secretary, who would almost certainly ignore such scraps of barely intelligible information, mis-spelt, and full of veiled allusions. For don't forget this not unamusing fact: that anonymous letters—and a good many have passed through my hands at various times in positions I've held—are written with the greatest possible caution. For the most part, their writers avoid like the plague any kind of formal charge, anything which can be verified. One's impression is that they are obsessed by a fear that they may be recognized, and think of nothing so much as keeping their line of retreat open.

"To be brief, local opinion quieted down. A few natural sceptics insisted, on principle, that the whole thing might have been due to a series of coincidences. Others soon lost interest in a story which did not really concern them. The majority were content to note with a sigh this incontrovertible fact, that in the twentieth century, given a cool head and an assured social position, a man may quite comfortably imitate the Borgias. . . . You know the sort of half-regretful way in which the ordinary decent citizen is so often tempted nowadays to moralize when confronted by drama of a different kind—for instance, the activities of profiteers and speculators: 'Really, one wonders sometimes why one remains honest—I suppose it's just that one is made like that.'"

"Precisely. . . . And so, I suppose, our pair of turtle-doves, their troubles over, as in the fairy-tales, lived happily ever after at their château in the Seine-et-Marne?"

"Ah, but I've not quite finished. . . . There's one final, and not unamusing, episode to relate. When the marriage was announced, your humble servant was not altogether comfortable in his conscience.

Said he to himself: 'Life becomes a bit too simple if one regards one's every judgment as rash, all action as headstrong and ill-considered. If the police are never to be given a hint it's quite obvious that justice will never be in a position to track down the less obvious sort of crime, which includes, of course, those of a particularly cunning and hateful type. There is a point at which the reticence of honest folk— always excused on the ground that the affair is none of their business —must be regarded as stupidity, to use no harsher word; and it is due, in the last analysis, to laziness and lack of courage.' I added that there was less excuse for me than for most people because, given my way of life, it was easy for me to get the ear of an important magistrate and to make him listen to me, always allowing, of course, that there was no reason why I should lodge any definite charge. I could trust the bench to proceed with the utmost circumspection. It would be up to the authorities to decide whether the preliminary evidence would be sufficiently disturbing to justify a more formal inquiry. It was open to the spiteful to say that I wanted to play a public role in the matter. But, in fact, that would have been going a great deal too far. To be perfectly frank, I was not altogether averse to setting the machinery of the law in motion. I had never had occasion to watch it operating at close range, and I wanted to see how it would handle the matter. . . . But that wasn't what really decided me to act. I was urged to intervene by the thought of the prize which would fall to my lot, and would be sufficient compensation for any little inconvenience I might cause myself. I found no difficulty about getting in touch with a magistrate who was willing to do me a good turn. He gave me an interview; he listened to what I had to say. Admittedly, he showed some surprise when he heard my story. He had expected something in which I had a more obvious personal interest. Roughly, I put the business to him as follows: 'I don't habitually do this sort of thing. But, thinking things over, it has seemed really very odd to me that a situation of this kind should be allowed to benefit from the forgetfulness and apathy of the public, without anything being done to establish whether suspicions of so grave a nature, shared by so many people and supported by so much seeming evidence, were really based on anything definite or were merely imaginary.' He made a number of notes, promised me that the necessary steps should be taken, that my plea for discretion should be borne in mind, and that I should be kept informed of the progress of the inquiry.

"All this happened at the beginning of November. I waited. I did not dare to give my magistrate friend a ring on the telephone. That would have looked as though I were attaching undue importance to the matter, as though my personal interest was too deeply involved. But at last my patience gave out, and I took up the receiver. With as much apparent indifference as I could muster, I said: 'I hope things are all right with you? I wonder if you remember a little chat we had three weeks ago? Has anything happened?' My friend remembered perfectly. He had reported the case at once, and was pretty sure that it had been taken up. But he had heard no more of it. Since I seemed in a bit of a hurry, he would inquire what was happening. He ought to have an answer in the course of a few days, and would ask me to call on him again."

"The same sort of game they played with me!" exclaimed M. Pouzols-Desaugues.

"Sure enough, a few days later my telephone rang. I went to see him. After refreshing his memory from a not very bulky file, he told me the result of the inquiry, or rather of the opening stages of the inquiry. I got the impression that the authorities had confined their efforts to getting a report from the police surgeon, summoning to Paris the doctor who had attended the two fatal cases, and making the sort of meaningless inquiries into the affairs of my landlord and the handsome concierge that a shop makes when one wants to open an account. They seemed to have been reassured by what they found out. The doctor—the same one had attended both cases—merely said that he had found nothing suspicious, nothing that would have justified him in refusing a certificate and demanding a post-mortem. He went further; he said that in the case of the woman he had seen the prescriptions supplied by her regular medical attendant, and that they had fully borne out his own diagnosis. He confessed, however, that, knowing nothing of local gossip, he had not connected the two fatal cases at all in his mind. I got the idea too, as a result of my talk with the magistrate, that the landlord was on terms of very considerable intimacy with the Municipal Council (though how and why the magistrate had been led to ferret out this detail I have no idea). Not that the authorities would have felt that to be any reason for not going on with the inquiry if there had seemed to be a case. But it was only wise to assume that our gentleman would not be fool enough to fall into a trap. They wanted to be more or less sure of the result before pressing things to the point of actually formulating a slanderous suspicion and starting a scandal. By this I think he meant me to understand exhumation and post-mortem. Naturally, I couldn't guarantee that traces of arsenic would be found in the two bodies. It was pretty obvious, however, that short of exhumation and a post-mortem we should never be able to prove criminal activities. Consequently it became at once quite clear that there was very little chance of our getting anywhere. After uttering a few platitudes with the object of saving my face, I did my best to make him believe that I felt the matter to be in good hands, and that I was sure no efforts would be spared, allowing for all necessary prudence, to discover the truth."

# Chapter

## SOCIETY IS SLOW-MOVING

"And, I suppose, from that day to this, you've heard no more?"

"Not a word—unless, of course, I find a message waiting for me when I get back to Paris. I should be considerably surprised if I did."

"So should I, my dear sir, so should I," said M. Pouzols-Desaugues in cheerful tones. "But if you do, I hope you'll be good enough to drop me a line. Your story has thrilled me. I should hate not to know the sequel—if there is a sequel. You and I, it seems to me, are bound together by the threads of crime. On my side, I promise to keep you faithfully informed of any developments in the Vaurevauzes business. The only way I can show my thanks is to put at your service, during your absence, what little influence I may have in the constituency, what few gifts for intrigue I may still possess."

Jerphanion declared that he was only too glad to accept the terms of this bargain, from which it was he, mainly, who stood to gain. At the same time he looked appreciatively round the dining-room with its beamed ceiling and its windows with their intricate curtain of creepers.

M. Pouzols-Desaugues went on:

"The experiences which each of us has had, if I may say so, of putting the law in motion, are remarkably alike despite differences in setting. . . . What conclusion can we draw from that fact? Having myself been a civil servant, I am always loth to condemn out of hand the official point of view. Few laymen can have any idea how much courage is necessary before even the slightest piece of business in a public office can be put through."

"That I believe," said Jerphanion politely. "And then there's another thing. The attitude of society to crime differs from that of the detective of fiction in being neither scientific nor sporting. It is strictly practical. What primarily interests society is not to know how crimes are committed but to deal out exemplary punishment to criminals once they are caught. In theory, it finds a certain pleasure in unearthing hidden crimes. But the machinery at its disposal is chiefly used in cases where the crime is established beyond doubt, is, indeed, fully illuminated by publicity, though the identity of the criminal remains unknown. But where the crime itself succeeds in remaining hidden, I rather think that society shows much less keenness. Where can you point to any organization devoted to the investigation of crime as crime—spontaneous, self-sufficient investigation? Investigation begins, in theory, as soon as a complaint has been filed or a charge laid; in other words, as soon as public interest is aroused and scandal begins. But experience has taught both of us that the keenness of the public is very moderate so long as interest in the crime is confined to gossip and the suspicion of individuals. For two pins the average man would quietly extinguish these incongruous sparks. Obviously, society is far from anxious to add to the number of known crimes—in other words, of crimes that weigh on its conscience. By remaining undiscovered a crime may be said to be less serious, because, by the mere fact of being undiscovered, it strips itself of the most dangerous characteristic of all crimes, that of throwing down a challenge to public morality and becoming an example of antisocial activity. It is hardly an exaggeration to say that Justice, asked to nose out some hidden crime, especially when it involves the more respectable classes, provided she could be absolutely certain that the crime would remain hidden and not, at some future date, explode into a glare of delayed publicity, would almost always rather refrain from bringing it to light, or at most would go through the motions of investigation only, like the customs-house official who longs for a quiet life and doesn't really want to find a box of cigars at the bottom of your trunk." (Jerphanion was using almost the words which, fifteen years earlier, the binder Quinette had used in pondering the lessons of his first experiments in crime. But with how different an intention! What comfort, too, would Quinette, in the tortured moments of those days, have derived from Jerphanion's interpretation of the facts!)

M. Pouzols-Desaugues admitted the ingenuity of this theory.

"We'll put it to a new test," he said. "You have filled me with the ardour of the chase in this matter of Vaurevauzes. I am becoming more and more inclined to hand the baby to my friend Doublet. It'll be fun to see how he'll manage to get rid of it."

The last fifteen minutes before they parted were spent in discussing election business. M. Pouzols-Desaugues gave his visitor a great many useful hints, showed by his tone that he was deeply interested in the outcome of the campaign, and promised further assistance when he had given the matter more thought. A stranger hearing them talk would have concluded that they saw eye to eye on all points of political doctrine, and that the only differences between them had to do with mere problems of tactics and timing.

# Chapter

## 17

### JALLEZ ENJOYS A
### SENSATION OF WELL-BEING

Jallez had got into the habit of interrupting his work rather oftener than was, perhaps, altogether proper, in order to enjoy his window. As a porter will treat himself to a glass of wine between jobs, so did Jallez treat himself to a "bit of window." No matter how often he looked at that view, his pleasure in it never grew less. It was a famous view: the side of the lake (only a strip to be sure, but there was enough of it to conjure up the rest), a bit of the lake itself, a bit of the city with just enough glimpse of monumental façades to establish the fact that the city was an important one; beyond it the nearer slopes, and beyond them, when the day was fine, Mont Blanc. It really was a staggering window, the remarkable nature of which could hardly have been guessed by anyone seeing it only from outside. From below it looked much like any other window, though the situation of the building to which it belonged was, to be sure, especially favoured. But in fact it constituted a really remarkable "find," because there was nothing to spoil the perfection of its outlook (not a single ugly or ill-proportioned object in the foreground), and because, though the definitely lovely elements brought together in the composition which it framed were few in number, each seemed to have been chosen as possessing genuine significance, and to have been arranged in relation to others with the happiest inspiration.

Much patience and cleverness had gone to its acquisition. He had pretended to resign himself to the disadvantages of a small office on the ground that it would be less cold, adding that he was by nature a chilly individual. He had been careful not to stress the importance which he attached to the window. The self-importance of his colleagues might lead them to express disdain of the temperature, but there was always a danger that they might develop an obstinate affection for the landscape.

Today was particularly lovely, the sort of day that one gets in Geneva at the beginning of winter. The light was such as one might have found on the Riviera, though with a spoonful of mist dissolved in it. Outside, there was probably a nip in the air, especially in the shade; but it was clear that there was no wind.

Jallez gave himself up to a sensation of general well-being. He did not attempt to disguise the fact that it depended upon a concatenation of circumstances which were held in a state of delicate equilibrium. They centred in a rather childish awareness of his own bodily presence. He was still of the opinion that when these springs of inner comfort showed a readiness to flush his consciousness, it was foolish to inquire too closely into their nature. But today he would not have felt averse to discovering a rational basis for his mood, and, in particular, to persuading himself that they were not altogether ephemeral nor wholly subjective. He told himself, for instance, that he loved this city with a calm, passionless affection which had in itself the seeds of a lasting satisfaction (as lasting as the beauty of the view from his window). He told himself that this city was well on the way to becoming, gradually, the capital of the world (though not as Paris, as Washington, is a capital), and that it was exciting to be alive at this period of history, and to be one of the many nonentities engaged on the task of making Geneva the capital city of the civilized world. Among the many jobs which a writer anxious not to prostitute his pen might accept with a clear conscience, this was certainly one of the most legitimate, and by no means one of the least well paid. If there was to be a future for humanity other than repeated massacre and catastrophe, Geneva, of all places, was where it might most probably be planned, and in that planning he had a part, however small, to play.

Viewed at close quarters, this great task was seen to be honeycombed with the mean and the tawdry. It involved rubbing shoulders with more chatterboxes than true believers, more sluggards and schemers than genuine apostles. But hadn't that always been the case? Even in the Catacombs there had been scepticism, envy, and self-seeking. . . . (And how had it been possible to prevent such elements from multiplying when the passages of the Catacombs had become the corridors of the Vatican? . . .) But taken all in all, and for the time being, the omens were not too bad . . . and, speaking of the Vatican, the new Pope looked, in spite of everything, like being a better sort of fellow than that old schemer Benedict XV. Not that it was a matter of supreme importance. But then, what event, seen in isolation, ever was? If conditions were to improve, it would only be as a result of piling up a number of weights, each tiny in itself, in the scale of goodness. The actual effect of each might have little positive value, but taken all together, they were rather more numerous than the weights at the other end. . . . The Ruhr agreement, taken separately, had little positive value. . . . To have succeeded in winning the United States over to the League of Nations would have been worth a great deal more than establishing the International Labour Office. Nevertheless, the International Labour Office was a good solid stone laid well and truly in the foundations of the temple, a massive stone firmly set in the earth. A few more of such crude, honest bits of country masonry, and there would be little fear of the whole building toppling over in the first high wind. He was not one of those who believed that a new world could emerge ready made from some vast subterranean explosion (all an explosion could do was to bring up new materials from the depths, or to thrust into the upper air the slimy, formless substrata of possible worlds). On the contrary, he was the kind of man who believed that the building of a world could be achieved only by trial and error and hard work. That being so, he had to admit the truth of such saws as "Sufficient unto the day is the evil thereof," and "This may not be the best possible, but it is better than anything else." He had to believe in the virtue of improvisation. . . .

Lenin, it seemed, was dying. Too early yet to judge his work, but if the Russian people, after passing through their revolutionary paroxysm, really showed a desire to become more human and rational, then the disappearance of Lenin would be a step towards liquidating the period of fanaticism. . . . And if that blusterer Mussolini had the good sense to slip on a piece of orange peel, then two, at least, of the centres of European conflagration would be damped down. . . . Perhaps the quiet wisdom of the country practitioner was the best, after all. "We here, meanwhile, will be making a normal life possible for the patient when he shall have got over the crisis. . . . There is nothing dramatic, to be sure, about our preparations. They don't involve a great deal of work, they don't set the walls trembling. Only too often our labours amount merely to being there, on the spot. But when it's a question of establishing a new institution, of getting it through its leading-strings stage, of persuading a mistrustful world to become accustomed to its existence, the mere fact of being there partakes of the virtue of planted and growing things. . . . What right have I to accuse others of being lukewarm? Of the hours which I spend by this window, more are devoted to my own writing and to my own dreams than to the League of Nations. . . ."

At this point in his meditation he began to think of Nice and of the view which he had had of the old town, when, in his little apartment in the avenue Félix Faure, he had sat, as today, pondering the right wording of a phrase, watching the urban scene, and thinking of world affairs. He accused himself of being too "self-indulgent," though scarcely had his mind formed the word when he realized how absurdly inept it was. Rather, he reflected, he accused himself of not giving enough of himself to objects which he knew to be of supreme importance, objects for which he entertained a genuine enthusiasm, even though that enthusiasm might not go beyond the awareness of an inner delight, a transport of the soul.

"That's where Jerphanion is so much better than I am. If he were here, in my place, he might see little more than I see myself; but having realized that he was playing his part, however modest it might be, in a great achievement, he would expend every ounce of strength on bringing it to a successful conclusion. He would clench his fists; he would not, as I do, between two moments of concentrated labour, permit himself the pleasure of long hours of care-free dreaming, of mental wanderings unconfined, of dallying with the timeless. Odette writes that at this very moment he is in his native mountains conducting his electoral campaign and that of his colleagues on the party ticket. I know him well enough to realize that having made his choice, he will never relax his efforts until his self-appointed task is finished. The danger he runs is that of exaggerating its importance. He lives in a constant state of noise and bustle, seeing the whole world in relation to his duty of the moment, and never ceasing to keep himself up to the mark by argument. If he pays any attention to his dear mountains—and I'm sure he does, because he is not an insensitive brute—it is to enlist their help. Them, too, he mobilizes among his supporters, like some army of myth or history. He dreams, but his dreams bear fruit in action. He does not fritter himself away in childish games. At heart, he is much more grown up than I am. . . ."

Lebail knocked at the door and, without waiting for a reply, entered the tiny office.

"Aren't you going to the inaugural session of the International Medical Commission?"

"Is it any concern of ours?"

"More or less. I'm sure that a good many departments who are less 'concerned' than we are will be represented. There's a general desire, I gather, to make the session rather a brilliant affair."

"Where are they meeting, and when?"

"Eleven o'clock this morning, in one of the university lecture-rooms —probably the Aula. I'll find out."

"I'm sorely tempted to send you in my place," said Jallez. "You look bursting with enthusiasm."

"That wouldn't be at all the same thing. You are the head of the department. . . . Besides, I don't know anything about medicine."

"Do I? Am I a doctor?"

"No, but you're full of miscellaneous information."

"Much miscellaneous information there'll be in the opening speeches of a medical commission!"

"You never know. . . . At least you could spy out the ground, decide whether we ought to send someone to keep a tag on their deliberations. Besides, there will be one or two eminent Frenchmen there who ought to be given a word of greeting."

"Presumably someone has gone to greet them at the station?"

"Naturally. But that's quite different."

"Have you got a list of the delegates?"

"Yes, it's on my table, I think. I'll get it."

Lebail returned with the list, which was arranged by countries. Most of the names were marked with a cross.

"What do the crosses mean?" asked Jallez.

"That the gentleman in question has actually come. The list was supplied to me by the general secretariat. They had marked off the arrivals for the purpose of getting the hotel accommodation right, and they transferred the crosses to the copy they gave me."

"And people say we don't work! . . . Congratulations on your initiative. . . . It makes one reason the more why you rather than I—" Jallez broke off. He had just seen on the list, marked with a cross, the name Viaur. "On second thoughts, I believe I will go. It might be interesting."

# Chapter

## 18

### REAPPEARANCE OF DR. VIAUR

Throughout the opening session Jallez kept his eyes fixed on Dr. Viaur. As soon as it was over and they were on their way out, he went up to him in the vestibule.

Despite the fact that the width of the room had been between them, he had picked him out fairly easily; but from where he was placed, and because Viaur had remained seated all through the proceedings, he had not really been able to take note of the changes in the man's physical appearance.

Now, however, he had a close view of him as he came bare-headed down the grand staircase.

Viaur was rather fatter and much more bent. Consequently he looked less tall than in the old days, though the traces of youth in his face stood out with startling clarity. His flesh was firm, his complexion pink. The trace of protuberance about his waist-line did not give an impression of unhealthy distension. Rather, it gave to his appearance a look of soft and kindly dignity. His fair hair was still thick, and the few silver streaks were not over-obvious. On the whole, there seemed to be more of it; it looked more wavy, more like a crown, than Jallez remembered. The short beard had vanished. The moustache had been reduced to a thin line. The china-blue eyes were unexpectedly vivid. Surely in the old days the colour had been less definite, the innocence of their expression less marked. For all that, there was shrewdness in their glance, and a hint of gentleness. The face, taken as a whole, the quality of skin and flesh, the discreet roundness of its contour, the way the man carried himself, the manner in which he descended the stairs and walked across the level paving of the hall, combined to produce an effect of kindliness, sympathy, and charm. Yes, charm was the word that best expressed the aura of this man seen now for the first time after so long an interval. Even when he had been an obscure doctor at Celle there had always been something pleasing in his unassuming modesty of demeanour. But there had not then been the same air of positive goodwill about him, embracing, as it now did, everyone in his vicinity, friend and stranger alike. Not that it was even now, strictly speaking, a conscious charm. It set itself neither to seduce nor to take by storm. It was the kind of charm of which the dominant characteristic was sweetness, quiet intelligence, and something that might almost be called humility.

"I wonder whether you recognize me, sir," said Jallez.

Viaur stopped, took a pace backwards, smiled. "Let me see, now. Why, of course, of course, you are, if I'm not mistaken . . ."

His voice had still the old full-toned gentleness.

"You are—Monsieur Jallez—am I right? Monsieur Pierre Jallez. How delightful to see you again!"

His face had come to life. A look almost of affection shone in his eyes. He pressed Jallez's hand warmly and held it for some moments in his own.

"I am deeply touched," said the latter, "to think that you have not forgotten me."

"You must forgive my momentary hesitation. It is not that you have changed—far from it—but it is so long since we met!" He gazed at Jallez with as much eagerness as though he had been a much loved and long lost friend.

"Does he behave like this to everyone?" wondered Jallez. "I'm inclined to think not." He too was smiling with a far greater show of friendliness than was customary with him on such occasions.

"And what are you doing here?" went on the doctor.

In a few words Jallez explained the position he held in the League of Nations.

"Excellent! Excellent!" exclaimed Viaur quietly. "Needless to say, I have kept up with your writings. I have watched your career with delight. It has already given you an honourable position—yes indeed, a worthy reputation compared with that of some I could name. . . . But I never dreamed that you carried on these other activities. It says a great deal for you that you have chosen to do so. I am not one of those who sneer at the League. It can't, obviously, be expected to perform miracles at once. But in the present state of our poor old world, it is our chief hope for the future—or so at least it seems to me. . . ."

He had spoken with the obvious intention of being polite, but his tone was simple and sincere. Then, with a change of voice and a smile in his glance, he went on:

"Look here, we mustn't just meet casually like this after so long. . . . I would like to make a suggestion, but I don't want to be a nuisance. I've got to get rid of some people with whom I've promised to have a word—I see one of them over there—but why shouldn't we lunch together at my hotel? The session arranged for this afternoon doesn't start until late. We should have plenty of time for a good talk. . . . They've put me in the Hôtel des Bergues—I gather that's where all the French go. . . . But perhaps you're engaged?"

"No, I'm not, and I shall be charmed. The only thing that might make me hesitate is the fear of occupying your time. . . . There must be any number of things you have to do—"

There was a look of mischief in Viaur's smile. "Luncheon invitations, you mean? I can assure you there are not. . . . I don't enjoy what you would call a fashionable reputation. . . . True, I noticed a few cards on the table in my room . . . and there may be one or two invitations among them. But I'm sure there is nothing for this morning. That's settled then, eh? In about half an hour at the Hôtel des Bergues? I'll do my best not to keep you waiting."

"He's a fine type," decided Jallez when they had parted. "It's nice to find that he's turned out so well after all these years." Then he added: "I can only conclude that that article of mine really did please him."

# Chapter

# 19

## THE BITTERNESS OF SUCCESS AND
## THE DISAPPOINTMENTS OF FAME

Their table stood by a window that gave onto the small square with a fountain in it. There was no one in their immediate vicinity. Viaur ordered the meal after asking Jallez what he would like. He insisted that his guest should drink wine.

"I won't take any myself, if you don't mind. My health is ridiculous —always running to extremes. There are times when I can eat anything and drink, if not like a trooper, at least like an honest Frenchman; and others when the slightest thing makes me ill. . . . So I stick to water. . . . It's a pity, because the Swiss wines are gay and attractive. . . ."

Then, averting his gaze, which had taken on an air of melancholy, he asked Jallez whether he remembered precisely when it was that they had last met.

With a little effort Jallez was able to give him the date to within a fortnight or so.

"Yes," said Viaur, "you're right. It all comes back to me now. I was passing through rather an unsettled time. Things have a way of becoming foreshortened in memory. And then some time elapsed between your visit to Celle and that article you wrote. . . . What an excellent article it was! I've kept it carefully all these years. Nothing half so good was written about the researches on which I was engaged in those days."

Jallez's protest was perfectly sincere.

"No, I mean it," went on Viaur. "You can take my word for it that no one else expressed himself with anything like the same fullness, the same dispassionate understanding, and, let me add, the same grasp of what I was after. . . ."

His eyes were still on the fountain. But quite clearly there was an element of sadness in the warm affection with which he spoke. Jallez, noting this, was surprised.

"In an essay of yours published later," continued Viaur, "devoted by no means entirely to my work—I don't remember its title, but I rather think it appeared in the *Nouvelle Revue Française*—you said a number of very amazing things—things which had a direct bearing on what I was doing. There may even have been some reference to me, of that I'm not sure—but the article itself was something to which my thoughts have often returned. Some of the forecasts you made in it were really extraordinary."

He gave a faint sigh.

Jallez was conscious of a desire to minimize the compliments being paid him. They seemed to him to destroy the relation that should have existed between them—the master on one side, the journalist on the other. At the same time a feeling of friendship prompted him to point out to this man how much to be envied he was.

"I should never have supposed," he said, "that you would have remembered so unimportant an incident. . . . Since those days you must have found so many reasons for satisfaction. . . . I have followed your career, though not, alas, as closely as I could have wished. . . . When one thinks of your age, when one looks at you now, the speed with which it has been built up is amazing. . . . People use the same tone in speaking of you as they do in referring to the best-known and most deeply revered heroes of science . . . and that flatters me retrospectively, because I was one of the first, as I fully realize, to adopt that attitude. . . ." His voice took on a new tone reflecting a sudden twist in his thought. "I should have liked to write about you again. But no suitable occasion arose, and then, too, I felt that I had become—how shall I put it?—even less competent than I had been."

"That, surely, is mere politeness," remarked Viaur with a smile. "Let us say, rather, less attracted."

"No . . ." Jallez uttered the denial very quietly. "I was perfectly well aware how important, how fruitful, were the directions in which your work was taking you. Nor was I forgetful of the fact that you were returning to your old love—you had spoken of it, you remember, at Celle when you showed me your various gadgets—returning, yes, and taking a further step forward. But, you see, I had always had to take up a rather general, a philosophic point of view, if only because I had not the necessary specialist training to do otherwise, and that meant that I should have had to explain your evolution, feel my way back to the line of your general advance. But for me, an outsider, that wasn't at all easy. There were certain steps in your development, even, which escaped me altogether. . . . And then the war came. . . . I know, of course, that I could have got into touch with you again, but —well, I didn't. To be perfectly frank, I have a feeling, even when I'm thinking these things out quite privately, that there are whole movements in your more recent phase that have to be represented in my mind by"—he smiled pleasantly—"large question marks." His words called forth from Viaur an answering smile which produced a network of small wrinkles round his eyes, though the same melancholy as before was still visible in their depths. For the moment, however, it seemed that he was not ready with an answer. Jallez went on: "So that at the moment, putting it rather differently, in spite of my contacts with you in the old days, I feel like a layman in the presence of a great scholar—terrified of mentioning your work for fear of saying something idiotic."

For a few moments yet Viaur remained silent, absent-mindedly munching his food. At last, with an air of modesty, almost of apology, so unexpected as clearly to be not deliberate, he said:

"Circumstances, as always, played no small part. In 1916—I was called up at the beginning of the war—in '16 it so happened that quite by chance I found myself practically in control of an important hospital in one of the back areas. A senior doctor, a regular, was nominally my chief, but he was an old fogy, and a sick man into the bargain . . . though, to be fair, he gave me my head. In fact, I was my own master. A great number of wounded passed through our hands. It was the year of Verdun. In spite of working at high pressure—I had a staff of young and competent assistants—I managed to isolate in a special pavilion several serious cases who were making a particularly slow recovery. Remembering the lines on which I had been working earlier, I had the idea of testing on them—with all due precautions, of course—some of the results I had obtained in the old days, before 1912, in my laboratory researches. The risk was not very great, because they were more or less desperate cases who would either die or survive only in a terribly mutilated state. I don't remember now how I managed to get the necessary equipment, or how we succeeded, my colleagues and I, in carrying out a whole series of experiments in time snatched from our routine hospital duties. All that part of the business must be classed among the inexplicable things that one does somehow get done in periods of extreme nervous excitement. All I need say now is that I was successful in getting a number of wounds to heal quickly, and even, in certain cases, of promoting the actual growth of damaged tissues. When you think of the primitive conditions in which a lot of our work was carried on, and the appalling groundwork of physical destruction on which we had to build, some of the results were little short of miraculous." He smiled.

"But there was no lack of opportunity for soft-pedalling my own and my colleagues' enthusiasm. Whenever one of the big noises of the medical world came to have a look at us, I always gave instructions to the staff that they weren't to make too much of a song and dance about what we were doing, but to take the general line that, on the whole, results were encouraging, though, of course, the experience we were getting was strictly limited. When I was asked about my special pavilion and the sort of work that was going on in it, I adopted a rather apologetic air and spoke as though I had taken on something that would probably turn out to be too big a job. I made it quite clear that I wasn't going to be tempted into making premature generalizations, that what I was after at the moment was to accumulate a small number of positive and significant results. The patients, however, were less discreet. They were as proud as Punch of the treatment I was giving them, and of whatever effects it was producing. Sometimes, too, the nurses disregarded my instructions about not talking too openly. I have since learned that one of them, a pretty little thing, as cheeky as the devil, would think nothing of taking our distinguished visitors aside and saying confidentially: 'I've worked in ten ambulance columns and five general hospitals . . . I've seen thousands of wounded. I know what I'm talking about. You can take my word for it that our doctor's achieving positive miracles. It's a crime that his methods shouldn't be applied on a large scale.'

"One fine day I was sent for and more or less compelled to take over one of the large back-area hospitals where I should have a full staff and equipment. I was asked to give a series of lectures. 'What steps,' said the authorities, 'do you think ought to be taken to get your methods applied to the largest possible number of cases?' I replied that the best thing would be to establish a research laboratory where, with the requisite number of assistants, I could set about preparing my special products in quantity, in particular certain organic extracts from living animals, as well as the quite simple equipment which I used in my treatment. Such an installation would give the opportunity of improving my methods. It would become a centre of distribution for the hospitals and dressing-stations. We should be able, too, to write up concise accounts of what we were doing, to be sent round to the medical officers of the various formations with the preparations to which they referred, so that the treatment could be applied with some knowledge of what it aimed at doing. . . . I got what I asked for, more or less, though, as you may imagine, there was a certain amount of paring down. By the time the war ended we had made a good deal of progress, though I won't go so far as to say that my methods were being applied anything like universally either in field-hospitals or in the rear. We hadn't, you see, the equipment to make that possible. Still, they had been used in some tens of thousands of cases, and the number of these was growing daily."

"They were based, if I remember correctly, on the same general principles as your earlier experiments at Celle, on certain facts that you had observed in relation to the growth and repair of tissues among the lower animals . . . in fact, generally speaking, on your researches into what I think you called 'sarcophilic' substances?"

"Precisely! Your memory is amazingly accurate. . . . To start with I had made use of those among the more or less 'sarcophilic' substances that had formed the matter of my earlier researches, which I could most easily get hold of—most of them inorganic. In treating my wounded I adopted the methods of application, in powdered form, for instance, which I described to you when I showed you my workshop. . . . The use of organic extracts, in the conditions of our work in war-time, was a very different matter. . . . Once installed, however, in my back-area laboratory, I was in a position to concentrate on the second aspect of the problem, which alone was capable of really positive development." He made a little grimace. "With the result that, by the end of the war, I was already on the track of my *Anaplastine*. Its later modifications are not without importance in the sphere of practical application, but the general theory remains what it was then"—he gave a slight shrug—"and so does the name! That name, I think, was a happy inspiration and did a lot to popularize the theory. Personally, I always thought it rather ridiculous, but I couldn't, at the time, think of anything better."

The tone of his voice was still quiet, friendly, detached. Once more he shrugged his shoulders, and continued:

"And that, my dear sir, was the beginning of what you have been kind enough to call my 'career.'"

"But—you speak of this work of yours, this discovery, with a sort of—I won't say contempt, but remoteness. From what I have read at various times, it was something of the first importance, something which goes to the root of the problem of life. . . . Already, in practice, it has had beneficial results, which themselves open the way to a further line of research, which should, too, in your eyes, have the additional merit of carrying a step forward, of crowning, as it were, the labours of your youth."

"Oh yes, I know all about that," said Viaur with a sort of ironic indulgence, which was not, however, overstressed.

"There is one question I should like to ask. . . . I have read a good deal about Anaplastine, but of a vague, general kind . . . and I'm not sure that my memory is very reliable. . . . The basic element—am I right?—was an organic product, something in the nature of a hormone, which you had succeeded in isolating in certain batrachia, among whom it explained the phenomenon of an amazingly rapid reconstitution of damaged tissue. Properly introduced into the human system, it is found to produce much the same kind of stimulus?"

"Yes, that's roughly the idea," said Viaur, and he proceeded to elaborate his explanation with a vague air of apology. "There are, in fact, two anaplastics, or rather two series of anaplastics. One of these is precisely the substance which I managed to isolate in a certain species of marine animal, though I afterwards found it to be present in related forms of life. That is the anaplastic of pure science. The other anaplastics—for there are several which differ slightly from one another in that they are more or less efficacious in the treatment of different kinds of tissue—are the anaplastics of the pharmacopœia. It has been my fate, unfortunately, to become something of a practising pharmacist . . . but don't condemn me out of hand. There are mitigating circumstances. In the course of my experiments in practical healing, and they were many and various, I became convinced that anaplastic does not produce its best effects—among human beings, that is—when used in its pure form. It benefits from an admixture of —but I'll spare you the technical details. I should explain, too, that the method of application is susceptible of variation, and that the composition and dosage differ according to whether it is used as a subcutaneous injection or is applied in powdered form to the actual wound. Well, the result of these later discoveries was that we have had to establish a whole scale of pharmaceutical anaplastics. . . . You will understand, of course, that all this meant a lot of experimenting, which in its turn raised a completely new set of problems.

"I am by no means a saint. When I first isolated this anaplastic I was proud to think that my name would be associated with its discovery. But I refused to derive any material benefit from it. I made a public exposition of the methods of extracting the substance in its pure state. It was open to anybody to make use of it. As was only natural, I made a present of it to science. . . . The next thing that had to be done was the manufacture of preparations for practical use, all of them highly specialized and involving an infinity of modifications. I made no mystery of this either, nor did I attempt to profit by it in a financial sense. But it was pointed out to me that a number of druggists, tempted by the growing fame of Anaplastine, were about to put similar products on the market. I was warned that many of these men were pretty unscrupulous, that not all of them were highly skilled, and that, in order to give their preparations a 'special' character, they would add Heaven knows what ingredients which might have very serious repercussions on the public and would bring discredit, which it had not deserved, upon my discovery. The only way of guarding against this would be by lending my name to what I considered the best formula and authorizing its manufacture only under my personal supervision. I have such a horror of certain kinds of commercialism indulged in by some members—and these by no means the least eminent—of the medical profession that for a long time I would have nothing to do with the suggestion. Finally I adopted the following solution: I refused to consider the offers made by the great wholesale druggists. Some of my younger colleagues joined with me in establishing a large private laboratory which was to be devoted partly to the preparation of Anaplastine according to our formula, and other supplementary 'sarcophilic' substances, partly to general research. The money was put up by our friends. . . . We fixed a sale price for our Anaplastine, which we kept as low as possible. All profits, after deduction of a dividend on our borrowed capital, reckoned at the low rate obtaining for state loans, were entirely devoted to the endowment of the research department of the laboratory. My colleagues and I received only a fixed salary, as did our assistants.

We had no interest whatever in the commercial success of the business. It's a matter of entire financial indifference to me whether we sell ten or ten million phials a day. In this way we are able to command ample resources for the purpose of research. Since, too, our plan has been drawn up in as liberal a spirit as possible, a number of young scientists have been given an opportunity of working, under satisfactory conditions, at the problems that really interest them. As a matter of fact, this policy of ours has had one result which we did not anticipate. The sale price of our products has turned out to be so low that our competitors, accustomed to a profit of a hundred per cent, have lost heart. Even the Germans have only been able to put on the market a preparation of inferior quality at a price slightly higher than our own. The laboratory is overwhelmed with orders . . . and most people imagine that *Anaplastine Viaur* brings in for its discoverer not only honour and glory, but a fortune to be reckoned in millions."

"So far as I can see," said Jallez with sly humour, "this organization of yours is run more or less on Soviet lines—using the word in its best sense."

"Maybe,—I hadn't given the matter a thought. It doesn't really interest me."

"I don't think there's much in your fear that people may suspect you of accumulating a fortune from your discoveries. That's certainly not the story *I* hear."

In Viaur's smile there was a hint of remorse, a taking back, as it were, of something he had said.

"You're probably right," he said. "The truth does sometimes get about, and ill will is not always blind. Many of my colleagues show a willingness to forgive me my success because it is not expressed in terms of villas, castles, and motor-cars. . . . Nor does my wife go in for large strings of pearls. . . . Why, as recently as last month my name was considered for the Academy of Medicine."

"So I heard . . . and for the Nobel Prize, I believe?"

Viaur made a little mocking grimace. "Something of the sort was in the wind, but nothing more. . . . I mention these matters to you only because I know that you attach no more importance to them than I do myself. I imagine you have a pretty shrewd idea of what my attitude is. . . . Well, last month, one of the bigwigs of the Academy, a man whose vote carries a lot of weight, asked me to call on him. What he said to me can be summarized more or less as follows: 'A suggestion has, I understand, been made that you put yourself up for election. It's perfectly right and proper that you should, young though you are. . . . Your reputation has preceded you, and a very fine reputation it is. It is very much in your favour that you live on the equivalent of a professor's salary when you could, if you liked, be a millionaire.' This was amusing, coming as it did from a man who has the reputation of having as sharp an eye for the main chance as any surgeon now practising. . . . You mentioned the Nobel Prize just now. Well, thereby hangs another not unamusing tale. . . . My name was proposed—very prematurely, I think, and without the slightest chance of being seriously considered. . . . But— and this will make you smile—the gentleman I mentioned just now gave me a pretty plain hint that this rumour, associating me with the Nobel Prize, would do me no good with the Academy. If I was wise, I would make it quite clear that what really mattered to me was being elected to the Academy, after a suitable delay. It would be time enough to think of the Nobel Prize later. Once I was safely installed in the Academy, my fellow members would no doubt be delighted to give me their influence. . . . If, however, I seemed to regard that body as merely a fifth wheel to my car, it would be thought to show a lack of proper feeling on my part. . . . In fact, I was being presented with a sort of ultimatum. But the bargain was somewhat one-sided, since even if I showed a due sense of unworthiness, there was no guarantee that my candidature would be successful."

"Still," said Jallez after a pause to consider what he had been told, "you must admit that it's all very flattering. Whatever value you may attach to official recognition—and, personally, I attach very little—the mere fact that your name has been put forward is not without its significance. I hope you will forgive me if I say that, seeing you again like this, I cannot refrain from setting side by side two pictures, one of which is immediately anterior in time to the other—that of the Albert Viaur whom I see sitting before me—"

". . . And that of the obscure doctor of Celle-les-Eaux, who was looked down on by all the leaders of the profession. You're saying to yourself that it's pretty cheeky, after all, for the obscure doctor to put on these cynical and almost complaining airs, are you not?"

For some time he remained lost in thought, his china-blue eyes turned towards the light. Then, in quite a different tone, he went on:

"I don't want to give you a false impression. . . . Nothing, I assure you, is further from my intention than to adopt the attitude of the man who is never content, who believes that life never breaks his way. In my case such an affectation would be odiously unjust. Don't run away with the idea that I'm not conscious of having had more than my fair share of good luck! The whole of my personal adventure has been one piece of good luck after another. Had it not been for the war—horrible though this confession may seem—I should have had neither the thousands of wounded I did have, with the vast opportunity for experience offered by their problems, nor perhaps even the idea of returning to my earlier researches in the field of medicine. In 1912 I was on the threshold of my discoveries relative to anaplastics, but it is very doubtful whether, without the war, I should have got any further. But for the war, again, even after I had discovered my Anaplastine—to confine the discussion to that single enterprise—and perfected it, I should have had no opportunity of trying it out on a large scale and of proving its value by an accumulation of successful cases, which, though each, taken alone, may have been no great matter, did, when taken together, produce a startling effect. I had, too, the advantage of that new sensibility created by the war, as a result of which people, including the leaders of the profession, found themselves saying: 'After all, the only thing that matters is the physical well-being of our poor dear soldiers. To hell with medals and decorations! It would be nothing short of criminal to stop a young doctor from helping thousands of wounded men, from saving their limbs and sometimes their very lives, just because he hadn't got the right number of markings on his sleeve!'

"And there's another point. In ordinary times the noise made, three or four years earlier, by my former investigations would have done me a terrible lot of harm. Everyone would have said: 'Having failed to take us in with one miracle, here he is trying to foist another one on us. The man must be either a charlatan or a lunatic!' In 1916 no one was in the mood to care about what had happened before '14. Besides, it was no longer the fashion to turn up one's nose at miracles, my own or the next fellow's. The War Ministry was ready to listen seriously to any manufacturer of pencil-sharpeners who could bring them the drawings of a shell which would smash the Boches. . . . Even when the war was over, the prevailing state of mind was all in my favour, for it had never been so sceptical of the professional expert in all fields, never so ready to pay attention to the independent and unorthodox thinker. Why, ten years ago the question could never even have arisen of electing to the Academy of Medicine a man of my age who was neither a university professor nor attached to one of the big hospitals. . . . The very accidental twists and turns of my character, which in other circumstances would have proved a severe handicap, have stood me in good stead. For instance, I am a shy man. My natural inclination is to efface myself as much as possible. Whenever I do have any little success in the great world, I am ready to let it go at that and to regard it as considerably greater than my deserts. Now, seeing how rapid my actual success was, how monstrous and excessive, nothing would have done me greater harm than an opposite tendency—a willingness to make the most of my triumph, to squeeze the last drop from it, and an inclination to behave arrogantly towards my colleagues. It wouldn't, I dare say, have prevented me from making a fortune, but it would most certainly have prejudiced my career as a scientist. It is so easy to say of a man: 'Oh yes, he ran a special line of treatment which had a good deal of success. He makes a lot of money, but that's no reason for making a god of him.'"

Once more Viaur relapsed into silent thought. Then:

"So you see, my dear sir, that I'm the last person in the world to have a grievance. . . . Far from it, for it seems to me that my actual success is out of all proportion to what has produced it. My discovery of Anaplastine was all very well in its way, but God knows it wasn't in any sense revolutionary. It has not opened to science one fresh vista which—well, you know what I mean. No new principle was involved. My discovery did no more than complete work done before me by thousands of labourers in the field. . . . What I've done since either has taken the form of elaborating the same central fact—has been good, honest routine research—or has wandered off onto new ground . . . but so far I have published no results, and, except for my most intimate assistants, no one as yet even knows about it. So, you see, that hasn't done much to add to my reputation. In fact, so far as reputation is concerned, I am still living on the capital represented by my Anaplastine. What on earth does the Academy of Medicine amount to? It's already chock-full of men who've spent their lives doing appendicitis operations or prescribing mineral-water cures! . . . But the Nobel Prize! . . ."

While he had been giving vent to these sentiments that came so oddly from the mouth of a favourite of fortune, Jallez had been watching him carefully. Throughout, Viaur's voice had retained its earlier note of gentle kindliness, though now and again a trace of bitterness, repressed almost as soon as it occurred, was faintly audible. It was marked, as of old, by a scrupulous concern to express exactly the thought that lay behind. (Each time that he could not at once find the correct phrase, he had a curious way of turning his right hand, the palm hollowed, the fingers extended and slightly bent, the joint of the wrist oddly flexible.) In the expression of the face and eyes there was that remembered look of disenchantment. Quite clearly, this was no pose intended to impress his interlocutor. There was little doubt but that he was making his old friend privy to moods which it had never occurred to him to confess to others. Not improbably he was conscious of a faint intoxication brought on by a sense of relief which led him to put into words rather more than his thoughts could have justified. Doubtless, too, he would have been less ready to betray his private bitterness if, instead of overwhelming him with the twin threats of the Academy of Medicine and the Nobel Prize, his contemporaries had decided to ignore his existence.

"One mustn't forget," said Jallez, "that every discovery, like every act of intellectual creation, has its social aspect; and that the value placed upon it by the public always differs to some extent from its real significance. Had rabies been merely some rare tropical disease known to none but a few specialists, discovery of its treatment would have demanded in Pasteur the same degree of genius, though it would have brought him far less public recognition. But rabies being what it is, Pasteur would have been assured of fame, honours, and veneration if he had been content to rest on those particular laurels until the day of his death. The best example of what I mean is the case of dear old Parmentier, who has become immortal, has been placed by the gaping mob in the same class as Réaumur and Lavoisier, simply for telling people that they ought to eat potatoes instead of leaving them to the beasts of the field; whereas some stupendous invention in the realm of mathematics will always remain something hidden in a mist of secrecy. . . . Nothing you can do will alter the fact that your Anaplastine, by its very nature, was bound to produce dramatic results, or that its discovery coincided with a moment in human history when the war inevitably multiplied those results and fixed on them the attention of everyone from specialists down to the man in the street."

"I know all about that," interrupted Viaur. He smiled politely. "I said as much myself a moment ago. . . ." He relapsed once more into melancholy reflection before continuing: "It's not really that I'm complaining of. . . . If I were, I should be guilty of affectation and of a lack of ordinary human feeling. . . . The men I envy are those investigators whose reputation, whether great or little, inadequate or excessive, rests on what they themselves know to be of genuine importance." Viaur looked Jallez straight in the eyes. "You are probably the only man capable of understanding what I'm after." His voice had become serious, and almost trembled.

"Oh, come now!" said Jallez embarrassed and no less moved than his friend.

"I mean it—the only man at this moment." He shrugged his shoulders. "The others—well, the others have forgotten—even if they ever really understood."

They both looked down at their plates, caught in an eddy of shyness. They said nothing. A few moments passed, and then Jallez, speaking with deliberate restraint and in tones of careful and affectionate thoughtfulness, remarked:

"I'm glad you referred to—the other thing. It has been occupying my mind ever since you began speaking, to the exclusion of everything else." He hesitated, then very quietly added: "What's happened about it?"

Viaur lifted his head, turned it towards the little square beyond the window, and raised his brows above the wide-open blue eyes with their subtle hint of pain.

"That's hard to say. . . . But for the war, what might not have happened? . . . I'm an obstinate sort of chap in my way . . . and a pretty hard worker. . . . No matter how ruthlessly I examine my conscience, I can't find that I have ever been impatient of success. . . . When I was a child, one of my favourite stories was that of Bernard Palissy. . . . There was nothing to terrify me in the thought of a long life of misunderstood application to study—far from it. . . . I know well enough that with the coming of age—and age, in this sense, comes quickly— But no, I hardly think—"

He was speaking more jerkily than was his wont.

"You see, the resistance one meets differs considerably both in weight and in importance. There are cases where it seems terrible but is, in fact, stimulating. There are others in which, after an initial period of hard fighting, people suddenly seem to get sick of putting up a struggle. They surround one, as it were, with a sort of protective barrier through which nothing can penetrate. . . . They behave as though one were an encysted abscess. One feels completely out of touch with everything. . . . I have often wondered what would happen if one of us modern scientists, complete with all his latter-day knowledge, were transported suddenly into a period of the distant past, to the twelfth century, for instance, or to Egypt under the Pharaohs. . . . Doubtless it would have the effect of an intellectual thunderbolt, but I am not at all sure that the presence of that thunderbolt would have any very lasting results, or any markedly noticeable result at all. However that may be, one thing is certain: for all his formidable load of knowledge, our man would not send the science of that distant epoch, or its ideas, flying in splinters. After a sort of flash-in-the-pan curiosity, a moment of scandalized and anxious fear, people would leave the thunderbolt to cool off by itself. The embarrassing stranger might, in accordance with the usages of the period, be sent to the stake or locked away in a dungeon. But I very much doubt whether the public would be sufficiently interested to proceed to such extremes. When, in the old days, a sorcerer was burnt, it was because there was a general feeling that he had attacked society in its own terms, by turning against it the ideas and the words with which it was familiar. Our thunderbolt would represent so abnormal, so totally improbable a peril, a peril so incapable of touching the life of the ordinary man or woman, that it would scarcely be felt as a peril at all. . . . Let me remind you of an essay of yours which I read once. It contained a number of admirable observations. . . ."

"Oh!"

"I'm serious. . . . I can't remember exactly how your argument ran, though I read the essay more than once and thought about it a lot. . . . In one passage you described truth as a wandering beggar, leading the life of a tramp without papers or means of identification. The explanations she gives to the policemen she meets are useless. She has no recognized place in society. She just doesn't belong to the world through which she moves. Her home is in a limbo of times and places empty of all other inhabitants—humanly deserted. You spoke of 'truths without a country.' A truer word was never spoken. The country in which the great truths dwell is a place of austerity, governed by laws which, beyond a certain limit of tolerance, are inflexible. Or rather, I should say, they dwell in a series of countries which succeed one another from age to age, and in each the point of view shifts slightly. It is only their own jealous authority that does not change."

After a short silence he went on:

"No, I can't say what I should have done had the war, with its abnormal conditions, never occurred. . . . If I had lived a little earlier or a little later—which, by the way, proves that one is a good deal less courageous than one imagines oneself to be. Or perhaps I should say that courage always carries in its heart a vague hope of victory. . . . But how can one hope for victory when one no longer feels that one is up against an enemy . . . when one has the impression that one is fighting nothing but one's own fantasies?"

"It may be," said Jallez, "that such courage as you speak of belongs only to those whom I may perhaps call 'professional failures' because in their hearts they know that they have nothing to lose. Every failure who refuses to give in is essentially a megalomaniac, and megalomaniacs are most at ease when there is no one to shake their faith in themselves. . . . But a really great man—if you will excuse the phrase—is dominated by the need not so much to win the recognition of others as to measure his strength on the battlefield, to give proof of his prowess . . . and, since every really great man is at the opposite pole from the fool, he tends to consider not what humanity thinks of him but the problems with which humanity is immediately confronted . . . and he ends by convincing himself that, after all, there is nothing dishonourable in measuring his strength against the difficulties presented by those problems. . . . It is, is it not, the case of the artist who works to order, harnessing his genius to the job of producing Last Judgments when really he wants to paint circles of naked girls on ball-room ceilings?"

"Yes, but the artist can always manage to work in his naked girls somewhere. . . . He accepts his subject, but, under cover of that subject, succeeds in secretly achieving what lies nearest to his heart, in expressing a view of the world as he sees it. . . . The case of the scientist is very different, as you'll see if you think for a moment. Except, possibly, in the field of mathematics, the subject is paramount. It absorbs all his efforts, becomes identified with the very labour of creation. He can't slip a forbidden subject into the sort of subject that is demanded, or at least accepted, by his age. I am in an even worse position. The forbidden subject happens to be a whole world in itself, and, as I see it, a world that has never been explored. . . . Not even the cleverest cheat can carry a world about at the bottom of his suitcase. . . . And so!" The gesture with which he accompanied the words seemed to sweep away the thoughts that obsessed him with a useless bitterness.

What he had said was so true, and went so deep, that Jallez felt that it was no good trying to argue against it. He was on the point of saying: "Perhaps greatness of conception is the only thing that really matters—the doing of something great, no matter what it may be"—a point of view almost identical with that of Strigelius. But suppose the playing of chess was the only free human activity permitted by society, should a man remain satisfied to do nothing but invent chess openings? And what if his gifts didn't lie that way?

He therefore said nothing. But a moment later, taking all his courage in both hands, and with an air of extreme shyness, he put, in a low voice, a question which had every appearance of being superfluous. He felt, however, that if he didn't put it fairly and squarely, there would always be a lurking doubt at the back of his mind. He wanted to turn the light full on the astonishing human situation with which he was confronted. He could not remain contented with the approximate, the half-truth.

"Then," he said, "if I am not mistaken—in this matter—this matter, I mean, of the phenomena which you were investigating when I knew you first, of their meaning, their extent—your views have not changed?"

Viaur looked him straight in the eyes and said with all the gentleness of which he was capable:

"No, they have not changed."

Then, as though checked by a scruple, and very confidentially, he added:

"What has happened in my case is that at times all that side of my life seems to be infinitely remote. I say to myself: 'Haven't I, perhaps, been dreaming? . . . I must have been dreaming . . . because the rest of the world behaves precisely as though that had never existed. . . .' But I start thinking, and five minutes later—"

"Yes?"

". . . I recover my sense of proportion."

That evening, when he got back, about midnight, to his tiny apartment on the Plainpalais, Jallez found the following letter:

Dear Sir:

We were so busy chatting that I quite forgot to say something to which I attach considerable importance. I am not altogether sure that you will agree, but you seem to take so excessive an interest in my affairs that I think I owe you this further evidence of my appreciation. Do you remember those words of the Tempter: "Ye shall be as gods"? I have often said to myself when thinking of the work I was doing between 1912 and '14, and especially of the developments that might have taken place as a result of it had the science of those years showed the same degree of passionate interest in what I was doing as in physical mathematics and physical chemistry: Wasn't I really suggesting that science should take those words of the Tempter as a program for future research? Wasn't I asking it to teach man to free himself from the bonds that hold him in blind servitude to the mechanism of the body, to subject that mechanism and, to some extent, the very substance of the body to the growing power of the spirit and the will—which might amount to tearing up by the roots the essential conditions of the human being in order to approximate him to a god? And isn't it possible that this is what ought to happen to humanity? Because, in spite of all its successes and all its pride, modern science has, up to now, done little more than multiply the achievements of the earliest scientists and experimenters. It has developed the purely human aspect of our species to an excessive, perhaps to a monstrously excessive, degree, but it has done nothing, really, to help mankind to escape from the conditions of its humanity. . . . I should like you to think this over. I mention it only because you have shown such remarkable sympathy and patience in all that concerns me, a sympathy and a patience for which I shall be eternally grateful.

Yours very sincerely,

ALBERT VIAUR

PS. I have checked and find that I am free the day after tomorrow in the evening. It will give me great pleasure, therefore, to dine with you at that tavern in the old town which you have so kindly offered to show me.

"How very odd!" said Jallez, when he had read the note through twice.

# Chapter

## 20

### A MAGISTRATE WHO WON'T BE RUSHED

Jerphanion was called to the hotel telephone.

"Monsieur Jerphanion?"

"Speaking."

"This is Pouzols-Desaugues. How are you, my dear fellow? Look here, if you're free this morning, what about a drink?"

"I could manage about noon, I think—a bit before, if anything."

"Right. I'll pick you up, say, at a quarter to. If you're not ready, I'll wait. Yesterday I saw that magistrate I mentioned, and I told him about our little business."

"In general terms, or did you go into details?"

"I gave him the whole bag of tricks!"

("He didn't want me to have the fun," thought Jerphanion, "of telling him the story myself. What a queer fish this Pouzols-Desaugues is! For months he doesn't stir a finger, and then suddenly . . .")

Aloud he said: "Did you mention our visit—Grousson's and mine?"

"Naturally. Shouldn't I have?"

"Oh, I don't mind. And the theory we have formed?"

"I sketched the main outline, but I don't think I gave you away."

"Good." There was a lack of enthusiasm in Jerphanion's voice. "Only, I can't see, in that case, what more I can tell him. . . . Still— Wouldn't it be as well to have Grousson there too?"

"I'm not quite sure. . . . I merely suggested to Monsieur Doublet that he should meet *you*. . . . He's very keen, in any case, to make your acquaintance. . . . I don't want it to look as though I'd engineered the meeting just for that. . . . I rather think that Grousson's presence would give a different slant to our conversation. Don't you agree?"

At a quarter to twelve M. Pouzols-Desaugues's limousine drew up before the hotel. Jerphanion was told of its arrival and came down at once.

"I've arranged to meet him at the Brasserie du Théâtre," said M. Pouzols-Desaugues. "We'll drive there."

"But it's no distance."

"The streets are full of snow. We should get our feet horribly wet."

"True." Jerphanion had a sudden vision of sitting about for half an hour with ice-cold feet gingerly resting on the frozen ground.

In the car, and later in the café, during the few minutes of their wait, M. Pouzols-Desaugues was bubbling over with advance information.

"I thought it best," he said, "to put him wise before he met you. I didn't know how long you could spare. It might have been tiresome, even a bit irritating, for you to have been forced to develop your—your impressions for the benefit of a man who didn't know the first thing about the business. . . . He promised that he would look up his predecessor's files at once. So, you see, he'll come primed with a certain amount of information. That'll make the meeting a good deal more interesting for you, I think."

"How did he react to the talk you had with him?"

"I thought he seemed to be listening very attentively."

"He didn't seem over-sceptical?"

"On the whole, no. . . . You've got to take him as he is—a charming fellow—with a passion for living—hates being bored, you know. . . . You mustn't expect him to show that fine zeal for his work which marked the old-time magistrate. He hardly symbolizes Justice running the criminal to earth." M. Pouzols-Desaugues uttered a faint sigh. "I can remember the time when the servants of the State liked to burn with a sacred fire . . . but that sort of thing went out of fashion with the frock coat and the top hat. The post-war generations may have lit the flame beneath the Arc de Triomphe—a charming thought, that, by the way—but I'm afraid it won't manage to kindle a blaze in the hearts of our civil servants." He laughed meaningly. "I ought to have told him more about the handsome widow."

"Why?"

"Oh, that's only my little joke—it might have increased his interest, though hardly his impartiality."

"Do I take it that he is susceptible to that sort of thing?"

"Extremely—though don't think I hold it against him. He hasn't got much to do, and there's not much in the way of relaxation to be found in Le Puy. He takes his fun where he can find it. . . . After all, at his age! He's pretty clever at finding it too, let me tell you."

"Is he?"

M. Pouzols-Desaugues leaned towards Jerphanion. His eye gleamed roguishly behind his monocle.

"Young women are the objects of his special study."

"Collects them by the shovelful, eh?"

"Oh, I wouldn't go as far as that—though, as I said before, he's a clever chap. . . . There are sportsmen who can start a hare in the most unlikely places. . . . Besides, he's not difficult to please." He lowered his voice. "I have heard it said that he's been seen on the watch outside a certain workshop on the road to Vals. Most of the girls there are ugly enough, but there are a few good-lookers among them. You remember the cigarette-makers of Seville?"—and M. Pouzols-Desaugues started to hum, in an odd sort of voice, a tune that might have been meant for something out of *Carmen*.

"And doesn't this form of sport cause him any awkwardness?"

"Not up to the present, so far as I know." He relapsed into silent thought for a few moments, after which: "I don't want you to think," he said, "that I spy on his movements. . . . I won't say that I don't envy him, but I certainly don't spy on him. . . . Since you have chosen to use the word 'sport,' let me follow suit and say that, in his own field, he is a 'lone hunter.' He works on his own, not in a gang."

Jerphanion guessed that these words contained a reference to some local joke to which he had no key. He uttered the kind of laugh which means that one wants to have the *i*'s dotted.

"You see," continued M. Pouzols-Desaugues without waiting to be pressed, "he's not the only man here with a liking for girls, but the others have adopted a different method." He spoke in a tone of playful seriousness. "The future alone will show which is the best. . . . Our friend Doublet can hardly be ignorant of what goes on in a pleasant establishment on the boulevard Carnot which, at first sight, would seem to offer better guarantees of secrecy. . . . But that kind of thing doesn't interest him. . . . It may be that he is planning a police raid one of these days. . . . Public morals must be protected! . . . It would be a bit odd, I must admit, but— Hush, here he comes!"

A high-complexioned man of about thirty-five came in at that moment, rubbing his hands and stamping his feet, from the snowy waste to which the Breuil had been reduced by the weather. He wore a very short beard, which with the intent but mocking glance of his eyes, and the faint protuberance of his stomach, gave him somewhat the appearance of a Renaissance nobleman.

With the first words he spoke he showed himself very cordial to M. Pouzols-Desaugues, very attentive to Jerphanion. He asked him whether he was pleased with the results of his trip, though he was careful to give the impression that he knew nothing of its political character. They discussed the countryside and the mountain-dwellers in general terms.

It was the squire of Brives who led the conversation on to the Vaurevauzes affair.

"Ah, to be sure!" said the magistrate, turning to Jerphanion. "I gather that you've been treating yourself to a fine slice of the picturesque. You've got the whole bag of tricks there—scenery, characters. . . . It'll be something for you to remember, if nothing else."

He seemed anxious not to depart from his tone of amused detachment, in which he allowed no hint to appear of his professional preoccupations. But M. Pouzols-Desaugues was in no mood to let him off so easily.

"Have you taken a look at those old files?" he asked.

"I did just turn them over this morning," replied Doublet without any show of enthusiasm. "They're not very bulky, you know. I'm not likely to lose my way in them. The only document of any real weight is the police report." He broke off with a look which said as plainly as words: "Is it really worth while going on? You know everything there is to be known." But the faces of the other two showed that they expected more than this; so he continued: "It gives the facts, to be sure, but in a way to reduce suspicion to the minimum. It is obvious that the officer in charge of the inquiry, however eager he may have been for promotion, didn't want to get it by unearthing a full-sized crime among his neighbours."

"Does the report give the Leblancs' version of what occurred?" asked M. Pouzols-Desaugues.

"It does."

"Is there any mention of the fact that the house is unhealthy?"

"Not in so many words," replied Doublet with a slightly increased show of interest. "They do say, at one point, that it is very damp, and that people living there get ill . . . that the father had never really recovered from a cold which he caught at harvest-time . . . but nothing more definite than that."

"Ah!" exclaimed M. Pouzols-Desaugues in a tone of justified innocence.

"The actual death is made to appear as having been a pure accident brought on by the effect of cold weather on a man who was no longer young, who was in a poor state of health, and who wouldn't look after himself. . . . That's all." The curiosity of the other two seeming in no way satisfied, he added: "I hardly think that the report could have encouraged my predecessor to nose out any dramatic possibilities. . . . Not that he ignored the matter. . . . There is a note in his hand asking for details about the death certificate, and the reply, which shows, incidentally, that the mayor didn't relish the idea of anybody treading on his toes. . . . There's a letter, too, which I was rather surprised to find in such a place in view of its apparently personal nature."

"Does it bear on the business?" asked Jerphanion.

"To some extent—for it shows that the writer had it in mind. This letter is signed by a young magistrate called Fachuel, a friend of Piard's. . . . I don't know him, but I rather think I have come across his name since, as that of a member of the Seine District Bench. . . . At the time in question he was serving in the Army, and Piard seems to have kept up a pretty regular correspondence with him—I gather that they were old school friends. Piard had almost certainly told him the Vaurevauzes story, presumably because of its picturesque details —the corpse in the snow, and all the rest of it . . . and Fachuel's reply takes the form, not of a letter of professional advice (for which the other had probably not asked), but of a dissertation, half serious, half fantastic, but, I must say, extremely well done, on the special conditions attending crime in out-of-the-way places, on the assistance afforded to such crimes by the mountain winter, and on the special advantages, from the criminal's point of view, of a state of war. I imagine that they wrote to each other about such things just for the fun of it." Doublet gave a little laugh. "Just as other men tell one another stories about women. . . . But perhaps if they had been writing about women, Piard wouldn't have left the letter in the file."

Jerphanion exchanged a glance with Pouzols-Desaugues. He felt that the magistrate with the little beard had not bitten very hard on the hook, either because he was not particularly hungry or because the bait was insufficient. He wondered whether when Pouzols-Desaugues had outlined the case to his friend the day before, he had gone into sufficient detail, had made clear enough the logical development of the arguments which gave them their strength, or whether he had merely given a few casual examples to illustrate the theory. "One ought always to do this sort of thing oneself," he thought. But it wouldn't be easy now for him to go over the ground again. There was a good chance that the other might interrupt his tale with "Oh, I know all about that. Monsieur Pouzols-Desaugues went into it all yesterday. . . ." And there was a grave danger that he might seem to attach to the business a degree of personal interest which would seem ridiculous. There is no reason why a gentleman who is busy organizing his party's electoral campaign in the district shouldn't amuse himself with a highly seasoned local story. But if he takes it too seriously, his sense of proportion may be called in question; besides, he may look too much like the kind of fellow who pokes his nose into all sorts of odds and ends, waking sleeping dogs, stirring up mud, and, in general, behaving in a way not likely to recommend him either to the various local authorities whose one concern is a quiet life, or to the many different kinds of petty delinquents, peculators, and people with their fingers in various odd pies, who make up the bulk of any constituency.

He was careful, therefore, to adopt a line of detachment, as though he had to make a considerable effort in order to flog himself into some show of interest in a matter of purely legal concern. "Are you hoping that it will be possible to take action?"

M. Doublet shaped his mouth, beneath its silky moustache, into a grimace that expressed but a moderate degree of enthusiasm.

"I shall see what can be done. It's rather difficult."

"Well, whatever happens, that fellow's got to stop running my house down!" said M. Pouzols-Desaugues with vigour. "If he goes on, and I'm forced to it, I'll get statements from witnesses and prosecute—which might be a good way, don't you think, of enabling you to probe more deeply into the whole business?"

"Possibly," said M. Doublet apathetically. "But I wouldn't let Leblanc's reflections on your house upset you too much. . . . When he spoke as he did to Monsieur Jerphanion the other day, it was really only to say something. Probably he's forgotten all about it by now. . . . As for probing more deeply into the affair, hm—it's a year, you say, since the most recent incident occurred, and six or seven years since the first? Picking up the threads after such a long interval isn't, you know, very easy. If one acts at once, one can always pick on some little irregularity, legal or otherwise, and make it an excuse for opening an inquiry which may seem quite innocent at first; and then, if one looks like getting results, it is always possible to turn on the heat. . . . But when there's been such a long delay, the whole thing takes on a serious aspect from the first. The legal authorities can't act irresponsibly. The thing's awkward enough, in all conscience, when one's dealing with nothing worse than tax-evasion, and even then one can act with a considerable degree of discretion, should such seem desirable, up to the very moment of preferring a charge. . . . And the same holds true, to some extent, in cases of moral delinquency. . . ." Once again Jerphanion and Pouzols-Desaugues exchanged a glance. It was only with the greatest difficulty that they kept from laughing. "But in a matter such as this—one could hardly reopen proceedings without first having a double exhumation—unless, that is, one were going only to touch their surface, as was done last time. . . . But an exhumation, and all that goes with it, is bound to cause something of a sensation. It's not the sort of thing one can keep between four walls, even if those walls happen to belong to a magistrate's chambers. At once there'll be a whopping great scandal, everyone'll start talking, and we, the authorities concerned, will have to go through with the thing to the end."

"This," thought Jerphanion, "is almost word for word what the magistrate of the Seine District said. Is there, I wonder, a sort of professional code which makes these fellows say precisely the same things whenever certain circumstances arise? Or is it that their general equipment of common sense dictates similar responses in cases of similar provocation?"

"And then," went on the magistrate, "seeing that most of the facts would be extremely hard to come by at this time of day, our own local police wouldn't be adequate for the job. We should have to get hold of some officer of experience, someone from the Sûreté, and a pretty able man at that. . . . It would be the devil of a business even in the case of an obvious crime which had already made a lot of noise and public clamour . . . but in the kind of circumstances we have to deal with, I could only call in the Sûreté with some show of justice if I was pretty sure that a crime really had been committed." He looked first at Jerphanion and then at Pouzols-Desaugues as though he had asked a question and was expecting an answer. "Of course, if the inhabitants of the commune had lodged a joint complaint, I should look at the whole thing very differently; or even if some one person had put in a demand for an inquiry duly signed by a notable of the district, and supported by definite charges. . . . But I doubt whether we can expect anything of that sort."

His two interlocutors made it pretty plain by their looks that he wouldn't get them to take the necessary initiative.

With the air of a man making a concession, M. Doublet continued:

"What I can do is to send someone up there to have a look round—" he gazed at the white expanse of the Breuil—"as soon, that is, as this snow's thawed a bit. I'd go myself, though I doubt—" he smiled— "whether that is a very practical suggestion. It's not very easy for me to disguise myself. But I could probably find some young fellow among my colleagues who could get a pretty fair idea of the lie of the land without causing undue alarm."

He looked at Jerphanion with the expression of a good-natured official who has just been asked to confer a rather exceptional favour, and who, after digging deep into his store of goodwill in the interest of the person making the request, concludes by saying: "So you see, my dear sir, I really am anxious to do what I can. You mustn't hold me responsible if nothing comes of my attempt."

Pouzols-Desaugues, addressing Jerphanion in his turn, said, in a conciliatory tone which, though it seemed to lack something of sincerity, implied that he recognized their joint defeat, and had an air of being a little too ready to accept the inevitable:

"You can rely on Monsieur Doublet. It may be that he will be able to do what he suggests before you leave. In any case I will keep you informed."

Noticing a somewhat ironic smile on the younger man's lips, he added with a greater show of firmness:

"Don't think for a moment that I'm going to abandon my inquiries into this fantastic story of a germ-ridden house and galloping consumption. You had a perfect right to tell me what you heard, and so have I to let it get under my skin and to use it as an excuse for going up to Vaurevauzes, where I shall be a little more insistent than I was on my former visit. If I'm to be told that my house has been responsible for killing people, damme, I've got to know rather more than I do at present about how those people died! . . . Don't worry; Monsieur Doublet and I will join forces." He felt for his monocle with the air of a man whose mind is made up. "Our friend Leblanc will make a great mistake if he thinks he can sleep quietly in his bed."

Though Jerphanion nodded his head in polite agreement, he turned on M. Pouzols-Desaugues a faintly disappointed eye.

# Chapter

## 21

### PULL YOURSELF TOGETHER

Among the people who had come down to the station to see him off, Jerphanion noticed M. Pouzols-Desaugues.

The "squire of Brives" was standing a little apart. He kept making expansive and faintly comic gestures for the young man's benefit, in which spine, arms, face, and monocle all had a part to play. Their message, roughly interpreted, was: "Carry on with your committee men. I'll manage to get a word with you at the last moment." It occurred to Jerphanion that, among the other men who thronged the platform, with their shorter, fatter figures and their quieter movements, M. Pouzols-Desaugues looked (and this was the first time that the comparison had been borne in upon him) like a conventional rendering of Punch; but of a Punch with something of the aristocrat in him.

Sure enough, a few seconds before the train began to move, M. Pouzols-Desaugues sidled up to him and, with an air of great mystery, said in a low voice:

"Our friend sends word by me that he is already on the track of something that has to do with the mountain folk. But that's not all. He thinks he's found an excuse for summoning the handsome widow to a private interview. He is convinced that a few words with her in his chambers will produce results"—with a smothered guffaw—"or at least will put him on the right scent. . . . I mentioned her again. . . . I aroused his interest. . . ."

"But are you sure," said Jerphanion, "that that really is the best way of setting him on to discover the truth?"

"One never knows. . . . We shall see what we shall see. . . . God

moves in a mysterious way. . . . I'll keep you posted. . . . I'll write.
. . . Count on me for that, and for everything else. In return, you'll
remember, won't you, to let me know what happens about your great
lady of the Seine-et-Marne? That's a bargain; don't forget, now!"

As the train emerged from the first tunnel, Jerphanion felt as
though he had shaken himself free of a smother of cloud. The sensation was similar to that of a man who breathes in the fresh air of the
street after spending a thick night with his friends. Or, putting the
matter a little differently, it came over him suddenly that a second,
an elder, self had been waiting for him at the exit to the tunnel and
now caught him by the sleeve with a "Pull yourself together, now;
you've wasted enough time." He was tempted to make a faint protest:
"It wasn't all wasted. . . . I've done some good solid work too. . . .
Oh, let's get on; what's the good of arguing!"

No more time to lose, and much to make up. He was conscious of
a mood of high lucidity, of icy, stern resolve. Every circumstance of
the present stood out for him with the distinctness of a diagram drawn
on a blackboard. The vista of his immediate future lay open to his
eyes clearly focused, as though the precise ordering of his actions in
the weeks ahead had been long planned and was now fixed beyond
the need of further discussion.

"My own seat is assured. To give more to it than the bare minimum
of necessary thought would be mere foolish fussiness. The first thing
I must do when I get back is to clear the decks—see that the names on
my party ticket are changed. If feelings are hurt, that's no concern of
mine. Bouitton is right. I'm the man to organize the party campaign,
to lay down its general lines, to settle its platform, as they say. No
good waiting for the others to make up their minds. The thing to do
is to present them with a *fait accompli,* so that all they'll have to do,
apart from changing a phrase here and there, an occasional comma,
will be to say amen. My speech to the teachers of Le Puy, reduced
to its essentials, will provide the necessary basis. The fun of deciding
on details of persons and candidates I'll leave to them, provided that

the too obvious fools and nonentities are kept out. If Bouitton agrees, I'll get myself nominated as vice-president of the party. That'll free me from the danger of being merely the power behind the throne and will give me authority in dealing with the die-hards. I must have a long talk with Herriot and Painlevé. I ought to see Léon Blum too, and find out exactly what we can count on in that quarter. There must be no resting content with vague expressions of goodwill. We must know accurately the points on which we see eye to eye and where we differ.

"Ought I to see Briand? . . . In theory, yes. But I don't think it's a matter of any very great urgency. What can he say to me that I don't know already? He won't feel inclined to do more than embark on generalities with a man of my age . . . to give me his pontifical blessing. . . . Gurau? Yes. He's never really found his niche. The very fact that he feels rather bitter will be an advantage when it comes to talking frankly with him. I shall be able to clear up my mental reservations—mental reservations almost as important as mental certainties. . . . When it comes down to brass tacks I like Gurau, even though I hardly know him. Can't help feeling he's a man with a soul. . . . Perhaps I may be able to help him later on. . . . When the elections are over and it's a question of constituting a new cabinet, I'll certainly manage to have my say. . . . The less I push myself forward, the more inclined will they be to listen to me. . . . I shall enter Parliament in company with a dozen or so men who will be in my debt, who will be already used to receiving their instructions either directly or indirectly from me. . . . We've got to liquidate the post-war period and get France back on the rails. Everything depends on how well established the peace is, and on how long it will last. The whole of our future depends on the peace. That's axiom number one, and we must never lose sight of it for a moment. The problem must be attacked from every side. The thing to do is to begin with a sort of scientific survey. We must draw up a profit-and-loss account of attempts, of obstacles, of results, of underlying causes. Nothing must be neglected which might throw light on the problem, nothing, however improbable, which might give positive results. What about having a word with Laulerque—why not? And Lengnau, and Jallez—get him to spill what he knows and what he guesses. Then I ought to get into touch with some of the sharks of big business, like Champcenais and Haverkamp, so as to get their point of view and have a clear idea of the strength of the opposition that they represent, of how much of it can be neutralized, how much used, how much must be destroyed.

"As soon as I've got a free moment after the elections, I ought to make a trip to America. The fellows over there have got a stranglehold on us. Maybe they don't mean badly, but they're too drunk with success to see straight. If they go on as they're going at present, they'll push the whole world over the edge, us first of all, naturally, and head-first. They're fools enough to think that Europe no longer counts except as a world of ruins ready for exploitation, as a Balkan peninsula on a large scale in which they can peddle their goods. If Europe crashes, they'll crash with her. They may laugh at her, but the world still stands on the old foundations. And France is the keystone. That, at bottom, is the simple truth, and it should be as clear as daylight.

"But as soon as I'm home, before getting under way, there's one act of faith I must accomplish. I must go up on the college roof again and have a good hour there, alone. I must recapture the old enthusiasm, see again the vision of true greatness. *Memento magnitudinis.*"

On a fine winter's day Jerphanion gets Félicien
Grousson to drive him from Saint-Julien-Chaptueil
to Le Puy. His electoral campaign of 1924 awakens in him ridiculous
memories of the Marquis de Saint-Papoul's candidature in 1910. News
of his parents. How Grousson, the wine-merchant, spends his days.
Jerphanion ponders the art of living as practised by his travelling companion. First reference to M. Pouzols-Desaugues.

Jerphanion makes a great speech at the luncheon of the Teachers'
Institute of the Haute-Loire. "Why I took up politics." Memories of
Laulerque in 1910. "The one great problem is how to avoid war."
What matters is the comparative urgency of the various questions
confronting society. Laulerque is always right. The treaty of peace
examined. America's great blunder. The behaviour of England. Democracy means, among other things, a chance for the man in the street
to have his say in foreign politics. Allusions to the more personal
concerns of his audience. The Russian experiment. France did not
manage to escape a war; she must escape a revolution. The good will
and wisdom of the Radical-Socialist Party. The matter of the Ruhr.
France's role.

Jerphanion is entertained by M. Pouzols-Desaugues. He admires the
view from his host's study windows. The latter's theories on foreign
politics. They are joined for luncheon by Mme Pouzols-Desaugues.
How an old diplomat would have dealt with the peace treaty. Jerphanion is conscious of a strange and fragile bond of sympathy between himself and his host. M. Pouzols-Desaugues gives a thumbnail
sketch of what he thinks may have been the criminal activities of his
tenants at Vaurevauzes.

Driving with Grousson, Jerphanion enjoys a curious sense of mental well-being. Why there are both Catholics and Protestants in Le Velay. A long discussion leads to the formulation of a plausible and ingenious reconstruction of the happenings at Vaurevauzes.

Jerphanion writes to Odette: The problem of his colleagues on the party ticket. His view of the part he will be called upon to play as a representative of the people. The problem of Jean-Pierre, and of the spoiled only child in general. Mankind's fear of the future.

Driving once more with Grousson, he goes into the Vaurevauzes crimes in detail and discusses how they were carried out. Grousson suggests a visit to the curé of Saint-Front. What a country inn can provide for luncheon. The curé of Saint-Front at home. His poverty awakens conscientious scruples in Jerphanion. The priest calmly sums up his views about the morals of his parishioners. It is not his opinion that human justice should altogether abandon the field to the justice of God.—Visit to Vaurevauzes: The handsome widow seen in the obscurity of a tunnel. Three women in a large, dark room. The man appears. He attributes the recent deaths to the fact that the house is unhealthful, and succeeds in sowing doubts in the mind of Jerphanion, who, despite a faint feeling of disappointment, persuades himself that his self-respect as an honest investigator will be saved.

Jerphanion addresses forty electors at Saint-Front. The story of Vaurevauzes gets mixed up with the phrases of his speech. He accuses himself of childishness.—He gets Odette's answer: Her advice. Her entertainment of her parents. Her views on large families. News of Jallez.—Jerphanion's second luncheon with M. Pouzols-Desaugues, whom he tells of his conversations in the car and of his visit to Vaurevauzes. "The squire" is indignant when he hears of the charges brought against his property. Jerphanion tells the story of the beautiful concierge and the Paris landlord. Society is quick to punish the criminal who is known as such, but shows considerable reluctance to bring concealed crimes to light.

Jallez, in his office at the League of Nations, with its window commanding a particularly lovely view, indulges in an orgy of spiritual well-being which he seeks to justify by objective reasoning. Like Jerphanion, he accuses himself of childishness.—Dr. Viaur at Geneva. Jallez, anxious to renew an old acquaintance, introduces himself. The changes in Viaur's appearance; his charm. The two men lunch together at the Hôtel des Bergues. How Viaur discovered "Anaplastine." Even a successful man can feel bitterness. He envies those whose reputation rests on work that is genuinely important. Truth without frontiers. A curious letter.

Pouzols-Desaugues arranges a meeting between a local magistrate named Doublet and Jerphanion. The former shows little relish for the Vaurevauzes affair.—Jerphanion leaves Le Puy: "Pull yourself together; stop wasting your time." He works out a plan of campaign which he intends to pursue as soon as he gets home.

# BOOK TWENTY-TWO:
# WORK AND PLAY

# Chapter

## 1

### HAVERKAMP SETS ABOUT REFURBISHING

"That must be one of them," said Haverkamp impatiently to his private secretary, who had just entered the "studio." "I think I heard the bell."

"It was my decorator friend. He's always on time. I've shown him into the drawing-room."

"Hasn't Turpin turned up yet?"

"No," replied the secretary with a rather affectedly self-conscious smile. "I've met Monsieur Turpin only once; but I certainly did not get the impression that punctuality would be his strong suit."

"And he hasn't rung up to cancel the engagement?"

"Not so far as I know."

"It's very tiresome. We're already ten minutes late."

"Wouldn't you like to have a few words with my friend while we're waiting?"

Haverkamp gloomily considered the suggestion.

"No, I don't want to have to say the same thing over and over again. Besides, as I've told you before, I like doing things in the proper order. We've got to begin with the architect, or at least that's how I see it. I agreed to see this decorator fellow at the same time because you seemed to want me to, and because if he's got any useful suggestions he'd better make them with the architect here. If they're going to start an argument, I want to be in on it. That's the only way I can make up my mind whether they're likely to be able to work together. . . . Ah, there's the bell! It must be Turpin this time. You see, he's not so late as you'd like to make out."

Henry de Belleuse, the secretary, delicately perfumed, and with the mincing gait of a diplomatic attaché, introduced Raoul Turpin and Serge Vazar, the interior decorator.

Turpin had not changed much since Celle-les-Eaux days. He had grown rather stouter, but the added weight of flesh was fairly evenly distributed over his whole body. His face was slightly more puffy than of yore. He still, in defiance of all fashion, retained his beard, but he was careful now to keep it clipped short. His hair too was shorter and thinner than it used to be. A wide patch of incipient baldness was visible running back from his forehead towards the centre of his skull. A few grey curls showed at his temples and above his ears. As a concession to the taste of the period—almost his only one—he wore a pair of large tortoise-shell spectacles. His suit of reddish English tweed was of rough texture. The general impression of the man was faintly ambiguous. The former art student, heavily disguised though he might be, still persisted in peeping through the new trappings. He might have been a stockbroker with a weakness for the studios of Montparnasse.

Serge Vazar was a good-looking young fellow in his thirties, slim, supple, undulating. He was beautifully shaved and powdered and his black hair shone with an oily lustre. A pair of heavy black eyebrows was the one note of rather brutal virility in his appearance. His sinuous movements, his carefully arranged smile, the pitch of his voice—the result, seemingly, of deliberate choice rather than of nature—and the languid singsong, alternating with little gushes of words, in which he spoke (it was difficult to determine whether his accent was faintly foreign or not), gave him a certain family resemblance to Henry de Belleuse.

The presence of these two young men in the uncompromising masculinity of Haverkamp's studio set Turpin staring. The hint of a smile peeped out from behind the tortoise-shell spectacles.

As soon as everybody was seated, Haverkamp, without wasting time on preliminaries, plunged straight into his subject:

"I have called you together, gentlemen, to consider a certain scheme which I have in mind. You, Turpin, old man, are a friend of long standing who knows my ways. I have not the pleasure of knowing you, Monsieur—Vazar, except, more or less, by name. Belleuse has spoken to me of you in highly flattering terms. . . . So far, so good." In what followed, he addressed his remarks chiefly to Vazar. "I want to make it quite clear at the outset that this meeting commits neither of you to anything definite. We have come together merely for a general exchange of views. Having heard what I have to say, you will each of you think over the proposal, though I trust that you will not take too long about making up your minds, because if we are to work together, I want to get going at once. Turpin knows me. I make up my mind quickly, but once it is made up, I have a horror of delays. If we can agree on general principles, I shall want the details to be worked out at once and the work carried through straight away. If either of you is engaged on other work, I should be obliged if he would tell me so at once and let me know how long it will be before he is free. . . ." (This remark, though ostensibly addressed to both, was clearly intended primarily for the newcomer.)

It was Turpin, however, who first replied. Quietly, but with a faint tone of mockery, he pointed out that, naturally, he had a number of jobs on hand. Haverkamp, he indicated, could hardly have expected it to be otherwise, and, speaking for himself, he rejoiced in the fact. He was getting too old, he said, to live happily on bread and water in a garret. Fortunately, however, he had assistants who were quite capable of looking after the work in hand under his general supervision. As luck would have it, there was nothing of major importance to occupy his mind at the moment, though he couldn't guarantee a similar state of affairs in, say, three weeks' time.

In a little spate of semiquavers alternating with impressive pauses, Serge Vazar explained that he had recently received a number of commissions, but that several of them, luckily, came from members of the old aristocracy, leisurely and fussy persons who could never let well alone, though this had the advantage that they could be kept waiting in such a manner that they would scarcely notice the delay. What it came to was that, once the "get started" signal was given, he was ready to go full-steam ahead on any scheme sufficiently important to justify priority treatment.

"Fine!" said Haverkamp with jovial heartiness. "I'm planning in a big way. You see, I'm sick of living in my trunks . . . I don't feel that my setting is worthy of me. Look at this studio, Turpin, old man. When you built it for me—about three years ago, it must be—nothing could have been more charming, given the taste of the period. But the two salons and the dining-room might, but for my Modiglianis and my Vlamincks, have been designed for my old aunt. The bedroom, I admit, would still pass, though. . . . And don't say that I could have the whole place made over. It's much too small. I can't find room to hang more than a third of my pictures. Besides, I don't see any fun in spending a lot of money just for the privilege of handing back the apartment, with all my improvements, to my landlord when the lease has run out. No, I want to feel that I've got something of my very own. And since it's going to involve a general upheaval and much waste of time, I prefer to get the whole thing done at one fell swoop and on generous lines. . . . Speaking generally, my idea is a house in Paris and a place in the country. I don't say necessarily 'build.' I am willing to consider any solution of the problem. The object of this preliminary meeting, as I see it, is to determine our methods of procedure whether we build or whether we don't. Let me repeat that I face the whole problem with an open mind."

"Knowing you as I do," said Turpin, with his air of mockery, "I confess that I should be very much surprised to hear that you had really been thinking in such vague terms. It's not your way of doing things. Surely you've already got something pretty definite at the back of your mind."

"Well, if I have," said Haverkamp, puffing out his chest, "few men have more right. I needn't remind you, Turpin, that I used to know a thing or two about house property. More than one person came to me in the old days for advice on that subject. . . . But you're right, I have given the matter some thought. Without wishing to influence you in any way, let me tell you how the whole thing looks to me. . . . You can put your own point of view later. . . . First of all, the house in Paris. . . . It seems to me that the best thing to do would be to buy some already existing example of a good period, and adapt it to modern requirements of comfort, being careful to keep our alterations in tone with the general spirit of the place. . . . It doesn't seem to me, Monsieur—ah—Monsieur Vazar, that there ought to be any insuperable difficulty about decorating and furnishing a house in the way I propose. Am I right? The trouble is that houses of a really good period are situated in those districts of Paris which it's fun to visit occasionally, but where I should hate to live. Most of them suffer from lack of air and light; they are difficult to get at; the surroundings are mean and grubby. How about the Île Saint-Louis, you'll say. Well, but what sort of choice are you going to get on the Île Saint-Louis? Even allowing that you do hit on two or three possible houses, what likelihood is there that they'll be for sale? Besides, it's at the other end of nowhere. All my business deals take place between the Étoile and the Bourse. I want to be able to lunch at home when the fancy takes me. No, we must dismiss the Île Saint-Louis from our minds. But in the possible districts, whether the Plaine Monceau or Passy, the houses are all of the worst possible period. Look at this avenue, for instance. I'm not going to shell out a million just to remodel some horrible lump of bricks and mortar which will never cease from stinking of Second Empire financiers or the Félix Faure demi-monde. What it comes to is that, for the time being at least, I lean to something new for the Paris end of our campaign. And when I say new, I mean really new and up to date, put just where I want it. The country place is different. There are lovely little gems waiting to be picked up all over France, of the best possible periods. Very often they cost no more than a suburban villa. There's a lot has to be done to them, I admit. They need thorough modernizing, for one thing. And there's always the problem of decoration: how to rejuvenate and brighten them up, while at the same time leaving the general character unspoiled. Still, given a little taste and people who know their jobs, one can achieve miracles.

"Early in the autumn the Duc de Prasle asked me down to Anjou for a bit of shooting. The château is a superb piece of pure sixteenth century. The Duchess—a woman of real charm and simplicity, and incidentally quite young still—seeing that I was interested, told me that when she and her husband were married, shortly before the war, they had found the château exactly as it had been left by the Duke's parents; that is to say, sound enough so far as roofs and walls went, but with only a couple of old-fashioned bathrooms, where half the time the water wouldn't run owing to defective pressure, an obsolete system of central heating, and electric lighting that was quite awful. Worst of all, she said, were the frightful, dirty wall-papers which they found everywhere, and the furniture, most of it dating from the period between 1850 and 1880. It was just a richer version, she assured me, of the kind of thing you see today in the houses of country shopkeepers and concierges' lodges. The few good old pieces were almost completely lost among the appalling ornamental vases, tapestry stools, and draped curtains. Well, I only wish you could see what she's managed to make of it all with the comparatively very small sum of money which she persuaded her husband to give her a year or two back. The total she mentioned was a hundred and fifty thousand francs! Most of that had to go on heating, light, and plumbing. She made a clean sweep of all the horrors, and kept only the one or two really good pieces. A certain amount of furniture she bought, the kind of good, solid stuff one can still pick up at local sales, which ran her into something between five hundred and two thousand francs. I don't mean to say it's anything remarkable—no museum pieces, you understand—but quite inoffensive, and in the general dignified setting of the house it looks pretty good. But where she has shown real genius is in the paintwork. She had the idea of doing the walls all over, from top to bottom, in broken white with a rough surface and picking out the beams and cornices in a dark wine-colour. You can have no idea what a feeling of space one gets with those great expanses of white wall, the thrilling quality of light in the rooms, the effect of rarity and beauty produced by the comparatively small quantity of not too large pieces of furniture, all of them carefully spaced instead of being jumbled higgledy-piggledy, and by several old mirrors and a sprinkling of gilded wooden frames set in relief against the white. . . . The Duchess told me that the idea had come to her after a trip to Spain. I know that the experts, the kind of people, I mean, who think of such things only in terms of period reconstruction, would have a fit. They'd say the whole thing was an outrage, that the colours were all wrong for the period at which the house was built. . . . But there were no charming seventeenth-century chests at the time of Francis I. All I can tell you is that any unprejudiced person of taste entering that ground floor for the first time, the great hall with its staircase, the two salons, and the dining-room, gets a genuine thrill. The extraordinary thing is how artistic and modern the effect is—yes, modern. How do you account for that? All the details are old—even the colour scheme; after all, we've known broken white and dark red since the year one. Yet the fact remains that as soon as you set foot in the place, you get a sense of something young, something absolutely of the moment. The whole effect is completely successful. So far the Duchess has been able to tackle only those parts of the ground floor I have mentioned and two bedrooms and a bathroom upstairs. 'I'll do the rest,' she said, laughing, 'when you've made a little money for my husband.' I took my cue and said that next time I put a deal through for the Duke, I should insist on twenty per cent of the profits being set aside for the Duchess's own special fund. . . .

"I've told you all this because it strikes me as an excellent lesson in what can be done. Just think what one could produce if one multiplied the Duchess's expenditure by five or by eight! But perhaps, Monsieur Vazar, I've horrified you. You're probably thinking that the Duchess and I are just a couple of barbarians?"

"Far from it! Far from it!" replied Serge Vazar with a great show of earnestness. "As a matter of fact, my mind was working in just the opposite way. The impression you got from that house shows a high, a very personal degree of sensitiveness. It is quite clear that the Duchesse de Prasle has a natural instinct for interior decoration. If you will pay my studio the honour of a visit, I will show you certain designs and models of arrangements which I have created for just such period settings. You will see what I, too, have done with large white surfaces; the way in which I have used old pieces of furniture and other objects as *accents,* bringing them freely together not because of any period relationship they may have, but in virtue only of certain plastic affinities. I have more than once actually got rid of period pieces of no particular interest just in order to achieve an effect of space." Serge Vazar sketched a few broad gestures with the flat of his hand, while his voice pursued a paradoxically sinuous line. "And then that sense of the modern to which you refer is really quite easily accounted for. You see, it is produced by the purity, by the stark quality, of the surfaces, by the clean colours, the vivid contrasts, the absence of clutter and half-tones, by the geometrical value of position and form which is the inevitable effect of objects carefully spaced against large expanses of abstract light. Fundamentally we are after the same thing; we play up and down the same scale no matter what the elements at our disposal may be. Let me make a little confession while Monsieur Turpin is out of earshot. The purely modern decoration of a purely modern building is a little too easy. One can get one's effects *too* completely. It is more exciting, in a way, to achieve a modern atmosphere with old elements, with shapes that one hasn't designed and is forced to accept, in an old setting that has been imposed upon one. Speaking for myself, so far from disapproving your idea of a country house, what I should really enjoy would be to deal with similar problems in some fine old town mansion in the rue de Bourgogne. I think that in the matter of light and gaiety I could provide you with some very pleasant surprises. Still"—with a smile of frank good-fellowship—"I don't want to be odd man in the crew. I don't suppose it would be much fun for an architect to have no more to do than knock down a few partitions in some old building. It's no part of my business to dissuade you from building, since that seems to be the direction in which your mind is working."

In spite of long training at the hands of his private secretary, Henry de Belleuse, Haverkamp found it difficult to adapt himself to the mannerisms of people like Serge Vazar. He was torn between a desire to laugh, a feeling of repugnance, and a consciousness of being intimidated. None of the three moods went very deep; they merely, as it were, tickled the surface of his mind. On the other hand, he had to admit that, beneath his comic exterior, the fellow was thoroughly sensible, nor was he deaf to the flattery to which he had been exposed. He turned to Turpin.

"You're very silent, my dear chap. What's the matter? Are you sulking?"

"When interior decorators start speaking their little piece, it's better for me to keep silent. I find them a bit too much of a good thing."

The insincerity of such a remark was patent. Haverkamp had not forgotten things that Turpin had said to him in the great days of Celle-les-Eaux. True, they had been spoken in a slightly uneducated accent, but they had been a good deal more staggering than any of the sentiments expressed by Serge Vazar.

"Come now, Turpin," he exclaimed, "for Heaven's sake, no jealousy! I know you're angry with me for having asked this gentleman to our first meeting . . ."

"Nonsense!"

"Oh yes, you are! You're saying to yourself that you would have been perfectly capable of arranging everything with me, including decoration, and that when it came to details, we could have found some working carpenter to carry out your designs. . . . No, don't interrupt! . . . I'm not forgetting for a moment that you designed this studio for me. . . ."

"Perhaps you'd like me to remind you, too, that only a couple of months ago I finished a night-club which the whole of Paris recognizes as a masterpiece of its kind."

"And I suppose you'd like to decide on what furniture I ought to have, and how the curtains should be hung?"

"Why not? A dwelling-house is an organic unity. The decoration and the furnishing ought to emerge as the result of a sort of internal secretion. If they don't flow naturally from the original idea, they're so much monkey excrement smeared on the walls."

"Hello, who's making speeches now? I'm just a simple chap, and I can't help thinking that decorators have some useful function to perform, if only because thirty years ago there were plenty of architects doing their own job, though they cared so little about things flowing from original ideas that, once their houses were finished, they let their clients paint the walls with sewage if they wanted to, and furnish the rooms like pigsties, and employ firms which had about as much artistic sense as a jackass. It's only since interior decorators came on the scene that we've got used to seeing rooms decently designed even when the owners are devoid of personal taste. . . . I should be the first to maintain that the architect is the captain of the ship. But why should he pretend to know more about the engine-room than the engineer? Be that as it may, I don't regret having arranged this meeting. As a result of my talk with this gentleman, I see now that the whole question of the actual building may be modified by decorative possibilities which one may have envisaged beforehand. Am I wrong, Monsieur Vazar?"

"Indeed no. You have expressed my views perfectly."

In tones no less elaborate than those of Serge Vazar, though quieter, Henry de Belleuse remarked that, it being the object of a house to be lived in, the dominating consideration should be the interior as planned by the man who was going to live in it. None of those present, however, seemed to consider M. de Belleuse's contribution as either necessary or decisive.

"Personal pride oughtn't to enter into the matter at all," said Haverkamp good-humouredly. "What I want is for each of you two to express his own point of view, and then, if agreement can be reached, to march forward arm in arm. Come now, Turpin, don't be a spoil-sport. Let's hear what you've got to say."

Turpin assumed an air of injured innocence:

"What do you want me to say? There's nothing of the yes-man about me. It seems to me that if people like you don't build a country house when they want one, it's a pretty rotten state of affairs."

Since he was by no means a fool, he managed to impart to his words a kind of affectionate deference. He went on:

"I can perfectly well understand an impoverished nobleman patching up some old family barrack, but not a man like you with original, creative ideas." He sighed. "I can fiddle about with a Renaissance château as well as the next man and stuff it chock-full of enough bathrooms and mechanical bidets to make Francis I wish he'd lived four hundred years later."

"And you agree that it's possible to achieve a gay and lively interior while at the same time retaining the general style of the period?"

"All things are possible. If this gentleman here"—he indicated Vazar with a movement of his head—"wants to put a Chinese vase somewhere, I'll arrange a niche for it at the end of a great vista of communicating doorways which will set all the ladies gushing about the wonderful eye the Renaissance had for perspectives on the grand scale. I'll run concealed lighting round the cornices and flood-light the outside of the house after dark. If you have a chapel, I'll fix up a phonograph and loud-speaker in the font and arrange for it to play Erik Satie when the door opens. . . . Oh, I can be modern all right!"

Haverkamp laughed loudly. Serge Vazar tried to laugh. Henry de Belleuse smiled.

"It'll all work out," said Haverkamp. "And now let's discuss the town house. You won't have anything to complain of there, because I've quite decided to build."

"Have you any idea of the size you want?"

"Not exactly. I want plenty of space . . . say three or four times, at least, the dimensions of this flat. There must be good reception rooms on the entrance level, set well above the street. Not too many storeys. A garage to accommodate three cars, and a garden."

"Modified modern or extreme modern?"

"Oh, extreme modern!" said Haverkamp with enthusiasm. But on second thoughts he added: "Though I don't want it to look like a joke now and an out-of-date monstrosity in ten years."

Turpin shook his head and remarked in a carefully exaggerated drawl:

"You remind me of the woman who used to keep the dairy where I fed sometimes in my student days. 'I'm partial to artists, Monsieur Turpin,' she would say; 'they're my favourite customers, they are; but they've got to pay on the nail.' I see exactly what you want—the latest thing in houses, which must manage to be at the same time a masterpiece of classic architecture. Good! I'll see that the cook is given special instructions. . . . How about a site?"

"I've got several pieces of real estate in Paris which happen to have been left on my hands. But I doubt whether any of them will do. I must have a list of them somewhere, complete with plans. Belleuse shall look them up. But don't worry about the site. We'll find something, never fear."

"This is where I'm going to be a bit difficult, I'm afraid. For all I know, this gentleman may be able to produce models of his interior decorations without first seeing the kind of house he's got to fit them into. But, speaking for myself, I quite definitely cannot start designing a building until I've seen my site." Anticipating an objection, he hurried on: "Oh, of course I can draw you a lot of pretty pictures, if that's what you want—cottage for large family to cost 85,000 in easy payments; elegant detached house, Neuilly type, at 250,000; town mansion, à la Passy, 783,902 francs . . . and so on . . . site provided by the client. . . . But that's not the kind of thing you've got in mind, I imagine?"

"Of course not, but—"

"The first thing to do, boss, especially in Paris, is to decide on the site. And I'm not thinking primarily of the shape, which is bound to put certain plans out of court and make it essential to solve some of our problems in definitely unavoidable ways. What I'm thinking of are the surroundings. The architect who dashes ahead without knowing whether or not he's going to have a seven-storey block as a neighbour, whether the street is wide or narrow, whether the main aspect is west or north, whether the windows will look onto a city square or over gardens—is a charlatan of the first water."

"But that stops us at the very outset," exclaimed Haverkamp with an air of disappointment. "I must say I thought you'd be able to make a few preparatory sketches while we were looking for the site . . . even if they had to be modified later. Besides," he added, with more firmness, "they would give us some sort of idea of the kind of site we ought to look for." His self-confidence grew with his words. "When I've decided that I want a thing, I get it. I don't waste time haggling about how it's to be done. If the only suitable site is already occupied, I'll buy the place and pull it down."

"Unless the tenant is protected by law or has a thirty-year lease to run."

"Naturally. That kind of thing would mean a damned lot of delay. All I meant," concluded Haverkamp with a princely air, "was that I don't want you to start on the job with the feeling that you've got to skimp or that you are up against insuperable difficulties. Go to it, my dear chap, give the horse its head. Don't you remember how you used to laugh at me in the Celle days?"

"I never laughed at you in my life."

"Oh yes, you have. You thought it a huge joke when I used to call the labourers, the house-wreckers, and the masons together every four or five days for a pow-wow. But who was right, eh? Now, please, my dear chap, no more obstructionist tactics from you. Let's agree to meet, you and I, tomorrow evening. I've still retained an interest in my old real-estate business, and I'll send Belleuse along there this afternoon. They'll let me have a list of all the suitable sites in the west end of Paris that they've got on their books. I'll tell them, too, to make inquiries of some of the other agencies. Then tomorrow evening when we meet I'll bring all the stuff along, together with a list of the odds and ends of ground which stand in my name. We'll go through the whole lot, checking the possibilities. Then the next morning I'll call for you in the car, and in two hours or so we shall be in a position to say definitely whether any of them will do or whether we've got to look farther. It might amuse Monsieur Vazar to come with us."

Turpin just visibly pulled a face.

Vazar accepted the offer. "I should love to," he said; "though I don't know whether at this stage I can give much useful advice. Any views I expressed would be merely a personal opinion."

"Well, come or not as you like. Belleuse will give you a ring. Meanwhile, Turpin, be a good chap and just jot down a few ideas."

"What do you mean by 'meanwhile'?"

"Between now and the day after tomorrow. The kind of thing you can do in five minutes. Just rough sketches, of two or three general types of house, so that I can see what you've got in mind. I only want something that'll give me a rough idea. We can look at them in the car. They'll make it much easier for me to come to a decision when I've got the site before my eyes."

"You really are a monster! I don't call that sort of thing work; it's—"

"Real life, that's what it is. I don't know how your mind works, but when I've got a problem to solve, the idea of attacking it from several sides at once doesn't bother me in the least. On the contrary, it stimulates my brain. There's nothing of the bureaucrat about me, nothing of the 'passed on to you for consideration' mentality. I've just been reading the published report on a scheme for the new city-planning lay-out on the line of the old Paris fortifications. It's enough to make a fellow cry. It's so obvious that the thing these chaps really enjoy is niggling away at plans, talking, scrapping the whole thing, and beginning again. They're none of them really keen to get on with the job. I don't mind betting that in ten years' time practically nothing will have been achieved, and that, as a result of all this shilly-shallying, irreparable damage will have been done before they even begin— there'll be a rash of horrible little shanties and speculative building. I wish they'd put me in charge, with dictatorial powers. You'd soon see how I would call the tune. Don't start telling me that a few sketches are going to give you brain fever. . . . If Monsieur Vazar decides to come too, he can go over them with us. And I'd like him to rough out a few designs, with colour indications, by, say, the middle of next week —an idea for the dining-room, the chief reception-room, and the smoking-room, for instance."

"But, good heavens!" groaned Turpin, half serious, half in fun, "the thing's impracticable. What's the setting of these rooms to be—the moon? Don't you see that until he's got my general plan to work on, he'll merely be thrashing round in a vacuum? He'll be just wasting his time to give you pleasure."

A retort was on the tip of Haverkamp's tongue, but Vazar hurriedly intervened, with a sort of courteous authority. His utterance had become much quieter as the conference wore on. It looked as though his earlier trills had been deliberately assumed with the object of making an effect. On the other hand, they may have been simply the result of shyness.

"I fully understand Monsieur Haverkamp's point of view," he said. "He's not asking us to commit ourselves to anything definite. What he wants is that we should all of us set our minds working, and working fast. My sketches, which I can certainly have ready by the middle of next week, won't be worth much, but they'll be something for Monsieur Haverkamp to work on, so that he can give us some idea of what he does or does not like, and perhaps furnish us with some useful hints. That'll be much more useful than any amount of talking in the void. Of course I could just show him some of my old models, but the art of interior decoration evolves day by day. What I mean is that each one of my creations marks a step forward on its predecessors. I don't go in for mass production. What I shall devise for Monsieur Haverkamp's town house will be quite different from what I might have designed a year ago . . . and, let me add, from anything I might have produced for someone else. You may think I'm talking highfalutin nonsense, but I do like to adopt the psychological approach; so much so, that when I have to work for somebody I don't know or have only met for a moment, I feel sort of paralysed."

He continued, speaking now directly to Haverkamp:

"I know you'll understand what I mean, sir, when I say that when I have to decorate and furnish a house for some actress who has made her career in the music hall, and her fortune in its purlieus, my mind and my imagination work quite differently from the way they would if my job was to create the daily background of living for a great lawyer or a famous author."

"That seems perfectly good sense to me," declared Haverkamp, who continued to regard Vazar with every sign of flattered approval.

"I'm not such a fool as to think that I really know you yet, sir," went on the other, "but I pride myself on having a certain amount of intuition, and these preliminary contacts which I have had the honour of making with you, taken in conjunction with the indiscretions of rumour and with what I have been able to learn about your activities, will guide me in drafting my designs. If, when we come down to brass tacks, nothing of them is left, that really doesn't matter. Time wasted? Very little, taken all in all. Besides, I don't think it will have been wasted."

Haverkamp made no bones about showing the satisfaction he felt at so marked and so unexpected a state of harmony between the rather precious Serge Vazar and himself. Nor was he unaware of the sulky and jealous expression behind which Turpin was now entrenched.

"You'll see," he remarked with brisk cheerfulness; "everything's going to go swimmingly. . . . In less than a week our plan for the town house will have made giant's strides. . . . In the next few days Belleuse and I, without prejudice to what we have arranged about sites, will do a little quick scouting among those Paris and provincial agents who might have country places for sale. At the end of next week the three of us will get together again. We'll make it a week-end, going off on Saturday morning and coming back Monday midday. In my car we can cover five or six hundred miles in that time, including time for looking over houses, without tiring ourselves in the slightest. That's more than we shall need, because I'm not interested in anything lying outside the quadrilateral formed by

Paris, Deauville, Saumur, and Montargis, and I don't suppose the possible bargains are all going to be at the four corners. With a little luck we ought to have my country place by Sunday evening."

"Well, I certainly can't manage it," grunted Turpin, who was still out of temper. "On Saturday I've got to go down to the yards and see some of my contractors, and on Sunday I've arranged to visit friends in the country."

Haverkamp got up, walked across the room, and touched him on the shoulder.

"Come, come! Remember Monsieur Vazar doesn't know you as I do; he'll get the impression that you're a difficult chap to work with, and that's not really true. You can see your contractors on Friday evening—I've dealt with them a good deal, a change of plans is nothing to them. . . . You can tell your friends: 'That beast Haverkamp has got me by the short hairs; I'm terribly sorry, but I can refuse him nothing.' We shall have four meals together. I promise you they shall be eaten in the four best inns we pass. You shall do the ordering; and you shall choose the wines too."

# Chapter

## 2

### HENRY DE BELLEUSE IS TAUGHT A LESSON

When the two visitors had gone away, Belleuse said to Haverkamp:

"He's nice, my decorator friend, isn't he?"

"Oh, quite. I should like to see his work before I say more about him. He's got a bit too much manner for my taste, but that may be the result of his job. On the whole, he made a good impression on me."

Belleuse savoured the compliment as though it had been addressed to him personally. He ventured on a daring sally:

"I, on the other hand, found Turpin terribly irritating."

To this Haverkamp said nothing, but he pulled a face. Belleuse began to feel his way more cautiously:

"Of course, I hardly know him. . . . I've no reason to suppose he hasn't done good work in his time . . . but I can't help wondering whether he isn't just a teeny bit—soured."

"And why should you think that?" asked his employer sharply.

"Oh, I don't know. . . . I shouldn't have said he was in the very first flight nowadays. That night-club he made such a to-do about, you know . . . well, I mean, surely a really *successful* architect who could pick and choose wouldn't risk his reputation with a thing like that. . . . People say— But I don't want to put you against him. I can't help feeling, nevertheless, that you could easily have found someone more contemporary, someone whose name would have carried more weight. . . ."

Haverkamp frowned.

"Now you listen to me, my lad. In the first place, I have a way of sticking to people so long as they don't forfeit my confidence. Do you see that portrait over there, stuck up on the bookshelves? I've never

told you who it's of. You probably thought it was some young cousin
or nephew. Well it isn't. It's the picture of a nice young chap who was
called Wazemmes, Félix Wazemmes. He worked with me in the early
days. I paid him damn little, and I jumped down his throat pretty
often. He was as smart as they made 'em, and he never played me a
dirty trick in his life. I was very fond of him, and I think he was fond
of me. I'd never have sacked him unless he'd been guilty of something
pretty serious. The odds are that he'd have been one of my chief
assistants by this time. Maybe my right-hand man. But he went off
to the war, and was killed in front of Verdun, at Mort-Homme, on
the 9th of April 1916, leading his pals—he was a corporal—and singing
the *Marseillaise,* while the rest of us —I speak for myself—were carrying on business as usual and making money. Each year on the 9th of
April I send his good old uncle—a workman called Miraud—a little
present, with a line in my own hand—I never dictate it to a secretary
—asking him to lay a few flowers on the war memorial in the Saint-
Ouen cemetery, in memory of poor young Wazemmes. His grave is
somewhere near Verdun, marked by a wooden cross. . . . Then
there's Turpin. . . . I'd like you to know that I've kept Turpin in
my time. . . . I gave him a big commission, far the biggest he'd ever
had, at a time when we were both of us just beginning life with little
but our courage and good humour to see us through. I gave him his
chance. He would probably never have got half, a third, of the work
he's had since if he hadn't been able to say: 'I built Celle-les-Eaux.'
You've been hinting that people don't think much of him now, that
there are other, more fashionable, architects. Do you really think that
matters a hoot to me? I'm going to get him to build me a house that'll
be a stunner, a house in which I shall entertain all Paris. I'll make him
fashionable again. . . ." Haverkamp was on his feet, his head turned
a little sideways, his great nose thrust forward. He thumped the table
with the flat of his hand. "Turpin, let me tell you, is a fine fellow. He
may have got on the wrong side of us just now, but I've known him
spend whole nights at his drawing-board when I was pressed for time.
He's never played me a dirty trick yet, and many's the time, when I

was feeling blue, though he didn't know it, that he's talked me back into a good humour. He's a great scout, don't forget that, a pal who knows how to laugh and how to drink. I rely more on him, let me tell you, than on your decorator friend to make the party go next Sunday week when we make our little trip. And there's something else: if things had gone badly with me, and I'd had to tramp the streets of Paris, I know that I could always have gone to Turpin. Perhaps he wouldn't have called me 'boss,' as he does now, but he would have said: Don't look so down in the mouth, old man. I'm going to take you in hand. Damn it if I don't find something for you before a week's out. To begin with, we're going to have a bite of lunch in a decent place I know where I'm on good terms with the proprietor.' And he would have found something, too—managing a hotel or running a theatre or being a floorwalker in one of the big stores; he'd have found it because he knows everyone, and everyone likes him, in spite of what you've been told—and because when it's a question of helping a friend he'll spend the whole day at the telephone, beard people in their own homes, and threaten never to see them again if they don't listen to what he has to say. . . . Since the war I've spent probably more than sixty thousand francs—and God knows I don't regret it—to say nothing of the jobs I've given or found—just to help Turpin's various protégés— painters, designers, scribblers. 'He's a good chap,' he'd say. 'We can't let him starve. Give him two thousand francs for those two watercolours or that manuscript.'"

He finished on a kindlier note:

"So remember, if you want us to stay friends, don't try to make bad blood between me and Turpin."

Henry de Belleuse was conscious that the force of the storm had spent itself. He had been in Haverkamp's employ for only six months, and he was sufficiently sensitive to realize the lurking danger of such outbursts. He now looked rather sheepish.

His chief gave him a look and proceeded to show, by a rather boisterous cordiality, that all was forgiven and forgotten:

"Don't look like a puppy that's done something it shouldn't on the carpet. . . . You'd be better employed reminding me that I'm lunching with my lawyer. It had almost slipped my mind."

Before resuming his seat he glanced out of the window. "Odd," he said to himself, "to think that fifteen years ago I should have thought this flat in the avenue Hoche the top of the world. . . . I remember when I came away from Ducatelet's . . . and now it's no more to me than a bachelor's diggings which I want to get out of and set up house seriously. Life's a funny business. . . . Let's hope the luck'll hold . . . and it will, of course it will. Why shouldn't it? But I mustn't let myself be forced to climb indefinitely, always higher and higher, because . . ."

# Chapter 3

## A ROOF-TOP PILGRIMAGE

No sooner had Jerphanion got off the train than he telephoned to Bouitton:

"Hello, sir, is there anything very urgent waiting for me?"

"Not specially—no. Why?"

"Because I don't particularly want to come to the office this morning."

(He had sworn to himself not to delay his pilgrimage to the College roof for any reason whatever. "If I let myself be caught up in the machine again, I shall put it off from day to day and all meaning will go out of it.")

"All right. It isn't even necessary for you to be here this afternoon. I shall be out myself, except for a very short while, so that there'd be no time for us to talk. And there's a good deal we ought to go over together, eh? Tomorrow morning, then, and don't worry."

Jerphanion went back to his flat on the boulevard Saint-Germain, kissed Odette, asked after Jean-Pierre, made a hurried toilet, and was on the point of leaving for the rue d'Ulm when a thought struck him. Odette would certainly be expecting him to tell her about his trip. The only real excuse he could have made for going out again so soon would have been the necessity of seeing Bouitton, and he didn't want to tell her a lie.

He said to her: "I shall have to go out later this morning, but there's no hurry. Won't you sit with me while I have a cup of coffee? I'd like to tell you my adventures."

They chatted away for a good hour. Then:

"Are you off to see Bouitton now?" she asked.

"No. I'm going down to the College. There's something there I want to see."

As he had a rather mysterious air, she refrained from asking him anything further about it.


To the caretaker, Belplanque, he said:

"I want to take a turn round the roof."

"Really? . . . You think—?"

"Is there any reason why I shouldn't?"

"It's not very safe up there."

"As safe as it used to be, I imagine."

"Yes, but—"

"You mean I'm not as young as I was?"

"Well, not so used to it."

"I take full responsibility."

They went upstairs. Jerphanion realized that he had forgotten the way. Belplanque led him to a small door. Jerphanion seemed vaguely to remember it. He turned to his companion.

"Thanks. Now I can manage for myself. I've taken up enough of your time."

"No, no. I haven't anything to do. I'll go with you."

"The devil he will!" thought Jerphanion. Aloud he said:

"Really, if you don't very much mind, I'd rather go alone. I'm making something in the nature of a pilgrimage."

A worried look showed on the other's face.

"I suppose he thinks I'm going to throw myself off!"


No sooner had he reached the roof than he found there to welcome him the Panthéon, Henry IV's tower, the Val de Grâce, and a surge of memories the solidity and intensity of which were quite unexpected.

He could see again in imagination Caulet with his cape, Caulet with his head ever so slightly bowed. He could hear again the recollected voice: "Like a flight of falcons out of their natal charnel-house. . . ." Caulet's words, flooding over him from the past, broke like a wave. Nothing so amusing, so redolent of youth, he thought, had ever been said, or ever would be. Some savour had gone from the world since those russet autumn days of 1908.

"What a rare chap Caulet was! How many times have I seen him since the war? What a mess we've made of life, all of us. . . . The world is a black darkness. A few points of light that are our friendships, a flaming, secret belt of stars like that of Cassiopeia, is all, probably, that compensates for such an eternity of empty space. If the truth be told, half of my friends are dead; the rest I have lost through negligence."

He had climbed the spidery stairs, had reached the narrow platform intersected by low traverses. "I'm just a little frightened . . . as I always was . . . neither more nor less. Haudromont has done nothing to diminish that sense of fear, nor to add to it.

"A fine place for the ambitious dreamer to walk and ponder. . . ." The same thought, in almost the same words, had come to him, years ago, in this very spot.

"What, really, is the point of this visit? Have I come here to recapture the old thrill . . . to live again those unrepeatable days when one was staggered by the sudden vision of truth? . . . Rediscover and recapture, as though the old days were back again, as though nothing had happened since?

"How well I remember saying, in a letter I wrote to Jallez from the Rhineland: 'I feel completely unattached. That is the war's one gift to me: a new start. All roads lie open to me as they did when I was twenty.'

"One day at Mainz I was crossing a large square. Round it were buildings of red sandstone; at the far end a church. I walked across the square all lit up, intoxicated by that thought. Since I had not been killed either at Haudromont or elsewhere, a present had been made me of a brand-new life, untouched, unsmirched, just waiting to be lived. I owed nothing to a soul. Every paper I had ever signed burned to cinders in a great fire of rejoicing. The zest of my twentieth year was with me once again; I had sloughed off my civic identity. If I had kept my name, it was only because I wanted to. If I had kept my wife and my child, it was because I wanted to. . . . The great fact burst on me like a dazzling truth, one of those truths one feels must never be forgotten, but evoked by some magic word whenever the need arises.

"And what does it all amount to now?—to recapture the old thrill. Does that mean that I am to deny the declaration of liberty which I made at Mainz? Take, for instance, this pilgrimage: what have I come here to find?—the domes, the roofs, the great flat vistas of the city; the wind; enthusiasm, a sense of wide views and generous ideals; the feeling that great tasks await me, tasks that shall match the vastness all about me; contempt for all mean, selfish thoughts and the reckoning of loss and profit?

"And does my Mainz declaration deny such things? No, surely not.

"Other things too I have recaptured: the old vision of a lever—yes —the sense of energy pouring from me, forcing that lever between great blocks of stone, feeling its way in, taking advantage of cracks, beginning to press upwards, irresistibly upwards, till the surface gives.

"All that I have recaptured . . . retrospectively. I no longer enjoy in anticipation the sense of making the surface fly. My hand no longer itches to prize up and shatter. Why? Because I am older? I swear I'm not. Because now, in all this vastness, there are interests affecting my own personal life, hatching out beneath the surface I would crack? Perhaps, but they amount to so little. No, why make myself out worse than I am? It is not my fault if now, when I look on this immensity, my gaze is not impatient as once it was, but preoccupied and anxious, not now seeking the cracks and crevices in an ecstasy of destruction, but solicitously, like that of a frightened mother caressing her child. . . . It is not my fault if I have learned fear of what may lie in wait for our present world. The war cured me of the desire to destroy; and what I have seen of revolution has not given back to me that earlier zest. I find no pleasure now in thinking of reason as an explosive charge. I've had more than my fill of explosives. I don't now wish that justice should confine herself to rummaging in a heap of burnt-out ashes. Certainly that drab forest of chimneys over there is a deformed and leprous growth; I would gladly pull it down, but with care and a sense of compassion, that something else may grow in its place. But then comes the thought that an aerial bomb might fall upon it all, and then I'm not so sure . . . I weaken, even the chimneys become dear to me. . . . I want nothing to be done in a hurry. . . . I realize that my heart is full of fear for this great city hive. I value the work of dead craftsmen. I know that what a century has built a moment may destroy. I realize that it takes twenty years to bring up a son, to plant in all the corners of his brain and body ideas and habits, skill and prudence, tenderness and a million subtle images; and that in a single second one shell can send it all sky-high in a spate of flesh and bone. I've seen it happen; no one need tell me. I am interested in the living man, not in the fœtus, and still less in the future plans of spermatozoa. The great masters of slaughter have ever been champions of the fœtus, panegyrists of the spermatozoa.

"On that autumn day of 1908 I had no fear for all this vastness. To-day I have. Because of all I have learned since, of all that I know. I realize that humanity is a drunken old hag; that weariness will sate her for a while, that she sleeps off her last war amid the snores and hiccups of a nightmare, but that, unless she is prevented, she will start it all again. I know that if she starts it all again, what happens will be worse (and I thought that I had seen the worst!), that perhaps it will be the end of everything. However that may be, it will certainly be the end of our heritage, of our terrestrial loveliness, of the accumulated riches of the past, the return of the ancient nudity of earth, of mankind once more in embryo.

"I am like the scientist of long ago who proved to his own satisfaction that the earth revolves or that the blood circulates. Reason played its part in the proof, as water in cement, but once the truth is established, the cement set, neither reason nor water can attack or disintegrate it. My certainty has become something heavy, stupid, peasant-like, taking no stock of quibbles, or subtlety, of 'never forget this . . .' or 'don't you think that . . . ?' It is what men call faith.

"I came here to recapture the old thrill—true enough—but by that I meant an eagerness of mind, not a handful of formulas, because what I want is to enlist the eagerness that once I felt in the service of my present faith. Soon I shall be a man of forty, alas! . . . But I won't grow older. I am now thirty-seven. When I make my bow to the Chamber I shall be thirty-eight. It is no part of my desire that the faith of this man of nearly forty shall be expressed with any less energy than if he were twenty. That's really what the whole thing comes to. Naturally, I should prefer that my job, our job, was to build a new world rather than merely to save the world that we already know. But history has chosen the part we are to play, and we shall be able to build in the future only if we have preserved in the present. True salvation can come only through building. A man who constructs a dike to protect a village threatened by the sea does more true building by that single act of his than the sum total of the village masons. The man who can build a peace that will endure for at least two generations—and by that time the habit of peace will be far more surely based—will by the sweep of his endeavour give shelter to the makers of laws, the menders and rejuvenators of society—namely, poets and scholars—the functioning alike of beauty and of justice, the whole army of blind, ungrateful workers who forget that catastrophe would send their world sky-high.

"Of that I am sure—absolutely sure."

But even while he was saying this to himself, he felt the stirrings of an anxious thought:

"But others before me have shared that certainty, either because, having been born into an earlier age, they could summon to their aid a greater body of thought and experience, or because, like Laulerque, their power of looking into the future was more precocious than mine. Why, then, were they able to do so little? Why, in God's name, couldn't they have prevented the concatenation of circumstances that sent me to the Valley of Haudromont? Why couldn't they so arrange that seven years after Verdun I should not be trembling for the fate of my little son, for the fate of the little son of that peasant who questioned me in the mountains, for the fate of the massed and mighty city here stretched below me with its chimneys and its domes, of its homes and of those who live in them?

"Is it that they did not know? That, at least, is what I must believe; but, further than that, I must find out why they did not know. I must question all those with whom I can make contact, just as an explorer, setting forth to discover the Pole, questions those who went before him on the same quest and failed. I must convince myself whether it was their faith that was lacking, or the means at their disposal, or the atmosphere that might have spelled success. The mere fact that something has not come to fruition proves nothing. Every human invention has started by finding itself up against a blank wall. Just because a plague has not been conquered, those of little faith argue that it is beyond the power of man to conquer. As often as I feel discouraged and prone to doubt, I must invoke this spot where now I stand, this present moment of my life."

# Chapter

## HUSBAND AND WIFE

Jerphanion returned from his expedition to the College roof in time for luncheon. (His old profession of teacher had bred in him the habit of lunching early—half past twelve at latest—and he still did so as often as the changes and chances of his new career made it possible.)

As soon as he was seated opposite Odette, he felt that she was, very naturally, waiting for him to give some sort of explanation of what it was that he had been so obviously impatient to accomplish. Though she was not suspicious by nature, a habit of mutual confidence had become so rooted in their lives that a silence on his part at such a time would inevitably have provoked questions.

But a feeling of shyness kept him from speaking. His pilgrimage had sprung from one of those excessively personal impulses that are apt to look foolish when brought from the glow of the heart into the light of common day. They have an air of childishness, or, if not that, of self-conscious oddity. How can one make them appear to another as genuine and as simple as they do to oneself? The fact that that other is closer to oneself than anyone else in the world does not make the difficulty less. A friend met casually at intervals of six months or so may very likely be less surprised at one's sudden introduction of the sublime into the affairs of daily life; for it is open to him to suppose that, since the last meeting, one's daily life may have become imbued and saturated with sublimity.

On the other hand, he disliked the idea of lying to his wife. He adopted, therefore, the kind of amused and trivial air with which one refers, laughingly, to some piece of irresponsible foolishness of which one may have been guilty.

"You know, I hadn't, as a matter of fact, anything very important to do at the College. I just took the opportunity of going up on the roof."

"How odd of you!" she exclaimed. "It was never very safe even in the old days. Think what might have happened if you'd slipped." She added, on a faint note of incredulous irony: "It would certainly never have occurred to me that your most urgent preoccupation on getting home from a journey would be to make an expedition to the College roof."

Jerphanion thought: "Knowing, as I do, the impulse that sent me there, I find that remark of hers just stupid. But that's my fault. How is it possible for her to realize my state of mind?"

He turned to Jean-Paul and said in a bantering voice:

"When you're bigger I'll take you up on the College roof. . . . But you mustn't get dizzy."

Odette looked at him. In spite of his attempt to seem frank and natural, he looked, she thought, rather worried—more so than he had before he started on his trip. Not that there was anything very surprising about that. The trip itself, tiring in many respects though it might have been, had been a kind of holiday. Now that he was back in Paris, he was faced by an accumulation of pressing business, by the prospect of new and extensive responsibilities. In a way, of course, they were flattering, but, for all that, they must be giving him some anxious moments.

"Perhaps," she said to herself, "this expedition to the College roof was a harmless sort of self-indulgence, an attempt to recapture the memories of his youth. That's something I find it very easy to understand. But it's foolish of him to keep it to himself like this."

"Tell me," he said, "do you think a black tie will be all right for that dinner-party next Tuesday?"

"At the Countess's? I don't know. I don't move in such distinguished circles."

Though the tone was deliberately indifferent, it held a hint, perhaps not of bitterness, but at least of mockery. There was a faint air of concern in the glance he turned on her.

"If you're afraid," she went on, "that a black tie and dinner jacket won't be suitable, why not wear your tails?"

"I don't want to be the only man in tails. Besides, my dinner jacket does fit me pretty well, whereas my tails look like nothing on earth. When was it I had them made—1920, wasn't it?"

"Yes, don't you remember, you wore them for the first time one evening that we went to the Opéra."

"Of course. Really, you know, I ought to have the price marked on it. It's so out of fashion now that it looks pre-war. It makes me look like a country bridegroom."

"He actually seems quite worried," thought Odette. "He's afraid he won't be smart enough for his grand new friends. How he would have laughed in the old days at the idea of a little thing like that putting him out!"

"I'd suggest your going to a good tailor and having a new coat made if there was time. But between now and Tuesday . . ."

He looked at her again to make sure that she was not laughing at him. Then, with a shrug, "In any case," he said, "I shouldn't feel justified in incurring an expense like that just now. But I've got to make up my mind pretty soon."

An appreciable silence fell between them.

"When you wrote asking me to telephone your acceptance," said Odette at length, "you said you thought you'd already met this famous Countess somewhere. Do you remember where it was?"

In spite of his irritation, Jerphanion assumed an air of ingenuous detachment.

"Yes, it was that time Bouitton took me to a cocktail party given by a mining engineer who lives somewhere near the Trocadéro, at the end of November. Bouitton has mentioned her once or twice since, and her husband too."

"But you've never spoken of her to me, have you?"

"If I haven't, it was because she made no particular impression on me."

"I shouldn't have thought that a countess would have deigned to set foot in the house of a simple mining engineer—to say nothing of rubbing shoulders with politicians of the Left." She accompanied her words with a little laugh as though to cover up their only too obvious insincerity. "I know, of course, that when Papa used to give big parties at La Rochelle, with the Prefect, the deputies, the senators, and all the local bigwigs, he managed, as a rule, to include some sort of countess to go through all the social tricks, but she'd be only some poor little country countess. . . . Still, I suppose yours isn't anything much to shout about, after all. . . . Foulion? It doesn't sound like one of the great names of France. I've always heard that these barons and counts with names like Lambert and Durand, without any 'de' before them, got their titles some time in the last century, and that their great-grandfathers were probably petty tradesmen."

"You may be right—though I gather from the experts in such matters that the 'de' means really very little. It wouldn't surprise me to learn that these Foulions were a quite recent creation. It's a matter of no interest to me, I can assure you."

"Then you're wrong. The only point about getting to know people like that, it seems to me, is that you may learn something about the genuine old aristocracy, about a social class, I mean, that is something quite on its own and beyond the power of the ordinary person to imagine—even after reading Proust."

"Let's be exact and say: after reading *bits* of Proust."

"I agree. But what I meant was that there's nothing interesting about the minor or the bogus aristocracy."

"What you forget," replied Jerphanion, striving hard to keep the discussion friendly, "is that I am not engaged in making a study of the great world."

"Then I don't see . . ."

"But you should. I am going to this party because I have been invited and because I happen to have good manners. Even if it doesn't turn out to be particularly thrilling, I don't suppose it'll be any more boring than most things of the sort. What you call the minor aristocracy might offer quite a number of points of interest. In its own way it might be highly significant. And anyhow I know that Bouitton would like me to go."

"Why? Is the Countess one of his numerous conquests?"

"Not so far as I know. He finds her attractive, and to that extent she has a claim on his attention. But the husband, if I understood him right, is mixed up with certain business concerns along with a number of Bouitton's friends. I've heard him say, too, that the Countess prides herself on being interested in politics. She has been flirting, I gather, with the Left, and since she is in the habit of entertaining some of the important men of the Right, it is quite possible that she might have a part to play in the case of certain eventualities . . . in short, that she might be useful, though I don't know how serious Bouitton is about it."

"You seem to be remembering all right now! I'd no idea that great political issues were involved!"

They became silent. The mocking smile in Odette's eyes set a faint quiver on her lips. Jerphanion felt that the effort he was making to discuss the matter calmly but truthfully only had the effect of making Odette suspect him of dissimulation and insincerity, or, worse still, that it was putting him in the light of the peasant's son whose head has been turned by the thought of dining with a countess, though he is doing his best to conceal the fact. No matter what he said now, it would only add to her feeling of provocation and grievance. If they went on bickering like this long enough, no matter how anxious he was to keep the peace, sooner or later he would have to say something unpleasant. The only sensible thing was to keep silent and let this beginning of a conjugal disagreement peter out of itself. He resigned himself to the necessity, though he could not overcome a sense of sincere regret. He had entered on married life with the conviction that two persons who loved each other, who had nothing serious with which to reproach each other, ought always to be able to discuss any difficulties that might arise in a rational manner. The stupid quarrels which are a blot on the lives of so many couples were due, he thought, to the fact that reason played too small a part in their daily dealings with one another. And it was the man who was chiefly to blame, because it was up to him to give a rational lead, conducting all discussions in a cool and sensible fashion instead of losing his temper.

But now he began to wonder whether he had not been guilty of presumption in believing that an age-old problem could be so easily solved.

# Chapter

## 5

### HAVERKAMP WISHES TO CARRY OUT
### REPAIRS IN HIS PRIVATE LIFE

Haverkamp's first idea had been to invite that eminent counsel Lévy-Sangre to lunch with him at Lapérouse. The early stages of more than one enterprise in the past, both successful and the opposite, were associated in his mind with meals at that restaurant. It was one of the little superstitions which he allowed himself. But second thoughts had brought a change of mind. "A first-class place, of course, but not so fashionable as it once was. Wouldn't it seem a bit odd as the choice of a man as up to date as I am? . . . The journey there and back would make me lose a good half-hour. . . . Besides, I've been there at least three times with Emma, and it might seem in rather bad taste." He decided finally to have a private room at Fouquet's, and Henry de Belleuse had been sent to make the necessary arrangements.

"I hope you won't think I've taken up your time unnecessarily," said Haverkamp.

Lévy-Sangre broke in on his explanations. "How can you say such a thing? You know what a pleasure it is for me to lunch with you."

"It's kind of you to say so. . . . And now I am going to ask you an idiotic question which I hope you will forgive. Have you ever appeared in a divorce case?"

"Most certainly I have."

"No doubt when you were beginning at the bar . . . but recently, I mean. . . . I ought to know that, of course, if I read the social columns of the papers more carefully."

Maître Lévy-Sangre stroked his beard and, in the tone of professional suavity which he so often employed in dealing with his clients, said:

"Please don't apologize. The fact is that I don't often appear in divorce cases. It is not the type of work I invite, and the solicitors know that. When people who are strangers to me ask me to act for them, I usually send them to one of my colleagues. But if some old client does me the honour to believe that I can be of service to him, I certainly don't put him off. To be perfectly frank, I rather like the change. Business and financial litigation is sometimes exciting, but not always. Too much of it dries one up. Normally, it is lacking in human interest. An occasional divorce is rather refreshing. One's feeling for psychological subtleties ought not to drop below a certain point, and that is one of the ways of keeping it exercised. It keeps one up to the mark, too, in the matter of oratorical style."

"So much the better. You make me feel less guilty. In any case, even if what I am going to say doesn't interest you professionally, you may be able to give me some useful advice."

Maître Lévy-Sangre raised his eyebrows and said, with a faint hint of polite embarrassment in his voice:

"It is my turn to ask a question which, to anyone knowing the terms on which we are, might seem excessively odd. Does this question of divorce concern you personally?"

"Unfortunately, yes," replied Haverkamp, passing the wine as though nothing untoward were occupying his mind. "I have recently made an important decision . . . about certain aspects of my private life. I feel that it ought to be in tune with my general circumstances. You see, I'm not getting any younger."

"You? For Heaven's sake don't let us start talking about age!"

"I appreciate the compliment, but unfortunately I can't forget the date of my birth. I'm well past the tale of years that begin with a 4, and I have no particular love for the higher numbers . . . especially since I have a strong feeling that I shall not make old bones."

"My dear friend, this is a you I have never seen before—a regular romantic stage hero, full of sighs and sadness à la Alfred de Musset!"

"Come, don't exaggerate! As a matter of fact, I feel perfectly well, as well as I ever did. It's not that. . . . All I meant was that I can't see myself living to be a very old man, nor do I want to. . . . The long and the short of the matter is that if I don't settle down now when I am at the height of my powers, it won't be worth my settling down at all. To come to brass tacks, I have made up my mind to terminate once and for all, and as soon as possible, a state of affairs which, for many years now, has been meaningless, but which I have very foolishly allowed to slide."

Maître Lévy-Sangre looked out thoughtfully from the thicket of his beard. "You may find what I am going to say rather extraordinary," he remarked, "but at least it will prove that I do not habitually meddle in affairs that don't concern me . . . I never even knew for certain that you were married."

"Really?" The satisfaction in Haverkamp's voice sounded even greater than his surprise.

"I mean it, though I confess to wondering how I could be so ignorant. The only explanation is that the question whether you were married never arose in our dealings together, or never in such a way as to fix my attention. It's quite possible, of course, that my secretaries had to find out about it—as a matter of necessary detail when completing certain formalities. . . . Gossip isn't a thing, you see, in which I take the slightest interest. Besides, I don't let my attention wander. I concentrate on essentials. I can even forget what isn't central to the point at issue. . . . It may perfectly well be that the fact of your being married may have passed through my mind some time or other, but if anyone had asked me straight out whether you were or not, I really shouldn't have known what to say." He paused, as though worried by some scruple of conscience, and then went on: "Or rather, let me say, I did have a vague idea—probably as a result of something I had half heard some time or other—that there was some woman in your life whom you hadn't been able to get rid of . . . but I suppose I assumed that she had figured in some old liaison of yours, and since you'd never mentioned the matter to me . . ."

"I find that very surprising. I must have mentioned it, but you probably weren't paying attention."

"Maybe, maybe . . . it didn't seem to have any bearing on the matter we happened to be discussing . . . so I forgot it."

"What you say," declared Haverkamp, his face lighting up, "rather pleases me. I always tried to put the whole thing out of my life, and I seem to have succeeded pretty well." He dropped his voice slightly. "I even did my best not to think of it. . . ." Then: "Not that that's a sign of strength of mind; as a matter of fact, it was uncomfortably like cowardice. God knows that as a rule I haven't played the ostrich where difficulties were concerned . . . but a man may think himself strong-minded, and seem so to others, and still be a coward on occasion. . . . Well, be that as it may, I have made up my mind at last to have done with the whole business, but I don't want to have to think about it more than is absolutely necessary. . . . In fact, my state of mind is more or less that of the man who knows he's got to have a tooth out."

Little by little Maître Lévy-Sangre's face had assumed all the suitable shades of expression which went with his profession: kindliness, concern, a stern patience, and the severity befitting one who has to conduct cross-examinations. (It looked as though the very exceptional piece of fish on his plate would be absorbed into his digestive system without in any way impressing itself on his attention.)

"But you'll have to think about it," he said, "and very closely, too. It will be necessary to give me a complete account of the situation, and in proper sequence; it'll be no good your just dropping disconnected bits of information into my lap and leaving me to put them together into a consecutive record. . . . If there are facts of that kind, so much the better. . . . But what I want to get from you is the general psychological background. In a commercial case that sort of background doesn't, as a rule, matter, but in this divorce of yours it may turn out to be absolutely essential. You are the only person who can supply me with both facts and emotional colouring, at any rate in the early stages. You must tell me everything, however painful it may be, and you must answer my questions just as though I were a doctor."

# Chapter

## THE STORY OF A MISTAKE

Haverkamp threw out his chest and smiled with an air of bravado.

"The whole story," he began, "is ridiculous . . . it's been the one major stupidity of my career. . . . But anyhow, here goes. You said that you want to know everything. Nevertheless, I shall spare you the details because, really, there can be no earthly point in resurrecting them. You know how I began . . . how I started a real-estate agency, which I tried to run on new lines. . . ." (Haverkamp never went further back in his life than this. He drew a curtain over his racetrack days.) "My staff was a small one and I treated my employees as friends. Among them was a young woman, Madame Genticœur. She was not particularly pretty, though she had a good figure, distinguished manners, and knew how to wear her clothes. She was thoroughly efficient at her job, was a keen worker, and never minded putting in an extra hour or two, because she was anxious that the business should be a success. She had married, two or three years earlier, some rotter or other who had made her unhappy, and she had left him. I was very fond of her. I valued her admirable qualities. It's always my way to get fond of the people who work with me so long as they deserve my consideration. I felt that there was more in her than just ordinary loyalty. She had allowed no other man to come into her life, and, quite obviously, she was in love with her boss. I don't mean that her feelings were seriously involved, but the mild sort of affection with which she regarded me served to fill an otherwise empty life. I was neither flattered nor embarrassed. I just took no notice, or rather I took just sufficient notice to go carefully. You know how it is when a naturally warm-hearted man, not otherwise attached, finds there to his hand a fresh and personable young female who is not likely to make a nuisance of herself. I was fully aware of the temptation and swore that I would not yield to it. It wasn't that I foresaw difficulties in the future, but merely that I realized how awkward it can be for an employer to take as his mistress one of his staff, especially when she happens to be indispensable to the business. To do so means that he risks losing his authority and creating a bad atmosphere in the office. The end of it usually is that he has to get rid of the woman, et cetera. . . .

"But a day came when I forgot all my good resolutions. I accepted the gift she offered. Foolish I may have been, but at first there was no great harm done. I was careful to keep my distance during working hours. We met outside, but not very often and not regularly. I never spent a night with her. The situation seemed to make her happy, but she made no attempt to get a hold on me, and never asked me for money. A few little presents and an occasional treat were all she wanted. . . . After a while I cooled off and gave up arranging to meet her. No doubt she shed a few tears in quiet, but so far as appearances went she accepted the new situation. . . . She didn't ask me to explain, and there was never the hint of a scene. Quite possibly she was afraid of losing her job. I raised her salary and gave her a handsome present. . . . In short, everything began to go smoothly again. My business grew and developed. Then came the war. I had to take on a lot of new people, but didn't get rid of the old. Madame Genticœur had by that time become a valued colleague and an old friend. I had nothing but praise for her.

"When young Wazemmes went, and later when he was killed—you remember Wazemmes, I've spoken of him before—I began to feel very lonely. I was making big money, or what in those days I considered big money. I tried to console myself with the people—some of them important people—with whom I came in contact in the course of my work, but for the most part they gave me a pretty mean idea of human nature. They helped me when it was in their interest to do so, but there wasn't one of them I could really call a friend. At the end of '16, or the beginning of '17, I took a hard knock. Disaster brushed me, as the saying goes, with its wing. I needn't tell you that all the bluff good fellows with whom I had had dealings began to keep their distance. Two of my chief assistants deserted me. . . . I still had no regular mistress. Why? That is a question I find it difficult to answer. I had very little spare time, and I've never been in the habit of running after women. I had no wish to take up with one of the ordinary type of 'kept' women. As a rule they're no better than whores engaged by the month, who think nothing of deceiving you with the first man who comes their way . . . I found the simple, honest professional far more to my taste. One knows where one is with them, and they don't play tricks. And one has the advantage of variety. When I was a young man I always found it more amusing to eat at all the different restaurants I could afford, instead of going always to the same boarding-house. . . . Well, to go back to that hard knock I mentioned. Madame Genticœur was magnificent. She worked any number of hours overtime, including Sundays, and wouldn't hear of my paying her extra. One day when she saw that I couldn't meet the wages of one of the big factories I had started, she said: 'I've got a few savings. They don't amount to much, but if they'd help you over this bad patch—' "

A slight change had come into Haverkamp's voice. He drank some wine.

"Another day I caught her crying. There was no reason why I should think she was deliberately putting on an act. I was quite convinced she wasn't. Well, you'll understand me when I say that a man is touched by a thing like that. I felt that she was very lonely, and so did she. Sometimes, when we'd been working late at the office, I used to take her out to dinner. One evening we became lovers again. It was quite spontaneous. I hadn't planned it any more than she. . . . Six months later my affairs had got straight, and, as a matter of fact, were going better than ever. I don't know what came over me. I asked her to marry me. We fixed everything up in three weeks. She had got her divorce a year or two earlier, but had never mentioned the fact. To realize what happened, you've got, I think, to imagine my state of mind at that time. In the first place, there was, as I have said already, my feeling of utter loneliness, my sense of being unable to rely on anyone. I had nobody round me but rivals, enemies, or the allies of the moment. . . . And then, the world was turning upside down at such lightning speed. The past no longer counted. I was well on the way to becoming a rich man. I was raking in money by the shovelful, and limitless prospects were opening up. I was growing older and getting sick of a bachelor existence without a home or any real comfort. I dreamed of settling down. To put it briefly, I was ripe for marriage. But with whom? Suppose I'd turned my mind to some young girl of good family. In the first place, I should have had to find her, and then I should have been involved in a lot of social fuss and bother. For that I had neither the time nor the taste. Besides, I knew that no young woman with such a background would have married me except for my money. . . . The question of dowry did not arise. I could have made as much in three months as the best that a good pre-war middle-class family could have offered me by way of dowry. I had no wish to saddle myself with some stupid shrew of a woman who would have been for ever reminding me that she had brought half a million as her portion. Then there would always have been her mother. I could hear, in imagination, the sort of things she'd say: 'With my daughter's dowry . . . with the money my daughter had. . . .' No, as you may well imagine, I found a woman who owed me everything infinitely preferable. But the thing that weighed most heavily with me was that sense of the world turning upside down. What point was there in sacrificing myself to convention? The society of tomorrow would bear no resemblance to that of yesterday. The former rich would be the new poor, or the new almost poor. The plums of life would go to those who had carved out a position for themselves in the space of a few years, and what would it matter to them whether I married a woman whom I had employed at two hundred francs a month, or the daughter of a retired colonel? The men of my sort who were still at the height of their powers wanted novelty above all else, modernity; were intent on ordering the latest thing in furniture, on buying the kind of pictures that would have outraged middle-class people of the years before '14; and if they'd got to festoon the necks of their legal spouses with ropes of pearls, they'd far rather that those women should have come from the ranks of the workers, knowing the difficulties of life at first hand, the anguish and the joy of battle, the awful days when bills fell due and one galloped about Paris or hung on to the end of a telephone, the champagne suppers to which one treated oneself in a night-club because that afternoon one had landed an order worth a couple of millions. . . . A woman drawn from that class would be more likely than any other to stay one's comrade and, most important of all, wouldn't be likely to mince along later with her airs and graces and superior ways to ask for ten thousand francs or so. . . . I knew better than most that there were serious disadvantages about Madame Genticœur. . . . She was about my own age, which means that, for a woman, she was no longer young. . . . True, when I married her she didn't show her age. I say 'when I married her.' On the other hand, she had been my mistress and had no longer the charm of novelty. . . . I grant you all that . . . but I'm not the sort of man who bothers about unimportant details once he's made up his mind."

He sighed and looked hard at his interlocutor. "I wonder whether I've succeeded in making my behaviour comprehensible."

"I find no difficulty in understanding it," the lawyer assured him. He had been listening intently, with an occasional nod of the head. "I'll go further and say that even at this distance of time, and without having myself been plunged in the atmosphere of those years, in the conditions of—how shall I put it?—of general upheaval, which you rightly regard as having had an influence on your decision—I find the step you took a perfectly natural one. . . ."

"I'm glad to hear you say that," exclaimed Haverkamp with an air of relief, "because I've got to admit that what I did then turned out in the long run to have been very foolish, and I hate to have to confess that it was foolish all along and that only an idiot would have failed to foresee what would happen."

"Let me add," said Lévy-Sangre with an air of cautious firmness, "that though I am not a specialist in divorce cases, I have had a certain experience of marital problems and can sum up as well as most men the chances of success or failure implicit in most unions. My feeling is that there was every reason to suppose that your experiment would work out well. What you tell me of the lady's character, and of what she had learned in the school of life, predisposes me in her favour. You knew her intimately, and she, on her side, was familiar with your ways and your temperament—"

He left the sentence unfinished. Haverkamp found himself wondering whether Lévy-Sangre wasn't formulating in his mind some such question as: "Isn't my client well on the way to behaving like a cad? Isn't it more than likely that the fault was all on his side? May it not just be that he simply wants to get rid of a woman against whom he's got no real grievance other than that she isn't any longer young and is inferior to the style of life which he has now adopted? Oughtn't I to make him think twice before letting him behave like a swine?"

As a matter of fact, Haverkamp thought pretty hard during the two minutes which it took for the waiter to change the plates. Then he said: "I must now try to explain to you what happened in the sequel, and it may rather surprise you. You may be tempted to think that I am distorting the past in the interests of my case. But that is not so. I don't pretend to be a saint. At times I can be pretty hard. I know that as well as anybody. I don't take obstruction well whether it comes from people or from things. But where my affections are involved I am loyal—anyone who knows me will tell you that—especially to those who have played a part in my life . . . unless they have seriously abused my confidence. But for certain scruples of conscience, I should have settled this business three, four years ago. . . . I have done my best to be just. I have tried every kind of compromise; no one can say that there has been any lack of goodwill or openness on my part."

"I am glad to hear you say that," replied the lawyer. "Please go on, I am all attention."

"Well, when people talk of a radical change coming over the attitude of a certain person towards them, one often feels that they aren't being entirely frank, are leaving out some element of the story, some essential fact that might explain their grievance. You won't have to complain of anything like that with me. No sooner had Madame Genticœur become Madame Haverkamp than she changed completely —I won't say in the space of a week, but certainly in not much more. It would perhaps be more accurate to say that she began to show a side of her nature to which my attention had not hitherto been drawn. It is possible that she herself hadn't fully realized its existence till then. I had imagined that she would be contented, more than contented. In saying that, I am not guilty of being fatuous. She had married a man still young, in excellent physical health, and with no unpleasant surprise, as she knew, to spring on her in the matter of fitness. She at once began to enjoy a standard of living twenty, thirty times better than she had known as a single woman. Nor could she plead that she had sacrificed her feelings for money, that she had taken a step which nothing could make up for, because in fact she had long been in love with him, had formerly given herself to him unconditionally, and had quite certainly been very unhappy when they had separated in circumstances which made it very unlikely that they would come together again. . . . No, in making such a marriage there can be no doubt that, from every point of view, she had seen an apparently hopeless dream come miraculously true.

"Well now, listen what happened. Barely a week after our wedding she was already behaving like a woman who had long been accustomed to luxury, to leisure, and to being waited on hand and foot. She assumed the airs of one who has become thoroughly bored with the pleasure to be drived from such amenities and now sees nothing but the trivial inconveniences, annoyances, and unavoidable frictions of daily existence. Every day brought some new excuse for complaining that things weren't as they should be. We went off for a fortnight's holiday on the Riviera. 'How intolerably noisy this hotel is!' was all she said, or 'There's something wrong with the hot-water tap in the bathroom.' The hotels I took her to were the best that could be found, the sort of hotels she could never in the old days have dreamed of frequenting. Later, it was: 'It's outrageous the way we're kept waiting for the new curtains,' or 'I hate the cook; she spoils everything and resents my criticism.' When I tried to pass the whole thing off as a joke, saying that things weren't as bad as she made out and that we ought to think ourselves lucky to find any servants at all at a time when most people were hunting in vain for them, she merely said: 'Oh, of course you would take their part . . . it's always I who am in the wrong! . . .' I persuaded Bertrand to let me have one of the first twenty-eight-horsepower cars he turned out after the war. I don't say it was all it might have been, but at that time it was as good as you'd find anywhere, and we were objects of envy to everybody who saw us. But I got nothing but complaints from her: 'How uncomfortable it is!' or 'Considering what it cost, I don't think it's very good on the hills,' or 'The colour's perfectly hideous.' I was very patient. I said: 'You know that to have got the colour you wanted would have meant waiting another six months.' More than once I felt inclined to say: 'If you don't like it you'd better go off and find your precious Genticœur. No doubt he could give you a much better car!' "

"Forgive me, but isn't it possible that in a fit of ill temper—very excusable ill temper, I agree—you may have said something like that rather—how shall I put it?—rather prematurely?"

Haverkamp protested vigorously:

"No, I swear nothing of the kind ever occurred. I'm not a man to hide what I feel, but I am not lacking in self-control. If I did say anything of the kind—and I was a great deal milder than you suppose—it was not until things had grown desperate. I've given you only a few examples of the way she behaved. If I liked, I could give you dozens. Whenever I came home tired from the office, wanting a little gaiety and relaxation, I would be sure to be met with some fresh jeremiad. I won't pretend that I didn't pretty soon let her see how irritated she made me. If only she'd had the slightest intelligence, she'd have realized that she was ruining my life out of sheer stupidity, and was well on the way to ruining her own. She ought to have known me well enough by that time. I'm an optimist by nature, and I needed my optimism to help me over my difficulties. I've always loathed whiners, but I'm not an unfeeling brute. When there's a really good reason for people bothering me, I don't expect them to laugh and be merry just for my sake. I look at things from their point of view, and do my best to help. But I've no time for those who are never contented with their lot, especially when it's a great deal better than they deserve. Only twelve months ago I sacked a butler who had been with me for two years. I had paid him two hundred francs a month more than he'd have got anywhere else, and was for ever giving him extra little presents. I shut my eyes to a lot of petty thieving, and I had told him that when he was tired of domestic service I would help to set him up in a restaurant or hotel. He went about the house with the look of a martyr, the sort of look that said as plainly as words: 'I'm only staying on to save the master unpleasantness.' It was maddening. I go out of my way to make my people happy, and I expect them to show a little appreciation." He added, as a sort of marginal comment: "That was what was so remarkable about young Wazemmes: he was always contented. Any little kindness I showed him he accepted with a smile, but his eyes seemed to say: 'Oh, boss, I really don't deserve it!' "

"In the case of Madame Haverkamp," asked Maître Lévy-Sangre with his air of incorruptible impartiality, "you don't think that if you had shown a little more indulgence, had handled her in the right way, you might have managed to build up a workable married life?"

For a few moments Haverkamp pondered this question as though to acquit himself at the bar of his conscience. Then, without a shadow of indecision:

"No," he said, "I have considered the question, at various times, from every angle. I used to say to myself, for instance, even after our separation: 'Isn't it a little hard to abandon her like this? By spending a little more I could so arrange matters that we might live together under the same roof and at the same time enjoy, each of us, complete liberty of action. Loneliness may by this time have taught her a lesson, and perhaps she realizes that, even though we can never return to the old intimacy, it would be pleasanter for her if she could share my life in the eyes of the world, could go with me to theatres and play her part in any dinners or parties we might give. . . .' But I saw that it was impossible. In the first place she had not the self-control necessary to behave decently and to spare me her lamentations during the times we should have had to spend together. . . . And then there was another thing. She had absolutely refused to have her hair cut and touched up. She's becoming very grey, and among a lot of fashionable women she would have looked like an old woman up from the country. I could hardly have been expected to take her about like that!"

Without giving any indication of what he thought about this particular grievance, Maître Lévy-Sangre remarked:

"How do you account, generally speaking, for the fact that this tiresome side of her character became so apparent? Or let me put it this way: how is it that you had never realized its existence during all the years during which you had been on intimate terms with her?"

"I'll try to explain how I see the matter. . . . It seems to me that there are a great many people in this world who are temperamentally made for obedience . . . who can live contentedly only when the conditions of life are imposed upon them from outside, even if those conditions are comparatively hard. In order to be reasonably happy they have got to be conscious of some sort of pressure, of limitation . . . of constraint. That is true particularly of women. Without that they become the slaves of their nerves, and things that ought to give them added pleasure merely increase their irritation. When Madame Genticœur was no more than a member of my staff, she suffered, no doubt, from moments of peevishness in her small flat. I expect her concierge or her gas ring were constantly upsetting her, but there was no one to listen to her. Besides, most of her time was spent at the office. To be perfectly frank with you, I had noticed these moods of nervous agitation, but they were caused by things that cropped up in the course of business; they were an expression of her professional conscience and, so far as I was concerned, were an asset rather than a liability. They were part and parcel of the day's work. I don't think they bothered her much, in fact, I am pretty sure that she was happy when she was at the office—as happy as she was capable of being. You see, at that time she had an object in life. The possibility that I might frown, or that, on the other hand, I might give her a smile of approval or a word of praise, imparted an interest to her every day. I don't like big words, so I won't say that I was her God, but that describes a little of what she felt. As soon as the god became a simple husband on a level with herself—whom self-pride dictated that she must regard as being on a level with herself—the charm vanished. When a woman's husband loads her with presents which before would have seemed to her fantastically excessive, she does not derive from them one tenth of the pleasure which a smile on the face of the god gave her. There is no longer the daily occupation of work, the discipline of the office which has forced her to be constantly pleasant to employer and customer alike, the presence of colleagues who will send her about her business as soon as she starts complaining or becomes a bore. She has all the time in the world in which to brood over her grievances, and it becomes a pleasure to unload them on her husband, whom she regards as being there for that purpose."

Haverkamp threw himself back in his chair. "I suppose my ideas on this subject are pretty extreme. I am a man of the people. I support the political program of the Left"—he started to laugh—"I made munitions to help on the triumph of democracy . . . but that doesn't alter the fact that, as the result of long experience, I am convinced that a great many human beings, men and women alike, are born to be slaves and to find peace of heart in a state of slavery. To condemn them to liberty is to condemn them to a life of drifting; and when that happens, the price, sooner or later, has got to be paid."

Maître Lévy-Sangre's only comment on this pronouncement was a movement of his bearded chin.

"Her case," he said, "may have been aggravated by the fact that she felt herself to be growing older. . . . Isn't it true that a woman's change of life is often accompanied by disturbances of that kind?"

"Possibly. . . ."

"She must have known that there was the danger of your being caught by a younger woman . . . and when a jealous woman is faced by that possibility, the result is often to draw down on herself, by sheer tactlessness, the very misfortunes which she dreads. And now that the subject has been mentioned, let me ask you this: are you conscious—I put the point so that we may know in advance what weapons the other side has—of having at any time since your marriage given Madame Haverkamp cause for suspicion?—I am referring to incidents which, though to you they might have seemed harmless, could have given some justification to her ill humour, could have nourished her desire to get back at you."

Haverkamp thought for a second; then, with an accommodating grimace:

"No," he said. "For more than a year I was not guilty of the mildest infidelity, and even after that they were adventures of the most passing description and produced no complications whatever. I am sure that she knew nothing about them. Long before that our life together had become impossible. . . . It was not until after our separation that I allowed myself consolation of a more obvious description."

"Tell me about the separation. We are getting to the heart of the subject now."

# Chapter

## 7

### HALF-MEASURES ARE NEVER SATISFACTORY

"Things moved by stages," said Haverkamp. "One fine day, when I saw that patience produced absolutely no effect, I lost my temper. A little of the old fear, the old respect, came back into her attitude towards me. I told her quite firmly that I had had enough, that I would buy her a place in the country, anywhere she liked. She had often said that she loved the country. One of her most constant grumbles had been about the life she was obliged to live in Paris, about the way in which life in Paris troubled and wearied her. Not that I hadn't always done my best to help. Whenever we gave a dinner or a party, even when things didn't go altogether smoothly, I congratulated her on her success." He sighed. "Well, she chose Biarritz—that was her idea of the country. The advantage for me in the arrangement was that there would be no risk of my coming across her every few days. I found a nice little place, not too big, between Biarritz and Saint-Jean-de-Luz. I made no conditions. 'You just get settled,' I said to her, 'and have a good rest. I'll come and see you from time to time. When you want a day or two in Paris, come and look me up. All I ask is that you should let me know you're coming. And do try to behave decently when we're together. I don't want to have any scenes.' "

"How did she accept the suggestion?"

"Not too badly. For the time being, I had once more become for her the boss, whom no one dared to contradict. No doubt, too, she argued to herself that by yielding to my wishes she would be assuring her future. I had made that fact fairly clear to her."

"And how did it all work out in practice?"

"She seemed perfectly resigned. She was once more in the position of having to submit to constraint, of having to obey, and I think that as a result she was able to get the better of her nerves. There was nothing tragic about her lot. I had bought her a car, and since she refused to drive it herself, she was provided with a chauffeur, who would also act as gardener, and with a maid and a cook. I made her a generous allowance which enabled her to run the establishment comfortably. For a former employée earning two hundred francs a month at pre-war rates, I don't think that was too bad, eh? I paid her several visits, though naturally they were short. She too came to see me in Paris, where she did her best not to show her real character. I think she must have done a good deal of thinking. She tried to prolong these periods of our being together. . . . On one occasion I did give in. . . . But nature was stronger than she. The old poison began to work again. Admittedly, I didn't much like having her there. I had grown a whole crop of new habits. At the end of four weeks I said, without any show of temper: 'You must go back. That's the only way we can remain on friendly terms.' She wept and sobbed. I expected her at every moment to start a real big scene, but her courage failed her at the last moment. . . . I took my hat. It didn't at all suit her to be left alone in the apartment. The servants hated her and would have ignored her completely. . . . She tried the same game again several times, but I nipped the attempt in the bud. There is one principle on which I always act. When I've proved to myself that there is a radical flaw in anyone's character, that he is temperamentally bad, I'm not such a fool as to believe in the possibility of improvement."

"And of course there was always the question of her hair, wasn't there?" put in Lévy-Sangre with sly humour.

"Oh yes . . . of course . . ." said Haverkamp, rather nonplussed. "I won't bore you by going into everything that happened. There was one occasion, for instance, when she appeared quite unexpectedly. It was particularly irritating. I had asked some friends to dinner that evening, and among them a young woman in whom I was very much interested. I didn't mince my words: 'I'm very sorry, my dear, but you didn't tell me you were coming as we'd arranged. Jean, take Madame's things'—and I drove her to a hotel. Luckily she didn't start smashing up the furniture or drawing a crowd, as she was perfectly capable of doing. At the last moment something stopped her."

"How long ago was her last visit?"

"About three months."

"Um!" Lévy-Sangre pulled a face. "Was it her habit, except on this one occasion which you have mentioned, to stay with you in your apartment?"

"Yes." Haverkamp looked rather anxiously at the face opposite.

"During these short periods did she act as your wife? So far as appearances went, I suppose, your conjugal relations were re-established?"

"From the point of view of appearances, certainly. Sometimes even—"

"Yes, what are you trying to say?"

"Only this, that when I wanted to be particularly pleasant, I did actually play my part as a husband. . . . Put it down, if you will, to politeness, or pity, or to the influence of happy memories. . . . I wanted her to go away in a good mood. . . . " He gave a little shame-faced laugh. "I don't see what difference that can make."

"I'm afraid it makes a good deal. It means that your separation, from the very beginning, however genuine it may have been in your eyes, is without validity in those of the law. It might have been regarded as legal desertion had it not been for the fact that it was interrupted on more than one occasion. It is perfectly open to your wife to claim that intimacy has never really been discontinued, and I don't see in what way we can deny a statement of that sort."

"What a nuisance!"

"It might be should Madame Haverkamp take it into her head to fight. . . . Have you ever mentioned divorce to her?"

"Yes, often. I tried to discuss the whole thing on a friendly footing. I said: 'Really it would be so much simpler and more sensible. The present position is ridiculous, and it's awkward for both of us.'"

"What was her reaction?"

"She shut up at once. She wouldn't discuss the matter. I didn't want it to look as though I were bringing pressure to bear—anyhow, not at first—so I just dropped the seed into her mind, so to speak, and hoped that it would grow."

"And I suppose it didn't, eh? But when you did bring pressure to bear, she must have said something?"

"Oh, she did. She said, for instance, that there was nothing with which she could reproach herself where I was concerned; that it was I who had decided on the kind of life we should lead; that she was perfectly prepared to resume normal relations; in short, that she saw no reason whatever for a divorce."

"She would, of course," said the lawyer with a sigh.

"How do you mean, 'of course'?"

"She's got a strong case, and if she decides to put a lawyer to work on it, he's going to have an easy job. From sheer good nature you've put yourself in a position in which all the appearances are against you. You've let your best weapons be broken before the battle has even begun. Your grievances, so far, don't make much of a showing: bad temper, an impossible temperament. I know that in fact nothing can be worse, but it wouldn't sound like much in a court of law."

"I'm perfectly ready," exclaimed Haverkamp, "to take all the blame. What I want is to be free."

"That would be all right so long as the other party was willing to have a divorce. But that, it seems, is not the case. . . . If we could bring any real charge against her, everything would be different. We might manage to make her change her mind. If there was a chance that the verdict might go against her, her attitude might become much more conciliatory. . . . Don't you think that if you instituted in-quiries—? . . . Her life at Biarritz, for instance—has it always been blamelesss?"

.Haverkamp shrugged. "I've never had her watched."

"Perhaps you were wrong not to. Divorce is a form of battle. It's no good relying on the enemy's chivalrous behaviour."

Haverkamp thought for a few moments. "There may have been

some gigolo, some dancing partner . . . but if there was, no hint has ever reached me . . . not even in the form of an anonymous letter. . . ." With a hint of affronted pride he added: "But I don't believe there has been anything of the kind. . . . A year or two back she did start gambling a bit, at the Casino. . . . I can understand that; she must have led a deadly boring existence. I realized that when she wrote asking me for money. She'd got a number of debts to settle— nothing very serious. But it strengthened my general case against her, so I coughed up without any fuss. . . . There have been two similar occasions since."

"What sort of sums were involved?"

"Three thousand francs the first time. The second was, let me see, two thousand; the third, five."

"We couldn't make much of that in court. . . . Have you kept any record of these payments? In particular, have you got the letters in which she asked you for the money and explained why she wanted it?"

"The payments could be traced through my old cheque-books, and at the bank. I don't think I've kept her letters. I must have destroyed them. I didn't want to hand them over to my secretary for filing. I suppose I ought to have put them away somewhere myself, oughtn't I?"

"It's a pity; not that they would have amounted to much in themselves, but they would have helped to build up a favourable atmosphere. . . . Now, one of the first things you must do is to have Madame Haverkamp watched by a private detective. That will give us some idea what cards we may hope to have in our hand."

An expression of distaste appeared on Haverkamp's face. "I don't much like the idea."

"It's an elementary precaution. We'll try to make it as little offensive as possible. . . . But tell me, when you discussed divorce with her, did you get the impression that you had pushed her back onto her last defences? . . . Do you think it might be worth while trying another friendly approach before we proceed to employ cruder methods?"

There was embarrassment in the gesture with which Haverkamp prefaced his reply:

"Look here, I've got rather a humiliating confession to make. When I'm engaged in a deal—and I don't need to tell you that pretty big sums are involved in my business—I can usually succeed in reading my adversary's thoughts, or my partners' . . . and they're pretty tough guys as a rule. But with her, though she is by no means a woman of outstanding ability, I simply don't know where I am . . . and that's the truth!"

"That, no doubt, is because you attribute rational methods of thought to the men you meet in business, because you assume that they will think as they ought to think. In the case of your wife, though part of her mind may work logically, there are other motives to take into consideration. It's all a question of intuition, of guessing what part reason plays in her ratiocination and what part instinct."

"But I think my intuition is pretty good."

"In dealing with women one has always got to make allowances for contradictions, for the capricious. There have been many occasions in my career when I've had to handle a woman client. Even when I have had her complete confidence, when there was no question of her wishing to disguise her intentions, I have often found myself compelled to say: 'What is it you really want? If I am to succeed in this case, I must know what result you are aiming at.' And not seldom she has burst into tears and replied: 'I don't know. . . . I did once, but I don't now. . . . Tell me what I ought to do.'"

Haverkamp remained silent, his lips pursed. It irritated him to find himself wandering in regions of human psychology with which he was unfamiliar, with which he was entirely out of sympathy. He seemed to be gazing into little puddles of agitated water, shallow puddles, unimportant puddles, and he felt that it was absurd that he should have to waste his time in such an activity. He ought to have been able to get rid of them with a single sweep of a broom.

The lawyer continued: "Please try to give me a plain answer to the following question: What is Madame Haverkamp's game? Does she want to remain your wife at all costs, or does she simply want to get as high a price as possible out of you for this divorce? . . . What form did your marriage contract take?"

"We each retain complete control over our own property, luckily," said Haverkamp. Lévy-Sangre made a gesture expressive of relief. "But," continued the other, "don't congratulate me on my far-sightedness. When I took her as my wife, I had no idea that things would turn out as they have done. As I have told you, I had just gone through a pretty bad time. 'In the kind of life I lead,' I thought, 'a similar situation may easily arise in the future. Since I've decided to marry, it would be foolish not to take advantage of the fact to put away a little something out of harm's way.' I settled eight hundred thousand francs on my wife, and later I increased this to a million. With an unencumbered million to fall back on, I could always start again if my business failed. You see, I had no suspicions whatever of her."

"Good. . . . You're sure that there was no clause to the effect that property acquired later should be held in common?"

"Quite sure. I wanted to make certain that, should my affairs get in a bad way, I could arrange, with as little delay and bother as possible, for further sums of money and further property to be held in my wife's name alone. I am perfectly clear in my mind about that."

"But in fact you have never found it necessary to take any such action?"

"Fortunately, no. I have never added to the million which I've already told you of."

"That's a tidy sum, but I suppose you've written it off a long time ago?"

"Of course. And then, you see, I shan't have the same expenses now. . . ."

"I'm afraid you're not going to get off so lightly as you think! . . . But to return to my question: what do you believe she is after?"

Pausing uncertainly now and then, in a manner very unlike his usual self-assured attitude, Haverkamp replied:

"I don't think she's a mercenary woman. I'm not saying that she

wouldn't, probably, have hesitated to take me if I'd been a beggar. . . .
But she has never nagged at me to make more money. On the contrary,
security was always much more important in her eyes. What I think
she would really have liked would have been for me to retire from
business at the end of the war with two or three millions safely invested, a little establishment in Paris, another in the country, no
worries and no risks. . . . She was blissfully ignorant of conditions
today which force a man to go on the whole time making more and
more if he isn't to collapse altogether. She didn't think on the grand
scale. . . . And she wasn't extravagant. If she took to gambling, it
was only because she was bored. I am pretty sure that she put money
aside when she was living at Biarritz, and that she paid some of her
losses out of her savings. . . ."

"I see. Is it possible that she wants to remain your wife for reasons
of sentiment or pride?"

"I can't say. It's possible. But I think the real reason is that she
wants to make a nuisance of herself."

# Chapter

# 8

## A PLAN OF ACTION

Maître Lévy-Sangre sat stroking his beard. He was apparently giving full play to his imagination.

"Please attend to me for a moment," he said. "I am going to put forward a hypothesis, and I want you to tell me whether in your opinion it holds water. Madame Haverkamp is a woman who sets more store by a moderate fortune combined with security than by the pleasures and dangers of the kind of life you have made your own. . . . Probably she still loves you, though, at a pinch, she can get along without you. She is not by temperament so intensely passionate that she is incapable of listening to reason. On the other hand, she would like, in some degree, to punish you, so to arrange matters that your desertion of her shall cost you fairly dear. But it is the idea of this act of punishment that really matters with her. The actual sum of money to be obtained from you is of secondary importance. Well, now, is she familiar with the state of your affairs?"

"No. I should say that she never has been. Before our marriage, when things were difficult, I tried to explain the situation to her in detail. I regarded her as my collaborator. Much correspondence, some of it of a very confidential nature, passed through her hands. She knew roughly that I was heading for a crash, but she never got an all-round view of my business, nor did she really understand how it worked. After our marriage she no longer worked at the office, and she made no attempt to keep up any connexion with it. At first I used to tell her things, but she never troubled to follow what I was saying. If I told her that it looked as though I should pull in an extra million, she would reply: 'That's all to the good; but do be careful.' Further than that she didn't try to go."

"I hope you didn't speak too often of an extra million, because a simple addition—"

"No, I was just as likely to say—'that swine So-and-So is trying to bear the copper market. He hopes I shall unload my holdings and drop half a million or so on the deal. . . .' Let me explain the situation to you a little more in detail. My affairs have become more and more complicated and difficult to grasp. It is not as though, for instance, I just owned a great factory or a big shop. . . . I've got a little of everything: real estate, industrial property, various bonds, stock and founder stock which you won't find quoted anywhere— which I shouldn't want to see quoted—and interests which give me control—often indirect control—of a number of companies. All this represents money, in many cases a tidy sum, but it is difficult to say how much in round figures. Stock and shares . . . but if they were suddenly flung on the market they probably would not realize more than a third of the value at which they stand in my books . . . short-term bills . . . and you know what they would be worth if they were called in . . . contracts, some of which I may farm out instead of executing myself, though I can't tell you how many . . . and a good many currency deals, mostly short-term affairs too. I can reasonably look forward to netting a profit of several millions, but one can never be sure. Then, I hoped at that time to make money on the mark. A pretty fair mix-up, by and large. Today even a man who owns a straightforward factory would be hard put to it to set an actual monetary value on his property. There is all the difference in the world between a factory in running condition and the same factory six months later when the owner has been forced to sell as the result of a crisis in his particular industry. If that happened his plant would be nothing but a lot of scrap, and he would be lucky to get the price of the building and the land on which it stood. You have appeared in endless cases as counsel either for or against big concerns, you have had any number of company books and reports pass through your hands, and I don't have to remind you what a poor showing some of the balance-sheets make, or what tricks a board of directors can play with them! . . . But leaving aside all question of jugglery, if you asked me in confidence to tell you the amount of my fortune, what I think I've got, I couldn't tell you within a thousand or so, not if you gave me a week to go into the figures. . . . It's so much a matter of mood. When I'm feeling optimistic I'm quite capable of adding ten million to the total. How, then, do you expect a woman from whom I have been separated for several years, and who has no head for business, to know what I'm worth?"

"Quite so. . . . This, then, is what I suggest. Some carefully chosen intermediary—we can decide whom later—must get in touch with Madame Haverkamp and explain that you want to do the decent thing by her, that you are prepared even to make such sacrifices as may be necessary, but that there is a limit to the price you are prepared to pay, if only because there is a limit to what you can afford. He will hint that your resources are not as great as they were, that your affairs are in a state of considerable confusion, that if you were compelled to liquidate, there might be some painful surprises, and that the future, anyhow, is very uncertain. He could add that while your income remains at its present level, you are prepared to pay out a considerable sum in alimony. But nobody can say what your position will be ten years from now, and Madame Haverkamp would be well advised to accept a reasonable figure now to be settled on her as a lump sum. If you are right in your view of her character, she will be tempted to accept. . . . She might even feel anxious to have the divorce put through at the earliest possible moment instead of waiting in the hope of making things uncomfortable for you. . . ."

Haverkamp did not look particularly pleased at the prospect, hypothetical though it might be, thus held out to him. There were things in it which he very much disliked hearing.

"But that isn't all," went on the lawyer. "We shall, at the same time, be carrying on with our little enterprise of private detection, and if luck favours us and we find out anything, we shall be in a position to indicate to Madame Haverkamp that we have weapons which we can use against her, however regretfully, should she decide to be unreasonable, and that if things took such an unfortunate turn, we should cite her in a case of divorce with damages, and take the necessary steps to get a verdict. She will have to decide between security for her future and the risk of losing her case."

"That's all very well, but who is to act as the intermediary? She wouldn't trust anyone chosen by us."

"The best person for the purpose would be her lawyer, as soon as she's decided to employ one."

"You're not suggesting that we should bribe him to act against his client?"

"No," replied Maître Lévy-Sangre with a fine show of delicacy. "Public morals may have deteriorated since the war, but we haven't sunk as low as that yet. But if our own solicitor knows his business—I can put you on to an excellent man—it will be easy for him to give his colleague, in the course of conversation, the impression that we are not bluffing, that we are perfectly serious, and that it will really be to the interest of his client to accept our offer. Naturally, we must be prepared to do a little bargaining, but a lump sum down is always attractive, and never more so than in these uncertain days. What would you be prepared to offer?"

"Over and above the million which I have already settled on her?"

"Yes."

"I don't know. I haven't thought about it. . . . To begin with, I should be willing to make over to her the house at Biarritz as a free gift. Fully furnished, it represents a pretty handsome sum."

"Yes, and after that?"

Haverkamp threw back his head and frowned. He seemed to be struggling with a disagreeable thought.

"You know me," he said crossly. "God knows I'm not stingy, but I hate letting people get the better of me. If it were merely a question of buying my freedom, I wouldn't stick at two, even at four million, but what really sticks in my throat is the idea of having to give all that money to a woman who doesn't deserve it, whom I took without a penny to her name and surrounded with the sort of luxury she can never have dreamed of, who has repaid me with never ceasing complaints, and who already, as my wife, is in receipt of a cool million of my money."

He broke off. There was a look on his face as though he were wrestling with a knotty problem. At length, without anger, but with quiet determination and in the tone he might have used to wind up some discussion at a board meeting, he said:

"No, she's not worth that."

"You mustn't forget," said Maître Lévy-Sangre very quietly, "that this woman offered you her little all when you were in a bad way."

Haverkamp went on as though he had not heard (a faint note of anger had come back into his voice):

"Even if you assured me that the result would be the same, I would far rather spend the money on the costs of a suit, on solicitor's and counsel's fees . . . on private detectives . . . on—oh, I don't know— on bribing witnesses and judges, and . . ."

"Don't let your imagination run away with you!" said Maître Lévy-Sangre, laughing into his beard. "A moment or two ago you were ready to kick at the idea even of having her watched."

"I was a fool. There's no doubt whatever that she means to get all she can out of me! . . . When people try to blackmail me, I see red! No blackmailer can boast that he's ever got a penny out of me. . . . Remind me some time to tell you a story . . ."

The lawyer broke in on the flow:

"My dear sir, if I had an eye to the main chance I should say: 'All right, let's go ahead . . . let us crush the enemy by sheer weight of our artillery.' But I belong to the old school. My first concern is the interest of my clients. Let us look at the matter coolly and calmly. If I asked you to mention a sum, it was because I wanted to know the limits within which her lawyer and I could work. What allowance do you make Madame Haverkamp now, roughly speaking?"

Haverkamp had grown slightly less excited:

"I've got the precise figures somewhere," he said. "One way and another, I suppose, leaving aside the cost of buying and furnishing the house, I gave her, the first year, or paid out on her behalf, some-thing between forty and fifty thousand. Since then it has risen to between sixty and seventy, to say nothing of the car, which was a present, and which I replaced last spring. I look after all her taxes, too."

"Let us take as a basic figure, then, eighty to a hundred thousand, including everything, and bearing in mind the continually increasing cost of living. We will assume that Madame Haverkamp invests the money you give her in gilt-edged securities at four per cent."

"Why not five, or even six? There are State loans which at present rates . . ."

"The more conservative we are, the more weight our proposals will have. To ensure herself an income of a hundred thousand, she will need, at four per cent, two and a half million of capital. One million is already settled on her. We will offer her another million, and reckon the house and its contents as making up the remaining half-million. . . . Don't interrupt. . . . I think we ought to add, before her lawyer starts arguing, that we are prepared to go further and to pay the additional half-million, either in cash or in bonds, the house to be a free and voluntary gift on your part. . . . Please let me finish. When solicitors and counsel get together, they can put things in such a way as to imply that a given offer is final, and that the other side can take it or leave it. If I explain to my colleague the basis on which we have built our calculations, and the spirit in which we have proceeded to frame our offer, if I tell him that it was I who dictated this figure to you because I thought it more than reasonable, even generous; if I add that we have assembled a powerful body of evi-dence against Madame Haverkamp, which, however, we do not wish to use, and that we should much prefer to see things settled in a manner satisfactory to all concerned; if I give him to understand, in the strictest confidence, that if I were his client I should most certainly accept, firstly because a refusal will exasperate you to such an extent that I, your counsel, could no longer persuade you to adopt a con-ciliatory attitude, and secondly because your financial future, like that of many other business men, is uncertain—there are nine chances out of ten that my colleague, or the solicitor, or both, will go back to their client and say: 'Accept! Don't try to get any more. If you do, you may get nothing.'"

Haverkamp tried to say something, but Maître Lévy-Sangre continued before he could get the words out:

"You told me that you used to deal in real estate. Haven't you often had to say to some client on whose behalf you were negotiating a sale: 'Accept. It's a reasonable offer. If you try to get more, he may walk out on you and we may never see him again'?"

"That's true enough," Haverkamp agreed: "I'd go further and say that I always made it a rule to do business on those lines."

"Well, then!"

# Chapter

### HAVERKAMP DISCOVERS THAT HE
### HAS BEEN RATHER STUPID

Later in their conversation Haverkamp had occasion to say:

"I'll tell Belleuse to get all the documents together and send them to you."

He noticed that a smile rippled, as it were, through Maître Lévy-Sangre's beard.

"Is that mischievous look of yours due to the thought of my secretary?"

"Oh, I really hardly know him!" But the lawyer's eyes continued to sparkle.

"To tell you the truth," said Haverkamp rather shyly, "I find him a bit comic myself, and I make no bones about laughing at him. But so far I've found nothing to complain of in his work. He's more serious-minded than he looks. I believe him to be discreet. He knows how to deal with visitors. . . . You'd agree, wouldn't you, that he's a man of the world, that he has good manners?"

"And good manners are more important than bad habits."

Haverkamp frowned. His surprise had every appearance of being sincere.

"What exactly do you mean?"

"You must excuse me," said Lévy-Sangre with some show of confusion. "I couldn't resist the pleasure of making an epigram, and an epigram which shows that I am not really up to date. It would be a brave man who would use the phrase 'bad habits' today in this particular connexion."

There had been no edge to his words. He was speaking lightly, as ordinary decent people do when they are chatting. But there was

338

nothing light about Haverkamp's reaction.

"You seem," he said, "to be alluding to something I ought to know. . . . You must think me a perfect fool, but—"

"Surely, you're pulling my leg?"

"Indeed I'm not."

"In that case I find myself in an extremely embarrassing situation. I felt so certain that you knew. . . . I thought it was just that you didn't give a damn—an attitude which I fully understand. . . . That is why I permitted myself the luxury of what I thought would be an innocent epigram. But now it looks as though I had wanted to blacken the lad's character."

Haverkamp's face expressed a medley of emotions: a lingering trace of surprise, a longing to burst out laughing, annoyance, and a touch of indignation.

"Let's stop beating about the bush. What it comes to is this: that my private secretary is a fairy, and that he is pretty generally known to be one."

"Never having had an ocular demonstration, I am not in a position to swear to the first point. To the second I feel compelled to say yes. . . . I am not, as you know well, given to gossip, and if the story has reached my ears, it must be going the rounds pretty freely. . . . But I do hope you won't let it influence you."

"Influence—that's hardly the word, but it certainly annoys me. I have an objection to being made to look a fool, and a still greater objection to being the kind of simpleton who is always the last to know what is going on under his nose. . . . I have a strong antipathy to the type. Nobody could call me a puritan, and it's not the moral aspect of the thing I mind, but simply that the idea gives me a sensation of physical disgust. . . ."

Maître Lévy-Sangre could not repress a smile, nor entirely keep from it a trace of irony.

"You're thinking, aren't you, that for a man who feels a physical disgust in the presence of people like that," said Haverkamp, "I'm not very good at recognizing them when I see them? This fellow, Henry de Belleuse, was warmly recommended to me by a friend whom I wanted to oblige and whom I have no reason to suspect in this particular connexion . . . unless, of course, his many mistresses are merely a blind. One never really knows where one is. . . . When the young man was first introduced to me, I did, I confess, think that his manners were a bit elaborate, and that he was overfond of his own voice. . . . But people are always saying that I have no manners myself, so I thought that if my secretary had too many, the balance would be redressed. I didn't see how I could very well turn him down for such a trivial reason. I thought I'd see how he turned out on the job, and, as a matter of fact, he turned out excellent. . . ."

"Then what are you worrying about? No one's going to imagine for a moment that you took him because you are yourself one of the brotherhood."

But Haverkamp would not let himself be appeased so easily. He kept on saying that he couldn't just dismiss the matter from his mind, that he would be made to look a fool even in his own eyes. His expression was that of a proud and powerful man who has been tricked and now broods on revenge. The lawyer began to get uneasy.

"Don't tell me that you're going to get rid of him for no better reason than that. I should feel horribly responsible."

"For no better reason than that! . . . I'm quite capable of telling him to his face what I think of him. . . . It wouldn't bother me!"

"And suppose he accuses you of a gratuitous insult; suppose he dares you to produce proofs, says that his private life is no more your concern than yours is his, challenges you to show that he has been inefficient at his job?"

"Yes, I see that . . . and there are plenty of people just waiting to have a good laugh at my expense. . . . Probably the best thing I can do is to let him see that I'm not taken in, and to let others see it too— in particular, the friend who recommended him. I like being credited with having an open mind, but I'm damned if I'll be taken for a fool. As to Belleuse, I'll wait until he's committed some bad blunder before I get rid of him—which reminds me—"

And he proceeded to give an account of the meeting which had been held that morning in his office.

"I'm beginning to understand," he wound up. "This fellow Vazar is another of them. That's why Belleuse brought him to me. When I remember how they behaved together, the whole thing's as plain as day. It's extraordinary how one misses the obvious if one's attention isn't drawn to it! . . . What a confounded nuisance it all is, just as I was getting on so well with that Vazar."

Maître Lévy-Sangre took this opportunity to turn the talk away from a subject which he regretted having so foolishly introduced:

"I gather that you are planning big changes which may have the effect of altering your whole manner of life, the way in which people regard you. . . . I haven't given the matter much thought yet, but I am inclined to wonder, judging from first impressions, you know, whether this is quite the moment."

"What makes you think that?"

"If you start spending on a big scale it's bound to be matter of public knowledge, and there's considerable danger that, as a result, the other side may step up their claims. It might give them an awkward weapon against us. It would make it more difficult for us, in our unofficial talks, to put the spectre of your future financial difficulties in a convincing light."

"I don't agree at all!" exclaimed Haverkamp with a return of good humour. "You can say that I'm suffering from megalomania and that this proves it. You can argue that I'm heading straight for disaster!"

"Mm. I'm afraid that even if they believed me, they would reason in some such way as this: 'We should be fools to hold our hands. What's two or three million to a megalomaniac?' The Courts, you know, are particularly sensitive to that kind of argument."

Haverkamp relapsed into his former mood of irritation.

"Don't tell me," he burst out, "that I've got to waste another year or two of my life, perhaps more, because of this woman! If I've got to wait until this case is through before I settle down—!"

The lawyer replied by a noncommittal glance.

Haverkamp went on in tones of sullen determination:

"I don't care what happens. I'm not going to give up my plans. I'm all for taking the offensive at once, before people begin talking about my building schemes. I could tell you of past deals in which I stood to lose a great deal more than I do now, and was up against adversaries of a very different calibre. But I beat them simply by not giving them time to get their breath."

## ADVICE FROM AN OLD HAND

"Well, my young friend," said Bouitton bluntly, when Jerphanion had given him a full acount of his trip, "one thing's certain—your business is all settled!"

"Oh, one can never be quite certain, sir. My inferences may be all wrong; I may have taken at its face value what was nothing but superficial politeness. I know nothing of all the sharp tricks that go with an electoral campaign. . . ."

"You're not so simple as you'd like me to believe. . . . I don't say there aren't difficulties ahead: there is, for instance, the problem of your colleagues on the party list. You don't, I know, find it much fun to work yourself to the bone for a couple of damn fools. But I think that can be arranged, though you'd better not let them think you're helping to cook their goose. You would only expose yourself to their 'venjunce.' . . ."

"You know perfectly well, sir, that they don't talk like that in my part of the country."

"You mean that the local brogue is more like that of Auvergne? . . . I don't know your part of the country very well . . . I'll try to have a word with Vincent. He is one of your senators, isn't he? We'll find a way out somehow." He relapsed into a thoughtful silence; a smile showed in his fine eyes. "In your place— It's no bad thing to be the big man of a department . . . and sometimes, even when one is out to do a serious job, it's better not to have to run in harness with intelligent but rather pushing colleagues who are for ever trying to feather their own nest. . . . But that's your affair."

He got out of his armchair and started pacing heavily up and down the office with the air of a man who has just remembered the beneficial effects of physical exercise. "Incidentally, let me congratulate you on the choice of a constituency. Big city electorates are the very devil. It may flatter a man's conceit to be a deputy for one of the divisions of Paris . . . or even of Lyon. But in the big cities personal loyalty is non-existent. The urban population catches the infection of every political epidemic that's going—boulangism, nationalism, communism—and when that happens, nothing else counts with it, neither services rendered nor the glamour of a reputation . . . not even, and that's really odd when you come to think of it, the force of habit. The worst place of all is Paris, because it's the biggest . . . and the least stable. If I were a Paris deputy, I should never feel that I had any freedom of action; I should have no inclination to take a long view of the future. I should always be saying to myself: in two years, perhaps in six months, some Tom, Dick, or Harry, some post-office clerk or gas-company employee, will have swept me into the political limbo. . . . The sole alternative is to be frankly reactionary, for the only constant political influence in Paris is that exercised by dowagers and butlers. No, give me every time a nice country constituency with, say, one good-sized town of about twenty thousand inhabitants. That's the ideal, and that's what you're going to have. How big is Le Puy?"

"Twenty thousand, almost exactly."

"And since, sooner or later, there will almost certainly be a redistribution of the electorate by districts—"

"You think so?"

"Certainly I do—you'll be able to sink back comfortably into a still more rural division with no more than a half or a third of Le Puy as its share of the city population . . . where, by that time, you'll be a well-known figure on terms of intimacy with every field labourer for miles, and then you'll have a nice, placid life. Once a country electorate has taken a man to its heart, it's not likely to let him go again short of finding that he's—oh, I don't know—killed his father and mother, or is too obviously wallowing in Panama stock. . . ."

He stopped, looked at Jerphanion with a smile, and then, noting a wry expression on his face:

"Don't," he said, "put on the airs of an offended incorruptible. What I've been saying isn't so disgustingly low as you seem to think. It's not a question of ensuring for any given individual a secure position complete with pension, as though he were a civil servant—far from it. What I'm arguing is that no one, be he ever so sincere, enthusiastic, and devoted to the service of his country, can hope to achieve any lasting or even serious work, can plan to enlist under the banner of any noble cause, unless he has some guarantee that his mandate won't suddenly be snatched from him. . . . People are always complaining of the instability of French governments . . . and they're right. But the instability of governments is not the worst of our troubles. A statesman of the first rank, with brains in his head, could always manage to make a career and jog along pretty happily in politics, through a whole succession of governments in which he might hold various portfolios, and between times he could be active on different commissions, in party organizations, and even in the lobbies of the Chamber. I could quote you several striking instances. The only condition necessary is that his electors remain loyal to him, and that the ground should not be cut from under his feet. He might occasionally be defeated at the polls, but he could always make a come-back, and while he was out, there would be nothing to prevent him from nursing the constituency. But things are beginning to be different now, as you'll see when you get into Parliament. A crack has developed in the political fabric, and you will find it affecting your own position. It can be mended, but the join shows for a pretty long time. Unless you happen to be one of the three or four party chiefs whom the country can't do without, you'll never again enjoy the solid security of the member who in the old days could keep his seat for twenty or thirty years without ever having to pay a visit to his electors."

Once again Bouitton glanced at Jerphanion in high good humour.

"I am telling you all this," he said, scratching his nose, "because you're going to be a newcomer, and there's always something you can learn from the old hands."

# Chapter

## 11

### TO WHICH THE NEWCOMER REPLIES

"Do you mind if I say something, sir?"

"Go ahead, my boy."

"I'm afraid you may not like it."

Bouitton looked anxious. "Never mind, let's have it."

"It's only an impression—and like many impressions, it may be unfair. You see, I'm very fond of you, and I should hate to think anything I didn't say straight out. . . . I've got a sort of a feeling—it's so difficult to put these things into words—one or two things gave me an idea—things often of no importance in themselves—for instance, what you said about constituencies . . . and that's not the only one . . . it's really more the general trend of what you've been saying . . . well, what it comes to is you make me feel that there's a good deal of scepticism and conservatism in your attitude."

"So that's it!"

"I'm sure you don't mean to—and anyhow, the words I used were very crude—let me try to explain. My feeling is all the stronger because, although I'm not yet in Parliament—touch wood—I've already, as you know, had a good deal to do with politicians, and perfectly sincerely I've always looked on you as one of the very few men in public life who still have genuine faith, a power of enthusiasm, and a really open mind where the future is concerned. . . . I remember, for instance, that when we were in Russia together, it was always you who were marked by an elasticity of mind."

"That's quite enough sugar . . . let's get to the pill . . ."

"It seems to me, hearing you talk of French political life, of the French system, and noting your attitude to the future . . . that you are more or less dominated by the idea—I don't say consciously; in your case it's a sort of reflex action—that our old habits of thought will go on just the same or will be given a new lease of life; that we ought to envisage as little change as possible . . . and that the safe course is to put up with a bad job." He hurried on in order to anticipate a possible interruption. "Please don't misunderstand me. I'm not forgetting for a moment that when you think calmly about these things, when you survey the general problem, no man of my acquaintance is more sympathetic to the heroic solution, and less likely to be easily frightened. It's as though, deep down in yourself, at the level of instinctive wisdom, you were persuaded that the only sensible thing, for France at least, is to go ambling along in the old rut of the Third Republic, bogged up to the ankles and carrying a lot of extra weight . . . that there is no need for us to modify our habits of thought, our prejudices, and our traditional vices. . . . "

Bouitton, very upright, his legs well apart, his hands behind his back, his head thrown back, his eyes fixed absent-mindedly on the window, choked back an angry protest. His nostrils still twitched from the effort of self-control.

"I was on the point of saying: 'Damn your cheek,' young man, but on second thoughts I'm not so sure that you haven't laid your finger on a contradiction in my nature. There's one side of me that believes in the need for changes, big changes, based on reason. I am convinced that certain deep-seated evils of the times can be cured only by violent remedies . . . or by drastic surgery. I feel this so strongly that when people ask me about the Russians, I find it difficult to argue that they could have got rid of the old system by less violent means. At the same time, being familiar with certain periods of history, not in a generalized, philosophical way, but as instances of the living, human adventure, I find myself forced to admit that mankind has had to pay a very high, sometimes an appalling price for revolutionary changes. When I see France, our poor France, in the state she is in as a result of the war"—with growing excitement—"and we must never forget, my boy—I can say this to you because we are both of us republicans to the backbone, both of us children of the Revolution—that France has never completely recovered from the shocks to which she was exposed between 1789 and 1815. I'm not thinking only of her population, of the fecundity of her people, of their zest for life, and the rest of it, but also of certain internal schisms, of the morbid and incurable violence of attitude between the Right and the Left. There are times when one is tempted to think that in making her Revolution, France was really working for the profit of the foreigner, that her neighbours have really got as much as she from the human benefits to which she gave birth with blood and sweat, without having to pay the same awful price. I'm always hearing young people of your generation saying that another violent political and social upheaval would give France back her vitality and set her feet firmly on the path of the future. . . . But I can't believe it. That sort of talk is all very specious, very heady . . . but my common sense protests."

At this point Jerphanion hastened to assure his chief that he was inclined, with certain minor modifications, to agree; that one of the things he most frequently said when addressing audiences which might be suspected of holding extremist views, was: "France failed, or didn't know how, to spare herself the horrors of war. Let her at least be spared the horrors of revolution. If further terrible experiences are necessary for mankind in its forward march—a by no means justifiable assumption—let us see to it that this time France shall be a pupil in the bloody school of others, weighing the arguments for and against, and wisely profiting from their lessons, herself undisturbed. She has earned a rest." But when he had spoken, awhile back, of an unconscious tendency to scepticism and conservatism, he had been thinking of a thoughtless, a dangerous, a heretical application of this legitimate doctrine of prudence. Surely there was a great gulf fixed between wishing to spare the country a revolution from which it might never recover, and seeing her slip back into the old rut, and, in particular, getting into the state of mind that regarded the accidental features, the peculiar vices, of the parliamentary system as laws of nature which it would be foolish to try to resist.

"Yes, I see," said Bouitton. "Like most old hands, I suppose I've got a certain attitude of indulgence, almost of tenderness, for the routine in which I have been brought up. And I can't altogether get out of my mind the conviction that the weaknesses and vices of which we are talking, and with the bad side of which we are only too familiar, would be replaced by others fraught with a danger no less for being at present unknown. Call it scepticism if you like. I should prefer to say modesty, but"—there was a hint of kindly mischief in his smile—"you've forgotten one thing. . . . In the electoral campaign of the party, in its future political program, and in the influence it may have upon events, you are going to play not a very dazzling part, perhaps, but a part that will be important and far-reaching. And to whom do you owe that? . . . Do you really think that if I were sincerely opposed to necessary changes and daring solutions, I should have pushed you forward as I have done? I'm not a fool. I've got a pretty shrewd idea of what kind of chap you are. You have your ambitions, but you are not merely an ambitious politician. You dream of doing great and useful things, not simply of making a brilliant career. I'm inclined to believe that the thought of a brilliant career plays no part in your mental make-up. That'll come of itself, but only in so far as you need it as an aid to your schemes. . . . In fact, what it all comes to is that you're a damn dangerous fellow!"

"I don't follow you."

"Oh, come! Descartes himself couldn't reason more lucidly. The man who is ambitious and nothing more is not, as a rule, dangerous, or not to his rivals. Why? Because, his object being merely to arrive, he puts all his energy into using what means he finds to his hand. Unless he's an embittered failure with nothing further to hope for from normal methods, it is not to his interest to send the rules of the game sky-high. The resulting chaos would merely leave him confronted by unfamiliar problems and unknown opponents thrown up by the convulsion. He would have to start planning all over again from scratch."

"He's putting into words almost exactly the thoughts I once had," said Jerphanion to himself. "How very extraordinary! . . . When was it, now?—I know, it was when I was up on the College roof that autumn day of 1908. . . ."

Bouitton went on: "Whereas a man who is working towards an impersonal goal which he feels himself destined to attain *is* dangerous. I don't think you can deny that, my boy?"

"You mean—"

"I mean that he is dangerous to all who in their heart of hearts mistrust any fundamental change, for the conservative-minded, to be precise, and for the sceptics. Since, then, I have pushed you, it follows that I must be a conservative, a sceptic, and a fool, all at the same time. You can hardly refuse to admit that I'm the last, since you have yourself told me that I am both the former."

Jerphanion felt both flattered and touched. He said quietly:

"You're perfectly right, sir. Please forgive me. I was unfair. I've never really doubted your fundamental beliefs. If I have seemed to, that is because I expressed myself badly. I was only wondering whether, sooner or later, political life didn't create, even in the best of men, a habit of accepting traditional errors, an involuntary and almost superstitious dislike of changes, however small. . . . I have more than once had occasion to discuss with public men of your generation certain obvious faults in the Constitution of 1875, very partial faults which could quite easily be corrected without tampering with the essential design of the structure. . . . All of them agreed with me in theory. All admitted that such limited changes as I suggested would cost little and would result in great improvements. But when I replied: 'What are you waiting for, then?' they one and all began to look terrified—began, in short, to look like conservatives."

"And very naturally, my boy. A constitution is very much like a young girl, who is respectable only so long as she is a virgin. But, unlike a young girl, the longer its virginity is left to mature, the greater the respect with which it is treated. Let but an impious hand be laid upon it, the sacred character disappears. All the restless and evil-intentioned individuals within sight begin to erupt. The heavens rain projects of reform each week. Why not this? And if this, why not that? Nothing can stand against the advancing hordes. Betterment specialists thrive like mites in a cheese. The responsibility which lies at the door of those who took the first step is no light one. A tendency to hesitate seems to me more than natural. This Republic of ours has already given signs that the central pillars of the structure are not too strong."

"All right, then; let us take a page out of the Church's book, and keep our hands from the sacred texts. But at least let us try to follow the Church's example by getting as much out of them as we can. What really infuriates me is to hear these same people screaming like a lot of frightened birds when I merely suggest that the Constitution of '75 be worked for what it is worth, which is no more than they are willing to grant in theory. . . . I am no friend of Millerand's. . . . I regard it as most unfortunate that he should have been elected President of the Republic. That's another story. But I maintain that he is fully justified in exercising without exception the powers which he holds by right of the Constitution. If his predecessors were a lot of nonentities and let them rust unused, so much the worse for them. If he takes them out and cleans them, more strength to his elbow, say I! It's up to us to choose better next time and get a man who will make a better use of them. But to talk, as people do, of a *coup d'État,* to nickname him the President of the 2nd of December, seems to me just stupid. . . ."

"Wait a moment, my friend! You forget that that is one of our deadliest electoral weapons. Poincaré enjoys now a popularity which he never had before—and why? Because the country sees him in the light shed by Millerand, by Millerand the *coup d'État* President, by Millerand who started out by betraying his socialist friends and would like to end by strangling the Republic. What a spring-board for our speechifiers, what a sure means of waking a sleepy audience to enthusiasm! . . . It's the very thing that gives our program its maximum driving power. . . . People never get so excited as when one can egg them on to demolish some Bastille or other. . . . Admittedly, Millerand isn't much as a Bastille. . . . His walls, at best, are of cardboard. But the good workman doesn't quarrel with his tools; let us have no nonsense of that sort, my lad!"

There was a note almost of bitterness in Jerphanion's voice as he interrupted the other:

"Well, it's a miserable state of affairs! It's not my idea of what the Republic stands for or of the way we should educate the democracy. In my view, we ought to tell the people nothing but the truth, to rouse it to enthusiasm or anger by using only such arguments as we ourselves know to be genuine. I loathe the bogus in no matter what form it may appear. . . ."

"My dear, earnest young undergraduate, come off it!"

"No, but when I spoke in the villages to my future constituents—and they weren't by any means 'undergraduates,' but just honest, simple souls—I told them nothing but what I took to be the truth. . . ."

"Hm!"

"You must believe that, please!"

"And again I say 'Hm,' not to be offensive, but because I don't want you to treat this truth of which you speak lightly. 'Thou shalt not take the name of the Lord thy God in vain.' I have never heard you speak in public, but could you, my dear boy, take a solemn oath that you have never overstressed an argument in order to give it more punch, never played on a single string when you thought that by so doing you could rouse your audience or get it where you wanted it? Can you even lay your hand on your heart and swear that you have never played on the Millerand note?"

Jerphanion, aware that his conscience was stirring uneasily, felt the colour rushing to his face. Hurriedly he tried to remember. Yes, during more than one of his public appearances, perhaps during all of them, he had mentioned the case of Millerand. Could he really say that he had never worked up facile effects of indignation? Had he not failed to distinguish between Millerand the man, who was rightly suspect, and the perfectly justifiable experiment made by the President to operate to the full the Constitution of the Republic, even when he had been talking to the school-teachers of Le Puy, who were perfectly capable of grasping the subtle difference, whom he had invited to follow the working of his own mind when engaged on many a different but no less delicate analysis? He dared not answer. Memory shirked the issue, memory mocked him.

"Of course," he said rather uncomfortably, "when one's talking on the spur of the moment, one can't always weigh one's words. . . . I admit, too, that sometimes one gets carried away by one's audience. . . . But there's the whale of a difference between a thing like that, which one can't avoid, and a deliberate staging of propaganda. . . ."

"Naturally, naturally! . . . But let me give you a word of advice. In your place I should be very careful not to make too much of these scruples of yours, and of others like them, when you are dealing with the fire-eaters of the party. Otherwise you may take the heart out of them. They will think that you are lukewarm, that you lack the fighting spirit." Bouitton's laugh was a shade more hearty than it need have been. "Come now, don't let an excess of puritanism spoil the chance which I've put in your way. . . . In any case, you're not a Protestant, are you, even though you do come from the Cévennes?"

"No, we're all Catholics where I come from. But we have Protestant neighbours, and there may have been a few among my antecedents."

"Really, now—and I suppose there are still traces of the poison in your blood! Ha ha!"

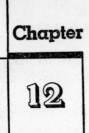
### THE FUTURE OF FRANCE

Once again Bouitton became serious.

"Now listen to me. We're playing for big stakes. It would be absurd to lose the fight for the sake of a few fine gestures better suited to the days when soldiers fought in lace and ruffles." He could see that Jerphanion was deep in thought, and he pressed his point. "I suppose you do agree that the stakes are big?"

"Of course I do. I was only thinking that the Chamber which emerges from the next elections is going to decide our fate and, indirectly, the fate of Europe, for a long time to come—for a far longer time than its own Parliamentary life. . . ."

"A historic Chamber, eh?" said Bouitton with a bellow of laughter.

"If you like to put it that way."

"Certainly it would be historic if you're in it."

Jerphanion, faintly riled by his leader's mockery, began again in the calm manner of a lecturer demonstrating a theorem:

"As I see it, this Chamber is going to decide whether France is to sulk in her tent and remain on the defensive, or whether she is to take the lead in the reconstruction of Europe. She will never have a better chance of 'declaring peace on the whole world,' to use Michelet's phrase. But what I'm thinking of is a declaration of peace that shall be as rich in consequences as a declaration of war; in other words, a declaration that shall be followed at once by energetic action and the throwing of every available man and machine into the battle. . . ."

It was Bouitton's turn to become thoughtful. He sat down again, biting his leavy lip and wrinkling his great forehead.

"You don't agree, sir?"

"Oh, I do ... I do...."

Jerphanion warmed to his task:

"I am going to ask you two or three questions, and I should like you to answer them with a plain yes or no. First: is or is not our civilization doomed if it lets itself be pushed into a new world war?"

Bouitton replied slowly:

"Probably, yes. ... Even if it struggles through once more, it will be at the cost of such agonies, such mutilation, that one is inclined to wonder whether the game will be worth the candle."

"Good. Second: do you feel, more than five years after the Armistice, that things are settling themselves, and that we've only got to keep alive to see all turn out for the best?"

"No, I would hardly go that far."

"Third: if France does not take the initiative, will other countries have the will and the means to do so?"

"That's doubtful. ..." Bouitton raised his eyebrows, and a change took place in both his tone and his expression. "What it comes to is that you want to make peace the chief plank in our political program?"

"If by that you mean a positive and well-organized peace, I can't say yes too strongly. I don't mean that the idea of peace should be our only plank, but that it should be the chief one. We shouldn't be timid about declaring that everything else is conditioned by it and secondary to it."

"Ye-es."

"You don't agree?"

"I think it might make a good fighting point. It'll win over the ex-service men and get an enormous amount of support from all elements of the population. ..."

"Look here, sir, you're getting me all wrong. I don't look on this matter as an electoral trick to catch votes. To me it's God's truth, and terribly urgent." His heart started to hammer. He hurriedly reflected: "If you can't move *him*, if I can't light a flame in his heart, good-bye to any hope. ... The rest of them will listen to me much more passively, will give much more thought to petty party tactics and petty personal interests. If I can't, it means quite simply that I don't know how, that I lack the necessary gift. . . . No subject could, in itself, have a stronger appeal."

"I'm going to speak quite frankly, my boy," said Bouitton in his most deliberate tones, and pulling at the end of his nose with his thumb and index finger. "I find it difficult to say exactly what I feel about it. I realize, to begin with, that it's a matter on which you speak with far greater authority than I can possibly claim—you, and the men of your generation. You were in the war. No one knows its horrors better than you. We, the people for whom I speak, the people of my age, failed miserably to prevent it . . . or rather we did nothing to compel our elders to prevent it—if, indeed, it was preventable. . . . We have a poor claim on the attention of our countrymen. And there's another thing: even when we feel tempted to believe that you are the victim of an illusion, or that you are setting out on a risky adventure . . . we feel a certain shyness about putting our thoughts into words."

"Do you really think that what I suggested just now means that I want France to set out on a risky adventure?"

"Don't, please, ask me to embark on a formal argument! It's only a sort of instinct I have. You mentioned my instinct awhile back. What it comes to is that I often feel things though I can't express them in words."

Jerphanion gave an incredulous little laugh. He was familiar with his leader's eloquence and knew that on great occasions he could rise to Ciceronian heights; with his gift of marshalling, illuminating, and demonstrating his ideas, often at the cost of an over-simplification, his power of managing his transitions and his contrasts. This attempt to hide behind his instinct was pure affectation!

"I'm perfectly serious," Bouitton went on. "I sometimes feel that my logic is defective. You accused me just now, very unjustly, I think, of being a timid conservative in my attitude to our political system. What, I wonder, would you say if you could look into my mind and see there the fears, or rather the prejudices, which dictate my attitude to foreign affairs. I really dare not be frank about it, especially before other people, because I am conscious of a deep sense of shame. . . . On the other hand, I can't bring myself to deny it, because I have a vague conviction that it proceeds from—I use the word again deliberately—an instinctive clarity of vision. I can't, for instance, stand the Germans. It's not a fashionable attitude nowadays, and it's rather funny to think of myself apologizing for it to you, who've got far more reason than I have for harbouring a grudge against them. It's just that I simply can't trust them, and any policy towards them which involves trust seems to me to be essentially vicious and the sheerest stupidity. . . ."

"But don't you see," interrupted Jerphanion, "that if we don't trust them we shall never achieve any real reconciliation, which means that we shall be stampeded blindly into a new war?"

"Possibly . . . but let me go on. I'm not defending my views, but merely telling you what they are. I have a great admiration for Briand; I know him well . . . and I think I've got a pretty good idea of how he has developed. . . . I always used to regard him as one of our most subtle realists, as a man who had a surer instinct, a greater sensitiveness, than any French politician for years. . . . Well, I feel now that he has parted company with the solid earth, that he's away into the clouds, that he has silenced his instinct once and for all, that he has said to it: 'Leave me in peace. You are a disturbing influence. I want to finish my life as an apostle. I can't sleep for thinking of Wilson's laurels and Jaurès's posthumous beatification. Apostles don't pay any heed to their instincts. They're busy listening to their heavenly voices.' One of La Fontaine's fables touched on the subject; but he used the word 'astrologer,' not 'apostle.' "

Jerphanion was slightly taken aback. His leader had never before spoken so frankly about these matters. He tried to laugh off his embarrassment, but all the while he was wondering what he should say. With a gesture of the hand Bouitton stopped him from speaking.

"Let me wallow in confession. . . . I know you'll keep it to yourself. . . . You see, quite apart from anything else, I stand firm for the Army. I believe in France's military tradition. The moments of the Revolution that thrill me the most are those at which it declared the fatherland to be in danger, set men to scrape together saltpetre from the cellers, and launched the soldiers of the Year II against the Kings. . . . There are things that persuade me in spite of myself that France, with her history, her geographical position, and the fact that she provokes envy among her neighbours, will have, for a long time yet, to be a country which inspires respect, a country with a strong army and a vital military spirit . . . that we shall make ourselves heard all the better, whether at the League of Nations or elsewhere, if the countries of the world feel that we are not to be challenged with impunity. . . ."

This time Jerphanion burst out laughing.

"Really, sir, your frankness tempts me to make a return in kind. . . . I'm not, for the moment, going to argue about fundamentals. . . . All I want to say now is that, listening to you, I could almost believe I was listening to Clemenceau, to Poincaré, to Millerand, each in his turn—to the Millerand of 1913, the man who sponsored the military pensions bill, as well as to the Millerand of the 'Cannes coup' of 1922. . . . I can't see what grounds you can possibly have for objecting to those two Millerands, or to the Poincaré who drove us into occupying the Ruhr. . . ."

Bouitton, staring at the ceiling, went on as though he had heard nothing:

"My blindness goes further than you'd ever guess for yourself . . . as far, for instance, as suspecting that our foreign policy has always been, more or less, dictated by the peculiar necessities of our situation —by, let us say, the need to cultivate, at the other end of Europe, whether in Turkey or in Russia, alliances devised with the object of dividing and containing the danger that threatens us. It was partly for that reason that I lugged you off—lugged us both off—to the land of the Soviets."

"You must, while you were there, have found yourself regretting the disappearance of Austria-Hungary."

"That situation is rather different where France is concerned, because Austria-Hungary has been more often our enemy than our ally, and it was in Austria-Hungary that the Germanic dream of world-domination had its birth. But I don't deny that I regard the destruction of that Empire as not unlike the opening of Pandora's box, and that I was rather surprised to find so many Frenchmen ready to express loud satisfaction at the event."

"I see. Once more, I'm not going to argue. But I confess that I find it difficult to understand your position on the political map. Your instinct ought, by rights, to have set you down among our friends opposite."

Bouitton opened wide eyes alight with laughter. There was laughter, too, in the tones of his strong, virile voice.

"My heart is on the Right, my brain on the Left, is that what you mean? Well, I shouldn't be the first who has suffered from that unfortunate ailment." He gave a loud guffaw. "But no, after due consideration I don't think you're correct in your diagnosis. I'm a 'Left chap,' as our friend Doumergue would say, from the crown of my head to the soles of my feet. I'm not the only 'Left chap' who's had thoughts of this kind in the privacy of his bosom. . . . Ask Herriot. . . . But I'm speaking now for myself and for nobody else. I've never, personally, come across a catechism of the Left, but if there is such a thing, its articles must have changed so much since the days of my youth that I feel it no part of my duty to know it by heart. I regard nothing as being forbidden to me. If I decide, before the bar of my own conscience, that something is just, I don't care two hoots whether it may seem just to Poincaré, to Millerand, to Louis Marin . . . or to Trotsky. It's only in public that I watch my step. But there I do. I'm not a dilettante, and I'm not the kind of man to play into the enemy's hands." He laughed more loudly than ever so that his belly shook. "I wouldn't, for instance, in public hesitate a single second"—with a wink—"to refer to Millerand as the President of the *coup d'État,* although I know perfectly well that he's only the President of a board of directors."

"You know, sir, you're not an easy man to understand."

Once again Bouitton scratched his nose. "I realize that. . . . I'm not sure that I always understand myself. . . ." He seemed intent now on self-examination. "One side of me thinks that we ought to stick to France and the Republic. I'm more nervous than you about international flirtations and high-sounding constitutional reforms. But there's another side which is less frightened than you are by social innovations. . . ."

"But look here, sir—"

"You as good as admitted the fact just now when you were talking about our trip to Russia. I agree that you did it in order to sugar the pill which you were about to administer to me, but I kept an eye on you while we were together, and you were a great deal more critical than I was."

"Let's get this straight. . . ."

"Quietly, quietly. What I mean is that your reactions were those of a self-respecting French shopkeeper."

"That's too much! In return for my compliments you fling in my teeth the worst insult that the citizens of the Soviet Union can think up!"

"*Your* compliments—I like that! Let me add: a highly intelligent, a generous-minded shopkeeper, who, however, would think that the end of the world had come if there was no more Crédit Lyonnais or Galeries Lafayette."

"You're damnably unfair!"

"I see that I'm making you angry, but there's a good deal of truth in what I say."

"When you have more time to spare—I'm not forgetting that your meeting is almost due to begin—I shall prove to you that you're quite wrong, that any reservations or fears that I may have in connexion with certain experiments proceed not from the timorous outlook of the shopkeeper but from the exercise of my critical faculties—it was you who invoked the name of Descartes—from my refusal to believe that all is gold that glitters; and this attitude of mine is part and parcel of a firm belief that we must observe a hierarchy, a scale of comparative urgency, in the tasks and perils that lie before us. But if you had not interrupted me when I was outlining what I think ought to be our electoral platform, you would have realized that when I demand that France shall abandon her attitude of sulky passivity, I am thinking as much of social reform as of foreign policy. My point is that the only safe way of combating Bolshevism is by making it super-fluous, not by drawing a sanitary cordon round the land of its birth. My idea is that in the reconstruction of Europe, in which I want France to take the lead, room must be found for a thorough overhaul-ing of our economic machinery. . . . What I'm really trying to make you see is that unless we can ensure a period of peace, anything we do will be tantamount to building houses in the middle of an earthquake."

Bouitton had been glancing at his watch, a large, handsome gold timepiece, secured by a chain of classic proportions. He leaned forward, stretched out his arm, and tapped Jerphanion on the shoulder.

"Don't let's waste our time accusing each other of being reactionaries. All I ask is that you shouldn't try to persuade our fellow countrymen that because France wants peace, other countries necessarily want it too. There are, unfortunately, a great many fools—and they are to be found as frequently in the working class as elsewhere—who seem to have convinced themselves that Poincaré and Millerand are the only trouble-makers in Europe. I realize that we of the Left are not entirely blameless. . . . Getting rid of Millerand and Poincaré doesn't matter so long as we can keep the strength of the country, including her finances, intact. I don't think you have given much thought to finance, dear dreamer. . . . It might be well if you realized that the fall of the franc is a matter of far greater importance to the mass of the electors than the reconstruction of Europe. . . ."

Jerphanion, indignant at the thought that his attitude on this point should be so completely misunderstood, broke in with "But, sir, do please listen," uttered in a tone of pathetic protest. But Bouitton checked him:

"Oh, I fully realize that it may be due to blindness on their part. But if your program says nothing, or not enough, about finance, we shall pay dearly for the omission; and if our adversaries choose to make capital out of our silence, and argue that the fall of the franc, so far from inconveniencing us, fits into our general schemes, and that it will be accentuated as soon as we are in power, because our only idea of financial policy is to turn out more and ever more banknotes from the State printing presses, then we shall be faced by imminent disaster. . . ."

"But I entirely agree with you!" cried Jerphanion, bursting with impatience. "I was constantly putting that point of view at my meetings. But if you think that it's a good thing to announce the sort of daring social innovations to which you attach such importance and at the same time to reassure the small capitalists, whether in the towns or the countryside, about the safety of their savings—I must beg leave to differ."

"We'll talk about that another time. I've got to hurry."

He got up and went into the anteroom. The appointment which he was leaving to keep was with the Finance Committee. While he was getting into his overcoat, and probably because he could see in imagination some of the faces opposite which he would be sitting, he said to Jerphanion:

"What I think worries me most is the low moral standard of the new men. It's not a question of party. There's a sort of family likeness about them all, including the war veterans, which is odd. There are times when I reproach myself for being out of tune with the old lot—though probably I'm not really. Oh, I know there were plenty of black sheep in pre-war politics, and a still larger number of men who kept just on the windy side of honesty. But there were big men too, both on the Left and on the Right. With the new men, Left as well as Right, no matter what their qualities may be as individuals, one has an uncomfortable feeling that they are all more or less contaminated by the period. . . . I could, for instance, give you the names of not a few members of the Committee who regularly speculate on the fall of the franc. You'll be in a better position to judge for yourself in a few months' time. . . . I only hope that your particular batch is of better quality grain. Meanwhile, if I may give you a word of advice, don't be too contemptuous of the old hands when you get to grips with our fighting leaders. You may at times be tempted to think them slightly ridiculous, rather old-fashioned. But they are the people among whom you are most likely to find what used to be called the republican virtues."

## THOUGHTS OF A SOFT-HEARTED JUDGE

"Does he really know how to look after himself? Isn't he letting them put too much on his shoulders?" Rather fearfully she completed the thought: "I only hope he has not taken the wrong road."

Ever since the days of their engagement, as she was too honest not to admit to herself, he had always talked about a future that should be more or less dedicated to action, about a future in which it would be his task to try his hand at accomplishing important and difficult things. He had never said in so many words: "I am going into politics, I am going to stand for Parliament"; still less: "I shall enlist under the banner of a party. I shall accept all the duties they may think me capable of performing. I shall regard it as my duty to obey the orders of my elders and my leaders." Whenever in those days he had referred to political parties, it had been always in tones of either tolerance or disdain.

She couldn't help being a little afraid of the future, couldn't blind herself to the possibility that it might contain more causes of bitterness than of joy.

"In a few months now he will be a deputy; of that, I think, there can be no doubt. In one year or perhaps two, an under-secretary of state or even a minister. Will his life be any the happier? At the moment he thinks only of what he will be able to achieve, of the authority and the influence which he will wield, of the exciting life he will lead from morning to night. But I know him so well. He takes things to heart so. He is extremely sensitive to disappointment, to the ill will and bad faith of others. He is incapable of imagining that people in whom he has trusted could do him a bad turn deliberately.

He is not used to being blackguarded and attacked. Poor dear! he's got many sleepless nights in front of him, and in what way shall I be able to help him?"

The example upon which she could most nearly draw for verification of her fears was that of Bouitton. Bouitton, of course, had succeeded. He was still short of fifty, and though, to be sure, he had not yet filled the highest offices, he was one of the leaders of the Left, and it was the general opinion of people in the know that after the next elections he would be, with Briand, Herriot, Painlevé—perhaps Gurau—one of the five or six men who would share between them the premiership, the presidency of the Chamber, and the chief ministerial portfolios (to say nothing of the presidency of the Republic). Within the Radical Party no one was more beloved, more readily listened to, than he. In the country at large he was one of the two or three outstanding men of his generation whose name was a popular rallying-point. The Socialists spoke of him with cordial approval as of a bourgeois who deserved the gift of grace. The Communists, because of his trip to Russia, and in obedience to the instructions which they received from Moscow, were careful not to heap insults on his head; if they came to power, Bouitton would be one of the last to be shot.

Nor had Bouitton much to complain of in the matter of a clear conscience. There was nothing with which he need seriously reproach himself—so far as Odette knew—in the course of a career which had already lasted a good many years. He had more than once effaced himself in the interests of comrades whose hunger for success was more urgent than his own, and the only revenge he had taken had been to utter a few epigrams, lightly phrased though terribly effective. In so far as a politician nearing fifty can maintain, without running the risk of seeming too great a simpleton, that in twenty years of mixed activities he has managed to win for his ideas, for what he is brave enough to call his ideal, some minor successes, Bouitton might justifiably declare, without undue exaggeration: "I have served the cause I had at heart." In short, if she called on his example to help her in imaging what sort of a future lay before Jerphanion, she would be neither wronging her husband nor loading the dice.

Not that Odette didn't realize how much more exigent her husband was when it came to ideals, how deeply humiliated he would have felt had he known that people thought he could rest contented with minor successes. But she knew, too, from having heard the melancholy confession of those who had a right to speak, that politics is a hard school of modesty, and that its pupils find reality harder to bend to their wills than do other men.

Well, was a destiny such as Bouitton's so very much to be envied, after all? Admittedly, he seemed happy. But wasn't that chiefly due to his temperament? If he had been happy in the role of a Minister, he would have been scarcely less so in that of one of the Ministry's doorkeepers (it was so very easy to imagine him receiving visitors, all paunch and heartiness); he would have been still more so as a country innkeeper (it was even easier to imagine him standing on his doorstep saluting the passers-by).

One day, when he happened to be alone with Odette in the little drawing-room of the boulevard Saint-Germain flat (Jerphanion had been off on a long expedition to a wine-shop on the boulevard Arago in search of a particular Chablis which he wanted the chief to taste), Bouitton had suddenly felt a need to indulge in confidences. He liked being with Odette. He never overstepped the limits of respect in his relations with her, but he made no bones about letting everyone see the mixture of admiration and tender affection which she inspired in him (an admiration not very usual with him; his liking for women did not prevent him from judging them with sharp severity). On this occasion he said, and there could be no question of his sincerity:

"I ought really, after my time at the École des Chartes, to have continued my studies, instead of letting myself be caught up in politics. My true vocation is for history—the history one reads, and writes. I was a victim of muddled thought. I had an idea that it would be more amusing to play a part in history in the making. That was the result of a profound illusion. It was as though a landscape-painter—a man like Troyon or Millet—should think that he would get more kick out of becoming a ploughman. . . . Had I followed my true vocation, I should have looked for a place as a librarian. Libraries are my spiritual home. I should have had plenty of time for my own work. The money wouldn't have been much, to be sure, but in those days my family was reasonably well off. My father, who detested politics, and who, when he saw that I wasn't attracted by the cognac business, had resigned himself to seeing me adopt the honourable career of a scholar, would gladly have given me an allowance of three or four thousand francs. That was my dream. I should have written one or two superb volumes . . . in particular, a history of Gaul—Jullian pinched the idea from me—and a history of the last years of the Western Roman Empire, something that would have been completely new, and chock-full of ideas which, so far as I know, have never been put forward by anybody. . . ."

"But which may have come to you later," Odette had ventured to suggest, "as a result of your active experience of politics?"

"That's an ingenious notion!" Bouitton had replied, "a very shrewd notion! There can't be many pretty young women capable of making so disconcerting a reply! . . . But I don't think you are right. I had had those ideas in my head for a long while . . . though, admittedly, certain lessons that I learned, more particularly during and after the war, strengthened and clarified them. . . . By this time I should have been a member of the Institut, less well known to the street-car conductors of Paris, but surrounded with a general atmosphere of respect. The *Echo de Paris* would not be saying that I am one of those responsible for the destruction of France—an awkward business, by the way, because my mother reads the *Echo de Paris*. . . . The *Action Française* would not be accusing me of carousing on money sent from Moscow, and violating little girls by the dozen as a wind-up to my orgies. . . . I am rather sorry that our code of behaviour does not smile on such exercises; I think I should derive a great deal of pleasure from them, and I doubt whether the little girls would take much harm. . . . The trade of politics today—and I trust that your husband entertains no illusions on the subject—provides none of those intoxicating opportunities enjoyed by caids and emirs, which I should find so very much to my taste. . . . By adopting that trade, I threw overboard, in return for just nothing, all the chances of more solid happiness which I might have had in some other walk of life. At the end of my life I shall not have even the consolation of saying that I have left a great work behind me. For we politicians have nothing to which we can give that name. To fight and juggle with circumstance, to achieve the very reverse of what one set out to do—a war, for instance, when one started out as a pacifist, the suppression of a general strike when one began one's career as a revolutionary—can hardly be called a 'work.'"

But even if fate dealt Jerphanion an equally good hand, he would derive from it a good deal less happiness even than Bouitton. He would worry far more. (Men who let themselves be easily worried ought to be more careful than most about adopting the kind of career in which occasions of worry are abnormally frequent.) Attacks would hurt him more. He would find it less easy to resign himself to the compromise solutions which life imposes.

Odette visualized his face. She knew it so well. Quite apart from the general effect produced by its expression, which was totally unlike that of any other, its every feature, line, and movement had for her a definite meaning. Only the mouth and chin had still the power of disconcerting her. She saw them now in thought sometimes with, sometimes without, a beard. The two pictures fought for supremacy in her consciousness, each fighting to suppress the other. In a curious way they seemed to have some spiritual significance, though she would have found it difficult to say precisely what it was. She only knew that mixed with other elements in her thought was the deadly sickness of those war years, the memory of that suspense so terribly like death which had hung in those days over almost every head. She felt that she must make an effort and choose once and for all. Which of the two pictures should she make her own? On the bearded, pre-war face humour and bitterness blended with a sweetness of expression which kept either from going its own way, from establishing its claim to ultimate verity, so that the general character of the physiognomy was more balanced, more reassuring. Today every subtle shade of feeling showed at once and plainly, the flicker of a smile, the lines etched by weariness. Odette was not yet expert in reading their precise meaning. Familiar though it might be to her from long years of intimacy, his face held some quality that remained for ever new and strange and oddly disturbing for the fixed habit of her love. Certain caresses, certain impressions of tenderness, of physical rapture, were associated in her memory with that older countenance. Driven back into a past which would never come again, they tended to disappear altogether, as for a man will disappear an accumulated richness of happiness and dreams when his wife decides suddenly to cut her hair. Sometimes at sight of his newer face she would be conscious of a vague sense of adulterous guilt that held for her at once a trace of terror, of repulsion, of delighted thrill, for there could not but be a certain thrill in such an experience won at so small a cost.

For his sake she feared the future which he had deliberately chosen. But what other future, what other fate, would she have preferred? From her mother she had learned—and she had had to make no great effort to absorb the lesson—that though money is indispensable to happiness, material comfort, given the bare minimum necessary for decent living, depends less on the size of an income than on the way that income is used; and had her own comfort alone been in question, she would have been perfectly contented to see him pursue the ordinary humdrum of a teaching career. Her views on happiness were perfectly definite, and she held that it could be best assured by keeping it independent of too many material conditions. Of the many celebrated men whose biographies she had read, those she could best understand and most truly envy, those whose lot she would really like to have shared as wife, were the scholars and writers who had managed to pursue their life's work in an atmosphere of calm and tranquil privacy diversified by a few, not costly pleasures and a certain amount of travel. The frenzied restlessness of the post-war years had passed her by. She had come in contact with not a few young women who had fallen victims to its infection, and these she had found pitiful or amusing according to the violence or otherwise of their symptoms. She would no more have dreamed of following their example than she would have dreamed of becoming a gambler or taking to drugs. Bred up in the provinces, she had a deep love of Paris, but she would have faced without dismay the prospect of long years spent with Jean in the country, broken by occasional trips to the capital or elsewhere. She would, for instance, wholeheartedly have approved, if her husband, worn out by too many classes and too shackling a routine of teaching, had decided, after taking a brilliant doctorate, to accept a professorship, even though such a step might have meant less money. The only thing that really mattered, as she clearly saw, was that in any career that he might choose he should be able to make his mark and accomplish the great things for which, she did not doubt, he had been destined from birth.

But though she had never dared to put her thoughts into words, and scarcely even to formulate them in the secrecy of her own mind, she could not help wondering whether he had not perhaps got a mistaken idea about what those great things were. He had persuaded himself that his vocation was for a life of political activity. No doubt he had, to an outstanding degree, many of the gifts necessary for such a career: he was a good and fluent speaker; he had the kind of voice that could thrill large audiences; he knew how to talk to the common folk without any display of vulgar humbug. He believed in his cause; he was rational and public-spirited; he could grasp problems of many different kinds and make them his own; he had a gift of practical common sense, a power of seeing what was probable or at least possible. He was tenacious, though never mulishly obstinate. Self-assured though he might be, he was not the man to persist in a mistake once he had been made to see it clearly. He had courage (he hated to have anyone mention his valour as a soldier in the field, declaring that that sort of courage was the commonest thing in the world, and that, anyhow, he had displayed it only much against his will; but he did admit that he was readier than most to take risks when it was a matter of braving public opinion or challenging those in power). One other gift he had, as mysterious as it is rare: the gift of authority, the art of getting himself respected and obeyed without using the weapons of command and sometimes without having them to hand. As a teacher he had never been "ragged," not even in his early years. He had gone whole terms without giving a single punishment (and how gentle most of the punishments of the modern schoolmaster were!). Speaking of certain famous ministers, he liked to say that they could not have kept order in a class of twenty boys. All who aimed at becoming the country's governors should, he maintained, be subjected to that test, since no profession depended more on the power of exercising natural authority than that of the schoolmaster, especially where large classes were concerned, in which everything favoured indiscipline—the lawlessness of youth, the uncurbed cruelty and mischievousness of human nature, long practice in plots and premeditated rowdiness, and the utter lack of any real means of compulsion. Compared to that, he used to say, the task imposed on an officer of getting his men to follow him, even when it was a question of going over the top—allowing for the various means of persuasion to which the military leader could have recourse—was the merest child's play. . . .

Having thus itemized all his qualities, so wholly suited did they seem to the work which he had chosen for his own, Odette felt tempted to say: "What more could one want? It's just prejudice on my part."

And yet the real answer came quickly to her lips. In the first place, Jerphanion was not sufficiently petty-minded. Odette had listened to the confidences of those who moved in the great world of affairs; she had heard stories, and she had drawn her conclusions. Without a certain amount of petty-mindedness, no one, she felt sure, could make a real success of politics. For that sort of success a man must have the gift of seeming to forgive while being in fact a stranger to forgiveness, of hoping that a rival would fail, and at times of discreetly making sure that he should. Jerphanion, too, was over-trusting; he liked to trust people, and to bind them to him by the mere fact of trusting them. He had found that the method worked both with schoolboys and with soldiers. It was less to be relied upon with his parliamentary colleagues. It would not, she reflected, really have worked even with his wife, had not that wife been naturally of an upright disposition. It was an admirable method for anyone in a position of leadership, provided always that those subordinated to him were prepared, even against their will, to recognize his right to lead, whether by reason of age, ability, or military rank. Where that condition obtained, the lad felt flattered by the leader's trust. But even so, it must never be blind. As the result of a few dozen political dinners and receptions, of an occasional visit in her husband's company to the lobbies and sittings of the Chamber, of her own fleeting impressions, Odette had very soon become convinced that natural leadership was a thing unknown in parliamentary circles. There were only the older members—into whose shoes the young were waiting to step, sponsors from whose temporary influence it was well to derive as much benefit as possible—and rivals, who must be got out of the way at the earliest possible moment.

Jerphanion accused her of being too harsh in her judgment, of taking things too much at their face value. "The same holds true everywhere," he said. "Remember what Jallez told us about literary circles." But Odette, thinking over his words, saw truly that the writer is always in direct contact with his work and with his public. So far as other writers are concerned, he can see just as much or as little of them as he wants. He does not live immersed in a parliament of literary folk. Unless he is a mere careerist without genuine merit, the fate of his work, his own position now and in the future, does not depend upon the attitude he may adopt, on each and every day, within the closed circle of his colleagues, upon the shake of a hand or a word uttered in debate or dropped in a lobby. His market price does not depend from day to day upon the noisy and suspicious activities of his competitors.

Jean was not made to show up at his best in a hurly-burly of competitors. He lacked the gifts of the man who can worm his way through crowds or speak soft and ingratiating words. The art of intrigue was hateful to him. When he felt sure that he was right in a certain course, he felt it degrading to bolster up the claims of reason with trickery and haggling. His scorn for the methods of the gutter and for the blundering of fools showed too clearly in his face. Bouitton undoubtedly shared that scorn, but he had an engaging way of passing it off with easy familiarity.

What it all really came to was this: if Bouitton at fifty, and with not a few gifts of fortune in his pocket, could confess to wondering whether he had not taken the wrong road, wasn't there some reason to suppose that Jerphanion, when he had reached the same age, might have even stronger cause to regret his choice?

What would she have planned for him if the choice had lain with her? He felt, she knew, that he had no vocation for pure literature. The stimulus of an active life was necessary to him; he had to have the assurance that, as the result of something that he had done, the details of his environment were actually being modified.

She tried to imagine what his life would have been like had he taken his doctorate and then almost immediately been appointed to an important chair at the university. After some years he would have published some work of theory—moral, political, or social—based upon his doctoral thesis and aimed at popularizing his views. It would have had a great success, would have been read by men of action, deeply pondered, widely discussed. Members of Parliament, wishing to be up to date, would have quoted it in their speeches. Orators at public meetings would have thrown at the heads of their audiences some one or other of his ideas, more or less digested, and accompanied by abuse; but the abuse would not have detracted from the idea. That was the point. Mud would have been flung, but it would not have stuck. There would have been no sneering, wounding asides. She would not have seen him slinking home, his spirit broken because some wild man in the Chamber had accused him of every villainy under the sun—conscious that his defence had drawn but half-hearted applause from his friends—or because he had had to give his adherence to some political compromise inevitable, perhaps, but none the less, in his eyes, dishonourable. Odette remembered hearing someone quote—she thought it was from Renan—a cruel epigram to the effect that "politicians are the camp-followers of philosophy"; yes, camp-followers with dirty hands and bent and burdened backs.

How often had she not heard Bouitton, or others, say in her hearing that everything achieved by the Third Republic had been but a makeshift attempt, usually incomplete, sometimes even dishonest, of some general principle long ago laid down by a few thinkers? Any praise there might be would go to the thinkers, not to their grubby-handed disciples.

Some time would pass, and then Jean Jerphanion would have given to the waiting world a second work destined to be as great a sensation as his first. His quiet academic life would have gone on, surrounded, illuminated, at a discreet distance, by the fame of his achievement. He would have avoided the drudgery, the affronts, which fall to the lot even of the man of letters. The thinker who works in seclusion from the great world is safe from abuse. The newspapers pay little attention to him, and if they ever refer to his activities do so with respect. Whatever jealousies he may arouse have a blunted edge.

A clear road would have stretched before him to the Collège de France. The careers of two men in particular had always filled Odette with admiration: that of Renan, four or five of whose books she had read with delighted amazement, and that of Bergson, whose work was known to her only at second hand. Only twice had she been to hear him lecture, but his face, the general impression which he diffused, had exactly fitted in with her idea of what a great intellectual ought to be like. She knew perfectly well that Jerphanion's career could not have been a repetition either of Renan's or of Bergson's. But what was there to prevent a professor of political theory, a creator of social dogma, from making a place for himself in the same high regions of the mind, from presiding there with a serenity no less than theirs, from exercising upon the events of his time an even more direct, an even more tangible influence? If Jaurès, of whom Jerphanion so often spoke in tones of tender veneration, had elected to be not a great tribune of the people but the Renan or the Bergson of Socialism, would he not, when all was said, have better served his ideal, known a greater happiness, have been spared much bitterness of spirit and a tragic end?

Now and again she would say to herself: "Perhaps I'm just being an egotist—an egotist for him and for myself." But she had not the courage seriously to take herself to task. She suspected that when people claimed to be sacrificing their personal happiness and that of their nearest and dearest to the call of duty in the world of action, they were, as like as not, mere victims of another kind of egotism, of a craving to influence and dominate others; that their sacrifice is but a sacrifice in words, the decorative façade to self-indulgence (as when a gambler says: "I sacrifice my nights and days to my duty at the card-table").

She was no less scrupulous in admitting to herself that in her fear of the future there was something of fear for her own happiness. Almost all members of Parliament, with scarcely a single exception, turned out in the long run to be bad husbands. Bouitton might, in this respect, be the most notorious, but he was by no means one of the worst. Their every step was beset with temptations and excuses. How could home life stand up to the politician's life of overwork, irregular hours, and scanty leisure? As a result of morning sessions prolonged beyond their normal time, of night sessions fixed at the last moment, of committee and group meetings not arranged beforehand or lasting longer than was expected—and of dozens of other like incidents—a husband gets the habit of being late for meals, then of telephoning that he won't be back, then of forgetting to telephone at all. Finally he thinks it perfectly natural to reach home at two in the morning without having sent a word of warning to his wife, full of a strange excitement which he finds it quite impossible to communicate to her, and so tired that the sight of an exhausted husband is the only kind of present she ever expects to receive at his hands.

Odette had to admit that so far her husband had not taken advantage of the many pretexts furnished by his work for Bouitton. He had, on the contrary, struggled hard to defend the sanctities of his home life. But how long would his courage last? For how long would he continue the struggle when the difficulties became greater? The moment of danger comes when the husband diminishes, by ever so little, his vigilance and begins to lose his sense of having to keep a watchful eye open to see that the precious values of his home life are duly protected. "Since he got back from Le Puy he hasn't once suggested making love to me. . . . I doubt whether the idea has even crossed his mind. . . . It's not that I don't understand. The two days since he returned have been one continual rush. . . . But it's the first time that such a thing has happened and"—a bitter line showed at the corners of her mouth—"that's how it begins." When a man's life became as full as his was now, it was always the happiness of the home that suffered. When it occurred to men so caught up in the whirl of everyday existence that they must, after all, take a little time off for the carefree happiness of love, it was not to their wives that they turned for relaxation.

And suddenly Odette began to think of the Countess's dinner to which Jean was to go without her, which was occupying his mind so much more than was reasonable, and so much more than he was willing to admit. She was aware of the extent to which, quite involuntarily, her mind was dwelling upon the subject. She smiled in an attempt to laugh herself out of her depression, but deep within her heart a small voice murmured: "That, too, is how it begins. This Countess or another. This time or another. . . ." But the voice brought warning only, not advice. What was there that she could do about it? Whatever a wife might do to meet such a situation was bound to turn to her own destruction. No precaution can have the slightest effect when it is a man's whole life that is set on a wrong course.

## JERPHANION WRITES TO LAULERQUE

On the very day that he was to dine at the Countess's, Jerphanion wrote and posted the following letter.

My dear Laulerque:

It is a long time since I gave you any news of myself, and you may be surprised by what you find in this letter. I know, fortunately, that you are not the sort of man to let yourself be seriously disturbed by so unimportant a matter.

The fact is that I want to have a long and confidential talk with you. Perhaps more than one. It is about something of high importance, involving grave matters. I am so full up with work at the moment that it is quite impossible for me to come and see you in Switzerland. I could not make such a journey for some considerable time. What I ask you now can be put into a few words: could you manage to come to Paris if you've got a day or two to spare? I am sending you with this letter a first-class travelling-pass and return from the Swiss frontier to Paris. I think you told me once that you yourself had railway facilities in Switzerland itself. The pass holds good for two months, but I sincerely hope that you will not delay that long. As soon as you have fixed the date, send me a wire. I'll see about getting you a room at a hotel.

I am going to look up Sampeyre in order to find out whether you are at your old address. He is gradually, but very, very gently, fading away. There is less and less flesh on his face, and he says himself that he is not long for this world. I only hope that he is wrong. He must be a great age, and he is unhappy—partly on account of himself (the growing cost of living worries him a lot), but chiefly on account of the times and of the years ahead. But he is still the same clear-headed, kindly man we knew of old. I couldn't help admiring something he said to me the other day: "I wish you'd tell me that my disillusionment and pessimism are primarily the effect of old age. That would help me to get the better of my gloom."

I hope that we can help in another way. What I want to talk to you about is rather to the point. It will remind us, too, of a certain night of long ago when we walked together under a fall of fine snow in the light of the street lamps.

Send me a line about the proposal I have made, even if you can't as yet tie yourself to a date.

Yours always,

JEAN JERPHANION

# Chapter

## 15

### BACK FROM THE COUNTESS'S

Jerphanion got home from his dinner at a quarter past midnight. His wife had gone to bed and was lying over on the right-hand side, as was usual with her, reading.

"Well, you see, I didn't stay late," said Jerphanion.

"No," replied Odette without any show of excitement. She finished the paragraph she was reading and then added: "Everything go off all right?"

"Splendidly."

"Many people there?"

"About a dozen guests—fourteen, to be exact."

"Quite an intimate little party."

"Two or three men and a married couple—old friends of the family —came in later."

"Did you know anyone there?"

"Hardly a soul. A deputy of the Right, called Filloteaux, whom I've met once or twice in the Chamber and at the Ministry, when I went there with Bouitton; and Pellen de Tracy, the Vice-President of the Municipal Council. Quite a nice chap. I've come across him once or twice at official ceremonies."

"If the political small-fry were of such noble birth, what did the rest of the party consist of? The fine flower of the aristocracy?"

Jerphanion did his best to follow Odette's lead in keeping their conversation on a level of easy good humour.

"You've said it, my dear. One Duchess, one Marchioness—"

"Complete, I hope, with Duke and Marquis?"

"Naturally. . . . A Count or two . . ."

Jerphanion began to undress. He took off his tie. Odette was still holding her book open in her hands.

"My poor dear, you must have been the only commoner present?"

"Very nearly. . . . My only companion in misfortune was a big industrial magnate from the north."

"With his wife?"

"No."

"Why wasn't she there? Hadn't she been asked?" Odette was careful to keep any suggestion of personal interest in the matter out of her voice.

"I don't know. . . ." He was on the point of adding: "I don't know whether his wife is with him in Paris, or even whether he has a wife . . . " but he resisted the temptation.

"And I suppose you were tucked away at the far end of the table, you poor darling."

"Not at all. I was given quite a good place."

"Who was next to you?"

He began to laugh. "I had a Marchioness on my left hand and a Countess on my right. . . . I'll try to remember their names, if it's a matter of interest to you, though I'm not at all sure that I haven't got them mixed up in my mind."

"Young?"

"Fairly."

"Pretty?"

"Dear me, what a lot you want to know! . . . The lady on my right wasn't bad-looking. . . . The other, the Marchioness, was a bit horselike, but extremely distinguished. Neither of them was much made up. I couldn't help feeling that if one or two ladies of our acquaintance who pride themselves on being very smart had been there in all their paint and powder, they'd have looked rather like chorus girls from the Folies-Bergère."

To this at first Odette made no reply. Jerphanion would have liked very much to talk more about his evening, but he did not want to seem too full of the subject. He waited, therefore, dawdling over his undressing.

"Why wasn't Bouitton there?"

"He may have been asked and not been able to go. I forgot to ask him. It's quite possible," he added, with an assumption of modesty, "that he was asked in the first place and suggested me as a substitute, a stopgap, because he couldn't accept."

"Is it a nice house?"

"Do you mind if I sit down a moment and have a cigarette? . . . You're not too sleepy?"

"Please yourself . . . but won't you be cold?" He was wearing only his trousers and, above them, a light undershirt.

"Oh no," he said. Then he slipped on the top part of his pyjamas, lit a cigarette, and sat down on the bed, not very close to her, his right leg cocked over his left, his left hand holding his right foot.

"I'm afraid I didn't take much notice of it," he said in rather deliberate tones of self-mockery. "I was much too busy trying to behave well and not make a fool of myself. There I was, you see, in that distinguished company, as a representative of the Third Republic and the political Left. . . . I only got a very sketchy impression. It's huge . . . not at all modern, but solid and dignified; not at all the kind of place that stinks of money. I suppose some of the furniture was good, though most of it seemed uninteresting. I don't get the impression that any attempt had been made to produce an effect—not even an effort of period decoration. I just got the feeling that I was dining in the house of people who'd had money for a great number of years."

"Is it a house standing in its own grounds?"

"Not exactly. It's part of one of those big, solid blocks dating from the early years of the century. That district of Paris is full of them. It has its own private front door and, I think, a bit of garden. I saw no more of it than the four reception-rooms on the entrance level: two largish drawing-rooms opening into one another, a smaller library and smoking-room combined, and the dining-room, which is really big. I think that the dining-room is furnished in the English style, but I'm no expert and don't take much notice of that sort of thing. . . . I noticed that there was a staircase leading from the hall to the first floor, where, presumably, the bedrooms are."

"Whom did you talk to most of the time?"

"During dinner, to my two neighbours. . . . Nothing very exciting. One of them, the Marchioness, talked about the Bourbonnais country, where she has some property. The other chatted about London, which she knows very well. . . . Afterwards, in the drawing-room, I talked to the deputy and the vice-president. Both of them were most friendly. We discussed recent happenings. The Filloteaux man had heard—though I don't know where—that I am a candidate at the next elections, and, even more surprisingly, that I am likely to play a big part in fixing the general campaign of the party. He didn't treat me as an insignificant beginner, but as a gentleman who pulls the strings and knows the secrets of the great. It's odd how even the most confidential information gets about in those circles—odd and rather unfortunate."

"Can't it be explained by assuming that Bouitton told the Countess? . . . You say they're pretty intimate, and he's an awful old gossip, you know."

"Possibly."

"And what about the famous Countess herself? Didn't she take any notice of you?"

"Oh yes. She made me sit down beside her later in the evening and asked me a whole lot of questions."

"What about?"

"You'll never guess! First of all, about Russia. She knew that I'd been there."

"You see, I was right. She must have got it all from Bouitton."

"Yes, I suppose so. . . . What amused me was to find how interested all these people are in Russia. . . . It's a form of snobbery. They're a bit frightened too, though they try not to show it. If some of the extreme Left enthusiasts had been there, they would have been surprised at the calm, the almost sympathetic way in which this Countess Foulion questioned me about the Soviet experiment. . . . I expected to find her full of prejudices, crammed with hair-raising stories, and was prepared to contradict her—though quite mildly, of course. But I was quite wrong. I almost had, I don't say to disillusion her, but to remind her that not all the criticisms of the Soviets are without some foundation, and that the new Russian way of life is not all rose-coloured."

"May it not have been that she was trying to pull the wool over your eyes, getting you to talk so as to find out what you really think, and be in a position to estimate the degree of danger which you, and people like you, represent?"

Jerphanion felt slightly vexed by this remark of Odette's, but he forced himself to keep all sign of irritation out of his voice.

"I don't think so . . . though I'm prepared to admit that my surprise at her open-mindedness may not have been wholly unpleasing to her, that she found it amusing to shatter any prejudices I might have had about the attitude of her class . . . and no doubt if I'd come out with a wildly enthusiastic account of the Soviets, she might have said to herself: 'If one of the fairly moderate political parties entrusts a fellow like this with the drawing up of its electoral program, it's a poor outlook for all of us! . . . Those of my friends who declare that these Left-wingers are nothing but Communists in disguise aren't so far wrong after all!' But I don't think there was more in it than that."

He paused, thought for a moment or two, and then continued with rather more animation:

"My impression was that these aristocrats have a feeling that they are a good deal further removed than the middle classes from these odd and terrifying realities about which they hear people talking, often as though the end of the world were at hand. The older people among them are content to bury their heads in the sand. Those who are still young, or fairly young, put it to themselves in this way: 'It would be nice to understand what it's all about.' I don't mean that their attitude is one simply of intellectual curiosity. No, what they mean is: 'We might just as well know precisely what sort of threat it is that we've got to face.' Deep down in their hearts they can't help hoping that things won't be so terrible, so infernal, after all. . . . They want someone to tell them that if the worst comes to the worst, or some part of it, the world will still be a place in which they can live . . . and they want that someone to be, not an obvious fanatic, but a man who knows how to behave at a dinner-table and seems to be a person of culture and good sense. . . . In that respect they are rather like the countrymen who questioned me in the mountain villages much as they'd have questioned a doctor—just in order to find out whether another war is likely to come along, whether it's safe for them to have another son without the constant dread of seeing him packed off to the battlefield when he's a grown man. . . . It's all very human!"

"Is this Countess of yours—young?"

"Yes—I should say about thirty-five."

"And now that you've had a chance of studying her, do you agree with Bouitton that she's pretty?"

"Not really, in the ordinary sense of the word. . . . She has a very live face, and her eyes are intelligent." The change in his voice seemed to betoken a slight shift in the direction of his thought. "You can't get away from it, you know, there's something extraordinarily simple about these people, about all of them, especially the women. . . . I kept being reminded of what I used to feel in the old days with the Saint-Papouls. . . . Most of the women we meet are so affected, so conventional, that one begins to wonder whether there is a grain of true feeling, of sincerity, in anything they say: 'I adore music . . . I adore Proust. . . .' Something is always sure to be 'perfectly splendid, absolutely divine' . . . something else 'too terrifyingly awful' . . . this man or the other is 'just too gifted' . . . you know the sort of thing. And then the sort of languid way they say it, the exaggerated enunciation, which they quite obviously take to be the mark of an aristocratic upbringing. . . . Well, the women I met tonight, with the possible exception of the Marchioness, who was guilty of just a trace of affectation, all of them speak quite simply—rather like Madame Hubert; you know whom I mean, the headmistress of the secondary school at Orléans, whose complete absence of any sort of pose, and complete ease of manner, used to strike us so forcibly. . . ."

"Still, I can't help thinking that when these marchionesses and countesses of yours started talking about Russia, there must have been, shall I say, a marked absence of sincerity."

Jerphanion pondered these words for a moment; then:

"Let me express what I mean by an analogy—rather an exaggerated analogy, perhaps, but it will serve. When a Racine heroine is having a dialogue with another character, it often happens that she has to dissimulate her real meaning, has to be crafty and cunning, has to say things not because she sincerely means them, but because she wants to force her interlocutor to show his hand. But for all that, the tone of her voice seems to us perfectly genuine, and it is not difficult for us to realize that under all the deliberate choice of word and phrase there is a sincerity of feeling. Even her lies are, in a sense, true. She is not merely unpacking her heart with empty words, not merely giving currency to a lot of fake sentiments. Hermione does not try to make us believe that she is a woman for whom love is all, a woman torn by passion and poetry, while all the time she is nothing, really, but a calculating little bitch. . . . It's that which makes the classics such magnificent reading. . . . Well, something similar is true of the women I've been describing. I'm not claiming that the average of their intelligence is especially high, nor that their culture is either wide or deep—far from it! . . . But there is something about them of the classic note. In days like these when the bogus rules the roost everywhere, I find something very restful about them. . . . Even in purely intellectual matters they can teach us a lesson in good taste."

"In fact, what it comes to," said Odette, not without a trace of bitterness, "is that you have come back from your dinner filled with enthusiasm for everything that happened."

Jerphanion showed his disappointment in the expression of his face. He was on the point of making a sharp rejoinder, but refrained. He got up and moved slowly towards the bathroom. As he reached the door he turned. He saw on Odette's face a look of genuine unhappiness, childish perhaps, lacking any real justification, weak and undignified, yet disturbing to his emotions just because it expressed something real.

He went across to the bed and put his arms round her. At first she resisted, sulking. Her eyes shone with something suspiciously like the brightness of tears.

He whispered in her ear:

"Don't you think you're being a tiny bit silly? . . . and giving the impression, too, that you think I'm even sillier than I am?"

A moment later:

"Are you terribly tired—so tired that you would hate me to make love to you?"

"What do you think?" she said.

# 16

## IN THE FOREST OF ARDENNES.
## A LOVER OF ISLAM

In the course of the previous September, as the result of a casual meeting, Sammécaud had reached a turning-point in his life.

He had gone to spend the first few days of autumn at the Château d'Ourthe, which had been recommended to him by friends. The Château d'Ourthe, standing in the middle of trees on one of the summits of the Belgian Ardennes, was a former residence of princes which had been bought by a business syndicate and turned into a country hotel likely to appeal to a very select clientele. Sammécaud had liked the name, which reminded him of the Forêt d'Othe. Nor had the resemblance been merely in the name. The actual place reminded him strongly of the Forêt d'Othe—certain smells of earth and rotting leaves, the way the clearings were cut, but, above all, the feeling it gave him of being in a very ancient and romantic piece of woodland, where once upon a time knights had ridden and jousted, where still, at times, the ear could almost catch the clank of armour. (The place had other and more recent echoes which it was a great deal harder to dress up in fancy clothes, echoes of the World War, traces of which were even now visible here and there. But Sammécaud did not allow himself to think of such things.)

Something else, too, had drawn him thither. Seven months earlier he had made a short trip to Egypt. There, in very sophisticated surroundings, he had renewed his acquaintance with the Coptic Princess, older now than she had been during those four days spent at Bruges in 1913, but still very charming, still making devastating play with her eyes. And once, when they were alone, she had said to him: "Promise me that, if you get the chance, you will make a little pilgrimage to Bruges as an act of joint devotion. You will, now, won't you?"

He had planned, therefore, to spend about two weeks at the Château d'Ourthe, to go on from there to Bruges through the autumnal countryside, and thence to travel back to Paris—a program which, in fact, he did carry out.

There were very few people at the Château d'Ourthe, and very little to disturb the peace of the place. The public rooms and terraces were almost empty. What few guests there were spent their time riding in the woods or hunting in the neighbourhood. A lazy man could sit and think undisturbed beneath a sky that showed sometimes golden, sometimes silver-grey, with nothing to distract him but a screen of waving branches.

At the end of a week Sammécaud had struck up an acquaintance with an American of about the same age as himself, and with similar quiet habits, called William P. Milne. Little by little, by dint of exchanging ideas, they became fairly intimate. Their lives were not without points of resemblance. William P. Milne came of a family of industrialists settled in Pennsylvania who had amassed a fortune in the eighties when the railways began to flourish and the age of the motor-car had not yet dawned. He had started life in his father's office and had later taken over the management of the family business. But he had got into the habit, very early, of taking long vacations. Very naturally, he had used these periods of leisure for travelling, and, no less naturally, most of his journeys had led him to the Old World, with many parts of which he was familiar. Between these trips he moved frequently about the United States in order, as he put it, to "check up." What he wanted to "check up" was an idea which had been gradually forming in his mind about the relative value of various civilizations.

His method was not that of the ordinary tourist. It was less superficial. Instead of rushing through a number of countries, trying to see a little of everything, like most of his compatriots, he would choose some particular spot which seemed to him to have a special significance, and settle down in it for as long as his vacation permitted. He tried to live the life of the natives, without, however, depriving himself of the amenities which even the most backward countries can offer to the foreigner. With the resources at his command, he could enjoy these without difficulty. In other words, he saw no reason to carry a passion for local colour so far as to shiver all winter in a palace of Seville, but was perfectly willing to accept the advantages offered by central heating. His particular problem took, therefore, approximately the following form: "Where does any particular civilization rank in the general scale of values, when seen in the best conditions possible, allowances being made for the heightening or modification of its own peculiar characteristics by the addition of contributions from outside, always assuming that those contributions do not too violently change the essential nature of the original material?"

For several years before the war he had managed to cut himself almost completely free from the obligations of his business life. He had retained an interest in various concerns, which, however, ran themselves without any active participation by him. He had spread his investments widely. So long as he kept himself in contact with his banks, and spent a few weeks of each year in America, he had nothing to worry about. He had, consequently, been able to carry his experiments several steps further. Some of these experiments he recounted to Sammécaud, and dwelt with particular emphasis on the general conclusions which he had reached. He insisted that these conclusions were valid only for himself, and was perfectly willing to admit that they might seem absurd to those who held a view of life other than his own.

After many and prolonged comparisons he felt convinced, he said, that the civilization of Islam was far preferable to any other. And of all Islam he knew of no corner more exquisite than Tunis and the surrounding district.

"I am perfectly well aware," he admitted, "that to some extent I have been influenced by a spirit of contradiction, or, let us say, the charm of contrast. I was brought up, and spent my best years, in a hard tradition; in a world where overwork and nervous tension were the rule, which was a stranger to all the graces and elegances of life, where men lived in a perpetual state of rush, never satisfied with the attainment of the ends they set themselves, and, for the most part, having no clear idea of what those ends were; a world over which brooded a dark heritage of Puritan morality from which they could escape only by dint of indulging in crude and shortlived dissipation. In Islam I found the precise contrary of everything I had hitherto known: tranquillity, leisure, a contempt for hustle, a conviction that in the search for pleasure and happiness lay the end and object of mankind. But I found that when the novelty of contrast had worn off, the charm still remained, and now that I have been settled there for some time, I am convinced that the people of Tunisia have found, and known how to preserve, the best of all possible ways of life, or at least the one that suits me best."

Sammécaud expressed some surprise that he should have picked on Tunis.

"Do you know it?" asked William P. Milne.

"Unfortunately, no. It is ridiculous that I should have to make such a confession. Chance alone has kept me a stranger to it, and I have planned more than once to make the trip. . . . I did once pay a hurried visit to Algiers—returning by way of Oran. I found it, I admit, amusing and very picturesque in spots, but nothing more. On the other hand, I know Cairo well . . . to say nothing of Alexandria, which I enjoyed, though it seemed to me to be more a city of Europe than of Islam. I should have thought that Cairo would have held more interest for you than Tunis. . . . Once, too, I did go to Constantinople and back. I had always meant to see it before the war, but unfortunately I waited too long. . . . Constantinople as Loti knew it must have been a place of extraordinary charm, and parts of it are still well worth seeing . . . but I fully realize that you would not find what you are looking for in the Constantinople of today."

William P. Milne explained how he had set out to explore Islam, conscientiously pursuing the program which he had drawn up for himself. He had approached it by way of North Africa and Tunis, and the effect upon him had been immediate and startling. He had been led, very naturally, to wonder whether, by travelling farther eastwards, he might not find still better-preserved examples of Islam, and even more characteristic samples of the life which so fascinated him. He had pressed his investigations far into Asia, had lived for a while in Cairo, in Jerusalem, in Bagdad, Damascus, Smyrna, and Constantinople. Every one of these cities, even Smyrna, had interested him. Many of them contained monuments of Islamic culture superior to anything to be found in Tunis or even in Kairouan (William P. Milne regarded Kairouan as a dependency of Tunis). But it was not an an art-historian that he had carried out his investigations. What he was after was to find some place in which a definite way of life had reached its maximum development, where the savour of that life could be found in its highest concentration. That being his object, the cities of Turkey offered few temptations, for though there might be much to attract in their composite character, they had never, in any period, exhibited the Moslem culture in its pure state, and were now evolving very rapidly towards something quite other.

In the other centres to which he had referred, the genuine atmosphere of Islam had undergone profound changes, some of them, as in Egypt, due to the awakening of nationalist sentiments, others, as in Syria and Palestine, the result of a mixture of races and religions and of the haphazard introduction of Western habits of thought and of Western industrial methods.

"But isn't that all just as true of Tunis?" Sammécaud had objected.

"Not to the same degree. Under French rule nationalist and political passions have continued to slumber. The European minority lives side by side with the Mussulman population, neither mixing with nor violently reacting against it. The appearance and the essence of the old way of life have been far better preserved in Tunis than in Cairo or Damascus. Modern life has not, as in those two places, elbowed the Moslem ideal into the gutter or torn it higgledy-piggledy in pieces. You, who have been to Cairo, have seen all those new streets dotted here and there with shoddy blocks built on the European model, while all between is a wilderness of demolition and empty housing sites. The whole heart of the Arab city has been ripped out without plan or purpose. It reminds me of those towns one sees near the old front line in France—long straight lines of ruins left behind by the guns. So far, nothing of the kind has happened in Tunis, where the European city has been content to develop round and outside the Arab core. I say nothing of Kairouan, which is a marvel of preservation—something the like of which is not to be found anywhere else in the world. Not being an archæologist, I am not interested in places where the life of Islam is in a state of decadence, victim of some hostile principle, decrepit, sad, and no longer certain of itself. That, for one reason or another, is the case almost everywhere you go. Nor do I like what you in France call *'la pouillerie'*—squalor—or only when it has a certain air about it of truculence and colour. . . . The Arab city of Tunis is full of gaiety, colour, and superb self-assurance. It would be difficult to find anywhere a more satisfying sight than the local *souks,* or markets. What a gloomy business, by comparison, is the great bazaar of Constantinople! . . . Of course, there is always Fez, in Morocco. I am very fond of Fez, but it has never occurred to me to settle down there. I feel sure that I should have died of boredom and loneliness if I had. Thanks to Lyautey, the town has been admirably preserved, more carefully even than Tunis. But there is nothing very Oriental about it. I find it lacking in brilliance and variety. Even the sky there is at times as overcast as you'd find it on the Atlantic seaboard. In my idea of Islam there must always be a feast of sunlight, a delight of vivid colours, glitter, and sweet scents . . . all the poetry, at once gorgeous with the splendour of pomp and racy of the soil, which one associates with the *Arabian Nights*. . . . And then there is always the question of climate to be considered. The climate of Tunis is far from being perfect. But it's as near anything Eastern as I can stick. . . . The three or four most oppressive months of summer I spend in Europe. All the rest of the year in North Africa seems to me to be perfectly delicious."

William P. Milne went on to explain the way in which he had ordered his existence. His house was not in Tunis itself, but on the outskirts, at Sidi-bou-Saïd, where the air is better, the temperature more agreeable, and peace and quiet more certain. He had bought a palace built in the local style, dating from last century, and had remodelled and modernized it. The cost had been small. He had six servants—not by any means an excessive staff. He then gave some account of his average day, of the general atmosphere in which he lived. Almost every morning he went to Tunis, to the Arab city, where he lounged away his time, visiting merchants of his acquaintance and sitting with them in their shops. Or he might be asked as a guest to some old palace the blank walls of which look onto a narrow lane. He had made several friends among those foreigners who lived the same sort of life as he did (two or three people settled at Sidi-bou-Saïd), but for most of his social life he was dependent on a small circle of rich and cultivated Arabs. With these he exchanged calls, and by them was invited to feasts that were at once intimate and brilliant, at the opposite pole from "our dreary social functions," and marked by the elegant and voluptuous traditions of the now almost mythical East. William P. Milne did not elaborate the details of these sumptuous entertainments. He was content merely to suggest.

"I'm no longer the same man," he concluded. "It's as though I were living on a different planet. When I come to a place like this, and especially when I visit America, I get a sort of feeling that I'm asleep and having a lot of dreams, rather nightmarish dreams too, about some period of my existence long past and done with. . . . I don't really come properly to myself till I'm back in Sidi-bou-Saïd."

Sammécaud, too, had indulged in a few confidences. While trying to avoid anything that might seem to be pretentious, he had mentioned his pet theory of "art made real" and "living the chapters of a novel," giving his new friend to understand that he had more than once put the theory into practice.

Encouraged by these confidences, to which he had shown himself visibly responsive, William P. Milne, in the course of one of their last talks together, had said to Sammécaud:

"You ought to come along and settle at Sidi-bou-Saïd. I'll find you a house. You, like me, have reached the period of life at which a man needs a certain sense of stability. You won't be able to go on living the chapters of novels for ever, and it's a tiring business, anyhow. I think I've got a pretty good idea of what you want from life. You'll find it at Sidi-bou-Saïd, to a degree you've never dreamed was possible."

Sammécaud let it be understood that certain family obligations, which didn't exist, or not to the same extent, in the case of William P. Milne, would make such a permanent arrangement impossible for him. They could, however, be adapted to his theory of "chapters."

Milne replied that he was married and had two sons and two daughters, all of whom, however, were old enough, and sufficiently settled in life, to do without him. Provided one had enough money, he said, that sort of difficulty could always be overcome.

"Neither my wife nor my children have any real need of my presence. If they were in serious difficulties, I should be told. . . . Anyhow, I don't see why you shouldn't make a trial trip. . . . Come and stay with me this winter."

They arranged to meet again in Paris during October, when the whole question could be taken up again.

# Chapter

# 17

## SAMMÉCAUD AT A TURNING-POINT

This chance encounter had occurred at the very moment in Sammécaud's life when he was most likely to respond to a jolt. For some time he had been playing with the idea of "settling things once and for all." Even before the catastrophe of 1914 he had dreamed of breaking free from his business ties. He had actually gone so far as to take definite steps to that end. At that time he was finding considerable pleasure in contemplating a long vista of "chapters" to come. But the war had blown all such plans sky-high. It had broken in pieces all the "chapters" already lived through, and all that he had hoped to live through at a later date. These, with many other charming things, had fallen in ruins at his feet. Further than that, it had meant a vast increase in his own business commitments, and in those of the group of industrialists who were associated with him. This increase he had had both the courage and the good manners to deplore, but it had delayed the hour of his final retirement as surely as if he had been a civil servant.

Now, however, the whole situation had changed. The petroleum industry, or rather the odd and often deceptive mixture of industry and market-rigging which went by that name, persisted in prospering beyond anything that could have been anticipated. But no claims of national duty could now be invoked to keep the nose of a man who had made millions to the grindstone if he wanted to break loose.

Sammécaud's daughter had married (a man who was neither an astronomer nor a poet). The eldest of his two sons, Didier, continued to waste his time in ways that were neither those of 1880 nor yet of 1900, and which his father regarded as quite incredibly vulgar. But he got through a good deal less money than he pretended. He had inherited an avaricious strain from his mother. He had even been persuaded to take a post within the organization of the cartel, which did not, however, claim much of his time, since it consisted of taking distinguished foreign visitors to restaurants and night-clubs. It was a job after Didier's own heart. He drew on the business for his expenses, with the result that his own personal pleasure-budget was considerably lightened.

The younger boy, Raymond, was following quite a different line. He had just finished at the Central School. He was engaged, and made it quite clear that he intended to take a prominent part in the family business. As for Berthe Sammécaud, she seemed to find her days happily filled by the concerns of her daughter's household, and by preparations for her younger son's forthcoming marriage. Her temper had improved. She still sighed at times over her husband's absences from home, but the sighs were more a matter of form than anything else. A more definite separation would certainly not break her heart.

His private affairs, therefore, presented no insuperable difficulty. So far as the business was concerned, the problem was ripe for solution.

A growing complication within the cartel had led to a general loosening up of the organization. The heads of the associated firms depended less than they had done on one another. Some of them, like Champcenais, had struck out into new fields so vast and so profitable that they considered themselves now to be only to a very small extent dependent upon the cartel. At the same time as this slackening of ties was taking place within it, new links were being forged between some of its member firms and foreign groups, for the most part American. In short, the old balance of power had changed.

Now was the moment, thought Roger Sammécaud, to break free— partially from the business, wholly on the personal side. He saw clearly what would have to be done if he was to achieve his object. It need not take very long. First of all he resigned from the key position which he had held in the cartel, a position which, though it had given him powers of co-ordination over all the associated enterprises, had long since ceased to be more than moderately profitable. Next, taking advantage of certain offers which had been in the air for some time, he disposed of such of his holdings as could be easily realized. In this way he greatly increased his capital. One part of these additional funds he spread over a great variety of new investments, keeping the rest in the form of liquid assets. The management of what remained of his own business he entrusted to his two chief assistants, Gardebois, who took over the technical side, and Lafeuille, who would be in charge of the general administration. Gardebois had been one of his real finds, a mannerless oaf with a remarkably clear brain and a quite unusual power of making decisions. He had the further advantage of not being out for money. He was the kind of man to whom the running of a business was far more satisfying than the making of high profits. There was no danger that he would ever get too big for his shoes. Sprung from the "people," and gifted with natural common sense, he realized that he had done better for himself than he could ever have dreamed of doing, and was well aware that an excess of ambition may well end in disaster. He was on excellent terms with his employer. The two men differed from each other in almost every respect, but each knew that the other was ideal for the job he had to do. "I'm rather like some king of ancient times," thought Sammécaud, smiling to himself, "who was lucky enough to find among the sons of his chief groom the very man he needed as chief adviser." About Lafeuille he did not feel nearly so warmly. He knew all the man's faults, and realized that there was no refinement of treachery of which he might not be capable. Time and time again he had sworn that he would not be so weak-minded as to keep him, but then one day it had occurred to him that if there had been no Lafeuille he would have had to invent him, and that it was far better to have him working in the same office with himself than to know that he had been snapped up by some rival firm. Then had come the war, from which Lafeuille had returned covered with glory. And though he may have deserved only some small part of the recognition accorded to him, the point was that he had been recognized, with the result that henceforward he would, it was to be hoped, see how much to his advantage it would be at least to wear the trappings of virtue. "I have no illusions about him. He shall be my Talleyrand. When one's working with fellows like that, the great thing is to see that there shall be no Waterloo. But should I decide, like Charles V, to abdicate at the height of my power and retire into a monastery, he might see that loyalty to the business would pay him best." With Gardebois and Lafeuille in control, and the knowledge that Raymond would soon join them, the future seemed reasonably safe, and any position he might see fit to retain for himself in the concerns of the cartel assured. Besides, after all, he had no intention of going into exile at the other end of the world. He could easily keep himself informed by letter of how things were going, and from time to time he would come, say, to Marseille or even to Paris for a board meeting.

"Putting things at their very worst," Sammécaud concluded, "it may cost me a million a year in lost profits or unexplained leakages. No good looking too far ahead; life is too short."

He was not far from his sixtieth birthday, and he was only too well aware that the "brief span of life" was far from being a mere literary expression. On the other hand, the years through which mankind had just passed had convinced him that the lovely and rare moments of this world had also but a brief existence. He felt it almost a duty to enjoy them to the utmost before they too should vanish in a welter of destruction.

He had had a second meeting with William P. Milne in Paris. The American, somewhat to his surprise, saw that the idea which he had casually thrown out, so far from seeming to Sammécaud a mere piece of empty talk, had taken firm root in his mind. He concluded that the French are less superficial than he had been led to suppose.

"Grand!" he said. "If you've got this far, you'll never know any peace of mind until you've at least made a try on the lines I suggested. . . . I shall be home again in a week. I'll get going at once about finding a place for you—some house which you could take furnished by the year. An apartment in the city or a hotel would be no good.

You'd see things from the wrong viewpoint. Better not try it at all than that. I say by the year because you won't get anything decent on a shorter lease, and if you did, it would cost you almost as much. I'll send you a cable and let you know the figure. Then you can make up your mind. . . . Pleasant position, comfortable quarters—you can trust me to know the sort of place. . . . I suppose you wouldn't mind if the landlord wanted the lease to date from the beginning of the season rather than from the time of your arrival. I think that's the usual arrangement."

"What do you think it will cost me, roughly?"

"You ought to get something pretty decent for five or six thousand. For ten or twelve you can have a palace."

"Don't let that worry you. All I want is something comfortable and nice to look at."

# Chapter

## 18

### EN ROUTE FOR A NEW LIFE

That was how it came about that, early in January, Sammécaud found himself on the way to Tunis.

He had taken the greatest possible care in preparing his departure. Even before William P. Milne had let him know the result of his inquiries, he had set about making arrangements to reorganize the business on the lines he had laid down. He had given endless instructions to Gardebois and Lafeuille.

He had thought it best to disguise the real nature of his proposed journey and the reason for it. In talking to his staff, he had given out various rather mysterious hints to the effect that somebody had put him on to a pretty good thing in Tunisia, near Cape Bon. In the vaguest terms he alluded to vast tracts of unexploited land—olive groves, and so on. He had, he said, the gravest doubts about the economic and even the social situation in France, and was not at all comfortable about the future of industry. It might be as well, therefore, to see whether the risks could not be covered by launching out in new directions. But the possibilities would have to be studied at length, and on the spot.

Neither Gardebois, Lafeuille, nor the other members of his immediate staff showed any surprise that they were not to be associated with him in this journey of exploration, since it lay, so obviously, outside the field of their activities. As to Berthe Sammécaud, she had by this time grown accustomed to having but the vaguest idea of what her husband was about. He found no difficulty, therefore, in getting her to accept his story.

"If it comes to that," he reflected, "what's to prevent me from actually buying a few hundred acres, once I'm there? They might be a very good excuse if I do decide to settle down in North Africa. Some people may think it a mad thing to do to neglect my business at home in order to go off and become a planter. But it won't be the first time that a man's had a bee in his bonnet. All that people ask is an explanation that they can accept."

He took a great deal of luggage, but nobody found that particularly surprising. He never travelled light, even when he was to be away only a short time.

He packed with loving care, bringing to bear on the task all the ingenious imagination of a young man and the experience of a seasoned traveller. He made his choice of what to take with him as though the shopping facilities of Tunis would provide nothing but celluloid combs and garters.

Said he to himself: "For all I know, this may be the beginning of a new life. Six months ago such an idea had never even occurred to me. . . . With any luck, I, too, may find that I'm living on a different planet. If only this wretched liver of mine behaves itself!" A few excesses committed about Christmas had given him cause for anxiety on that score.

Sitting in a window at Basso's, he looked out on the old harbour at Marseille. A few stationary street-cars prevented him from seeing the Château d'Yf landing stage.

"Life," he thought, "isn't really so bad—just rather ridiculous and unfair. To me, and to a few others like me, it gives the marvellous opportunity of tasting one of the last surviving miracles of loveliness. I feel rather like a man who has gone down into his cellar after an earthquake and found a single bottle preserved by the merest chance. . . . Up above, thousands of his fellow men are still struggling in a world of blood and destruction, or mourning their dead. But what would be the good of sharing a single bottle among so many?"

He felt wildly happy, intoxicated by the prospects offered by a confused but delicious future. Kindly, generous thoughts, touched by a mild philosophy, took shape in his mind.

"I think I read somewhere that one of the rules of Islam is that the rich should give a tenth part of their wealth to the poor. If I really do settle down there, if I share in the pleasures of Islam, I will make that rule my own. One half shall go to the poor of Tunis, one half to works of charity in France. A tenth part of my income, if I make the reckoning honestly, is not to be sneezed at. . . . Quite apart from what Berthe and I give away already. . . . Oh well, there'll be time enough to think about that later."

His thoughts turned to the ship awaiting him at the Quai de la Joliette. The exciting prospect was not without its more sombre side. Sammécaud had a dread of sea-sickness. Partly because of it, rich though he was, he had reached his present time of life without ever having travelled widely. When, a year or two earlier, he had decided to take a trip to Constantinople, this same dread had led him, stupidly enough, to make the journey both ways by Orient Express. The crossing from Alexandria—he had had perfect weather both ways, except for a few hours in the Gulf of Lions—had put him on good terms with himself. Unfortunately, a considerable part of his journey to Tunis would be in the Gulf of Lions.

# Chapter

## 19

JERPHANION CONSULTS LAULERQUE
AND FINDS HIM ALMOST TOO MUCH
DISENCHANTED

The telephone rang while they were having breakfast. Jerphanion got up to answer it.

"Who was it?" asked Odette when he came back.

"You'll never guess!—Jallez! He would choose the morning I've
got to meet Laulerque at the station. And six months without a
glimpse of him. He was speaking from his hotel."

"Has he been travelling all night?"

"No, he made the journey yesterday. He only just didn't come by the
same train as Laulerque. It only needed that to make the coincidence
complete. But that's only my joke; he couldn't have. Laulerque must
have come by Pontarlier."

"What did you say to him?"

"Asked him to come around about noon and stay to lunch. I thought
you wouldn't mind, as we're expecting Laulerque anyhow. . . . I
only hope I shall be back by the time he arrives."

"Of course you will!" exclaimed Odette; "unless Laulerque's train
is terribly late."

"I'm not so much thinking about the train. I want to take him
along to the Quai de Béthune first. I thought you'd rather have us
out of the way, and we've got a lot of talking to do. . . ."

Odette was on the point of saying: "About what you mentioned
to me?" A few days before, when he had spoken of Laulerque's forthcoming visit (without mentioning that it had been suggested by himself), Jerphanion had added: "I'm going to take advantage of his
being here to ask him about certain forms of subterranean activity
with which he was closely connected in the old days. . . ." But he

had not enlarged on the subject, and the thought came to her now: "I mustn't be curious."

"I'd forgotten this view," said Laulerque, walking over to the window. "It really is superb. Unfortunately, it's a bit overcast today. When I was here last, there was just a touch of sun. . . ."

"Were you ever here? I'd forgotten."

"Of course I was—with Clanricard, that time we were discussing a trip to Russia." He chuckled ironically and pulled a face.

"Of course. . . . Take this chair so that you can see out of the window. Bouitton always sits there when he comes in for a chat. . . . Sure you're not too tired after your journey?"

"What do you think!"

"Have a cup of coffee, then. The cook can easily make it; she's got nothing to do. Bouitton's out and won't be in to lunch."

He rang the bell and asked the maid to bring coffee. Then he sent for Suzanne, the stenographer-typist, and said:

"If anyone telephones, say that both Monsieur Bouitton and I are out; and the same if there should be callers. Just take their names."

Then, turning to Laulerque:

"Like that, we shan't be disturbed. . . . I want to have a really serious talk with you. . . . I warned you that I should when I wrote. What I have to say may surprise you a bit—but no, on second thoughts I don't think it will."

He sat down behind his desk. His expression, his whole attitude, was that of a man getting his thoughts in order, of a man who wants to express himself clearly and forcibly and is not quite sure how to begin. Laulerque waited, a look of curiosity on his face. He, too, was preparing himself for what was coming, so as to grasp at once what his friend was about to say. The jerky way in which he opened and shut his eyes, the manner in which his face twitched in an attempt to control the almost excessive mobility of his features, gave evidence of the degree of his concentration.

"I needn't bore you with a long preamble," said Jerphanion, folding his arms before him on the desk and leaning forward. "You remember that evening in January 1910 which I mentioned in my letter? . . . The date came back to me when I thought about it a bit. . . . It all started in a café on the Place Clichy. . . . You were there with Clanricard and Mathilde Cazalis. . . ."

"Yes, I remember. . . ."

"You said that there was something even more urgent than the Revolution . . . and that was to put a stop to the coming war. We shouldn't put a stop to it, you said, by just crossing our arms and sitting back. You were obsessed by your idea . . . and then, later, you and I wandered together through the dark streets. . . ."

"I remember it all very clearly. I have often thought about that evening since. For some reason or other, it has stuck in my mind as an occasion of quite peculiar significance."

"Good. Then I suppose you remember what we talked about on our way home?"

"Indeed I do."

"It was then that you first mentioned to me the curious suggestion that had been made to you."

"Yes. . . ."

"Well, I'm in much the same state of mind now as you were then. . . . Odd, isn't it?"

Laulerque raised his eyebrows.

"Is someone suggesting that you should join an organization of the same kind?"

"No, that's not it. What I mean is that I am obsessed—agonizingly obsessed—even as you were then, by this idea: 'At all costs a new world war must be avoided. Whatever other difficulties the future may hold for us, whatever dangers, are nothing if we can keep the peace. But if peace goes, then everything goes.' This self-evident truth haunts me more even than it haunted you in 1910, if that be possible. Between then and now I have seen what war is like for myself, and I have taken an oath that I will do everything in my power to prevent another. It was chiefly for that reason that I went into politics, and wholly for

that reason that I am sticking there—that I am putting all my eggs in
the political basket. As I see it, the Peace of the World is the only
foundation upon which any Great Work can be built; in times like
ours, it is the one Great Work worth doing. For the last few months
I have been going about like a man who has seen the light. If we were
living in the days of Jeanne d'Arc I should say that I hear voices. . . .
I want to stop people in the street, and shake them and shout in their
ears: 'Don't you realize that it's the only thing that matters?' . . . I'm
going to be called upon to play an important part in the electoral campaign and in shaping the program of the Radical Party. I hope to play
a part, too, in the Chamber, if I'm elected. It's now, then, that I must
get my point of view fixed once and for all and plan my line of action.
What I am chiefly concerned about at the moment is to make a sort
of survey of all the ways in which mankind has tried to preserve peace
in the past—whether successfully or not isn't so much the question.
I don't want, *a priori,* to neglect a single possibility. That previous
schemes have failed doesn't prove anything. They've got to be studied
again in detail. If they broke down once, that may be because they
weren't suited to the purpose, or because they were wrongly employed
. . . or because people expected too much of them. . . . It may be
that several schemes will have to be combined. . . . Do you see what
I mean?" There was an almost audible tremor in his voice. "Whenever
I think about it I find myself clenching my fists. I'm like a peasant
with a grievance. It goes over and over in my mind from morning to
night. I won't let myself be discouraged.

"I believe in the energy of the human spirit—as you believed then,
as you may still believe today. I tell myself that if it has great potentialities for evil, it has also great potentialities for good. We have examples before us which you never had before you. Think of the story of
Lenin. Think of what has been set going by Mussolini and his doctrine of Fascism. What was Mussolini ten years ago?—an obscure
country schoolmaster, a petty Socialist agitator. If I'm not wrong,
Germany at this moment is swarming with adventurers of the same
stamp, men whose strong cards are energy, a belief in the power of

the human will, and a fixed idea. Why should we let these men have a monopoly of belief in the human will and of fixed ideas? Must an idea, just because it is approved by the reason, be vacillating and soft? You will tell me that these people exploit the passions of their audiences. My reply is that the people have passionate need of rest, prosperity, and peace. . . . Laulerque, there is still truth in the old image of the runner who passes the torch to his friend to carry on. What matters it if he falls in his course? The torch still burns. A sceptical observer might find something absurd in the thought of me, in 1924, taking up again with an idea, an obsession, which was yours in 1910, after all that has happened in between, after such a huge weight of disillusion and disaster to bring it into disrepute. . . . But once a man decides to take the heroic view of life, the case is altered."

Laulerque was now intensely serious, which meant that the twitching of his face had grown worse, while his eyes shone with a hot and restless light.

"And what do you expect me to do about it?" he asked.

"For the moment, I want nothing from you but a word or two of advice. But that advice must come from your very guts. . . . I know that you have had an odd and unusual experience of certain aspects of the problem. One day last year, if you remember, when we happened to meet and chat, you told me a few things you remembered from the days when you belonged to that famous Organization. . . . You said, I think, that you no longer felt yourself pledged to secrecy . . . and that, anyhow, you'd already spoken of it to Sampeyre, and perhaps to others as well."

"I don't think I said anything about others."

"Not even Clanricard?"

The suspicion of a blush showed on Laulerque's cheek. "No. . . . I may have dropped a hint or two in his hearing . . . but I certainly never let him have any detailed account of the matter, as I did you."

"I take your word for it. Some of the episodes you described were quite extraordinarily—let me say, thrilling. But I'm not asking you today for more details or for a more consistent account of what happened to you in that connexion. What I'm after now is something I've never had from you yet—a considered statement of your views. Bring all your wisdom to bear, Laulerque; forget your love of paradox and the spirit of contradiction . . . as well as any personal bitterness. Tell me quite frankly, is it your impression that, without prejudice to other forms of activity, something might still be done along more or less similar lines?—I mean, through a secret organization, recruited with the utmost care . . . and benefiting from past experience and former mistakes . . . a sort of order of chivalry, a kind of monastic body, diffused throughout the world. . . . Many of the historical orders had to contend with obstacles; others were still-born. No one has ever hit on the right formula at the first go. Many schemes came to nothing, many honourable attempts have been made to influence the course of history, some of them without success, but the fact remains that the world has had its Templars . . . its Teutonic Knights . . . its Jesuits . . . its Freemasons. . . . Or do you think that all that kind of thing should be relegated to the scrap-heap of childish romanticism?"

Laulerque squirmed in Bouitton's chair as though he were sitting on a red-hot stove. He seemed to be having trouble with his eye-glasses. At last:

"You put me in a terribly difficult position," he said. "You've no idea how difficult. All the time you were speaking, I felt the old flame burn hot, as though someone had been blowing on the dead ashes of a wood fire. . . . For many years now, and especially during the last two, I have done my best not to think of those old days. I said to myself: 'I regret nothing. Thinking as I did then, it was my duty to take a chance. There's nothing to be ashamed of in that. But it's time now that it was all decently buried.'"

"But you didn't seem to me to be avoiding the subject that day last year?"

"Oh, I recounted certain incidents, described a few curious scenes, because you appeared to find them amusing. You had started me on the subject, I don't quite know how, and your interest in it encouraged

me to go on. Ah, yes, I remember now, we had been talking about
your trip to Russia, about your friend Jallez's adventures—and from
that we went on to discuss the Russian character and then the peoples
of central Europe. What seemed to attract you then was the picturesque side of my adventure. I don't remember that you questioned me
much about essentials."

"That may be. My mind wasn't at that time occupied by the particular problem. But how comes it that you are so anxious to forget that
period of your past?"

"Put yourself in my place. Do you think it's really a memory in
which I take any particular pride—an episode much to my credit?
Try to remember the enthusiasm with which I embarked on it, my
faith in direct action. I won't say that I was ever tricked into doing
anything diametrically opposed to my convictions. But the general
impression left on me was one of frustration, of utter uselessness, of
having been caught up in a children's game. There were times when
what I chiefly remembered was that I had been nothing but a silly
little man who had been pressed, quite ignorantly, into an army which
was fighting in the interests of an Austro-Hungarian quarrel which
he didn't know even existed. The whole thing had just been a bad
joke . . . and the less I thought of it, the better. There are times when
I suddenly get a clear vision of myself sitting opposite Karl (I've spoken
of him before, I think) in some Bern beer-garden during the war.
The very face of the man comes back to me vividly at such times, the
convinced and honest look in his eyes. I can hear him telling me of
some plan that was to put an end to all the slaughter and bring reconciliation to the peoples of Europe, to usher in a time when there should
be neither conqueror nor conquered, and the seeds of revenge should
have withered. . . . At such times I feel myself invaded by a mingled
sensation of retrospective enthusiasm and terrible regret. I say to
myself: 'We were within a stone's throw of success; it needed only a
scrap more will-power, another ounce or two of pressure. . . . That
was one of those brief moments in history when man finds himself
inside the engine-room of fate, almost in the central room where sits

the engineer in charge, only a few paces from the controls. . . . If the luck had been a little more on our side, what might the results not have been? . . . Two million fewer deaths! And how much ruin avoided! While all the post-war problems would have been infinitely easier to solve.' . . . I think you will understand me when I say that such thoughts are less easy to bear even than those others of which I have spoken; worst of all when, as often happens, they come to me in Bern, where I constantly have to be on business. . . . And then I take a look at myself, at the man who has borne the full weight of those memories, and what do I see?—an obscure member of the middle classes no different from a hundred others like him, who makes a bit, saves a bit, does no particular harm to anybody—and does nothing, just nothing at all, to forward any of the causes in which he once believed. . . . However you look at it, that kind of brooding is thoroughly morbid . . . and so I take refuge in flight."

Jerphanion nodded his head.

"Yes, I understand," he said, "I understand. . . . But now that I have made you think of it—and I ask your pardon for having done so —can't you take advantage of the opportunity to give me the considered opinion for which I asked? It might be so useful to me, and to others."

Laulerque's agitation grew more marked. "A considered opinion, you say. I don't know that I have one. I still believe that some such piece of mechanism—somewhat modified, perhaps—might achieve something of the right kind. But one would have to be in complete charge, to determine the ends for which one was working, to draw up the slogans. . . . One would have to build the whole thing from the beginning, determine who should and who should not be recruited. . . . That, surely, must be obvious." He sighed. "I am a good deal more modest now than I was. Twelve or fifteen years ago I thought I was no end of a fine fellow. I felt that I was burning with the divine fire. I pitied the poor devils who could find satisfaction in a few hours' talk at some debating club. . . . I liked hearing my friends say that I was a bit mad. I knew that by madness they meant precisely that faculty of believing wholly in an idea and matching one's actions to one's beliefs. . . . Nowadays I see more clearly. I see that I was never quite mad enough. And if, Jerphanion, you'll let me say so, I don't believe that you are, either."

A worried look appeared on Jerphanion's face. "I'm not sure," he said, "that I quite understand you."

Laulerque forged ahead:

"You mentioned Lenin just now. . . . It's ridiculous, of course, to compare myself to a man like Lenin, but you must remember that I've had Lenin sitting opposite me as you are now; I've argued with him, man to man; there have been times even when I've almost lost my temper with him. . . . He was so sure of himself and, not seldom, so infuriating. . . . By the bye, I suppose you saw that he's dying— he's been quite helpless for a long time now. . . . To go back: if what I'm going to say is to have any sense at all, I must keep the comparison confined to a certain level. . . . When I compare myself to Lenin, when I look back at all that he has done in his life in the way of enlisting followers, imposing his discipline upon them, baffling the police of more than one country, amassing the sinews of war, and so on—and I am speaking now only of his preliminary exploits—I tell myself that he must have possessed an obstinacy, a power of standing up to discouragement, a confidence in final triumph, which, set against my poor little touch of madness, have all the marks of lunacy in very truth. . . . When I try to see myself faced by his problems—it's rather as though you were to ask me to lift a piano from the floor in one single movement and hoist it on to my shoulders."

Jerphanion's head had drooped. When he spoke, his voice was lower:

"Then you think that with a deep, rational faith and average tenacity one could never hope to do much in the way of changing the course of history, not even if one wasn't alone? And you don't believe that a strong dose of intelligence can ever make up for short measure in lunacy?"

Laulerque grimaced with nose and lips.

"Frankly, no, I don't believe it. What you and I think about war in the modern world is so obvious to the eyes of reason that the vast majority of mankind must be of our opinion. Clearly, then, the danger of war can't come from the reasoned conclusions of humanity. No, my friend, it comes from the vast and inexhaustible reserves of man's lunacy. Lunacy can be cast out only by lunacy—and a pretty large dose of it at that. The question of nationality also plays no small part in the matter. We, in France, have not the gifts necessary for that sort of thing. That was a favourite idea of Mascot's—the man, you know, who induced me to join the Organization."

Jerphanion straightened his back and grasped the desk before him, his thumbs beneath the edge.

"I suppose you realize, Laulerque," he said slowly, "that in giving me your views on the one method of which you have had personal experience you could scarcely be more discouraging?"

"And there's another thing," went on Laulerque as though he had not heard. "We've all of us got the poison of the frontiers in our veins."

Jerphanion all but burst out laughing. "That I can well believe. But I don't see what bearing—"

"You will in a moment. Let us assume, for the sake of argument, that some such attempt is set on foot again—some kind of more or less secret international organization—and that I join it. Knowing what I do, how could I help saying to myself each time that I ran up against a foreign member: 'How do I know that he isn't working for his own country? He may be carrying out the orders of his government. Perhaps he is hoping to make use of me for purposes of espionage, in order to provoke weakness and disorder in my country.' What it comes to is that I should be, half the time, in a state of acute suspicion, always afraid of being made use of. That will always be so while frontiers exist and, behind those frontiers, sovereign governments controlling unlimited means of bringing pressure to bear, as well as a lot of poor devils, like you and me, imbued, in spite of themselves, with nationalist passions, who, however free they may think themselves of that particular prejudice, find it soon enough when they see their country in danger, or when it occurs to them that they may be playing into the hands of the foreigner, the foreigner of today who may be the enemy of tomorrow."

Jerphanion had been listening with an expression of anxious attention.

"Yes, I see all that," he said slowly. "It's a very serious objection. It derives its strength—where mere nationalist sentiment is insufficient —from the dislike shared by all men of being made fools of. The attitude of our own Socialists at the beginning of the war is a very good instance: 'So the Kaiser's Socialists think they can do what they like with us, do they! We'll soon show them!' It's all very sad. . . . But not to scheme for the preservation of peace until there are no more frontiers is merely to get caught up in a vicious circle. It's worse, it's to be guilty of the rankest stupidity! . . . And when all's said and done, the frontiers weren't drawn yesterday. In the past, men have plotted internationally for great causes. Surely I needn't remind you of that old argument of yours that history can be interpreted in terms of secret societies?"

Laulerque sighed. "Oh, for Heaven's sake, stop! When you remind me of the vital, thrilling view I took of things when I was young, it's as though you were speaking of some paradise from which I have been shut out for ever. I feel sick with nostalgia. . . . Still, I can make some sort of answer to your charge. In the first place, frontiers formed a less serious obstacle in the old days. Scarcely anywhere did they coincide with the lines of demarcation existing between peoples. The shape of nations seemed to be much more a matter of the ruler's personal whim, with the result that his subjects had only a modified and conditioned sense of patriotism. And then when you talk of plottings having been carried on sometimes internationally—that is, across the frontiers—it is important to realize that it was not across the frontiers as we understand them. The divine concept of 'the nation,' in so far as it can be said at that time to have existed at all, was never directly threatened. There was no danger that the zeal of the conspirators for their cause might find itself in conflict with their patriotism."

"All right; but isn't Communism today, inspired by Moscow and spreading throughout the world, a sort of universal plot which takes no account of frontiers and may at any moment find itself in conflict with the emotion of patriotism?"

"The aim Communism sets itself is to transcend individual national-isms—which reminds me of something else Mascot said: he was a man whose brain was always chock-full of bright ideas, you know."

"Why do you speak of him in the past tense? Is he dead?"

"No; but it's ages since I saw him."

"Why?"

"When we last met we rather irritated each other. There didn't seem to be any point of contact left between us." Laulerque shrugged. "Well, one of his pet theories used to be that our great mistake had lain in not presenting the cause of peace to the peoples of the world as a positive aim . . . but only as the negation of an evil. No ordinary man finds that sort of thing exciting. You can only work him up—and this is especially true when he happens to belong to a nation of rather un-balanced visionaries—when you give him the task of building some-thing—good or bad doesn't matter, so long as it is something on a bigger scale than he is normally used to. World-wide Communism appeals, even to the mind that cannot rise above the petty details of conspiracy, as something new, as something bigger than the mere idea of nationalism, as a goal for the attainment of which separate nations should be sacrificed." He gave a sigh. "I have felt the fascina-tion myself. There was a time—or rather, I should say, there have been times—when I longed with all my might to be a Communist."

"And what prevented you?"

"Sheer common sense. I may be a bit mad, but, for all that, I'm a man of common sense. Or let us put it a little differently and say that I'm a realist. I saw that Communism could never succeed."

"Go on, this is very interesting."

"It enlists too many forces against it. A day is bound to come, and it may not be far distant, when throughout Europe and the world all the sources of possible support will have been exhausted. It will have reached saturation-point. And when that happens, we shall suddenly realize that all this time it has roused, concentrated, and solidified against itself very numerous and very varied forces, superior to its own in quality and weight, forces which, but for the threat and fear of Communism, would never have submitted to discipline. Take what has happened in Italy, for instance. I am constantly being told in Switzerland, by people who travel a lot to and from Germany, that Communism is well on the way to producing a similar state of affairs there. Very soon now it will find that it has swept into its net all the available man-power of the German industrial proletariat. It will have sucked Social-Democracy dry of its supporters, and maybe it will find it not very hard to smash the German Republic in pieces by a sudden uprising. But since, meanwhile, it will have had the effect of alarming, outraging, and infuriating the whole German middle class, upper and lower alike, as well as all the parties of the Right, it will find itself up against an enormous coalition, far richer than itself in men and money, and it will be just swept out of existence. . . . That, at any rate, is my view of what's going to happen. . . ."

"I think you may very likely be right," said Jerphanion. "My own thoughts frequently work along much the same lines. . . . But knowing, as I do, your liberal opinions, I'm a bit surprised, I confess, to hear you talk in that strain."

After a moment's thought Laulerque replied: "When you in France hear Communism abused, you assume at once that the attack comes from the reactionaries, from people of a past generation soon to be elbowed aside by the surge of events. But Switzerland, where I live, is essentially a democratic country; nine tenths of the inhabitants would claim to be workers having no connexion of any kind with large-scale capitalism, and consequently with a clear conscience on that score. They regard themselves as adult-minded, thoroughly modern persons with as much right to think about the future as anybody. You won't frighten them by saying that they're the representatives of an outworn convention; on the contrary, such language merely makes them shrug their shoulders. Well, almost every Swiss without exception regards Communism with bitter detestation. Extremist propaganda leaves them cold because they are well-educated and thoughtful people. They loathe Communism because they don't want, at any price, the kind of life it imposes. They far prefer their own, with all its imperfections, which, incidentally, they hope to mend by degrees. I imagine that the same is true of all the more advanced countries of Europe. How can Communism ever hope to overcome resistance so based? At the moment it is dormant, but any threat of danger might well make it active." He paused, then added on a note of deep seriousness: "Really, it all rather frightens me."

"How do you mean?"

"I've got an idea that the next war—if there's to be a next war—may spring from what we've been talking about."

"I don't understand."

"As a result of the massing of the forces of opposition. Do you follow the oratorical gymnastics of Mussolini and his gang? We in Switzerland have got front seats for that particular show. . . . You may say it's a lot of Italian hot-air. Perhaps you are right, but I don't like the way things are shaping. Just assume for a moment that the fear of Communism, and the exploitation of that fear, result in a crop of Fascist movements in other countries—and the thing's beginning—successfully establishing themselves. Fascism implies a recrudescence of militarism and the warlike spirit. It doesn't have to apply the bellows: the spark's there and will quite easily grow into a flame without encouragement. These movements grow by their own impetus. What starts in speechifying ends by assuming political forms. And now suppose that meanwhile Communism becomes stabilized in its own natural home, which is Russia, though still not wholly abandoning its dream of universal domination . . . suppose the Red Army becomes a force to be reckoned with. . . . I'm afraid I'm expressing myself badly, but it's all so confused in my mind. The one thing I'm absolutely convinced of is this: that Communism could have established a régime of permanent peace only if, immediately after the war, it had swept across Europe and the world, conquering every country at once, either by dint of peaceful persuasion or by the stunning effect of surprise. . . . It's hardly worth while pointing out how highly improbable any such development would have been . . . but now that it has given the forces opposed to it—and they are extremely numerous and not by any means all stupid—time to rally and unite, there are only two possible courses open to it: either it can take up the challenge and begin a fight to the death—which means not only another but a total war, something that has never before been seen, a sort of world war and civil war combined—or it can withdraw into itself, though even then, since it must have adequate defences not only against internal enemies but against external ones as well, who will lose no opportunity—witness the efforts of Denikin, Wrangel, and Kolchak—of attacking it, should it show the slightest sign of weakness, it will have to go ahead with what Trotsky began, and become a formidable military power. And the result of that will be that every other country in Europe will have to remain, or become, a formidable military power as well. . . .

"Now, we know from experience what, sooner or later, always happens in Europe when a number of its countries become formidable military powers. . . . Of course, there is always the League of Nations, and the hope that Russia may be induced to become a member. Everything depends on how efficient the League can be made, and on how sincere those countries may be which will decide, from time to time, to join it. . . . Nor, if you are making up a balance-sheet of chances, must you forget what is generally known as 'revisionism,' or, in other words, the desire of those who were defeated in the last war, sooner or later, and in some form or other, to revenge themselves—an attitude which Fascist Italy would dearly like to champion, since by so doing she could make things very uncomfortable for her former allies, with whose later attitude towards herself she is profoundly dissatisfied, and because Fascism is by nature out for adventure and is more likely to find it in that way than by tagging along at the heels of France and England. . . . No, turn where I will, I don't see how we can hope to find a bulwark of peace today in Communism . . . or anywhere, for that matter, in the state of affairs which has been directly brought about by Communism and the reaction against it."

It was a very melancholy Jerphanion who answered him:

"If it were only a question of what was going to happen to Communism—for which I have no special feelings of tenderness—I shouldn't care two hoots. But it is a question of what is going to happen to peace, and of something even more fundamental still, of what is going to happen to our hopes of ever being able to influence, by the exercise of the human will, the blind forces that shape events. . . . When I think of the Laulerque I once knew . . . with his fulminations against the preachers of inevitability . . . his theory of the 17th Brumaire and of what might have happened on the 18th . . ."

Laulerque was within an ace of blushing. For a while he remained silent; then suddenly he thumped the arm of his chair three times with his clenched fist. "Oh, for God's sake, stop! You needn't rub it in! I know I'm finished, I know I'm nothing but a dirty skunk!"

Jerphanion burst out laughing. "I wouldn't go so far as to say that!"

"Then you ought to!" replied Laulerque in tones of profound unhappiness. "Disenchantment, the lessons of experience, the bludgeoning we've all had at the hands of this hateful period—oh, I know there are plenty of excuses. But if the old flame still burned there!"—and he struck his chest. "Do you remember that famous line: 'Death caught the stripling poet—the man lived on'—I don't know whether I've got the quotation right—but if ever those words were true of anyone, they are true of me! Once I was a poet dreaming of heroic deeds; what am I now?—a slippered pantaloon! . . . But I'll tell you something else —health has had a good deal to do with what has happened to me, though not in the way that one usually means when one says that. At the time you knew me first, I thought that at most I'd got a few years to live. Consequently I didn't much care what happened to me and would have welcomed a chance of martyrdom. I was only too ready to plant a bomb somewhere, and be blown sky-high in the process. . . . But now I've got an idea that my Swiss doctors have cured me, or almost—touch wood—and I know something of what I'm talking about. I've had through my hands the records of hundreds of cases like my own. Looking at the whole thing dispassionately, I should say that I'm through the worst, that I've weathered the stage at which the patient usually dies, if he's going to die. From now on my lung-trouble looks like being an unimportant and not very tiresome ailment which will keep me company until I'm sixty, or perhaps even seventy, provided I live a rational sort of life. . . . One of our old patients dropped in to see us the other day. His cure dates from a time before the present sanatorium was established, but it was our doctor in charge—then quite a young man—who was responsible for his recovery, and the methods of treatment have improved out of all knowledge since then. The man I'm talking of must be seventy-four if he's a day, a dried-up old chap with a wrinkled face. But his eyes sparkle and his optimism is something to be envied. He seems rather proud than otherwise to have had the disease, and speaks of it as you might speak of hay-fever. . . . Well, all this means, don't you see, that I've grown to love life. I tell myself that with any luck I ought to be able to reckon on another twenty-five or thirty years. The doctor in charge even goes so far as to say that a mild form of tuberculosis, by helping certain eliminations and concentrating the defence-mechanism of the body along a few fixed lines, sometimes actually preserves people from many of the ailments which we associate with old age. . . . Nowadays I look up at the blue sky with a feeling of tenderness which is quite new to me. Twenty-five years may not be a great deal; but if one knows how to make the best of one's time—and when one's reached our age, one does know—one doesn't indulge in foolish waste. . . . I suppose you think all this is pretty degrading, eh?"

Jerphanion replied in measured, gentle tones:

"Why should I? It seems to me a profoundly human attitude. But even from that point of view, you must want the world to be a place fit to live in during the twenty-five or thirty years that remain to you."

"An unnecessary question—there's nothing I hope more ardently.

If only I could see how to help you! . . . But there you are, you asked me for an honest opinion on the lessons I learned from a certain experience which I once had. Well, I've given it to you. Apart from that—surely it's not my fault if I don't see a break in the clouds. . . . Only—look here, I've not finished yet, but I'm afraid you'll begin to think I've got a real bee in my bonnet and see everything in terms of my own medical history—I can't help thinking that the best thing we can do about these times of ours is to keep them going. The world has just passed through a terrible crisis; it has been spitting blood by the pailful. It's still as sick as sick can be. What we've got to do is to spare it all unnecessary shocks, wait until the wound heals over and the centre of infection becomes dissipated. Don't let's get into a panic if another one forms elsewhere. The only thing is to rely on the healing effects of time, to go on saying to ourselves that every fatal attack staved off is a step in the right direction. I'm for ever seeing doctors at work. It is very rare indeed that they are called upon to take a heroic stand, to do something definite, to face the adversary in the open field with the determination of fighting to the last man. As a rule they adopt a workable compromise, avoid making the trouble worse. They say: 'Let's get through the winter and then see.' You're going to be a deputy, a minister—oh yes, you are, I've no doubt whatever of that. Well, you'll find that your job is remarkably like the doctor's."

Jerphanion shook his head. The words reminded him of the way his own mind had worked—on days when his chameleon-like optimism had temporarily adopted the protective colouring of prudence. Had Jallez, in an attempt to reconcile the claims of mental lucidity and emotional well-being, talked like that, he would have felt a great deal less surprised than he did. Truth to tell, this rather retiring, disenchanted, and seemingly realistic way of appealing to "time the healer" was becoming a favourite gambit with quiet, decent-minded folk—or rather a sort of high-class consolation prize. It didn't strain the powers of illusion too far, and did put off the evil day of despair. Was all this a form of weariness, or due to a feeling that we were living in a period about which nothing at all could be done?

"I've got only too many people round me," said Jerphanion, "ready to tell me to live for the day, not to take risks, to wait and see how things will turn out—the very circumstances of my life are for ever preaching the same sermon."

Laulerque looked rather crestfallen. "I know I'm too impulsive," he said at last. "Sampeyre always used to accuse me of being a slave to my impulses. My mind works by fits and starts. I didn't really digest your question, but just gave you the first answer that came into my mind. Probably when I get back to my room this evening, I shall spend a lot of time telling myself that I fobbed you off with a lot of nonsense . . . which had nothing much to do with what I really think . . . a caprice, a burst of temper. And after you had brought me here for a serious talk, too! . . . What a fool I am! I'm going to sit down and see whether I can't think things out a bit better. Let's knock off for today—you'll only be wasting your time with me in my present mood. We'll meet again tomorrow, shall we? And do, please, forgive me—I'm just impossible!"

Jerphanion watched the play of winter sunlight on Laulerque's face, while, dimly reflected from the river outside, a train of ghostly ripples ran across the ceiling. The mingled smell of water and of Paris was strong in the room. That all too mobile face had lost none of its old power to charm. How easy to forgive it for masking so many contradictory emotions! Life, after all, would be much less interesting if it didn't, occasionally, bring one up against the unpredictable and the disconcerting. So few things in this world were ever really clear-cut! If one was to keep track of every fleeting pointer to the changes and chances of existence, it might be no bad thing to let the mind play freely, released for a while from the leading-strings of logic. In times, too, like the present, so stripped of all that brought comfort or certainty, one must learn to find a sort of pleasure, a kind of intoxication, in the very trembling of the earth beneath one's advancing steps. Even the horizon that marked one's journey's end was never still, but showed as a distant mirage, shone for a moment, and was gone again.

# Chapter

## ODETTE AND JALLEZ HAVE A CONFIDENTIAL TALK

Jallez, preceded by Odette, entered the little drawing-room, furnished in the style of Louis XVI.

"Jerphanion not back yet? I'm afraid I'm rather too early."

"No, he's not back, but you certainly aren't too early. I'll keep you company until he appears. I'm sure you won't mind if I pop into the kitchen now and then. Anything out of the ordinary upsets my maid completely. But I don't dare get rid of her because of the appalling difficulty of finding anyone else. You must just make allowances for the meal."

They sat down. Jallez looked round the Louis XVI room. Not that he had forgotten it, but his memory of it, in the intervals between his visits, modified the details in his mind. At times he thought of it as larger, at times as smaller, as gayer or more sombre. Each time he entered it he was conscious of a little shock of surprise. Today it seemed to him rather smaller than he had remembered, but rather gayer, too. The way it was arranged, though not startling, was certainly neither too conventional nor unpleasing.

"It really is nice here," he said.

Odette thanked him with a smile in which there showed a hint of incredulity, and answered:

"Please don't be polite! As a matter of fact, it's beastly. In the first place we need more space. Jean-Pierre has to sleep in my husband's study, on a little couch behind a curtain. Think what that means! Fortunately, he sleeps like a top and Jean manages to work evenings without disturbing him. But it means that he's got to walk on tiptoe. He hardly dares so much as to move a book. The whole thing's quite ridiculous. We've tried to find something else. They're asking terribly high premiums for all the older apartments. My father has offered to help, but Jean won't let him. He thinks that my parents have lost quite enough money already. Besides, it makes him furious to think of paying out money for no good reason. He regards the whole thing as a form of blackmail. . . . Anything in the newer blocks, with more than three rooms, brings huge rents, and there's not much available to choose from. . . . Jean doesn't get much, you know—less than he did when he was teaching."

"But that won't always be so, I suppose?"

"Perhaps not. But then our expenses will go up. . . . Still, we must make up our minds. What kept us from moving earlier was the fact that we were tempted into a lot of foolish expense here just after the war. We thought it absolutely essential to have running water, and to put a tiny bath into our diminutive dressing-room. The lay-out of the apartment made it all difficult, and the alterations cost us a small fortune. But Jean was so pleased! . . . Then there was the electric light, though that cost less. . . ."

"If you let it, though, you'll be able to ask a premium too, won't you, since premiums seem to be the fashion?"

"We've got a very disagreeable landlord; I think he must be a perfectly horrid man. He knows that we want to leave, and he has already promised the apartment to some people he knows. But the arrangement he proposes is that we should leave all the fixtures and not get a cent for them. When he gave us leave to make all those improvements, he stipulated that they should remain his property. When it comes to business, Jean will never really take a stand. When it's really necessary, he can lose his temper, but never for long. If the other man digs in his toes, Jean just says: 'Oh, have it your own way; let's get the thing done with!' "

The conversation wandered to other subjects. Odette asked whether anything new had been happening to Jallez, or was likely to happen. He replied that he was getting sick of Geneva, but that he found it easier to note the fact than to do anything about it.

"It's not really that I've got anything against Geneva as a place. It's more my manner of life that is getting me down. . . . I'm beginning to see that I need roots, a place to call my own—if you see what I mean," he added hurriedly. He spoke with a suggestion of embarrassment and seemed anxious that she should not misunderstand him. "I want some place, some collection of objects, that I can regard as my own and no one else's, something with an air of permanence about it, a nice comfortable rut which I might grow fond of. . . . I feel the need, and yet all the time I'm struggling against it."

"But why should you?" Odette asked him. Her surprise was perfectly genuine, although she was aware that Jallez's words had expressed that mysterious side of his nature of which she had always obscurely felt the presence.

He gave her a deprecating smile. "Because of a theory I formed long ago about the kind of life I wanted to live . . . and because, too, of the signs and portents of the times. . . . I've got a strong feeling that we're all of us, more or less, condemned to death. We're like a lot of stormy petrels, and if we're to be ready for what is coming, it's no good becoming too settled, is it?—too fond of things." At sight of a sudden shadow that dimmed Odette's eyes, he realized that his words might have caused her pain. He continued, therefore, in a more cheerful tone: "As a matter of fact, I am rather more settled than I was. I've taken a tiny apartment in the Upper Town—it really is tiny— half of an old middle-class house which has been divided. . . . It has a lovely view over the old walls to the mountains. . . . I've got together some odds and ends of furniture. . . ."

While he was speaking, Odette had been trying to imagine the apartment and the kind of life he led there. Did he share it with some woman who, perhaps, had begun by being his mistress, whom later he had installed there, though without any intention of marrying her? Jallez's emotional life was one mystery among many. Even Jean had only had glimpses of it, and since, in such matters, he felt bound by a sort of dutiful reticence, he had not passed on to Odette the little he did know.

It was this thought that prompted her next question. She spoke lightly, trying to mask her curiosity under a faint show of mockery:

"You're still not married, then?"

His answer was less immediate and less assured than she had expected it to be:

"No—though I'm not, probably, quite the declared enemy of marriage you might think me . . . or that I ought to be with my peculiar views about stormy petrels. Truth to tell, I've never met the right person."

"You probably demand too much."

"I certainly demand a lot. A successful marriage seems to be man's crowning achievement, and far rarer than a great friendship. You see, it has to solve so many more small problems, is so much more closely bound up with daily existence. I place it very high, but, for that very reason, think that only very exceptional people can undertake it with any real hope of happiness." As though to minimize the seriousness of his words, he added with a laugh: "I expect I shall meet my fate one of these days!"

Without waiting for her answer, he hurried on, in an apparent attempt to keep her from continuing with the subject:

"Probably if I lived in Paris I should have a less confused view of the situation—of my real needs, I mean. I get terrible fits of depression in Geneva. I feel that I've been abandoned by the world. . . . That wouldn't be so here, for many reasons."

"Have you no friends in Switzerland?"

He thought for a moment, before replying:

"Oh yes, I've got friends, companions, let us say, acquaintances, though I've never succeeded in becoming really intimate with anyone there. It's my fault, I expect." He paused again for reflection. "No," he said, "that's not quite fair. I do see a good deal of two French couples, the Gambiers and the Lejeunes. The husbands work, as I do, in the League of Nations. They're charming people, and we spend quite a lot of time together . . . make expeditions and things like that. But somehow, I don't quite know why, our chief bond seems to be a longing for Paris. That's especially true of the young women and me. We play a sort of game of 'exiles' together. We encourage each other to brood on the fact that we're not where we ought to be."

Odette went off to pay one of her visits to the kitchen which she had warned him would be necessary. On her return she said:

"I can't think why Jean is so late. . . . He went to meet Laulerque at the station."

"Yes, he told me he was going to, when I rang up this morning."

"Funny, isn't it, that you must have arrived almost at the same moment? Do you ever see anything of Laulerque in Switzerland?"

"Absolutely nothing, more's the pity. I think I've only run across him once, on the Lausanne station platform. I don't move about much, you know, and when we come to Paris we probably travel by different routes. . . . As a matter of fact, I don't know him at all well, though Jerphanion's told me a good deal about him. . . . I should dearly like to meet him again."

"I know that they had a lot to talk about. Jean must have taken him to his office on the Quai de Béthune, and they may have dropped in at the hotel on the way. It's quite likely, too, that Jean may have found some unexpected piece of work waiting for him at Bouitton's."

Jallez thought that he detected a faint note of resentment in her final words, though the circumstances seemed hardly to justify it.

"Does he often let you down by being late?" he asked with a smile.

There was a lack of frankness in her reply. And then, with amazing suddenness, the whole expression of her face changed. It was as though some ill-considered word had stirred to activity a swarm of complaints and grievances that had been lying dormant in her mind. Her voice took on a more gloomy note. A little pulse started to beat on either side of her throat. Jallez, looking intently at her, found himself wondering whether there were not tears in her eyes.

After a few stammered words, which had little apparent bearing on the emotional disturbance which accompanied them, she suddenly burst into a flood of speech. She needed no encouragement, and Jallez confined his part in the conversation to looking sympathetic and making occasional comforting noises.

"It's not a question of his being occasionally late, or of anything one can put one's finger on. . . . I'm not difficult, and I'm not a fool. . . . It's what's going to happen in the future. I'm terribly worried. I can tell you, because you're such an old friend, his best friend. I know you won't misunderstand. . . ."

Jallez was deeply moved by her confidence in him. He felt sure, from the note of uncertainty, of fear, in her voice, that she had never spoken like this to anybody else, probably not even to her parents. Odette was not the sort of woman to wear her heart on her sleeve or to play the part of the misunderstood wife.

She went on:

"I'm anxious about the kind of life he's leading. It's not doing either of us any good. You may tell me that I'm taking a childish view of marriage, though I don't think you will, to judge by what you were saying just now. . . . Up to now we've been so happy together, so united. Of course we've had our little quarrels, but they don't matter. I'm more experienced now than I was, I've heard other women talking, I've kept my eyes open, and I know what a rare and precious thing a marriage like ours is. Once one's tasted that sort of delight, no other life seems possible. Unless one can rely on that close, intimate happiness in the home, one can't take pleasure in anything else. . . . If that goes, everything goes. Don't forget that we had to endure nearly five years of war separation . . . and that meant a sacrifice that is quite indescribable, the sacrifice of our youth . . . of all the hours we might have spent together and which nothing can ever bring back to us. Those five years might so easily have built a barrier between us, or, if not that, have broken the charm, as they did in the case of so many other couples. . . . Thank Heaven we were spared that! But just because we were spared it, the years after the war were even lovelier than they might have been. . . . I'm expressing myself badly. If you weren't so sensitive and understanding, you might be tempted to think that I'd got something definite to complain about, which I haven't. It's just that—oh, in the vaguest possible way—I'm afraid of the future."

Jallez looked at her. Never before had he studied her so closely. Her pretty, deep-set eyes beneath arched brows were markedly round in shape. The irises showed a rich brown, the whites were clean and pure in tint, the lashes long. She had a straight little nose, ever so faintly tip-tilted, and her finely chiselled lips gave evidence of a gay and valiant spirit. Her skin was smooth and mat, her complexion a golden rose. The general impression was of someone in love with life, a complete stranger to bitter introspection. There was no sign in her, as yet, of that fullness of contour which comes with maturity. Odette was still a young woman with all her life before her. And here she was, afraid of it!

He said: "What is it that you fear?"

She bit her lips; then:

"That the kind of exhausting life he's leading may dissipate his energies, and bring him much disappointment and bitterness of heart. . . . But that's not really the point." The pulse in her throat became more accentuated, as though she were stifling the beginnings of a sob. "No, what I really fear is that, gradually, it may estrange him from me."

His voice now was very gentle:

"I understand so well this clinging to happiness, this constant vigilance lest it may escape. It's so much wiser to take precautions than to wait until the threat assumes form and substance. . . . Still— tell me, are you quite sure that nothing has happened, however trivial, that would justify your feeling of anxiety?"

She wrinkled her forehead and raised embarrassed eyes to his. "No. . . . As I told you before, it's only that I'm vaguely uneasy, that I have a presentiment."

"But there must be some foundation for such a feeling; not necessarily anything serious in itself, but something that may perhaps foreshadow serious consequences in the future. Or am I quite wrong?"

Odette struggled painfully to reply. Her agitation betrayed itself by little movements of her face, her hands, and all the upper part of her body.

"You'll laugh at me!" she said at length. "But I can't help it if you do! I'd rather you laughed at me than that you went away with a wrong idea of what I mean—it's so difficult to explain—but, well, let me give you an example. . . ."

And she started to tell him, speaking very rapidly and interrupting her narrative with little nervous laughs which gave the measure of her confused state of mind and of the need she felt to apologize for her words (but also of her need for some reassurance, if only in the form of good-natured mockery), how, a few weeks earlier, Jerphanion had been asked to dine by a certain Countess who had not included her in the invitation, and was, apparently, in complete ignorance of her existence. Jerphanion had accepted, and had come back from the dinner more dazzled than he had altogether been willing to admit. Then later, on the pretext that the Countess ran a "day" and that he would meet in her drawing-room certain men of the Right who were not too firmly fixed in their political principles, and with whom, in the interests of the party, he ought to keep on good terms, he had gone once or twice to see her. On these occasions he had stayed rather longer than mere politeness demanded and had come home in a new and rather odd mood which had shown itself in brooding fits of ill-disguised excitement.

"I don't mean that he has ever deceived me in the sense of telling me definite lies. He admitted quite frankly, for instance, that the Countess had paid him very special attention, had had a long and intimate conversation with him, had asked him to explain what part he expected to play in the forthcoming elections, and what plans he had for the future . . . and that she had shown an intelligent and sympathetic interest in what he said, which at times amounted almost to enthusiasm. . . . But he has been guilty of deception in pretending to attach no particular importance to these things, and in talking as though they were no more than the natural behaviour of a woman of the world who wanted to be polite to a stranger."

"But mightn't he be sincere in such a view?"

She shook her head. "No. . . . This new world into which he has stepped, this Countess, and the various other women he meets in her house, have thoroughly unsettled him, more, perhaps, than he realizes himself."

"May it not be that there is safety in numbers?" asked Jallez in an attempt to laugh her out of her mood.

She gave him an obedient little smile, but it was rather mechanical. "I'm not saying that there is any real danger in this particular business, though of course one can never be sure. But the same sort of thing may happen again, may go on happening. . . ."

"But surely there have been similar incidents in the past? . . . And they didn't end in disaster?"

"That's quite different. Jean's not the sort of man who's always out for adventures. Unless I'm very wrong, the initiative rarely comes from him. On the other hand, up to now, women who are out for that kind of thing haven't set their caps for him—women, I mean, of a certain social standing. I'm not afraid of the other sort. He's not likely to lose his head over merely physical charms. Whereas a woman who chose to play him up by pretending enthusiasm for a cause, who sympathized with him and quite obviously admired him, who had the prestige which comes of education, refinement, and perfect manners, as well as the merit of having overcome the prejudices of her world in order to share his convictions—he would be less likely to mistrust the motives of such a woman and to stay on his guard. . . ."

Jallez, who had been following her with the greatest attention, smiled. Odette, he felt, was showing a remarkable capacity for subtle analysis. The immediate danger might be less acute than she imagined, but she wasn't so very far wrong in the view she took of her husband's character.

"You see," she went on, "when we were first married, my husband offered no temptation to a woman of that type. What was he?—an obscure school-teacher. Any haunter of society ballrooms would have been more to her taste if she had just wanted to amuse herself. But now people are beginning to talk about him as a coming star in the political firmament. I can just imagine the kind of things Bouitton says here and there: 'That boy'll go far; you see if he doesn't.' And that makes all the difference, doesn't it? That kind of woman's always deceiving herself. She might not dare to run after a man simply because he was young and happened to have taken her fancy. She wants some kind of excuse. And what better excuse could she have than to become the inspiration of a rising statesman, and through him"—she gave a little nervous laugh—"to influence the future destinies of France?"

"My dear Odette"—Jallez put all the seriousness he could muster into his words—"I'm not going to say that you're crazy. I've been much struck by the excellence of your reasoning. But there is such a thing as what the mathematicians call the coefficient of probability. I don't think that in the present case it is very strong. I'm not denying that the kind of danger you have so ably described may exist, but unless you have kept back some piece of definite evidence—"

"I have kept back nothing."

". . . I don't think it likely that it will emerge from the realm of theory. And you must be careful not to help it to emerge. It's quite possible, you know, to spoil your happiness by showing an excessive, or a premature, zeal in its defence. Men don't like women to be too jealous. And when they think that the jealousy is unfounded, that, instead of being grateful to them for having shown unusual common sense—yes, Odette, very unusual—their wives reproach them more violently, and display more ill temper than they would have done if they'd caught them in some sordid little affair, they are apt to become easily irritated. Some of them get into the way of thinking: 'Well, if that's how she feels, I may as well be hung for a sheep as a lamb.' "

The doorbell rang twice.

"There they are!" she said, and added hastily, in a low voice: "Promise you won't say a word to him!"

"Not even indirectly?"

"No, no, please!"

"I certainly won't say that you have been talking to me. But the right word dropped at the right moment might make him think a bit."

They could hear the noise of the door opening, and then the sound of voices in the hall.

"No, I beg of you! Promise that you won't say anything at all."

"All right, then," he said, rather perfunctorily.

The door of the drawing-room opened, and Jerphanion, with his hand on the knob, stood aside to let Laulerque come in.

# Chapter

## 21

### A PARTY OF FOUR.
### MISSED OPPORTUNITIES

The luncheon was gay and animated. No one appeared to be indulging in secret thoughts under cover of the general conversation. Neither Jerphanion nor Laulerque made any allusion to the subject of their long talk earlier in the morning. A good deal of light chatter went on about Switzerland and about the different ways in which Jallez and Laulerque spent their time there. The two men compared impressions, narrated typical experiences, and discussed the comparative merit of various Swiss cities. But Laulerque was able to draw on a greater fund of information than Jallez, who was entirely ignorant of a number of places and had only had a glimpse of others in passing.

"You make me regret my lack of enterprise," he said. "I see now that often, when I was bored stiff in Geneva, I could so easily have taken the train and gone off on a voyage of exploration. One's so often guilty of that kind of stupidity in the course of one's life, don't you think? Just because one doesn't happen to like the place in which one has been compelled to live as the result, very often, of reasons that have nothing to do with the place itself, one neglects to take advantage of the unexpected and unique opportunities it offers. One sort of takes it for granted. One lets the days slip by without trying to get the best out of them, for no better reason than because one has made up one's mind that it's no good making any effort. How bitterly one may regret that attitude later! Fifteen years from now I shall probably kick myself because, when I had the chance, I didn't explore the villages of the Hauts-Grisons in midwinter, or take a trip along the Austrian frontier or in the Valais, which I'm told is well worth while. Instead, I just gloomed the time away between my four walls. I don't know, Jerphanion, whether you remember something extraordinarily true you once said. It was when we were walking somewhere near the Tuileries, before the war. . . . It all comes back to me now; it was in the Tuileries Gardens. You said: 'There is a particular science, or art, rather, which is still awaiting development—the art, I mean, of learning to use our time to the best advantage, of being able to pick out at first glance the things which in ten or twenty years will still have a meaning for us, will still have power to make our hearts swell with emotion and fill us with a sense of intolerable regret, while others, which, at the time, seemed infinitely more important, will appear in the light of memory as so many tiresome bits of routine, things that took a lot of useless energy and turned out to have been mere waste of time or worse. . . .' I remember vividly the sound of your voice as you said 'or worse.' That's precisely the problem I'm up against now. Down there in Geneva, I ought to be able to foresee the severity, the feeling of having missed my opportunities, with which I shall judge myself later, when I realize what chances I missed of exquisite enjoyment lying ready to my hand. And yet I think that, on the whole, I am a good deal less shortsighted and blundering in such matters than most men."

"You've taken the words out of my mouth!" broke in Jerphanion. "When I feel like that, I always find myself thinking of you and of the example you set. I have always regarded you as a master of that particular art."

"I'm afraid you flatter me! But, to revert, there's a fellow I know slightly in Geneva who was stationed for two years in Persia. He was so bored there, or rather he had made up his mind in advance that he was going to be so bored, that he never even tried to see anything of the country. I'm not sure that he bothered about getting to know even Teheran. He spent his afternoons at the bar of a big hotel, yawning, playing bridge, and complaining of his exile, in the company of an Englishman and two Americans."

Jallez and Laulerque expressed considerable surprise that they had not met oftener. They discussed in detail the single occasion on which they had run into each other in the Lausanne station. When exactly had it been? Where had they both been coming from? Laulerque said that there was another occasion on which he had caught sight of Jallez. It had been at Geneva, on the Quai du Mont-Blanc, but he hadn't had the courage to make himself known. Jallez reproached him for the omission, and they undertook to see a lot of each other in the future.

"It's very easy for me," said Laulerque. "I have a free pass and the use of a car as well. I could meet you in Lausanne without any difficulty, or pick you up in Geneva."

They exchanged addresses and telephone numbers, and explained which days and times were best for them, how they could most easily take a few hours off from their work.

"I'll show you villages in the Oberland and in the Canton of Glarus," said Laulerque, "which you didn't know existed. One can always manage to reach them even when the snow's on the ground, and there are plenty of sunny days in the winter. We can always leave the car somewhere—one can go pretty high if one uses chains—and take a sleigh. We'll pay a visit to some people I know who live in a mountain chalet of the real old-fashioned kind. They'll give us cheese soufflé to eat, and scrambled eggs and thin slices of smoked ham."

And so they went on, playing a sort of sonatina together, in which the twin themes of friendship and opportunities missed (but not in the days to come) recurred and mingled.

"Missed opportunities," said Jallez, "are the curse of existence. They are like moth-holes in the fabric of life. . . . In love, too, they are not unknown. But in that case there is consolation in the thought that they could not, perhaps, have been taken without, sooner or later, causing pain to someone else and destroying his happiness. . . . The victim is not always there on the spot, but there are very few occasions on which there is not a victim of some sort."

Though Jerphanion and Odette felt rather out of the conversation, they listened with a good grace, intervening now and then in support of the argument. It pleased them to think that their table had seen the birth of a friendship which was to make up for so many missed opportunities and which held the promise of so much happiness for the future.

When luncheon was over, Jerphanion took Jallez aside.

"Have you a moment to spare?" he asked.

"What, now? At once?"

"Yes."

"I'm terribly sorry, but I'm afraid I've got to rush away."

Jerphanion's disappointment showed in his face.

"Will what you've got to say take long?"

"Yes, rather long."

"What a nuisance it is! If only you'd told me when I telephoned, I could have arranged things."

"It didn't occur to me," stammered Jerphanion with ingenuous candour. "You see, I thought—I suppose I was a fool— Well, it can't be helped."

"I could give you all the time you want tomorrow morning."

"Right you are, then. Let's make it tomorrow morning." There was the suspicion of a sigh in Jerphanion's voice.

"What time and where? Here? Or at the Quai de Béthune?"

"Anywhere you like. . . . Let's say ten o'clock here, if that suits you. I'd thought that as the weather was so lovely today we might have discussed what I've got to say walking about the streets as we used to do. . . . There's no knowing what it'll be like tomorrow!"

He looked like a child who has been cheated of some expected pleasure and can find no comfort in promises, however gorgeous, since they cannot undo the sense of disappointment in his heart.

"Good!" said Jallez, not altogether untouched by a sense of sadness. "I'll come for you at ten. Perhaps it will be a fine day. Why not? I shall be prepared for any kind of weather, and we'll make the best of what the gods send."

Laulerque, too, tormented by a variety of regrets, arranged for a private chat with Jerphanion.

"The more I think things over," he said, "the more sure I am that I talked a lot of nonsense this morning. I made a disgusting exhibition of myself. Don't pay any attention to what I said. I'll ring you up early tomorrow—that all right?"

It was not without a feeling of melancholy that Jerphanion saw Laulerque and Jallez going off together.

# Chapter

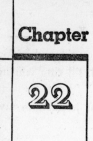

## TWO MEN AT ODDS WITH THEMSELVES

They walked westwards along the boulevard Saint-Germain, saying little as they went. Laulerque had fallen into one of those day-dreams of his which found expression not so much in words as in movements of the head and facial grimaces.

After they had gone some way in silence, he said without warning: "Have you got a good memory?"

"I?" exclaimed Jallez, surprised. "Well, that depends. I don't think that as a piece of automatic machinery my memory's up to much. It's very unreliable, apt, you know, to drop a whole lot of things which I may need later but which don't happen to interest me at the moment, or in which I have tried to interest myself though in a rather half-hearted fashion. It has its own arbitrary methods of classification, which are a mystery to me. I suppose that's more or less the case with everybody, though some people do seem to have a memory which functions more or less automatically."

"Perfectly true . . . but what I'm really after is this: do you fairly often find yourself caught up in the memory of some emotion, some impression, which had a strong effect on you in the past? Some emotion, I mean, which, without quite knowing why, you regarded as being more than usually significant. Do you feel that if only you could recapture it entirely, you would have the key to all sorts of problems, that you would no longer accord the same degree of importance to this or that incident, that you would know better what to do in order to win happiness, and so on . . . only to find that the memory in its necessary completeness slips through your fingers? It's as though a veil had dropped before my memory. As soon as I make a conscious effort to recapture the sensation that's plaguing me, it goes clean away. . . . So far, of course, what I've said is the flattest of commonplaces. . . . It's on the next stage that I should value your views. . . . You're pretty certain to have experienced the original emotion in some one, definite spot. You can see it clearly in imagination, and there is nothing very remarkable about it. You'd been there often before the date of your special experience, and have visited it often since. It follows naturally that you find it all the harder to fix, even approximately, the date of the original occurrence. . . . You've got a vague sort of idea what time of day it was, the state of the light. . . . Well, now, if you quite honestly want to get that memory back, how do you set about it?"

"In the first place, I should think that if you tried, at different times, to think back deliberately, to isolate in your mind certain details which your memory reproduced, even though in a fluid form, connected with the original happening, you might arouse an associated memory which would help you to fix the date. . . . And then, as a result, it ought to be possible to reconstruct the circumstances which surrounded it. I don't say that that would necessarily reproduce the emotion, but you never can tell."

"Of course," went on Laulerque, as though he had not heard, "there are other vivid impressions out of my past which I find no difficulty in recovering. I can remember the place, the hour, the approximate date, the people who were with me, if there were any, and also, to some extent, the ideas and feelings which I had at the time, and the reason why that particular memory seems so significant, so thrilling. Only this morning, when I was with Jerphanion in his office, an instance of that kind came up, of which he himself had reminded me. But the worst of the other sort, the sort I was telling about before, is that you get only one or two vague hints, and try and try as you will, nothing definite comes at all."

"Have you tried going back to the place in question, at approximately the same time of day—since you say you usually have a pretty vivid recollection of the state of the light, the time—and hanging about to see whether anything happens?"

"Yes, I have hung about there more than once since I began getting curious in the matter. It's only fairly recently that the thing has become an obsession. But at first it was all very vague. 'It's odd,' I said to myself. 'What is it that this place reminds me of, and why does it seem so important?' One evening, about two years ago, I had just left Clanricard—that was how it all began, but nothing definite emerged. . . . I didn't try to force my memory. Since then I've found myself passing the spot two or three times, but the time of day has been different, and I have probably had my mind filled with other things. . . . I think you're right. I'll try."

Then they relapsed into silence.

Just as they reached the boulevard Saint-Germain, they stopped in front of a news-stand.

One of the magazines had a cover showing the picture of a young woman in colours (probably a photograph, or a drawing executed with photographic realism). She was elegantly dressed for winter walking in clothes of the latest fashion: felt hat, fox fur, tailored suit. The picture ended at the waist. The expression of the woman's face had a look of insolent pride. Her figure was swathed in fur, her pretty, wide-open eyes looked straight out from the page. There was a hint of condescension in the smile on the reddened lips.

"Pictures like that, nowadays, tug at my heart-strings," said Jallez.

"Why?"

Jallez pointed. "There is something so fragile about it, it's got so little basis in reality, so little solidity."

"What has?"

"Look at her expression, the assurance, the pretty disdain with which she gazes at us . . . her self-confidence. . . . It's all so charming; she's so happy to be alive, to be just what she is, to be afraid of nothing. . . . Each time now that I find myself looking at pictures like that, full of feminine grace and a sort of queenliness that somehow doesn't irritate one, the kind of face that used to fascinate me and make me feel slightly inferior, I think of all the similar faces that have watched a firing squad line up in front of them in some country or other which

I have recently visited . . . or at least have wept in a vain attempt to soften the hearts of the warders in some concentration camp . . . that have frozen in terror at the sound of police officers in the hallway or at sight of a tribunal of bawling fanatics . . . of all the faces of those women who have had it suddenly borne in on them, in a split second, that no amount of disdainful smiling, no coquettishly raised eyebrow, no queenly glance, is going to avail them anything, that all this parade of challenging eyes, of impudence and invulnerability, of 'I'll never do what you want' or 'You'll have to do what I want if you don't want me to get angry,' is just a hollow mockery, something brittle as a seashell that will break at a touch, a theatrical convention that worked only when there was still room in life for elegance of living. Once the jack-boot has started tramping, once the world has become a place of Kommandanturs and Chekas and machine-guns . . . when nothing is left but naked force, and it has become the only reality . . . what hope is there for all that pretty play-acting? Yes, I want to cry out: 'Oh, you poor darling!' "

They crossed the boulevard.

"Don't misunderstand me," Jallez went on. "My feeling has nothing to do with a desire for revenge, has no connexion whatever with the savage grin of the sansculotte who says to the former noble: 'No more of your la-di-da airs now, my fine lady!' or 'You won't look like that much longer!' Just the contrary, in fact; it seems to me perfectly horrible that we should have once more reached a time when the sight of a little too much self-assurance on a woman's face makes us want to cry."

He added: "We're all in the same boat. We've all got some photograph of ourselves tucked away which shows us looking as though we were on top of the world. There are moments now, moods, when to look at it gives us the shivers."

They reached the open space in front of the Odéon. Jallez saw the time on a clock.

"I'm late," he said. "I must take a taxi. Let's meet again before you leave. I've got your address."

A little farther on, Laulerque saw a motor bus marked with an H. "I'll take it," he said to himself. "I'll get off at the Place Clichy and sit at Wepler's till it gets dark and the lights come out in the dusk. Then I'll go towards the Caulaincourt Bridge. I'll concentrate. I'll see if I can't get what I'm after."

He had no idea how long he had spent in the café. He had tried to find the corner where he had once sat with Jerphanion, Mathilde, and Clanricard. But he couldn't be certain which it had been. It seemed to him that the place had changed.

He let the memory of that evening drift into his consciousness. Little by little the pieces fell into place. He found that no deliberate effort was necessary to reconstitute the scene. Mathilde's laugh sounded in his ears, something said by the bearded Jerphanion of those days. He could see again Clanricard's thoughtful face and astonished eyes, and the Clanricard of his memory had still two arms. All around him the square, the streets, the underground passages of the Métro, filled gradually with the fashions of 1910.

He felt the old flame of those days rekindle in his breast. What had been true then was true now. What had been more urgent than anything else in those days was still more urgent than anything else. What had deserved the tribute of enthusiasm and sacrifice deserved them still.

"Why did I speak as I did to Jerphanion this morning? Is my spirit of contradiction as self-assertive as all that? Certainly not as a rule. But it did seem rather absurd to hear someone else, so long afterwards, trotting out all my pet theories. I felt just a little irritated, and that made me want to deny even the thoughts that I had had, the thoughts that had lain nearest to my heart. It was as much as I could do not to exclaim: 'It's taken you long enough, in all conscience!' . . . as though that mattered! It took our Jerphanion four years of war to teach him that the high-strung little schoolmaster was right. But who am I to throw that in his teeth? . . . Four years of war, and his first grey hairs. Yes, he is going grey on the temples. So am I. But mine aren't so obvious. Besides, I'm going bald pretty fast, and the odds are that most of my hair will have fallen out before the change is noticeable. There's justice even in these matters!"

But there was something indistinct about this uprush of 1910 memories. Something deep within himself refused to come to terms with them. Something seemed to be distracting his attention, something at once futile and fundamental. "I didn't come here for that!" What he had come for was to see the fading daylight and the first lamps.

When the dusk had made it difficult to distinguish the roofs of the houses opposite through the café windows, and the lights of the moving traffic had begun to weave a pattern with the fixed lights of the street-lamps, he got up, left the café, and started to walk along the strip of ground that ran down the middle of the boulevard, towards the beginning of the rue Caulaincourt.

The hour was well chosen. The quality of the dusk, the mingled effect of darkness and lamplight, was just as it had been on that day of long ago. One thing only was not just as it should have been: the state of the pavements, an effect, perhaps, of dampness. Yes, that was it. The dark gleam of wet pavements was absent, the atmosphere of a holiday spoiled by rain. Absent, too, was the shimmer of almost imperceptible drops around the lamps. The light striking from the shops at his right hand was a little too violent, unless it was that the illumination of those days had become dimmed in memory.

Were the street sounds as they had been? Memory said no. But was its message true? Instead of the unbroken swish of motor tires, had there really been, on that evening long ago, quite so many sounds of horses' hoofs, quite such a crowded clip-clop, as he seemed to remember, all along the street and over the bridge, becoming muted with distance; a soft, muffled diminuendo in the moist air, fading into a perspective of silence? Or was his imagination merely adding its quota to the remembered facts, as when the mind in a dream strives to supply the local colour of a period?

He walked as slowly as possible. He stopped in front of a shop

443

window, but without looking in, because he knew that the objects displayed would not be the same, nor, indeed, the window itself, and so would not help his reverie.

"Approximately when was it? What was I doing here? . . . The thought of Mathilde keeps coming into my mind, of meeting Mathilde at the other end of the bridge. And the thought, too, of Margaret-Desideria. A lot of different memories are muddled up in my head. Mathilde played no part in the particular impression I am trying to recapture, nor did Margaret. No single individual did."

As he drew nearer to the bridge (and he had to exert much ingenuity to keep from reaching it too soon, so short was the distance), he felt himself brought up short by a painful sensation of frustration. This powerlessness of the human spirit to seize and hold something that was its own by right, something much desired and probably of great worth, struck him as a miserable infirmity. "Even should it turn out to be nothing at all, I want to be sure that it is nothing and so free myself of the obsession."

He had already passed the first criss-cross girders that form the sides of the bridge, and had almost begun to lose hope, when he became conscious that something had happened, something so slight as to be with difficulty identified, like a faint puff of wind on his cheek or the sudden shudder of a clearing mist. Even before he had succeeded in grasping, however vaguely, the nature of the impression just on the point of taking form, he realized that it would be precisely what he sought, and at the same moment he was aware of a tiny sense of disappointment: "Is that all, then?"

The scene became detached from himself; the things round him, the actual world, at the point where it impinged upon his consciousness. A gulf seemed to open at his feet, but it had the curious quality of diminishing in no wise the dimensions of the phenomena involved. They were not, as it were, drowned in the receding darkness. On the contrary, everything became extraordinarily vivid, astonishingly interesting. Not a detail was superfluous or vague. The whole thing took on the perfection of something seen under glass in a museum. It was like one of those carefully built-up period rooms in a museum, in which you can see everything, in complete comfort, without losing a single detail, each flower in the carpet and the gold hand on the clock-face; but between the exhibit and yourself is stretched a velvet cord which you make no attempt to cross. It separates you from the scene within. On one side of it lie the various objects, all of them in the frozen perfection of things dead and done with, which, if they move at all, do so only within that closed circuit of the past; on the other, you, the observer, situated in a totally different dimension of time.

But from it all there spreads a still subtler emanation holding at its heart a note of counsel—like some magic formula, written on a folded scrap of paper and slipped into your hand.

There, before you, is something complete in itself, achieved and perfect in the completeness of the past. But no less perfect, in a sense and partially, is the perfection of the present. And as soon as you realize that, you will never again suffer torment on its behalf or your own; never again be troubled, for you will be set free from all the terror of the times to come. The future can no longer appal, no longer stain the present with its shadow or fright it with its sombre vulture's wings. For the present has become the past and, as such, is now invulnerable.

You cannot force the passers-by to know it, to live as though their world were set in the tranquillity of completion. But you, who are a visitor of some other species, fresh from some other world, with all about you, like the air you breathe, the dimension in which you live—you mingle with these others and move with them, enjoying what they enjoy with a keener sense. You long to whisper in the ears of all those men and women: "If only you could realize how calm and inoffensive it all seems, seen from where I see it!"

But over and above this there was a sense for Laulerque that the earlier scene was, as it were, superimposed upon the present. But this complication was without importance. In a sense, neither of the two scenes was anterior in time to the other. Both had been plunged into the protective fluid of the past. Some degree of exchange between them seemed right and natural. The clip-clop of horses' hoofs, muted by the distance, drew out the pattern of their sound upon the road made dark and glistening by the fallen rain of long ago where now was audible the swish of motor tires. What here obtained was a brotherhood in the formed and finished, a change of features and a mingling such as the dead know in the cemetery that raised its mounds over there to the right.

When he reached the farther end of the bridge, he asked himself again: "Is that all it was?" and, without pause, replied: "Yes, all. . . . But there is more yet to be found, and I will seek. I hold the key, but know not yet how best to use it. I am still feeling about for the lock."

Just as he entered the rue de Maistre, a sudden craving for a trivial point of exact knowledge teased his mind: "I still haven't discovered when exactly it all happened, nor in what connexion." The picture of Mathilde flickered ghost-like between the corner of a wall and a street-lamp. He cut his brooding short: "That's absurd! What had Mathilde to do with it? I'm getting everything mixed up."


The following night, about two hours before dawn, Jerphanion woke suddenly from sleep. At first he was conscious only of a sensation that partook at once of anxiety and peace, a confused mood of urgency and regret. Then he began to follow out a line of detailed thought, though not knowing to what extent it carried on his dreams or whether what had wakened him might not have been their vivid reality.

"I have no friends now . . . in the sense that once I understood or that one finds in books. Jallez is my best friend. But of what does our friendship consist? How casual and incomplete it is! More and more it seems lacking in all it should contain of a deep mutual knowledge, of shared and unbroken intimacy. . . . When we were at the College, it still held something of that quality . . . when he used to tell me, for instance, the story of Hélène Sigeau . . . or when he called on me to get him out of his difficulties with—what was the fellow's name—Maurice Ezzelin. In those days, too, there was the fact, of capital importance, that all our daily life was shared, so that we lived in common each incident and thought of every hour, and even made one in the secret brooding of our minds. But already there was over-much of privacy. There were many things he never told me of! There was never a time when I could really have built up a convincing picture of a single week in Jallez's life, even approximately. But now! Yesterday evening Odette told me of the half-questions she had put to him, and what he had replied. She hinted that I almost certainly knew more of his secret life; that if I pretended to be no less ignorant than she was, that was from loyalty to the claims of friendship. But what do I know?—that Jallez lives in Geneva when he is not travel-ling, that he is engaged in some occupation about the nature of which I am still extremely vague. When has he ever described to me in detail the place in which he works, the people who are his colleagues . . . the way he spends his time? Presumably he takes his meals in a restaurant, but even of that I am not sure. And in what kind of restaurant? Is it always the same one? He has alluded in my hearing to his apartment in the Upper Town, but he has never gone into details. And yet he knows that I am a good listener and that I am interested in other people's activities. I learned more about him at luncheon yesterday when he was talking to Laulerque than I had known before. And what about the more intimate side of his life? Since he is my best friend and I am his, surely I ought to know every-thing, or almost everything, about that? In fact I know strictly noth-ing at all. If I try to visualize him in his apartment, I am reduced to making the mildest guesses. Does he live alone or, as Odette sug-gested, with some woman whom he does not want to parade in public? And if so, what kind of woman and where did he pick her up? Do they sit down of an evening at a small table in his study and eat a dinner that she has cooked? Or would it be truer to imagine a dis-creet knocking at his door, and a woman slipping in—well dressed, perfumed, and furtive? For the life of me, I can't say which hypothesis is the more probable. I feel that our friendship has become a poor thing, that there is emptiness where there should be substance. All very well to say that what we share are the important things, the great ideas and noble preoccupations of our lives. All bunkum! As though the intimate things, the secret things, were not just as important, or even more so; as though they didn't bite more deeply into human sensibilities, exercise more power than anything else over the means to happiness. One can share ideas and noble preoccupations with anyone, and frequently one does; which only goes to show that we do not regard them as constituting the most jealously guarded part of our selves, which we can share with others only when we have proved, by means of the severest tests, that they are worthy of the confidence.

"That's what makes the idea of marriage so important. Marriage may involve all kinds of perils and enslavements, to be sure, and it is rarely a success . . . its importance lies in the fact that it makes necessary just this complete community in little things. As soon as that community ceases, the ties of marriage begin to work loose. . . . I know that that condition has its own dangers; it means that each party to the union has to be privy to the other's each and every trouble, no matter how trivial—a stomach-ache, the loss of a button or a cuff— and gradually one gets into the habit of keeping secret all the graver problems, the small store of sublime preoccupations which one creates for oneself in the course of the week, hoarding them as a bee its honey. The life of the heart is difficult. . . . One must see to it, maybe, that the sublime is not eaten up by the daily round. But it is no less a duty to guard against emptiness and the cold winds of the desert. A friendship from which all day-to-day concerns are banished becomes no more than an allegory. . . . It's a matter for sorrow that circumstances have made it necessary for Jallez to live so far away. Nothing can compensate for lost proximity. Friends, as I understand friendship, should meet every day, even if only for a moment. They should be in a position to telephone to one another: 'How about an hour this evening, before dinner? At what café shall we meet?' or: 'Come and dine with us if you're doing nothing.' Friends go walking together . . . friends share one another's amusements, even those which promise to be of no particular interest, in which they indulge merely to pass the time. It is essential that friends should be often together, even when nothing particular is happening. Boredom endured together, labour shared, has a virtue all its own. But the real point is that nothing that affects one, however unimportant and insignificant, nothing that may change one's way of living or touch one's happiness in any way, should remain unknown to the other. I fully realize that all this implies, on either side, a degree of friendship far above the average. But anything less . . .

"Take Caulet, for instance. The quality of his friendship is not of the highest order, but that is no reason for my neglecting him as I do. When he was appointed to the Lycée Voltaire last October, he came to see me. Can I put my hand on my heart and say that I made him really welcome? . . . I know that we asked him to stay to dinner. . . . I thought him looking fatter, rather pot-bellied and shining. I noticed that he had clipped his moustache (as though he had not as much right as anybody else to be in the fashion and clip his moustache), thought him too well shaved to fit into the picture of him I had carried about in my imagination, and, if not well dressed, at least excessively respectable (as though he must be condemned everlastingly to frayed trousers and dirty collars, just so that my legendary picture of him should not be falsified!). He was much struck with Odette, whom he scarcely knew, and seemed particularly anxious to make a good impression on her. He was always one for the women, but in a rather clumsy, dubious manner, like one of those old fellows who like to take their fun in a corner and pick up the scraps from other men's plates. How many times had he met Odette before that evening? Four or five at the most. Once, if I'm not mistaken, before the war, and once during . . . or perhaps twice. Once or twice since. . . . He did his best to make himself pleasant, within the bounds of good manners. But good manners are not his strong suit. He's only really himself when he lets himself go. I didn't do much to help him. My cordiality must have seemed rather absent-minded and a trifle patronizing. When he left we made a vague undertaking to meet again. And since that evening I've not given him so much as a sign of life. Odette, who has never seen him in his wilder moments or witnessed his displays of fireworks, found him, I think, rather awkward. When I quote instances of his high spirits, she thinks that I am embroidering on memories of an old companionship. . . . There can't be many people as amusing as Caulet. I certainly have not met his equal in fifteen years of living. Fabre was a great stand-by in the trenches. But his waggishness wasn't in the same class. It never touched me so nearly, or called forth so many responses. One makes so few friends in the course of a lifetime, while the bores, the sham buddies, the seekers after favours, are thick. Not that I should ever think of picking on Caulet as my best friend. In a sense, I should have to keep too close an eye on him, though, to be sure, the women to whom he is dangerous are of the type to which all men are dangerous. The great thing is to have a subtle sense of friendship, to know precisely what may or may not be expected of any man. There are many wise men who regard the world as a hodge-podge of brigands, through which we pass because we must, trying to collect as few kicks as possible. But there is another view of the art of living, which consists in cultivating a small number of friends, each for the quality that is his special own, and sticking to them till death."

His heart began to beat violently. He felt as though a hand were feeling round his throat, seeking to strangle him. Soundlessly he repeated the words *"fugit irreparabile tempus,"* without asking himself into which precise aspect of his meditation this idea of fleeting time would fit. But of the fact there could be no doubt whatever. Time was passing for him as it had never passed before. If he were to use his life aright, there were things needing urgently to be done and errors to be corrected, without the loss of a single moment.

Had he not been afraid of disturbing Odette, he would have got up there and then, run to the telephone, and rung up Jallez: "I can be ready in half an hour, and in three quarters I can be at the Place du Châtelet, if that's convenient, waiting by the little column, or, if it's raining, inside the street-car station. . . . I've got so many things I want to talk to you about. There'll never be enough time for all I've got to say. Oh yes, I know it's still dark, but why should we bother about that? We don't often have a chance of seeing a winter dawn in the open streets. We'll have a cup of coffee at some counter with the market porters. We'll tread on a carpet of cabbage leaves."

But his courage failed him, and the fact that it did so deepened the worried mood in which he looked out at the world. "In the old days I shouldn't have hesitated. It's growing older, really, that does it. It's not that the body would be more reluctant, or only very little, or the mind either, if that were all I had to think about. . . . It's the growing complexity of life that hampers one's movements, convention, this and that preoccupation, the fear of making a fool of oneself. And what would Jallez, snug in his hotel, reply? Probably he would tell me, with a yawn, that I'm an ass, that I had dragged him from a lovely sleep, that he has no wish to stand shivering in the drizzle of early morning, and that it'll be time enough if we meet as we arranged to do. Hasn't he grown older too?"

# Chapter

## MONSIEUR POUZOLS-DESAUGUES
## GIVES SIGNS OF LIFE

Nevertheless, Jerphanion got up earlier than usual.

Odette, whom, in spite of every precaution, he had wakened, said rather peevishly:

"What is the matter with you? It can't be time yet. I bet that the cook isn't even down."

"Nothing to worry about," he whispered. "Go on sleeping. I want to get going a bit earlier, that's all . . . but there's no earthly reason why you should get up. The contrary, in fact."

He finished dressing as quietly as possible. That done, he had to admit that he had got up simply because he was restless, and that he hadn't the ghost of an idea what to do with himself in order to fill the time until Jallez's arrival.

He went to the front door himself when the concierge brought up the mail. One of the letters bore the postmark "Le Puy." The contents ran as follows, and at the end he read the signature of M. Pouzols-Desaugues.

January 20, 1924

Le Marolle
Brives-Charansac
Tel.: 7
Dear Sir:

I have news for you, though less definite than I had hoped. But one has got to take what comes.

The interview between the fair widow and our friend D. has taken place. I gather that the lady showed herself to be no fool. She appeared to be much upset at the idea that her husband's death had given rise to gossip. Quite of her own accord she said that something of the same kind had occurred when her father-in-law had died. Why that should have been she couldn't say. So far from wishing to pull wool over the eyes of justice, she would, for two pins, have demanded an exhumation of the two bodies. All she wanted, she said, was for everything to be dragged out into the full light of day and settled once for all. Our friend concluded that she had no reason to be nervous, and that the people up at the farm, whether guilty or not, felt pretty safe. He is more than ever anxious not to start anything unless he can see his way clearly.

In urging the meeting I suppose I let my mind work either too subtly or too simply. Events have failed to bear out my anticipation. I must wait until some better opportunity occurs.

Our friend G. has started that little retrospective inquiry for which, if you remember, I thought he would be so admirably suited. But the results, unfortunately, have been meagre in the extreme. The old folks remember one case of death, but there seems to have been nothing dramatic about it—just the kind of thing that happens in the most healthful of houses. My farm gets away with a perfectly clean bill of health.

Don't forget our bargain. I am waiting impatiently for news of our gentry of the Seine-et-Marne. When I get it, I will write to you of less important matters, notably of the progress made hereabouts by the candidature of a certain young political leader whose acquaintance I recently had the great pleasure of making. My wife wishes to be most kindly remembered to you.

Believe me, dear sir,

> Yours very sincerely,
> H. Pouzols-Desaugues

As he read this letter, Jerphanion was conscious of a sense of irritation, though it did not banish from his mind the vision of climbing roads along which, in the cold air, he had driven and talked and dreamed. "He seems to think that I have time to waste."

Which was precisely what he did have after he had finished his early breakfast. The thought of his coming meeting with Jallez and of all the things he wanted to say to him prevented him from turning his mind to any serious work. "I may as well answer Pouzols-Desaugues at once. Then it'll be out of the way."

He wrote as follows:

Dear Sir:

I too was impatient for news, though, to be perfectly frank, I have not, perhaps, been quite so seriously at grips with the problem as I should have been. My mind has been distracted by others which affect me more nearly. But though I haven't altogether played my part in the matter, I am only too glad to profit by the work of others.

I never really understood, I admit, what exactly you hoped to gain by bringing our friend D. and the fair widow together. Not being in the secret of your subtle planning, I am scarcely surprised at what you report. But you don't seem to have lost all hope, and I confidently await future developments.

On my side, I have even less to tell you. I did telephone a few days ago, but the only effect of my questions seemed to be to rouse the authorities from a twenty-year sleep. "What! Still got the bee in your bonnet? The thing's becoming an obsession with you!"

As soon as I'm through with some rather urgent business, I'll try what a personal visit will do.

Thank you for being so meticulously faithful to the letter of our bargain. Even what you refer to as—quite rightly—"less important matters" are of considerable interest to me.

Please thank Madame Pouzols-Desaugues for her kind message, and believe me

Yours very sincerely,

JEAN JERPHANION

Short though the letter was, it contained two or three misstatements either of fact or of feeling. For instance, the telephone call to the magistrate was pure invention. There was a time when he would have hesitated to adopt such methods of getting himself out of a difficulty. But he had grown used to putting off tiresome callers of Bouitton's with this kind of yarn. The time was not far off when he would have to make use of similar devices on his own account: "I've been over to the Ministry at least three times to look up those papers of yours, my dear sir. . . . They're perfectly appalling people to deal with!"

# Chapter

## 24

They had waited a long time on the curb. Once or twice they had stepped off into the roadway, only to beat a hurried retreat before the oncoming traffic.

"Don't you think," said Jallez, "that walking in Paris since the war has become far less pleasant than it used to be? I've got no rooted objection to noise and crowds, but they pursue one all the time. It's become a regular problem how to get anywhere. Every street-crossing is a puzzle that's got to be solved. I've got the feeling, too, that people hustle one more than they used to, even in those parts of town where one could stroll so happily in the old days. The result is that conversation suffers. One's constantly being separated and torn away from one's companion, constantly having to feel one's way back. . . . The world's suffering from a sort of spatial ague."

Jerphanion's reply was absent-minded. For the last half-hour he had been saying to himself, over and over again: "I ought to be discussing matters of real importance with him. That was why I was so anxious that we should meet. But I shan't have the necessary peace of mind until I've first got off my chest the thoughts that worried me all last night. I must find some way of saying: 'Friendship's only a sham when two people know practically nothing about each other. Actually, I'm almost completely ignorant of how you live. Talk to me a little about yourself. In return I'll answer any questions you like to put.'"

But the right moment never seemed to come. Even between old friends the right moment is essential if certain things are to be said. They must crop up naturally in the course of conversation, must seem to be involuntary and not the result of premeditation. It may often

456

happen that one's interlocutor is not deceived, but he is not so ill mannered as to take the talk in bad part. The rules of the game have got to be observed. Since he himself contributes something to the course followed by mutual discussion, he is in some degree responsible for any indiscreet question which may rise to the lips of his friend, and under a certain obligation to answer it. If he takes refuge in reticence, then it is he who is responsible for suddenly introducing an element of caution and mental reservation into the free and natural processes of friendship. In fact, he shows himself a bad player at the game of confidences.

Jerphanion waited patiently, but somehow the right moment would not come. Yet the scene around them seemed admirably suited to intimacies. A wide stretch of pathway ran down the centre of the road, planted with trees and dotted with benches. The surge of the traffic was confined to the thoroughfare on either hand; the bustle of the pavements was, as it were, drawn off into the side-streets. Nor was the noise continuous, but throbbed with an irregular note between the low-built houses. In the spacious avenue, beneath the high-arching sky, it had the effect of being thinned and dissipated. The style of the buildings was that of fifty or a hundred years ago. The general sense was one of a middle-class suburb which had been gradually encroached upon by the spread of Paris. The sounds and jinglings of the street, filling the air and clustering about advancing feet, were not deafening, but gentle. For all their note of modernity, they fitted well with the sweet old names of Reuilly and of Picpus. The weather was not as good as it had been on the previous day. The sky sagged, and the touch of the winter's day was too reminiscent of the nuzzling of a melancholy dog. It needed but the onset of a few personal troubles to bring a sense of shivering discomfort. On the whole, however, the sadness of the material setting was not without a certain pleasurable quality.

It was Jallez who broke the silence:

"Sometimes," he said, "I'm sorry that I'm not five or six years older. You'll never guess why."

"No; tell me."

"Because in 1900, at the time of the Exposition, I was only a child. My powers of appreciation were limited, I had no knowledge of life, no freedom of movement, and no pocket-money. If I were five or six years older I should have been then—yes, I should have been about the same age as I was when you and I first met. The Exposition, instead of merely leaving on my mind a vague impression of rather frightening, rather crude bigness, without overtones or any stimulus to thought, would have taken in my memory the place it deserves—that of an event rich in a sort of pathetic majesty . . . a vast sunset glowing for ever in the shadows of my past."

"Are you pulling my leg?"

"Not at all. The more I think of it, the more convinced I become that the Exposition was a great firework display heralding the end of a period . . . the final cry of that period's sense of joy and triumph. And the period had, in fact, been a particularly splendid one, marked by a belief in liberty, in progress, in science, in machinery, and in universal brotherhood. It died, not at once, but a few years later— ten or so—but the intervening time saw its gradual decadence and the slow increase in the intensity of its death agony. If only I could have strolled, not once, but hundreds of times, both by day and by night, about that Universal Exposition, a man full-grown! If only I could have rubbed shoulders with that polyglot crowd, the like of which has never since been seen, nor ever will be, feeling its happiness, its belief in the future (never so great as then) . . . its expectation that perhaps a few days would see the declaration of Universal Peace . . . its certainty that the years to come held a limitless perspective of great works, that the peoples of the earth would march forward in friendly competition, that the world would turn out, after all, to be of centaur breed, part power, part justice, in which we should see capitalism and socialism miraculously united. But as things turned out, I missed all that!"

"And so did I. You, when all is said, did manage to get a glimpse, however blurred and imperfect, whereas I was even more miserably out of luck, for I was never one among those millions of undistinguished provincials whom the excursion trains decanted into Paris. The children of farm labourers came, but not I. I have never forgiven my parents for that . . . but, poor souls, it wasn't their fault. In the spring of that year my father was seriously ill. He had double pneumonia with complications. They had to spend a lot of money. Doctors in out-of-the-way country places are expensive luxuries. My father remained weak for several months. Both he and my mother dreaded the idea of so long a journey and the fatigues that would await them at the end of it. In short, despite the temptation, despite the special arrangements made by the railways and an invitation given me by my uncle—the one who used to live close to the Gare de Lyon and who died last year—I never saw the Exposition. I was miserable at the time, but chiefly because most of my school friends were in better luck. But I never fully realized what I had missed. Now, listening to you, I see it all. . . . As you say, it was a moment of apotheosis, and the more tragic, I think, just because it didn't mark the actual, the dramatic end of a period . . . wasn't, in your words, a sunset. That final comment of yours strikes in me an answering chord. As I see it, humanity was taken up into a high place and shown a brilliant present with, beyond it, a future into which it might step at once towards horizons of increasing splendour. 'See what your possibilities are! Things that you have never yet had are within your power to attain —you have but to stretch forth your hands!' And then the thunder crashed. Apotheosis flamed into apocalypse. For me, the sequel to the Universal Exposition, which I never saw, was Verdun in flames, which I did see."

He realized that the theme thus incidentally announced by Jallez had drawn from him an almost exaggerated response. But still it had not sounded the right moment for which he hungered. "We could go on endlessly playing variations on our thoughts as in the old days. Such easy chat would be delightful in its way. But it happens that I have matters of importance to discuss with him. And he seems to have forgotten that I told him so yesterday. He goes on weaving his lace-

like meditations in a mood of calm detachment and never for a single
moment thinks of giving me the chance I need. Well, one subject is
as good as another as a point of departure. But I must make up my
mind to take the plunge."

Of the two problems which occupied his mind, he chose the one
that would jar less obviously on his companion's mood, because it
had but little personal application.

"I wanted to ask your opinion on a matter which has been much,
and increasingly, on my mind."

He spoke of how he had for months past been thinking about the
state of the world; of his sense of an increasing urgency that overcame
him when he realized that very soon now he would be called upon
to play a part in politics.

"You must forgive me if I repeat the commonplaces of the moment,
if I speak of the things that everyone, more or less, regards as obvious.
But there are dead ideas by which people are as little inconvenienced
as they are by corns, and there are living ideas which tear the heart
out of one's body. Mine is torn by this conviction that the world must
be saved from a new war, that we've got, at once, to find, with that
object, not fine words for speeches, but means of action, surveying all
possibilities, picking out those most worth while, concentrating our
attention upon them . . . and finding new ones if we can."

He explained why, and in what words, he had questioned Laulerque.

"That was why he was lunching with us yesterday. I don't suppose
you guessed it?"

"Of course I didn't. I thought he had come to Paris on business
connected with his sanatorium, or just for a holiday."

"He didn't say anything when he left with you?"

"Not a word."

"I suppose," went on Jerphanion, in a tone that betrayed something
of his anxiety, "that you must think this effort of mine to start a sort
of *a priori* scientific inquiry instead of doing something straight off

the reel pretty stupid? You probably regard it as all very academic, very intellectual, in the bad sense of the word?"

"Not at all. Everyone knows that an engineer can't build the simplest bridge without a great deal of preliminary work, without studying how similar problems have been solved in the past. How, then, can one be expected to start reconstructing the world except on a basis of much laborious thought? . . . Those who laugh at the unwillingness of intellectuals to commit themselves prematurely don't know what they're talking about. . . . What was Laulerque's answer?"

Jerphanion smiled. "Do you mind if I don't tell you at once? I want to hear your opinion first, uninfluenced by the thought of anybody else." Then, seeing a look of surprise on Jallez's face, he added: "Actually, Laulerque said things that might so easily have come from you, or so, at least, I thought . . . and I don't want that fact to stand in the way of your repeating them. . . . Do you see what I mean?"

"Yes . . ." Jallez spoke thoughtfully, "although I don't quite see . . ."

Jerphanion interrupted him with the news that he had been to see Lengnau the previous week, and had asked for his views on the problem.

"What an extraordinary notion! . . . I don't suppose if you hadn't mentioned him that I should ever have given so much as a thought to Lengnau again. . . . Don't you find him almost too much of a museum piece? . . . But there, I suppose I mustn't ask questions."

Jerphanion smiled once more.

"His case and Laulerque's are not quite the same. . . . It is not very likely that what you may have to say to me will coincide with the views of Lengnau. I haven't the same fear that your spontaneity might be influenced."

"Then you'll admit me to the secrets of the oracle? But before we begin on that, tell me, how is he these days? Is he still living at the same place?"

"Yes—rue Guy-de-la-Brosse—just round the corner from me. That was one of the reasons that decided me to go and see him: it was so easy."

"Hadn't you ever met him since the old days?"

"No."

"Since when, actually?"

"Wait a minute—it must have been, yes, some time during our second year—1910, I suppose, pretty early in 1910—roughly, about this time of the year. Fourteen years! What an appalling thought! Fourteen years! How they have flown! In another fourteen years we shall be a couple of old dotards! And what shall we have accomplished in the meantime?"

"He must have changed a good deal—grown older?"

"Not as much as you'd think. What should you say his age is now? It hadn't occurred to me to wonder—sixtyish, I imagine. He's got rather a dried-up appearance. His hair has turned white and his face is paler than it used to be, but he's still a good-looking fellow. The general impression is that of a rather battered gentleman of the old school. His manner is even more detached than it was, but his mind is as clear and fresh as ever, though there is a trace now of cliché in his talk."

"He must have been very much surprised to see you."

"Not excessively so."

"But surely, after all this time?"

"I had warned him that I was coming. He took a couple of seconds to fit my face into his memory of me . . . then he accepted me as though we'd met no longer ago than last year. . . . I got the impression that the passing years affect him less than they do us. It is natural for him to see things 'sub specie æternitatis.' . . . It's an attitude, too, that I think he cultivates. . . . His room looks exactly as it always did—the same pitch-pine pigeonholes, that I swear; the same books on the same shelves . . . the big map still where it always was. . . . I found all that rather appealing. So many things nowadays are upside-down."

"What did he say to you?"

"In that, too, I could see no change. He behaved precisely as though we were taking up a conversation where we had left it a few months ago. To what, I wonder, is that due? To a remarkable memory? To the fact that he is always thinking of the same things and can find his way about in them without effort?"

"Why not to the remarkable impression which you produced on him?"

"Oh, shut up! . . . Almost the first thing he said, with a smile of indulgent superiority, was: 'Well, you see, it wasn't the end of the world after all.' I must say, that brought me up short."

"Was he referring to something you had said in 1910?"

"I think it was probably a sort of gloss on that 'Well, what about it?' of his—you remember?"

"Yes, I remember."

"I think I had been talking about the fear of some catastrophe hanging over the world which some of us had in those days. I was still under the influence of my recent talks with Laulerque. But I'm sure that I never used the words 'end of the world.'"

"When he quoted them to you the other day, what exactly did he mean?"

"Oh—that the processes of history as he sees them are not deflected by such trivial incidents as a four-year world war . . . something like that, I imagine."

"And he didn't deign to explain himself?"

"Not in so many words. He embarked almost at once on a severe criticism of the general situation, but all conducted in the tone of a man set aloof in lofty isolation, to an accompaniment of contemptuous allusions. He made no attempt to build up a reasoned argument. . . . There was a time when he had a great belief in Wilson, had seen him—or that is the impression I got—as one of those heroes of history marked out by fate to further the Great Work. He has nothing good to say of either Clemenceau or Lloyd George. He speaks of Clemenceau, in particular, as a bishop might speak of some notorious unfrocked priest. . . . He drew my attention—speaking with irony and an air of contempt—to the fact that the peace, which might have sounded the death-knell of nationalism and of frontiers, had, in fact, strengthened and, above all, multiplied both, had given them a new lease of life of which no man could see the end."

"But what about the problem which you've got most at heart? Did you press him at all on that point? By the way, what did you expect him to say?"

"I wanted to make him admit, in the first place, that neither Masonry nor any other international institution had succeeded at all in preventing the catastrophe or in shortening it, once it had occurred, and that the serious apprehensions entertained by people like myself had, in fact, been exceeded. . . . Then I wanted to ask him whether he didn't think that there might be something to hope for from that angle so far as our future now is concerned, whether we mightn't look for a reawakening, a new sense of urgency stimulated by the appalling check to which the progress of humanity has been exposed . . . a new type of Masonry, for instance, with a strengthened sense of its mission, reformed, rejuvenated. That sort of thing has happened, you know, in the past to religious orders. I wasn't allowing myself to entertain many illusions, just asking for information. It didn't seem to me that I had any right to neglect that particular possibility. And where should I find an answer to my question delivered with greater authority?"

"Well?"

"I think I shook him. He is still riding that old hobby-horse of his, still believes in a possible alliance between all soldiers of the Spirit. He alluded to certain very secret negotiations which, it seems, are about to begin in Rome between the Church and the Masons, and especially with that branch of Masonry which Lengnau himself adorns. The Jesuits are to act as go-betweens, and one Jesuit in particular. He said: 'I could mention names if I wished.' How much truth there is in all this I don't know. A little later he remarked: 'It was in 1910, wasn't it, that you came to see me? Well, if you had repeated the visit a year later, I could have given you proof that the Masons, acting

464

through the channel of Italian Masonry, were making superhuman efforts in Rome to prevent the outbreak of the Turco-Italian War. We knew only too well that it would lay a train which would set off other wars, and that the conflagration would ultimately involve the whole world. We're not, you see, just simple-minded dreamers. . . . And don't run away with the idea that we should have remained inactive in '14, in '18, or, above all, in '19. But by that time the torrent had become irresistible. Even the Church, with all the means and the men at its disposal, was just as helpless as we were.' And that brought him back to his particular hobby-horse—a general mobilization of Spiritual forces. Incidentally, he has no particular love for Bolshevism. He admires 'Lenin and his gang,' as he calls them, for having turned the Communist Party into an Order so vigorous and so well disciplined that, actually, a handful of men is at this moment in a position to rule a vast country. I got the impression that our friend Lengnau would dearly love to see the Masons exercising in France and elsewhere—in the name, I need hardly add, of the highest possible principles—the same sort of power. What wonderful benefits for mankind might not emerge from such a situation? . . . He hinted, in this connection, that Mussolini and almost all the Fascist leaders are renegade Masons; that they have betrayed the Masonic ideal and would unhesitatingly persecute its representatives. Which only goes to show, he maintains, what Masonry could achieve if it could command in support of its true ends the organization and the methods of the Fascist Party. To go back to the Soviets, what Lengnau hates about them is that they stand for the triumph of an utterly inhuman and aggressive form of materialism. They claim to have realized by their revolution the Unity of the Human Race. But it is a caricature of true unity, a piece of soulless machinery, a devilish imitation of the real thing. He actually used the word 'devilish.' And when I remember the flippant way in which, 'way back in 1910, he brushed aside the charge of diabolism levelled at Masonry, I can't help reflecting with a smile that every devil finds a devil worse than himself upon whom to concentrate the arts of the exorcist."

"It would be true, then, to say that he offered you nothing really useful?"

"He made me think more seriously than I have done hitherto about the possibility of organizing a Party as closely disciplined and as full of enthusiasm as a religious order, which might concentrate in itself the ideals and the strength of a whole nation, acting, as it were, as that nation's nervous system. That was not exactly what he set out to do."

"Nor what you had gone to see him for."

"No. . . . But that's enough of Lengnau for the moment. I have told you of my visit because it has a certain documentary value. What I want to know is what you think."

"On what point, precisely?" The tone in which Jallez asked this was not very encouraging. His manner was distinctly evasive.

But this time Jerphanion refused to let himself be intimidated.

"Don't tell me that you have no particular right to speak. You've travelled a great deal in Europe. You live in a world where you see and hear many things which closely concern the future of the world. However much you may pretend otherwise, you must have some idea, some feeling, about what is or is not possible. Put yourself in my place. You are sufficiently intuitive to guess my state of mind, the kind of things I dream of doing. What lesson have you drawn from your experience which I might find instructive?"

"I understand what you mean," said Jallez slowly; "I think I understand. But I can tell you little that you don't know already. You know my feelings about the League of Nations. I won't yield to the temptation of making superficial judgments of a derogatory nature, which come easily to a man like me, living on top of it all. . . . The League is composed of men, after all, and I've got a pretty good idea of what goes on in their minds. I still believe in the League, but—oh, how shall I put it?—it seems to me that, so far from saving the peace, it is peace that will save it."

"But that's a very serious thing to say . . . or is it merely a very obscure one?"

"You must take your choice. I don't believe that the League, as it is at present constituted, can do anything to stop a lot of wild men once they have decided to make war. But the longer peace can be maintained, the more powerful will the League become—or so at least I hope. A moment will arrive, once the period of growing-pains and consolidation is over, when the League of Nations will become the central instrument of peace. Then men like you will no longer have to go looking about for extraordinary and heroic ways of salvation. Peace then will be merely a job of administration—like the running of traffic police."

Jerphanion pulled a face. "But until that happens, isn't it up to us to hold back the avalanche and to fight our way out of the mess with any weapons we may find to our hands? . . . I can't say you are very encouraging. . . . Don't you believe at least that the spirit of internationalism is growing? Don't you think at least that the people you meet in Geneva and elsewhere, feel, no matter how much their minds may be filled with diverse preoccupations, that, whatever happens, we mustn't fall back into the old imbecilities, that the first essential is to preserve the common heritage?"

"A few—yes—anyhow, in words. . . . There is a lot of childishness to be found at Geneva. . . . The representatives of the new nations, for instance, are all more or less intoxicated with the idea of cutting a dash. They act as though the eyes of the world were upon them. It's a wonderful life for some of them: a Congress of Vienna which, with an occasional break, will last indefinitely . . . although, I must say, Geneva is rather a temperance society's idea of Vienna. . . . It is very rarely, you know, that one finds a man like you who is really serious, really earnest, about an idea. As a rule, petty interests, daily worries, vanity, and the desire to put on an act, to get oneself talked about at all costs, are the things that dictate a man's activities—except when he's making a speech. I've thought a good deal about the part played by speechifying in the world in which I live. It provides a perpetual alibi."

# Chapter

# 25

## HAPPINESS, TOO, IS WORTH DEFENDING

Jallez lowered his voice and spoke in a confidential undertone:

"It's easy to say all that, but the fact is I haven't sufficient courage to pass summary sentence on them. . . . What power, after all, have we to influence events? Our responsibility is so small, so very small! Occasions do arise, of course, which permit of our exercising some influence, but only within a strictly limited field. Take Debussy, for example. He has influenced music—one corner of the music of his time, and just for a few years. . . . But such instances are almost always incalculable and unforseeable . . . and the influence which any one man may exercise, even in the most favourable circumstances, is scarcely ever the sort of influence he hoped to exercise. Nor is it always lasting. Some counter-influence comes along and sweeps aside everything that he has done. The longer I live, the more conscious I become of being carried along with the current. All I can do is make myself as comfortable in the water as possible. . . . After all, we didn't choose to be born into this period, did we?"

The tone of his voice was steady, however disconnected his thoughts might seem to be.

He continued:

"When it acts foolishly or criminally, it doesn't ask our advice. It's just another case of our not being really responsible for anything. . . . Apart from those few moments in which I allow myself a certain degree of optimism, I prefer, so far as events are concerned, to expect the worst. That done, I find it more convenient not to bother my head about them."

"Isn't that a little too easy?"

"If it comes to that, it's not very easy, is it, to be even reasonably happy with the world in its present state."

"What do you mean by 'with the world in its present state'? I may, on the whole, agree with you, but I should like to know what it is that makes you say that."

"Well, I say it because the world today is nothing but a confused series of shocks. It is only in settled periods that mankind has a chance of organizing his happiness. . . . I concentrate all my efforts in an attempt to make myself as small and as light as possible in order to avoid the worst effects of those shocks." He gave a melancholy smile. "And then, you see, I haven't a great deal of happiness to defend. . . ."

As he said this, he raised his eyes. There was a break in the clouds above the roof-tops. How soft the sky was (if only one didn't demand too much)! How indifferent, or, better still, how tolerant, the boulevard seemed with its muted roar!

"What do you mean by that?" asked Jerphanion with considerable surprise.

"Oh, nothing—only, I suppose, that I am a lonely and rather restless man with little to cling to, and even that little not very important. I can make my ration of happiness into a very small parcel, small enough to be carried slung on the end of a stick. If it gets lost in the course of my wanderings, it's no very serious matter." He looked at Jerphanion. "Now, you are in an altogether different case. Your happiness is worth some effort to defend. It is something complete in itself, something that has been built up only by dint of struggling . . . I mean that its achievement has been the result of a rare concatenation of chances. You probably don't fully realize how rare such happiness is. . . . I approve of your determination to give your life to great causes, but, whatever you do, don't neglect your happiness. One never knows what great causes will lead to, especially when they involve a life of action. Ten to one they will result in nothing but a mixture of disappointments and success. . . . And what a fool you will be if you let happiness slip just for that!"

A troubled look showed in Jerphanion's eyes. He could not make out whether Jallez's words were no more than an expression of wisdom in general terms or whether they concealed some more precise implication. Jallez and Odette had had a long talk on the previous evening. Was it possible that Odette had voiced any grievances?

He was on the point of saying: "Do you see any danger in particular that threatens my happiness?" But second thoughts stopped him. "It would be a bit too much if, after deciding to question him about his private life, I started an argument on mine." As when, in a skiff, one of the oarsmen redresses a movement started by the other, he brought the conversation back to generalities.

"Of course I agree with you there. But if the whole of our period lies under a cloud of danger, any mere personal happiness is bound to be involved. Even if there is a risk, oughtn't one to take it? When we had to take what was coming to us in the trenches, the point at issue was, at bottom, the same for all of us—to save our common future. . . . Is the risk any greater when personal happiness alone is at stake?"

Jallez did not reply at once. He felt that he was in a false position. What he wanted to say to his friend was perfectly simple and direct: "You're just making difficulties for yourself." For some moments longer he remained silent. Then he pretended that his attention had been distracted by what was happening in the street. They had taken a turning to the right. He looked at the street-sign set on a corner.

"Rue Marsoulan—never heard of it. . . . It's a terrible thing, you know, but I'm forgetting a whole lot of street names. Sometimes, in my little apartment in Geneva I suddenly ask myself the most humiliating questions, such as: 'What's that street which leads from such and such a square to such and such another? I must have been along it hundreds of times.'"

"Haven't you got a map of Paris?"

"Yes. But I don't like having to consult it. I sometimes wait for days at a time in the hope that I shall remember."

Jerphanion was quick to seize his opportunity:

"You must often feel pretty lonely in that little apartment of yours. . . ."

It was Jallez's turn to reflect silently: "Odette must have told him of our talk." He pretended not to have heard the last sentence. "And while we're on the subject," he said, "what's the name of that church in the rue de Bagnolet? You know the one I mean, like a village church. Isn't it Saint-Blaise?"

"Possibly. You know that kind of thing much better than I do."

"No, I don't. I forget. That's the trouble. . . . I've got a vague impression that if we go along this rue Marsoulan, keeping uphill, we shall come out close to Saint-Blaise. Shall we try? I seem to remember that just below it there are a number of bars, also rather like what you'd find in a village street. How about having a drink at one of them?"

"Just as you like," said Jerphanion in the tone of one dismissing an aside, and then returned, with an air of easy mockery, to what he had been saying a moment before: "Yes, you must often feel lonely, unless, of course, you have managed to discover agreeable compensations for your solitude. I find it almost impossible to believe that you have condemned yourself to a completely hermit-like existence." He brought his courage to the sticking-point. Rather too lightly, with an almost excessive assumption of spontaneity, he added: "You really ought to let me in on it. . . . There was a time, if you remember, when we used to tell each other everything. So far as I am concerned, the same holds good now. The trouble is that there's nothing in my life worth telling. All there is to be known about it you know already. Come, there must be some nice little Swiss girl?"

Jallez seemed ill at ease.

"For some time I did carry on a half-hearted sort of *affaire*," he said, "but it was rather dreary, just a matter of satisfying physical needs. There wasn't much feeling involved on either side, and no real sense of comradeship. The loneliness of my rooms in the Upper Town, since that is what you're talking about, remained as unbroken as ever.

The lady in question visited me there perhaps twice, and then only for a few hours. It's not so easy as you might think to lead a life of vice in Geneva. The comings and goings of tenants are watched with a very jealous eye, and the problem where women are concerned—women, I mean, who have a reputation to lose, which isn't always the case—is almost insuperable. I have two or three women friends, to be sure, but there's nothing that needs hiding where they are concerned—and nothing to tell."

"But don't you feel the need of something more settled and definite?"

"Do I not! I was saying so only yesterday to your wife. Unfortunately, the more experience one gets, I find, the less willing one becomes to embark lightly on anything that will restrict one's liberty. . . . That's what makes me—how shall I put it?—so concerned about a case like yours, like yours and Odette's. I don't think you realize quite how lucky you were to meet each other. In love, almost more than in friendship, the part played by free choice, by fundamental preference, counts for so little. It's all really a matter of chance. Do you remember what we said once about all the initial choices and eliminations which went to modify the sheer accidents controlling a friendship like ours? The ideal state of affairs is when the final spark which sets off a love-relationship is struck in an atmosphere of pure chance which, in itself, is the product of very unusual elements. . . . Your being thrown together with the woman who became your wife seems to have been the last stage in a whole complex of initial selections. Don't, no matter what the pretext, treat such a successful achievement lightly. . . . Don't ever get used to what, in fact, was a remarkable piece of good fortune. I've nothing against your devoting your life to politics; even assuming that I should have liked to see you embark on another kind of career, I have no right to try to argue you out of what you regard as your vocation, your mission. But the life of a man who gives himself up to politics is full of dangers to his happiness, especially where that happiness is of the very precious, very fragile kind that involves two persons. Odette, I assure you, has made no complaints. I am pretty sure that she has none to make. But I have a strong feeling that she is already feeling uneasy. You mustn't put that down to feminine intolerance, to the woman's instinct of possessiveness. Your Odette has more than her share of intuition. She is a very wise woman. Her ideas about life are extremely sane. She knows you well. Don't make it difficult for her to protect your joint happiness."

Jerphanion walked on with his head bent. He felt something like a lump in his throat. It did not occur to him for a moment to think: "What business is it of his?" or "*I* don't give *him* advice." Rather, the trend of his thoughts was: "Where we two are concerned, it is I who have most to lose in the matter of personal happiness. Any mistakes he may make can very easily be put right. . . . It's I who need advice, I whose life gives rise to concern. . . . I might say that I don't give a snap of my fingers for personal happiness, that I have more important things to think about. . . . But that wouldn't be true. . . . There are so few things in life of which one can be certain. . . ."

When they had climbed the hill as far as Saint-Blaise, they decided to rest awhile before visiting the church. Two bars, not far apart, offered competing attractions. They chose the one that had the most old-fashioned look. Entering, they found themselves in a rather dilapidated, rather down-at-heels establishment, which soon, alas, would vanish to make room for some more modern bar, all bright with chromium urns. They sat down, however, and ordered some white wine, which the proprietor assured them was a genuine product of the Loire. They drank without exchanging more than a few words. But their silence was the silence of friendship.

# Chapter

### A TEMPTING PROPOSAL

When they came out of the church they went to have a look at the graveyard which surrounded it—a real country graveyard. They might have been standing on a hill above some village of the Île de France, with the main road running past its foot. All week a Sunday quiet lay about the houses. When the church clock sounded, the creaking of its supports was clearly audible.

The distant sounds of Paris presented, as it were, a problem to the understanding. Many of them came from very far away, seemingly confused and mingled, creeping up the slope and forming eddies in the misty air. From the summit of that little country hill, with its church and its graveyard, in the paths between the scattered tombstones, the watcher could hear the sounds of Paris, not as the warning of an ever present reality, but as things evoked against a remote background by the meditation of some human mind in love with contrast.

"By the way," said Jallez, "I'm due to meet Bartlett in a few days—you know whom I mean?"

"That nice chap we met in Moscow?"

"Yes. . . . He's coming to Paris on purpose. . . ." He smiled, hesitated, and then:

"For a long time now," he said, "we've been playing with a rather fantastic notion. . . . Do you recollect my once mentioning a man called Torchecoul?"

"You and Bartlett used to talk about him in Moscow. He was a sort of standing joke with you—'Torchecoul's second law,' 'social stratification.' . . . I got the impression that he was some young thinker with no sense of humour. Later you explained it to me. Surely you haven't forgotten that? I can see us still, all three, sitting in a kind of inn not far from the Tverskaia. It was already very late. We had been talking about private jokes and key phrases, and I had quoted that saying which was so popular with us at the front: 'throwing ourselves into the enemy ranks. . . .' "

"Yes, it all comes back to me."

"At first Bartlett didn't quite grasp what I was getting at . . . but I went over it all again, and told stories about Marchand and Fabre to illustrate what I meant. . . . I remember that Bartlett started chuckling and didn't stop for three minutes (just as Fabre and I used to do at Verdun, but with us it didn't last more than three seconds— we had other things to think about) . . . gasping in a way that I found very endearing . . . pursing up his little mouth into an O and giving a series of gentle thumps on the table with his fist as though he wanted us to summon first aid. I took a great liking to him from that moment. A fellow who could react like that, said I to myself, would make an ideal travelling companion. I understood then why you had chosen him as such. . . . I thought: 'What fun they must have had together!' and felt rather jealous!"

"And when he got his breath back, Bartlett told you, in his turn, all about our 'Surely that's Poliapof?'. . . and the story about the attack in the ravine . . . and our meeting with Poliapof on the boat."

"And he told it all with a delicious air of mock innocence . . . it was first-rate clowning. . . ."

"Well, this notion of ours which we have been playing with for so long is nothing less than that of paying a visit to Torchecoul— 'my master Torchecoul,' as Bartlett so admirably describes him—at his Burgundy château. . . . We must have told you, too, all about his marriage and his château?"

"Yes indeed. . . . Some of the details I have forgotten, but I've got the general outline clear."

"Good. You realize, then, the sort of value we attach to this pilgrimage?"

"I think I've got a pretty good idea. . . . I haven't become completely oblivious of certain old-established, though non-Kantian categories: such as 'the incomparable way of life,' 'the comic-sublime,' 'the dionysiac trivial.' . . ."

"You've got it exactly! Well, that is the pilgrimage we are about to undertake. We kept putting it off because we never seemed to be free at the same time . . . though that's not much of an excuse! But now we have taken the great decision. . . . Bartlett will be here in about ten days, fifteen at the outside."

"Is he coming from London?"

"Yes, from London, with a little car which he owns. . . . Until he arrives I shan't stir from Paris, no, not even if the League of Nations is burned to the ground! We shall set off by road for the Château d'Aubepierre near Grobois-sous-le-Mont. Torchecoul has been warned of our coming. We have mentioned no precise day, but he has given us his word that he will not go more than a mile from home for the whole month of February. At some moment or other, not yet fixed, we shall descend upon him. And he will be there, waiting for us, with his wine."

Jallez saw on Jerphanion's face the expression of a sort of uneasy pleasure which vanished almost immediately before the onset of an almost childish disappointment. For a moment he remained busy with his thoughts, then, as they came down the steps from the Church of Saint-Blaise:

"If you were the man you used to be," he said, "do you know what you'd do? You'd come too . . . with Odette, of course. . . . What fun that would be!"

Jerphanion, taken entirely by surprise, began to stammer:

"It would be pretty difficult. There's my work . . ."

"Don't talk nonsense! Aren't you always saying how much you despise the kind of man who can't get free of his obligations when there's a chance of doing something extra special and unforgettable?"

"Then Odette would hate to leave the boy alone with the maid."

"Pack him off to your parents-in-law. They'd be only too delighted."

"Then there's this job I've taken on. You don't seem to regard it

very seriously, but I do. It's much more than a journalistic survey—
it's a question of getting my thoughts in order as a preliminary to
action. I've worked myself into the right mood . . . and I don't want
to interrupt the process. . . ."

"There's no question of your having to interrupt any process. You'll
have plenty of time, between now and our leaving, to get well ahead
with your survey. And then while we're driving you can let it all
simmer, so that by the time you get back, you'll have everything cut
and dried in your mind."

Jerphanion went straight to the difficulties of carrying out the plan—
without further developing the argument upon which he had embarked—a good sign:

"But how could we manage? I don't suppose Bartlett's car will hold
four?"

"Nor do I . . . but you've got a car, too."

"It's only a poor little Citroën," said Jerphanion with indulgent
modesty. "It won't take more than two."

"That's all right; the cars can follow one another."

"But we shouldn't be together."

"Yes we should; it's only a question of the rear car not getting lost.
I think it would make the trip all the jollier."

"I must think it over," said Jerphanion. The desire to say yes showed
through his tone like beads of sweat on the forehead of a man in a
state of high excitement. "I must talk to Odette."

"I'll say a word to her, too," remarked Jallez with the air of one
who can exercise some special pull over a friend. "I shall be very much
surprised if she doesn't agree."

# Chapter

## 27

### LAULERQUE REPENTS

Jerphanion received the following letter by the evening post:

My dear Friend:

I had a bad night and got up this morning thoroughly disgusted with myself for having talked such a lot of nonsense to you yesterday.

If I had behaved like a rational being, this is what I should have said:

A secret international organization, designed to promote direct action, would be as useful today as it was fifteen years ago. If it is at all possible, we must create, or help to create, such an organization; but in doing so we must profit by the lessons of past experience.

1. Its members must be few in number, but of high quality.

2. At its head we must have, not champions of the old way of looking at things, left-over romantics whose hearts are bigger than their heads, dreamers liable to be easily discouraged or taken in, but thorough modernists, well trained in science and philosophy, and of a high intellectual level.

3. Our objective must be far more inclusive than it was before, involving the complete reconstruction of the world as it is today. It will be for the leaders to determine what single practical problem takes precedence of all others, and to concentrate the efforts of all our members on finding its solution.

4. They must give careful study to the technique of *cells*. As a matter of fact, this played some part in the organization of which I have spoken to you, but has been far more intelligently developed since then by the Communists. It would keep us from wasting our efforts in an attempt to carry through schemes too big for us, and

would form a guarantee of secrecy and internal discipline.

When I get back to Switzerland and can give more thought to the business, I will jot down some sort of scheme. If it comes to anything I will send it to you. In any case, whether or not it has value in itself, it will serve to clarify my ideas, and may give you a few concrete suggestions.

I should like to finish this letter with some sort of fighting slogan, a modern version of *"Écrasons l'infâme."*

I need hardly say that if anything comes of all this, I want to be in on it. I want to show you that though I may be a vacillating thinker, I can be firm enough when it comes to acting.

I hope we shall meet again before I leave Paris. Even if we talk about something totally different it would give me the greatest pleasure.

Please give my respects to your wife.

Yours affectionately,

A. LAULERQUE

# Chapter

## 28

### HAVERKAMP, CONFRONTED BY THE WORK IN PROGRESS, REALIZES THAT THERE IS A LIMIT

Haverkamp had got up early. The evening before, in the course of a meeting with Turpin and Vazar which had lasted only a few minutes, he had said, turning to the former:

"I'd like to see how the work is going on. . . . Tomorrow's a very full day for me . . . but if I hadn't known you were the champion lie-abed, I'd have said: 'Meet me here on the stroke of eight and then we can put in a good hour and a half on the site. I've been over your plans, and several ideas have occurred to me.' . . . But as it is—!"

"You talk as though eight a.m. was a prodigy of earliness. It's pretty obvious that you aren't often about at that hour. As it happens, I've already got an appointment for half past. But I can easily put that off, in which case I should be free until ten."

Haverkamp had then addressed Vazar:

"My dear sir, I feel rather badly about getting you up so early, especially as the points we shall be discussing won't really concern you."

"I can always listen," Vazar had replied. "If you decide on certain modifications, it's just as well that I should be there. I might be able to help you a bit by pointing out how your decisions will affect the decorative scheme. You can count on my being ready at eight—that's to say, if you're sure I shan't be in the way."

Realizing, as he did, that he had got into the habit of dawdling over his dressing, Haverkamp had the satisfaction of being ready at ten minutes to the hour. While waiting for the others, he glanced at the morning papers. He read an article about the changes taking place on the Champ-de-Mars. Discussions of that kind always interested him deeply. "I might," he thought, "have looked for my site in that neighbourhood. After all, it's about half-way between the faubourg Saint-Germain and Passy. One of these days it will become fashionable. But, on second thoughts, no. I don't want to live for years with building and road-making going on all around. And I could never stand having the Eiffel Tower on top of me."

At precisely eight o'clock Vazar, the interior decorator, was announced. He was at great pains to let it be seen that he had not hurried. His appearance was that of a man who had been up and about for hours and was well set in the rhythm of his day.

"I don't expect," said Haverkamp, "that Turpin will keep us waiting long."

Vazar showed him some new designs. As the minutes went by, Haverkamp betrayed signs of impatience. Turpin was starting the day badly by slowing down the tempo set by his employer. Haverkamp still felt responsible for him where Vazar was concerned. He regarded his failure to turn up in the light of a personal grievance.

"I'll telephone his flat," he said.

Scarcely had he taken up the receiver when the doorbell rang. The clock standing on the desk showed fourteen minutes past eight.

Turpin entered with the air of a man who has just taken part in a Marathon race.

"What a darned awful elevator you've got here!" he said. "Why, I can get from my place to Père-Lachaise in the time it takes to climb from ground level to this floor!"

"If it took fourteen minutes," said Haverkamp very calmly, his eye on the clock, "that certainly is a bit thick. I'll complain to the landlord."

They started off. The chosen site (it was Turpin who had found it) was on the avenue Bugeaud. On the way there Haverkamp began wondering, with that anxious intensity to which he was naturally prone, whether the choice had been a wise one.

"You don't think," he said to Turpin, "that we've made a mistake in settling on this place?"

"Certainly not. It's an ultra-smart neighbourhood—you're no more than a hundred yards from the Bois, and the exposure couldn't be better—south-south-west to a hair's breadth."

"But isn't that right-hand party wall going to be a nuisance?"

"Not if we treat it in the grand manner. In the old days I'd have tackled the problem with a few bogus columns, a portico, and a statue of Diana at the far end, parading her nipples in the distance. . . . As things are, that wouldn't go very well with a modern-style house. . . . We must see what can be done. That's where 'M'sieu' Vazar comes in." Then, turning to Vazar and carrying off his shyness with an air of raillery, he added: "What's there to prevent you from trying the same kind of fake with a sort of up-to-date pergola? I'm sure you can make a pergola look ever so modern."

"Certainly I can," said Vazar.

"And there's no rule of the Snobs' Academy, I believe, against treating a modern motif in terms of scenic perspective—at least, so far as I know?"

"I've never heard of any."

"And instead of a Diana we'll fake a Maillol, though her thighs will be a damn sight thicker, and her nipples not nearly so alluring."

Haverkamp gave no indication whether he had heard this last exchange of remarks. A few minutes later he said to Vazar:

"Do you know Sévelin? Jacques Sévelin, the playwright?"

"Yes, quite well."

The question was almost unnecessary. Every time that Haverkamp had had occasion to ask Vazar whether he knew somebody, Vazar had replied: "Why, yes," adding, as the particular case demanded: "very well," "quite well," or "a little." But the answer had always been given in a modest tone of voice, no matter how important the person in question might be. Vazar's unuttered comment seemed always to be, not: "See how famous I am!" but "In my job one meets all sorts of people. There's no particular merit in that."

"What do you think of him?"

"He's a very talented man, though perhaps a bit unequal. There were a lot of good points in that play of his which Copeau did two years ago. I didn't so much care for the one Baty put on last season. Taken all round, though, he's been pretty generally successful."

"Is he the kind of fellow one can trust?"

"In what way do you mean?"

"In matters of business."

"I didn't know," said Vazar very quietly, "that he dabbled in business."

"He doesn't exactly—not directly, that is. What I meant to say was this: would it be safe to assume that a deal in which he was to some extent interested was honest and above board?"

"I imagine so. As to the technical value of his advice, that would depend, of course, on the nature of the deal in question and whether he was competent to hold views about it. Is it something to do with the theatre?"

"Yes."

Vazar went on, picking his words with care:

"I don't think it would be worth his while to get mixed up in anything shady. He has had a certain amount of experience on the practical side. I'm told that he put up some of the money for his last play, which must have cost a good deal. Whether it was his own money or whether he found a backer, I don't know. In any case, I don't suppose it was lost."

"You've never heard of anything against him?"

"No. . . ." After a momentary hesitation Vazar added: "Everything would depend, wouldn't it, on the people who were in it with him? . . . It's not easy to venture an opinion of this sort without knowing the details. . . ."

In spite of the hint contained in these words that he should be more precise, Haverkamp said nothing.

The visit to the site was rather dull. Each time he had been there, Haverkamp's first impression had been one of faint disappointment. The work was always at a less advanced stage than he had expected.

Besides, the work actually in hand at the moment was scarcely of a kind to fill the spectator with immediate enthusiasm. A gang of house-wreckers was at work knocking down the old mansion. Labourers were digging up that part of the ground which was not built over. The method was the same as the one he had employed at Celle-les-Eaux. But while, at Celle-les-Eaux the general impression had been one of almost lyrical bustle, of a sort of spring burgeoning wherever the eye rested, a brave defiance of routine, here, in this narrow plot of Paris earth, the mind was oppressed by a sense of frustration, a consciousness of chaos, a feeling of congestion.

There was something else, too, that worried Haverkamp. "In the old days," he thought, "when I went to have a look at one of the undertakings at Celle-les-Eaux and found that things weren't going as they should, I flew into a temper. I shouted more than I do now. But fundamentally I was in a far better mood. What really mattered then was that I was floating on a strong tide of delight. Can it be that I'm getting old?" He hated to think that he was getting old. Any other reason for his present state of mind was preferable. In the first place, the field of his business activities had grown so immeasurably, that this building of a house could rank as little more than an incident, a momentary whim. There is no reason why a great captain of industry shouldn't get excited over a collection of rare plants, but it can only be a hobby. It cannot stir the same depths in him, involve such burning faith, as did those early enterprises on which his fortune had been founded. "Besides, I'm not in such close contact with the work now. When I was getting things going at Celle, I was perfectly capable of taking a hand with a pick myself, even though I never actually did. If things got behindhand, or unexpected obstacles were encountered, I always had the feeling that I was lending a hand, was exerting bodily pressure in an effort to get it out of the way. And this sense of taking a part in the actual job of building made me optimistic and confident; I felt strong. It's all very well saying 'I' still (*I'm* going to clear that corner, *I'm* going to have that wall down, *I'm* going to shove three more cartloads of stuff over there), the fact remains that I'm gradually getting farther and farther away from the real job in hand, from the actual spade-work. The result is that I haven't the enthusiasm I once had, the same confidence in the task next to hand, the sensation that my impatience will have a direct and immediate issue in results."

These thoughts led him to a rather vague but no less staggering conclusion: "One shouldn't have too many irons in the fire at once. There is a point beyond which nothing is important enough to get one really excited; no success sufficiently thrilling to carry one out of oneself. Because there are always all the other things, and all the other things can't burn at the same high degree of temperature, but merely flicker and simmer at a dead average level. . . . To be really happy, one ought to have just one thing on hand on which one can expend all one's energies. And it mustn't be on such a scale as to prevent one from getting the maximum of enjoyment from it. Because if it is too big it becomes too remote, too impersonal. One can no longer be involved in its every detail."

This idea of a point beyond which it was unwise to go was new to him, and rather overwhelming. He very nearly felt his head with his hand just to make sure that everything inside it, and in the world around, was as it should be.

"I say, boss," said Turpin with a faint tone of anxiety, "why this gloom? Do you think things aren't going fast enough?"

"Do you?"

"Of course I do. They're doing their best. It isn't the demolition that takes time, but the clearing of the site. A lump of stone like that over there, or a girder weighing half a ton, can't be shifted with a shovel. Look at that cart; it's already full, and what of? Not a third part of all this mass of rubble. . . . You must have a little patience. Just wait a week and see what a change there'll be. Come over here a moment. Something rather tiresome's happened."

"What, again?" Haverkamp frowned. "Oh, you mean that pump? Have they struck water?"

"That's nothing. At least, I don't think it's serious. . . . No, here. You too, Monsieur Vazar."

He led them across a number of trenches, at one of which he stopped. "Look at that."

"What of it?"

"Don't you see how the soil deteriorates? Look, Monsieur Vazar. About two feet from the surface. I've never seen anything so odd in my life! I don't know what the people who last had this place were up to; but stuff's been dumped there all right, all sorts of rubbish; looks like some kind of rubbish heap. How deep does it go? Hanged if I can make out. Funny thing is that the top layer looks all right. The ground rises in a kind of mound. Doesn't look right to me."

"Yes, I see that . . . but what's bothering you about it?"

"Hell! Don't you see that we shall have to go deeper? If I'd suspected anything of this kind, I should have treated my foundations differently, put in a layer of cement, for instance, at any rate in this section."

"Is it too late to do it now?"

"It's never too late to do what one wants. But considering the work that's been done already— I should have arranged my walls differently too. It would mean working out all my calculations again. It'll be simpler to carry on as we were."

"But won't it mean extra work, and more delays?"

"You've got a good eye for realities, boss."

Haverkamp said nothing, but walked away a few paces with a look of annoyance. The other two joined him. He said:

"I really wonder if we aren't making a big mistake. To begin with, the place is too small. We need at least another four hundred yards. There's nothing I hate so much as lack of space, and here I am, saddled with a house and garden all jammed together anyhow. I told you how it would be when you first worked out the dimensions. But you over-persuaded me!"

Turpin almost lost his temper.

"You're arguing like a child, boss. Here you go wandering about this rubbish dump where there's hardly room to put one's feet, and you think it'll always be like that!" He shrugged his shoulders angrily. "Wait till it's cleared! *My* dimensions! It gets me down to hear you talk like that. They'll give you room and to spare, see if they don't! Space in itself is nothing. An artist can make it expand or contract at will . . . according to his creative genius. He uses it like gold-beater's skin. . . . Have you never heard how Michelangelo—and you'll agree that he wasn't a nit-wit—undertook to put the biggest dome in the world over the Pope's head in such a way that the good father shouldn't feel crushed by the weight of it . . . so that, for all its size, the enclosed space should give an impression of devout and intimate smallness? . . . I promise you all the grandeur you want. Don't start measuring up my dimensions with a foot-rule. Wait until I pop you down at the entrance to your great drawing-rooms."

Haverkamp smiled and nodded his head once or twice.

"What is your opinion, Monsieur Vazar?"

"I agree with Monsieur Turpin that we've got to produce an impression of size. I shall tackle my part of the problem."

"You think it's possible?"

"Certainly—to a very great extent, that is."

# Chapter

## MISTRESS AND WIFE

Haverkamp dropped Turpin and Vazar at the corner of the avenue du Bois and the Place de l'Étoile. "There's a little job of mine in the rue Képler I want to look at," Turpin had said. "It'll do me good to walk. When I've finished there, I'll pick up my car, which I left parked in front of your place. I'm beginning to put on fat, and I've got to keep an eye on myself. I've tried doing exercises every morning with a chest-expander, but it's an awful bore."

"If you don't mind," Vazar had put in, "I'll go with you. We can talk on the way."

"They seem to be getting on a little better," thought Haverkamp. "Just as well to give them this chance for a mild flirtation."

He looked at his watch. Ten minutes to ten. "I was so afraid of not having enough time that I've given myself too much. I'm not meeting those theatre people till eleven. How about dropping in on Sylvie?"

He told his chauffeur, René, to drive him to the rue de Lubeck. René betrayed some surprise. His master had showed a trace of indecision in giving the order.

"René's a bit taken aback at the idea of my going to see Sylvie at this time of day. Maybe it is something that's not done. She'll only just be up. Whatever I do, I mustn't give her the idea that I'm a jealous lover. But I've got a good excuse: she and I ought to have a final exchange of views before my meeting at eleven. I'm not spying on her. But if I do catch her doing something she ought not to, it's her funeral."

The look of surprise with which the maid received Haverkamp was rather more marked than René's had been. But there was no hint in it of genuine embarrassment.

488

"Mademoiselle is still in bed," she said. "I only brought out her breakfast tray five minutes ago."

"I don't want to disturb her too much."

"Oh, I don't think you will, sir. She's learning her next part. I'll go and tell her you're here."

"Her next part?" wondered Haverkamp, wrinkling his forehead.

He was not kept waiting long, but was shown almost at once into her bedroom. Sylvie Préval was sitting up in bed, wearing a sky-blue bed-jacket. With quick dexterity she was manipulating powder-puff, comb, and lipstick almost simultaneously. A paper-bound book was lying open on her knees.

"Good morning, Sylvie darling. I must apologize for coming at such an unearthly hour. If I'd been told you were asleep I wouldn't have come in."

"I wasn't sleeping. I was going over my part."

"Your part?"

"Yes, the part I'm playing. I noticed last night that I slipped up once or twice. Savoir was out in front and remarked on it—very nicely, you know. But I hate being caught like that. It's my fault, really. The words aren't particularly difficult, but they're not coming automatically. My memory's playing tricks with me. There are one or two bits of dialogue which I've got to try out over and over again before I can be sure of them. They won't stick in my mind. What's the trouble— nothing serious?"

She spoke rapidly and with a trace of ill temper in her voice. There was something almost metallic about the sharp edge of her articulation. Her short hair was artificially blond.

"Oh no, nothing serious at all. But I've got this meeting hanging over my head with Sévelin, Haudebert, and somebody else they're bringing with them. I was wondering whether anything had occurred to you at the last moment. I don't feel altogether at home with those chaps. I'm not at all sure that it wouldn't be a good thing if you were there too. You'd be able to ask the sort of questions which would never occur to me, and you'd be in a position to prompt me if necessary."

"Not on your life," she replied with determination. "My position is quite delicate enough as it is. Up to now I've managed my career single-handed. I've no wish to be taken for one of those gay young things who only get parts because they're kept by one of the backers." She spoke now with a quiet reasonableness. "They want to interest you in running a theatre. You, on your side, want some sort of guarantee that the thing will be a success. That's natural enough, since you're going to find the money. What you're particularly anxious to get clear is that they shouldn't make the usual mistake of experimental theatres, that they should get their female roles well played. You want them to have at least one woman who's had experience on the boulevard. You're perfectly entitled to make such a stipulation, and to insist on having a voice in the casting. You may have some particular actress in view, though you can't be sure that she'd be interested in the proposition. There's no reason why you shouldn't offer to make yourself entirely responsible for that side of the business. She may be someone with whom you are on terms of intimacy; she may also have ideas of her own on the sort of career she wants. But you've got to make them realize that she's not just snatching at any job that comes along. You see the subtle difference? If she was sitting there beside you, the thing would at once take on the appearance of a piece of crude bargaining."

"You think, then, that I should be perfectly frank about stressing the connexion?"

"Don't worry your head about that. You'll find that they can take a hint."

"Suppose they say: 'It all depends on how much she asks'—do you want me to mention an actual figure?"

"Certainly not. You're supposed not to have mentioned money yet. . . . I think, on the whole, that your best line will be to say you have just casually mentioned to me the possibility of such an offer . . . that you have sounded me on the likelihood, other things being equal, of my being willing to come in on the deal. So far I haven't committed myself either way. You don't want to discuss terms with me. That's their affair. But you're willing to bring friendly pressure to bear on me if I look like hesitating, or to get me to see sense if I ask too much, because, naturally, if you put money into the business, you expect to see profits. . . . At the same time, you must make it perfectly clear that you are not likely to be interested in a theatrical venture in which I'm not involved."

"I've got my lesson pat, darling. You see how lucky it was my turning up like this."

He laughed. The subtlety displayed by the young woman filled him with admiration. Whenever, thanks to someone else, he had his attention drawn to some new complexity of business in a field hitherto strange to him, he was always conscious of a feeling of surprise, of the pleasure experienced by the amateur, of a desire to try his hand, with all due respect for its difficulties and awareness of his inexperience, at this novel game.

He got up and kissed her.

"When the meeting's over, I'll give you a ring. I've got a very full day. I'll try to come round to your dressing-room this evening."

"Between the first and second acts?"

"No, I shan't be able to manage that. Better make it after the final curtain."

He felt for his latch-key, but at the same time pressed the bell twice. He was just turning the key in the lock when the door opened. The face of Honoré, his man, appeared. It expressed the need for unusual caution.

"Madame is here," he whispered.

"What's that?"

"Yes, sir. She must have arrived this morning by the night train. She's got a handbag with her, and one suitcase."

"And you let her in?"

"You had given me no orders, sir."

"I told you always to say that I wasn't at home.

". . . and to try to get her to go away. That's what I did. But I had no instructions to prevent her coming in."

"The truth is, it never occurred to me that she'd come. Where is she?"

"In the big drawing-room, sir."

"Oh hell!—and I've got people coming in a few minutes. Did she say anything to you?"

"Yes, sir. I gathered that she had received a letter from the lawyer. She is aware of your intentions, sir."

"I bet she is!" Haverkamp had advanced into the entrance-hall. He was very nervous. He led Honoré towards a narrow passage at the far end. He spoke in a whisper.

"Listen to me, Honoré. You must get her out of here at once. I'm going down to the concierge's to telephone from there. You must tell her that I've just rung up from my office in the Champs-Élysées, that you told me about her being here, and that I want her to go at once to Maître Lévy-Sangre's, where I'll meet her. You must give her his address."

"But your car's outside, sir. Won't Madame smell a rat?"

"I'll tell René to drive round the block. Explain that I'm sending the car for her."

"You won't let her see you, sir?"

"I'll keep an eye on the house from a distance. I won't come back until the car's driven off."

"Are you really going to Maître Lévy-Sangre's, sir?"

"We shall see. In any case, I'll telephone him and say that I've been prevented."

"But will Maître Lévy-Sangre be at home, sir?"

"Pretty sure to be. He's expecting me to give him a ring after my meeting with these gentlemen. It's twenty to eleven now. We must move quickly."

"I'm only asking all these questions, sir, just to make sure you've forgotten nothing, and so I shan't be caught in case—"

"Yes, yes, that's all right. The main point is that you get her out of this house and don't let her come back under any pretext whatever."

"But what about the handbag and the suitcase?"

"As soon as she's gone, call a taxi and take them round to Claridge's. Take a room in her name. If I meet her I'll explain the arrangement . . . otherwise, I'll telephone. If she comes back here, you must do the explaining. But whatever happens, she must not cross this threshold."

"And if she insists, sir?"

"You must say that those are my lawyer's instructions. Did she see Monsieur de Belleuse?"

"No, sir. I warned Monsieur de Belleuse in case, sir. But he stayed in his little room."

"Good. Now get going. I'm off downstairs to telephone."

Haverkamp ran down to the entrance-hall of the building without waiting to summon the elevator. For all that he was put out, he felt gay. It was as though he were twenty once more and performing an acrobatic feat in order to avoid the attentions of an importunate mistress.

# Chapter

## A THEATRE DEAL

He finished making his arrangements a bare five minutes before his visitors were announced. A great deal of argument had been necessary before Mme Haverkamp would consent to leave, and once that problem had been solved he had had to ring up his lawyer in order to explain what had happened.

It was Jacques Sévelin's card that was brought to him. The name of Octave Haudebert had been added in pencil, as well as that of a third person, which was difficult to read and conveyed nothing to him. He summoned Henry de Belleuse. "Who is this fellow?"

"Just a moment. . . . It looks like Weiner or Werner, with a P. in front of it. It must be Pierre Werner."

"And what do you know of Pierre Werner?"

"Oh, he's a chap who has had a finger in various theatre deals. He was part author of a play at the Mathurins, and has done dramatic criticism for various papers."

"Why has he come to see me?"

"I've no idea."

Neither spoke for a few moments. Then "Do you want me to be present at the meeting?" Belleuse asked with rather too obvious an air of a man who is the soul of discretion.

"Of course—that is to say—yes, of course. . . . I assumed all along that you would be. Do you object?"

"Not at all."

Sévelin and his two companions were shown in. Sévelin was a pale, spare man of forty, with fine eyes and a moustache worn slightly longer than fashion dictated. Haudebert was a great hulk of a fellow with thin, fair hair. He stooped a little and seemed to feel the cold.

Above his waistcoat he wore a woollen pull-over, which, obviously, had been carefully chosen to match his suit. There was quiet distinction about his tie. Pierre Werner was a short, bustling, affable little man. His hair was even fairer than Haudebert's, and the colour of his eyes was indeterminate. He was probably a Jew, though the racial characteristics were not very marked.

In a gentle voice, and with a courtesy that had something almost formal about it, Sévelin introduced Werner. He apologized for bringing him, adding that it would soon be apparent why he had done so.

At first the conversation went rather limpingly. From what Sévelin said, it appeared that certain "fresh developments" had taken place, that things had been "taken a step or two farther."

Haverkamp took the floor. "I remember the general trend of our last talk, gentlemen," he said, "but I'm not quite clear about the details. My impression is that we came to no definite decision. But now, if I understand you aright, things are moving. If you don't mind, Monsieur Sévelin, I should like you to give me a brief résumé of the situation, just as though I knew nothing whatever about it. I am a very busy man, and I have a way of only half hearing what is said to me. All sorts of proposals are made to me every week. But when I'm really interested I don't miss much. And I'm interested now. Will you take notes of our conversation, Belleuse?"

Sévelin hesitated a little in his speech, but there was nothing vague in the matter of his remarks, and he outlined the situation with remarkable clarity.

Two main points emerged at once: a theatre and a producer happened to be available at one and the same moment. The theatre was in the rue du Colisée. It was of good average size, capable of holding about eight hundred people. That would mean good receipts if they had a success; and if a play was slow in capturing the fancy of the public, quite a small audience could be made to look like a well-filled house. The dimensions of the stage were convenient. It had a wide proscenium opening, but was not very deep. That, however, didn't matter; they weren't, after all, planning to put on opera. The only serious disadvantage was the scene-shifting equipment. The place had been built as an "intimate" theatre to house three-act plays produced with a single set. They would have to exert a good deal of ingenuity. It might be possible to make several structural alterations which would improve matters.

"If we agree to proceed," said Haverkamp, "I'll put Turpin on the job. He's a wizard at getting out of difficulties, and he likes tackling the problems set by a limited space."

The producer in question was Octave Haudebert. A Parisian like Haverkamp didn't have to be told who he was, and in the course of the talks that had already taken place he had had, no doubt, an opportunity of summing him up. It should be unnecessary to remind him that Haudebert had been responsible for several productions in many different theatres. All of them had attracted public attention. Two of them had been outstandingly successful. Haudebert was not a producer in the ordinary meaning of the term, not the usual kind of stage director. What he did was to give life to his author's script, to "realize" it in three-dimensional terms. He had what was lacking in so many of the people who had started experimental theatres, people like Copeau, Jouvet, Baty, Dullin, and Pitoëff—an instinct for "box-office," a feeling for the practical possibilities of up-to-date methods through which the producer could get in touch with his public and impose upon it a taste and a curiosity about things theatrical which it hadn't had before. The fact that he did not concern himself with the details of a production was far from being a disadvantage. It meant that he didn't have to limit himself to one particular style or any definite method. He could afford to have wider interests than the normal producer, because he could approach the problems of a production with an open mind and without the prejudices which inevitably hampered a man who was wedded to one special technique. As a matter of fact, he had quite extraordinary gifts as a producer, but he preferred not to make use of them. What he did was to visualize how a play should be put on the stage, in what style, in what atmosphere, and by whom. His instinct in these matters was infallible. He had travelled a great deal and consequently was a master of the comparative method. He was the kind of man who would say: "The man for this comedy is the chap who produced a play I saw last year in a little theatre in Vienna. I'll look up his name." And then it would turn out that the producer in question was a young man who regarded Paris as his Mecca, and asked nothing better than to get a chance of making his reputation there on very modest financial terms. Haudebert was a marvel at that kind of bargaining. He knew just how to appeal to people's enthusiasm and ambition, and could get them all worked up over his schemes. In fact, Sévelin had no hesitation in saying that if the advanced theatre ever ceased to depend for support on a public of intellectual snobs and became really established on a firm basis of popular favour, it would be entirely owing to Haudebert.

Haudebert listened to all this with an air of rather anxious interest, as though he personally were not involved at all. His light, rather prominent eyes blinked a good deal. From time to time he scratched his right armpit through the thickness of his woollen pull-over. He kept his eyes more particularly on Haverkamp, watching him as he might have watched a man who was undergoing some curious electric treatment, anxious not to miss any significant change in his expression. Pierre Werner, in a rapid, lisping voice, interrupted once or twice with some example which served to illustrate and stress what the dramatist was saying. Henry de Belleuse, sitting with his elbows resting on one corner of the big table, kept his pencil and pad ready. So far, however, he had not thought it necessary to make any notes. The telephone had rung three times during the course of the conversation, and Belleuse had taken the calls. Apparently they were of no particular importance or urgency, and he had dealt with them quickly.

So far, went on Sévelin, Haudebert had suffered from not having a theatre of his own. Employed on all sorts of stopgap productions, and at the mercy of backers who had unaccountably failed, he had had several by no means negligible successes, and he had made money. But he had had no opportunity of building up a solid reputation or of methodically enlisting the interest of the public.

And now this Heaven-sent chance had come his way. He had been offered the long lease of this theatre in the rue du Colisée.

At this moment the telephone rang again. Belleuse lifted the receiver and then passed it to Haverkamp, saying:

"Maître Lévy-Sangre. . . ."

Haverkamp listened for a few moments; then, in a low voice, he replied:

"No, I can't do that . . . and I don't think it at all desirable that I should. Tell her that I've been kept by an important conference, but that I'll do what I can. . . . Send her packing if she becomes a bore. . . . What's that? You'd have preferred . . . yes, I know it was all rather irregular . . . but I didn't know what to do . . . hadn't any time, you know, to think what would be best. If it's a nuisance, stick to vague generalities. . . . The important thing is that she shouldn't have any doubt in her mind. I must hang up now. I'm in the middle of a business discussion. Ring me again later if you think it's necessary . . . yes, in half an hour."

This theatre, continued Sévelin, belonged at the moment to a man called Dubief who had got a long lease of it, just after the war, on ridiculously easy terms. The contract wouldn't expire until 1939. Dubief had tried running the place himself. But he knew nothing whatever about the entertainment business and had lost money. As a result of this experience he had agreed to sub-let. But his tenant, who was an adventurer, had soon gone bankrupt. Taking advantage of this double disaster, Haudebert had induced Dubief to transfer the lease to him until 1939 at the comparatively low rent of 140,000 francs a year. Dubief, of course, was pocketing a handsome profit. The original rent, Sévelin thought, had been in the neighbourhood of 60,000. But against that should be set the fact that Dubief had made certain improvements. Besides, values had changed, inevitably, since 1919, and the district had become increasingly central. All together, it was a wonderful chance. Haudebert could easily sub-let again at a handsome profit, but that was not what he was after. He wanted to establish a theatrical enterprise, to work with first-rate authors, and to build up a professional future.

What Sévelin's suggestion amounted to was that a limited-liability company should be formed with a small number of stockholders, having as its object the founding and running of just such an enterprise. Haudebert would transfer his sub-lease to the company, receiving in exchange a certain amount of stock. It went without saying that he would be appointed director of the proposed theatre. It was important that the company should be incorporated as soon as possible. Haudebert's agreement with Dubief would come into operation on the 1st of April. But that wasn't the only reason. Dubief had burned his fingers badly as a result of his failure, and was demanding an advance of 70,000 francs on account of rent, to be refunded when the sub-tenancy came to an end. The agreement would come into force on the 1st of April only if this advance had been paid before that date. Haudebert could not lay his hands on the necessary capital, and it would be for the company to find the money between now and then. They hoped that M. Frédéric Haverkamp would be willing to subscribe about half the total capital required, that he would consent to be chairman of the board, and, above all, that he would put his very great experience and the authority of his name at the service of the enterprise.

"What have you in mind, roughly, as the amount needed to capitalize such a company?"

Haverkamp hated all vagueness in matters of business. Never, even for a moment, was he prepared to work on a basis of merely approximate figures. Without waiting for an answer he began to work out the sum in his own mind: "Anything, I suppose, from one to two million. My contribution, therefore, would, at most, be a million. But I should probably have to put my hand in my pocket more than once. That's certainly more than a trifle . . . still . . ."

"If it weren't for this advance on account of rent," said Sévelin rather nervously, "I think we could float the whole business with a hundred thousand, to be paid up in two instalments. . . ."

Haverkamp started. Sévelin continued:

"But as it is, I don't see how we can say less than a hundred and fifty thousand, and with this advance hanging over our heads, I think two thirds of that amount will have to be paid up at once. . . . Do you agree?"

Haverkamp could not restrain his laughter. He felt as some engineer might, taking a walk on the seashore, who had been asked to give his professional advice to a lot of children building sand castles. But suddenly an idea struck him: "They can't be serious. The actual sum is not worth bothering about, but it's never a good thing to let oneself be made a fool of. But then again, if these fellows simply want to take a few banknotes off me, why on earth should they choose such a roundabout way of doing it?" As politely as he knew how, he said:

"I think I must have got you wrong. How on earth can you expect to start that sort of business on such a minute capital? Am I to take it that you regard a hundred and fifty thousand as your ceiling? Why, the rent alone comes to a hundred and forty thousand, and then there's this advance of seventy thousand to be paid. What about your overheads? What about the costs of production? What'll it cost to put on your first production, for I'm assuming that you do mean to produce something?" (He really began to doubt it. Perhaps the whole thing was just a joke.)

It was Haudebert, this time, who answered. His voice had more quickness, more gaiety, than Sévelin's. There was in it an undertone of well-bred sarcasm, and it seemed clear that its owner could be insolent should the need arise. In dealing with Haverkamp, however, he was properly deferential.

"I realize that the smallness of the amount must cause you some astonishment. Let me ask your attention while I establish a rough balance-sheet. Let us assume, for the sake of argument, that a hundred and fifty thousand is the total agreed upon, and that two thirds of that total are paid up at once. That gives me a hundred thousand with which to start operations, and that is all I shall need."

Henry de Belleuse was busy taking notes.

"How do you make that out?" said Haverkamp.

"I shall want seventy thousand of it for the advance. That leaves thirty thousand. I plan to open on the 2nd of April, not a day sooner or later. The 1st would look too much like a joke. Dubief has agreed to give me possession a month earlier so that I may have time for rehearsals and for carrying out essential alterations. The theatre is in a very clean condition. He has let it for a few evenings in March, but that won't inconvenience me. I shall rehearse in the afternoon. By the 1st of April I shall have spent scarcely a penny of my thirty thousand. I shall have had to make a few payments for rehearsals, given one or two of my actors advances on their salaries, and settled up with my stage-manager for the first month . . . two or three odd items of that kind. I myself shall draw no emoluments until the 1st of April."

"But what about scenery and costumes—and all that sort of thing? . . . What about posters and newspaper advertising?"

Haudebert smiled:

"You're not suggesting that I pay for these things in advance? If I were someone completely unknown, fresh from Budapest or Warsaw, I might. As it is, I undertake to put on a production costing a hundred thousand francs without spending so much as a centime before we ring up. No, I'm exaggerating. It is possible that some small firm I wanted to use because their price was lower than anybody else's might ask for payment at once, not because they didn't trust me, but because they had expenses of their own to meet. But that wouldn't be a serious matter. In the world of the theatre" (a note of pride crept into Haudebert's voice) "we all know one another; and we're all of us willing to give the next fellow a run for his money, always provided, of course, that his reputation is reasonably good. Generosity's the rule, and a man is given credit for doing his best when he's been in for a run of bad luck." He surreptitiously touched the wood of his chair.

"If he can't settle with all his creditors, they're prepared to wait till he's doing better. It's not regarded as an adequate reason for refusing credit."

"I take your word for it; not that we are proposing to run into debt. Please go on."

"As soon as the run has begun I shall start at once paying off my various bills by degrees—so much each week, say, over a period of three months. Don't forget that in the theatre business, money comes in each night—and good, honest coin at that. We don't have to go out and get it. . . ." As he said this, Haudebert once more touched the wood of his chair.

"On what sort of takings do you think we can reckon?"

"A maximum of fifteen thousand, which, quite likely, we may never reach. An average of five to six thousand, perhaps even seven if the show's a success, in other words, fifty thousand each week of eight performances. If it's a flop, we may come down as low as two or three . . . or thirty thousand a week. But even if that happens I can still pay my running expenses and settle up for scenery and costumes somehow."

"It's just that 'somehow' that I should hate if I were in your place."

"Oh, that doesn't bother me!" laughed Haudebert. "It's all a question of what one's used to. I think that if I had too much money in the bank I should feel uncomfortable."

"A bit of tightrope-walking is no bad thing in the theatre," said Sévelin. "It stops one from going to sleep. Most of the really active theatre people I've known have spent a good part of their lives wondering how they're going to get to the end of the month. . . . An old fellow once told me that there is a good deal to be said for working with limited capital, and he seemed to know what he was talking about. I had to take the statement on trust, having no knowledge of finance myself."

The telephone rang again. Belleuse took up the receiver and then handed it to Haverkamp.

"Monsieur Bouitton."

"Ah! . . . Good morning, my dear sir. How are you? . . . Yes, that's how we left it. I shall be expecting your colleague at half past four. I've got a board meeting at half past three—nothing of any importance. If I should be so unlucky as to be late, my secretary will be here, and he can start discussing matters with your colleague. . . . So long. We must dine together one of these evenings."

He hung up, and glanced at Haudebert and Sévelin as though he were summing up his impressions of them for the first time.

"I don't think they're twisters. I've given them their heads. . . . If they're merely trying to get money out of me— Perhaps it's just that they don't see things on a big enough scale. . . ."

Out loud he said:

"But what if you suddenly found yourself up against some big money crisis—a run of bad receipts, for instance?"

Haudebert shrugged his shoulders. "I should explain matters to the people who'd made my stuff. They know life. They're not savages."

"Besides," put in Sévelin with a smile, "in such a case, the stockholders, who are all friends, would realize what had happened. It would be a sad thing if two or three of them couldn't find the ten or twenty thousand francs required to get us out of our difficulties without inconveniencing themselves too much."

Haverkamp merely smiled. It was to him, he imagined, that such an appeal would most probably be made. There was nothing very alarming in the prospect. The amounts mentioned were not of a size to make his flesh creep. He was not a gambler, but there had been occasions when he had gambled, just to keep up appearances, and he had often lost more than that in a single evening without seeming to feel it. He had always dreamed of being a "patron of the arts" and knew that such an ambition had more to it than investing in a few modern pictures; that it probably meant dropping a good deal of money in various ways. He felt at once disconcerted and rather touched by the modest financial dimensions of these theatre enterprises which make so much noise and occupy so large a place in the world of Paris. "These fellows could balance their budget after a bad season for what it would cost to give a necklace to a pretty lady. It all seems very odd to me."

Sévelin noticed that he was deep in thought and imagined that he was hesitating. He entirely misconstrued the nature of his private thoughts.

"We should like, too," he said with well-bred courtesy, "to discuss with you the question of the casting. Haudebert has got his eye on a number of actors and actresses whose capabilities he knows at first hand, who are accustomed to working together and who have the added advantage of being cheap. Naturally, you will be told who they are. But he thinks we ought to have one man and one woman whose names would be a box-office draw. Sylvie Préval has occurred to us as a possibility. She will be free as soon as Savoir's play comes to an end, and that, probably, will be at most in six weeks' time. She has been approached for a production which is billed for the latter part of the season, but we have reason to believe that she hasn't signed up yet. The trouble is that she's a bit expensive. Haudebert is thinking of offering her fifty francs less than she's getting now. She's a good trouper, and it's quite possible that she may accept, especially as we want to have a yearly contract with her and not engage her only for the run of a single piece. Actresses who love their work prefer that sort of arrangement. . . . But a word from you, we feel sure, would carry great weight with her."

Haverkamp was filled with admiration. "The interests which these people handle are miscroscopic compared with mine, but what a technique they've got! The tact of that last remark was something worth hearing! In such matters I'm the merest child beside them!"

"I think I ought to make it clear," put in Haudebert, "that it's not so much the actual fifty francs—though I'm determined to keep salaries as low as possible—as the effect they might have on the rest of the company. Too great a discrepancy in pay is bad for the esprit de corps. We must bear that in mind, and I'll make a point of it when I talk to Sylvie Préval."

"The amount involved is so small that there's no reason why I shouldn't give them my answer straight away," thought Haverkamp. "I shouldn't like them to have a bad impression of me."

"Gentlemen, I ask nothing better than to be allowed to help you. How much do you want me to put up? I think you mentioned something about half the capital? In other words, assuming that we take our present estimate as definite, seventy-five thousand francs. With your permission we will call it seventy thousand. In that way it will not look as though I had so arranged matters as to have a majority of the holdings under my personal control. That would be an uncomfortable situation both for me and for my colleagues. If you are in any difficulty about filling the gap, I can lay hands on a friend of mine, within five minutes, who will provide the balance. Then there's this question of Mademoiselle Préval. I agree with you that she would be a valuable addition to our company. I suggest, Monsieur Haudebert, that you go and put the whole thing to her quite frankly. Meanwhile I will mention it myself."

"The reduction of fifty francs," he thought, "makes very little difference when she's getting seventeen hundred a month. It's not worth talking about. But a generous gesture on her part will look well."

His visitors expressed their thanks with becoming dignity. Then Sévelin asked whether he would agree, as they all hoped he would, to act as chairman of the board.

Haverkamp smiled, but hesitated before replying. He was a prey to considerable embarrassment. His feelings as a man of the world were flattered by the idea of adding to his other, more substantial titles that of chairman of a theatrical enterprise, more especially since the theatre in question was to rank as "advanced." On the other hand, wouldn't his enemies say that his meddling in this sort of thing was evidence of frivolity and declare that the big concerns in which he held the controlling stock were no more sound than this trivial toy?

"What is to be the name of this company?"

"We thought of calling it the Société du Théâtre du Rond-Point."

"That's not at all bad. And who, if you'll forgive me for asking, are the other stockholders? You mentioned certain names, but I should like to get the matter quite clear in my mind."

Sévelin handed him a short list. After each name was a series of figures (in most cases five thousand francs) and several of these were followed by a question mark. Haverkamp's name headed the list, but the space for the figures had been left blank. The largest sum, twenty thousand francs, was attached to a well-known and respected name in the world of banking.

Haverkamp commented upon its presence and privately congratulated himself on the fact. The other names, though a couple of them had a "de," could not be called particularly brilliant.

"Yes," said Sévelin; "and his subscription's absolutely certain. As you see, there is no question mark. If necessary, the Baron will give a further five thousand. It was Pierre Werner who got him interested, and who represents him here."

Haverkamp looked at Pierre Werner.

"But why not ask *him* to be chairman? His position in the world of business makes him obviously the right person, and if he accepted, it would be a great feather in our caps."

Pierre Werner, whose lisping accents fell on the ear like the snipping sound of a nervous barber's scissors, and who had suddenly assumed an air of importance, declared that the Baron would certainly refuse. It was not even certain that he would agree to be a director.

"Why not?" asked Haverkamp, slightly ruffled.

"Oh, the reason's perfectly simple, and casts no slur whatever on us. The Baron knows that you will be the biggest stockholder. He actually said to me: 'It's only fair that Monsieur Haverkamp should be your chairman. Besides, he's a man who succeeds in everything he touches. He'll bring you luck.'"

Haverkamp felt very proud to think that the famous financier had shown such flattering knowledge of his existence. His attitude now was one of polite deference.

"I am deeply touched," he said. "But why should the Baron hesitate to be on our board?"

"He is very scrupulous in matters of this kind. 'I don't feel that I

shall be in any way indispensable'—those were his very words to me—
'so long as you have Monsieur Haverkamp. Besides, I should have to
be absent from a good many of your meetings. You had much better
find somebody who can give more time to your business.'"

"Try to persuade him, Monsieur Werner. Tell him he need only
come when it's convenient. With so few stockholders we can always
find room on the board for anyone else who wants to take an active
part in our deliberations."

He looked at the paper before him, wrote in pencil after his name
the figures 70,000, and added up the various sums.

"Yes," he said, "that comes out about right."

And it was not without a certain inward glow of satisfaction that
he saw on a list which bore the name of the famous Baron followed
by the figure 20 (what the object of the list was didn't much matter;
the world, if it came to that, was a mere matter of signs and symbols)
his own followed by 70.

# Chapter

## HAVERKAMP ENTERTAINS JERPHANION

"That, I think, will be Monsieur Haverkamp," said Henry de Belleuse.

Jerphanion had just spent half an hour with the brilliant secretary in his employer's studio. Contrary to all expectation, that half-hour had passed very pleasantly and had been most instructive.

Had it been because he found pleasure in tracing a certain analogy between their respective positions? Henry de Belleuse had, from the very beginning of their interview, treated Jerphanion like an old friend, and his rather exotic manners, so far from obscuring his intention of familiarity, made it, on the contrary, only more obvious and, as it were, more odd.

But there was a great deal more in the attitude adopted by Henry de Belleuse to cause him surprise. For a long time now Jerphanion had been planning to find out what kind of person Haverkamp really was, to treat himself to an inside view of his position in the social scene, to examine his methods and to determine precisely how far he was to be trusted. He had said to Bouitton: "I should very much like to take on this job, now that you have prepared the ground. The man interests me. I've already put a few questions about him to several people in the know. It's very difficult to reach any conclusion, to make up one's mind. It's quite extraordinary how lazy people are when it comes to getting a clear view of somebody, or in putting that view into words even when they've got it. I'm hoping that this meeting will give me a good deal more to go on than I could pick up in the course of a single supper-party in Moscow. I shall continue to tap my outside sources. But I hope it is clearly understood that in the event of my unearthing anything really discreditable, we shall call a halt—

even if he has given a definite promise of money, even if he has already paid it into the funds. In the latter case, the party must return his cheque with a polite letter which I shall draft."

Jerphanion had taken advantage of his private talk with de Belleuse to put a few questions. But he had been careful to give them the appearance of innocent curiosity and did not expect to be able to press them very far. Henry de Belleuse had answered them with surprising frankness. So far from avoiding the issue, he had, of his own accord, furnished certain details for which his visitor had not asked. "You are not, I imagine, familiar with this type of financial operation?" he had said, and had then proceeded to explain it in detail, illustrating his remarks with examples which were far from discreet. What, precisely, had been his object in all this? Was it just a way of saying: "We are sitting here in a house of glass. My employer's activities, which strike terror into a lot of fools who know nothing at all of the matter, merely exemplify the modern technique of big business. It is important that an intelligent man like yourself should get the thing straight in your mind." Had bravado played a part in his attitude? Or a desire to show off by demonstrating, with casual ease, the working of a system which was commonly supposed to be appallingly complicated? How pleased would Haverkamp himself have been could he have overheard his secretary's confidences?

Jerphanion's surprise made it difficult for him at times to take in the new ideas which were being poured out for his benefit. The difficulty was increased by the nature of the impromptu and far from academic lesson to which he was being treated. Belleuse, it seemed, was intent on dazzling his hearer rather than on leaving him in doubt. He adopted a kind of shorthand method, assuming knowledge where it did not exist. Jerphanion could not take notes. Nor could he ask the secretary to elaborate still further explanations which he was already somewhat embarrassed at having provoked. He asked himself: "Shall I ever be able to get all this into reasonable shape so that I can repeat the essentials to my boss tomorrow morning? I don't suppose he is much more informed than I am."

"I shan't be needing you, Belleuse. Please take any telephone calls that may come in. Don't bother me with them unless they're very important. See you later. . . . And now, Monsieur Jerphanion, please sit down. I'm afraid I'm very late. I'm not usually late, and I beg your pardon. I had to attend a board meeting which was summoned to discuss some not very important details, and then somebody started a hare. . . . I hope Belleuse looked after you?"

"He was most pleasant."

Haverkamp, still on his feet, shot a sidelong look at Jerphanion. There was a hint of interrogation in his next words:

"He's rather a curious type, but he's by no means a fool. . . . It's not always easy to find the right kind of man to work with one."

He sat down, looked more squarely at Jerphanion, then suddenly:

"Surely," he said, "I've already had the pleasure of making your acquaintance? Wait a moment, now. . . . Weren't you with Monsieur Bouitton in Moscow that evening when we had supper together after the opera?"

"Certainly I was. I thought Monsieur Bouitton had mentioned the fact when he arranged for me to call on you."

"No," replied Haverkamp with a laugh; "he spoke only of the object of your call." Then he went on more quietly: "I expect he forgot. But I am very glad to be reminded of it."

He made a few very ordinary and rather absent-minded remarks about his recollections of Russia and about Russia itself. It was obvious that it was not of his travels that he wished to speak at the moment. The only time he seemed to show any real interest was when he said:

"Lenin has just died. Three years ago such an event might have produced far-reaching changes. . . . But now?—I wonder! . . . I feel rather as though I were watching a game of roulette. There are those who say: 'The return to normal will be speeded up.' Perhaps they're right . . . perhaps not."

The tone of his voice changed. He assumed an air of light-heartedness marked by somewhat crude bursts of jocularity.

"However that may be, I don't mind betting that Bouitton's glad enough to find that there are still a few capitalists in France, and that some of them can see beyond their noses! If they were all cautious, it wouldn't look any too healthy for the party funds!"

He thought for a while in silence and then gave another guffaw.

"I can't see you going to Champcenais with such a proposal! You remember Champcenais? If I'm not wrong, he was with us that evening?"

"Yes, indeed; I remember him perfectly."

"We lunched together a few days ago. He wanted me to meet General Duroure—you know whom I mean?—the hero of the Woëvre. He was furious, of course, at not being made a marshal. . . . In the case of Castelnau there may have been political reasons. But would that apply to Duroure? . . . Admittedly, it's largely a matter of luck in the Army. . . . With Champcenais there, the conversation turned, naturally enough, on the coming elections. I told him that, all things considered, I hoped the Left would win . . . that if necessary I would contribute my mite to that end. He thought me completely mad. . . . I tried to make him understand. . . ." He chuckled. "I realize that some of the arguments I used couldn't exactly be trotted out on a public platform. But it was a private party, and you don't need me to tell you that when it's a question of convincing somebody, one's got to speak his language. . . . He said, I remember, that the victory of the Left would accelerate the fall of the franc, and I replied: 'All right, let it fall!' . . . "

Jerphanion was on the point of entering a protest, but on second thoughts it occurred to him that it would be wiser to listen.

" '. . . Do you really think,' I said, 'that the fall of the franc would be such an unmitigated tragedy? Was Germany any the worse off when the mark collapsed? I know I got caught, and rather badly too; but that's not the point. I shan't get caught twice. The next time I speculate in currency I shan't be such a fool as to gamble on a falling market. The money market's got nothing to do with Stock Exchange values. Much bigger and simpler influences are involved. . . . But speculation in currency is a side issue. You're a big industrialist,' I said, 'and though you may have spread your investments pretty widely, the greater part of them are still in France. You employ thousands of workers. The fall of the franc means cheap labour for you, and since your concerns are based on world prices, your margin of profit will go on increasing. The English and Americans,' I added, 'who, at this very moment, are launching a terrible offensive against the franc for purely political reasons, with the object, in fact, of making us loosen our grip on the Ruhr . . .' "

"That's not just a story, then?" Jerphanion interrupted. "There really is such an offensive, and it's not the work of mere speculators? It's a more or less deliberate act on the part of the governments in question?"

"There's no doubt about it. They are carrying out a systematic campaign of strangulation. I'm pretty well placed to know what I am talking about."

"A charming state of affairs!"

"Well, to go back. 'Our good friends,' I said to Champcenais, 'will realize sooner or later that there is a reverse side to the medal. By crushing the life out of us they are helping to lower still further the cost of labour in France—in other words, to make the competition of our tariffs more dangerous in the future than it was in the past . . . assuming, of course, that our producers are not such fools as to fail to take advantage of the situation.' 'And what,' he replied, 'about strikes and the raising of wages?' I replied, what is true, that the rise in wages is slower than the fall in money value, that there is always a time-lag. I added that there was nothing to prevent him from investing part of his profits in real estate, houses, for instance. That, I think, is precisely what he is doing, and it gives him a second source of profit, because the nominal rate of land values does not become adjusted at once to the fall of the franc."

Jerphanion listened to all this with a certain sense of alarm. Replies sprang to his lips, but they were not of a kind that could be aired without his losing his temper. Indignation would introduce a note of sentiment into the discussion, and what purpose, in this case, would indignation serve?

"All these fellows," went on Haverkamp in a thoughtful tone of voice which was part of his carefully cultivated attitude of serene detachment, "live in constant terror of the future. Champcenais, Duroure, they're all the same, no matter what their sphere. Everyone I meet is in a state of trembling panic. Some of them are frightened of Communism, others of a general collapse due to causes which they can't grasp. They are making more money than they ever dreamed of making. Their businesses are booming without their having to raise a finger. They can indulge their every whim and drink champagne every night if they want to. And yet they are shaking in their shoes. It's an odd state of mind. Now I," he went on with carefully assumed aggressiveness, "have no fear of the future, and that for the very good reason that I don't let myself think about it."

"Still, I should have thought that a man operating on such a large scale as you do would have to look forward?"

"That's not the same thing. You can anticipate, calculate, in matters of detail as much as you like. What's bad is brooding about the future as a whole, filling it with imaginary demons, when you can't stir so much as a finger to prevent what you think is coming—as in a nightmare. When I'm tempted to worry, I always fall back on one remedy: I start something new—an undertaking, a company, an enterprise in some field into which I've never yet ventured. That gives me something definite to worry about, a new obstacle to overcome, a goal toward which to work. I don't have time to torment myself with vague fears."

"A cynic would say that you are running away from them, that you are constantly seeking something that will keep you from looking the future in the face."

Haverkamp shook his head. He had no desire to look in the face the idea suggested by his visitor's words. He brushed them aside as an interruption of no importance.

"And there's something else, something positive, something scientifically certain. Each time I start a new business, I widen the sphere of my operations, I increase my floating surface. . . . I know as well as anybody that we are living in a time when not all concerns are equally sound. But everything's not going to collapse at the same moment. I've sunk so many roots that I can't go to smash unless the whole caboodle goes to smash."

Jerphanion smiled in spite of himself. Somewhat to his surprise, he found himself relishing this mixture of megalomania and cunning. He was about to venture a mild objection, but Haverkamp got in before him.

"And then," he said more quietly, in the tone of a man who knows the ways of this world, "there is the human side of the question. I take my own case an an illustration, but the point remains generally true. The more people you can involve in your fate, the more props you have. Your ruin takes on the aspect of a public, even of an international catastrophe. . . . Don't you agree?"

It was on the tip of Jerphanion's tongue to say that international catastrophes did occur, that many of them were extremely grave, but that the fact of their gravity did not make their occurrence impossible. He decided, however, to limit his remarks to a few harmless observations on the instability of the times. That, surely, to some extent excused the nervousness of those who feared the future?

"But don't you think," said Haverkamp, "that the same thing could be said of every period? I doubt whether the world was ever arranged like the neatly ruled lines on a piece of music paper. Don't you think that people have always lived between two catastrophes, and that the fearful have always anticipated the end of the world? The only sensible thing is to realize that that is the normal condition of humanity, and to pick one's way as best one can through the general confusion." A faintly contemptuous expression showed for a moment on his face. "What is really abnormal is the kind of period through which I lived as a young man. People had grown so used to a state of calm that when they were confronted with a Panama scandal or a Dreyfus trial, they completely lost their heads. The pace, too, was slower then, even for men of energy. When I think of the distance I have covered since the war . . . yes, in less than six years!"

He relapsed into thought. Some secret process, which he did not confide to Jerphanion, seemed to be going on, for when he next spoke the direction of his thought had changed:

"I'm not such a fool as to deny that Communism is a danger. But it is not confined to France. Italy has got rid of it for the time being—true. . . . Champcenais and Duroure swallow Mussolini hook, line, and sinker. It remains to be seen whether they are right. . . . There's one thing that gives me a good deal of pleasure. I am not personally an object of hatred. In the eyes of thousands of workers Champcenais, for instance, is the very type of villainous employer, a millionaire several times over, an exploiter, a blood-sucker, a cursed capitalist. . . . The same is true of Bertrand, though he's really a decent fellow. Up to the end of the war I, too, was regarded as a bad employer. Now I'm no longer in the foreground of my various concerns. I control them, but from a distance. Only those in the know realize that. I am not an enemy of the people, if only because the people don't know anything about me. If my name means anything to them, it is only very vaguely. I've become a sort of legend to them."

He burst out laughing and looked Jerphanion straight in the face.

"So much of a legend have I become that even in business circles . . . see for yourself if it isn't so. Try turning the conversation on me. . . . Ask anybody you like to tell you something about me. . . . You'll see their faces take on an expression as though they were going to talk about some Hindu magician with his sleeves full of tricks, or about the mathematician—what's his name?—Einstein, yes, that's it" (he pronounced it Ennstenn) "—whose calculations are so abstruse that only about three persons in the world, I gather, can follow them. . . ."

He shrugged his shoulders in a magnificent gesture and offered Jerphanion a cigarette.

". . . And yet it's all very simple. I have two or three agents abroad who deliberately envelop themselves in an atmosphere of mystery.

They give the impression that no one can follow the details of my operations. . . . It's all a matter of bluff. I'll guarantee that a man like you could get the hang of them in five minutes."

Jerphanion was on the point of saying that he was only too anxious to understand, or, rather, to verify the extent to which he had grasped the explanations given him by Henry de Belleuse. Such a confession, however, would have been beset by many difficulties. He remembered, too, that he was paying this visit with a definite object, and that though it might be tactful to encourage a preamble of general conversation, he must be careful to see that Haverkamp didn't suddenly jump up with a "Good God! I had completely forgotten that meeting of mine! You must excuse me, my dear sir. Let us continue our conversation another day."

Truth to tell, however, Haverkamp seemed to enjoy taking his time like a man who has all day before him. His mind worked by curious fits and starts. There was nothing for it but to accept the fact with as good a grace as possible.

"I believe I've got my finger on the pulse of our times. The essential thing is to take it as one finds it. There are a great many people about who deplore the prevailing state of disorder. As though one can't find plenty of uses for disorder! When it touches our own country, that's quite a different matter. If it's at all possible, we ought to do every-thing in our power to save France from the ultimate consequences of chaos . . . But are we thus bound in the case of other countries? The chaos in Russia is a splendid opportunity for us, which few Frenchmen have been intelligent enough to turn to their advantage. Champcenais and General Duroure, for instance, were in complete agreement the other day on the necessity of encouraging the return of Germany to an ordered way of life—to a régime of the mailed fist— so long as it is not the mailed fist of Communism. They said: 'What a pity it is that Ludendorff is a bit mad.' I don't know what your views may be. *I* think that way of talking is sheer idiocy."

His visitor expressed polite acquiescence, and he continued:

"With Duroure it is sheer professional stupidity. He has heard people saying that matters are not going well in Germany, that the soldiers, or the men who are playing at soldiers, think that they can restore order. As a soldier himself, he is on the side of the soldiers, even though he did fight against them. Champcenais's vision goes a bit further. He is afraid of universal infection. His great argument against the Left-wing coalition is that you fellows are going to be the forerunners of the social revolution. He maintains that Painlevé, Herriot, and Bouitton are so many Kerenskys. Kerensky, like them, was all right in himself, but because he opened the door which, as things turned out, let in Lenin, he did as much damage as though he too had been a fanatic. It's not hard to follow that line of argument. Champcenais has not yet recovered from his Russian trip. He's damned frightened, and I don't suppose he'll ever get over it. But, being a man of taste and cultivation—you knew, of course, that he prides himself on being literary, that he writes verse?—he says that it is not for the fate of his own millions that he's frightened, but for the future of civilization. What he saw in Russia gave him the heebie-jeebies."

Haverkamp threw back his head, turning his great nose a little sideways, and smiled at the far wall.

"I may be a fool to seek my political friends on the Left. But it is hard to change the habits of one's youth. . . ." He sat for a while silently thinking; the beginnings of a smile showed once more on his lips. "Not that I have any very great belief in ideas. . . . Now you, I suppose, have?"

"I believe that ideas can have a great deal of influence on mankind, both for good and for ill. Consequently I attach great importance to the triumph of those ideas which seem to me to be good and just."

Haverkamp made an indulgent grimace. "Yes—in a way your job demands such an attitude. A financier would find himself unemployed if money didn't exist. A man whose business is politics has need of ideas, for they are his field of activity." Haverkamp looked keenly at Jerphanion as though he were trying to take him in as a whole.

"Speaking for myself, I think it is personality that counts. There are a certain number of men—pretty few, on the whole—who have got something in them. They see to it that they show their mettle—whether it's in manipulating the money market, stocks of copper, or ideas. There are others"—he laughed on a note of rather crude heartiness—"well, who are usually a damned nuisance when they speak out of their turn."

Quite suddenly he changed direction:

"Look here; Bouitton's already dropped me a hint about what you've come for. The party funds are going to have to cough up a good round sum. I realize that. . . . Now, even if this had been one of the times when I'd had a good deal of liquid capital, I couldn't have afforded more than half a million; perhaps, if I'd made a great effort, a million, not a penny more. Unfortunately, I've had to face a considerable drain on my resources. I've got to settle a matter connected with my private life to which I attach considerable importance, and that means that I may have to find several millions at short notice. That's the only way I can see it through successfully. Then, I've committed myself to a course of action which will involve me in more heavy expense—oh, it's sheer self-indulgence and luxury on my part, I admit that . . . but one's got to live, and I feel that there is a certain obligation on me to contribute what I can to the general brilliance of the period . . . fact is, I'm building a house in Paris, and making over a château in the country. . . . Well, however large a fortune one may have, one can't lock up several millions without producing a certain amount of friction in the machine. I'm sure you realize that, whatever my capital may be, it's not exactly liquid. . . . To cut a long story short, this is what I propose. The State still owes me five million. It wasn't so long ago that it owed me eight. . . ."

"I remember that you talked about it when we met in Moscow."

"That so? Well, perhaps I did. . . . As a matter of fact, I agreed to a compromise. The Treasury paid me a million last year, in return for which I wrote off two. In recognition of this the State is willing to recognize my claim to the balance of five million. This is my offer:

if you can arrange for me to get all or part of that five million at once, I'll turn over to the party funds half of everything I receive. . . . How's that for an offer?"

"I think it's very generous," said Jerphanion, with a smile that might have meant anything. "Very generous indeed . . . but I find that phrase 'arrange for me to get' rather embarrassing, and so, I think, will Monsieur Bouitton."

"Come now, let's put our cards on the table! You're not going to tell me that Herriot, Bouitton, and the rest haven't got enough influence with the government to get me my money? I'm only asking for the period of waiting to be shortened, for priority treatment, in fact. There's no question of anything illegitimate. I'm claiming something that's my right, after all, and a right that I have already agreed to cut down considerably."

"I think you forget that it would mean asking the present government to furnish us with the weapons we need to overturn it . . . and suggesting to the party leaders a manœuvre which they might, quite possibly, regard as—"

"Not quite honourable?"

"Let us say morally displeasing, not quite compatible with the dignity of the party."

"Bah! Bah! . . . I should be obliged if you would transmit my offer to Monsieur Bouitton. Give him a chance to think it over, to consult his friends. But don't influence him." He got up. "All you need tell him is that I am making a big sacrifice for the cause, and that if the party declines my offer, I shall be compelled, in view of the circumstances, to contribute the merest pittance—a bare hundred thousand, say—and that, really, would be the end of the world, now, wouldn't it?"

# Chapter

## 32

### AN OFFER OUT OF THE BLUE

As he shook Jerphanion's hand at the studio door, Haverkamp smiled suddenly as at some secret thought, glanced at the ceiling, and then, cloaking his nervousness beneath a hearty manner, said:

"My dear fellow, I'm going to say something which may come to you as a bit of a surprise . . . you may even find it rather improper, in view of my friendship with Bouitton . . . but that's my responsibility. . . . Is your present job entirely satisfactory?"

"My relations with Monsieur Bouitton," replied Jerphanion, somewhat put out, "have always been excellent, I can almost say affectionate. But my job, as you call it, is merely a temporary arrangement."

"Ah, just as I thought! . . ." He went on quickly: "Now, see here, I'll come straight to the point. I imagine that the material side of your contract with Bouitton is not particularly brilliant. That is not his fault. At the same time, you are interested in your work, in the people with whom it brings you in contact. . . . I don't want to say anything against politics, but, frankly, you are worth more than that. You will very soon find that there are fields of activity compared with which politics look a little like a country fair. . . . I don't know what Bouitton gives you, but I'm willing to double it, and if we find that we can work comfortably together, things won't stop there. The post I'm offering you is that of my private secretary, or rather, let us say, secretary general, because if I get the right man for what I have in mind, he'll have to handle most of my dealings with the outside world. If that is not the case at present, it's because the man I've got at the moment lacks breadth of vision. . . . I need hardly point out that I've got a technical secretariat with someone in charge of it. It's no part of my intention to burden you with a lot of routine administration. . . . You would be my closest collaborator, that's what it comes to, the confidant of my most secret thoughts. . . . And you needn't have any scruples about Belleuse. I've been meaning to get rid of him for some time . . . or if I do decide to keep him, it'll be merely to look after my social engagements. . . . I expect the suddenness of all this must seem a bit odd to you. The fact is, I flatter myself that I know a good man when I see him. When I've made up my mind to do something, I do it, without beating about the bush. That's always been my way, and it's always succeeded up to now. I took Belleuse against my will, to oblige a friend. . . . And don't run away with the idea that I act on impulse, that I get sick of people as quickly as I take to them. Ask those who have worked with me since the beginning. I am extremely loyal." He turned towards the book-case. "There's just one photograph there, as you will notice; it's of a young assistant of mine, the first alter ego I ever had in the old days, a little guttersnipe who was killed at Verdun. If he'd lived, he'd have been the person whom you'd have found here when you came today. . . . If you like having things in black and white, I'm ready to give you a written contract here and now . . . and, as I said before, I'll undertake to make it right with Bouitton. You said yourself that your arrangement with him was purely temporary. I'll explain the whole business to him. I'll take full responsibility. You needn't even speak to him about it. He'll do all the speaking necessary when he and I have had our chat. Bouitton's an intelligent chap, and he's good-natured too."

Jerphanion had had time to get over his first surprise, to decide on what attitude he should adopt, and to prepare his answer. The offer was not quite so flattering, perhaps, as Haverkamp imagined. Still, however that might be, it had been made on a generous impulse, and it implied a degree of feeling not always to be found in human relationships.

"My dear sir," he began in a tone of real sincerity, "I am deeply touched by what you have been saying. I realize just how much spontaneous esteem such an offer, coming from a man like yourself, betokens, and I shall long remember it with pride." He continued with marked modesty: "My use of the word 'temporary' has, I fear, caused a certain amount of misunderstanding. If I felt that my true career lay in doing the kind of work I am doing now, I should most certainly not dream of leaving Monsieur Bouitton, for whom I have a feeling of deep affection, so long as he needed me, no matter what advantages I might be offered elsewhere. But it so happens that I became his assistant more or less by accident, and in order to serve my political apprenticeship under his wing—an apprenticeship which it was not intended should last long. I was—I still am—a university professor; I took my degree at the École Normale Supérieure. Politics have always interested me. When Monsieur Bouitton became a Minister, he asked me to run his office for him. Since it was my intention to stand for Parliament at the next elections, I stayed with him when he resigned his portfolio, instead of looking about for another teaching post. I have now been adopted as a candidate, and my campaign has already begun. I am assured that my chances of being returned are very good."

Haverkamp stared; he looked crestfallen.

"That puts an entirely different complexion on the matter. You must forgive me. I had no idea—"

"Did Monsieur Bouitton never mention the fact to you?"

"No. . . . As I said before, he is often very forgetful . . . or rather he thinks he's said things when he hasn't. I certainly was under the impression—I can't help being sorry, you know, that a man of your calibre should meddle in politics . . . and I am certain that if you had been willing to work with me you would have found a far wider field for your abilities, wider and more exciting than you imagine. But I fully realize—"

"I think," said Jerphanion, accentuating the modesty of his tone, "that I ought to mention one other detail that will take from my refusal any lingering suspicion of discourtesy. I have just been appointed vice-president of the Radical Party. . . ."

"Vice-president?"

"Yes . . . and it puts both Monsieur Bouitton and me in a rather difficult position. Monsieur Bouitton thinks it rather embarrassing that a vice-president of the Radical Party should hold a subordinate position in the service of a man who, for the moment, is merely a deputy. Consequently I am going to resign my post of assistant."

"I must say, I've made a proper fool of myself!"

"Please don't talk like that. After all, you couldn't know all this by merely looking at me. There is nothing offensive in your estimate of my potentialities—far from it."

Haverkamp went back with Jerphanion to the door. As he shook his hand in farewell, he said:

"It has been a great pleasure for me to know you better, Mr. Vice-president. I have a feeling that many things will throw us together in the years to come. Please explain to Monsieur Bouitton the proposal I have made—about the party funds, I mean. I suppose that as vice-president you will have something to say in the matter?"

"It was discussed between you and Monsieur Bouitton before I was appointed. I have acted merely as his agent. Besides, the decision will have to be taken by our finance committee, of which Monsieur Bouitton is at present the chairman, and on which I have no seat. But you can rest assured that I will faithfully interpret all that you have said."

# Chapter

## 33

**JERPHANION MAKES HIS REPORT.
ALGEBRA A LA HAVERKAMP.
BOUITTON LOSES HIS TEMPER**

"Well, how did your visit to the master bandit go off?"

"It was all rather odd. But I at least learned one thing."

"What?"

"I think I'm beginning to see rather more clearly how he reached his present position of power. It had always seemed to me a somewhat dizzy and fantastic achievement."

"Good. You speak as though your conclusions were intellectual rather than practical. But I shall be interested to hear what they are, all the same. They may give us something to go on with."

"It was as I was leaving his house yesterday evening that the conviction first dawned on me. I flattered myself that I had the whole business at my fingers' ends. At that moment I could have made a first-rate speech on the subject. But this morning I'm beginning to wonder whether I haven't lost the thread. You know how it is when a friend explains some amusing arithmetical problem. You think you have it firmly fixed in your mind, and then, somehow, next day—"

"Who gave you this explanation? The master bandit in person?"

"No, his references were of a very roundabout nature. It was his private secretary who gave me the facts—a fellow of infinite subtlety, and rather a queer fish to have a job like that. He was lavish with the most confidential information . . . stuff of the sort I should never have dared to ask for. Funny, isn't it?"

"And what, precisely, was the arithmetical problem?"

"Just a minute. . . . It's all terribly complicated because, you see, his personal and particular method depends upon the interlocking of his various 'operations.' If I'm not careful I shall lose my way in a bewildering mass of detail. I'll try to describe a single instance to you, simplified and laid out as scientifically as I can manage—provided that I can remember what he said, and, still more, that I really did understand what he was getting at. The whole process might be called —the Wedding at Cana [1] Up to Date, or the Multiplication of Millions."

"And a very alluring title, too. If the process is genuinely practicable, I hope to learn something that I can turn to advantage."

"Well, here goes, then. Haverkamp, through his intelligence service, gets to hear of some industrial or commercial concern which was once a good thing, but is now in a bad way. He buys up some of its outstanding debts. He doesn't have to buy many, and he gets them pretty cheap because the creditors want, at all costs, to avoid bankrupting the concern in question. Next he arranges for some of its stock to be taken up by one or two groups which he already controls, or by certain banks whose boards of directors he can twist round his little finger. The business is done privately, not in the open market, with the big holders, who are prevailed upon to sell at a very low figure by having it pointed out to them that if they don't listen to reason, the company's scrip will be forced down to zero by means of secret unloading, or by the sudden calling in of debts on a large scale, and so on. As soon as he has got into his own hands, by this underhand method, the amount of stock he thinks necessary, Haverkamp lets it be known that he is interested in the company. The business world is not slow to realize the significance of that. He becomes a director himself or so works it that some of his cronies shall be elected to the board. It is announced that the company is about to enter on a period of unheard-of prosperity. At once a new capital issue is made, and Haverkamp acquires a large amount of the new stock in return for the debts he has purchased. This, taken together with the stock which he has already acquired

---

[1] Presumably, Jerphanion, less familiar with the Bible than with French politics, meant the Miracle of the Loaves and Fishes.—Translator's Note.

or which he controls, gives him the whip-hand of the concern. The market price rises, partly as a result of his own manipulations on the Exchange, partly because the general public flocks to buy.

"As soon as the business is put sufficiently on its feet again and revalued, even though the market quotation may be wholly ficti-tious, Haverkamp floats a new company, the object of which may be totally different, but which has at least a vague relation, some sort of connexion, with the activities of the original company. . . . Sup-pose, for example, that the original company has to do with street-cars, the new one will deal in electric motors, or in various products or operations more or less connected with tramways, and on which they depend for their existence. It becomes, in fact, what is known as an omnium company. Or the whole racket can be worked the other way round. In any case, Haverkamp subscribes, or gets sub-scribed, a large part of the capital required by the new company, which he arranges to pay up in the form of stock in the old, refloated concern, valued at a figure approximating to the market quotation. I need hardly add that this apparently genuine quotation has been 'bulled' by the manipulation of Haverkamp and his gang. In coun-tries where this kind of financial operation is not allowed—for you mustn't forget that our friend operates on an international scale, and that corporation law varies more or less in different parts of the world—an intermediate stage is necessary. (I don't know whether that is the case in France.) In short, what happens is this: Haverkamp de-posits the stock of the refloated company in one of the banks which he controls, as security for advances calculated on a scale as liberal as though the stock were absolutely gilt-edged and the quoted price indubitable evidence of public confidence. Since, too, Haverkamp can always manage to get his hands on a nice little parcel of stock in the new concern—he can always trot out some sort of pretext; I gather, for instance, that his desk is crammed full of patent certificates of all kinds, bought for a song, which he can always palm off in return for stock in the companies which he floats, provided the patents can be made to appear even a little relevant to their activities—in this way he can fairly easily gain control of the new concern. That done, he uses its scrip as a means of getting hold of still another company, or of something fresh which he sets about floating.

"It really is, you see, a case of multiplying the loaves. And yet it's not pouring water into a sieve, not a building up of purely fictitious values which a flick of the fingers can send tumbling to the ground. For each one of the operations which I have attempted to describe represents real money which has been subscribed by others—by friendly capitalists or by the public—or, should we say perhaps, by the gullible members of the public? And this real money, taken in conjunction with the fake stock, makes up a comparatively substantial whole, as sound and as honest as most financial operations today can claim to be, and capable of tremendous development. Of all these complicated transactions Haverkamp remains the real master. They develop as he develops, and with him their influence penetrates into every corner of the financial world at a speed exceeding anything of which our fathers even dreamed. In his hands they represent power rather than an actual fortune. What that fortune is it is impossible to express in terms of figures, or rather any statement of it would have to be algebraic. You see, it has less relation to the fixed quantities of arithmetic than to the equations ruling in a system of curves. The thousands of stock certificates in this or that which Haverkamp holds are not so much *values* in the sense understood by an old-fashioned middle-class man of business or by a lawyer as in that of the mathematician who writes that value $m$ is a function of value $t$. If you asked Haverkamp for a statement of the exact size of his fortune, the most he could do would be to give you a page filled with equations. But as to substituting recognizable figures for the $x$'s, the $y$'s, the $t$'s, and the $m$'s—well, anyone wading through that page would find it a very different pair of shoes, and Haverkamp himself wouldn't undertake the job without a pretty cynical wink. And that, sir, is the sum of what I understood or deduced from what I heard. I may have made a lot of howlers. Please tell me if you spotted any."

"No, I can't say I did," replied Bouitton with good-humoured modesty. "But, then, even though I am president of the party finance committee, I'm no more familiar with these high matters of the money market than the coal-dealer at the corner. Your explanation dazzled me. I seemed to be taking in all the details as you mentioned them; but damned if I'd care about trying to recapitulate them now! What a hodge-podge! My dear fellow, you're a positive marvel. Make a speech like that in the House two years from now, and though all but four or five of the members will think it just a piece of oratorical fireworks, I'd bet that when it next comes to forming a government, you'd get the portfolio of finance! . . . But don't tell me that the master bandit's private secretary spilled the beans to that extent. Or if he did, he was guilty of an abominable act of betrayal!"

"No, I did a good deal of putting two and two together, though I tried to keep myself out of the picture as far as possible."

"Do you mean to say you just took it in your stride—put your two and two together on the way home?"

"I'd given a good deal of thought to the subject beforehand. I've been worrying this thing out for some time now, and trying to guess the answer to a lot of questions. But, as I said before, this fellow Belleuse behaved all through our talk with an assumption of frankness which really was rather odd. I shouldn't wonder if he wasn't getting revenge in some way or other, or possibly he may have stumbled on the fact that his employer means to get rid of him. His attitude may have had some connexion with something that happened later—I'll tell you about that in a minute or two."

"Go ahead. You seem to have a whole lot of things to tell me that haven't very much to do with the party funds."

"Oh, I'm coming to them all right."

And he proceeded to give an account of the suggestion which Haverkamp had asked him to pass on. Bouitton heard him in silence, biting his lip. Jerphanion was all agog to see how he would react. When he had finished:

"I see—yes, I see . . ." said Bouitton, still biting his lip.

"It's not such a stupid move on his part as you might think," went on Jerphanion. "He may put as brazen a face on the matter as he likes, but I'm pretty sure he's far from easy in his mind about the chances of getting his five million, or at least he's afraid that if he does touch his money it'll have been shaved down a good deal and anyhow won't come home to roost for a long time yet. And he's not the kind of man who cares about long-term loans. He likes doing business, when he can, on a cash basis. It's quite likely that he is a bit short at the moment. Two and a half million, or even less, paid now would mean more to him than the whole amount later. He's offering us a commission, that's what it comes to. And if things turn out as he hopes they will, he'll figure as one of the biggest supporters of the party. No future government of the Left will be in a position to refuse him anything. So, you see, he gets it both ways."

"Yes . . . yes . . . yes."

"You're not being very communicative, sir."

"I was thinking."

"You don't regard it as an improper proposal and that we ought to refuse?"

"If I had only myself to consider . . ."

"You think that the others—?"

"I think that the prospect of two and a half million will make them open their eyes a bit, and that they'll howl their eyes out if we suggest refusing such an offer."

"But there's a long way to go before those two and a half million actually materialize. I can hardly believe that the Treasury, hard put to it as it is at the moment, will agree to pay Haverkamp on the dot."

"Well, but—for people who are juggling every day with sums running into billions, a few million extra aren't much."

"But the whole thing's like a bad joke! Do you really suggest that we should go to the Poincaré government with a proposal that they should give Haverkamp preferential treatment and cough up 'a few million' which are going to be employed to ensure the defeat of its majority and to drive it out of office?"

"The suggestion would not be made on those grounds."

"But surely they'd pretty soon guess what was in the wind?"

"Odder things than that happen in politics, my lad. The parties, after all, are always to some extent playing a game and striking bargains —duellists saluting one another. . . . I'll scratch your back, you scratch mine. . . . For the moment I can't make up my mind. I shall have to think it over for a day or two. . . . Whatever happens, we shall have to submit the problem to our friends."

"I've still got a surprise up my sleeve," said Jerphanion; and he gave an account of the second proposal which Haverkamp had made to him.

"Well, of all the damned pieces of cheek!" exclaimed Bouitton without waiting to hear what answer Jerphanion had made. "A fake-company promoter, a conjuror, to try to sneak you away under my very eyes, just because he can afford to pay more than I can! The damned rascal!"

Jerphanion hurriedly explained how he had received the offer.

"You did perfectly right, my lad, and just what I should have expected of you. And anyhow the dirty trickster was getting a misfire for his pains, because anyhow I've got to let you go. But he didn't know that. It doesn't alter the fact that he behaved like a swine."

He got up and started pacing up and down the room, brooding in silence. At last:

"I know," he said, "what I shall say to our friends. It's not half what he gets from us that he'll have to turn over to the party funds, but two thirds. Two thirds or nothing. If he says yes, we'll manage to make the Treasury give him his five million down. I see how the old fox's mind is working. He thinks he'll get only partial payment before the elections, and that we shan't claim anything on the balance even though we do get it for him without undue delay. Well, he's got a surprise coming to him!"

# Chapter

## 34

### THE EXQUISITE DELIGHT OF A
### PROJECT REALIZED

Jerphanion and Odette had invited Jallez and Bartlett to dine and spend the evening with them. Bartlett
had been introduced to the young Mme Jerphanion the night before
at the Café des Deux-Magots. He had been a great success.

"He's a thoroughly pleasant, warm-hearted young man," had been
Odette's comment to Jallez. "For all his shyness, there is a glint of mischief in his eye, and I find the combination charming. I should think
he's an absolutely loyal friend. This trip we are going to make together
looks like being tremendous fun. I confess that I was a bit nervous
when I first heard that he was to be included, but now that I've met
him I feel perfectly happy about it."

The meeting at the apartment had been arranged with the object
of settling the last-minute details. A "staff conference," they called it.
Bartlett had nodded approval of the phrase, being clearly much impressed by the idea of the "staff."

They plunged into their discussion as soon as dinner had started.
All four of them found pleasure in treating it with the utmost seriousness. Though the point had never been previously discussed between
them, they were in complete accord about the necessity of giving the
most careful thought to the choice between alternative routes, each
of which might have an almost equal claim. Whenever this particular
problem arose, every conceivable argument and conjecture had to be
stated before the final decision could be reached. Bartlett entered
whole-heartedly into the game.

The first point to be settled was the date of their departure.

"It's now the end of February. The days are already reasonably long.
The first green ought to be showing in the woods. The weather, since

yesterday, seems to have set in to be fair. Is there any point in waiting? Besides, it's easier for me to get away now than it would be a week from now."

"Let's get off tomorrow!" said Jallez.

Odette protested. It wasn't Jean-Pierre who was the difficulty. It had been settled what was to become of him. Bouitton had offered to take him in at the Quai de Béthune, where he would be overwhelmed by the combined attentions of the maid, the cook, Suzanne, and Bouitton himself. The boy was thrilled at the idea of spending a few days in such a lovely apartment, with which he already had some small acquaintance. But there were one or two details which still had to be seen to. Odette could not leave home without first giving a number of instructions to her maid, who was not blessed with a quick intelligence. Jean-Pierre must be taken to Bouitton's. If they were to start the next day, Odette couldn't possibly get off before midday, which would be a pity.

Their hesitation was considerably increased when Bartlett announced that his car had developed "trouble." He didn't think it was much, but the man at the garage had said he couldn't do anything about it before morning and wasn't sure of having the car ready until the evening.

"Then let's make it the day after tomorrow, early."

That settled, they discussed the route. Jerphanion had got a pile of maps ready on the sideboard.

"Which way were you thinking of going?" he asked.

"It's not hard to answer that," said Jallez. "The direct way is by the main Dijon road, through Melun, Sens, Tonnerre, and Montbard. After Montbard we've got a choice, but I don't think we shall have much difficulty in making up our minds, do you, Bartlett? . . . It'll be possible, you see, for us to follow Jérôme Coignard's itinerary all the way to the Torchecoul country; and that's an advantage not to be lightly abandoned."

Jerphanion replied that the precedent set by Jérôme Coignard had not occurred to him. He agreed that it weighed heavily in the balance.

But unless it was to be considered as being absolutely decisive, he would like to suggest an alternative route. He knew the main road No. 5, by Melun, Sens, and Montbard, very well indeed. It was not without a certain beauty. It was a typical French main road. But it was monotonous.

"I think you'll agree with me. One can go nearly two hundred miles without noticing any appreciable change in the landscape. We shouldn't really get the feeling that we were exploring. My idea was to take a less direct road. It may be a bit longer, a bit more winding, but every yard of it is crammed with interest, and the country changes all the time. When you get to the other end, Monsieur Bartlett, you will feel that you've travelled through counties and kingdoms."

Bartlett declared rather shyly that he would be delighted to travel through counties and kingdoms, and at a cost, too, of such a very small amount of gasoline.

"Let's have the details," said Jallez. "I imagine you've got them all cut and dried."

Jerphanion unfolded his maps. They made a pleasant sound. They soon covered table and dishes alike, and as Jerphanion laid them out the room was filled with the sound of the wind in the trees and of whirring wings.

"It isn't really very complicated," he said in conciliatory tones; "at some points the two routes coincide. We leave Paris by the Porte d'Italie and take the Fontainebleau road, going through Juvisy, Essonnes, and Ponthierry, where there is an entertaining zigzag stretch up and down hill among the trees and houses. In honour of Monsieur Bartlett I propose to go through Fontainebleau instead of by-passing it. . . ."

"Do we go through the forest, too?" asked Bartlett.

"Certainly."

"I've only been there twice. It'll be jolly to see it again. I know the château, but the town hardly at all."

"We'll take a look at it. From Fontainebleau we go to Moret. Do you know Moret, Monsieur Bartlett?"

"I'm not sure. . . . I'm a bit mixed up. . . ."

"I think you'll like it. A little farther on we rejoin Route 5, and follow it along the valley of the Yonne. Do you know Sens, Monsieur Bartlett?"

"I've passed it in the train several times, but I don't really know it."

"Then we must make a point of having a look at it. At Sens we leave Route 5 and continue up the Yonne valley . . . as far as Joigny. The valley there begins to take on a character all its own. One feels that the country has personality. After Joigny things become a bit more complicated. Look carefully. As far as Migennes we're still on what one may call a main road, but after Migennes we turn off into a much narrower and more tortuous road . . . winding here and there, giving one a sense of being in close contact with the countryside . . . and it's a countryside with a past, let me tell you."

Bartlett declared that he liked little winding roads up river valleys, but that he never dared take them when he didn't know the country, for fear of losing himself. It would be delightful, he said, to embark on such an adventure behind a guide like M. Jerphanion. He imagined that when they reached this point in their journey they might be said to be in the very heart of those counties and kingdoms which had been dangled so temptingly before his eyes.

"Precisely. Now, this name here, would you mind reading it, Monsieur Bartlett? Does it convey anything to you?"

"Chablis?" Bartlett nodded his head very gravely. "Can my eyes be deceiving me?"

"No, they have told you true."

"And may we stop the car there just long enough to drink a glass of the local wine in honour of my master Torchecoul?"

"You may rest assured that we shall join you in that toast. I plan to take you on from Chablis to Lichères and Nitry, where the road begins to climb towards Avallon, winding still through wooded valleys, and still in the land of counties and kingdoms. Do you know Avallon, Monsieur Bartlett?"

"I'm not sure. I'm a bit mixed up."

"So much the better; we shall have the pleasure of showing it to you."

"Failing the ghost of Jérôme Coignard," said Jallez, "we shall have that of Auguste Dalville, the hero of *The Dairymaid of Montfermeil* by Paul de Kock."

"Paul de Kock!" exclaimed Bartlett. "I had a great-uncle once who had several of Paul de Kock's novels. He loved them, but he always refused to lend any of them to my father, on the ground that they were highly unsuitable reading for a clergyman."

"You'll be quite at home, then! A few miles beyond Avallon, we turn off into a side road which brings us to Semur-en-Auxois. Ah! there's a treat in store for you! As one comes into Semur by that road—but no, I won't go on. I don't want to spoil the effect! From Semur we take the Pouilly road until we reach a fork, and then about a mile farther on there's Grosbois-sous-le-Mont, which must not be confused with Grosbois-en-Montagne; and I shouldn't be surprised if the Château d'Aubepierre were somewhere in the rectangle of country lying between those two places. The map shows no road to the château, but there must be one."

"You mustn't forget," put in Jallez, "that when Bartlett and I first planned this expedition—it was at a wine-shop in Rome—we had a clear vision of ourselves asking the grocer or the postmistress of Grosbois-sous-le-Mont how to get to Aubepierre. There was no question of just going stolidly on with our noses glued to the map. This rather anxious but pleasing inquiry made in the gathering darkness is all part of the ritual!"

"You regard the gathering darkness as essential?"

"I think it is certainly indicated, don't you?"

"Undoubtedly."

"On condition that we arrive at the château before nightfall. . . . But the château must almost certainly be built on a hill, so that it will be light up there even when it is already dark in the village, which lies in a valley."

"And so we come to the question how long all this is going to take."

They agreed that it would be possible to make the journey in a single day. But that would mean starting very early, having to curtail their visits to places of interest, rushing through the counties and kingdoms, and taking the risk, in view of possible breakdowns, of arriving in pitch-darkness.

"My car runs well," said Jerphanion with ill-concealed pride, "but she's small, and slow on the hills. I can't maintain a high average, and I'm afraid I may keep you back."

Bartlett protested. All he'd got, he said, was a small English car. "It's you who'll have to wait for me. On steep hills I'm always being passed by cyclists . . . and going down, too, because I'm an excessively careful driver."

"Whatever happens, we must stick together. Otherwise the trip will lose half its point."

"You lead, Monsieur Jerphanion, since you know the road. But you must look back now and then just to see that I'm following. If I find that you're gaining on me too much, I'll sound my horn."

The final arrangement was that they should take two days. Jerphanion suggested that they should sleep at Chablis, and this was agreed upon.

"Ought we to let Torchecoul know that we're coming?"

"I've already done so. He knows that four of us will turn up."

"Yes, but only quite vaguely. . . ."

"It would be more fun if our arrival had something unexpected about it, don't you think, Bartlett? We want, as it were, to tumble on him out of the sky. And we shan't do that if we find him at Grosbois-sous-le-Mont, standing in the middle of the street, watch in hand, waiting for us."

"You're dead set on that moment of delicious uncertainty in the grocer's shop!"

"To be sure I am . . . and also on the note of joyful surprise in Torchecoul's voice when he cries: 'There they are! There they are! . . . Give me my hat, Gertrude—or Aurélie!' I don't know Madame Torchecoul's name."

"The solution would seem to be—since he mustn't be made privy to the plot—that when you leave here you go to the Central Post Office in the rue du Louvre and send off a telegram in forceful but not too definite terms—something like: 'Arriving shortly . . .' 'Arriving next few days.'"

"That's the very thing. It'll keep him on tenterhooks."

"Where is your car?" asked Jerphanion.

"In a garage on the boulevard Montparnasse."

"I'd like to have a look at it. The garage man may be up to tricks; or he may say tomorrow evening that it's not ready yet. What about meeting there tomorrow morning at ten? Give me the address. We can take her out for a trial run. I've had a pretty long experience in doing repairs on the road!"

# Chapter

## 35

### ALL SET FOR THE COUNTIES AND THE KINGDOMS

They had arranged to meet on the next morning but one at ten o'clock precisely, in front of the house on the boulevard Saint-Germain in which the Jerphanions' flat was situated. At half past nine Jerphanion went to get his car, which he kept in an old coach-house in the rue du Cardinal-Lemoine. As he opened the door, he was conscious of a faint sensation in the pit of his stomach. True, he had spent the early part of the previous afternoon in seeing that everything was in order, but the motorist never forgets that he is watched over by jealous gods. Everything, it seemed, was as he had left it. . . . None of the tires had gone flat. At his third pressure on the starter the engine came to life with a rhythmical roar that was music to his anxious ears. He turned the switch, and the headlights went on; when he pushed the Klaxon, it responded with a pleasant, though somewhat muted bray. By ten minutes to ten the car was in front of the house, the two suitcases duly stowed away. Odette and the maid would bring down the handbags.

At five minutes to, Jerphanion began to show signs of restlessness and anxiety. If only Bartlett's car hadn't had a relapse! The previous morning Jerphanion had looked it over and tried it out. He had soon discovered that the "trouble" was due to the presence of water in the carburettor, which, in spite of the garage-man's mocking look, had there and then been taken down and cleaned. A fresh trial had triumphantly vindicated this treatment, but there could be no guarantee that other drops of water, lying about, perhaps, at the bottom of the tank, might not have got once more into the carburettor.

At five minutes past the hour his heart gave a jump. The little English car had just turned into the boulevard. It contained Jallez as

well as Bartlett, who proceeded to pull up immediately behind the
yellow Citroën [1] with every sign of the most extreme caution. He
apologized for being late, explaining that the Paris streets terrified
him, and that having to drive on the right went against all his instincts.

It was a quarter past before Odette appeared. For a woman, Jallez
remarked, that was not too bad.

Jerphanion, who, as had been arranged, was to lead the procession,
explained that he was going to drive as far as the city boundaries by
a route which, though rather roundabout, would be easier than the
direct way because it kept to the main streets, the quays, the boulevard
de l'Hôpital, the boulevard Saint-Marcel, the avenue des Gobelins,
and the avenue d'Italie. Bartlett expressed his gratitude.

They reached the Paris toll at half past ten. The Fontainebleau road
was fairly empty. The only trouble they had was in getting clear of
the Villejuif bottleneck, which was a maze of heavy street-cars.

"Are they following all right?" Jerphanion asked Odette.

"Yes, but Bartlett just missed getting run into by the last tram. Go
slowly."

The Juvisy road opened before them, straight and empty. The
weather, which, ever since the start, had given Jerphanion considerable
cause for anxiety, seemed to be looking up. Behind the clouds away
to the left, there was quite definitely a hint of sun. Jerphanion began
to feel thoroughly happy. He was doing forty-five, which was a comfortable speed for the five-horse yellow Citroën.

"Are they still following?"

"Yes, they're all right now. I even think they could manage to go
a bit faster."

"So could we, if it comes to that!"

But pride of ownership did not urge him to any reckless display
of prowess.

They reached the edge of the forest a little before midday. At the
first big road-junction to the west of the town Jerphanion pulled up.

[1] Throughout these chapters the French text contains a play on the words "Citroën"
and "citron" (lemon) which cannot be rendered in English.—Translator's Note.

Bartlett's car came to a stop a few seconds later, with admirable precision, immediately behind him.

"Everything all right?"

"Yes," cried Jallez and Bartlett in unison.

"Listen; I'm going to drive slowly through Fontainebleau to give Bartlett an opportunity of looking about him. But I don't think we ought to get out. It would make us too late. How about lunching at Moret? I know a hotel there."

"Splendid. I'm going to drive until we get out of the town, so that Bartlett can be free to satisfy his curiosity."

At twenty past twelve they drove under the gateway of Moret, which Bartlett greeted with several flattering exclamations of "Oh!"—which proved that he was no stranger to the artless courtesy of the tourist.

At the inn they were told that luncheon would not be ready for a quarter of an hour. They filled up the interval by taking a short walk. They showed Bartlett the place's not very exciting beauty-spots, and the view over the river. He was a pleasant person to take around. He admired just the right things, and had a way of opening his eyes, pursing his mouth, nodding his head and giving little grunts of satisfaction, which absolved him from any charge of indulging in merely polite exclamations of wonder. He said little, but what he did say gave pleasure to his hearers.

"If Shakespeare had not lived at Stratford," he remarked on their way back to the inn, "this would have been just the place for him. I must remember to put the point to Ernest Torchecoul, though I am not at all sure that it will fit in with his attitude to the problem of Shakespeare, about which he once spoke to me."

They asked him what Torchecoul's attitude to the problem of Shakespeare might be. Bartlett confessed that it was so terribly subtle that he had forgotten, after this long interval, what precisely it was. All he could remember was that it ran counter to every accepted theory.

They made a good honest meal, though it could hardly be said to escape the mediocrity of the typical suburban restaurant. They started out again shortly before two.

"We're really clear of Paris now," said Jerphanion, "and getting into open country."

Just beyond the river junction they entered the valley of the Yonne which at that point is flat and without any clearly marked natural features. Under the bright winter sky, however, with its promise of sun, it was redolent of a gentle lyric quality which insensibly affected their minds and lulled them into a pleasing condition of drowsiness. Trees stood at the side of the road, sometimes in clumps, sometimes in scattered isolation. The sky above them was of an even tint. A train came towards them, showing black in the landscape and trailing a long plume of smoke.

At Pont-sur-Yonne they found themselves in a maze of twists and turns which give to the little town the appearance of a fortress with carefully contrived approaches. At the far end of the bridge Jerphanion waited for their companions. In a few minutes the little English car appeared. Jallez waved encouragement. Bartlett's face bore an expression of pride.

They had promised that he should be allowed to explore Sens, but it was three o'clock before they got there.

"We can't spare more than ten minutes," said Jerphanion. "I suggest that we drive to the Cathedral and just have a hurried look round the interior. Apart from that, we must be content with going slow through the town and taking in what we can of it from the cars. As a matter of fact, almost everything worth seeing is in the main street."

"If we had tried to do the trip in one day," said Bartlett with a meaning look, "our sightseeing would really have had to be cut a bit short."

They left Sens at ten minutes past three, reached Joigny about four, and wasted a good deal of time looking for the road to Migennes.

"Is this where the counties and kingdoms begin?"

"Their most mysterious fastnesses, into which no traveller can penetrate without a beating of the heart."

Odette was implored not to take her eyes from the map. They mustn't miss the winding road which struck off to the right at Migennes and went from there to Chablis. They did miss it, however, but the error was soon noted and repaired. The two cars acquitted themselves nobly. After leaving Migennes they had to turn back on their tracks, and this, owing to their small size, they managed to do with triumphant ease.

"That was the first blunder of the day," said Jerphanion, who was jealous of his reputation as leader.

"The country's becoming very difficult," said Bartlett enviously.

Once on the side-road they had no difficulty about finding their way. The twists and turns were numerous. There were several road junctions. But through all the complexity there ran, as it were, a thread, a general line of advance, and only the very unintelligent could have missed the indications provided in plenty for those with a sense of direction. It was not even necessary to keep an eye open for the number of the road painted on the milestones.

The country now had the appearance of being constructed on a small scale. Hills and dense woods closed them in on every side. They felt tiny, an insignificant little party nosing its way adventurously forward, creeping along grooves cut deep in the landscape, taking advantage of openings in the hills. There were grass meadows and woods in plenty, copses that were almost woods, enough pines and firs scattered here and there to give an impression of greenness, and among the leafless timber trees a sufficiency of branchy arabesques to catch the eye and to suggest to the imagination the lovely secrecy of deep, mysterious forests where a man may hide.

Jerphanion was completely happy. He was like a child absorbed in a game with other children, for whom nothing is real outside the limits of their game. "What delight lies round each hidden corner, what adventure breathes in every yard we cover!" he said to himself. "What fun it is, just we four being here together! It needed only that to make everything marvellous! How delicious, how stimulating and suggestive is that clump of bushes to the left! I must point it out to Odette, to my dear, adorable Odette who sits there with the map on her knees, so seriously intent on her pilot's duties! . . . I want to shout it to the other two, that they may share my pleasure! Dear old Jallez, just as he used to be when we tramped the streets of Paris; and that nice fellow Bartlett, who enters so understandingly into the elaborate pretences of this game of ours about life's incomparable moments. We shall spend the evening all in the same inn, sleep all beneath the same roof. We shall drink plenty of new Chablis. To-night Odette and I will be making love together in a rather cold room; but the cold won't matter, because we shall have a feather bed, an eiderdown, and, within us, the warm Chablis. Tomorrow morning we shall set off again, all four of us together, the batteries well charged, our grand little cars on their best behaviour!"

They reached Chablis with daylight to spare, and put up at the Hôtel de l'Étoile, though they thought the prices a trifle exorbitant. A disappointment awaited them in the matter of the wine. The land-lord refused to serve them with that year's Chablis on the ground that it was not yet drinkable, and made them take '21 instead, for which he had the cheek to charge them twelve francs a bottle.

"What a damned swindle!" exclaimed Jerphanion. "For the last six weeks I've been getting this year's from my little wine-merchant in the boulevard Arago—at five francs the litre, not the bottle, mind you! You drank it at dinner the evening before last. Didn't you think it pretty good? As a general rule, Chablis is delicious in its first year, and the '23 vintage is particularly fine. It will be a historic year. It's hardly worth the trouble of coming all this way to drink a '21 Chablis at the place of its birth, and paying through the nose for it, when we could have had the same wine at half the price at any café on the boulevards!"

But except for this disappointment, everything else at Chablis fully came up to Jerphanion's expectations.

## CHÂTEAU d'AUBEPIERRE BY GROSBOIS-SOUS-LE-MONT

At a little after half past four the next evening they were driving up a valley which rose before them in a gentle gradient. The road twisted a good deal and was only just wide enough to permit their passage. It was bordered on the left by a steep, wooded slope, on the right by a succession of copses leading down to a river which, though they could not see, they could just dimly hear.

A few seconds earlier Jerphanion had slowed down and, pointing to the undergrowth, had shouted to the second car:

"Look! There are leaves coming out on the bushes!"

The others appeared to doubt his words, and he challenged them to get out and see for themselves. They were forced to admit that he was right. Two twin bushes, braving the Burgundian winter through which they had just passed, were, in fact, displaying a few tiny, half-unfolded leaves of tender green.

A lane appeared, leading off to the left.

"According to the map," said Odette, "that should lead us to Grosbois-sous-le-Mont . . . a little more than a mile. But there's no signpost."

All four expressed their pleasure, but not without some uncertainty. They held a hurried conclave, each in turn examining the map. Finally they agreed to take the chance.

The spot in which they found themselves was all that they could wish. The winding valley up which they had just come had brought to a fine point their sense of partaking in a voyage of discovery. The country gave them more and more a sense of cosiness, with, here and there, a vista opening onto distances of fold after fold of hills; a hollow, secret land in its wider stretches, with smaller, self-contained areas which looked, and were, withdrawn and hidden. And now here was this little lane upon their left to give the last touch of perfection to a lovely picture, creeping up a deep defile that was steeper and narrower than the valley they had left. It might, they felt, end in a tangle of crooked paths, a dead end of woods and bubbling springs. What more suitable setting could they have imagined for Grosbois-sous-le-Mont?

Driving along it, they noticed a milestone, but it had been freshly painted, and stood there gleaming white and innocent of all inscription, like a gift of Heaven set on the grass-green verge.

A village came into sight, and soon they reached it, a place of white walls and grey roofs, with here and there a damp patch showing on the houses as befitted such a sunk and smothered place, and silent but for a voice suddenly raised, the ring of an anvil, the chatter of a motorcycle engine from somewhere near the church.

They met a man who told them that this was indeed Grosbois-sous-le-Mont. They could have asked him the way to the Château d'Aubepierre, but the ritual of their journey necessitated a rather anxious halt for inquiry at some village shop or post office.

There was no post office to be seen. But they noticed a village shop— the perfect village shop. It was painted a faded brown, and was approached by a much worn but very high flight of steps.

Such was their impatience that they all four entered the shop.

"The Château d'Aubepierre?" was the reply to their inquiry; "nothing could be simpler. Go as far as the church and there, on the left, you will see a road that takes you straight to it. It's not more than a kilometre distant."

The grocer came out into the street to give the final touches to his instructions. A fresh breeze was blowing off the sides of the valley; a faint mist mingled with the gathering darkness, and suddenly there was a sense in the air of the gentle melancholy that hangs over village streets at nightfall.

Five minutes later the five-horse yellow Citroën and the little English car, after traversing a road which, though free of stones, was slightly rutted, drew up before a large and elongated building. It had two storeys, two towers, an excessive number of windows, and a flight of stone steps. Beyond all possibility of question it was a château. Bartlett, throwing his habitual discretion to the winds, could not resist glancing at his companions with a movement of the head which clearly meant: "Well, I haven't dragged you here for nothing, have I?"

Then they heard, and a moment later saw, an old man who came out on the topmost step, shouting and gesticulating:

"Adélaïde, here they are! Adélaïde, give me my hat, here they are!"

# Chapter

## 37

### ERNEST TORCHECOUL DOES THE HONOURS OF HIS CHÂTEAU

Jean and Odette Jerphanion were the only members of the party who had to be introduced. Ernest Torchecoul recognized Jallez, though he admitted that, had he not been forewarned, he would have found it difficult to put a name to him. Then:

"As for you, Bartlett," he said, "I am going to ask your permission and that of your friends to give you the accolade"—which he proceeded to do. To the others he remarked: "You see, I regard Bartlett as no ordinary friend. He is my faithful disciple." Bartlett grunted a shy protest. "Some of his early articles demonstrate my theories with a happiness of phrasing of which I should never myself have been capable. They are among my treasured possessions"—and he let Bartlett go with a great guffaw of laughter. "I look on him almost as a son."

"I recognized you at once," said Jallez. "You have hardly changed at all."

"You are too kind. I am an old man now. I have passed my sixty-eighth birthday."

"I had no intention of flattering you. If anything, you seem to me more vigorous even than you did in the old days."

"Perhaps, perhaps," replied Torchecoul in gratified tones. "I keep pretty fit. But there's no particular merit in that. I lead a very healthy life. . . ."

"Your—diabetes no longer troubles you?" asked Bartlett in a low voice.

"Never. I drink a bottle regularly at every meal . . . though I must admit I have cut out cocktails—except on special occasions. My doctor

547

swears that I break all the rules of the diabetic. . . . So much the better, say I. . . . No need for me to ask any of you how you are. Your faces speak for themselves."

Two maids approached, one of them fairly young, the other middle-aged.

"Take this lady's and these gentlemen's things," said the master of the house.

They had by this time entered a huge gallery which seemed to command the whole interior arrangement of the château. Their first impression was of an intense but gentle warmth, quite unlike the usual atmosphere of a country house. Then they noticed that the whole of the space between a double door on the left and the bottom of the staircase was filled by a vast stove, square in shape, faced with tiles, fitted with a fine brass door, and surrounded by a tiled bench.

"I see that you are looking at my monument," said Torchecoul with gay good humour. "Yes, it is one of the major achievements of my reign. You'll hardly believe me when I say that it eats about twenty tons of good Burgundy coal bricks. We have to use a good deal of wood to warm it up, but once that's done—! . . . There's a special opening direct into the dining-room. . . . The heat is diffused more or less all over the house; it even reaches the upper floors. With open wood fires, we can make the place really quite tolerable."

"And when you're feeling chilly, all you have to do is sit on that bench."

"Exactly. No attack of rheumatism can stand up to it for more than a quarter of an hour. I don't say it's as efficient as central heating, but to have installed that in a great barrack of a place like this would have cost a fortune. . . . And then, you see, we can get all the wood we want from the estate."

Bartlett's English prejudices led him to declare that he would exchange all the central heating in the world for such an obviously healthy method of warming a house.

"And now, I'll show you your rooms. . . . Jeannette, Eugénie, follow us. . . . If you'll allow me, I'll lead the way."

He took the lamp which Eugénie held out to him, and began to climb the noble flight of stairs with a firm step. The first-floor landing was furnished with a few ancient armchairs and chests of drawers. Mirrors and portraits adorned the walls.

"All very feudal!" murmured Jallez to Bartlett, who inclined his head in, as it were, grateful recognition of the words.

"This way!" He led them into a corridor so high and so wide that the lamp failed to illuminate it entirely. The warmth of the stove was noticeable even here.

"This is Monsieur and Madame Jerphanion's room. . . . Eugénie, put some more logs on the fire. . . . It's not, I trust, too cold. We've had the fire going since we got your telegram. Please say, madame, if there is anything you require. The accommodation of Monsieur Jallez and Monsieur Bartlett has, I fear, presented something of a problem. . . ." He went a few steps along the corridor and opened a door opposite. "This is quite a good room. . . ." It was, in fact, huge and filled with old-fashioned country furniture. It contained two large beds, one set against the wall of the corridor, the other against the wall dividing the room from its neighbour, and facing the fireplace, on which a pile of logs glowed red. "We have kept a fire going in here too. If you don't mind sleeping together, this, I think, is where you will be most comfortable. I can give one of you another room, but the fire's not been lit in it. The chimney has been partly demolished, and it'll be rather cold."

Jallez and Bartlett hastened to assure him that they would rather share a room.

"It's an enormous house. . . ."

"Yes, it's much too big, really. We don't use some of the rooms at all. There's so little coming in from the estate!"

"Are the grounds equally extensive?"

"They're pretty big. We've a lot of woodland, which is nice for us, and since the war it's become very profitable. In addition there's a certain amount of arable and pasture land, enough for two farmers, each of whom keeps from eight to ten cows. There's a small farm which supplies most of our produce. It's run by a family, and the man acts also as gardener. The estate as a whole is not too big to look after fairly easily. It keeps me occupied. . . . I'll show you round tomorrow—and the following days, for I hope you're going to stay some time. Oh, but I insist! You can't imagine what a delight it is for me to have you here. It is many years since I've had a chance of talking to people like you. I put up pretty well with a life of isolation, but when a gift like this comes my way—!"

He instructed the maids to sort the bags out into the various rooms. "I expect you want to clean up a bit. You'll find hot water in the jugs, and if you want more you've only to ask for it. If madame would like a bath, Eugénie will show her the way to the bathroom—the only one, I'm sorry to say!"

"Please don't bother . . . tomorrow morning will be quite time enough. . . . We can manage beautifully like this for tonight."

"When you want to put your cars away, I'll show you the stables. I've enough room to house six cars! We don't run one ourselves. I know it's absurd, and one of these days we shall have to make up our minds to it. If we want to drive out we've got two old carriages and a couple of sturdy horses, and that's all we really need. . . . Besides, I like walking. . . . Well, I'll leave you now. You'll find my wife and me in the drawing-room. My wife will be delighted to make your acquaintance. . . . Don't hurry. . . . We'll have a glass of something before dinner. We dine early here. . . . Seven, or a quarter past. . . . I hope you don't mind? You must remember, dear lady, that you are in the country."

# Chapter

# 38

## A FAMILY PARTY

"With your permission, gentlemen, I propose to give the place of honour to our friend Bartlett. He is our guest in more senses than one, as I think you will agree. . . . Adélaïde, will you put Monsieur Jerphanion on your left? . . . Madame, may I have the honour? . . . I ought to tell you that my right ear is deafer than my left. The arrangement has its advantages. As for you, my dear Jallez, I shall treat you with an absence of formality which is, I think, justified by a friendship which goes back to our old Closerie days."[1]

There was a charm about Torchecoul's ceremonious manners. He carried his good fortune with just that lack of pompousness which it had pleased Bartlett and Jallez to evoke when they used to discuss him in their Roman restaurant. While his guests had been in their rooms, he had changed his clothes and now wore a dark suit, a very clean white shirt with a turn-down collar, and a flowing tie. With his long hair, which had grown much whiter since 1910, but was better looked after (it was difficult now to see the slightest sign of scurf on the collar of his coat), he might well have been some old astronomer or Assyriologist dividing his time between the bars of the Latin Quarter and the Institut. His wife, Adélaïde, was a large lady of some sixty summers, whose superfluity of flesh had become concentrated on hips and bosom. Since, however, it had spared her stomach, she could still show a passable feminine contour. She had the face of a jolly barmaid. Her big black eyes still retained a sparkle, her kindly voice was hoarse and at times slightly shrill, and her

[1] The Closerie de Lilas is one of the most famous of the Quartier Latin cafés.— Translator's Note.

speech was marked by the rounded *r's* and *a's* of the patois of Burgundy. Her laugh was frequent and filled the echoing vastness of the dining-room—a full-throated laugh, rich with accumulated experience, and readily provoked by sallies of gay obscenity. Anyone hearing it through the closed door would have imagined someone of mature years witnessing a rather daring performance and undisturbed by moral qualms.

But in fact nothing of the sort was occurring. The behaviour of those sitting round the table was free of formal constraint but perfectly decent. The talk was philosophical rather than broad, and the mistress of the house would have found in it little enough to excite her laughter had she not been at pains to interrupt it with an occasional remark, by the relation of some local incident scarcely suitable for a manual of etiquette. The way in which she managed these asides had something in common with the technique of the old classical authors who knew how to give a twist to any seemingly irrelevant turn of the conversation and mould it to their purpose.

"If it is not an indiscreet question, my dear master," said Jallez, "how do you spend your time?"

"I read a little. I walk. I try to clarify on paper ideas which I have been turning over in my mind for many years. But I have never been much of a hand at writing." He laughed. "Bartlett knows that well enough. My medium has always been, by preference, conversation. . . . Sometimes we go out in the carriage. My wife is too lazy to join me often in my walks."

"For which I am duly punished. It's always when he's alone that adventures happen to him."

"They are very few and far between."

"So *you* say! At least twice he has come across couples using our woods for the most abandoned purposes! Do you call that nothing? I'd give a lot for a front seat on such occasions. Ha ha ha!" Mme Torchecoul leaned over towards Odette. "He tells me about them afterwards, but that's hardly the same thing."

"And were these couples personally known to you?"

"I should say they were! . . . I hope you find these *vols-au-vent* all right?"

"They're perfectly delicious."

"I get the cases from the baker-pastrycook of our town. But it's his wife really who makes them. She was one of the ladies whom my husband surprised in the middle of one of her more pleasant diversions . . ."

"Now, Adélaïde, nothing personal, please!"

"That scarcely seems to have been the attitude of the gentlemen in question! . . . But the whole thing was a blessing in disguise so far as I am concerned. The lady seems to think that she is in my power. We never used to have anything like the *vol-au-vent* cases she sends us now!"

"What you might almost call blackmail, eh, Bartlett? . . . Taken all round, then, dear master, you can hardly be said to lead a boring existence?"

"When you've reached my age, time goes very quickly. But it will be many, many years, dear lady, before you realize that. . . . Why it should be so, I can't say. Possibly the mind grows calmer as one gets old, and worries less about how to fill the passing moments. It has learned by experience, you see, that the longest days slip by all too swiftly, and the years, too. . . . No, I'm not bored, but I'm conscious, sometimes, of an overpowering sense of loneliness; I feel that I have to go too long without distraction. My wife puts up with that kind of thing better than I do."

"He would like to whisper sweet nothings to the country maidens, but he doesn't dare!"

"You wrong me, Adélaïde! And before my chief disciple, too! Before the man who may perhaps write my biography—and in English, too!"

"When your husband speaks a little too much of some woman he has met, don't you feel rather suspicious? Don't you remember,

Ernest, how last summer you talked day in and day out of that young girl Hortense who was looking after the cows down in the birch meadow?"

"If I did, it was merely as one human being of another, and in perfect innocence."

"He used to say, for instance: 'It's surprising how grown-up she's getting. Her figure will be quite lovely one of these days!' Ha ha ha!"

"Such frankness," said Jallez, "is in itself a proof of the purity of the speaker's intentions."

"Nonsense! I know him too well not to realize that his intentions are far from pure! Luckily, he confined himself to talking! I think you'll agree with me, madame, that the art of a lawful spouse lies in her being able to change the object of such intentions?"

"My dear, when I was a bachelor I certainly took considerable interest in the shop-girls and news-venders of the boulevard Montparnasse. I have no hesitation in saying that the development of their figures did not, in those days, find me wholly indifferent . . . when there was anything to develop. Though I think you'll agree, Bartlett, that my habits were above suspicion? Please, Monsieur Jerphanion, help yourself to wine. It's in the decanter at your elbow. I hope you like it?"

"It's my ideal of what a table-wine should be. I only wish we'd found this last night at Chablis."

"Go on, then; drink it up! It comes from our own vineyards. Yes, we have a few acres. It's by no means a great wine. It resembles Pouilly as a younger brother resembles his elder. Do you realize that we're only about five miles from Pouilly as the crow flies? But don't slake your thirst entirely. When we come to the roast, I'm going to give you a Chambertin which—I'll say no more now, except that I hope you will approve of it. It is of one of the great years. My wife had it in her cellar when I married her. There are about four dozen bottles left, I think, eh, Adélaïde? I should tell you that if I take occasional interest in handsome figures, my wife has always had keen discrimination in matters of wine—a rather unusual taste in women."

"You'll have our guests believing that I'm just an old soak! . . . Naturally, I have never been particularly interested in handsome figures, not being blessed with the perverse instincts of certain Parisian women of letters. Ha ha ha! But, thank God, there are other things in life besides wine that can set me dreaming!"

"My dear, you are becoming slightly immodest!"

"I am merely defending my reputation."

"I believe, my dear sir, that you have, to some extent, been pursuing your investigations? May I ask whether the events of the last few years, the new situations which have arisen, have in any way modified your point of view? I should very much like to know how you react to the problems of the present and of the immediate future."

"Our friend Jerphanion would find your opinion particularly interesting, since, as you know, he is taking an active part in political life. He is running in the coming elections."

"So Bartlett told me in his last letter. Let me drink a glass of Chambertin to your success . . . and to our good luck in having men like you taking a hand in our affairs. . . . You ask for my opinion? My gift, as you know"—he spoke with a chuckle—"is more descriptive than anything else. I try to understand the ways of the world. I watch them carefully, and, as a rule, I find them amusing enough. . . . My opinion is probably worthless, but at least I can say that I am neither a preacher nor a prophet."

"Still, you can hardly prevent your ideas from playing their part in contemporary thinking . . . you must, to some extent, define your position" ("I'm burbling," thought Jallez; "it's the fault of this Chambertin.") . . . "as Jerphanion, Bartlett, and I discovered in the course of our conversations last year with the Russians."

"It amazes me to hear that the Russians even know my name. There must, I think, have been some confusion of identity." He laughed. "My knowledge of Marxism is of the most superficial kind. It has never attracted me. I have been told that my views have something in common with it, because of the importance I attach to the economic factor. But my impression is that Marxism attributes to economic structures an absolute value and sees in their evolution the central influence of all history; that it regards moral values as mere concomitants, as having no vitality of their own, as being interchangeable. My own view is that structures are no more than effects, indications, intellectual counters which the mind finds it easy to manipulate. I have given some care to the study of the stratification of society because, in my opinion, it represents a tangible formalization of a great many influences which, though real in the deepest sense of the word, are, in themselves, not easy to grasp. It provides us with evidence about the health of the body social."

"I take it, then, that you are not indifferent to that health? May we know what view you take of it?"

"You are an embarrassing questioner, young man! If you insist, let me say that the kind of social stratification which I approve is one that operates with the maximum of freedom. I regard that society as really healthy, really vital, in which individuals play their part in accordance with their, if I may so phrase it, specific gravity and natural affinities, with a minimum of resistance and time-lag. Anything within the framework of a given society tending to lessen the friction which may impede the free working of these forces, I regard as good; anything increasing it, as bad. I believe in a society which can maintain itself in a condition of fluidity . . . and the same is true of individual happiness. . . . Did you notice our maid Eugénie, the elder of the two?"

"Not especially."

"I trust that her manner towards you was good, that she brought your bags and your hot water cheerfully?"

"Indeed, yes," put in Odette. "I was struck by her readiness to do all she could for us."

"Good. At one time she kept an inn. In those days she had every fault under the sun, including envy. She envied people who had nothing to do with her, on whom she was in no way dependent. She grumbled at her servants and treated them with great harshness. Fundamentally, she was a thoroughly unhappy woman. Her business never prospered. Today she has found her rightful place in society. She has become a servant herself; and as such she is loyal and efficient. She obeys our orders cheerfully, and for the most part, I must say, they are reasonable enough."

"You're not always there when she gets her restless fits. You didn't have to put up with her rudeness that time when she was in love with the factor."

"Perhaps not. Love introduces entirely new elements into the social machine which may upset all our calculations."

"Factors of disturbance!"

"As you say, my dear . . . To go back to the question of stratification. When it operates ill over too long a period, when its free play is interfered with, when people have to overcome too great a resistance in their attempt to assume their rightful functions, revolutions break out. My dear Monsieur Jerphanion, if you and your future colleagues can only see to it that our society remains fluid, I can guarantee that we shall have no revolution in France!"

"I ask nothing better. . . . Have you ever put those ideas of yours on paper, ever published them?"

"Good heavens, no!"

"That's a pity. They are most interesting . . . though I won't pretend that I don't find in them a faint flavour of conservatism."

"Do you really?"

"If Monsieur Ernest Torchecoul had not been inspired by the spirit of conservatism," said Bartlett with an affectation of Tory solemnity, "I should never have become his disciple."

"It may be a hasty impression on my part, due to an entirely superficial analogy. Listening to you, I am vaguely reminded of certain theorists of the Right, like Le Play, though I must admit that I know very little about him."

"Others would say that I am a dangerous revolutionary. For to lessen resistance to the natural processes of stratification is tantamount to threatening all acquired positions in society, to dissolving privileges, to throwing open, with excessive speed, the ranks of the élite to the free play of the winds of heaven. My idea of a fluid society is, in a sense, a revolution that never becomes stabilized." He relapsed into silent thought, his eyes still twinkling with suppressed laughter. "You have quoted Le Play against me. . . . I am really as close to Fourier as I am to him."

Jallez saw in imagination the statue of Fourier which stands in the middle of the boulevard Rochechouart, at the end of the rue Vaulaincourt, and the inscription on its base which used to mystify him so greatly whenever he had read it as a child. He remembered Hugo's phrase: "Once upon a time in a garret there lived an obscure individual called Fourier. . . ." He was seized by a retrospective tenderness for that Fourier in bronze, sitting there in his frock-coat, thoughtfully leaning on a stick, which he had seen in the old days whenever he went home from school "the long way round."

Out loud he said:

"My dear master, you are perfectly right. There is something in you of a Fourier gone realist, having at his finger-tips all the details of rent, salaries, and the value of shop property in every district in Paris."

"I fear my facts have gone rusty since I became a country gentleman. I realized the other day that I was quite incapable now of analysing the budget of a working-class family of the Pantin quarter of Paris. I really am completely ignorant of many items in today's cost of living. . . ."

An hour later they were still at table. The stock of Torchecoul's Chambertin had been reduced by several bottles. More than once Adélaïde Torchecoul had warmed up the sociological atmosphere by hilarious references to the scandals of Grosbois-sous-le-Mont. Odette found the large lady quite adorable, and was unable to stop laughing though her head ached and she was dropping with sleep. Bartlett searched his memory for improper stories, but could think only of Scottish ones which, though funny, were not improper and therefore were unworthy of being offered to Mme Torchecoul. Besides, when-

ever one did come into his mind it was always in English, and he had
never found French words so elusive, a fact which he attributed to
the Chambertin. Jerphanion and Torchecoul were the soberest members of the party. Jallez was convinced of his own drunkenness as he
had been convinced of few things in his life. He was delighted to
find himself in such a condition. It seemed to him that in the present
state of the world, to be drunk in good and pleasant company represented one of the least illusory of mankind's achievements.

Obedient to a sudden impulse, he rose to his feet.

"I ask for one minute of your attention. . . . I rise to propose a
toast to Tellière and Gentilcœur. One of them is dead . . . he was
killed. The other is still living, but he might just as well be dead.
Together they had contrived a formula of a high and lovely way of
life. Jerphanion knows something of what I mean."

"Very little. . . ."

"Still, he is not entirely in the dark . . . while the rest of you, I
fully realize . . . I'll explain it all to you tomorrow if you think it
would interest you. Tonight—no—it's all too complicated. . . . Tellière and Gentilcœur ought to be here with us under the roof of our
charming hosts. That is all I have to say. May our thoughts be with
them . . . and reunite them, if such a thing be possible!"

Torchecoul's large face, under its mop of white and fluffy hair,
with its large and kindly eyes, wore an expression which showed that
he had fully caught the gist of Jallez's words. He had no idea who
Tellière and Gentilcœur might be. But he gave no sign of being in
any way put out by that simple fact. His mind caught, with a sure
instinct, at the speaker's intention. It was clear that he considered
Jallez's outburst the most natural thing in the world.

And Jallez, as he resumed his seat, looked fixedly at him. There
was an element of real greatness, he thought, about Ernest Torchecoul.

## SUMMARY

Haverkamp outlines to Turpin and Serge Vazar his intention to build a modern house in Paris and to adapt an old house in the country. Turpin shows a good deal of ill temper, but Vazar displays an unexpected similarity of views with Haverkamp.—The latter reads Henry de Belleuse a lesson which is not lost on the young man.

Jerphanion, on his return to Paris, makes an expedition to the College roof. He no longer wishes to bring the world toppling about him. He is frightened for the vast, spreading city at his feet.—Jerphanion at the dinner-table between his wife and his son. The Countess's forthcoming party causes some friction between husband and wife.

Haverkamp entertains Maître Lévy-Sangre to luncheon at Fouquet's. He wants to divorce his wife without any unnecessary fuss. How and why he came to marry Mme Genticœur. The radical change that took place in that lady's character; how is it to be explained? How they have been living since their separation. Maître Lévy-Sangre makes a suggestion. The conversation turns on the queer tastes of Henry de Belleuse. Haverkamp does not want to be taken for a fool.

Bouitton tries to give Jerphanion the benefit of his own early experiences, but Jerphanion reproaches him. Can he fire his employer with some of his own enthusiasm? Bouitton admits that contradictory influences pull him different ways. Emotionally he belongs to the Right, intellectually to the Left.

Odette is worried about the direction in which her husband is heading. She fears that he is doomed to disappointment. The case of Bouitton. The career she would have chosen for Jean. She fears, too, for her own happiness.—Jerphanion asks Laulerque to come to Paris.—On his return from the Countess's dinner he tells Odette of his impressions; Odette thinks that he has been dazzled.

Sammécaud meets William P. Milne in Belgium. Mutual confessions of two dilettanti: Tunis as the fine flower of Islamic civilization, and the philosophy of the "novel transported into real life."—Sammécaud's present position: his family, his business.—He halts at Marseille on his way to Tunis.

Jerphanion takes Laulerque to his office at the Quai de Béthune. He is obsessed by the idea that another war must be avoided at all costs. Laulerque is not very proud of the part he once played in the Organization; a touch of madness is, he thinks, indispensable; his nostalgia for the views of his youth; what he thinks of Communism and its possible dangers; the world must be nursed like a man suffering from tuberculosis.—Odette entertains Jallez, who tells her something of his life in Geneva, without, however, ceasing to be somewhat mysterious. She confesses her fears to him; her theory of how the countesses of this world seduce the politicians of the Left.—A friendly luncheon: Jallez and Laulerque, in the kindly atmosphere of the Jerphanions' flat, talk of Switzerland and of all the opportunities they have missed. They walk part of the way home together. Jallez explains the feeling of terror inspired in him by the sight of self-assured young women. Laulerque at Wepler's; his memory of an evening in 1910. Later, on the Caulaincourt Bridge he recaptures a mysterious sensation, the key to which he has vainly sought for many years. Jerphanion has a sleepless night. He sees friendship as a threadbare relationship.—M. Pouzols-Desaugues is under the impression that Jerphanion is still interested in their little game of make-believe.— How Jallez and Jerphanion used to walk the streets of Paris when they were still students at the College. Jallez regrets that he is not older: the Exposition of 1900. Lengnau's point of view has scarcely changed at all. Jallez no longer believes in the power of the League of Nations. He feels anxious about the Jerphanions' happiness. On the hill of Saint-Blaise. A project worthy of the "incomparable life."—Laulerque repents of his defeatism.

Haverkamp, accompanied by his architect and his interior decorator, pays a visit to the site he has chosen for his house. He feels less enthusiasm than he did in the old days of Celle-les-Eaux. He realizes that there is a point beyond which material achievement ceases to bring a man pleasure.—Sylvie Préval gives him a new angle on business. Inopportune arrival of Mme Haverkamp.—Sévelin, Haudebert, and Werner call on Haverkamp to discuss a theatrical deal. Haverkamp is struck by the modesty of the sums involved. The tactful behaviour of theatre folk. He finds his name coupled with that of a famous financial baron.—Belleuse gives Jerphanion a great deal of unexpected information. Haverkamp, too, behaves in a very forthcoming manner: chicken-hearted gamblers; the fall of the franc. A suggestion relative to the party funds, and another one that concerns Jerphanion personally. Jerphanion explains to Bouitton the nature of Haverkamp's special brand of algebra and tells him of the two suggestions. Bouitton loses his temper.

Bartlett, Jallez, and the Jerphanions lovingly sketch their itinerary. —All set for Burgundy: happiness on the road; the two gallant little cars; the wine of Chablis.—Everything goes according to plan.—Ernest Torchecoul, country gentleman of Aubepierre, entertains with becoming dignity his favourite disciple and his friends.—An excellent dinner: Mme Torchecoul's decidedly broad sense of humour; Torchecoul dilates on the problems of the day; effects of a fine Chambertin; Jallez proposes a toast to Tellière and Gentilcœur.

# INDEX OF CHARACTERS
## THIRD INSTALMENT
### Note regarding the use of this INDEX

This Index will figure at the end of every volume, and will be extended as necessary. An Index of the characters in the first five volumes will be found at the end of the fifth volume, *The Earth Trembles*. An Index for Volumes VI to X will be found at the end of Volume X, *The New Day*.

Large roman numerals refer to the Book.

Small roman numerals refer to the chapter.

Arabic numerals refer to the page.

If there is *no page reference,* this means that the character takes part in the *whole* of the chapter indicated.

When a chapter or a page is given *in brackets,* this means that the character is involved, but does not take part personally in the action.

EXAMPLES

I, x. Refer to Chapter x, Book I, where the character plays an important role.

I, xviii, 149. Refer to page 149, Book I (Chapter xviii), where the character appears only incidentally.

II, (xi). Refer to Chapter xi, Book II; a chapter which, as a whole, involves the character, though he is not personally present.

II, xv, (391). As above; the character is involved only on page 391. In the case of important events the reference is preceded by a brief summary of the event.

Proper names extraneous to the action, and intended to remain so, are not included in the Index.

ASTIER, MADAME, XXI, (x).—XXI, xi, 170.—XXI, xii, (188).

BARON, the well-known, XXII, xxx, (506–7).

i

ᴸᴇᴛᴛ, Stephen, XXII, (xxvi). Dines at the Jerphanions', where they plan the trip into Burgundy, XXII, xxxiv.—Drives his little English car over the French roads, XXII, xxxv, xxxvi. —Received by Torchecoul as his favourite disciple, XXII, xxxvii.— At dinner at the Château d'Aube-pierre, is unable to remember any improper stories, XXII, xxxviii.

Belleuse, Henry de, XXII, i.—Receives a veiled warning from Haverkamp, XXII, ii.—XXII, v, (307).—Lévy-Sangre jokes about his peculiar manners, XXII, (ix). —XXII, xxix, (493).—XXII, xxx.—Gives a good deal of information to Jerphanion about his employer's affairs, XXII, xxxi.— Haverkamp sets about to replace him, XXII, (xxxii).—XXII, (xxxiii).

Belplanque, the caretaker, XXII, iii, 295.

Bertrand, XXII, vi, (318).

Blum, Léon, XXI, x, (161).—XXI, xxi, (265).

Bonial, XXI, i, (4).

Bonnefoux, Dr., XXI, i, (6).

Bouitton, XXI, ii, (43).—XXI, viii, (136).—XXI, x, (161).— XXI, (xiii).—XXI, xxi, (264).— XXII, iii, 294.—XXII, iv, (303, 305).—Has a long conversation with Jerphanion on his return from Velay: his experience with electioneering questions; his internal contradictions; his attach-ment to the old routine of the Third Republic; his prejudices, his instinct in matters of foreign politics, XXII, x, xi, and xii.— XXII, (xiii).—XXII, (xv).— XXII, xix, (404, 408).—XXII, xx, (426, 430–1).—XXII, xxiii, (455).—XXII, xxx, (502–3).— XXII, (xxxi).—XXII, (xxxii).— Jephanion reports to him about his call on Haverkamp; he gets angry, XXII, xxxiii.—XXII, xxxiv, (532).

Briand, Aristide, XXI, ii, (40). —XXI, iii, (79).—XXI, xxi, (265).—XXII, xii, (357).—XXII, xiii, (365).

Cabirol, Abbé, XXI, i, (24).

Candidates on the ticket with Jerphanion, suggested, XXI, viii, (133–4).—XXI, xiii, (193–4).— XXI, xvii, (228).—XXI, xxi, (264–5).—XXII, x, (343).

Castaing, Dr., XXI, i, (6).

Caulet, XXII, iii, (295–6).—XXII, xxii, (449–50).

Champcenais, Count Henri de, XXI, xxi, (266).—XXII, xvii, (396).—His state of mind in 1924, XXII, (xxxi).

Chauffeur, the Pouzols-Desau-gues', XXI, iii, 74.—XXI, vii, (iii).

Clanricard, Édouard, XXII, xix, (404, 405, 407).—XXII, xxii, (440, 442).

Clanricard, Mathilde (née Ca-

theatre; preliminary conversation, XXII, xxx.—Reveals certain of his ideas to Jerphanion, XXII, xxxi. —Offers him a position, XXII, xxxii.—His methods, according to Jerphanion, XXII, (xxxiii).

HERRIOT, ÉDOUARD, XXI, i, (8).— XXI, x, (161).—XXI, xxi, (265). —XXII, xiii, (365).—XXII, xxxi, (517–19).

HONORÉ, XXII, xxix.

HUBERT, MADAME, XXII, xv, (384).

HUSBAND OF THE GOOD-LOOKING CONCIERGE, THE, his suspicious death, XXI, (xv).

ISLAM, its civilization preferred by William P. Milne, XXII, (xvi).

JALLEZ, PIERRE, XXI, i, (6, 8, 17).— XXI, ii, (52).—XXI, x, (156). —XXI, xiii, (196–7).—XXI, xiv, (200).—In his office at the League of Nations enjoys a sense of well-being, XXI, xvii.—Meets Dr. Viaur again, XXI, xviii.—Has lunch with him, asks him about his career recently, expresses his sympathy and understanding, XXI, xix.—XXI, xxi, (266).— XXII, iii, (296).—XXII, xiii, (372).—XXII, (xix).—Listens to Odette's confidences, gives her sympathetic advice, XXII, xx.— Has lunch, together with Laulerque, at the Jerphanions', XXII, xxi.—Leaves with Laulerque, XXII, xxii.—Jerphanion feels the insufficiency of their friendship, XXII, (xxii).—XXII, (xxiii).— Takes a walk with Jerphanion as in the old days; recalls the Exposition of 1900; how he sees the future of the world, XXII, xxiv. —Wishes to save his friend's happiness; his own not worth the trouble, XXII, xxv.—Invites Jerphanion to join Bartlett and him on a visit to Torchecoul, XXII, xxvi.—Discusses with Jerphanion the route to take to Torchecoul's, XXII, xxxiv.—On the way to Burgundy in Bartlett's car, XXII, xxxv, xxxvi.—Received by Torchecoul at the château, XXII, xxxvii.—At dinner, joins in the general pleasure, proposes a toast to Tellière and Gentilcœur, XXII, xxxviii.

JAURÈS, JEAN, XXI, ii, (49).

JEANNETTE, XXII, xxxvii.

JERPHANION, FATHER OF, XXI, i, (5; his health, his lapses of memory, 11–15).—XXI, ii, (26).—XXI, viii, (137).—XXII, xxiv, (459).

JERPHANION, JEAN, preparing for his election campaign in Le Velay, in December 1923, travels about with Grousson in his car, XXI, i. —Makes a political speech at a luncheon of the Teachers' Association of the Haute-Loire, XXI, ii.—Lunches with the Pouzols-Desaugues; talks with the head of the house and hears Vaurevauzes mentioned for the first time, XXI, iii, iv.—On the way to the mountain with Grousson, XXI, v.—

Saint François-Régis, XXI, vi.—Much excited by the supposed crimes at Vaurevauzes, discusses at length their hypothetical origin with Grousson, XXI, vii.—Writes to Odette; gives her news of his campaign and his trip; anxiety about Jean-Pierre, XXI, viii.—Goes into the problem of poisons with Grousson, XXI, ix.—Calls on the curé of Saint-Front, questions him discreetly, XXI, x.—Finally becomes acquainted with Vaurevauzes and its inhabitants, XXI, xi.—Gives a short talk to his constituents at Saint-Front and reproaches himself for childishness, XXI, xii.—Receives Odette's answer, XXI, xiii.—Lunches again at the Pouzols-Desaugues'; makes his report on Vaurevauzes, XXI, xiv.—Tells the story of the landlord and the good-looking concierge, XXI, xv.—Reaches a disillusioned verdict on the zeal of justice, XXI, xvi.—XXI, xvii, (227-8).—Meets the magistrate Doublet, XXI, xx.—On the train taking him back to Paris, dismisses distractions and draws up a plan for his future action, XXI, xxi.—Back in Paris, goes to find again the old thrill on the College roof; is filled with fear for Paris, for "all the men and all the houses," XXII, iii.—Lunches at home; gives his attention to the dinner at the Countess's; slight conjugal bitterness, XXII, iv.—Has a long talk with Bouitton, makes some remarks on his attitude and his words; his doubts; foreign politics, XXII, x, xi, xii.—Object of Odette's anxious thoughts; has he taken the right road? XXII, (xiii).—Writes to Laulerque inviting him to come to Paris, XXII, xiv.—With Odette after the dinner at the Countess's, XXII, xv.—Asks Laulerque anxiously for his conclusions about the Organization and his other experiences, XXII, xix.—Odette fears that his new life will estrange him from her, XXII, (xx).—Entertains his friends Laulerque and Jallez at lunch, XXII, xxi.—Thinks feverishly of the problem of friendship, XXII, xxii.—Receives news of Vaurevauzes from M. Pouzols-Desaugues; his reply, XXII, xxiii.—Takes a walk with Jallez as in the old days; the Exposition of 1900; confesses his anguish, tells him of his call on Lengnau, XXII, xxiv.—His happiness preoccupies Jallez, who finds it rare and precious, XXII, xxv.—Strongly tempted by a plan for a trip, XXII, xxvi.—XXII, xxvii.—XXII, xxx, (503).—On an errand to Haverkamp for the party funds, XXII, xxxi.—Haverkamp offers him a position, XXII, xxxii.—Reports to Bouitton; Haverkamp's algebra, XXII, xxxiii.—With Jallez and Bartlett, settles on the plan for their trip into

Burgundy, XXII, xxxiv.—Thoroughly enjoys the pleasures of the journey, XXII, xxxv, xxxvi.—Received by Torchecoul, XXII, xxxvii.—Takes part in the general gaiety at dinner, XXII, xxxviii.

JERPHANION, JEAN-PIERRE (previously called JERPHANION, the baby), gives his parents some anxiety, XXI, (viii).—XXI, (xiii).—XXII, iii, (294, 300).—Has lunch with his parents, XXII, iv.—XXII, xx, (422).—XXII, xxvi, (476).—XXII, xxxiv, (532).

JERPHANION, MOTHER OF, XXI, i, (3, 12–13, 14).—XXI, ix, (146).—XXII, xxiv, (459).

JERPHANION, ODETTE (née CLISSON), XXI, iii, (84–5).—Her husband writes to her, XXI, (viii).—XXI, x, (156).—Her reply to Jephanion; her advice; her distractions, her ideas about large families, XXI, (xiii).—XXI, xvii, (228).—XXII, iii, 294–5.—Shows a certain bitterness about the dinner at the Countess's to which her husband has been invited, XXII, iv.—Torments herself on the subject of Jerphanion's chosen career; what she would have dreamed for him, XXII, xiii.—How she receives Jerphanion after the dinner at the Countess's, XXII, xv.—XXII, xix, 403–4.—Pours out her anxieties to Jallez; her fear for the future, XXII, xx.—Entertains Laulerque and Jallez at lunch, XXII, xxi.—XXII, xxii, (447–50).—XXII,

xxiii.—XXII, (xxv).—XXII, xxvi, (476–7).—XXII, xxvii, (479).—Entertains Jallez and Bartlett at dinner, XXII, xxxiv.—Acts as pilot in the car with her husband, XXII, xxxv, xxxvi.—Arrives at the Château d'Aubepierre, XXII, xxxvii.—Laughs heartily at dinner; is a little intoxicated, XXII, xxxviii.

JOUVET, LOUIS, in Knock, XXI, xiii, (195).

KARL, MONSIEUR, XXII, xix, (409).
KREUZ, MARGARET-DESIDERIA, XXII, xxii, (444).

LAFEUILLE, PIERRE, XXII, xvii, (397–8).—XXII, xviii, (400).
LANDLORD, JERPHANION'S, his love-affairs and his possible criminal complicity with the good-looking concierge, XXI, (xv).—XXII, xx, (423).—XXII, (xxiii).
LANDLORD OF PANDREAUX, XXI, i, (9, 11).
LAULERQUE, ARMAND, inspires Jerphanion in his speech at the luncheon at Le Puy, XXI, (11).—XXI, xxi, (266).—XXII, iii, (299).—Invited to Paris by Jerphanion, XXII, (xiv).—Pressed by Jerphanion, gives vent to all his disenchantment regarding means of direct action, XXII, xix.—XXII, xx, (426), 432.—Lunches with the Jerphanions, XXII, xxi.—Leaves with Jallez, goes to Wepler's, then to the Caulaincourt Bridge, in

search of a state of mind, XXII, xxiii.—XXII, xxiv, (460–1, 463). —Regrets the disenchanted attitude he had shown Jerphanion, XXII, (xxvii).

LEAGUE OF NATIONS, THE, abandoned by the United States, XXI, ii, (41–3).—Discussed by M. Pouzols-Desaugues, XXI, (iii, iv).— Daily routine, XXI, xvii.—XXI, xviii, (231–2).—XXII, xix, (417).—XXII, xxiv, (466–7).

LEBAIGUE, MONSIGNOR, XXI, i, (24).

LEBAIL, XXI, xvii, 228–9.

LEBLANC, THE CHILDREN OF THE YOUNGER SON, XXI, (iv).—XXI, (vii).—One of the children, XXI, xi, 174, 179.

LEBLANC, THE ELDER SON, XXI, (iv). —XXI, (vii).—XXI, (ix).—XXI, xi, (184).

LEBLANC, THE FAMILY, M. Pouzols-Desaugues first alludes to them, XXI, (iv).—XXI, (v).—How Jerphanion and Grousson suppose they perpetrated the crimes, XXI, (vi).—XXI, (vii).—XXI, viii, (135–6).—The possible role of poisons, XXI, (ix).—XXI, (x).— Jerphanion, driven by Grousson, finally makes their acquaintance, XXI, xi.—XXI, (xiv).—XXI, (xx).—XXI, xxi, (263).—XXII, (xxiii).

LEBLANC, THE FATHER, XXI, (iv).— XXI, (vii).—XXI, (ix).—XXI, xi, (184).—XXI, xx, (257–8).

LEBLANC, THE MOTHER, XXI, (iv).—

XXI, (vii).—XXI, (ix).—XXI, xi.—XXI, xii, (190).

LEBLANC, THE WIFE OF THE ELDER SON, XXI, (iv).—XXI, (vii).— XXI, (ix).—"The fair widow": in the entrance of the tunnel and in the large room, XXI, xi.—XXI, xii, (190).—XXI, xiv, (202–5).— XXI, xx, (255).—XXI, xxi, (263). —Seems to have nothing to fear, XXII, (xxiii).

LEBLANC, THE WIFE OF THE YOUNGER SON, XXI, (iv).—XXI, (vii).— XXI, (ix).—XXI, xi.—XXI, xii, (190).

LEBLANC, THE YOUNGER SON, XXI, (iv).—XXI, (vii).—XXI, (ix).— His meeting with Jerphanion and Grousson; blames the house at Vaurevauzes for the deaths of his father and brother, XXI, xi.— XXI, xii, (190).—XXI, xiv, (205–11).—XXI, xx, (259, 262).

LEJEUNES, THE, XXII, xx, (425).

LENGNAU, XXI, xxi, (266).—Jerphanion, after fourteen years, pays him a call; what he has become in 1924, XXII, (xxiv).

LENIN, XXI, ii, (62, 63).—XXI, xvii, (256–7).—XXII, xix, (406, 411).—XXII, xxxi, (510, 517).

LÉVY-SANGRE, MAÎTRE, XXII, ii, (293).—Invited to Fouquet's by Haverkamp; doesn't know that Haverkamp is married; makes his client tell all about his marital life; reveals his plans for getting a divorce on the best terms; jokes about the manners of Henry de

Belleuse, XXII, v, vi, vii, viii, ix.
—XXII, xxix, (492).—XXII, xxx,
(498).

Lézarnauds, Dr., XXI, ix, (147).

Lloyd George, XXI, ii, (44–5).—
XXI, iv, (92).—XXII, xxiv,
(463).

Magistrate of the District of the
Seine, a, XXI, xv, (218–20).—
XXI, xx, (260).

Marchand, XXII, xxvi, (475).

Mascot, XXII, xix, (412, 414).

Milne, William P., introduced; his
mode of living; praises Islam and
the charm of Tunis to Sammécaud, XXII, xvi.—XXII, xvii,
398–9.—XXII, xviii, (400).

Miraud, Victor, XXII, ii, (291).

Mussolini, Benito, XXI, ii, (29–
30).—XXI, xiii, (198).—XXI,
xvii, (227).—XXII, xix, (406)—
XXII, xxxi, (515).

Organization, the, has become one
of the subjects about which Laulerque prefers not to think, XXII,
(xix).

Pages-Vernet, Monsieur, XXI, i,
(4–5).

Painlevé, Paul, XXI, x, (161).—
XXI, xxi, (265).—XXII, xiii,
(365).—XXII, xxxi, (517).

Paris, sites for private residences,
XXII, i, (277).—Seen from the
College roof; a city to protect, a
city for which one fears, XXII, iii.
—Walking there has become difficult, XXII, xxiv, 456.—Country
church and graveyard, XXII, xxv,
xxvi.

Party, the Radical-Socialist, Jerphanion is its candidate in the
parliamentary elections of 1924 in
the Haute-Loire; what he thinks
of it, XXI, (1).—Its good will and
good sense, XXI, ii, (68–9).—
XXI, xiii, (194).—XXI, (xxi).—
XXII, xi, (349).—XXII, xix,
(406).—XXII, xx, (429).—So-
licits a subscription from Haverkamp, XXII, xxxi.—Jerphanion
vice-president, XXII, (xxxii).—
XXII, (xxxiii).

Peasant of Le Velay, a, XXI, viii,
(139–40).—XXII, iii, (300).

Pellen de Tracy, XXII, xv, (379).

Piard, Judge, XXI, iv, (100).—XXI,
xx, (257–8).

Poincaré, Raymond, XXI, ii, (28).
—XXII, xii, (358).

Poliapof, Dmitri, XXII, xxvi,
(475).

Pouzols-Desaugues, Madame, has
ruined her husband's career, XXI,
(iii).—Entertains Jerphanion at
lunch, XXI, iv.—XXI, viii, (134).
—XXI, x, (162).—XXI, xiv,
(200).—XXII, xxiii, (453, 454).

Pouzols-Desaugues, Monsieur,
XXI, i, (23–4).—Receives Jerphanion; his estate; description of
him; his career, his political ideas,
XXI, iii.—Talks to him of the
peace treaty and of the crimes at
Vaurevauzes, XXI, iv.—XXI, (v,
vi, vii).—XXI, viii, (134, 135).—

# INDEX OF CHARACTERS

XXI, x, (162–3).—XXI, (xi).—Hears Jerphanion's report on Vaurevauzes, XXI, xiv.—Relishes the story of the landlord and the good-looking concierge, XXI, xv.—XXI, xvi.—Introduces Jerphanion to the magistrate Doublet, XXI, xx.—Bids Jerphanion goodbye at the Le Puy station, XXI, xxi.—Sends him news of the fair widow, XXII, (xxiii).

PRASLES, DUC DE, XXII, i, (278–9).

PRASLES, DUCHESSE DE, XXII, i, 278–80).

PREFECT OF THE HAUTE-LOIRE, THE, XXI, i, (24).—XXI, iii, (81, 83).—XXI, viii, (134).

PRESIDENT OF THE HAUTE-LOIRE TEACHERS' ASSOCIATION, THE, XXI, ii.

PRÉVAL, SYLVIE, still in bed, studies her part; description of her; gives Haverkamp some advice, XXII, xxix.—XXII, xxx, (504–5).

PRINCESS, THE EGYPTIAN, XXII, xvi, (387–8).

RENÉ, XXII, xxix.

SAINT-PAPOUL, MARQUIS DE, Jerphanion's "boss"; his position in 1923, XXI, (1).

SAINT-PAPOUL, MARQUISE DE, XXI, i, (6).

SAMMÉCAUD, BERTHE, XXII, (xvii).—XXII, xviii, (400).

SAMMÉCAUD, DIDIER, XXII, (xvii).

SAMMÉCAUD, RAYMOND, XXII, (xvii).

SAMMÉCAUD, ROGER, meets William P. Milne at the Château d'Ourthe, XXII, xvi.—The situation in 1923 of his family and his business; disposed to make a lasting solution, XXII, xvii.—En route for Tunis, XXII, xviii.

SAMMÉCAUD, THE DAUGHTER OF, XXII, (xvii).

SAMPEYRE, XXII, (xiv).—XXII, xix, (407).

SÉVELIN, JACQUES, XXII, xxviii, (482–3).—XXII,(xxix).—Sets before Haverkamp the plans for the Théâtre du Rond-Point; description of him; his tact, XXII, xxx.

SIGEAU, HÉLÈNE, XXII, xxii, (446).

SUZANNE, XXII, xix, 404.—XXII, xxxiv, (532).

TEACHERS' ASSOCIATION OF THE HAUTE-LOIRE, THE, XXI, i, (22).—Hear Jerphanion make a speech; their state of mind, their reactions; various groups, the man with the moustache and eyeglasses, the wearers of the Croix de Guerre, the women, the table of extreme Leftists, XXI, ii.—XXI, iii, (78).

TELLIÈRE, XXII, xxxviii, (559).

TORCHECOUL, ADÉLAÏDE, XXII, xxxiv, (536).—XXII, xxxvi, 546.—XXII, (xxxvii).—Her looks, her gaiety, her broad jokes; serves a fine dinner to four visitors, XXII, xxxviii.

TORCHECOUL, ERNEST, XXII, (xxvi).—XXII, (xxxiv).—The Jerphanions, Jallez, and Bartlett drive to his place, XXII, (xxxv, xxxvi).—Receives them like a country gentleman; his appearance in 1924, XXII, xxxvii.—Offers them a magnificent dinner; his attitude towards actual problems; Jallez finds an element of greatness in him, XXII, xxxviii.

TURPIN, RAOUL, is disgruntled at being associated with Serge Vazar, XXII, i.—Haverkamp praises his qualities as a friend and a jolly companion, XXII, (ii). —At the building site in the avenue Bugeaud, with Haverkamp and Vazar, XXII, xxviii.— XXII, xxix, (488).—XXII, xxx, (496).

UNCLE OF JERPHANION, THE, XXII, xxiv, (459).

VAUREVAUZES, the house, XXI, (iv). —XXI, (v).—XXI, (vii).—XXI, viii, (135-6).—XXI, (ix).—XXI, (x).—Visited by Grousson and Jerphanion; blamed for murder, XXI, xi.—XXI, xii, (190).—XXI, (xiv).—XXI, (xx).

VAZAR, SERGE, description of him, his manners, his art of pleasing, XXII, i.—XXII, (ii).—XXII, ix, (341).—At the building site in the avenue Bugeaud, XXII, xxviii. —XXII, xxix, (488).

VEIL-BERGER, DR., XXI, viii, (136).

VIAUR, DR. ALBERT, XXI, xvii, (229).—At Geneva, is approached by Jallez, XXI, xviii.—Lunches with him; reveals incidents in the last ten years of his career, particularly the discovery of anaplastine; shares his success and his bitterness with him; writes him a curious letter, XXI, xix.

VIAUR, MADAME, XXI, xix, (241).

VINCENT, SENATOR, XXII, x, (343).

WAZEMMES, FÉLIX, always alive in Haverkamp's heart, XXII, ii, (291).—XXII, vi, (312, 319).— XXII, xxxii, (521).

WERNER, PIERRE, represents the famous Baron at a meeting of theatre people in Haverkamp's studio, XXII, xxx.

WIFE OF THE LANDLORD, THE, her suspicious death, XXI, (xv).

WILSON, PRESIDENT WOODROW, XXI, ii, (40-1, 44).—XXI, iv, (92).— XXII, xii, (357).—XXII, xxiv, (463).

# MEN OF GOOD WILL

Volume    I. MEN OF GOOD WILL
          The Sixth of October
          Quinette's Crime

Volume    II. PASSION'S PILGRIMS
          Childhood's Loves
          Eros in Paris

Volume    III. THE PROUD AND THE MEEK
          The Proud
          The Meek

Volume    IV. THE WORLD FROM BELOW
          The Lonely
          Provincial Interlude

Volume    V. THE EARTH TREMBLES
          Flood Warning
          The Powers That Be

Volume    VI. THE DEPTHS AND THE HEIGHTS
          To the Gutter
          To the Stars

Volume    VII. DEATH OF A WORLD
          Mission to Rome
          The Black Flag

*Volume VIII.* VERDUN
> The Prelude
> The Battle

*Volume* IX. AFTERMATH
> Vorge against Quinette
> The Sweets of Life

*Volume* X. THE NEW DAY
> Promise of Dawn
> The World Is Your Adventure

*Volume* XI. WORK AND PLAY
> Mountain Days
> Work and Play

## A NOTE ON THE TYPE IN
## WHICH THIS BOOK IS SET

*This book is set in Granjon, a type named in compliment to ROBERT GRANJON, but neither a copy of a classic face nor an entirely original creation. George W. Jones drew the basic design for this type from classic sources, but deviated from his model to profit by the intervening centuries of experience and progress. This type is based primarily upon the type used by Claude Garamond (1510–61) in his beautiful French books, and more closely resembles Garamond's own than do any of the various modern types that bear his name.*

*Of Robert Granjon nothing is known before 1545, except that he had begun his career as type-cutter in 1523. The boldest and most original designer of his time, he was one of the first to practise the trade of type-founder apart from that of printer. Between 1549 and 1551 he printed a number of books in Paris, also continuing as type-cutter. By 1557 he was settled in Lyons and had married Antoinette Salamon, whose father, Bernard, was an artist associated with Jean de Tournes. Between 1557 and 1562 Granjon printed about twenty books in types designed by himself, following, after the fashion of the day, the cursive handwriting of the time. These types, usually known as "caractères de civilité," he himself called "lettres françaises," as especially appropriate to his own country. He was granted a monopoly of these types for ten years, but they were soon copied. Granjon appears to have lived in Antwerp for a time, but was at Lyons in 1575 and 1577, and for the next decade at Rome, working for the Vatican and Medici presses, his work consisting largely in cutting exotic types. Towards the end of his life he may have returned to live in Paris, where he died in 1590.*

THIS BOOK WAS COMPOSED, PRINTED, AND BOUND
BY H. WOLFF, NEW YORK.